The Noel Streatfeild Omnibus

Noel Streatfeild's first book must be one of the most
famous in children's literature – *Ballet Shoes*. It made
her a household name overnight, so much so that there
were times when she wished she had never written it!
But for Noel, *Ballet Shoes* was just the beginning, for
she went on to write more than thirty children's books.

Here in this single volume are three of her best-known
and best-loved titles – *White Boots*, *Ballet Shoes for Anna*
and *Thursday's Child*. All three have been in print since
they were first published, a tribute to Noel's remarkable
ability to write the books that children want to read!

"*White Boots*. Author: Noel (*Ballet Shoes*) Streatfeild.
And you know we might very well leave it at that – for
what higher recommendation is wanted? Noel Streatfeild
has that happy, skilful knack of turning her characters
into real people – something which only really good
novelists can do. A first-rate book." Derek McCulloch,
BBC Children's Hour

31 29-3-1996.

CONTENTS

To: Julie.

Happy tenth birthday

Lot's of Love.

Auntie Peggy.

x x x x .

First published in Great Britain 1995
Collins is an imprint of HarperCollins*Publishers* Ltd,
77-85 Fulham Palace Road,
Hammersmith, London W6 8JB

1 3 5 7 9 10 8 6 4 2

ISBN 0 00 675179 2

The author asserts the moral right to be
identified as the author of this work

Printed and bound in Great Britain by
HarperCollins Manufacturing Ltd, Glasgow

WHITE BOOTS

Illustrated by Milein Cosman

First published in Great Britain by
William Collins Sons & Co. Ltd 1951

Copyright reserved Noel Streatfeild 1951

CHAPTER I

THE JOHNSONS

★

EVEN when the last of the medicine bottles were cleared away and she was supposed to have " had " convalescence, Harriet did not get well. She was a thin child with big brown eyes and a lot of reddish hair that did not exactly curl, but had a wiriness that made it stand back from her face rather like Alice's hair in *Alice in Wonderland*. Since her illness Harriet had looked all eyes, hair and legs and no face at all, so much so that her brothers Alec, Toby and Edward said she had turned into a daddy-long-legs. Mrs. Johnson, whose name was Olivia, tried to scold the boys for teasing Harriet, but her scolding was not very convincing, because inside she could not help feeling that if a daddy-long-legs had a lot of hair and big eyes it would look very like Harriet.

Harriet's father was called George Johnson. He had a shop. It was not a usual sort of shop, because what it sold was entirely dependent on what his brother William grew, shot or caught. There had been a time when the Johnson family were rich. They had owned a large house in the country, with plenty of land round it, and some fishing and shooting. The children's great-grandfather had not been able to afford to live in the big house, so

he had built himself a smaller house on the edge of his
property and let the big house. When his eldest son, the
children's grandfather, came into the property he could
not afford to live even in the new smaller house, so he
brought up the children's father, and their Uncle William,
in the lodge by the gates. But when he was killed in a
motor accident and the children's Uncle William inherited
the property he was so poor he could not afford to live
even in the lodge, so he decided the cheapest plan would
be to live in two rooms in the house on the edge of the
property that his grandfather had built, and to let the
lodge. When he had thought of this he said to his brother
George, the children's father, " I tell you what, young
feller me lad " . . . he was the sort of man who spoke that
way . . . " I'll keep a nice chunk of garden and a bit of
shootin' and fishin' and I'll make the garden pay, and
you can have the produce, trout from the river, and game
from the woods, and keep a shop in London and sell it,
and before you can say Bob's me Uncle you'll be a
millionaire."

It did not matter how often anyone said Bob's your
Uncle for George did not become a millionaire. Uncle
William had not married, and lived very comfortably in
his two rooms in the smaller house on the edge of his
estate, but one reason why he lived so comfortably was
that he ate the best of everything that he grew, caught or
shot. The result of this was that George and Olivia and
the children lived very leanly indeed on the proceeds of
the shop. It was not only that William ate everything
worth eating, which made life so hard for them, but people
who buy things in shops expect to go to special shops for
special things, and when they are buying fruit they do not
expect to be asked if they could do with a nice rabbit or

a trout, especially when the rabbit and the trout are not very nice, because the best ones have been eaten by an Uncle William. The children's father was an optimist by nature, and he tried not to believe that he could be a failure, or that anything that he started would not succeed in the end, also he had a deep respect and trust for his brother William. " Don't let's get downhearted, Olivia," he would say, " it's all a matter of time and educating the public. The public can be educated to anything if only they're given time." Olivia very seldom argued with George, she was not an arguing sort of person and anyway she was very fond of him, but she did sometimes wonder if they would not all starve before the public could be taught to buy old, tired grouse, which had been too tough for Uncle William, when what they had come to buy was vegetables.

One of the things that was most difficult for Olivia, and indeed for the whole family, was that what would not sell had to be eaten. This made a great deal of trouble because Uncle William had a large appetite and seldom sent more than one of any kind of fish or game, and the result was that the family meals were made up of several different kinds of food, which meant a lot of cooking. " What is there for lunch to-day, Olivia ? " George would ask, usually adding politely: " Sure to be delicious." Olivia would answer, " There's enough rabbit for two, there is a very small pike, there is grouse but I don't really know about that, it seems to be very, very old, as if it had been dead a long time, and there's sauerkraut. I'm afraid everybody must eat cabbage of some sort to-day, we've had over seven hundred from Uncle William this week and and it's only Wednesday."

One of the worst things to Harriet about having been

ill was that she was not allowed to go to school, and her mother would not let her help in the house.

" Do go out, darling, you look so terribly thin and spindly. Why don't you go down to the river ? I know it's rather dull by yourself but you like watching boats go by."

Harriet did like watching boats go by and was glad that her father had chosen to have his shop in outer London in a part through which ran the Thames, so she could see boats go by. But boat watching is a summer thing, and Harriet had been unlucky in that she was ill all the summer and was putting up with the getting-well stage in the autumn, and nobody, she thought, could want to go and look at a river in the autumn. In the summer their bit of the Thames was full of pleasure boats, and there were flowers growing on the banks, but now in October it was cold and sad and grey-looking, and only occasionally a string of barges or a small motor launch came by. But it was no good telling her mother about the river being dull ; for one thing her mother knew it already and would only look sad when she was reminded of it, and for another her mother heard all the doctor said about fresh air and she did not ; besides she was feeling so cotton-woolish and all-overish that she had not really got the energy to argue. So every day when it was not raining she went down by the river and walked drearily up and down the towpath, hugging her coat round her to keep out the wind, wishing and wishing that her legs would suddenly get strong and well again so that she could go back to school and be just ordinary Harriet Johnson like she had been before she was ill.

One particularly beastly day, when it looked every minute as if it was going to rain and never quite did, she was coming home from the river feeling and looking as blue as a lobelia, when a car stopped beside her.

"Hallo, Harriet. How are you getting on?"

Harriet had been so deep in gloom because she was cold and tired that she had not noticed the car, but as he spoke she saw Dr. Phillipson, who ordered the fresh air, and quite suddenly everything she had been thinking about cotton-wool legs and fresh air and not going to

She went down by the river and walked drearily up and down

school came over her in a wave and she did what she would never have done in the ordinary way, she told the doctor exactly what she thought of his treatment.

"How would you be if you were made to walk up and down a river in almost winter, all by yourself, getting colder and colder, and bored-er and bored-er, with absolutely nothing to do, and not allowed to stop indoors for one minute because you'd been ill and your doctor said you'd got to have fresh air? I feel simply terrible, and I shouldn't think I'll ever, ever get well again."

The doctor was a nice, friendly sort of man and clever-looking. Usually he was too busy to do much talking, but this time he seemed in a talking mood. He opened the door of his car and told Harriet to hop into the seat beside him, he had got a visit or two to do and then he would take her home.

"I must say," he agreed, "you do look a miserable little specimen; I hoped you'd pick up after that convalescent home the hospital sent you to."

Harriet looked at him sadly, for she thought he was too nice to be so ignorant.

"I don't see why I should have got better at that convalescent home."

"It's a famous place."

"But it's at the top of a cliff, and everything goes on at the bottom of the cliff, sea-bathing and the sands and everything nice like that. I could never go down because my legs were too cotton-woolish to bring me back."

The doctor muttered something under his breath which sounded like "idiots," then he said:

"Haven't you any relations in the country that you could go and stay with for a bit?"

"No, we've only Uncle William; he's only got two rooms and use of a bathroom and one of his two rooms is his kitchen. He shoots and catches and grows the things Daddy sells in the shop. Mummy says it's a pity he wouldn't have room for me because he eats all the best things, so all that food would do me good, but I don't think it would because I'm not very hungry."

The doctor thought about Harriet's father's shop and sighed. He could well believe Uncle William ate the best of everything for the shop looked as if he did. All he said was :

" You tell your father and mother I'll be along to have a talk with them this evening."

Since she had been ill Harriet was made to go to bed at the same time as Edward, which was half-past six. This was a terrible insult, because Edward was only just seven, whereas she was nearly ten, so when Dr. Phillipson arrived only Alec and Toby were up. The Johnsons lived over the shop. There was not a great deal of room for a family of six. There was a kitchen-dining-room, there was a living-room, one bedroom for the three boys, a slip of a room for Harriet and a bedroom for George and Olivia. When Dr. Phillipson arrived Olivia was in the kitchen cooking the things George had not sold, Alec and Toby were doing their homework at one side of the table in the living-room, while on the other side their father tried to work out the accounts. The days when their father did the accounts were bad days for Alec's and Toby's homework, because accounts were not their father's strong point.

" Alec, if I charge ninepence each for four hundred cabbages, and twopence a pound for four dozen bundles of carrots, three and sixpence each for eight rabbits, and thirty shillings for miscellaneous fish, and we've only sold a quarter of the carrots, half the cabbages, one of the rabbits, and all the fish but three, but we've made a very nice profit on mushrooms, how much have I earned ? "

Toby, who was eleven and had what his schoolmaster called a mathematical brain, was driven into a frenzy by these problems of his father's. He was short-sighted, and had to wear spectacles, and a piece of his sandy-coloured hair was inclined to stand upright on the crown of his head. When his father asked questions about the finance of the shop, his eyes would glare from behind his spectacles, and the piece of hair on the crown of his head would stand bolt upright like a guardsman on parade. He would be in such a hurry to explain to his father that he could not present a mathematical problem in that form that his first words fell out on top of each other.

" But-Father-you-haven't-told-Alec-the-price of the mushrooms on which the whole problem hangs, nor the individual prices of the fish."

It was in the middle of one of these arguments that Olivia brought Dr. Phillipson in. In spite of having to cook all the things Uncle William sent which would not sell, Olivia succeeded in looking at all times as if she was a hostess entertaining a very nice and amusing house party. In the kitchen she always wore an overall but underneath she had pretty clothes ; they were usually very old because there was seldom money for new clothes, but she had a way of putting them on and of wearing them which seemed to say, " Yes, isn't this pretty ? How lucky I am to have nice clothes and time to wear them." As she ushered Dr. Phillipson into the living-room it ceased to be full of George, Alec and Toby all arguing at the tops of their voices, and of Alec's and Toby's school books, and George's dirty little bits of paper on which he kept his accounts, and she was showing a guest into a big, gracious drawing-room.

" Dr. Phillipson's come to talk to us about Harriet."

The Johnson children were properly brought up. Alec and Toby jumped to their feet murmuring, "Good evening, sir," and Alec gave the doctor a chair facing George.

The doctor came straight to the point.

"Harriet is not getting on. Have you any relations in the country you could send her to?"

George, though he only had two, offered the doctor a cigarette.

"But of course, my dear fellow, my brother William has a splendid place, love to have her."

The doctor was sure George would not have many cigarettes so he said he preferred to smoke his own. Olivia signalled to Alec and Toby not to argue.

"It's quite true, Dr. Phillipson, my brother-in-law William would love to have Harriet, but unfortunately he has only got two rooms, and he's very much a bachelor. All my relations live in South Africa. We have nowhere to send Harriet or, of course, we would have sent her long ago."

The doctor nodded, for he felt sure this was true. The Johnsons were the sort of people to do almost more than was possible for their children.

"It's not doing her any good hanging about by the river at this time of year."

Toby knew how Harriet felt.

"What she would like is to go back to school, wouldn't she, Alec?"

Alec was very like his mother; he had some of her elegance and charm, but as well he had a very strongly developed strain of common sense. He could see that Harriet in her present daddy-long-legs stage was not really well enough for school.

"That's what she wants, but she's not fit for it, is she?"

"No, she needs to exercise those legs of hers. Do they do gymnasium or dancing at her school?"

"Not really," said Olivia. "Just a little ballroom

dancing once a week and physical exercises between classes, you know the sort of thing."

The doctor turned to George.

" Would your finances run to sending her to a dancing school or a gymnasium ? It would have to be a good one where they knew what they were doing."

George cleared his throat. He hated that kind of question, partly because he was a very proud father who wanted to give his children every advantage, and who, except when he was asked direct questions by doctors, tried to pretend he did give them most advantages.

" I don't think I could manage it just now. My father left me a bit, and Olivia will come into quite a lot some day, but just now we're mainly dependent on the shop, and November's a bit of an off-season. You see, my brother William . . ." His voice tailed away.

The doctor, who knew about the shop, felt sorry and filled in the pause by saying " Quite." Then suddenly he had an idea.

" I'll tell you what. How about skating ? The manager of the rink is a patient of mine. I'll have a word with him about Harriet. I'm sure he'd let her in for nothing. There'd be the business of the boots and skates, but I believe you can hire those."

Alec nodded.

" You can. I think skating's a good idea. If you can get your friend to give her a pass we'll manage the boots and skates."

The doctor got up.

" Good. Well, I've got to go and see the manager of the rink to-morrow ; I'll have a word with him ; if he says yes I'll arrange to pick Harriet up and drop her off and introduce her to him. It's no distance, she could have a lot of fun there, plenty of kids, I imagine, go, it's a big, airy place and she can tumble about on the ice and in no time we'll see an improvement in those leg muscles."

George showed the doctor to the door. While he was out of the room Olivia said in a whisper :

" Alec, whatever made you say it would be all right about the skates and boots ? What do you suppose they cost ? "

Toby answered.

" We know what it costs because we went that time Uncle William packed that goose by mistake. They're two shillings a session."

Olivia never lost her air of calm, but she did turn surprised eyes on Alec. He was usually the sensible, reliable one of the family, not at all the sort of person to say they could manage two shillings a day when he knew perfectly well they would be hard put to it to find three-pence a day. Alec gave her a reassuring smile.

" It's all right, I'll find it, there's a lot of delivering and stuff will want doing round Christmas and in the meantime I saw a notice in old Pulton's window. He wants a boy for the paper round."

Olivia flushed, it seemed to her a miserable thing that Harriet's skates and boots had to be earned by her brother instead of by her father and mother.

" I wonder if I could get something to do ? I see advertisements for people wanted, but they always seem to be wanted at the same time as I'm wanted here."

Alec laughed.

" Don't be silly, Mother, you know as well as I do you couldn't do any more than you do."

Toby had been scowling into space ; now he leant across to Alec.

" How much do you suppose boots and skates cost ? If a profit can be made on hiring out a pair of boots and skates at two shillings a session. How much would it cost to buy a second-hand pair outright ? "

Alec was doodling on his blotting paper.

" With what ? "

At that moment George came back.

" Nice fellow Phillipson, he says this skating will be just the thing for Harriet. It's this skates' and boots' money that's worrying me. Do you suppose we could do any good if we opened a needlework section, Olivia ? "

He was greeted by horrified sounds from Olivia, Alec and Toby. Olivia got up and put her arms round his neck.

" I adore you, George, but you are an unpractical old idiot. You haven't yet educated the public to come to you for trout, and be prepared at the same time to buy a bag of half-rotten apples, so how do you think you're going to lure them on to supposing they would also like six dusters and an overall ? "

Alec looked up from his doodling.

" What sort of needlework did you mean, Dad ? "

George looked worried.

" Certainly not dusters and overalls. I seem to remember my grandmother doing some very charming things, fire-screens I believe they were."

Olivia laughed.

" I'm not much of a needlewoman, and I can promise you even if I were to start to-day it would be two years before you would have even one fire-screen, so I think you can count the needlework department out."

Alec put a bundle of newspapers under the arm of the figure he was doodling.

" It's all right, Dad, I'm going to tide us over to start

with by a newspaper round. Old Pulton wants somebody."

Toby had been doing some figures on paper.

" If a newspaper boy is paid two shillings an hour. Reckoning one hour in the morning and one hour in the evening daily for six days, with one hour on Sunday at double time. How long would it take him to earn second-hand boots and skates at a cost of five pounds ? "

Alec said :

" If a boy and a half worked an hour and a half for a skate and a half . . ."

Olivia saw Toby felt fun was being made of a serious subject.

" I'm afraid, Toby, you're going to grow up to be a financier, one of those people who goes in for big business with a capital ' B '."

Alec finished his drawing.

" It wouldn't be a bad thing, we could do with some money in our family. If you were thinking, Toby, I might get Mr. Pulton to advance five pounds for my services, it wouldn't work because I might get ill or something and you're too young to be allowed to do it."

" That's right, darling," Olivia agreed. " It wouldn't be practical anyway to buy boots because Harriet's growing, and probably the moment Alec had bought her the boots they'd be too small. Feet grow terribly fast at her age, especially when you've been ill. I wonder if she's awake ? "

George got up.

" I'll go and see. If she is I'll bring her down. It'll cheer her up to know what's planned for her."

Harriet was awake, and so was Edward. Edward was the good-looking one ; his hair was not sandy like the rest of his family, but bright copper, his eyes were

enormous with greenish lights in them. Strangers stopped
to speak to Edward in the road just because they liked
looking at him, and Edward took shameless pleasure in
his popularity.

"It's disgusting," Alec often told him. "You're a
loathsome show off."

Edward was always quite unmoved, and merely tried
to explain.

"I didn't ask to be good-looking, but I like the things
being good-looking gives me. I was the prince in the
play at school." Toby, when he heard that, had made
noises as if he were being sick. "All right, make noises
if you like, but I did like being the prince. There was
special tea afterwards, for the actors, with ices."

"But you can't like people cooing and gurgling at
you," Toby always protested.

Edward seemed to consider the point.

"I don't know. There's you and Alec off to school and
nobody knows you've been, and nobody cares. There's
me walks up the same street and everybody knows. I
think it's duller to be you."

"It's no good," Alec would say to Toby, "wasting our
breath on the little horror."

"Just a born cad," Toby would agree.

But Edward was neither a horror nor a cad, he was
just of a very friendly disposition, a person who liked
talking and being talked to. Already, although he had
only been seven for one month, he had a good idea of
the sort of people he liked talking to and the sort of
people he did not. He was explaining this to Harriet
when George came up to fetch her.

"It's those silly sort of ladies with little dogs I don't
like, and people like bus conductors I do like."

George went into Edward's room.

" You're supposed to be asleep, my son. Turn over and I'll tuck you in. I'm taking Harriet downstairs."

Edward sat up.

" What for ? She's supposed to be in bed and asleep too."

George pushed Edward down.

" We've got something to tell her." He could feel Edward rising up under his hand to protest that he would like to be told too. " Not to-night, old man, I dare say Harriet'll tell you to-morrow."

It was a cold night, so George not only made Harriet put on her dressing-gown but he rolled her up in an eiderdown and carried her down to the sitting-room. Harriet was surprised to find herself downstairs. She looked round at her family with pleasure.

" Almost it's worth being sent to bed with Edward to be got up again and brought downstairs. What did Dr. Phillipson say ? "

Olivia thought how terribly thin Harriet's face looked, sticking out of a bulgy eiderdown. It made her speak very gently.

" He wants you to take up skating, darling."

Nothing could have surprised Harriet more. She had been prepared to hear that she was to go for rides on the top of a bus, or do exercises every morning, but skating was something she had never thought about. George stroked her hair.

" Dr. Phillipson is arranging for you to get in free."

Alec said :

" So the only expense will be the hiring of your skates and boots, and that's fixed."

Toby looked hopefully at Harriet for some sign that

she was working out the cost of skates and boots, but Harriet never worked out the cost of anything. She just accepted there were things you could afford and things you could not.

" When do I start ? "

Olivia was thankful Harriet seemed pleased.

" To-morrow, darling, probably, but you aren't going alone, the doctor's going to take you."

Harriet tried to absorb this strange turn in her affairs. She knew absolutely nothing about skating ; then suddenly a poster for an ice show swam into her mind. The poster had shown a girl in a ballet skirt skating on one foot, the other foot held high above her head, her arms outstretched. Thinking of this picture Harriet was as startled as if she had been told that to-morrow she would start to be a lion tamer. Could it be possible that she, sitting on her father's knee rolled in an eiderdown, would to-morrow find herself standing on one leg with the foot of the other over her head ? These thoughts brought her suddenly to more practical matters.

" What do I wear to skate, Mummy ? "

Olivia mentally ran a distracted eye over Harriet's wardrobe. She had grown so long in the leg since her illness. There was her school uniform, but that wanted letting down. There were her few frocks made at home. There was the winter party frock cut down from an old dinner dress which had been part of her trousseau. Dimly Olivia connected skating and dancing.

" I don't know, darling, do you think the brown velvet ? "

Harriet thought once more of the poster.

" It hasn't got pants that match, and they would show."

" She must match," said Toby. " She'll fall over a lot when she's learning."

Olivia got up.

" I must go and get our supper. I think to-morrow, darling, you must just wear your usual skirt and jersey ; if you find that's wrong we'll manage something else by the next day."

George stood up and shifted Harriet into a carrying position.

" Come up to bed, Miss Cecilia Colledge."

Harriet's skating ceased to be a serious subject and became funny. Olivia, half-way to the kitchen, turned to laugh.

" My blessed Harriet, what is Daddy calling you ? It's only for exercise, darling."

Alec drew a picture of Harriet on his blotting paper : she was flat on her back with her legs in the air. Under it he wrote, " Miss Harriet Johnson, Skating Star."

Toby gave Harriet's pigtails a pull.

" Queen of the Ice, that's what they'll call you."

George had a big rumbling laugh.

" Queen of the Ice ! I like that. Queen of the Ice ! "

Harriet wriggled.

" Don't laugh, Daddy, it tickles."

But when she got back to bed Harriet found that either the laughing or the thought of skating next day had done her good. Her legs were still cotton-woolish but not quite as cotton-woolish as they had been before her father had fetched her downstairs. Queen of the Ice ! She giggled. The giggle turned into a gurgle. Harriet was asleep.

CHAPTER II

MR. PULTON

★

ALEC called on Mr. Pulton after supper. Mr. Pulton had been born over the newspaper shop and so had his father before him, and likely enough rows of grandfathers before that. Nobody could imagine a time when Pulton's newsagents had not been a landmark in the High Street. By luck, or because Pulton's did not hold with meddling, the shop looked as if it had been there a long time. It was a little, low shop with a bow-fronted window, and there were the remains of some old bottle glass in one pane. Nobody knew Mr. Pulton's Christian name, he had always been just Mr. Pulton to speak to, and C. Pulton when he signed his name. There was a lot of guessing as to what the C. stood for ; local rumour had decided it was Carabas, like the marquess who was looked after by Puss in Boots. There were old men who were at school with Mr. Pulton, who ought to have known his name, but they only remembered he had been called Pip Pulton. This was so unlikely a name for Mr. C. Pulton that nobody believed the old men, and said they were getting on and had forgotten. It was true they were getting on, for anyone who had been at school with Mr. Pulton was rising eighty.

Alec went to Mr. Pulton's back door for the shop was

closed.. He knocked loudly for Mr. Pulton was a little deaf. After a moment there was a shuffling, grunting, wheezing sound, and Mr. Pulton opened the door. He was a very thin, very pale man. His hair was white, and so was his face, which looked as if it had been a face for so long that the colour had been washed out of it, and it had been battered around until it creased and was full of wrinkles. His hands were pale too, long and thin and spidery ; he wore clothes that nobody had ever seen anyone else wear ; a little round brown velvet cap with a tassel hanging down on one side and a brown velvet coat and slippers embroidered with gold and silver thread. His paleness and thinness sticking out of the brown skull cap and brown velvet coat made him look like a delicate white moth, caught in a rough brown hand. There was, however, nothing delicate or mothlike about Mr. Pulton's mind, that was as quick and as tough as a lizard. This showed in his extraordinarily blue, interested, shrewd eyes. His voice was misleading for it matched his body and not his mind. It was a tired voice, which sounded as if it had been used such a lot that it was wearing away. Mr. Pulton looked at Alec and his eyes showed he was remembering who he was, and anything that he knew about him.

" What can I do for you, young man ? " Alec explained that he had come about the paper round. There was a long pause, not a pause of tiredness but a pause in which Alec could feel Mr. Pulton was considering his paper round, and whether he was the sort of boy who could be trusted to deliver papers without bringing dishonour to Pulton's Newsagents. Evidently his thoughts about Alec were nice, for suddenly he said a very surprising thing. " Come inside."

Alec had never been inside Mr. Pulton's house before, and neither, as far as he knew, had anybody else. He had often wanted to go inside, because leaning across the counter waiting for his father's paper he had sometimes seen glimpses of a back room, which seemed to be full of interesting things. Now he was inside the room and he found it even more interesting than he had thought it might be. It was a brownish kind of room, so evidently Mr. Pulton was fond of brown. There were brownish curtains, and brownish chair covers, and brownish walls. There was a gay fire burning, but in spite of it the room was dark because Mr. Pulton had not yet got around to electric light, and could not be bothered with lamps, so he lit his home with candles, which gave a queer, dim, flickering light. In spite of the dimness Alec could see the room was full of pictures, and the pictures were all of horses, which was amazing, for nobody had ever thought of Mr. Pulton as being interested in horses. There were dozens of portraits of horses : race-horses, hunters, shire horses, almost every sort of horse. As well on the top of a bookcase, on brackets and on tables there were bronze models of horses. It seemed such a very horse sort of room that Alec thought it would not be rude to mention it.

" I say, what a lot of horses, sir."

Mr. Pulton picked up a candle. He walked slowly round his walls, his voice took on a proud, affectionate tone, though it still kept its frail, reed-like quality.

" Old Jenny, foaled a Grand National winner, she did. There he is, his portrait was painted the day after, so my father heard, you can see he was proud ; look at him, knows he's won the greatest test of horse and rider ever thought of. That's Vinegar, beautiful grey, went to a

Mr. Pulton picked up a candle

circus, wonderfully matched greys they were. Now there's
a fine creature, you wouldn't know what he was—Suffolk
Punch. It takes all sorts to make up a horse's world, just
as it takes all sorts to make our world ; Suffolk Punches
are country folk, simple in their ways, not asking much
nor wanting changes. Now there's a smart fellow :
Haute École they call that, see his feet ? That's fine
work, that is, takes a clever horse for High School."
He paused by a bronze cast of a horse which was standing
on a small table. He ran his hand over the back of the
cast as if it were alive. "You were a grand horse,
weren't you, old fellow ? My grandfather's he was ; used
to hunt him, he did. My father used to say you were
almost human, didn't he ? Whisky his name was ; clever,

couldn't put a foot wrong. And how he loved it. Why, there's mornings now, especially at this time of year, when there's a nip of frost in the air, and the smell of dropped leaves, I can fancy old Whisky here raising his head, and I can see a look in his eye as if he were saying, ' What's keeping us ? Wonderful morning for a hunt, let's be off.' "

Alec was so interested in the horses and the little bits of their history that Mr. Pulton let drop, that he forgot the paper round, and it was quite a surprise to him when Mr. Pulton, holding up his candle so that he could see Alec's face clearly, said :

" Why do you want my paper round ? Not the type."

" Why not ? I'm honest, sober and industrious."

Mr. Pulton chuckled.

" Maybe, but you haven't answered my question. Why do you want my paper round ? "

Alec, though privately he thought Mr. Pulton was a bit inquisitive, decided he had better explain.

" Well, sir, it's to hire boots and skates for my sister Harriet, who's been ill and . . ."

Mr. Pulton held up a finger to stop Alec.

" Sit down, boy, sit down. At my age you feel your legs, can't keep standing all the time. Besides, I've got my toddy waiting in the fireplace. You like toddy ? . . . No, course you wouldn't. If you go through that door into my kitchen, and open the cupboard, you'll see in the left-hand corner a bottle marked ' Ginger wine.' Nothing like ginger wine for keeping out the cold."

Alec went into the kitchen ; it was a very neat, tidy kitchen, evidently whoever looked after Mr. Pulton did it nicely. He found the cupboard easily, and he brought the bottle of ginger wine and a glass back to the sitting-

room. Mr. Pulton nodded in a pleased way, and pointed
to the chair opposite his own.

" Sit down, boy . . . sit down . . . help yourself. Now
tell me about your sister Harriet."

Mr. Pulton was an easy man to talk to ; he sat sipping
his toddy, now and again nodding his head, and all the
time his interested blue eyes were fixed on Alec. When
Alec had told him everything, including how difficult it
was to make the shop pay because of Uncle William eating
so much, and how Dr. Phillipson thought he could get
Harriet into the rink for nothing, he put down his glass
of toddy, folded his hands, and put on the business face
he wore in his paper shop.

" How much does it cost to hire boots and skates ? "

" Two shillings a session."

Mr. Pulton gave an approving grunt, and shook
himself a little as if he was pleased about something.

" Morning and evening rounds. Good. The last boy
I had would only do mornings, no good in that, never get
into my ways. I pay ten shillings a week for the morning
round, and four shillings for the evening round ; there's
not so much work in the evenings, mostly they buy their
papers from a newsboy on the street, nasty, dirty habit.
Never buy papers from newsboys. You can have the
job."

Alec was reckoning the money in his head. Harriet
would only go to one session of skating a day, that meant
for six days, for there would be no skating on Sunday,
which would cost twelve shillings. That would give him
two shillings over for himself. Two shillings a week !
Because of Uncle William's mixed and irregular supplies
to the shop, it was scarcely ever that he had any pocket
money, and the thought of having two whole shillings a

week made his eyes shine far brighter than Mr. Pulton's candles.

" Thank you, sir. When can I start ? "

" To-morrow. You said your sister was starting skating to-morrow. You'll be here at seven and you'll meet my present paper boy, he'll show you round. You look pleased. Think you'll like delivering papers ? "

Alec felt warm inside from ginger wine, and outside from the fire, and being warm inside and out gives a talkative feeling.

" It's the two shillings. You see, Harriet will only need twelve shillings for her skates, and you said fourteen."

Mr. Pulton had picked up his hot toddy again.

" That's right. What are you going to do with the other two shillings ? "

In the ordinary way Alec would not have discussed his secret plan, the only person who knew it was Toby ; but telling things to Mr. Pulton was like telling things to a person in a dream ; besides, nobody had ever heard Mr. Pulton discuss somebody else's affairs, indeed it was most unlikely that he was interested in anybody's affairs.

" I've no brains. Toby has those, but Dad and Mother think I'll go on at school until I'm eighteen, but I won't, it's a waste of time for me, at least that's what I think. I'd meant to leave school when I was sixteen, and go into something in Dad's line of business. You see, it's absolutely idiotic our depending on Uncle William. Dad doesn't see that, but of course he wouldn't for he's his brother, but you can't really make a place pay when for days on end you get nothing but rhubarb and perhaps a couple of rabbits, and one boiling hen, and then suddenly thousands of old potatoes. You see, Uncle William just rushes out and sends off things he doesn't like the look of, or has got too many of. Now what I want to do is to get a proper set-up. I'd like a pony and cart to go to market and buy the sort of things customers want to eat. What we sell now, and everybody knows it, isn't what customers want but what Uncle William doesn't want. I think knowing that puts people off from buying from Dad."

Mr. Pulton leant back in his chair.

" It'd take a lot of two shillings to buy a pony and trap."

" I know, but I might be able to do something as a start. You see, if I put all the two shillings together, by next spring I'd have a little capital and I could at least try stocking Dad with early potatoes or something of that sort. We never sell new potatoes, Uncle William likes those, so we only get the old ones. If the potatoes went well I might be able to buy peas, beans, strawberries and raspberries in the summer."

" You never have those either ? "

" Of course not, Uncle William hogs the lot."

" You'd like to own a provision store some day ? "

" Glory no ! I'd hate it. What I want is to be at the growing end ; I'd give anything to have the sort of set-up Uncle William's got. There's a decent sized walled fruit and vegetable garden, where you could do pretty well if you went in for cloches, and there's a nice bit of river and there's some rough shooting."

" How does your Uncle William send his produce to your father ? "

Alec looked as exasperated as he felt.

" That's another idiotic thing, we never know how it's coming. Sometimes he has a friend with a car, and we get a telephone message, and Dad has to hare up to somebody's flat to fetch it; mostly it comes by train, but sometimes Uncle William gets a bargee to bring it down; that's simply awful because the stuff arrives bad, and Uncle William can't understand that it arrived bad."

Mr. Pulton had finished his toddy, he got up.

"I am going to bed. Don't forget now, seven o'clock in the morning. Not a minute late. I can't abide boys who come late." He was turning to go when evidently a thought struck him. He nodded in a pleased sort of way. "Stick to your dreams, don't let anyone put you off what you want to do. All these . . ." he swept his hand round the horses, "were my grandfather's and my great grandfather's, just that hunter belonged to my father. When I was your age I dreamed of horses, but there was this newsagency, there's always been a Pulton in this shop. Where are my dreams now? Good-night, boy."

CHAPTER III

THE RINK

*

OLIVIA went to the rink with Harriet, for the more Harriet thought about the girl on the poster, standing on one skate with the other foot high over her head, the more sure she was that she would be shy to go alone to a place where people could do things like that. Dr. Phillipson was very kind, but he was a busy, rushing, tearing sort of man, who would be almost certain merely to introduce her to the manager by just saying, "This is Harriet," and then dash off again. This was exactly what happened. Dr. Phillipson called for Harriet and her mother just after lunch, took them to the rink, hurried them inside into a small office in which was a tired, busy-looking man, said, "This is Harriet, and her mother, Mrs. Johnson, Harriet, this is Mr. Matthews, the manager of the rink. I've got a patient to see," and he was gone.

Olivia took no time to make friends with Mr. Matthews. She heard all about something called his duodenal ulcer, which was why he knew Dr. Phillipson, and all about how Dr. Phillipson had taken out his wife's appendix, and of how Dr. Phillipson had looked after his twin boys, who were grown up now and married, and only when there were no more illnesses left in the Matthews' family to talk about did Olivia mention skating.

" Dr. Phillipson tells me you're going to be very kind and let Harriet come here to skate. He wants her to have exercise for her leg muscles."

Mr. Matthews looked at Harriet's legs in a worried sort of way.

" Thin, aren't they? Ever skated before ? " Harriet explained she had not. " Soon pick it up, I'll show you where you go for your skates and boots. Cost two shillings a session they will." He turned to Olivia. " I'll have a word with my man who hires them out, ask him to find a pair that fit her ; he'll keep them for her, it'll make all the difference."

The way to the skate-hiring place was through the rink. Harriet had never seen a rink before. She gazed with her eyes open very wide at what seemed to her to be an enormous room with ice instead of floor. In the middle of the ice, people, many of whom did not look any older than she was, were doing what seemed to her terribly difficult things with their legs. On the outside of the rink, however, there were a comforting lot of people who seemed to know as little about skating as she did, for they were holding on to the barrier round the side of the rink as if it was their only hope of keeping alive, while their legs did the most curious things in a way which evidently surprised their owners. In spite of holding on to the barrier quite a lot of these skaters fell down and seemed to find it terribly difficult to get up again. Harriet slipped her hand into her mother's and pulled her down so that she could speak to her quietly without Mr. Matthews hearing.

" It doesn't seem to matter not being able to skate here, does it, Mummy ? "

Olivia knew just how Harriet was feeling.

" Of course not, pet. Perhaps some day you'll be as grand a skater as those children in the middle."

Mr. Matthews overheard what Olivia said.

" I don't know so much about that, takes time and money to become a fine skater. See that little girl there."

Harriet followed the direction in which Mr. Matthews was pointing. She saw a girl of about her own age. She was a very grand-looking little girl wearing a white jersey, a short white pleated skirt, white tights, white boots, and a sort of small white bonnet fitting tightly to her head. She was a dark child with lots of loose curly hair and big dark eyes.

" The little girl in white ? "

" That's right, little Lalla Moore, promising child, been brought here for a lesson almost every day since she was three."

Olivia looked pityingly at Lalla.

" Poor little creature ! I can't imagine she wanted to come here when she was three."

Mr. Matthews obviously thought that coming to his rink at the age of three brought credit on the rink, for his voice sounded proud.

" Pushed here in a pram, she was, by her nanny."

" I wonder," said Olivia, " what could have made her parents think she wanted to skate when she was three."

Mr. Matthews started walking again towards the skate-hiring place.

" It's not her parents, they were both killed skating, been brought up by an aunt. Her father was Cyril Moore."

Mr. Matthews said " Cyril Moore " in so important a voice that it was obvious he thought Olivia ought to know who he was talking about. Olivia had never heard of anybody called Cyril Moore but she said in a surprised, pleased tone :

" Cyril Moore ! Fancy ! "

At the skate-hiring place Mr. Matthews introduced Olivia and Harriet to the man in charge.

" This is Sam. Sam, I want you to look after this little girl ; her name is Harriet Johnson, she's a friend of Dr. Phillipson's, and, as you can see from the look of her, she has been ill. Find boots that fit her and keep them for her, she'll be coming every day."

Sam was a cheerful, red-faced man. As soon as Mr. Matthews had gone he pulled forward a chair.

" Sit down, duckie, and let's have a dekko at those feet." He ran a hand up and down Harriet's calves and made disapproving, clicking sounds. " My, my ! Putty, not muscles, these are."

Harriet did not want Sam to think she had been born with flabby legs.

" They weren't always like this, it's because they've been in bed so long with nothing to do. It seems to have made them feel cotton-woolish, but Dr. Phillipson thinks if I skate they'll get all right again. I feel rather despondent about them myself, they've been cotton-woolish a long time."

Sam took one of Harriet's hands, closed it into a fist and banged it against his right leg.

" What about that ? That's my spare, that is, the Japs had the other in Burma. Do you think it worries me ? Not a bit of it. You'd be surprised what I can do with me old spare. I reckon I get around more with one whole leg and one spare than most do with two whole legs. Don't you lose 'eart in yours ; time we've had you on the rink a week or two you'll have forgotten they ever felt like cotton-wool, proper little skater's legs they'll be."

" Like Lalla Moore's ? "

Sam looked surprised.

" Know her ? "

" No, but Mr. Matthews showed her to us, he said she'd been skating since she was three. He said she used to come in a perambulator."

Sam turned as if to go into his shop, then he stopped.

" So she did too, had proper little boots made for her and all. I often wonder what her Dad would say if he could come back and see what they were doing to his kid. Cyril Moore he was, one of the best figure skaters, and one of the nicest men I ever set eyes on. Well, mustn't stay gossiping here, you want to get on the ice."

" Mummy, isn't he nice ? " Harriet whispered. " I should think he's a knowing man about legs, wouldn't you ? He ought to know about them, having had to get used to having one instead of two."

The boots, with skates attached, that Sam found were new. He explained that new boots were stiffer and therefore would be a better support to Harriet's thin ankles. Sam seemed so proud of having found her a pair of boots that were new and a fairly good fit that Harriet tried to pretend she thought they were lovely boots. Actually she thought they were awful. Lalla Moore's beautiful white boots had made Harriet hope she was going to wear white boots too, but the ones Sam put on her were a nasty shade of brown, with a band of green painted round the edge of the soles. Sam was not deceived by her trying to look pleased.

" 'ired boots is all right, but nobody can't say they're oil paintings. If you want them stylish white ones you'll have to buy your own. We buy for hard wear, you'd be surprised the time we make our boots last. Besides, nobody can't make off with these."

Olivia looked puzzled.

" Does anyone want to ? "

" You'd be surprised, but they don't get away with it. If Harriet here was to walk out with these someone would spot the green paint and be after her quicker than you could say winkle."

Olivia laughed.

" I can't see Harriet walking out in these. I'm going to have a job to get her to the rink."

Sam finished lacing Harriet's boots. He gave the right boot an affectionate pat.

" Too right you will. I wasn't speaking personal, I was just explaining why the boots look the way they do." He got up. " Good luck, duckie, enjoy yourself."

If Olivia had not been there to hold her up Harriet would never have reached the rink. Her feet rolled over first to the right, and then to the left. First she clung to Olivia, and then lurched over and clung to a wall. When she came to some stairs that led to the rink it seemed to her as if she must be killed trying to get down them. The skates had behaved badly on the flat floor, but walking downstairs they behaved as if they had gone mad. She reached the bottom by gripping the stair rail with both hands while Olivia held her round her waist, lifting her so that her skates hardly touched the stairs. Olivia was breathless but triumphant when they got to the edge of the rink.

" Off you go now. I'll sit here and get my breath back."

Harriet gazed in horror at the ice. The creepers and crawlers who were beginners like herself clung so desperately to the barrier that she could not see much room to get in between them. Another thing was that even if she could find a space it was almost certain that one of the creepers and crawlers in front or behind her would choose that moment to fall over and knock her down at the same time. As a final terror, between the grand skaters in the middle of the rink and the creepers and crawlers round the edge, there were the roughest people. They seemed to go round and round like express trains, their chins stuck forward, their hands behind their backs, with apparently no other object than to see how fast they could go, and they did not seem to mind who they knocked over as they went. Gripping both sides of an opening in the barrier Harriet put one foot towards the ice and hurriedly took it back. This happened five times. Olivia was sympathetic but firm.

" I'm sorry, darling, I'd be scared stiff myself, but it's no good wasting all the afternoon holding on to the barrier and never getting on to the ice. Be brave and take the plunge."

Harriet looked as desperate as she felt.

" Would you think I'd feel braver if I shut my eyes ? "

" No, darling, I think that would be fatal, someone would be bound to knock you down."

It was at that moment that Olivia felt a tap on her shoulder. She turned round. Behind her sat an elderly lady looking rather like a cottage loaf. She wore a grey coat and skirt which bulged over her chest to make the top half of the loaf, and over her tail and front to make the bottom half. On her head she wore a neat black straw hat ; she was knitting what looked as if it would be a jersey, in white wool.

" If you'll wait a moment, ma'am, I'll signal to my little girl, she'll take her on to the ice for you."

" Isn't that kind ! Which is your little girl ? "

The lady stood up. Standing up she was even more like a cottage loaf than she had been when she was sitting down. She waved her knitting.

" She's not really mine, I'm her nurse."

From the centre of the ring the waving was answered. Harriet nudged her mother.

" Lalla Moore."

Lalla cared nothing for people who went round pretending they were express trains, or for creepers and crawlers, she came flying across the rink as if she were running across an empty field.

" What is it, Nana ? "

" This little girl, dear." Nana turned to Harriet. " You won't have been on the ice before, will you, dear ? "

Harriet was gazing at Lalla.

" No, and I don't really want to now. The doctor says I've got to, it's to stop my legs being cotton-wool."

Nana looked at Harriet's legs wearing an I-thought-as-much expression.

" Take her carefully, Lalla, don't let her fall."

Lalla took hold of Harriet's hands. She moved backwards. Suddenly Harriet found she was on the ice.

" You'll have to try and straighten your legs a little, because then I can tow you."

Harriet's knees and ankles hadn't been very good at standing straight on an ordinary floor since she had been ill, but in skates and boots it was terribly difficult. But Lalla had been skating for so long she could not see anything difficult about standing up on skates, and, because she did not find anything difficult about it, Harriet began to believe it could not be as difficult as it looked. Presently,

Lalla skating backwards, had towed her into the centre of the rink.

"There, now I'll show you how to start. Put your feet apart." With great difficulty Harriet got her feet into the sort of position that Lalla wanted. "Now lift them up. First your right foot. Put it down on the ice. Now your left foot. Now put it down."

Lalla took hold of Harriet's hands

Nana, having asked Olivia's permission to do so, had moved into the seat next to her. First of all they discussed Harriet's illness and her leg muscles. Then Olivia said :

"Mr. Matthews pointed out your child to us. I hear she's been skating since she was a baby ; you used to push her here in a perambulator, didn't you ? "

Nana laid her knitting in her lap. She could hear from Olivia's tone she thought it odd teaching a baby to skate.

" So I did too, and I didn't like it. I never have held with fancy upbringing for my children, and I never will."

" But her father was a great skater, wasn't he ? "

" He was Cyril Moore. But maybe your father was a great preacher, ma'am, but that isn't to say you want to spend all your life preaching."

Olivia laughed.

" My father has a citrus estate in South Africa, and I've certainly never wanted to spend all my life growing oranges and lemons."

" Nor would her father have wanted skating as a baby for Lalla. Bless him, he was a lovely gentleman and so was her mother a lovely lady."

" What happened to them ? "

" Well, he was the kind of gentleman that must always be doing something dangerous. He only had to see a board up saying ' Don't skate, danger ' and he was on the ice in a minute. That's how he went, and poor Mrs. Moore with him. Seems he was on a pond ; they say there was a warning out the ice wouldn't bear, but anyway they both popped through it, and were never seen alive again."

" Oh, dear, what a sad story, and who is bringing little Lalla up ? "

Nana's voice took on a reserved tone.

" Her Aunt Claudia, her father's only sister."

" And she was the one who decided to make a skater of her ? "

" It's a memorial, so she says. Lalla wasn't two years old the winter her parents popped through that thin ice. I'll never forget it, her Aunt Claudia moved into the house, and the very first thing she did was to have a glass case made for the skates and boots her father was drowned in. She put it up over my blessed lamb's cot. 'With all respect, ma'am,' I said, 'I don't think it's wholesome, we don't want her growing up to brood on what's happened.' And do you know what she said? 'He's to live again in Lalla, Nana, he was a wonderful skater, but Lalla is to be the greatest skater in the world.' "

Olivia, enthralled with the story, had forgotten about Harriet. She turned now to look at the two children.

" I don't know whether she's going to be the greatest skater in the world, but she certainly seems to be a wonderful teacher. Look at my Harriet."

Nana was silent a moment watching the two children.

" We'll call them back in a minute. Harriet shouldn't be at it too long, not the first time. They say Lalla's coming on wonderfully, she's got her bronze medal, you know, and she isn't quite ten."

Olivia had no idea what a bronze medal was for but she could hear from Nana's tone it was something important.

" Isn't that splendid ! "

" It's a funny life for a child, and not what I expect in my nurseries. She has to do so much time on the ice every day, so she can't go to school or anything like that ; governesses and tutors she has as well, of course, as being coached here every day by Mr. Lindblom."

" It must cost a terrible lot of money."

" Well, what with what her parents left her, and her Aunt Claudia marrying a rich man, there's enough."

" She has got a step-uncle, has she ? "

Nana was knitting again ; she smiled at the wool in a pleased way.

" Yes, indeed. Her Uncle David. Mr. David King he

is, and as nice a gentleman as you could wish to find, I couldn't ask for better."

Olivia was glad to hear that Lalla had a nice step-uncle because somehow, from the tone of Nana's voice, she was not certain she would like her Aunt Claudia. However, it was not fair to make up her mind about somebody she had never met, and anyway probably Lalla enjoyed the skating.

" I expect the skating's fun for her, even if she has to miss school and have governesses and tutors because of it."

" She enjoys it well enough, bless her, I'm not saying she doesn't, but it's not what I would choose in a manner of speaking." Nana got up. " I'm going to signal the children to come off the ice, for, if you don't mind my mentioning it, your little Harriet has done more than enough for the time being ; she better sit down beside me and have a glucose sweet the same as I give my Lalla."

The moment she sat down Harriet found her legs were much more cotton-woolish than they had been before. They felt so tired she did not know where to put them, and kept wriggling about. Nana noticed this.

" You'll get used to it, dearie, everybody's legs get tired at first."

Olivia looked anxiously at Harriet.

" Perhaps that had better be all for to-day, darling."

Harriet was shocked at the suggestion.

" Mummy ! Two whole shillings' worth of hired boots and skates used up in quarter of an hour ! We couldn't, we simply couldn't."

" It can't be helped if you're tired, darling. It's better to waste part of the two shillings than to wear the poor legs out altogether." Olivia turned to Nana. " I'm sure you agree with me."

Nana had a cosy way of speaking, as if while she was about nothing could ever go very wrong.

"That's right, ma'am. More haste less speed, so I've always said in my nurseries." She smiled at Harriet. "You sit down and have another glucose sweet and presently Lalla will take you on the ice for another five minutes. That'll be enough for the first day."

Lalla looked pleadingly at Nana.

"Could I, oh, could I stay and talk to Harriet, Nana?"

Nana looked up from her knitting.

"It'll mean making the time up afterwards. You know Mr. Lindblom said you was to work at your eight-foot one."

Lalla laughed.

"One foot eight, Nana." She turned to Harriet. "Nana never gets the name of the figures right."

Nana was quite unmoved by this criticism.

"Nor any reason why I should, never having taken up ice skating nor having had the wish."

"Harriet would never have taken up ice skating, nor had the wish either," said Olivia, "if it hadn't been for her legs. I believe two of my sons came here once, but that's as near as the Johnsons have ever got to skating."

Lalla was staring at Olivia with round eyes.

"Two of your sons! Has Harriet got brothers?" Harriet explained about Alec, Toby and Edward. Lalla sighed with envy. "Lucky, lucky you. Three brothers! Imagine, Nana! I'd rather have three brothers than anything else in the world."

Nana turned her knitting round and started another row.

"No good wishing. If you were to have three brothers,

you'd have to do without a lot of things you take for granted now."

"I wouldn't mind. I wouldn't mind anything. You know, Harriet, it's simply awful being only one, there's nobody to play with."

Olivia felt sorry for Lalla.

"Perhaps, Nana, you would bring her to the house sometime to play with Harriet and the boys; it isn't a big house, and there are a lot of us in it, but we'd love to have her and you, too, of course."

"Bigness isn't everything," said Nana. "Some day, if the time could be made, it would be a great treat."

Harriet looked with respect at Lalla. Even when she had gone to school she had always had time to do things. She could not imagine a life when you had to make time to go out to tea. Lalla saw Harriet's expression.

"It's awful how little time I get. I do lessons in the morning, then there is a special class for dancing or fencing, then, directly after lunch, we come here and, with my lesson and the things I have to practise, I'm always here two hours and sometimes three. By the time I get home and have had tea it's almost bedtime."

Olivia thought this a very sad description of someone's day who was not yet ten.

"There must be time for a game or something before bedtime, isn't there? Don't you play games with your aunt?"

Lalla looked surprised at the question.

"Oh, no, she doesn't play my sort of games. She goes out and plays bridge and things like that. When I see her we talk about skating, nothing else."

"She's very interested in how Lalla's getting on," Nana explained, "but Lalla and I have a nice time before she goes to bed, don't we, dear? Sometimes we listen to the wireless, and sometimes, when Uncle David and Aunt Claudia are out, we go downstairs and look at that television."

Olivia tried to think of something to say, but she couldn't. It seemed to her a miserable description of Lalla's evenings. Nana was a darling, but how much more fun it would be for Lalla if she could have somebody of her own age to play with. She was saved answering by Lalla.

"Are your legs better enough now to come on the rink, Harriet?"

Harriet stretched out first one leg and then the other to see how cotton-woolish they were. They were still a bit feeble, but she was not going to disgrace herself in front of Lalla by saying so. She tottered up on to her skates. Lalla held out her hands. "I'll take you to the middle of the rink but this time you'll have to lift up your feet by yourself, I'm not going to hold you. Don't mind if you fall down, it doesn't hurt much."

Olivia watched Harriet's unsteady progress to the middle of the rink.

"How lucky for her that she met Lalla. It would have taken her weeks to have got a few inches round the edge by herself. She's terrified, poor child, but she won't dare show it in front of Lalla."

Nana went on knitting busily, her voice showed that she was not quite sure she ought to say what she was saying.

"When I get the chance I'll have a word with Mrs. King about Harriet, or maybe with Mr. King, he's the one for seeing things reasonably. It would be a wonderful thing for Lalla if you would allow Harriet to come back to tea sometimes after the skating. It would be such a treat for her to have someone to play with."

"Harriet would love it, but I am afraid it is out of the question for some time yet. I'm afraid coming here and walking home will be about all she can manage. The extra walk to and from your house would be too much for her at present."

"There wouldn't be any walking. We'd send her home in the car. Mrs. King drives her own nearly always, and Mr. King his own, so the chauffeur's got nothing to do except drive Lalla about in the little car."

Olivia laughed.

"How very grand! I'm afraid I'll never be able to ask you to our house. Three cars and a chauffeur! I'm certain Mrs. King would have a fit if she saw how we lived."

"Lot of foolishness. Harriet's a nice little girl, and just the friend for Lalla. You leave it to me. Mrs. King has her days, and I'll pick a good one before I speak of Harriet to her or Mr. King."

Walking home Olivia asked Harriet how she had enjoyed skating. She noticed with happiness that Harriet was looking less like a daddy-long-legs than she had since her illness started.

"It was gorgeous, Mummy, but of course it was made gorgeous by Lalla. I do like her. I hope her Aunt Claudia will let me go to tea. Lalla's afraid she won't, and she's certain she won't let her come to tea with us."

"You never know. Nana says she has her days, and she's going to try telling her about you on one of her good days."

Harriet said nothing for a moment. She was thinking about Lalla, Nana and Aunt Claudia, and mixed up with thinking of them was thinking about telling her father, Alec, Toby and Edward about them. Suddenly she stood still.

" Mummy, mustn't it be simply awful to be Lalla ? Imagine going home every day with no one to talk to, except Nana, who knows what's happened because she was there all the time. Wouldn't you think to be only one like Lalla was the most awful thing that could happen to anybody ? "

Olivia thought of the three cars and the chauffeur, and Lalla's lovely clothes, and of the funny food they had to eat at home, and the shop that never paid. Then she thought of George and the boys, and the fun of hearing about Alec's first day on the paper round, and how everybody would want to know about Harriet's afternoon at the rink. Perhaps it was nicer to laugh till you were almost sick over the queer shop-leavings you had to eat, than to have the grandest dinner in the world served in lonely state to two people in a nursery. She squeezed Harriet's hand.

" Awful. Poor Lalla, we must make a vow, Harriet. Aunt Claudia or no Aunt Claudia let's make friends with Lalla."

CHAPTER IV

LALLA'S HOUSE

★

LALLA'S house was the exact opposite of Harriet's house. It was not far away, but in a much grander neighbourhood. It was a charming, low, white house lying back in a big garden, with sloping lawns leading down to the river. Where the lawn and the river joined there was a little landing stage, to which, in the summer, Lalla's Uncle David kept his motor launch tied. Lalla's rooms were at the top of the house. A big, low room looking over the river, which had been her nursery, was now her schoolroom, and another big room next to it, which had been her night nursery, was now her bedroom. As well there was a room for Nana and a bathroom. Her bedroom was the sort of bedroom that most girls of her age would like to have. The carpet was blue and the bedspread and curtains white with wreaths of pink roses tied with blue ribbons on them, and there was a frill of the same material round her dressing-table. The only ugly thing in the room was the glass case over her bed in which the skates and boots in which her father was drowned were kept. The nicest skating boots in the world are not ornamental, and these, although they had been polished, looked as though someone had been drowned in them, for the black leather had got a brownish-

green look. Underneath the case was a plaque which
Aunt Claudia had put up. It had the name of Lalla's
father on it, the date on which he was born, and the date
on which he was drowned, and underneath that he was
the world's champion figure skater. Above the case Aunt
Claudia had put some words from the Bible : " Go, and
do thou likewise." This made people smile for it sounded
rather as if Aunt Claudia meant Lalla to be drowned.
Lalla did not care whether anybody smiled at the glass
case or not, for she thought it idiotic keeping old skates
and boots in a glass case, and knew from what Nana had
told her that her father and mother would have thought
it idiotic ; in fact she was sure everybody thought it
idiotic except Aunt Claudia.

The schoolroom, which Lalla sometimes forgot to call
the schoolroom and called the nursery, was another very
pretty room. It had a blue carpet and blue walls, lemon-
yellow curtains and lemon-yellow seats to the chairs, and
cushions to the window seats. It still had proper nursery
things like Lalla's rocking-horse and dolls' house, and a
toy cupboard simply bulging with toys, but as well it had
low bookcases, full of books, pretty china ornaments, good
pictures and a wireless set. The only things which did not
go with the room were on a shelf which ran all down one
wall, this was full of the silver trophies that her father
had won. It is a very nice thing to win silver trophies,
but a great many of them all together do not look pretty ;
the only time Lalla liked the trophies was at Christmas,
because then she filled them with holly, and they looked
gay. Although every trophy and medal had her father's
name on it, where he had won it, what for, and the date
on which it had been won, Aunt Claudia was afraid Lalla
might forget to read the inscriptions, which was sensible

of her because Lalla certainly would not have read them, so underneath the whole length of the shelf was a quotation from Sir Walter Scott altered by Aunt Claudia to fit a girl by changing " his " and " him " into " her ". " Her square-turn'd joints and strength of limb, Show'd her no carpet knight so trim, But in close fight a champion grim." When Aunt Claudia came to the nursery she would sometimes read the lines out loud in a very grand acting way. She hoped hearing them said like that would inspire Lalla to further effort, but all it did was to make Lalla decide that she would never read any book by Sir Walter Scott. Sometimes Lalla and Nana had a little joke about the verse ; Lalla would jump out of her bed or her bath and fling herself on Nana saying " Her square-turn'd joints and strength of limb " and then she would butt Nana with her head and say " That butt never came from a carpet knight, did it ? "

On the day that Lalla met Harriet she and Nana had an exceptionally gay tea. Nana had let Lalla do what she loved doing, which was kneeling by the fire making her own toast, instead of having it sent up hot and buttered from the kitchen, which meant the top slice had hardly any butter on it because it had run through to the bottom one. They talked about Harriet and the rink. Lalla in an excited way and Nana rather cautiously. Lalla laughed at Nana and said she was being " mimsy-pimsy " and asked if it was because she didn't like the Johnsons. Nana shook her head.

" I liked them very much, dear ; Mrs. Johnson's a real lady, as anyone can see, and little Harriet, for all she's so shabby, has been brought up as a little lady should. But I don't want you to go fixing your heart on having her here. You know what it is, your Aunt Claudia has got strict ideas of who you should know, and I don't think, if she was to see Harriet, she would think she was your sort, not having the money to live as you do." Nana could see this was going to make Lalla angry, so she added : "Now don't answer back, dear, you know I'm speaking sense. I don't think it matters about what money a person has, no more than you do, but your

Lalla was kneeling by the fire making her own toast

Aunt's your guardian, and she sets great store by money, and you know you've been brought up never to want for anything, so you must be a good girl and not mind too much if you're not allowed to have Harriet here."

"But I want to go to Harriet's house. I want to be in a family."

"I dare say, but maybe want will have to be your master. The one that pays the piper calls the tune, and the piping in this house is done by your Aunt Claudia, and you know it."

Nana had only just finished saying this when the door opened and Aunt Claudia walked in. Nana was swallowing a sip of tea, and she was so upset at Aunt Claudia having so narrowly missed hearing what she had said that she choked. Lalla thought this funny and began to giggle. Aunt Claudia did not like either choking or giggling, and her voice sounded as though she did not. She was a very nice-looking aunt in a hard sort of way. She had fair hair that looked as if it had been gummed into place, because there was never one hair out of order ; her face was always beautifully made up, so that cold winds, hot weather, even colds in the head, never made any difference to it. She wore beautiful, expensive clothes and lovely jewels. Although she felt annoyed to find Nana choking and Lalla giggling, she did not let it show on her face, because she knew that made wrinkles. The only place where it showed was in her blue eyes, which had a sparkish look.

" Good-evening, Nurse. Can't you control that noise, Lalla, I don't think you should find it funny when Nurse is choking." She waited till Nana's last choke died away, and Lalla had stifled her giggles. " I don't seem to have seen you all the week, and I've got a few minutes before I go out, so I thought I'd hear how your skating is progressing. Have you mastered the one foot eight ? "

Lalla was not being very quick at the one foot eight because she was not trying hard enough.

" It's not right yet, at least not right enough for Mr. Lindblom, but I'm working at it, aren't I, Nana ? "

Nana was glad that after Harriet had gone she had sent Lalla back to work at that figure. It would have

been difficult for her to sound convincing if what she
could remember was Lalla holding up Harriet while
Harriet lifted first one foot and then the other off the ice.

" She worked nicely to-day, ma'am. I'm sure you
would be pleased with her."

Aunt Claudia pulled up an arm-chair to the fire and
sat down.

" Why to-day? Surely every day. You are so lucky,
Lalla ; how many thousands of girls throughout the
country would envy you your opportunities to learn, and
your gift ? "

Lalla had heard this kind of thing so often that it went
in at one ear and out at the other.

" They're awfully difficult figures for the inter-silver."

Aunt Claudia beckoned to her. Lalla came to her unwillingly. Aunt Claudia drew her down to sit on the
arm of her chair.

" That's not the eager face I like to see. I know you
don't care for figure skating as you do for free skating,
but you know as well as I do that you've got to know
all these figures to perfection before you can become world
champion."

Lalla wriggled.

" Suppose I never was world champion, it would seem
mean to have spent such ages learning figures."

Aunt Claudia forgot her make-up and frowned. Her
voice was severe.

" Lalla ! You know I don't like that kind of talk. You
will be a world champion. Already you're the most
gifted child in the country. I know that in your heart
of hearts you live for nothing else but your skating, but
sometimes you say things which hurt me very much. You
are dedicated to follow in your father's footsteps and you

know it." She raised her eyes to the silver cups. Lalla,
knowing what was coming, looked over her shoulder at
Nana and made a face. Aunt Claudia took a deep breath
and raised her voice: " ' Her square-turn'd joints and
strength of limb, Show'd her no carpet knight so trim,
But in close fight a champion grim.' " Nana's reverent
" And very nice too, ma'am," sounded almost like Amen.

Aunt Claudia got up and shook out her skirts.

" Well, I must be going to my cocktail party." She
held Lalla's hand and led her towards the door. At the
door she turned and pointed again to the cups.

" Cyril Moore's daughter. Lalla Moore, world
champion. We'll make his name live again, won't we,
dear? Good-night. Good-night, Nurse."

After Aunt Claudia had gone Lalla came back to the
table to finish her tea, but it wasn't a gay tea any more,
the toast didn't taste as good as when Aunt Claudia
came in. Nana saw Lalla was playing about with her
toast.

" It's no good worrying, dear. You can only do the
best you can."

Lalla stabbed at her toast with her knife.

" You say that because nobody thought when you were
nearly ten that you had got to be a world champion at
anything."

Nana thought back to her childhood. She saw herself
and her eight brothers and sisters sitting round the table
at the lodge of the big house where her father was
gardener, and she heard him, in her memory, say as he
had said very often when she was little : " I don't mind
what work any of you do as long as you have your feet
under somebody else's table." This meant they should
take jobs where their homes were provided, and their

breakfast, dinner, lunch and tea, so that all the money they earned, even if it was not very much, they had to spend on other things besides living. She remembered the cosy feeling it had given her when her father had said that, because she had always meant to go into service, to work in a nursery, so what her father wanted she wanted, and nothing could have been nicer. She was sorry for Lalla ; she thought it must be terrible to have to be the best lady champion skater in the world, and sometimes trembled to think what would happen if Lalla did not manage to be. Lalla loved skating when she could do what she liked, but Mr. Lindblom often had to scold her about the way she did figures, and sometimes she had heard him say : " You are not trying, Lalla. You could do it if you worked." Every time he said things like that Nana's heart gave a jump, and she thought how lucky it was that Aunt Claudia was not at the rink to hear him. She got up.

" I'll clear the tea. What are you going to do till bedtime ? That jigsaw puzzle ? "

Lalla turned on the wireless, but there was nothing happening that she was in the mood to hear, so she turned it off again and wandered out into the passage, feeling cross and loose-endish. She hung over the banisters and watched Aunt Claudia go downstairs dressed for a cocktail party. She admired Aunt Claudia's clothes very much and thought how nice it would be to be grown up, going to parties whenever you liked, wearing a mink coat. She heard Aunt Claudia speak to the parlourmaid. " Tell Mr. King I did wait, will you, Wilson, but I went on without him, and will he please follow me, he knows where the party is." Wilson said, "Yes, ma'am," opened the front door and then shut it. Lalla liked Wilson, so she slid down the banisters to her on her tummy. Wilson watched her arrive and made clicking, disapproving sounds.

" If I was your Nana I'd take a strap to you if I saw you doing that. Look at the front of your white jersey ! "

Lalla put her arm through Wilson's.

" Do you think Uncle David's going to the cocktail party ? "

Wilson's eyes twinkled.

" Not if he can help it, he won't. You know what he thinks of them." She lowered her voice. " I didn't say so to your Aunty, but when he was going out this morning he said to me, ' I think I shall be kept at work to-night, Wilson, so I'll be too late to go to the party Mrs. King's going to, you'd better put drinks in my study.' "

Lalla gave a pleased skip.

" Good. I shall come down and talk to him."

On the days when Aunt Claudia was out alone, Lalla often came down and talked to her step-uncle. Uncle David was a long, thin man with dark hair and blue eyes. He had always wanted to have a daughter, so he was pleased that Aunt Claudia had a baby girl ward. From the very beginning he had been fond of Lalla, and as she grew older and became more of a companion, he got fonder still ; but he had to keep what friends he and Lalla were a secret from Aunt Claudia, for from Aunt Claudia's point of view he was not a suitable friend for Lalla, for he had a great failing. No matter how often Aunt Claudia explained to him about Lalla's father, nor how often she repeated to him the praise and nice things people at the rink said about Lalla, she could not make him take Lalla's skating seriously. He was the sort of man who thought skating, like games, was a lovely hobby, but a nuisance when you tried to be first-class at it. Obviously, feeling as she did about skating for Lalla, Aunt Claudia did not like that sort of talk in front of her, so she did not let her see more of her step-uncle than she could help.

Uncle David was sitting on the leather top of his fender, drinking a whisky and soda, when Lalla came in. He was pleased to see her.

"How's the seventh wonder of the world this evening?"

Lalla did not mind being teased by Uncle David. She sat down next to him on the top of the fender, and told him about her afternoon and how she had met Harriet.

"You can't think how nice she is. She's just the same age as me, but taller, but that's because she's been in bed for months and months, so her legs have got very long. She is so thin." Lalla held up her hands about twelve inches apart. "Even the thickest part of her is not thicker than that, and she's got the most gorgeous mother called Mrs. Johnson and she's got three brothers and a father. Oh, I do envy her, I wish I had three brothers." She looked up anxiously at Uncle David. "I want awfully for her to come to tea with me, and me to go to tea with her; Nana thinks I won't be able to because she isn't rich like we are. Can you think of any way which would make her being poor not matter to Aunt Claudia?"

Uncle David was a sensible sort of man, he never treated Lalla as if, because she was a child, she was more silly than a grown-up. He lit a cigarette while he thought over what she had said.

"What's the father?"

Lalla lowered her voice.

"Nana doesn't know, but it's some sort of a shop."

Uncle David whispered back:

"You and I don't care how anyone earns their living,

do we, as long as it's honest? But I don't think your Aunt's going to cotton on to a shop."

"I think it's rather an odd sort of shop. Harriet said they only sold things that their Uncle William grew or shot or caught on his land in the country. And that was why they were so poor, because her Uncle William eats a lot so they only get what's left."

Uncle David was gazing at the carpet, as if by looking at it very hard he could see into the past.

"William Johnson. William Johnson. That strikes a note, I suppose Harriet didn't say what her father's Christian name was?"

"It's George. Harriet said that Alec, the eldest of her brothers, real name's George, but he's called Alec because he couldn't have the same Christian name as his father."

Uncle David got up and began pacing up and down the carpet.

"William and George Johnson. Shiver my timbers, but that strikes a note somewhere." Suddenly he swung round to Lalla. "I have it! You ask your Harriet where her father went to school. There were a couple of brothers at my prep. school, William and George. If it's the same we might be able to do something."

Lalla looked puzzled.

"Would it make it better that Harriet's father has a shop because he went to the same school as you?"

Uncle David nodded.

"I can't tell you why, but it does." He looked at the clock. "You'd better be skipping, poppet, don't want to blot your copybook by your being caught in here." He gave her a kiss. "I like the sound of your Harriet; I'll have a word with Nana about her, and if it's the same George that I knew, I'll talk your Aunt into letting you

know her. It's time you had somebody of your own age
to play with."

Lalla rushed up the stairs, her eyes shining, and flung
her arms round Nana's neck.

" Oh, Nana, if only it was to-morrow afternoon now.
Uncle David thinks he was at school with Harriet's
father, and if he was he's going to make Aunt Claudia
let me know her. Isn't that the most gorgeous thing you
ever heard ? "

CHAPTER V

AUNT CLAUDIA

*

HARRIET'S father had been at the same school as Uncle David. It did not take Lalla long to find this out, but it took what seemed to Lalla months and months, and was really only three weeks, before Uncle David had managed to see Harriet's father. Although Lalla thought Uncle David was being terribly slow, he was really doing his best. First of all he went to Nana and asked what she thought of Harriet, and on learning that Nana had liked both her and Olivia, he made inquiries about the Johnsons and the shop. He tried to find some way in which he could meet George Johnson in the ordinary way, for he was certain that if he could produce Harriet's father as an old school friend, and not as somebody who kept a peculiar sort of shop, it was much more likely that Aunt Claudia would think Harriet a good friend for Lalla. Meanwhile, whatever Aunt Claudia might think, Lalla and Harriet met every day at the rink, and every day they became greater friends.

Apart from meeting Lalla, Harriet was beginning to enjoy the rink. Every afternoon, just before the session started, she arrived, saw Sam, collected her skates and boots, put them on and was waiting, her eyes on the entrance, for Lalla and Nana several minutes before they

64

could possibly arrive. If there had been no Lalla, Harriet would have taken twice as long learning to enjoy skating. Probably, if there had been no Lalla, she would still have been at the stage of creeping on to the rink, afraid to move far for fear of being knocked down. Because of Lalla's lessons she had discovered quickly that moving about on ice was not really frightening, and that even cotton-woolish legs like her own could make skates move in the direction they wanted them to. Lalla was determined to make Harriet a skater. She could not spare much time from her own practice to give her a lesson, but she took her round with her to get her used to moving on skates, and she saw she only rested when there was dancing, and spent the afternoon moving round by herself.

" I know it's dull just moving along like that, but you've got to do it, Harriet, or you'll never get on to anything more interesting. Your legs look heaps better since you've come skating, honestly they do."

Harriet knew that not only her legs, but all the rest of her looked better since she had come skating. Everybody at home remarked on it, and Dr. Phillipson, when he came to see her, was so pleased that he said he should visit Mr. Matthews an extra time as a thank offering. Harriet thought that was a very odd sort of thank offering, because she would not have wanted a visit from the doctor as 'a thank-you present herself; but she was glad Dr. Phillipson was so pleased that he wanted to thank Mr. Matthews, and if Mr. Matthews liked a visit from the doctor she was glad he should have it. The person who was most proud of Harriet looking so much better was Alec. He felt as though it was he who was making her well, for after all it was his two shillings which paid for the skates, and so when it was wet and cold while he was on his paper round he did not mind as much as he might have done.

" It'd be much worse the weather being awful," he told Toby, " if Harriet wasn't getting any better, I should feel then it was all for nothing."

Toby peered at Alec through his spectacles.

" Mathematically speaking, if Harriet was not getting well, that fact would be cancelled out by the two shillings weekly towards vegetables for the spring."

Alec told Toby to shut up with his mathematical nonsense, but all the same he agreed with him about the two shillings a week. Two shillings a week adds up quickly when it is put in a money-box. Besides, to Alec it was more than two shillings a week, it was adventure, the capital that was to start him out on a magnificent career. On scraps of paper in his pockets, in his bedroom and in his desk at school were plans of how he intended his father's shop to look. There were arrows pointing to piles of fruit and vegetables. Each plan covered a different season of the year, and each was so ambitious that had he been able to buy all the things for his plan his father's shop would have looked like an exhibition of fruit and vegetables at a flower show. His vision of what he would buy in the spring was helped by Mr. Pulton, who sometimes said to him when he paid him on Saturdays :

" Twelve shillings for your sister's skates, and two shillings for your dreams."

The way Mr. Pulton said " two shillings for your dreams " dedicated the two shillings for the money-box. Although he wanted many things Alec was not tempted to spend because, apart from wanting a full money-box for himself, he would have felt he had let himself down in Mr. Pulton's eyes if he knew he had been buying anything.

What with Harriet's skating, and Alec's paper round there was a lot to talk about in the evenings. After the first week's skating Harriet looked so much better that the indignity of going to bed at half-past six with Edward came to an end, and she was allowed to stay up till seven o'clock. Edward was rather annoyed about this.

" I liked Harriet coming to bed the same time as me. I don't think there ever ought to be a minute in anybody's day when they can't be talking to somebody. Now there's me all alone, waiting and waiting for somebody to talk to, and I don't like it."

One night when Harriet had been skating just over three weeks, George came in from a meeting of the ex-serviceman's association to which he belonged. He told Harriet that he had met Lalla's step-uncle there, and what a nice man he seemed to be. Of course everybody in the Johnson family had known every single thing about Lalla since the first day Harriet had met her, and each day had been a continuation of the Lalla story. What Lalla had worn, what Lalla had said, how Lalla had skated, and what Nana had said. The only part of the Lalla story the Johnsons had not heard was the part that Harriet did not know, which was that the reason it was taking so long for Lalla to come to Harriet's house or Harriet to go to Lalla's, was because Lalla's Uncle David thought Aunt Claudia might not approve of a shop, for of course Lalla had not told Harriet that. If the Johnsons had known that Aunt Claudia might not have approved of the shop they would have thought it very funny, first because they would have thought it silly of Aunt Claudia to be so snobbish, and secondly because they did not like the shop themselves.

" He hasn't changed much," George told Harriet. " I remember him perfectly. He told me that Lalla has done nothing but talk about you, and he thought I was going to turn out to be the George Johnson he had been at school with, and that he came to the meeting to-night especially to meet me. He's going to talk to Lalla's Aunt about you because he thinks it would be nice now that you're skating every afternoon if you could sometimes go to tea with Lalla, and that she might sometimes come here."

After Harriet had gone to bed, and while the boys were out of the room, George told Olivia a few other things.

" He remembered William quite well too, he asked after him and called him by a nickname which I had forgotten ; he called him ' Guzzle Johnson.' "

Olivia laughed.

" I wish I could tell the children, they would simply love to call him Uncle Guzzle."

George did not answer that, because he knew that Olivia knew he was fond of William and would not have him called " Uncle Guzzle " by anybody.

" I gather that Lalla Moore's aunt likes the child's nose kept to the grindstone ; she's got the makings of a champion skater, and she's not been allowed friends because there's not much time for them."

Olivia thought of the conversation she had had with Nana.

" Poor little pet, she had to start skating when she was three. Imagine, she was pushed there in a pram."

" It's difficult, I gather, for David King to interfere, only a step-uncle, but he's very fond of the child and would like her to have a better time. I rather gather he's going to suggest to his wife that Harriet would be a good influence for Lalla, skating enthusiast and all that."

Olivia, who had not seen Harriet skating since she started, laughed.

"Poor darling Harriet . . . a skating enthusiast ! When she is on the ice she grips Lalla as if she was the only branch to catch hold of before she dropped over a cliff."

Uncle David, having seen George, did not waste his time. That very evening he told Aunt Claudia about him.

"Met a nice fellow to-day at a meeting. I was at school with him. Seems his child is a skating friend of Lalla's."

Aunt Claudia was surprised.

"Really ! I never knew she had any skating friends."

"This child, Harriet Johnson, had been ill and was advised to take up skating for her health, never been able to talk of anything but skating since."

Aunt Claudia looked thoughtful. A child who had been ordered to take up skating by her doctor, and had become keen in spite of having to skate whether she liked it or not, sounded an excellent friend for Lalla. Uncle David had not said how long Harriet had been skating, so she pictured her an experienced skater being trained under a good instructor and entering for tests, though, of course, taking them a long way behind Lalla, and not passing them with the same distinction. Later that evening she said :

"I shall ask Nurse about this child, Harriet Johnson. A skating friend might be useful to Lalla. She's getting on well and they are naturally proud of her, but sometimes I think she isn't as ambitious as she ought to be.

If Nurse says this child is suitable in every way she shall be asked to tea and I will have a look at her."

Uncle David wished Lalla had been there to wink at, but he answered gravely :

" Any child of George Johnson's is sure to be suitable in every way. Nice fellow."

Every day after breakfast Lalla's governess arrived. She was called Miss Goldthorpe. Alice Goldthorpe had been the sort of girl who had, when young, been expected to finish up in a blaze of glory as headmistress of a big school; but Alice Goldthorpe had never wanted to be head of anything. What she liked was teaching and she detested the bother of having teachers under her and being asked to decide things. Because of this she had taught in a great many schools, for sooner or later in whatever school she taught somebody noticed how brilliant she was, and tried to make her take a grander position. Each time this happened, with a shudder of horror at the thought of a grander position, Alice Goldthorpe said she was sorry but she would have to leave. Then she would go to a scholastic agency and ask them to find her a new school in which to teach.

One day two things had happened to Alice Goldthorpe : she noticed she was getting fat round the middle, which is called middle-age spread, and an uncle died and left her some money. In his will the uncle said it was enough money to keep the wolf from licking the paint from off her front door, but not enough to allow her to fritter away her life doing nothing. Alice Goldthorpe had laughed when she read the will, because even had the uncle left her lots of money nothing would have induced her to do nothing. All the same she was grateful for a little bit of money, because it meant that she could look round and find the sort of teaching that she would like to do. Some school where nobody would send for her to say something which began with, " Miss Goldthorpe, I have been noticing your work, and it's most satisfactory, most." Safe with her uncle's legacy Miss Goldthorpe went to the scholastic agency which always found her schools to teach in, and asked them to find a school which would never want her to take a grander position, and she said she could wait while they found it, because now she had got money behind her.

The head of the agency, although Miss Goldthorpe gave her trouble by changing schools so often, had grown fond of her and was pleased to see her. She was especially pleased to hear about the money that would stop a wolf from licking her front door paint. She had jumped up and fetched a letter, and had told Miss Goldthorpe that she believed she had exactly the job for her. The letter was from Aunt Claudia, explaining about Lalla, how she was to be a champion skater and asking if the agency could find a really good governess to undertake her education. Aunt Claudia wanted a governess who would see that in spite of spending her afternoons on the rink Lalla did as many lessons as other children of her age, and passed the necessary examinations at the right time, and—and this was underlined—the governess must be someone who, having accepted the position, was prepared to stick to it. Aunt Claudia did not want to entrust her niece's education to someone who was always moving on.

" There," said the head of the agency, " that ought to be perfect for you. This Mrs. King is never going to ask you to take a higher place."

Miss Goldthorpe had frowned at the letter.

" Poor child ! What a dreadful life ! I don't think I

shall like teaching her. I expect she's a horrid little thing full of self-importance. However, I will go for an interview and find out for myself, there's no harm in an interview."

All this happened when Lalla was seven. From the first moment that Miss Goldthorpe had seen Lalla she had known she would like to teach her, and from the moment Lalla had seen Miss Goldthorpe she knew she would like to be taught by her. More extraordinary still, for that had not been easy, Nana had approved of Miss Goldthorpe. Nana had said she could feel in her bones no governess would be satisfactory, that she had never been one for liking governesses in her nurseries, it never worked. Miss Goldthorpe had known in a minute that Nana's bones would tell her things like that.

" You mustn't forget I've always taught in schools, so I'm not used to teaching in private houses and am likely to make mistakes ; please help me because I'm sure I'm going to like teaching Lalla."

Nana thought saying " Please help me " showed a nice spirit on the part of Miss Goldthorpe, and, though it took time, she came to like her, and in the end to be very fond of her.

The morning after Uncle David's talk with Aunt Claudia, Miss Goldthorpe was giving Lalla a history lesson when Aunt Claudia came upstairs. Lalla touched Miss Goldthorpe's arm. She spoke in a whisper :

" I'm sorry to interrupt, Goldie. Listen ! There's Aunt Claudia. She never comes up in the morning. What can she want ? "

Miss Goldthorpe had heard all about Harriet.

" You don't think Mr. Lindblom has complained that instead of working you're giving Harriet lessons, do you ? "

" You know, Goldie dear, it doesn't matter how often

I tell you things you always get them wrong. I've told you and told you Max is an absolute angel, he wouldn't think of spying on me and telling Aunt Claudia."

Miss Goldthorpe looked anxiously at the door.

" It's a very unusual time for her to come up, and after all Mr. Lindblom has himself to think of, he's a young man, and you're his star pupil. He's expecting to get famous when you do."

Lalla drew a little skating figure on the edge of her exercise book. It was no good explaining skating to Goldie, she just would not understand. It was perfectly true that she was Max Lindblom's star pupil, and that Aunt Claudia had promised that he should have the entire training of her, so that when she became famous he would be famous for having taught her, but that did not mean he would be so mean as to complain about her to Aunt Claudia.

" He wouldn't say I hadn't worked, and anyway it wouldn't be true because I have, any more than you'd go to Aunt Claudia telling tales. You know you told her the other day I was well up to the standard for a girl of my age, although you knew that my arithmetic gets worse and worse, instead of better and better."

Miss Goldthorpe looked ashamed.

" I didn't specifically mention arithmetic, dear, and there's plenty of time yet to coach you before you need take your School Certificate, in fact you might take an alternative subject." Suddenly Miss Goldthorpe remembered they were supposed to be having a history lesson. " Oh dear, what would your aunt say if she came in ? Now, Lalla, I was explaining to you how the Wars of the Roses started."

In Lalla's bedroom Aunt Claudia found Nana. Nana

had been tidying one of Lalla's drawers. She heard the
door open and, thinking it was the housemaid, did not
turn round. It made her jump when she heard Aunt
Claudia's voice.

"Good-morning, Nurse. Mr. King met a friend
yesterday with whom he was at school, a man called
Johnson. I understand he has a daughter called Harriet,
whom Lalla meets skating. What kind of child is she?"

Nana wished she knew exactly what Uncle David had
said to Aunt Claudia about Harriet's father.

"A very nice child, ma'am."

"Does her nurse bring her?"

Nana knew Aunt Claudia would not approve of
children of Harriet's age going to a rink unaccompanied.

"It's her mother I've met, ma'am. A very pleasant
lady."

"Is the child a pupil of Mr. Lindblom's?"

Nana swallowed. How awful if she forgot herself and
said she was a pupil of Lalla's.

"No, ma'am, she is not having lessons at the moment.
She's been ill and it's the exercise she comes for."

Aunt Claudia readjusted her ideas. She very nearly
asked if Harriet was a good skater, but luckily for Nana,
whose conscience would not have let her tell a lie, she
asked instead if Harriet was fond of skating.

Nana beamed.

"She is indeed. Talks of nothing else. Of course
Lalla doesn't get much time for talking, what with her
lessons and the time she has to do alone on the private
rink and all, but the child talks to me. Naturally she
thinks Lalla wonderful, and not the only one."

"Do you think this child's enthusiasm and admiration
will make Lalla work harder?"

Nana tried to answer honestly, and luckily she was able to do so. In order to squeeze in time to give Harriet a lesson, and take her once or twice round the rink, Lalla was concentrating very hard indeed on the figures Max Lindblom was teaching her.

" I do, ma'am. You know how it is, a child likes to do well in front of another child, and of course poor little Harriet, all legs as she is after her illness, can't begin to do what Lalla does nor never will."

Aunt Claudia asked if the illness had been catching, and on hearing that it was not, said that if it could be arranged Nana could bring Harriet back to tea after skating on the following Friday, and she would make a point of being in to meet her. Nana said, " Yes, ma'am," then opened the door respectfully and came to the top of the stairs and waited until Aunt Claudia had reached the ground floor before she hurried to the schoolroom. She knocked. Both Miss Goldthorpe and Lalla thought it was Aunt Claudia knocking, because Nana seldom came in during lesson time. Both their faces showed how pleased they were it was Nana.

" I know I shouldn't interrupt you, Miss Goldthorpe dear, but it's such good news I thought you wouldn't mind." Nana turned to Lalla. " Your Aunt says, if it can be arranged, we can ask Harriet back to tea on Friday."

Lalla jumped up. She flung her arms round Nana.

" Giggerty-geggerty, my most beauteous Nana." Then she hugged Miss Goldthorpe. " Angel Goldie, Harriet's coming to tea ! Harriet's coming to tea ! The next thing is I'll go to tea with Harriet and meet her brothers. It'll be just like having a family of my own."

On Friday Harriet came to skating in her brown velvet

frock. It had been a nice frock, but since she had been
ill she had outgrown it. When she heard she was going
to tea with Lalla she and Olivia had studied the frock to
see if the hem would let down, but they had decided
against it. Olivia said she was afraid the let-down place
would show badly. Harriet agreed and said the velvet
of the turned-up bit under the hem would be much
pussier looking than the rest of the frock, where the
pussiness had got rubbed off by being worn so much. To
make it suitable both for skating and for going to tea
with Lalla, Olivia made some more or less matching pants
to go with it. Because of the new pants and because the
brown velvet, even if it was outgrown, was her best winter
frock, Harriet felt quite well-dressed when she met Lalla
and Nana, but to Nana she did not look well-dressed at
all. " The poor little thing," she thought, " she really
looks better in her old skirt and jersey. Velvet must be
good to look right."

Lalla, now that Friday had come, was so pleased she
did not notice what Harriet had on ; in any case she was
not a very clothes-minded child. She had wardrobes full
of frocks chosen by Aunt Claudia and put out for her by
Nana, but many days, if you had caught her with her eyes
shut, she would not have been able to tell you what she
was wearing. This was something that Harriet did not
know, and she was a little disappointed when they were
on the ice that Lalla said nothing about her dress. Instead
Lalla warned her about Aunt Claudia.

" You mustn't mind, Harriet, the way she talks. She's
my aunt but people can't help what their aunts are like,
and for goodness' sake don't laugh if she recites Sir Walter
Scott. There's a piece of him she's written under the
cups Daddy won, and she recites it at me." Harriet, busy

with her feet, could only make an inquiring grunt, but
Lalla interpreted it as a question. " It's to make me
prouder in case I don't want to be the greatest skater
in the world."

To Harriet Lalla's skating was too wonderful to be real.
As well, the fact that she had special coaching with Max
Lindblom, and special practice every day on the private
rink, made her an important child in the rink world.
Harriet was not envious, but since she had been coming
to the rink she had thought it must be fun being Lalla
Moore.

" How could you be prouder? Anybody would be
proud being you."

Lalla saw Max Lindblom looking at her.

" I've got to go now." She gave Harriet a push to
start her off by herself. ." I didn't say I wanted to be
prouder, I said that was why Aunt Claudia would recite."

Max Lindblom took Lalla to the small private rink.
He was a tall, fair, rather silent, serious young man. He
looked upon the business of training Lalla as a very
important matter. Himself, he had thought and dreamt
of a skating career ever since he could remember. He
found himself puzzled by Lalla, and he did not like to be
puzzled by children. He knew all about her father ; he
had books about him and pictures of him, and though he
could never have told anyone, to him he was a hero and
a god. It had been the happiest day of his life when he
was given Lalla as a pupil, and as he watched her
developing as a skater, he thought he was a very lucky
man. Lalla had a natural gift for skating, and was able
to give an immense amount of time to it, nor was the time
spent at the rink all the training she had. There was
ballet for grace and balance, and fencing to make her

strong and supple. In his dreams Max Lindblom could see Lalla's name known all over the world, and his name being known too because he had trained her. But sometimes he worried. Why was this little girl with everything, talent, money to spend on it, and first-class training not getting on as fast as she should? Max hoped he was wrong, but sometimes it seemed to him the reason was that Lalla did not care enough. Then he would laugh at himself; he must be mistaken; the daughter of Cyril Moore must live to skate. He had watched her friendship with Harriet; she had never had a friend on the ice before. He wondered if it was going to be a good thing, for he had to wonder about everything that happened to Lalla. As they walked towards the private rink he asked:

" The little friend is improving? "

Lalla smiled up at Max, glad he had noticed Harriet.

" Yes. I started her going backwards two days ago, she's unsteady still, but that's mostly because she's got legs like a spider because she's been ill."

Max saw how pleased Lalla looked.

" She is going to have professional lessons? "

Lalla explained to him how poor the Johnsons were, and how Harriet was only skating to get her legs strong, and how her boots were hired by money earned by Alec on a paper round.

" Anyway I don't think Harriet would want lessons, she's awfully keen to skate, but that's to get her legs strong and because it's fun."

Max thought perhaps it would be a pity if Harriet stopped coming to the rink when her legs were strong. It might have helped if she could have got on so well that she could share Lalla's interest and understand what she was trying to do.

" That is a pity, she is well-built, that little girl, and she has a something . . ." He broke off, never being good at words and finding it hard to explain the " something " he thought Harriet had was mostly a usefulness to Lalla.

When Harriet came to Lalla's house she thought Lalla's room too lovely to be true. She even admired the glass case with the boots and skates in it, and the silver cups and trophies on the shelf.

" I think it's rather nice having things your father won and his skates. My father never won anything much, except a little cup once for golf, but if he was drowned like yours I think I would like to have the little cup."

Nana looked more approvingly at Harriet than ever. A child who could agree so completely with Aunt Claudia must surely be an admirable friend for Lalla.

There was always a good tea at Lalla's, but because Harriet was coming there was a special tea with three sorts of sandwiches, chocolate biscuits and a cake covered with pink icing. At home if there had been such a tea everybody would have said how scrumptious it was, but Lalla seemed to take lovely food, like she took a lovely house and lovely clothes, for granted. She sat down at the table looking at the food with no more interest than if it had been bread and jam.

Harriet had not eaten a great deal since she had been ill, but the tea was so nice that she found herself suddenly hungry. She ate four sandwiches, and a piece of pink cake, and was just going to finish up with a chocolate biscuit when the door opened and Aunt Claudia came in. Nana stood up so Harriet stood up too. She was never expected to stand up at home when visitors arrived, though of course the boys had to, but she did have to stand up for visitors at her school, so she thought perhaps that at Lalla's you behaved as you did in school. It was lucky that she stood up because it pleased Aunt Claudia. She smiled.

" So you're Harriet ; I hear you are skating."

Harriet was not usually shy with strangers, but Aunt Claudia was much grander and more glittery than anyone she had ever met before. She hesitated before she answered.

" It's because of my legs, they got wobbly after I was ill, and Dr. Phillipson thought . . ."

Aunt Claudia was not in the least interested in Harriet's legs unless they were useful to Lalla.

" You enjoy skating ? "

" Awfully."

Aunt Claudia studied Harriet. She saw only the top half of her because of the table ; the top half seemed to have a great deal of reddish hair and very large eyes in a pale face. She noticed there seemed a neat though shabby brown frock. The child seemed to her to have pretty manners and to speak nicely. She thought that it might be worth while seeing whether she made a suitable friend for Lalla, but if she was to be that she was to understand how wonderful it was for her to be allowed to know Lalla, and what an important child Lalla was. She signalled to Nana and Harriet to sit.

" Go on with your tea." She settled herself in an arm-chair by the fire. " My brother, Lalla's father, was Cyril Moore, you know. Lalla will have told you how he was drowned. I was his only sister ; he left me Lalla's guardian and from the beginning I knew what I must do. I must make my brother live again in Lalla."

Lalla was sitting with her back to Aunt Claudia, with

Harriet facing her. Aunt Claudia never took her eyes off Harriet to see that she was taking in what she was told. While she was talking Lalla behaved very badly. She did not move her body at all, but she moved her face, giving a rude imitation of Aunt Claudia. Lalla's face, as Aunt Claudia said that her father had to live again in her, was so silly that the corners of Harriet's mouth began

Aunt Claudia studied Harriet

to twitch, and there was an awful heaving feeling in front as if she must laugh. Nana saw this. She spoke in the kind of voice that would kill any laugh before it started.

" Get on with your tea, Lalla, I want none of your nonsense messing the food about. And you eat nicely too, Harriet, there's no need to stop eating. Mrs. King wouldn't wish that."

Aunt Claudia had seen the twitch of Harriet's lips, but she knew there was nothing at all about which Harriet could laugh, so she thought she was nervous. She nodded at her kindly.

" Yes. Go on with your tea. You can eat as well as listen."

Nana put another large slice of pink cake on Harriet's plate, and though Harriet had really meant to have a chocolate biscuit, she ate the cake thankfully, glad of something to do, which meant she need not look at Aunt Claudia. Aunt Claudia went on with her story.

" You must understand that Lalla has never been treated as an ordinary child. All of us who are round her are striving for the same goal, and look upon our lives as dedicated to that goal. First of all, of course, there is Nurse ; you have never thought any trouble too great that improved Lalla as a skater, have you, Nurse ? "

Nana's face was respectful, but her voice was not quite so respectful as her face.

" Nice manners and ladylike ways and a healthy child, that's what I like to see in my nurseries."

Aunt Claudia was used to Nana.

" Quite, and a strong body and ladylike ways are part of Lalla's training. When she travels all over the world, as she very soon will for international championships, she will not be little Lalla Moore, she will be Lalla Moore, her country's little ambassadress."

Harriet by mistake looked up and saw Lalla making the face of a little ambassadress. She choked over her piece of cake, which luckily gave an excuse to drink her milk.

" Miss Goldthorpe, Lalla's governess, gave up a wonderful scholastic career to take over her teaching. ' Mrs. King,' she said, ' I feel any sacrifice is worth while if I may be allowed the privilege of educating a child with such a future before her.' "

Harriet felt Aunt Claudia expected an answer, so she said very politely :

" Yes, Mrs. King."

Aunt Claudia nodded approvingly.

" As well there is Alonso Vittori. He has more pupils than he can manage, but when I asked him to teach Lalla ballet he kissed my hand and said that he would be proud. Then there's Monsieur Cordon for fencing, another devotee, isn't he, Lalla ? "

Nana saw that Lalla was going to spoil her chances of being allowed to know Harriet by saying the wrong thing, so she answered for her.

" Indeed yes, ma'am."

Aunt Claudia got up.

" And now perhaps Lalla is going to have a friend of her own age, but being a friend of Lalla's is rather a special privilege ; it means being very ambitious for Lalla and taking as much interest in her success as her teachers. Are you interested in Lalla's success, Harriet ? "

Lalla had never mentioned Alonso Vittori, Miss Goldthorpe or Monsieur Cordon. She had spoken vaguely about a governess but there had been nothing to suggest the whole collection of teachers waiting to do nothing else but teach her. Harriet felt as if she was in the pages of a story book. She had never supposed in real life that anybody was treated like Lalla, not even princesses ; she could not think of the right sort of answer to make to Aunt Claudia and her face got quite red with trying. Aunt Claudia had made her see a new Lalla, a Lalla travelling all over the world, awfully grand and awfully famous, a lucky Lalla who was able to be grand and famous by doing something so nice as skating. The thought of this made her eyes shine. She spoke with real sincerity.

" I think it must be simply gorgeous to be Lalla, I wish I was her."

If Aunt Claudia had been on the right side of the table to do it she would have patted Harriet's head. Admirable child, what a stimulant for Lalla to have a friend who was not only admiring but envious ! She nodded approvingly, then looked at the silver cups and trophies. She took a deep breath.

" ' Her square-turn'd joints and strength of limb, Show'd her no carpet knight so trim, But in close fight a champion grim.' "

Harriet understood what Lalla said about the reciting but she had no feeling of wanting to laugh. Aunt Claudia made her feel as if she had been out in a very strong wind and had no breath left to do anything. She heard Nana's reverent amen-like " And very nice too, ma'am," and with eyes round with amazement watched Aunt Claudia walk towards the door, and it was only when her hand was on the door handle that she got her wits back enough to remember the very important thing her mother had told her to say.

" Please, Mrs. King, Mummy says might Nana bring Lalla to play with me on Sunday and stay to tea ? "

There was complete silence for a moment, so complete that the clock could be heard ticking, and a piece of coal drop in the fireplace. Six eyes were fixed on Aunt Claudia. Nana tried not to make hers look pleading, but Lalla's were and so were Harriet's. At last Aunt Claudia nodded.

" I think we may say yes, don't you, Nurse ? "

CHAPTER VI

SUNDAY TEA

★

OLIVIA said it was no good making special preparations for Lalla's and Nana's visit on Sunday.

"And don't look so anguished, Harriet darling, you know I always give you the nicest tea I can on Sundays as it is."

Harriet thought her home the loveliest place in the world, and her family the nicest family, but she did think on the Sunday morning, before Lalla came, that it looked shabby compared with Lalla's home. She knew Lalla would not mind a bit what it looked like, but Nana would and Nana was the one who would count.

The boys had heard so much about Lalla that they had got tired of her. To show how tired they were they mimicked Harriet before she had a chance to say what she had done at the rink. First Alec and then Toby would ask "How's little Lalla to-day?" or "What did Lalla say to-day?" To mark the fact that Lalla, her grand home and her beautiful skating meant nothing to them, both Alec and Toby had meant to be out on Sunday afternoon. This would have been what is known as cutting off your nose to spite your face, for they had a great deal they wanted to do indoors on Sunday, and nothing they wanted to do out of doors. Luckily for them

Sunday turned out to be the nastiest, wettest day anybody could imagine, and not even decent rain but a sort of dirty, damp sleet. So when Lalla and Nana arrived they found the whole Johnson family in the sitting-room waiting to meet them.

Nana came in first. She took a quick glance round. She saw that the furniture was what she called " been good once." She saw that the taste, though not of the sort that she fancied herself, was the kind that Aunt Claudia would approve. As well she saw, and this meant far more to her than the furniture, that the Johnson boys had been brought up nicely, for they all got to their feet the moment she and Lalla came in. Lalla, almost for the first time in her life, was silent. Coming from her big home, with so much space for everybody and so few people to talk to, Harriet's home seemed gloriously cosy and full of people. Olivia saw what she was thinking.

" Bless you, we surprise you, don't we ? You aren't used to a big family, are you ? " Then she signalled to the boys to come over. " This is Alec, Lalla."

Harriet did not want Lalla to get muddled about whom she was meeting.

" He's the one who earns the two shillings for my skates, you know I told you."

" And this," said Olivia, " is Toby." Toby blinked at Lalla through his glasses. Lalla thought, though he said " How do you do ? " politely, that Toby was looking at her rather as though he wished she was not there. What Toby was doing really was wondering whether he could find out how much Lalla was costing to train, and then work out how much was spent on each cubic inch of her. " And this," said Olivia, " is Edward."

Edward had been looking forward all day to Lalla's

coming ; the more people there were in a room the better
he liked it. He gazed at Lalla with his enormous, beautiful
eyes, and Lalla and Nana, just as Edward knew they
would, looked at him with the same pleased faces strangers
always wore when they met him.

"I'm so glad that you've come to tea. I've been
hoping and hoping you would."

Nana thought what a pity it was such looks should
have been wasted on a boy. They would have been so
useful to Harriet, poor little thing.

"That's very nice of you, dear, and Lalla's been
looking forward to coming, haven't you, Lalla ? "

Edward beamed at Lalla.

"I'm afraid you won't get tea here like the beautiful,
beautiful tea you gave Harriet."

Because Edward was so good-looking and so friendly
Lalla might have forgotten what Aunt Claudia would say
if she asked Edward to tea without permission, but Nana,
though Edward was the sort of child she would have been
proud to have had in her nurseries, was never carried
away by a child's looks. She said briskly she was sure
there would be a very nice tea, and in any case food wasn't
everything. Edward was disappointed ; he had meant
to be asked to tea with Lalla.

"Food's a great deal, especially when it's a cake with
pink sugar on it and chocolate biscuits."

"I hope Harriet's told you about Edward," Alec said.
"He's a born cad ; we do our best, but we can't do much
about him."

"I'm not," said Edward. "I like nice things to eat
and people being nice to me. It's much duller being
someone like you who doesn't tell anyone what he
likes."

Olivia laughed, and told Edward he was an insufferable child, then she took Nana and Lalla into her bedroom to take off their things.

At first it seemed as if the afternoon was going to be difficult. It would have been all right if only Lalla had been there, but having Nana to entertain too seemed to make it awkward, but Olivia soon arranged things so that people of different ages in a small room did not seem to matter at all. She got out some playing cards and suggested that George should play with the children, then, while Lalla was being taught how to play Slippery Anne, she sat down beside Nana and discussed knitting. Not that Olivia was a good knitter, she was not, but Nana had her knitting with her, and liked talking about knitting, and was soon deep in describing all the knitted things she made for Lalla, and how many sets of everything she had to have.

Lalla, who was quick, soon picked up Slippery Anne and found it the most exciting game. Sometimes she and Miss Goldthorpe played patience, for Miss Goldthorpe was good at patience, and sometimes she persuaded Nana to play Snap, but otherwise she had played no card games, certainly not a family card game, with everybody trying to do down the rest of the family, and roaring with laughter when they succeeded ; but after tea, when Nana insisted on helping Olivia and George to wash up, was the time she enjoyed best, for it was then that the Johnsons sprawled across the table and talked, and told her things which made her feel not Lalla Moore, who had come to tea for the first time, but Lalla Moore, part of the family. She heard all about Mr. Pulton and the paper round, and how much money there was in the money-box and what it was meant to be spent on. Toby told her that in the spring when Alec had enough money to start buying things for the shop he was not going to trust him with the accounts, or in no time there would be nothing left. That on Alec's capital outlay a profit had to be shown and that he was going to keep a proper profit and loss account book. Lalla had never thought where vegetables came from, or what you paid for them, but quite soon she was as deep in the discussion of whether it would be better to start spending Alec's capital on early forced lettuces, or wait for the peas and beans period and strawberries, as any member of the family. Alec drew for her a plan of the sort of nursery garden he intended to have when he had so increased his capital that he could afford to buy a nursery garden, and Toby got out an atlas and showed her whereabouts that nursery garden had to be so that the consumption of petrol used up by a lorry bringing in the fruit, vegetables and flowers did not absorb more than the fruit, vegetables and flowers could support.

"You mustn't mind him," Alec said, "he's got a mathematical mind, he can't help it."

Lalla looked respectfully at Toby.

"Miss Goldthorpe wishes I had. I can't do sums at all."

Toby thought this was a pity. So expensive an education being given to somebody and she could not do sums.

"What else do you do besides skating?" Alec asked.

Lalla was puzzled.

"I do lessons."

Toby saw she had not understood.

"Alec didn't mean that, he meant what other things do you like doing? I play chess, and I collect stamps, and Alec paints pictures, and he's awfully good at games."

Edward felt he was being neglected.

"And I sing. I'm going to get a scholarship and sing in a choir school, and I'm the best at acting in the family, I was the prince in the school play, and I'm going to be another prince this Christmas."

Alec rubbed Edward's hair the wrong way.

"Not because you can act, you little show-off."

"It's because of his looks," said Toby.

His family looked sorrowfully at Edward.

"We're worried about him," Alec explained. "If he goes on as he is now he's bound to turn out a spiv."

Edward had heard that before.

"I needn't. I can't help it if people like me. They talk, and I talk back."

Toby gave Lalla a look as if to say "you see."

"We'll be lucky if he's only a spiv, we think he'll be a confidence trickster." Then he remembered that Lalla had not answered their question. "What else do you do but skate?"

Lalla tried to think. There were her books, but she was not what Miss Goldthorpe called "a great reader."

"I listen to the wireless sometimes, and on Sundays, if nobody's in, Nana and I look at television."

Harriet saw that her brothers thought this a very poor answer. She flew to Lalla's defence.

"She goes to Alonso Vittori for ballet, and she fences, and she wouldn't get time for the sort of things we do."

Toby drew a piece of paper towards him.

"What time do you get up? How many hours lessons do you do? How many hours skating, dancing and all that?" Lalla told him. In the quickest possible time he had got the answer. She had two hours of her own every week-day and almost the whole of Sundays. What did she do with those hours?

It was the first time that Lalla heard anyone suggest that skating by itself was not enough to fill anybody's life. She looked first at one Johnson and then at the other, and saw, to her amazement, that they did not think it was enough. They thought just doing one thing very dull indeed. Ever since she had been pushed in her pram to the rink, Lalla, at the rink and at home, had been quite a person and she was unaccustomed to eyes looking at her in a reproachful way; eyes in her life had usually been filled with envy. Suddenly she felt a need to make Harriet's brothers see how important she was; without knowing it she spoke in rather an Aunt Claudia voice.

" It's dull doing things alone. I was never allowed a friend before I met Harriet."

It was not only the boys who were surprised, but Harriet too, for it did not sound a bit like Lalla talking.

" No friends? " said Alec. " Why? "

Toby did not believe her.

" You must have some, everybody does."

Edward beat on the table with his fists to attract attention.

" I've simply hundreds and hundreds."

More and more Lalla felt a need to be grand.

" My Aunt Claudia didn't know any who were suitable."

" Suitable for what? " asked Toby.

Lalla's face was red; she knew she was being silly but she could not stop.

" For me; she thinks a skating champion, I mean somebody who's going to be a skating champion, ought only to have friends who talk about skating."

Toby began reckoning in his head.

"How many good skaters are there at your rink? I mean of your sort of age?" Lalla thought there might be about ten, fairly good but not as good as she was. Toby wrote the figure ten on a piece of paper. Then he put down the number of towns in England. Then he guessed the number of rinks per town. Then he gave each rink ten promising pupils. "It's impossible to get a true figure, but if I were you I'd tell your aunt that your chances of becoming a champion skater are much less than one in a thousand." He could see that Lalla did not know what he was talking about. "I mean if there were a thousand girls in a row, all skating about as well as you do, and about the same age, it's unlikely any one of them would be a champion skater."

Lalla lost her temper.

"You're very rude. I'm going to be a world champion. Everybody knows it. You see, my father was."

Toby was about to explain that it was not that he was being rude, but that her facts were wrong, and he thought she ought to know, but Alec stopped him.

"Shut up. If Lalla isn't a champion skater she ought to be, seeing how many people are trying to make her one."

"And you've never seen her skate," said Harriet. "She skates gorgeously, everybody says so."

Alec saw that they had upset Lalla; he thought it was pretty silly to think you were going to be a champion something before you were, but he supposed you got like that if you had as many people poodling around you as Lalla had. All the same she was Harriet's friend and their guest, so he tried to change the subject.

"All he meant was that it seemed pretty miserable to

have nothing else to do except skate. I mean you can't skate at home in the evenings, and we meant what do you do then? Before Harriet was ill she collected things, and she's always making things, aren't you, Harriet? "

Lalla felt that none of them liked her as much as they had, and she was sorry. She did not want to leave with the boys despising her, but the truth was that there was not much she could say; outside skating there was nothing she could think of that she did do. She had a garden, and the boys would have been interested in that, but they would despise the way she looked after it. However, a garden was better than nothing. She mentioned it cautiously. As she had supposed Alec and Toby were interested at once. They wanted to know how big it was and what she grew in it. Lalla saw it was no good pretending so she told the truth.

" It's a piece of a side border, the end bit. I've got all the proper things for it, a fork, a trowel, a rake and a water-can and a wheelbarrow. I used to plant seeds and things; once I made my name in flowers, but Nana stopped helping me; she doesn't like gardening she hates bending, and she doesn't like getting earth on her hands, and it's dull doing a garden alone, so I don't."

" Then what happens to it? " asked Toby.

" It's still mine, but the gardener does it. It really looks like the rest of the garden, but as it's mine I can pick the flowers in it."

Alec thought having a bit of garden was the nicest thing that could happen to anybody.

" Do you mean to say you don't plant anything ever? "

Lalla was by now completely honest.

" No. You try digging and digging by yourself, it's awfully dull. Besides, if I did, neither Miss Goldthorpe or Nana are interested, though they pretend to be, so they don't really care what flowers come up." Then suddenly, looking at Alec, Lalla had an idea. " Alec, why shouldn't you grow things in my garden ? "

Slowly, in the way the best ideas behave, Lalla's idea took possession of them all. It was not decided that Sunday afternoon exactly what Alec would grow in Lalla's garden, but it was decided that it should be made use of, and that one Sunday when Aunt Claudia was out he and Toby would come round and look at it, and decide what to plant in the spring. Almost at once a fierce argument went on between Toby and Alec. Alec wanted to try forced lettuces, but Toby, putting down figures and adding them up, tried to make him see that lettuces were out of the question, as they had to be grown under glass, and if you grew lettuces under glass you had to grow an enormous number of them to pay for the glass, and Lalla's garden was only a piece at the end of a border and not a field. He said :

" We'll have to measure the ground before we can tell how the space can be most economically used."

As Toby said that, Lalla thought of her garden. What a surprise it was going to be to the gardener when, instead of the grand flowers he grew or the candytuft and the nasturtiums and things that she had grown, he saw tomatoes and cucumbers coming up. He would be so surprised he would be almost certain to talk about it.

" Don't say anything to Nana yet, she'll have to know, of course. It's better to tell her things slowly, she doesn't like me to do anything unless Aunt Claudia says I may."

Alec had got up and was walking up and down the room. In his mind Lalla's garden was growing larger and

" You stand on her other side, Alec, and show her what we do "

larger, with splendid rows of green peas, and broad beans, and even new potatoes. He was brought back from the new potatoes by Harriet pulling his sleeve. She pulled him down and whispered in his ear. When she had finished he was laughing.

" Harriet thinks that Lalla's garden is a family secret, so we ought to make our pledge over it, and as Lalla's a part of it she ought to make the pledge too."

Harriet danced across to Lalla.

" We've always done it, it's to do with our Uncle William. The one that eats the things Daddy would like to sell in the shop." She linked her little finger through Lalla's. " You stand on her other side, Alec, and show her what we do."

Alec linked his little finger through Lalla's.

" It's a family thing but we've always done it. I speak
the pledge, and then you say with the others ' Guzzle
guzzle guzzle, quack quack quack,' and as you say it we
lift our hands above our heads, linked together like this."
Lalla felt honoured ; she had no idea what a pledge was,
but she was glad she was being allowed to make it. Alec
spoke in a solemn, growly voice. " We Johnsons and Lalla
swear on the stomach of our Uncle never to divulge what
has taken place to-day." They lifted their hands, and all
said solemnly :

" Guzzle guzzle guzzle, quack quack quack."

" That guzzle part," said Alec, as they broke away and
came back to the table, " is the most secret family secret.
Dad doesn't know that we know that our Uncle William
was called ' Guzzle ' at school."

" When we found out," Toby explained, " it was the
beginning of a secret society, it had to be. That's when
we made up the pledge."

" When anything important's going on like your
garden," said Harriet, " we do our pledge."

Alec patted his front.

" We vow on our Uncle's stomach, because it's probably
the best filled, and therefore the most important stomach
we know."

Harriet looked proudly at Lalla.

" And nobody ever, except the Johnsons, made that
vow before, so it almost makes you one of the family."

Edward rubbed his cheek against Lalla's sleeve.

" I shall like you being one of the family."

Alec gave him a shove.

" Shut up, sloppy. As a matter of fact you've a right
to share the vow, Lalla, because your garden's going to
be a very family thing. It's not only going to pay for

Harriet's skates, but it's going to be the foundation of
the fortunes of the house of Johnson."

Driving home Nana thought Lalla looked solemn.

" Enjoyed yourself, dearie ? "

Lalla wished she could confide in Nana. She would
have liked to have told her that the Johnsons, at least the
Johnson boys, were not very impressed by her being a
champion skater, in fact Toby did not think she would
be one, but Nana would be shocked, because that was
just the kind of thing that Aunt Claudia did not want
anyone to say ; and she would have loved to have told
her about the garden, but that would have to wait. Nana
would not approve of Alec and Toby coming to look at
it when Aunt Claudia was out. But she could answer
about the afternoon.

" It's been simply gorgeous. Oh, giggerty-geggerty, it
was the nicest Sunday I've ever, ever had."

CHAPTER VII

INTER-SILVER

★

THAT Sunday afternoon at the Johnsons' had a great effect on Lalla's skating. She had often said things like "Who wants to be a champion anyway?" but she had not meant them; it was like a person saying "Who's afraid of the big, bad wolf?" when a headmaster or mistress sent for them. But hearing Toby say "One chance in a thousand" did something to her. She did not believe she was not going to be a world champion; nobody who has been told they are going to be a world champion since they were three years old could believe such a statement, but it made her want to hear people like Max Lindblom praise her and say how well she was getting on. And it made her decide to pass her inter-silver so brilliantly that not only Max Lindblom would say nice things but everybody else at the rink, and then Harriet would go home and tell the Johnsons, and they would laugh at Toby and tell him what an idiot he had been.

With the fine training she had behind her, all Lalla needed to make her do the figures well that she had to do for the inter-silver, was to care that she did them well, and to work hard. Quite suddenly she was caring and she was working hard. Max Lindblom, smiling in his shy way, came to Nana.

" Lalla does well. I am very pleased with her. You will tell Mrs. King."

" I will, Mr. Lindblom, and I know she'll be pleased. Very set she is on this skating."

Max was used to Nana, and knew how she felt about skating, and was used to her saying " this skating " in a despising voice ; but he knew too she worried if Lalla was not getting on well, and would be glad to tell the aunt that he was pleased.

Nana not only told Aunt Claudia but she told Wilson, who told the cook who told the housemaid and she told Miss Goldthorpe. Miss Goldthorpe, who took Lalla to fencing and dancing, told Alonso Vittori, and Monsieur Cordon, so in the end everybody who had much to do with Lalla knew how well she was doing and smiled at her in a proud way.

A month after Lalla's tenth birthday the inter-silver test took place. The judging was held on the small private rink and while it was going on skaters who had not been called practised on the big rink. It had been arranged that Harriet should come to the rink that morning, so that Lalla would have someone to talk to while she was waiting. Lalla did not need someone to talk to, for she was not nervous before a test, but Harriet was quaking at the knees. She looked at Lalla flying round in a new white kilt, jersey and bonnet, and because it was a test, white gloves, and she thought how awful it would be if she got her figures wrong, or fell over, or did something to lose marks, so she would not pass. Because the test was happening in the morning, and the mornings were her time, Miss Goldthorpe had brought Harriet to the rink. She thought skating rinks nasty, cold, damp places, and she could not imagine why anyone, unless forced like Lalla to do so, wanted to spend their time going round and round on ice, when they could spend it reading interesting books. She had not met Harriet until that morning but, as Lalla's friend, she had been wanting to meet her. The first thing that struck her was that Harriet looked worried. " Why," she thought, " should a child of that age look worried ? "

" Is anything the matter, dear ? "

Harriet sat down beside Miss Goldthorpe. She put her hands into her coat pockets to keep them warm.

" I feel peculiar inside for Lalla, I expect you do too, don't you ? "

Miss Goldthorpe had not thought of feeling peculiar for Lalla but she was always interested in new ideas. She thought this one over.

" I don't think so. Should I ? "

" It's a test. It'd be simply awful if she failed."

" Why ? "

Harriet stared at Miss Goldthorpe. Could it be possible that somebody who had met Aunt Claudia could ask why ?

" Well, she expects to pass, Mrs. King expects her to pass, and so does Mr. Lindblom."

" How old are you ? "

" I was ten just before Lalla was. Lalla gave me a simply lovely skating book, and Nana knitted me this beautiful jersey, and, of course, I'd lots of other presents besides."

Miss Goldthorpe said she was glad Harriet had had so nice a birthday, and remembered that Lalla had told her about it. Then she explained that the reason that she asked how old she was was to know if she was old enough to have taken any examinations. Harriet explained that until she had been ill she had been at school, and there had been examinations at the end of each term. Miss Goldthorpe said that she quite understood that, but it was not end of term examinations she was thinking of, but bigger ones.

"I taught in schools until I taught Lalla, so I was always coaching girls for examinations; of course it was important that they should pass, but I found it didn't really matter what they knew. Lots of people pass examinations who don't know very much, and lots of people can't pass them who do. Once I got used to this idea I never worried about examinations again; I did my best to make my pupils pass, I couldn't do more. If they didn't they didn't. I imagine a test's very like a school examination, and that Mr. Lindblom feels about Lalla much as I felt about my pupils."

Harriet hugged one of her knees.

"But Mr. Lindblom doesn't feel like that, nor does Mrs. King, nor does Lalla. She's simply got to pass, it'd be the most awful thing that had ever happened if she didn't."

Miss Goldthorpe took a small tin out of her pocket.

"Blackcurrant jubes, they're not at all bad though really they're medicine. You suck one, and don't worry. If Lalla knows her figures she will pass. She's that sort of child. If she doesn't know them she won't, and there's nothing either you or I can do about it. Now tell me about yourself; what lessons have you been doing since you've been ill?"

Miss Goldthorpe was the good teacher that she was because she was really interested in the girls she taught. She thought about them and nothing else. Now, sitting on the side of the rink, she was really interested in Harriet, and Harriet, feeling this, told her everything. About being ill, and the convalescent home, and Uncle William and the shop, and the boys, especially Alec's paper round, and it was quite a surprise when Lalla skimmed across the ice and leant over the barrier and said :

" I've been watching you two. Jabber, jabber, jabber. I knew you wouldn't care about my skating, Goldie, but I thought you'd watch me, Harriet, but you didn't, and I've practised all my test figures, and everyone was watching me except you."

Harriet started guiltily, but Miss Goldthorpe was quite unmoved.

" Harriet and I have been having a nice talk, dear. While she was watching you she was getting quite nervous for you, and I told her it was unnecessary."

Lalla nodded.

" So it is, but you can think of me now because I come next."

" I'll hold my thumbs," said Harriet. " I always hold my thumbs when anything's happening in the family. It's the best thing you can do to help anybody."

" All right, hold them," said Lalla. " But watch me. I don't want you two gabbling while I'm doing my test."

Harriet and Miss Goldthorpe stood next to Max Lindblom, Harriet tightly holding her thumbs, but Miss Goldthorpe, who did not believe in thumb-holding, had her hands in her pockets, and so did Max Lindblom. Harriet had never seen a test before, and she had the sort of respectful feeling she had when she went into a church. The two judges, though they looked ordinary, became, as Harriet watched their faces, taller, bigger and more important every minute. They were a man and a woman and they wore almost identical teddy bear

coats and fur boots; the woman judge had a scarf tied
over her head, and the man was wearing a cap, both
carried pencils and cards. Lalla seemed surprisingly at
home with them; she searched about on the ice for a
clean piece where no previous skaters' skates had left a
mark, and then stood, her hands at her sides, waiting to
be told to begin, as calmly, Harriet thought, as if she
were waiting to cross the road.

Lalla seemed surprisingly at home with the judges

As neither Miss Goldthorpe nor Harriet knew a well-
skated figure when they saw one, they could only stare
at Lalla and hope for the best. Miss Goldthorpe thought
it peculiar to be able to skate, so while she watched Lalla
she did not see the child she taught but a new Lalla,
whose talent was as weird as the talent of a chimpanzee
who could ride a bicycle. Harriet had been shown by
Lalla over and over again what she had to do, and she

understood just enough to know which edge she was on, and when she was doing the same figure on a different edge, or backwards instead of forwards. She tried to discover how things were going by glancing at Max Lindblom's face, but she got nothing from it until Lalla had finished her figures. Then he smiled. When later Lalla's one and a half minutes of free skating were over Harriet could bear the suspense no longer. She pulled Max Lindblom's sleeve.

" Was she good ? "

He was moving towards Lalla but he paused.

" Very good. I am well pleased. I shall ask if we may know her marks."

Lalla, after a charming smile from both the judges, came flying towards Max, her hands outstretched. He held them in both of his, beaming at her.

" That was good, Lalla. You have done well."

In a few minutes, that Lalla had done well, was known all over the rink. The top marks she could have been awarded for figures were fifty-four, and the marks she had earned were forty-eight. Better marks for figures than anybody had hoped, and extraordinarily good for someone who was only just ten. For free skating top marks were twelve and Lalla had been given nine point three. Lalla was enchanted with herself. She rushed on to the big rink and let off steam by spreadeagling all the way round it, and, in spite of Miss Goldthorpe waving and beckoning, she would not come off the ice. In fact she would have gone on going round and round if Max Lindblom had not caught her and pushed her to the barrier.

In spite of understanding that Lalla felt mad-doggish, and knowing people did feel like that after passing examinations well, Miss Goldthorpe had to make her voice sound severe.

"Come along, dear, it's time we were going home."

When they got to the cloakroom Lalla sat down on a stool next to Harriet, leant back against the wall and, in a lordly way, put a foot in Harriet's lap.

" Take my boot off for me, Harriet. A person who has got 48 marks out of 54 doesn't feel like taking off her own boots."

Harriet started to unlace the boot, but Miss Goldthorpe stopped her.

" I'm sorry a person who's got 48 marks doesn't feel like taking off her boots, but she's got to for no one's going to take them off for her."

Lalla felt as though Miss Goldthorpe had tugged her down from the clouds to a common everyday world.

" You are mean, Goldie. Why shouldn't Harriet take them off for me? She's got nothing else to do."

Miss Goldthorpe could see Harriet would be proud to take off Lalla's boots, but she knew that Lalla, who had always had everything that she wanted, could very easily turn into a spoilt little horror, so she answered in a really severe voice.

" Lalla. Take your foot off Harriet's lap at once, and unlace your boots."

Lalla thought Miss Goldthorpe was being horrible, but she knew there was no arguing when she used that voice. She unlaced her boots and took them off, but while she was doing it she kept up a running commentary under her breath.

" Such a fuss . . . you wouldn't think it would hurt people who've had nothing to do all the morning but watch other people doing things, to take off a boot . . .

it's mean . . . nobody would think here was somebody
who'd just got 48 marks out of 54."

Miss Goldthorpe said nothing while Lalla was mutter-
ing, but when she had changed into her outdoor shoes
she buttoned her into her coat and gave her a kiss.

"Shall we celebrate your success? Let's go to a shop
and have a bun and something to drink."

In one second Lalla was back in her mad-doggish mood.

"Gorgeous Goldie, you always think of nice things.
Can Harriet come? Can it be that sort of fizzy lemonade
that makes your nose tickle?"

"Of course it could, and of course Harriet's coming.
But if Harriet's sensible she will choose hot chocolate,
for it was cold by the rink."

They found a very nice shop and Lalla had lemonade,
Harriet chocolate and Miss Goldthorpe a cup of coffee,
and they all had buns. While they ate and drank Lalla
described every moment she had been on the ice taking
her test. Neither Miss Goldthorpe nor Harriet understood
much of what she was saying, but Miss Goldthorpe managed to look interested, and Harriet really was. Interested
faces were all that Lalla needed and she enjoyed herself
more and more each minute. When Miss Goldthorpe
went to a desk to pay the bill she suddenly remembered
an extra nice thing.

"Oh, Harriet, I've thought of something. The very
first second you see him you've got to tell Toby about
me. How many marks I got, and every single thing you
can think of. That'll show him that he's absolutely wrong
saying I won't be a champion."

A few days after the test there was more excitement for
Lalla. Max Lindblom thought that, as she had passed
with such flying colours, it would be good for her to have

the experience of skating before an audience. He went to see Mr. Matthews. Mr. Matthews was drinking a glass of milk and swallowing tablets for his duodenal ulcer. He listened to what Max Lindblom had to say with a surprised expression.

" But I've been wanting the kid to skate in public for years. We've got that big charity do in January. Nothing could suit me better. But you've always said you wouldn'1 allow it."

Max nodded.

" I do not like a show being made of a small child. A small child does a pretty exhibition badly, but people do not know she is bad, they think it wonderful she can skate at all, so they stamp and scream and applaud. How then can I say to that child, you are a naughty one, that was a bad display last night. The child has heard the applause, and she cocks a snook at me."

Mr. Matthews looked shocked.

" I hope not, I shouldn't like any of our youngsters behaving that way."

" I do not mean they cock a snook with the hand, I mean they cock a snook inside the head."

Mr. Matthews did not care what happened inside the head, so he went back to the discussion of Lalla giving a skating exhibition.

" D'you think that aunt of hers would agree ? "

Max explained that Aunt Claudia would have liked Lalla to have skated in public long ago, but she had agreed to wait until he said that she was ready for it. He thought now the time had come ; she had passed her inter-silver very well indeed, which meant she had mastered those figures well, and he thought she might perform an exhibition of free skating now and again to give her a sense of showmanship. He wanted her to understand how a free skating programme was made up. That the movements were chosen, and the jumps and spins arranged to show her to her best advantage, please the audience, and yet be well inside her range. The only question was who should write to the aunt. Should he do it or should Mr. Matthews. Mr. Matthews said he thought he ought to write. After all, he was arranging the performance for charity and he would say that Max had suggested it.

The result of Mr. Matthews' letter was that one morning Aunt Claudia came up to the schoolroom just as Lalla was starting lessons. It was easy to see, as she opened the door, that nobody had done anything wrong, for she looked like a cat just after it had drunk a large saucer of cream.

"Forgive me for interrupting, Miss Goldthorpe, but I have some exciting news for Lalla. Mr. Matthews asks that you may give an exhibition, dear, at his big charity performance in January. I think we may say yes, don't you?"

Lalla was as surprised as Mr. Matthews had been, for she knew Mr. Matthews had always wanted her to give exhibitions and Max had never allowed it.

"Does Max say I can?"

"Mr. Matthews says he suggested it. Now when you go skating this afternoon I want you to find out what sort of programme he is arranging, because we've got to see that you have a really lovely skating dress for the occasion. I think the first skating frock for our little star ought to be white, don't you, Miss Goldthorpe? With perhaps a sprinkling of silver stars or something pretty like that."

When Aunt Claudia said "our little star" Miss

Goldthorpe's inside felt as if it was milk about to curdle. She did not approve of that sort of talk. Time enough, she thought, to call Lalla a star when she was one. However, it was no good talking to Aunt Claudia ; she had to say things like that, poor woman, she did not seem to be able to help it. So she answered politely, though in rather a governessy, stuffy sort of voice, that she thought white would be very nice indeed.

Aunt Claudia sat down.

" The other thing I want to speak about, Lalla, is your food. Now that you're really on the threshold of success, we must do something about your diet. A skater should be slim, and there are a few naughty curves I should like to see disappear. Don't you agree, Miss Goldthorpe ? "

Miss Goldthorpe looked at Lalla's round face, coloured like a nice ripe peach, and her mass of shining dark curls, and her nicely-made, solid body, and Aunt Claudia or no Aunt Claudia, she had to speak her mind.

" Lalla's not fat, she's nicely covered, and I like to see a child nicely covered."

Aunt Claudia smiled at Miss Goldthorpe in a you-and-I-understand-each-other way.

" An ordinary child, yes. But we can't treat Lalla as an ordinary child, we must treat her as a little race-horse."

Lalla was startled. A race-horse ! She had been wondering what sort of diet she was to have, for the only kind she knew was the sort known as " starve a fever," which happened when she had measles, chicken-pox, and influenza.

" Do you mean I've got to eat oats ? I have those in porridge."

Aunt Claudia tried not to look impatient, but she

thought Lalla was being slow and her voice showed that she thought that.

" Certainly not oats. We have to increase the proteins and reduce the starchy foods." She turned to Miss Goldthorpe. " There's to be no bread with her luncheon, nor potatoes, and there'll be no starchy sweets. I've told cook it's to be stewed fruit in future. For tea and breakfast rusks instead of bread, and no cakes at present."

Lalla gasped.

" Rusks for tea ! But I like toast. No cakes ! "

Aunt Claudia used her reciting voice.

" Not for the moment. We don't mind any sacrifice, do we, to achieve our end ? "

Lalla did mind, and she minded Aunt Claudia saying " we." She thought to herself, " I bet she has cakes and toast, and it's only me that's got to eat rusks." But she kept these thoughts to herself, because she wanted to give the skating exhibition and if Aunt Claudia was cross she might say she was not to do it.

" I thought I was to have square-turn'd joints and strength of limb. I won't have those on rusks."

Aunt Claudia gave her a kiss.

" Naughty child. You know I'm only planning this diet because I have to. And believe me, it's not an easy thing to do. With meat rationed as it is, it's going to mean a sacrifice all round to see you have sufficient."

There was a little silence after Aunt Claudia had gone. Miss Goldthorpe was wondering what Nana was going to say when she heard about the diet. Lalla was listening to hear that Aunt Claudia was out of hearing. Presently her bedroom door shut, but all the same she spoke in a whisper for safety.

" She's gone to tell Nana, but I'll get round her.

Nana'd never be so mean as to stop me making toast. Do you think I'm too fat, Goldie ? "

Miss Goldthorpe struggled to be loyal to her employer. " Well, dear, I know nothing about skating." Then she broke off and her real feelings got hold of her. " No, I don't dear. However, if you've got to have a diet, you've got to have a diet, and there's the end of it. Now come on, we've wasted too much time. Where's your atlas ? Open it at North America."

In Lalla's bedroom Nana listened to Aunt Claudia's description of Lalla's diet with a respectful face but a turbulent heart. Never had there been a diet in her nurseries except when a child was ill. There had been trouble in the past because a child would not eat, but never when it could.

" Lalla's been brought up to eat what's put in front of her, ma'am, and so she does, bless her. I don't hold with interfering with children's food."

Aunt Claudia tried to be patient.

" But you see Lalla's not an ordinary child. As I've just been saying to Miss Goldthorpe, we've got to treat her with the same care as we should a little race-horse."

" Race-horse ! I don't like to speak against poor dumb animals, but I wouldn't wish it to be said that I would treat a race-horse better than one of my children. Same care as a race-horse indeed ! Lalla couldn't have had better attention since I had her when she was a month old, if she was Princess Anne."

Aunt Claudia wondered, as she had sometimes wondered before, if Nana were getting past her work. It would be awkward getting rid of her, for she had been chosen by Lalla's mother and there was some money to come to her if she stayed with the family till Lalla was grown up. The lawyer who looked after Lalla's money was a fairly reasonable man to deal with, but she had a feeling he might be difficult if she tried to get rid of Nana.

"This is not a discussion, it's an order; but I shall need your help over tea. It would be easier if you would eat rusks too; it's a temptation to the child if she sees a loaf on the table." Aunt Claudia could see by Nana's face that she was never going to agree to eat rusks, so she hurried on. "Now, to a much more exciting subject. Lalla's going to give a skating exhibition in January, so this afternoon I've told her to talk to Max Lindblom about the sort of display it's to be. Perhaps you would talk to him too. I thought her very first special skating dress should be white. What do you think?"

Nana, as usual when she had been interviewed by Aunt Claudia, opened the door for her and saw her down the stairs, then she came back to Lalla's room and went on with what she had been doing, which was tidying drawers. Suddenly she stopped, one of Lalla's socks in her hand. Little race-horse! What a way to speak of one of God's creatures! Rusks indeed! "I've never starved my children yet and I'm not starting now. The moment I see Lalla looking peaky, it's hot dripping toast for her tea and plenty of it."

CHAPTER VIII

CHRISTMAS

★

AT Christmas Aunt Claudia and Uncle David went
away to spend Christmas with Uncle David's sister.
Always before they had spent Christmas at home, because
of Lalla. This year's going away was not something which
happened accidentally, as Lalla supposed, but happened
because of a talk Uncle David had with Nana.

One day Harriet brought Lalla an invitation to spend
Christmas evening with her and the family.

" We'd have such fun, the Christmas tree, and dressing
up, and games, and it'll be twice as nice if you're there."

Lalla looked longingly at Nana.

" Nana, do you think Aunt Claudia would let me ? "

Nana hated to say no, but she had to.

" Not Christmas Day, dear. You have your own tree
that evening."

" But there's only me. It'd be much more fun at
Harriet's tree."

" That's as may be. But your aunt plans a nice day
for you, and would be upset if you asked to go out."

Although Nana had to say no to Lalla at the time, she
thought it a great pity that Lalla could not have a family
Christmas for once, so that was why she asked Uncle
David to help.

" I don't know if there's anything you can do, sir, but it's lonely for a child, being just the one. It'd be a treat for Lalla, and she's been working very hard, and eating those nasty rusks and all."

Uncle David was fond of Nana, and he could see she was worried.

" This diet nonsense isn't disagreeing with her, is it? She looks splendid."

Nana thought it all wrong that a child should look splendid while having a diet, and her voice showed what she thought.

" Not at the moment, sir, and I'll soon put a stop to it if it upsets her. I don't want a skeleton in my nursery. No, it's not the diet, it's all work and no play and too much being the only one, it isn't right."

" She has fun at the rink with Harriet, doesn't she?"

" Not really, sir. That poor little Harriet's not a skater like Lalla, nor never will be. She tries hard, and gets on wonderfully, but she doesn't have proper lessons."

" Doesn't she come to tea here sometimes?"

" Just twice she's been, and Lalla the once to her. It's not been easy, what with fittings for Lalla's skating frock and that."

Uncle David knew what Nana's " and that " meant. Aunt Claudia had taken to asking for Lalla to come to the drawing-room when she had visitors. " This is my little niece. She's becoming quite a skating star. You must take tickets for her performance in January." Lalla found it a bore being dressed up in a party frock, but she did not mind meeting the visitors. It was a change from being in the schoolroom with Nana. As well, when cocktails were served, she got nice things to eat, which, now she was on a diet, she appreciated. Aunt Claudia

would tell her to take the least starchy of the canapés.
" Lalla has to be careful what she eats, poor child, you
have to pay for success." But Lalla generally managed
to have a good feed of everything that was going. She
was expected to hand round and she usually manœuvred
something into her mouth each time her back was to
Aunt Claudia.

" You don't approve of her coming to the drawing-
room ? "

Nana looked more worried than ever.

" For most children I'd say yes, sir. It's good for
children to be used to meeting people, answering prettily
when they're spoken to, but it's not right for Lalla. She's
just a bit of the little madam, if you know what I mean,
sir, and always was. What she needs is being with a
nice family like the Johnsons. The Johnson boys are
properly brought up, but they won't stand for any
nonsense from a child of Lalla's age. You have to take
extra care when there's only one in a family. Three's
what I like ; there's the size of family a home has a
right to expect."

Uncle David patted Nana's arm and told her to stop
worrying, and that he would see what he could do. The
first thing he did was the arranging that he and Aunt
Claudia went away for Christmas, and the next was a
splendid idea which was not really his at all. It came
accidentally from Miss Goldthorpe.

Miss Goldthorpe had been thinking a lot about Harriet
since she had met her at the rink, and so when one day
she met Uncle David in the road, and he asked how
Lalla was getting on, it was no surprise when Harriet
came into the conversation. It started by Uncle David
asking if Miss Goldthorpe knew if Lalla had done any-

thing about presents for the Johnsons for Christmas Day. Miss Goldthorpe explained that Lalla had made grand lists of what she wanted to give them, but so far there had been no shopping because there was not time.

"I think she's going to trust me to get everything. You see, unless she takes time off from her skating or special classes, she's never free when the shops are open."

The thought of somebody of ten never being free when the shops were open sounded to Uncle David depressing. He could not, of course, interfere as Lalla was not his ward, so instead he told Miss Goldthorpe that he would like to help to make Lalla's Christmas pleasant and that he did not suppose she had enough money to get all the presents she needed, and Miss Goldthorpe could ask him for anything extra. Miss Goldthorpe looked as pleased as if she had had a present.

"That will please Lalla. She wanted so very much to give Harriet some good skates and boots, but, of course, they'd be too expensive for her. I myself think there are many things Harriet needs more than skates and boots, but Lalla is certain that skates and boots of her own would make Harriet happier than anything else."

Uncle David looked at Miss Goldthorpe's plain, kind face and bulgy figure, and thought what a nice person she was.

"I wish Lalla could see more of Harriet. Nana tells me they don't have much time together on the rink and of course Lalla's day is so full. It's none of my business, but I'd like to see her have more fun."

Miss Goldthorpe nodded vigorously.

"So would I. Sometimes when I see her sitting alone at the schoolroom table I wonder if I ought not to try and persuade her aunt to send her to a day school. I should miss her terribly, and of course there are difficulties in the way. Her curriculum does not really allow for a school life, but I feel I should do something, she does spend so much time alone."

Uncle David stared into Miss Goldthorpe's face, and between them the idea was born. Uncle David said it would take some handling, and Miss Goldthorpe said it would be splendid, just what Lalla needed, and she was sure that competition would be good for her work. They both agreed that Nana would be delighted.

" I wonder if the Johnsons would approve."

Miss Goldthorpe nodded again even more vigorously than before.

" They would. The day I met Harriet she told me all about herself, and it seems that she misses going to school. She was not allowed to go after her illness, because she was not considered strong enough, and now that she is strong enough her doctor won't let her go until the winter's over. He says schools are full of germs and draughts. In Lalla's schoolroom there are no draughts, and between us Nana and I can take care of her."

Uncle David thought for a moment.

" Say nothing about this to anyone. You know how I'm placed, I'm only her step-uncle, but I'll think the matter over, and see if I can persuade Mrs. King. It'd be a wonderful plan."

If Lalla and Harriet had known what Uncle David and Miss Goldthorpe were scheming for them, and what Uncle David was going to try and talk Aunt Claudia into arranging, they would have been even more excited about Christmas than they were. As it was they were mad-doggish. Once it was arranged that Aunt Claudia and Uncle David would be away for Christmas it was decided that Lalla should spend all Christmas Day at the Johnsons' house. She was to go there first thing in the morning, and not to come home till after supper. At tea-time both Nana and Miss Goldthorpe were invited for the Christmas tree, games, dressing up and for supper.

"And nobody's to mention diet on Christmas Day," said Lalla. "I'm going to eat everything I want to eat, plum pudding and mince pies, and Christmas cake, and as many helpings of everything as I can get in."

There would have been, of course, no chance of a turkey in the Johnsons' house if Lalla had not been going there for Christmas. Uncle William did not keep turkeys, and if he had he would have eaten them all. But part of Lalla's spending Christmas at Harriet's was a hamper from Uncle David to George. So that Olivia would not worry about Christmas things Nana told Lalla to tell Harriet that a hamper was coming. "And right and proper that it should be, seeing your uncle and Mr. Johnson were such friends at school."

The hamper came two days before Christmas. Olivia saved up opening it till all the family were home. It was an enormous hamper with a big red bow on the top of it, with a sprig of holly through it. Inside was everything Christmasy that was ever heard of ; as one thing after another was unpacked and laid on the kitchen table there were gasps and Oohs and Ohs from the family. Edward rubbed his face against Olivia's sleeve.

"Mummy, it's almost Christmas. Couldn't we have one teeny crystallised fruit to-night ? "

Olivia explained that the glories of the hamper must wait until Lalla could share them, because her step-uncle had sent the hamper. Toby said :

" I suppose as Lalla is going to share Christmas and her step-uncle has sent Dad all this, we ought to keep it, but it's unsound policy. We should sell most of this, especially the turkey, which will fetch a lot, and we should eat what Uncle William sends."

The family moaned with horror, but Olivia laughed.

" No, Toby, for one glorious day nothing is going to be eaten out of the shop, except possibly some vegetables, and we wouldn't eat those only I can't be bothered to go out and buy some anywhere else."

Out of doors Christmas Day was dull and grey, but in the Johnsons' house it was so gay it seemed as if the air was glistening. In the morning almost before the Johnsons had finished breakfast Lalla arrived, and behind her came the chauffeur with his arms full of presents to go under the Christmas tree. While Olivia cooked the turkey George took the family to church ; it was a nice service with all the proper carols, including *The First Nowell, Hark! the herald angels sing,* and *O come, all ye faithful.* When they got home again the table in the kitchen dining-room was laid for Christmas lunch. Olivia had made it look lovely, with two red candles, lots of holly, and in the middle something which had come out of Uncle David's hamper ; Father Christmas in his sledge, driving six remarkably prancy-looking reindeer.

The food was so good and there were such lovely things in the crackers, including a lot of indoor fireworks, that Christmas lunch was hardly cleared away and the fat feeling it had brought on had only begun to work off when Miss Goldthorpe and Nana arrived for Christmas tea. In spite of the splendid Christmas cake, nobody could eat much, for not only were they full of Christmas food already but the sooner they stopped eating the sooner they would get to the great moment of the day, presents and the tree.

Lalla had been so happy all day she had not supposed she could have felt happier. Everything was amusing ; the family jokes at lunch had seemed to her radiantly funny, helping to wash up and dry, a bore to the Johnsons, was the greatest pleasure to her, but when she was waiting for the Christmas tree to be lighted, she found a new sort of happiness rising in her which gave her a swelling-up feeling inside. Always before Christmas Day had been arranged for her, and though, of course, she gave presents to everybody in the house, it had been her presents that had mattered, and everybody in the house had stood round to admire and be interested when she opened her parcels. But now she had the thrill of parcel giving. Her inside sort of turned over each time she looked at her special parcels done up in holly-trimmed paper and scarlet bows. " Oh, giggerty-geggerty, wouldn't they all be pleased ! "

Lalla had to wait for the opening of her parcels. Guests first was Olivia's rule, and she rummaged amongst the parcels, picking out one for Miss Goldthorpe, one for Nana, and one for Lalla. They were all presents from Aunt Claudia. Nana had a grand new work-basket, Miss Goldthorpe an umbrella, and Lalla the latest book on skating.

" Very nice, I'm sure," said Nana.

The first of Lalla's presents to be opened was Alec's. A big book on cultivating vegetables. There was a card inside, which nobody would read except Alec, on which was written : " There are six closhes (I can't spell it) as well you know where. Guzzle guzzle guzzle quack quack quack, Lalla." Alec was pleased with the book, but when he read what was on the card he gave Lalla

*The great present was Harriet's and it took her
quite a time to unpack*

a hug, and as he shoved the card into his pocket he
whispered, " Quack quack quack."

For Toby there was a new fountain pen to use when
he was working out mathematical problems, Edward
had a Meccano set that he had been wanting for ages,
but the great present was Harriet's. The boots and the
skates had been packed in boxes, and the boxes were
wrapped in brown paper, and on top of that Lalla had
used her Christmas paper and bows, so they took Harriet
quite a time to unpack. When at last she saw what her
present was, her face was so pleased that it stopped looking
thin, and seemed swollen with smiling.

" Darling," said Olivia, " I didn't know you wanted
skates and boots so badly. Are you getting fond of
skating ? "

Harriet hugged the boots and skates to her and almost
sang.

" My own white boots and skates. Proper white boots!"

Lalla had forgotten what giving the skates and boots to Harriet would mean to Alec, but Toby saw the moment the boots came out of their box.

" You won't give up your paper round, Alec, will you? Imagine all that money is for you to save."

Alec, who was looking at his vegetable book, said " No " and gave Toby a wink. Harriet remembered her manners. She danced across to Lalla.

" Oh, thank you, thank you, Lalla. My own boots and such lovely skates. I'll be an absolutely proper skater now."

Miss Goldthorpe put the boots back in their box.

" I believe they'll fit you perfectly, dear. But Sam, who got them for us, said you were to keep them clean and bring them in to-morrow for him to make sure they are the right fit, if not he'll change them."

Harriet hated to see her boots shut up in their box even for one day, but she knew that skating boots ought to be properly fitted, and she had a great respect for anything that Sam said, so she let them be put away, though for the rest of the evening she went to the box every now and again and lifted the lid just to be sure they were there.

Mr. Pulton had told Alec to call on him on Boxing Day. Alec found him in his sitting-room wearing his brown velvet coat and cap, and his slippers embroidered in gold and silver thread. He welcomed Alec in his fading, tired voice, but his blue eyes were twinkling and pleased.

" Good-morning, young man. This is Boxing Day, do you know why it's called Boxing Day? " Alec said he did not. Mr. Pulton smiled. " It's the day set aside for the giving of presents or boxes to employees or messengers. I think a boy who carries round papers is a messenger, don't you ? "

Alec felt embarrassed. In the Johnson family if you received a present you gave a present ; he had not sent Mr. Pulton even a Christmas card, and he had not expected to receive one from Mr. Pulton, and it had never crossed his mind there might be a present. Mr. Pulton seemed able to read what Alec was thinking.

" Boxing Day is only a day for giving presents to those types of persons ; a present from an employee or a messenger to the employer would be most unseemly, most."

Alec glanced round the room ; it looked very un-Christmasy, not a piece of holly, a decoration or a little bit of paper and string to show where a present had been. He wished he had sent at least a Christmas card ; a Christmas card with a horse on it would have been nice ; Mr. Pulton would have liked that. Mr. Pulton pointed with his finger to the kitchen.

" If you go through there you'll find some plum cake, and port for myself and ginger wine for you. Employer and messenger should drink a glass of wine together at this season."

The kitchen was as spotless as when Alec had last seen it ; on the table was a tray, on which stood a decanter of port, two glasses, one filled with ginger wine, and some slices of plum cake. He carried the tray carefully back to the living-room, and put it on the table beside Mr. Pulton. Mr. Pulton filled his glass with port, and signalled to Alec to take his ginger wine. He held the port up to the firelight, so that it glowed like a ruby in his hand.

" Tell me, how is that vegetable garden shaping ? "

Alec sipped his ginger wine, it was good and warming and Mr. Pulton looked interested and encouraging, so in no time he was telling him everything, even about Lalla and her piece of garden, and the cloches. Then he explained that he would be able to do things now on a far greater scale than he had anticipated because Harriet's Christmas present had been skates and boots.

" You see, sir, that means fourteen shillings a week instead of two for my money-box."

Mr. Pulton was a man who respected money ; he said :

" Fourteen shillings ! " in a voice which showed that he appreciated what this meant.

" With this fortune do you intend to give up the idea of growing things in your sister's friend's garden ? "

" Not really, but she's only got a small bit I think. We haven't seen it yet, but you can't do much with a small bit. I think in March I shall start spending some of my money on stuff I shall buy at Covent Garden. If we could get a few people used to coming to Dad for decent vegetables regularly it'd be a start. I rather think my first buy will be new potatoes, but Toby's working that out. He's the mathematical one."

Mr. Pulton sat silent for quite a while, drinking his port and thinking over what Alec had said. Then a coal dropped in the fireplace, and brought him back to the present. He leant over the arm of his chair and picked up a parcel that was on the floor at his side.

" Here is your box." It was a cash box, a funny, old-fashioned-looking one made of leather, with little iron bars down it, and imitation iron studs all over it. " It's a copy of a very old chest, my boy. Fine craftsmanship. Smell it . . . beautiful leather."

Alec smelt, and found the box had a lovely smell.

Then he turned the key and lifted an iron hinge and found how splendidly it was made. Inside there were compartments divided by leather walls. Because it was such an original box it was nice to think of savings being kept in it.

" I say ! Thanks awfully, sir."

" That's all right, young man. When you were here before I spoke to you of horses." He swept his hand round the horses in the room. "And you told me about a pony and trap and vegetables and how some day you wished to be a market gardener. It will be an admirable start if you buy at Covent Garden, but you should not neglect growing things yourself in that piece of garden." He raised his glass. " To your dreams. May you follow them as I never followed mine."

Because of this talk with Mr. Pulton, Alec told Harriet to ask Lalla if he and Toby could come over and look at her piece of garden before Aunt Claudia came back. Because Aunt Claudia was away and it was Christmas time it was easy to arrange. The gardener was not coming, or if he came probably he would sit in the kitchen, and have tea and Christmas cake. The weather was cold, and Nana never came into the garden in the cold weather. The only person to worry about was Miss Goldthorpe. In the Christmas holidays Miss Goldthorpe came as usual, but it was not to give lessons, but to take Lalla for walks and to her special classes, so Miss Goldthorpe had to be told. One of the surprising things about Miss Goldthorpe was that you never knew what she would think about a thing. When she heard that Alec and Toby were coming over she did not understand why it had to be a secret.

" But very nice, dear. It's not really gardening weather, but it'll be healthy for you out of doors, but I shouldn't let Harriet come, she ought not to get her feet wet."

They were sitting by the schoolroom fire, roasting chestnuts, which would have shocked Aunt Claudia if she had seen them, because chestnuts were fattening. Lalla pushed a chestnut nearer the flames.

" But, Goldie, you do see, don't you, that it's got to be a secret ? I mean, Aunt Claudia doesn't know that Harriet's got any brothers, and she mustn't know that they come here. Nobody can come here unless she says so, you do know that."

Miss Goldthorpe sighed. She did indeed know. But she had thought Harriet's brothers just looking at the garden would be an exception.

" I can't believe she'd mind, dear. After all, any-body can be shown round a garden, though I don't think there's much growing at this time of year, is there ? "

Lalla took a chestnut off the fire and pinched it to see if it was done.

" You don't understand at all, Goldie. And I can't explain absolutely because it's a secret. It's nothing wrong ; as a matter of fact it's something good, so good it couldn't be gooder, and it's something nobody but Aunt Claudia could mind. Please, Goldie, would you know where I am if Nana asks, but not know the people I'm with. Nana gets in such a fuss if she thinks I'm doing something Aunt Claudia mightn't like."

Miss Goldthorpe thought of Uncle David's and her own scheme. It would be terrible if it was all muddled up because Harriet's brothers came to the garden and Aunt Claudia found out, though why the child should not be allowed to garden with Harriet's brothers she

could not imagine. Still, Aunt Claudia was queer,
everybody knew that.

"Very well, dear. But they're not to come without
you telling me, when they come you must let me know,
and you can slip out to the garden, but I don't like all
this secrecy."

The visit to Lalla's garden was a huge success. The
piece of bed which belonged to Lalla had been marked
out by stones, and though the gardener had taken most
of the stones away, there were enough to see where it
used to be.

"The first thing we must do," said Lalla, "is to put
the stones back, and if we sneak a little bit of extra
garden I shouldn't think anyone would notice, and if
anyone did it would be the gardener, and I expect he
would be pleased because it would be less for him to dig."

While Lalla and Alec collected stones to mark out the
bed, Toby measured the ground and put figures down
in a note-book. He said he thought that they might try
their luck at early lettuces, anyway the seeds would not
cost much. It was a pity they had not started in the
autumn, because a paying thing would have been strawberries. They would not be able to grow much of anything, but then it was not going to cost anything once it
was planted out, so that would not matter.

To her surprise Lalla found that putting stones round
the garden with Alec was fun. She had not thought it
could be fun grubbing for stones in damp earth, but it
was when there was someone to do it with. So when
Alec said that the difficulty was going to be getting the
bed looked after, watered and weeded and all that, Lalla
found herself offering to help.

"I think Uncle David could get Aunt Claudia to let

you come and give me gardening lessons. We could call
it that. Aunt Claudia thinks gardening good for me, it's
being out of doors and exercise both at once. But when
you can't come I won't mind watering sometimes."

Toby looked at her over his spectacles.

" It would be a very good thing if you took up gardening. It's always a mistake to count on just one thing.
It'll be all right if you are a skating star," he put enormous
weight on the word " are," " but if you're not you might
be very glad to get a job in Alec's market garden."

Lalla, safe in the knowledge of how well she had passed
her inter-silver test, looked at him with scorn.

" It's no good talking like that, Toby, my boy. Here's
someone who is almost a champion. If you don't believe
me you'd better come and see my exhibition, it's two
weeks from Wednesday."

CHAPTER IX

SKATING GALA

★

UNCLE DAVID had partly suggested to Aunt Claudia his and Miss Goldthorpe's plan for Lalla and Harriet. He knew that with Aunt Claudia it was a good idea to suggest something and then let the suggestion simmer. This idea took a lot of simmering, for Aunt Claudia could not put her mind seriously to anything until Lalla's exhibition was over. The nearer it got to the skating gala day the more excited she got. She made all her friends take seats, and found herself looking forward to the night more than she had looked forward to anything for ages. Her friends said, " Dear little Lalla, of course we'll take seats, especially if it's for charity." Aunt Claudia let them think that Lalla was just a dear little child giving her first skating exhibition ; it would be such a moment when the friends saw what Lalla's skating was really like. Already in imagination she could hear the buzz of admiring remarks and congratulations which would shower on her. She listened to Uncle David's idea and brushed it aside. It might be a good plan, she didn't know, she would see what everybody said ; if it was thought helpful for Lalla she might consider it. She would not go further than that.

Uncle David had wanted a good moment for George

and Olivia to meet Aunt Claudia. He knew it would be
a failure if Aunt Claudia met them in their own house,
because she was the kind of person who expected houses
to be large and grand. He thought the skating exhibition
would be his opportunity, so he bought three good seats
fairly near Aunt Claudia's and sent them to George, with
a letter. In the letter he said that he did not imagine
this sort of thing was much in George's line, but he
would be glad if he and Olivia would bring Harriet,
because it would be an opportunity for the two families
to meet.

Olivia never bothered very much about clothes; she
always managed to look nice, so she took dressing for the
skating gala quite casually, but not Harriet. The moment
she saw the tickets she fussed.

" Mummy, what shall we wear ? "

Olivia was busy at the time and answered vaguely.

" Our thick coats I suppose, it'll be cold, darling."

Harriet saw that her mother had not appreciated the
importance of the occasion.

" But, Mummy, it's fur coats and fur boots. Lalla told
me so. She said that Aunt Claudia had said on the
telephone to somebody just a smart warm dress under a
fur coat, and, of course, fur boots."

Olivia laughed.

" I've not got a fur coat, darling, and neither have
you, and we've no smart, warm dresses, and we've not
got fur boots, so I'm afraid we'll have to watch Lalla in
our ordinary winter coats, with a rug over our knees to
keep us warm."

Harriet confided in Nana.

" Mr. King has sent Daddy the poshest seats, and he
wants Mummy and him to meet Aunt Claudia, and that

would mean me too. Lalla says people wear fur coats and fur boots to things like that, but Mummy and me haven't those."

Nana was as usual knitting. She made soothing, clucking sounds, but her mind was on the problem. It was very important how people looked when they met Aunt Claudia.

" Anything your mother wears is sure to look nice, dear, she's one of the sort who looks dressed no matter what they wear." She paused and knitted half a row. While she knitted she thought about Harriet. Harriet's winter coat was in Nana's opinion only fit for the dust-bin ; it was navy blue and it fitted her before she was ill, now it was too loose, much too short in length and, worse still, much too short in the arms. It had too a saggy hang about the pockets, and there were worn patches where the material had a whitish look. If Harriet took the coat off Nana was sure she would be wearing her brown velvet. If possible, in Nana's view, the velvet was worse than the coat. The coat was just plain and shabby, but the velvet should have been smart. If there was one thing Nana could not abide it was clothes that had once been smart and now were shabby. " There's a pink coat Lalla has grown out of ; it's nice in the length but she's a bit square in the shoulders for it. It would fit you nicely, dear."

" But wouldn't Aunt Claudia know it was Lalla's ? "

" No. You see, Lalla's got so many things. Besides, even if she'd notice it in the ordinary way, she never would on a night like that. You ask your mother if you can borrow it, and if she says yes I'll bring it along and an extra warm sweater of Lalla's to wear with it. It's a spring coat really, and not thick enough without something warm under, and you want warm knickers, the ice strikes up very cold, you don't want to catch a chill."

The night of the skating gala every seat at the rink was taken. It was an annual event, in aid of local charities, and was always a big occasion. All types of skating celebrities gave exhibitions; professionals, championship soloists and pairs, champion figure skaters and champion dancing pairs. As well there was usually an exhibition by promising local children. Sometimes it was a skating ballet arranged for a lot of children, sometimes it was a pair of children ice dancers, and now and again it was a solo exhibition.

Lalla, as her father's daughter, and an unusually promising child, was given a star place on the bill. She was to come last in the first half before the interval. Nothing that could contribute to Aunt Claudia's approval of the evening had been forgotten. Mr. Matthews met her in the entrance and gave her a beautiful bow, and told her how proud she was going to be of Lalla in a loud enough voice for all the people coming in to turn round and look at Aunt Claudia. He himself took her and Uncle David to their seats, which were the best placed at the rink, and stayed a few moments saying polite things. When he had gone Aunt Claudia looked round, and found her friends were trying to attract her attention by waving their programmes. One of the many things that pleased her most about the evening was that Uncle David had not only agreed to come but came willingly. This had been a great surprise. Willingly to a skating gala ! He who said about watching skating, " I'm blessed if I'm going to pay to have cold feet ! " She thought how good-looking he was, and guessed how envious everyone must be of her ; such a handsome husband and a niece the star child of the evening. She did not know that Uncle David being there was part of a scheme and that while Aunt Claudia was waving to her friends he was waving to George and Olivia.

" Is that your friend David King ? " Olivia asked.

George nodded.

" Not a friend really, you know. Surprised he remembered me."

Harriet, feeling very grand in Lalla's nice-fitting pink coat and snug in her pink jersey, pulled at her mother's arm.

" The lady beside him is Lalla's Aunt Claudia."

Olivia was going to say that nobody could suppose the grand lady in mink was anybody but Lalla's Aunt Claudia, when she looked at Harriet. Pink was not her colour, poor pet, it did not go with reddish hair and rather a pale face, Harriet was getting on splendidly, but she still had too much eyes for the rest of her. She was so proud in her pink coat, and so in awe of Aunt Claudia, whom presently they had to meet, that Olivia knew it was not the moment to speak jokingly.

" Isn't she grand, but no grander than you look, darling. I shall feel as though I ought to curtsey when you two are speaking to each other."

The performers in the gala waited for their entrances on the small rink, so that they could warm and limber up before they went on. Nana had a seat reserved for her at the end of the rink next to Miss Goldthorpe, but she was not going to use it until Lalla went on. In the meantime she sat and watched her, holding her white ermine coat on her knee. Nana did not really hold with what she called " making a show " of Lalla. A little private theatricals was nice for a shy child, but Lalla was. not shy and did not need bringing forward, so she was being kept up past her bedtime for no purpose, so Nana was a little disapproving. But as she watched Lalla practising the disapproving feeling wore off and she felt a little proud. Lalla was wearing a white ballet dress, with a bodice of white satin, and net and tarlatan skirts which glittered with silver stars. On her head, in place of the bonnets she usually wore, was a small cap of diamanté, which held her curls in place. Nana saw that the grown-up skaters watched Lalla with pleased faces, thinking how sweet she looked, which she did, the pretty lamb. Nana still disapproved of dieting her, but Lalla did not seem any the worse for it, and now that she was dressed in her ballet dress, she thought, with that tight satin bodice, it was a good thing she didn't stick out in front as she had done a week or two back. Aunt Claudia had succeeded in buying a pair of the most beautiful nylon tights. When Nana had first seen them she had been most sniffy about them.

"Nylon tights! Lot of foolishness, catch her death. She should be wearing her white wool same as usual."

Lalla had giggled.

"Silly Nana! I couldn't have worn wool anyway, with a ballet dress, it would have to have been bare legs. Nobody could wear wool tights with a ballet dress."

Now that Lalla had the tights on Nana saw that she was lucky to have them. Many of the skaters had bare legs, and very cold Nana thought it looked, giving a nasty bluish tinge to the skin. If a child had to do a foolish thing like stripping to go on the ice in midwinter, then it was better to wear nylon than nothing at all. One thing she had seen to, and it comforted her to know that she had seen to it, Lalla was wearing good wool next to the skin, wool knitted by herself. She did not hold with ice, nasty, damp stuff, but she defied any ice to give a chill to a child who wore wool knitted by herself next to the skin.

Max Lindblom had arranged a programme for Lalla to fit into a specially orchestrated mixture of music from *Where the Rainbow Ends*. A few bars were played before her entrance, then, as she skimmed on to the ice, she was picked out by a frosted spotlight. The fairy music and Lalla's fairylike appearance, and the magic quality of the cold, blue light on the ice, was enchanting ; her entrance got a spontaneous burst of applause.

Lalla had not felt nervous before she came on ; she enjoyed free skating and was happy performing the routine Max had arranged for her. It included most of the jumps she liked best and, as well, spread-eagling, which she adored. She was enchanted at receiving a round of applause, smiled gaily and settled down to enjoy herself. The programme Max had chosen was not difficult, and no knowledgeable person would be fooled into thinking that it was ; equally the knowledgeable preferred seeing children performing a programme well within their range. What was noticeable about Lalla was her gaiety ; that she was finding every minute of her exhibition fun bubbled out of her and made the audience think it was fun too. When, at the end, she skimmed down the rink in an arabesque, her arms outstretched and curtseyed to the best seats, which really meant curtseying to Aunt Claudia, the audience not only clapped but they cheered. Lalla had to take six calls, and on the sixth Mr. Matthews, very nervously because he was not wearing skates and was afraid of falling down, came on the ice

and presented her with an enormous bouquet of pink
carnations.

Olivia turned to Harriet, her eyes very bright and her
cheeks very pink with pleasure.

"Darling! How lovely Lalla is! The pet can skate,
can't she?"

Mr. Matthews presented Lalla with an enormous bouquet

Harriet glowed; being Lalla's friend was almost as
grand as being Lalla.

"And she can do much more glorious things than
that, terribly difficult things that lots of people who've
learnt skating for years and years can't do."

George lit a cigarette. He was watching Uncle David
with Aunt Claudia. He turned to Olivia.

" I doubt whether King will be able to make that introduction. Look at the aunt." They all looked.

Aunt Claudia was in a dream-come-true world. She had always known that Lalla could skate, always known that she would be a star, but this was the first time she had felt what it was like to own Lalla. Years ago she had found it made her important that she was Cyril Moore's sister, and she had liked the feeling, and had missed it when he was drowned. But being Cyril Moore's sister was a mere nothing to being Lalla's aunt and guardian. Everybody that she knew and lots that she did not, flocked round her saying all the nicest things, and the nicer the things they said the grander Aunt Claudia felt. It was only just as the interval ended that Uncle David managed to introduce the Johnsons. By this time a smile had become part of Aunt Claudia's face, and a rich graciousness so much part of her voice that it was almost as if she were talking with a piece of cream out of a chocolate bar lying on her tongue.

" This is my friend George Johnson, Harriet's father," Uncle David explained, " and this is Mrs. Johnson, Harriet's mother. How do you do, Harriet? You and I haven't met before, but I've heard a lot about you."

Aunt Claudia was too carried away by the glory of the evening to see anybody as clearly as usual, but not so carried away but that some part of her mind said to her that Olivia, though obviously poor, was charming in every way, that David's school friend George seemed presentable, and that Harriet looked better dressed than when she had last seen her, though the colour chosen for her was unfortunate, and that it was curious that somebody who obviously knew how to wear clothes, even if she had not got any nice ones, should dress her daughter

in that shade of pink, which was obviously wrong for her
colouring. Because she was feeling pleased with everyone
and everything, Aunt Claudia was in the mood to say
nice things, and as she looked at the Johnsons the
suggestion made by Uncle David at Christmas came back
to her. She smiled kindly at Harriet.

"I hear this child has not been going to school since
her illness. It might be possible for her to have lessons
with Lalla. Of course nothing can be arranged in a
hurry, naturally everything planned for Lalla has to have
great thought, but perhaps I might give you a ring
sometime, and you would come to tea and discuss it."

The idea of Harriet doing lessons with Lalla was so
new to the Johnsons that they stared at Aunt Claudia in
silence. Then Olivia rose as usual to the occasion.

"What a lovely idea, but of course it would want
thinking over."

As soon as she was back in her seat Harriet put her
hand into her mother's.

"Mummy! Do you think she meant it? Lessons with
Lalla and Goldie every day? Wouldn't that be simply
gorgeous!"

Lalla's success at the skating gala made Lalla less nice
to have as a friend than she had been. Lalla had what
is called a vivid personality, which was the part of her
that made her remembered and stand out from other
skaters. Because she had this the skating correspondents
of the newspapers had noticed her, and wrote about her
in their papers, and photographers took photographs of
her. If Nana and Miss Goldthorpe could have had their
way Lalla would never have read about herself in the
papers, or looked at the photographs, but Aunt Claudia
thought reading about herself and looking at pictures of

herself would stimulate Lalla to further efforts. Many days she had her down to the drawing-room after tea and read her press notices out loud to her.

"Little Lalla Moore, Cyril Moore's daughter, is a skater of remarkable promise, of whom we should hear more." "Little Lalla Moore, the daughter of figure skater Cyril Moore, was the star of the evening." "Little Miss Lalla Moore, for whom a great future is predicted, won all hearts," and in the Sunday papers, under pictures, "A young skating star." "A winsome child skater." "A pretty little queen of the ice."

The more press cuttings Aunt Claudia read or showed to Lalla the more prancey, and difficult to deal with, Nana and Miss Goldthorpe found her. It was difficult to get her back from what Nana called "Being above herself." Aunt Claudia wanted her to be above herself. Wilson, the cook, and Helen, the housemaid, did not mind her being above herself. They cut out photographs of her, and stuck them up in their bedrooms, in their sitting-room, and on the kitchen mantelpiece, and liked it when she came in and told them all about the gala.

Harriet tried not to side with Nana and Miss Gold-thorpe against Lalla, but she did wish she would stop being grand. Lalla was always inclined to tell Harriet to do things for her, but after the gala she treated her rather as though she existed for no other purpose than to wait on her.

"Don't you give in to her, dear," said Nana. "The way she goes on you'd think you were no more than a heathen slave that she'd bought. You want to say no to her sharp and plain, same as I do."

Miss Goldthorpe said :

"I do hope Mrs. King will soon come to a decision

about your doing lessons with Lalla, Harriet dear. It's going to be so good for Lalla to have someone to work with, and you must not give in to her, she needs a friend who doesn't give in."

Nana's and Miss Goldthorpe's great supporter in putting Lalla back to being an ordinary girl who skated rather nicely was Max Lindblom. He spoke to Nana most seriously about her.

" It is not good that Lalla is shown these press cuttings. She thinks now she is so clever she need not work, but I tell you that she must work harder than ever before if she is to pass the test for her silver medal in May. I cannot make her concentrate on her brackets."

To Nana a bracket was something hung on a wall, on which ornaments stood, but she was accustomed to Lalla and Max using words which meant nothing to her.

" I'll speak to her about it, Mr. Lindblom. She's been a bit of a madam lately, but it should be passing off soon. Children are apt to get above themselves occasionally, but I'll tell her plainly that you're not pleased, and she's to think of those brackets, or we'll have to be bracketing her."

Lalla was not the only member of the household to get above herself after the skating gala, Aunt Claudia was above herself too. Often she thought about that night, about the way the manager at the rink had received her, the applause, and the admiration and envy of her friends, of sitting watching the rest of the entertainment with Lalla's bouquet on her knee, and people whispering about her, pointing her out and saying who she was, of leaving the rink, and the strangers who came up and said nice things. It was a new sort of world to her, and she wanted the same excitement to happen again very soon. She went

to Mr. Matthews. Mr. Matthews had been having a bit
of trouble with his duodenal ulcer, but when he heard
that Aunt Claudia wanted to see him, he swallowed two
dyspepsia tablets with a little milk, and went out to meet
her, trying to look like a man who did not know what a
troubled inside was. He brought Aunt Claudia into his
office and sat her in his best arm-chair, and told her how
pleased he was to see her, and how proud he was of the
success Lalla had made at his gala. Aunt Claudia leant
forward.

" It's about that I've come to see you. I think an
experience like that is good for Lalla. You won't believe
it, but there have been times when I've felt, not exactly
a lack of enthusiasm, but a lack of ambition. Now I
see why. The child needed a taste of success and
applause."

Mr. Matthews looked at Aunt Claudia politely, but
inside he was surprised. He was used to skating mothers,
pushing forward their own little darlings, and if another
child was given a chance that their child did not have,
making a fuss, but he had not placed Lalla's aunt as the
type. He had looked upon her as a strict guardian, who
saw in Lalla a child who might follow in her father's
footsteps and become a fine skater, and who was prepared to spend a great deal of money to achieve this. An
Aunt Claudia who wanted Lalla made a show of, giving
public performances, was a new idea to him, but he was
a business man and quickly saw two things. One, that it
would bring credit on his rink if Lalla were allowed
occasionally to appear for charity, and the other that
Max Lindblom must not be told what was planned. Mr.
Matthews picked up any gossip that was round his rink
as if he were a vacuum cleaner picking up dust ; that

Max thought Lalla's skating success had gone to her head was gossip that had blown in from every quarter. He drew a diary towards him.

" There will not be many important events before the season ends, but there are two, at which I should be glad if you would allow Lalla to perform. One is in London, and one away. Of course you will have no trouble with the arrangements, the hotel bookings for the away date will be made by the management of the rink concerned."

Aunt Claudia had a vision of herself, Lalla, and Nana walking into a large and expensive hotel, herself being pointed out as Mrs. King with her niece, the little skating star. She saw herself returning in the evening, carrying Lalla's flowers, and allowing her fellow guests to crowd round her and congratulate her. She told Mr. Matthews that she thought they could manage the two dates, and she would see about Lalla's frocks right away.

" I must plan quite a skating wardrobe for her before the winter season starts."

Mr. Matthews put his fingertips together and asked cautiously if Mrs. King had discussed these additional public appearances with Max Lindblom.

Aunt Claudia felt Mr. Matthews was not asking from idle curiosity, so she said " no," and asked why.

Mr. Matthews pressed his fingers more tightly together than ever, and hoped he was being tactful.

" Skating instructors are apt to think that only work on the figures for the tests is advisable before a test. With her silver test in May I think you may find Max Lindblom difficult to deal with."

Aunt Claudia, having decided that public appearances were good for Lalla and knowing they were good for herself, was not prepared to let Max Lindblom spoil things. She gave the sort of laugh that means "who cares?"

"Then I shan't tell him; I think I know what's good for Lalla, and I'm sure you do."

After Aunt Claudia had gone Mr. Matthews telephoned to the managers of the two rinks which were having charity performances about Lalla. After that he sat down meaning to get on with some other work, but the thought of his talk with Aunt Claudia kept interrupting him, and quite suddenly he said something out loud which surprised him very much, because it was "poor little kid."

When Max Lindblom heard that Lalla was going down to the south coast to skate at a charity gala he was very angry indeed. It happened to be a day when Miss Goldthorpe was at the rink, so she heard all that Max thought about it. Except when she was talking to Harriet, Miss Goldthorpe filled up her time at the rink with her favourite occupation, reciting Shakespeare in her head. She was a great lover of Shakespeare's plays, and could recite them for hours on end and never repeat herself once. That particular day she was with Henry V. She was saying to herself "O For a Muse of fire" and imagining the rink had turned into "this wooden O" and that she was breathing the casque-filled air that did affright at Agincourt, when Max sat down beside her and spoke rapidly in her ear. Miss Goldthorpe took her time to come back from Agincourt and missed the first part of what he was saying. When she could give him her attention she found that about Lalla he and she had ideas in common.

"That one exhibition, yes. I had thought it was good for Lalla, I myself suggested it. But it was not good. Now she is the great star, she knows everything. 'Do not bother me, Max, I'll do those silly old brackets in plenty of time for my test.' But I tell you," and here Max thumped his chest, " that she will not do them unless she works and works. There is no time for her to go away skating, and if she does she'll be even more difficult to train. Applause goes to her head like the glass of wine. This must not be."

Miss Goldthorpe looked at Max, and thought what a pity it was that such fire and earnestness should be wasted on so poor a cause as skating.

" I'm sure you are right, Mr. Lindblom, but you are wasting your energy being angry with me. I have nothing whatsoever to do with Lalla's skating. I educate her."

Max became even more frenzied.

" Then you know how I feel. You must go to this aunt, and you must say Lalla may not perform in skating galas because it interrupts her education."

Miss Goldthorpe looked again at Max. What a pity that such agile legs should not be allied to an equally agile brain. Clearly this young man's brain was not only not agile but scarcely a brain at all, else why, having met Aunt Claudia, should he suppose that she, or anybody else, could tell her what Lalla might or might not do. Such volubility wasted on such mistaken thinking made Miss Goldthorpe sad. She patted Max's knee.

" Keep calm. Now think. You know Mrs. King will not be told what is best for Lalla, she is the only one who knows. If you or I or anybody else tried to argue with her all that would happen would be that we should cease to teach Lalla. I have on many occasions given notice to schools at which I have taught, but so far no one has given notice to me, and I don't intend that they should.

Partly because I should dislike the sensation, and partly because I'm fond of Lalla."

Max put his head in his hands.

" Then all is finished."

Miss Goldthorpe felt sorry for him, for he seemed to her pathetic and no older than Lalla. She spoke briskly as she would to a child who was upset.

" Nonsense. Now take your head out of your hands and listen to me. You can't prevent Mrs. King allowing Lalla to skate at charity performances however regrettable it may be, but you can do something to help Lalla. Her old nurse says that Lalla has got above herself, and that describes it exactly. Now the remedy I suggest is the company of another child. Mrs. King is already half-wedded to the idea of Harriet spending the day with Lalla and doing lessons with her. If you, quite on your own, would suggest that Harriet would be a help to Lalla's career I think the affair could be settled. There's nothing so good for a spoilt child as the company of another child of her own age."

Max raised his head and looked at the rink. It was the few minutes that Lalla gave to Harriet before her practice and lesson with Max. Lalla was watching Harriet struggling with what Max's eye recognised as forward outside threes, and Miss Goldthorpe supposed was the sort of playing about which would end by Harriet falling on the ice. As Max watched the two children he began to look less distraught, then after a bit, the sort of cheerful that people look when they are thinking about something they like to think about.

" I shall see Mrs. King. I will tell her that I think it is good for Lalla that her friend Harriet should take lessons, and be on the small private rink when Lalla practises her figures. I have watched the little friend, she wastes no time, she is absorbed that one, she will not be able to know how a bracket should be, but she can watch Lalla, and be interested, and then˜perhaps Lalla will work."

Miss Goldthorpe was glad that Max could grasp so quickly what she had in mind, and began to think better of his brain. Probably, since he was the skating instructor, Aunt Claudia would pay more attention to what he said than to what she might say. It would be a good idea that he should be the one to propose that Harriet should work with Lalla. When Max got up to go she asked when he intended seeing Mrs. King, and was delighted to find that he not only moved fast on his legs, but evidently moved fast in things that he did.

" I go to Mr. Matthews now. By to-morrow it will be arranged."

Not by to-morrow, but by the day after, it was arranged. Mr. Matthews telephoned Aunt Claudia and asked if she would see Max Lindblom, and he explained what it was about. That same evening Uncle David telephoned George and asked if Olivia could come to tea the next day to discuss the whole thing, and told him what it was about. Finally Aunt Claudia told Lalla and Nana, and Olivia told Harriet. Harriet was breathless with pleasure.

" All day ! Tea too ? "

Olivia kissed her.

" Lalla's aunt wanted you to go to tea every day, but I wasn't having that. We should never see you at all, darling. Sometimes, of course, you can go back with her, but often, I hope, you'll bring Lalla and Nana to tea here."

Lalla asked the same question.

" And tea, and after tea a bit ? "

Aunt Claudia looked annoyed.

" That's the one tiresome thing. For convenience's sake, so that you have someone to play with, I invited Harriet to come back to tea every day, but her mother said that would mean they wouldn't see enough of her. I've had to agree that now and again you may go to tea there as a change. I understand that it's a treat for the Johnson family to have you, which I suppose is natural, they don't know any other celebrities to be."

The night when everything was decided Lalla and Harriet danced their way to bed.

" Mummy," said Harriet hugging Olivia, " you do know I'll miss being with you all day, but skating lessons ! It's probably the most gorgeous thing that'll ever happen to me."

Olivia put her arms round her.

" Is it, my pet ? You are a funny little scrap. Who would have thought that less than six months ago you'd never seen a skate ? "

Lalla butted Nana, who was trying to tuck her up, with her head.

" You wait and see my square-turn'd joints and strength of limb after I've had Harriet almost to live with me. They'll grow so square-turn'd and so strong they couldn't be squarer or stronger."

Nana kissed Lalla good-night.

" Lie down, and let's have no more foolishness. You don't want to get any squarer than you are or there'll be more of that banting."

CHAPTER X

SILVER TEST

★

LESSONS for both Lalla and Harriet became fun, and Miss Goldthorpe enjoyed them enormously. The two girls were not only almost exactly the same age, but much of a muchness at lessons. Lalla was good at things like grammar, and remembering dates, and geography, and Harriet, which was a great pleasure to Miss Goldthorpe, loved reading. Both girls were bad at, and detested, sums. But it was fun being bad at the same thing. Lalla found even adding money, which she thought the nastiest kind of sums, could be pleasant if it meant she beat Harriet when she got them right. She did not like Harriet's and Miss Goldthorpe's taste for literature, especially not their fondness for Shakespeare's plays.

"I wouldn't have thought it of you, Harriet. You don't look the mimsy-pimsy sort of person who could like hearing about that silly Viola and that awful Malvolio."

At eleven the door would open and Nana would come in with glasses of milk for the girls and a cup of tea for Miss Goldthorpe and biscuits for everybody. Sometimes she would bring her own cup as well, and while she drank her tea would give a running commentary on how things were going in the house.

148

" Your aunt's out for a fitting for her clothes for that Ascot. Cook has a chip on her shoulder this morning. She meant to go out with her sister this evening to the pictures, but now Wilson's brought a message from your aunt to say there'll be two extra for dinner. The sun's coming out beautifully, the gardener says you ought to come down and see his crocuses, proper sight they are on the lawn."

When Nana mentioned the gardener Lalla and Harriet would exchange looks with Miss Goldthorpe. It was time the boys came over and dug up that bed, and put in their lettuce seed. According to Alec it should have been planted some time before, and the little plants growing under cloches.

Usually Nana would finish with a bit of news for Harriet. She would say she had been going through Lalla's drawers and cupboards and had found this thing or that thing which would be useful to her. The things she found were always worn in the house, they never went back to Harriet's house. Nana had not talked to Miss Goldthorpe about Harriet's clothes ; it was no good talking to Miss Goldthorpe about clothes, she never knew what anyone had on, or cared what she looked like herself, but now and again she had confided in her about the Johnsons.

" They haven't any money, poor things, and Mrs. Johnson so nice and all. I don't want her knowing, but never knowing when Mrs. King will pop in and out of the schoolroom, and knowing how she expects the children to look, I find the easiest thing is to use Lalla's clothes for both. As soon as Harriet comes I say, 'Take that off, dear, we don't want it spoilt,' and I've popped her into something of Lalla's before you can say Jack Robinson."

Usually Nana's news for Harriet would come just as she was picking up the tray.

" After your dinner, Harriet, I'd like you in Lalla's room. I've an old frock of hers, more than good enough for lessons, it will fit you nicely if I take it in and let it down."

At twelve o'clock on Mondays and Thursdays Miss Goldthorpe walked the children round to Alonso Vittori's studio for Lalla's dancing class. Alonso Vittori was a leading stage dancer, but as well he took a few private pupils. He had been teaching Lalla for some time. He did not have to give her a strict ballet training, more a good grounding, so that she learned to hold postures and move her body and hands gracefully. As well, of course, ballet exercises were very good for her legs. Alonso was fond of Lalla as a person, but not really fond of teaching her dancing, because, although she liked Alonso, Lalla thought learning dancing a waste of time. " Not that beastly exercise again, Alonso darling. Why should I have to do it, I'm a skater? On my skates I couldn't do that, so why should I learn it on a floor ? "

To begin with, after Harriet had joined Lalla for lessons, she had watched her being taught to dance with the same open-eyed admiration she watched her skating. How extraordinary for legs to do that. How clever of Lalla to have legs that did that. At the end of the third lesson, at which Lalla had been particularly tiresome about barre exercises, Alonso noticed Harriet's admiring face. He had lived all his life in the ballet world, and had met any amount of young Lallas in his day, with admiring mothers and aunts who called them geniuses, and he had known what had happened to Lalla the very first lesson she came to him after the skating gala. Other

Harriet felt rather shy trying to do what Alonso told her

people might think Harriet too big in the eyes, and too
thin in the legs, but Alonso admired her; he liked her
thin look, and thought it a pity that now Lalla had
Harriet to work with, for of course he had heard about
Harriet ever since Lalla had first met her, she should be
a devoted admirer instead of an ordinary critical friend.
So he went across to her.

"Why don't you join the class next time?"

Harriet blinked at him in astonishment.

"Me! But I couldn't."

Alonso told her not to be silly.

"Take off your hat and coat, put on Lalla's shoes and
go over there."

Harriet felt rather shy standing all alone in the middle
of the room in ordinary school clothes, trying to do what
Alonso told her, while Lalla and Miss Goldthorpe looked

on, but Alonso did not think too badly of her. Just before he finished with her he called Lalla over.

" Have a look at that. Harriet's never learned but she's holding her hands better than I've ever succeeded in making you hold yours."

It was not absolutely true, but it was near enough true for Alonso to think he might say it, and it certainly had the desired effect on Lalla. She had never been jealous but she had never had cause to be. She gave Harriet a push, and told her to take off her shoes, and told Alonso he was only saying that to annoy her. He knew Harriet could not be as good as she was. Alonso laughed, rumpled Lalla's hair, and told her that from now on Harriet was to attend his classes, and he expected she would have to work hard to keep up with her.

Lalla had never needed to be told to work hard at fencing. She liked it, and found it fun, but Monsieur Cordon had often thought it would be good for Lalla to have a child of her own size to fence with. He ran his fencing classes with the aid of his sons, and they had a great many pupils, and it was not always convenient for him to fence with Lalla or to spare one of his sons to give his full attention to her for half an hour. So when he discovered that Harriet was always coming to watch his classes, he decided she should learn to fence too, and he told one of his sons to instruct her. He explained what he was doing to Miss Goldthorpe.

" It is nice that Lalla should have her little friend fencing too. Fencing for her is for the good of her figure, and for quick movement. She will never wish to study it seriously. If her friend fences that will be admirable for all."

Miss Goldthorpe recited Shakespeare to herself through

both ballet and fencing classes. Usually the clash of the
foils took her mind to the more fiery scenes. On that
day she was in imagination present at the duel between
Hamlet and Laertes. She was hearing the king say :
" Let all the battlements their ordnance fire " ; when
Monsieur Cordon spoke. She liked Monsieur Cordon,
as she liked the other odd people who instructed Lalla.
To her it was past comprehension why an apparently
pleasant Frenchman and his two pleasant sons should
waste their time playing about with foils, when duelling
had gone out of fashion years ago, but she tried never to
let him know that she thought he was frittering away his
life. She only caught half of what he said, but it was
enough for her to understand that he was suggesting
teaching Harriet. She began to wonder if she could be
misjudging Lalla's teachers ; they were all showing more
sense than she had anticipated. She smiled at Monsieur
Cordon and thanked him, and said nothing could be
better for Harriet, whose legs needed strengthening
because she had been ill.

On Wednesdays and Saturdays, when there were no
special classes, Lalla and Miss Goldthorpe were supposed
to go for walks or visit places of educational interest. But
Wednesday and Saturday mornings when there was
nothing to do were few. There were fittings for all Lalla's
clothes that were not knitted by Nana. There were
walking shoes to be made, and gloves to be bought.
Shopping was a loathing that Miss Goldthorpe and Lalla
shared.

" Goldie darling," Lalla would say hopefully, " the
sun's shining. When lessons are over do you think we
could go and look at the lock ? I think seeing how a lock
works is an educational subject, don't you ? "

Miss Goldthorpe usually agreed that anything Lalla wanted to look at was an educational subject, because she thought that for Lalla anything that used her eyes and head instead of her feet was educational. But they seldom did the things they planned to do. Presently there would be a tap on the door and Wilson would be there to say that when Lalla had finished her lessons, she and Miss Goldthorpe and Harriet were to go out with her for a fitting for a skating dress, or Nana would say apologetically, " I don't know what was planned, but I'm afraid you'll have to call in at the shoemakers, they've telephoned to say that Lalla's shoes are ready for fitting."

On Saturdays, to make up for the hours when she should have been doing lessons and spent at the rink, Lalla was supposed to work in the mornings, but Miss Goldthorpe interpreted the word "lessons," as they referred to Saturday mornings, in the widest possible way. She tried to make Saturday mornings adventure mornings, when they learned things out of doors. Some days it had been trees and flowers, and some days old buildings, and some days following a map, but whatever it was it was a nice thing to do, and there was always a good alternative for indoors in case it rained ; special things to look at in museums, pictures to see in a gallery, the under-cover animals to visit at the zoo, or they would go to Madame Tussaud's.

Aunt Claudia had always known in a vague way about Lalla's Saturday mornings, and had not minded provided they were educational and would help to get Lalla through proper examinations at the proper time. But after Harriet joined Lalla for lessons, Aunt Claudia began to steal Saturday mornings. They suited her. On Saturday mornings she could have Lalla for much longer than the odd hour on Wednesday mornings, and she would drive her to Garrick Street, which was the theatrical part of London, where Lalla's skating dresses were made. She did not as a rule take Harriet and Miss Goldthorpe with her, and Lalla found Saturday morning fittings an awful bore. It was not so bad while her frocks were being fitted, and the designer and fitter were looking at her and deciding whether there should be a little bit of silver here or whether she should stick out more there, but it was afterwards she got bored. She would stare out of the window at the London traffic, while the designer and Aunt Claudia discussed spangles, and tu-tus, and pleated chiffon. At luncheon she would describe these talks to Nana and Harriet.

" Goodness, you can't think how awful it was. Talk, talk, talk, jabber, jabber, jabber. I can't think why grown-up people like talking about stuff. The man who makes my frocks showed me some pale blue silky stuff, and asked if I liked it, and I said ' yes.' But, do you know, Aunt Claudia and him talked for hours and hours about it after that."

Miss Goldthorpe went home to lunch on Saturdays, and officially had her Saturday afternoons to herself, though sometimes she stayed on for the rink and took Lalla there to save Nana, when Nana had what she called " trouble with her knees." Miss Goldthorpe looked forward to her Saturdays. Often she would go to see one of Shakespeare's plays. There was not always a play in the West-end, but there were usually performances that could be reached by bus or tram in some outlying part of London. When there was no Shakespeare for her to see she would either go to a concert or stay at home reading. She cherished her Saturdays just as anyone treasures a Saturday, when

they work hard all the week, but when she saw Lalla's
Saturday mornings being sneaked by Aunt Claudia she
was sad, and decided that she must make a sacrifice. She
would give her Saturday afternoons to Lalla. After all,
she told herself, I'll have my Sundays left, and that ought
to be enough for anyone. So one day when she had taken
Lalla and Harriet to the rink because of Nana's knees, she
caught Max Lindblom's eye to show she wanted to speak
to him.

"You remember when we planned you should teach
Harriet as well as Lalla it was because it was good for
her. Now I want you to plan something else which will
be good for her." She lowered her voice for, though there
was no one near her, she felt like a conspirator in one
of Shakespeare's plays planning a dark deed. "I want
you to arrange to teach Lalla on Saturday mornings
instead of Saturday afternoons."

Max Lindblom was surprised.

"But it is nice for Lalla on Saturdays. There are
many people there and after her lesson and her practice
are finished I allow her to dance. Why is it that you
wish to change this?"

"Because the shops are shut on Saturday afternoons."
Miss Goldthorpe saw he did not follow what she was
talking about. "Lalla used to enjoy her Saturday
mornings, but lately she has to go to fittings, poor child,
and she finds them very fatiguing. You could easily
arrange that, couldn't you?"

Max's eyes twinkled. He did not say in words you and
I will plan things together to help Lalla, but he held out
his hand and, as his shook Miss Goldthorpe's, he said they
were friends, which meant the same thing.

Aunt Claudia agreed to changing Lalla's skating

lessons on Saturdays from the afternoon to the mornings.

" I don't quite know why Mr. Lindblom thinks the mornings will be better," she said to Miss Goldthorpe, " but anything that he wants we must fall in with, mustn't we ? "

Miss Goldthorpe agreed that they must in a polite way, and began thinking about Saturday afternoons. Miss Goldthorpe was not, as a rule, a person who pushed for the things that she wanted, but Saturday afternoons were different. It seemed to her terrible that Lalla's life was empty of the sort of things of which she thought a life should be full. No music, no plays, not even many books. Miss Goldthorpe could not imagine a world in which a person did not read ; it was not altogether Lalla's fault, she knew, for it was not easy for her to settle down to a book in the evenings when she came back from skating, but she was determined that somehow she would get books into Lalla's life ; it would be terrible if she grew up with no other interest but skating. The first thing she did towards Lalla's Saturday afternoons was to see Olivia. She called on her one day after Nana had taken Lalla and Harriet skating. Olivia was wearing a washing-up overall and asked Miss Goldthorpe to excuse her looking a mess, and would she come and sit in the kitchen-dining room. Miss Goldthorpe did better than that, she dried up.

" I'm not very domesticated, I'm afraid, but I can dry up without dropping things."

Olivia looked round the kitchen-dining room with a disgusted face.

" It's been a particularly nasty day. I expect you've heard from Harriet all about her Uncle William, and of course it is not a good time of year, but even so he is sending us the weirdest things. We can't possibly sell them, so we have to eat them. There's no real market, you know, for frost-bitten mangold-wurzels, nor for stored apples that haven't kept. Last year he tried an unfortunate experiment with eggs ; it was supposed to make them keep longer than most, but it hasn't worked and it's very depressing. Sometimes I open twenty bad ones before I come to one good. I dare say you can smell them."

Miss Goldthorpe had been wondering what it was she was smelling, but she didn't say so. She changed the subject to Lalla.

Olivia was a lovely listener. Even though she was washing up at the same time she kept turning her face, which showed how interested she was, to Miss Goldthorpe. Because Olivia was so interested Miss Goldthorpe found herself saying a great deal more than she had meant to say, about how fond she was of Lalla.

" She really is a dear little girl, Mrs. Johnson, but it's hard for her not to become spoilt because of the way she's brought up. It's made a wonderful difference to her having Harriet to work with her, but I'm afraid that Harriet is inclined to be an admiring audience rather than an outspoken friend."

Olivia washed a saucepan before she answered.

" Harriet is naturally a bit carried away by Lalla's glamour at the moment. You see, just now skating is very important to her. Of course she'll never be a skater, poor pet, but you can imagine, to her, being a good skater like Lalla seems a very important thing to be, which of course, if you're as good as Lalla, it is. I must say I took quite a different view of skating after I had seen Lalla at that skating gala. The child is really lovely to watch. But I don't think you need worry that Harriet will be nothing but an admiring friend ; after all, she's growing up, she'll be eleven this autumn, and she's used to being part of a family who speak their minds."

" Good, I'm glad of that. But that's not really what I came to see you about. You know the skating's been changed from Saturday afternoons to Saturday mornings?"

" We're pleased, we hardly seemed to see Harriet, and now we can have her on Saturday afternoons."

Miss Goldthorpe leant against the sink.

" That's what I've come about. I want to make something different for Lalla of Saturday afternoons ; not until after her next skating test, but we ought to make plans. You see, if I don't do something Lalla is going to grow up knowing nothing at all outside the skating world, which would be really terrible."

Olivia had finished washing up. She let the water out of the sink, dried her hands and put an arm through Miss Goldthorpe's.

" Come into the other room and tell me how I can help. I'll love to do anything I can, and I'm sure together we shall manage it."

Everybody in Lalla's house was gay that spring, because Aunt Claudia was happy. Now and again cook muttered to Wilson and Helen when she saw Lalla's diet sheet, that it was all a lot of nonsense, and that for twopence she would send up a nice cake to the schoolroom made with six eggs. Sometimes Nana, especially on days when her knees were bad, complained that Lalla was looking thin, which was not true, but on the whole everybody was pleased and one day slipped into another in a nice way. It was quite easy for Miss Goldthorpe to persuade Aunt Claudia that Alec and Toby might come along one Wednesday to give Lalla a gardening lesson, and as the days grew longer they could come in the evenings when she came back from skating. Miss Goldthorpe put the request suitably, saying she thought that Lalla would take more interest in botany if she learned by gardening than if she learned it from a book. Aunt Claudia agreed ; apart from botany she was sure gardening was good for Lalla, because it meant stooping. Aunt Claudia had faith in stooping, she stooped and touched her toes twenty-five times before breakfast every morning to be sure she kept her beautiful waistline.

The two skating galas were as big a success as the first one had been. Lalla got applause, cheers, a bouquet, paragraphs in the papers, and was photographed, and Aunt Claudia got envy, nice things said, and a creamy purr and smiling look became part of her.

"We must make big plans for the autumn, Lalla darling. I think little Miss Moore is going to be in great demand, don't you ? "

But behind the ordinary goings-on of the house and the pleasedness of Aunt Claudia there was a little nag of worry inside Harriet. It was surprising what a difference proper lessons from a teacher like Max Lindblom made to her skating. Nobody watched her or saw how she was getting on ; she was still at the very early figures, but, unlike Lalla, she adored figures. Once she had grasped the tracing her skates should leave on the ice she did not mind how long she went on working to get it right. Max Lindblom would watch her almost with tears in his eyes. "Look at little Harriet, how she works. If only I could make Lalla do that." Because she worked hard and loved skating, and because her skating lessons were only provided so that she would be able to take an intelligent interest in Lalla's skating, Max taught Harriet how to do figures that usually he left for a later stage. When he taught her curves he meant only to show her how to do them forward on the outside and inside edge. But because it might help Lalla, and because she worked so hard, he found himself showing her how to do an outside curve backwards. She had none of Lalla's verve, speed, and gaiety, but worked slowly, seriously and methodically, so only sometimes did Max realise she was enjoying herself, as when, during a lesson he asked if she was tired, and she looked up with shining eyes and said that of course she wasn't tired, nobody could be tired skating.

But the more she knew about skating the more Harriet worried about Lalla. She was always on the private rink when Lalla was supposed to be practising her brackets. Harriet could not do a bracket, but Max had drawn her pictures of how the different tracings of brackets ought to look, and as well he had done them for her on the ice, so that she could see for herself how the tracings were made. It was all very well for Lalla to look proud and grand and say " Silly old brackets, you watch me, Harriet, this is how I finished at that gala, I'll show you me taking my bouquet." Harriet knew that never when she watched Lalla do a bracket were her tracings right, they were nearly right, but were they right enough to pass a silver test, which was a very difficult thing to pass ? Also she thought Max Lindblom was worried. Often he asked her if Lalla was practising ; it was difficult for Harriet, she did not want to be a sneak, and say no, but she did most dreadfully want Lalla to pass her test. Lalla knew for certain that she was going to pass ; she had always had everything that she wanted, and now, after her success

at skating galas, she wanted to fly through her silver test
with the same ease that she had passed her inter-silver.
Harriet hoped that she was fussing for nothing, that Lalla
would pass, because nobody could imagine Lalla failing
at anything, but she did wonder when she was going to
work to make sure she passed. It seemed odd that she
could pass with only trying the figure once or twice at a
practice, and spending the rest of the time at her jumps
and the other sorts of skating that she liked doing. Sometimes she wondered what would happen to her if Lalla
did not pass. She was learning skating which must cost
a great deal of money, because having someone to skate
with was supposed to be good for Lalla. If Lalla failed,
would Aunt Claudia come up to the schoolroom and say,
" Go home, Harriet Johnson, you haven't done any good
at all. You can't do lessons with Lalla any more, or go
to skating, fencing, or dancing. Lalla never failed at
anything in skating until you came into the house."

As the day of the test grew nearer, Harriet nearly
had a quarrel with Lalla. It would have been quite
a quarrel only it was all Lalla having it, and it
takes two people to have a proper quarrel. Lalla was
doing an Axel. Axels were what she called her grandest
sort of skating, and she liked doing them and meant to
perform them in every free skating exhibition she gave,
and she was doing one in her three minutes free skating
for her silver test. Ever since she had skated in public she
had liked an audience. She loathed being made to
practise on the little rink. She thought it was much more
fun in the middle of the big rink, where lots of people
could see what she was doing, but since she was made to
practise on the small private rink somebody had to watch
her. She would have liked either Nana or Miss Gold-

thorpe to watch, but they were disappointing watchers.
Nana was always looking at her knitting at the wrong
moment, and would say " Very nice I'm sure, dear, but
don't slip and hurt yourself." And Miss Goldthorpe
would look and say " Splendid, dear," but as Lalla told
Harriet, you could see she was not watching, she was
thinking of one of those nasty old plays of Shakespeare's.
The only audience left being Harriet, Lalla insisted on
having her attention. Every few minutes she would call
out " Look, Harriet," " Watch this, Harriet," " I bet
you wish you could do this, Harriet." It was when she
watched Lalla's fourth Axel that Harriet felt she had to
say something.

" I thought that was awfully good, but oughtn't you
to be doing those brackets ? You haven't done them yet,
and it's only thirteen days to your test, I counted this
morning on the calendar."

Lalla knew she ought to be working at her brackets,
and though she was certain she could work at them for
the last few days, and then do them easily on the test day,
she still did not like to be reminded about them. It
was so gorgeous doing things fast, and so dull doing
brackets and studying tracings. Because she knew Harriet
was right, and did not want her to be, she lost her
temper.

" I wish you'd leave me alone. Fuss, fuss, fuss. I'll
pass my silver test, but if I didn't it would be your fault.
It's very bad to keep worrying a person, Goldie told me
that. She said before examinations and things you ought
just to forget, and then you did much better."

Miss Goldthorpe was not at the rink, but if she had
been she would have been very surprised indeed to have
heard this description of what she had said. Harriet knew

Miss Goldthorpe had not said anything about not working before her test, and hoping to get through on the day, but she did not want to make Lalla crosser, so she said in as nice a way as she could :

" I didn't mean you wouldn't pass. I only meant those brackets are awfully difficult, you told me so. And you are supposed to work at them every day, and to-day you haven't. I was only reminding you."

Lalla felt angrier than ever.

" Well, don't remind me any more. I don't want any reminding from anybody, especially not from you who doesn't know any more about skating than Nana does, and never will."

Nana, knitting as usual, had been disturbed by Lalla's raised voice, and had heard the last part of what she had said.

" What's that, Lalla ? Come over here both of you." She waited until they reached the barrier. " What were you saying to Harriet, Lalla ? "

Lalla leant on the barrier.

" I was telling her to leave me alone. She was fussing me about my practice."

" And why shouldn't she ? Isn't she having lessons, and put on this private rink with you, to see that you work ? What were you wanting her to do, Harriet ? "

" Brackets."

Always when that word was used Nana saw in her mind's eye some brackets that had been in her home when she was a little girl. They had been made of wood, covered in a pinkish plush, and on each bracket stood photographs of relations. To her it meant nothing what sort of skating Lalla did, one figure was the same as another, but she had grasped that something called brackets, though not made of pink plush, was part of the silver test, and had to be practised.

" And Harriet's quite right. I was thinking we weren't seeing much of those brackets myself. Now back you go on the rink, and let me see them right away, or I'll go outside and call Mr. Lindblom and tell him how you're behaving."

As they skated back across the ice Lalla, her temper quite gone, squeezed Harriet's hand.

" I'm going to imitate you doing curves. As I finish them you are to clap and say what lovely brackets they were."

Lalla was very good at imitating people. Standing ready to start, looking serious, she stopped being Lalla and became Harriet ; almost she looked as thin as Harriet. Harriet forgot that she ought to be cross with Lalla, because she still had not practised her brackets, and laughed and laughed. It was very painful sort of laughing, because it had to be done inside where Nana could not see it. Nana watched Lalla being Harriet doing curves for a few moments, then she nodded in a pleased way : " Very nice too, dear," and went back to her knitting.

As the day of the test grew nearer and nearer Harriet worried more and more. It was not that she thought Lalla would not pass exactly, but even if she only just passed everything nice might come to an end. Aunt Claudia was sure to say that Lalla was doing worse instead of better since she had known Harriet, and stop her going to lessons with her, and that would mean no more fencing, no more dancing and, worst of all, no skating lessons from Max Lindblom. When Harriet thought of that happening a lump came in her throat.

No more lessons from Max Lindblom ! It would be the most terrible thing that could happen to anybody.

As the date of the test grew nearer Harriet stopped reminding Lalla about practising her figures ; for one thing, Lalla was practising them without being reminded ; it was not the sort of practising Max expected her to do, but she did practise them for a bit, and then dash round the rink in a mad-doggish way, and then come back and practise them again for a few minutes. The other reason why Harriet stopped reminding Lalla was because of what Miss Goldthorpe had told her when they were waiting for Lalla to be called for her inter-silver test. That lots of people passed examinations who did not know much, and people who knew a lot sometimes failed. Lalla was the sort of person who passed even if she didn't know a lot, and it was no good worrying her now that it was almost test day ; it was much better for her to go on feeling certain that she would pass with almost full marks, as she had passed the inter-silver.

That Harriet was worried was noticed at home.

" Hallo, Long-face," Alec said.

Harriet flushed, for she did not want anybody to notice she was worried.

" I haven't got a long face."

Toby looked up from a sheet of figures on which he was working.

" You haven't usually, but lately you've seemed as if it had been raining for weeks and weeks."

Edward was lying on the floor, making something out of the Meccano set Lalla had given him for Christmas.

" This morning a lady said that seeing me was as good as the sun coming out."

Alec made a face at him.

" One more word like that and we'll drown you. You get more loathsome every day."

Olivia looked at the clock.

" Put that Meccano set away, Edward. I dare say you make strangers think the sun is coming out, but you make me think it's time you were in bed."

Edward gazed reproachfully at Harriet.

" If you hadn't looked miserable I wouldn't have remembered what that lady said, and then I wouldn't have been sent to bed for another ten minutes, would I, Daddy ? "

George was doing accounts. He murmured, " Two rabbits, ninety-two sacks of winter greens, eight of them too decayed to sell, a rook that probably got in by mistake . . . what was that, Edward ? " Then he turned to Olivia. " A rook should cook nicely with a rabbit, shouldn't it ? "

" I shouldn't dream of cooking the poor rook. You can give it to the cat up the road if you like. We were saying Harriet looked worried. Are you worried, Harriet ? "

George looked at Harriet.

" Seems all right to me. Has the doctor seen her lately ? "

Harriet was standing by George ; she leant against his chair.

" Not as a doctor, in the street. He said I was his walking advertisement."

George said " Good " and was going back to his accounts but Toby stopped him.

" All the same she is looking worried. I suppose it's because she thinks Lalla won't pass that skating test."

Hearing Toby say her worst thought out loud like that

made Harriet feel as though she had the wind knocked out of her. She glared at him.

"Of course I'm not worried. She's going to pass just as easily as she passed her inter-silver, probably better."

Toby shrugged his shoulders.

"All right, keep your hair on, but if she's going to pass I don't know what you're getting in such a flap for."

"I'm not in a flap."

Olivia was helping Edward put away his Meccano set. She smiled at Harriet.

"It's natural you should worry for her, darling. Everybody worries when people are going in for examinations, but I'm sure you needn't."

"Of course you needn't," said George. "I thought the child was a genius when I saw her. Passes my comprehension how you spin round like that on a pair of skates, bad enough to do it on the floor."

"Anyway," said Alec, "you haven't long to wait. I wouldn't get into a state if I was you."

Olivia had finished clearing up Edward's Meccano set. She stood up and gave Harriet a kiss.

"I shall be very glad when that test is over, because Miss Goldthorpe is planning some nice Saturday afternoons for you two this summer."

Harriet was surprised.

"Saturday afternoons, but . . ."

Olivia shook her head.

"Don't ask me, it's a secret until after the test, but it's something to look forward to, I promise you that."

Because all the family seemed so sure that Lalla would pass, and Lalla herself knew she would pass, Harriet did worry less, and came to the rink on the test morning not feeling too scared.   Miss Goldthorpe was the perfect person to wait with, when you were scared of something. She thought it unimportant if Lalla passed or not, though she did realise that other people thought it important, so she was happy and calm.   She knew Harriet would not feel happy or calm, so she did not bury herself in one of Shakespeare's plays, but talked to her about ordinary things.

They were using the big rink for the tests that morning, so part of it was roped off, and on the other half Lalla and the other people going in for tests were practising. Lalla, as usual, was wearing a white kilt and jersey and white bonnet, and because it was a test, white gloves. She looked calm and unconcerned, but presently she skated over to Miss Goldthorpe and Harriet.   She leant on the barrier.

" You won't forget about holding your thumbs, will you, Harriet ? "

" Of course not. I was going to anyway."

Lalla looked at Miss Goldthorpe.

" Haven't you anything you can do to bring people luck, Goldie ? "

Miss Goldthorpe was just going to say that she did not believe in luck, but believed in knowing your subject before the examination and then hoping for the best, when she saw that Lalla was fidgeting in a nervous way with one of her gloves. Lalla never fidgeted in a nervous way, for she was never nervous. Seeing her nervous surprised Miss Goldthorpe and made her sorry, so she tried to think of something which would help.

" I shall sit on my handkerchief. When I was a child I remember hearing an aunt say when she was playing whist and was having bad luck she would improve it by sitting on her handkerchief. As soon as it's your turn I shall sit on mine."

" Did your aunt win after that ? "

Miss Goldthorpe took her handkerchief out of her pocket.

" Of course. That's why I remember it, it seemed such a simple thing to do."

Lalla hesitated, as if she would like to say something else, instead she nodded as if she were satisfied, and skimmed back across the ice to her practice.

Half an hour later it was Lalla's turn. There were two judges, as there had been for the inter-silver. This time they were two women, one fat and one thin. They both seemed to know Lalla and greeted her with friendly smiles. Lalla, just as she had done when she went in for her inter-silver test, seemed completely at ease. She found a piece of ice with no tracings on it and stood calmly waiting to be told to start. Standing by the barrier close to where she and Miss Goldthorpe were sitting Harriet saw Max. His eyes were on Lalla, but he was looking quite at ease, his hands in his pockets. " He doesn't seem fussed," thought Harriet, grasping her thumbs, " so I shouldn't think there's anything to fuss about." At that moment Lalla was told to start her first figure, and Max's attitude changed. Harriet saw that his face looked grave and she could see by the bulge it made that he had clenched the hand in the pocket nearest to her. She turned to Miss Goldthorpe.

" You are sitting on your handkerchief, aren't you, Goldie ? It's now."

Miss Goldthorpe patted Harriet's knee.

" Of course I am. Don't worry."

Harriet knew more about skating than she had when

she watched the inter-silver. But the place Lalla had chosen on which to skate was near the centre of the rink, and she could not see the tracings. She watched the faces of the two women judges, as they stooped down and examined the tracings, and tried to gather from their faces, and from the way they wrote on their cards, how Lalla was doing, but people like judges, she discovered did not have faces that told you things. Because she had watched Max giving Lalla lessons, and because for the last two or three days the lessons had been a run through of exactly what she had to do in her test, Harriet knew when the figures were finished. She let out a gulp of breath.

" She's finished the figures, Goldie. She'll do her free skating presently, she likes that better."

But Lalla had not finished her figures. The two judges called her to them and told her something. It was clear from Lalla's way of standing that she was surprised at what she heard ; she threw up her head so that her chin was in the air, and clearly was answering in a proud way. Max moved up so that he was standing next to Harriet.

" It is those brackets. She must do her forward inside again."

" If she does them right this time will she pass ? "

Max had his eyes on Lalla. He spoke as if he were talking to himself.

" How can she do well if she will not work ? "

It seemed as if everybody round the rink was holding their breath. It felt to Harriet as if Lalla took hours and hours doing the two repeat figures. When at last she had finished Max, who was wearing his skates, went across to hear the results with her. The judges seemed to take a long time adding up. Harriet, who remembered exactly how everybody had looked when Lalla had got good marks for her inter-silver test, saw that things were different this time. The judges smiled, but it was a different sort of smile from the ones she had got last time, and Lalla did not dash over to Max and hold his hands. Instead, she said some quick thing, which Harriet could not hear, threw her chin in the air and skated towards herself and Miss Goldthorpe. As she reached the barrier she said in a be-sorry-for-me-if-you-dare voice:

" It will surprise you to know that Miss Lalla Moore has failed her test."

Miss Goldthorpe said :

" I'm sorry, dear. But not by much I hope."

Lalla looked prouder than ever.

" If you want to know, very badly indeed. I needed fifty-four marks to pass, and all I got was forty-one."

CHAPTER XI

PLANS

*

IT was awful for Lalla going home after her test. Miss Goldthorpe tried to talk about other things, but nobody answered ; Harriet kept looking at Lalla's face, and answers to Miss Goldthorpe dried up inside her mouth. She was sure, if it had been her who had hoped to pass and had failed, she would have cried, but Lalla did not look a bit like crying, she looked much more as if she might bite somebody. Her face was pink, her lips pressed together tight, and she had a very angry look in her eyes. Just before the car reached the house Lalla, still speaking in a proud voice, said :

" No one is going to tell Aunt Claudia instead of me. I know I ought to have passed, it was those silly old judges who were wrong."

Miss Goldthorpe looked worried. Too often in the past she had heard girls blaming the examiners when they did not pass examinations, but she did not say so. It was not the moment to make Lalla feel worse than she was feeling already. Instead she said that of course Lalla must tell Aunt Claudia, and explain that Max Lindblom had said she would try again in the autumn. She and Harriet would go straight up to the schoolroom and Lalla could find Wilson and ask when her aunt would be in.

Aunt Claudia was not in but Wilson said she thought she would be in for lunch, then she looked at Lalla.

"What's the matter, dear? You passed your test all right, didn't you?"

Lalla was standing on the bottom of the stairs leading into the hall; she swung on the banister rail so that her back was turned to Wilson.

"Actually I didn't, but I ought to have. It was the silly old judges' fault."

Wilson, like everybody else in the house, had got so used to the idea that Lalla was destined for great things in the skating world that she was sure, if she had not passed a test, it wasn't Lalla's fault.

"What a shame, but I wouldn't worry if I was you, dear; skating as prettily as you do I don't see what you want with any old test. Look at the lovely pieces in the paper about you."

"You have to do figures, that's the awful part. Do you know, Wilson, I hate, hate, hate figures." Lalla sat down on the stairs. "I shall wait here for Aunt Claudia. I want to get telling her over."

Wilson knew just how Lalla felt; when she had to tell Aunt Claudia something had gone wrong she would hang about waiting to get it over; but it was not the best way to please Aunt Claudia to be found sitting on the stairs in your outdoor things.

"I know how you feel, dear, but if I was you I'd run up to Nana and change into something pretty; you know the way she likes you to be dressed up. The moment she comes in I'll ring Nana's bell three times."

Lalla got up slowly.

"All right, I'd much rather sit here, I don't want to

tell Nana, still Aunt Claudia would rather I was dressed up, so I'll do it."

Miss Goldthorpe and Harriet had not told Nana that Lalla had not passed, but of course Nana knew. She had said the moment they had come in, " Where's Lalla ? " and when they said that she was downstairs waiting to see Aunt Claudia Nana had made upset, clucking noises, and gone into Lalla's bedroom thinking, " Oh dear, there'll be trouble about this."

When Lalla came in, still looking as though she would bite if anyone spoke to her, Nana said nothing about skating. She took Lalla's coat and hung it up in the cupboard and was just her usual cosy self. Because she was her usual, cosy self and not looking sorry or worried, Lalla stopped feeling angry, and the moment she stopped feeling angry she felt miserable and had to cry. She flung her arms round Nana, and sobbed and sobbed. Nana sat down in an arm-chair and took her on her knee, and heard, between the gulps and the sobs, that Lalla was shamed for life, that Aunt Claudia would be so angry that she would probably kill her, that she ought to have passed, that it was the judges' fault; that she would be the greatest skater in the world and then they would be sorry ; and, as the tears grew a little less, that Aunt Claudia would say she had not worked very hard, and the awful thing was that it would be true, that she hated those old brackets and she thought she could do them without working, and now, because she had not passed, Harriet would not be coming for lessons any more, and nothing nice would ever happen again.

When at last she finished crying and explaining Nana stroked the hair out of her face, and lent her a handkerchief to blow her nose.

" Now come along and wash, we don't want your aunt to see you swelled up like that. It would never do. You know, dear, you've been a bit of a madam lately, as often I've told you. You had to know best, you wouldn't listen to that Mr. Lindblom when he said you weren't working at those nasty brackets, but you'll be able to try again, won't you ? " Lalla agreed that she would in the autumn. " Well then, what are these tears for ? If at first you don't succeed, try, try again."

Lalla choked back a sob.

" But I'm not used to trying again, I'm used to doing things right away."

" I know, dear, but pride comes before a fall. Now come along, let me get you tidied up, and then you run down to your aunt and tell her quietly what's happened, and that you're expecting to do well in the autumn, and I'm sure she'll be very nice about it."

Lalla was at her basin turning on the water to wash her face.

" You don't think that, Nana, you're only saying it to make me feel better. She'll be awful about it, you know she will." Lalla's lips began to wobble again. " Oh, what will I do if she says Harriet can't come here any more ? Harriet only comes here to make me work harder, and now I've failed at my very first test after she's come. I just couldn't bear it if I had to go back to doing things alone again."

Nana was laying a frock on the bed so her back was to Lalla. Lalla could not see, but her face was worried. It was only too likely that Aunt Claudia would say that lessons with Harriet were to stop ; she had always said that a child like Lalla was best kept by herself, not mixing with other children, and now at last, when they had managed to get her a friend, look what had happened. To Nana that Lalla had not passed her test mattered nothing, unless it meant that Lalla once more was made to work alone.

" Did Wilson say what time your aunt would be in ? "

" She just said she'd be in for lunch."

Nana looked at the clock.

" It's only just gone half-past twelve, she's not often in before one. Do you know what I'd do if I was you ? I'd telephone your Uncle David at his office and tell him what's happened, and ask him the best way of explaining things to your aunt. Gentlemen, having business heads and all, are good at knowing how things had best be put." She gave Lalla a little push. " Run along down, dear, and do it right away before he goes out to his lunch, you can tidy for your aunt after."

Uncle David was just leaving his office when the telephone rang. He was going to signal to his secretary to say he was out, when he heard that it was Lalla. His cheerful voice came down the line.

" How's the child wonder this morning ? "

" Not a wonder any more." Lalla's voice rose in a wail. " Uncle David, I've failed."

Uncle David laughed.

" Failed in your figures ? Isn't that shattering ! "

" I knew you'd laugh, but Aunt Claudia won't. And Nana said I was to ask you how best it was to be put, so Harriet wouldn't be sent away."

At once Uncle David grew serious. He had not thought of that. He had been glad that he had arranged that Lalla had Harriet to learn things with and play with, and had not thought of it coming to an end, but now he saw what Nana meant. How best could it be put ?

" Half a moment, poppet, while I think." He sat down at his desk, the receiver in his hand, and doodled on his blotting paper, which always helped him to get ideas. He drew Lalla on skates. Then he drew Aunt Claudia. As he drew Aunt Claudia he knew the only thing that would make it safe that Harriet was not sent away. He spoke carefully, because it was a difficult thing to explain. " You know how important Aunt Claudia thinks this skating of yours is, and she's brought you up to think as she does. But, of course, really skating is like a game; it's grand to be a first-class tennis player or cricketer, but it isn't wrong for somebody not to want to be first-class."

" But I do want to be a first-class skater. I'm going to be the greatest skater in the world."

" Do you think Harriet's going to help you to be that ? "

Lalla remembered all the times that Harriet had tried to make her practise.

" It wasn't her fault I failed, she tried to make me practise my brackets and I wouldn't."

" Harriet sounds fine. I should think you'd listen to what she said next time, wouldn't you ? If I were you, if Aunt Claudia says that Harriet is to go away, I should tell her that if Harriet goes you don't want to skate any more." He heard Lalla gasp. " Well, it wouldn't be as much fun, would it ? It's nearly summer and you don't skate much in the summer anyway, and I think you would find that Aunt Claudia wouldn't want you to stop skating, and when she hears you would rather not skate than let Harriet go she will let Harriet go on working with you. In the autumn you can work so hard that you can show her what a help Harriet's been."

Lalla came back to her bedroom looking solemn. She

told Nana what Uncle David had advised. Nana made fussed noises with her tongue against her teeth.

" What a thing to ask a child of your age to say ! Don't want to skate any more ! Whatever next ! Still, you don't skate regular in the summer. Mind you, he's right, there isn't no more reason why you should skate than why I should ride a donkey."

That made Lalla laugh.

" Silly Nana ! Think of you on a donkey ! " Nana was putting Lalla's frock on. When Lalla's head came out through the top she was serious again. " Do you know, I think Uncle David really and truly doesn't think it matters if I skate. I thought before, when he said things like that, he was teasing, but I think he really doesn't think it matters. That makes me feel very peculiar."

Nana buttoned the frock.

" He's right, dear, you won't be eleven till the autumn. There's no reason a child of your age should be set on anything. Of course, with your father behind you and your aunt so fond of the skating and all, it's got into you."

Lalla moved to the dressing-table for Nana to brush her hair.

" I feel like Alice in Wonderland felt when she fell down the rabbit hole. I mean, it's like me having fallen down a rabbit hole and found things were different at the bottom. At the top everybody knew I had to be a great skater, and at the bottom people like you and Uncle David say it doesn't matter much." Nana's bell rang three times. Lalla looked at Nana. " I'll make Aunt Claudia let Harriet stay. But you and Uncle David aren't going to make me think skating doesn't matter, so there."

Aunt Claudia had a lot of afternoon engagements, and

had hurried home for a quick lunch before changing for them. She had no time to waste, but when she saw Lalla she wanted to hear how many marks she had got in her test.

" Did you do well, darling ? "

Lalla, having screwed herself up to confessing, did not waste time.

" Very badly. I failed."

The word " failed " made Aunt Claudia flinch as if someone had thrown a stone at her.

" Failed ! But, Lalla, that's impossible."

" It was not impossible at all, and if you want to know I failed badly. They let Max have my marks. I only got forty-one, and the reason I didn't pass was because I was bored with brackets and wouldn't work at them. Max tried to make me, and Harriet tried and tried but I wouldn't."

Aunt Claudia had come in thinking what a lovely day it was ; she was happy and she felt that Lalla was deliberately spoiling everything for her. She so believed in Lalla's skating future that she found it hard to take in what she had said. Failed ! Failed badly ! Forty-one marks, it was impossible. Everybody knew the child had a brilliant future. Then she remembered that in the afternoon she was going to a bridge party, with some of the people she had persuaded to take tickets for Lalla's first skating exhibition. Since that night they had been interested in Lalla and had asked after her. She had told them that this morning Lalla was to take her silver test, and that she was extraordinarily young to try for it, and they had said they hoped she would pass, and she had laughed and had said : " I don't think we need worry about that." They were sure to ask how Lalla had done.

It made her feel quite ill to think that she would have to admit that Lalla had failed. As she thought of her bridge party her voice grew cold and hard.

"Come into the drawing-room. We'd better have a talk about this."

Lalla was frightened by the tone in Aunt Claudia's voice, and it made her sound a little rude.

"Talk as much as you like. I've told you what happened, and it's me that minds most, not you."

In the drawing-room Aunt Claudia dragged a full description of the figure test out of Lalla. Because she had taken an interest in skating when Lalla's father was learning, and because of Lalla, she knew more or less what Lalla was talking about. She grasped how bad Lalla's tracings must have been, and she felt convinced that Lalla could have done them perfectly if only she had worked. Obviously something must be done to make her work in future. She had got to get through these tests before she could enter for the open championships, with all the fun and the excitement that those would mean.

"I must see Max Lindblom; you must, of course, have extra lessons so that you pass easily in the autumn, and I must arrange somehow for your lessons to continue throughout the summer."

"You can't. Max goes home to Sweden every summer. He sees his family then."

"We shall see. Then clearly you're having too many distractions. I was never sure if it was a good idea having Harriet to work with you; I knew what it would be, you'd play about and fritter away your time. I'll telephone to Mrs. Johnson and explain that the arrangement must finish."

Lalla was trembling inside and this made her speak in an extra loud voice, so that it would not tremble too.

"If you do that, I won't skate any more."

Aunt Claudia was as surprised as she would have been if a worm had turned round in the garden and told her to look more carefully where she walked. She repeated what Lalla had said in a shocked voice.

"You won't skate any more!" Then, as the words made sense, "Lalla! Child! You don't know what you're saying. That isn't my Lalla speaking. Why, ever since you were a baby you've thought of nothing but skating. I can see you now, insisting on holding your first little boots and skates when you were so small you had to ride in a perambulator. Not skate any more! Silly child. Why, you couldn't live without skating."

Lalla had heard what skating meant to her ever since she could remember, but as Aunt Claudia spoke she felt glad to hear it again. It made her feel more ordinary than hearing Nana and Uncle David say that it was possible she could give it up. But she was not going to give in about Harriet.

"I only said I wouldn't skate any more if you took Harriet away."

Aunt Claudia had been badly frightened. She had been looking forward for so long to the fun that she was going to have when Lalla was a star that even the suggestion that it might not happen made her feel as if the sun had gone in for ever. She did not want to give in to Lalla, but, small though Lalla was, she could see that she meant what she said. The only thing to do would be to agree that Harriet went on sharing Lalla's classes and speak to Harriet. Harriet must be made to feel her responsibilities. She was getting this wonderful chance

of sharing Lalla's expensive classes and she must understand that she was only being allowed these privileges if
they were good for Lalla.

"Come here." Lalla came unwillingly. "Don't look
cross, darling. You know I'm only thinking of you. I
know what a great gift you have and what a wonderful
future you're going to have, if only you work. Everything we've planned is for that. We'll say no more about
to-day as a set-back, but we won't let it happen again,
will we? We'll just be more determined than ever . . ."
She was going to say "more determined than ever that
Lalla should be world champion," but Lalla was sure
the quotation was coming and said it for her.

"That my square-turn'd joints and strength of limb,
will make me a champion grim. I know I've been a
carpet knight to-day, but I won't be any more if you
won't say anything more about Harriet going away."

Aunt Claudia kissed her.

"That's the spirit, now run along up to the schoolroom,
it's lunch time."

The rest of that skating season passed quickly. If Max
was upset that Lalla had failed to pass her test, he did
not tell her so. In spite of Aunt Claudia suggesting that
Lalla should have extra lessons, he refused to give them
to her; in fact, before the season came to an end, he
stopped giving her lessons. He said she could just enjoy
herself on the ice and forget about figures because
she was getting stale. In the autumn, when he came
back from two months in Sweden, they would get down
to her training and work really hard. To Harriet he
said :

"And you too must work in the autumn. After
Christmas you will be taking your preliminary and bronze

tests. I think it good that you and Lalla should both be working for tests at the same time."

Harriet was terribly pleased Max thought she was good enough even to try to pass a test. She had not thought of herself as the sort of skater who would enter for tests. She decided, if she was going to try for them, she was not going to wait for the autumn to start working. The rink would be closed for a month, but right up to the day it closed, and on the day it opened again, she would be there for her usual afternoon practice. She was surprised that Max thought it a good idea for her and Lalla to work for tests at the same time, but perhaps Max did not know that Lalla always wanted an audience, and that you couldn't watch her bracket tracings and practise figures yourself at the same time. Then, of course, Max did not know what Aunt Claudia had said. Harriet had not understood absolutely everything that Aunt Claudia had said herself, but she had understood how lucky she was to be allowed to work with Lalla, and that in exchange she must see that Lalla passed her silver test in the autumn with almost full marks. Harriet did not need to be told to want Lalla to pass with a lot of marks in the autumn; she wanted it without any telling, but she did wish Aunt Claudia did not think she could arrange it. Lalla had worked really hard for a bit after she failed in her test, which was why Max told her not to work any more in case she got stale, but Lalla was not the sort of person to go on working like that. If ever she thought she knew a figure and did it well, she would go mad-doggish and probably not work again for weeks and weeks.

Luckily that summer lots of nice things happened which stopped both Lalla and Harriet thinking about skating tests. Miss Goldthorpe's Saturday afternoons were

lovely. She arranged trips by river steamer to Green-
wich, and in Uncle David's motor launch to places like
Windsor and Hampton Court. She took them to
Wimbledon to watch the tennis championships, and to
matineés of Shakespeare's plays in Regent's Park. Sometimes she invited Alec, Toby and Edward to come too,
which she could do without permission because they were
her parties. At first, after she had failed at her test, Lalla
did not want to see Toby in case he said something rude
like " I warned you."

" You can tell him I passed my free," Lalla told
Harriet, " but I didn't exactly pass the figures."

Harriet had not had to say anything. Her family were
not interested in skating tests unless they worried Harriet.
Harriet went skating to grow strong and look less like a
daddy-long-legs, and Lalla because it was going to be her
profession, and that was the end of that. Everybody
knew they both went to the rink every afternoon, and
both had lessons from somebody called Max Lindblom,
so there was nothing to talk about.

That summer Alec's dream began to come true. In
consultation with Toby he spent the money he had made
on his paper round on fruit and vegetables bought at
Covent Garden. He and Toby would get up very early
and go to Covent Garden on the Underground. They
would be there so early that they saw the fruit and
vegetables arrive, smelling quite different from Uncle
William's fruit and vegetables. They would watch the
stuff unloaded and sometimes, when it was carried on a
cart drawn by a pony, Alec would nudge Toby and say :
" That's the sort of pony and cart I'm going to have."
They could not go to Covent Garden every day because
getting up so early made them sleepy at school, and Alec

terribly stupid on his evening paper round, so that unless
he was careful he put the wrong papers in the wrong
letter-boxes. But they usually managed to go on Tuesdays
and on Fridays. Tuesdays to get some of the good stuff
that had not been picked on Sundays, and Fridays
because Saturdays were holidays and it was possible to
make up sleep missed by getting up early. Toby made an
arrangement with George about Alec's fruit and vegetables. They were sold separately from Uncle William's,
and the money they made was put on one side for Alec.
George found the arrangement worrying at first because
he never could do accounts but Toby helped him.

" If you have five pounds of Alec's strawberries at two
shillings a pound, and ten pounds of green peas at one
and twopence, and five pounds of broad beans at one
and fourpence, and you've sold all the strawberries except
half a pound, all the broad beans except two pounds and
all the peas except one pound, you have to give Alec
twenty-three shillings and sixpence, and you are holding
four shillings and tenpence in convertible stock. It's
quite easy, Dad."

George never found it easy, but he did see that for
some reason the shop was doing better. Having good
vegetables and fruit on regular days brought people into
the shop who might not otherwise have come, and when
they were there, seeing a rabbit hanging up or some trout
in a basket, made them wonder whether they could use
rabbit or trout. In the same way they might come in
to buy Alec's good green peas and then notice some
unripe peaches which had fallen off Uncle William's wall,
and think, " Well, stewed peaches will make a change."

Of course there were days when what Uncle William
sent nobody could possibly buy. He had read somewhere

that there was a form of edible toadstool which was
nourishing, so several days running he went out with a
sack and picked every toadstool he could find. He sent
the sacks to George with a note saying, " Sort these out,
I believe some of them are good for eating, somebody
ought to know." George, trusting his brother William,
did try to sort the first lot of toadstools but luckily Olivia
spotted what he was doing.

" George ! Put those loathsome things back in the
sack, and burn the lot. I should think you've got enough
poison there to kill everybody for miles around."

Because more customers came to the shop things were
easier for Olivia. Quite often she would say, " Imagine !
I've had to buy everything for supper this evening, there
was nothing left over. You can't think what fun it is
choosing food, instead of cooking what the shop can't
sell."

In July Uncle David and Aunt Claudia went to stay
with friends in Canada and Nana went to visit her sister
in the Midlands. In August Nana and Lalla were going
to an hotel in the Isle of Wight, so while Nana was away
Miss Goldthorpe moved into the house and took charge.
It was while Nana was away that the exciting thing
happened about Lalla's garden. That summer Aunt
Claudia had engaged a new young gardener. His name
was Simpson and he was not only a good gardener, but
a proud one. It had worried him very much to see his
best herbaceous border finishing up with tomatoes,
lettuces and some ridge cucumbers. He had spoken about
it to Aunt Claudia. Aunt Claudia was not really garden-
minded, but when Simpson pointed out that vegetables
were not really right in an herbaceous border she could
see what he meant. She told Simpson that it was Lalla's

garden, but if he could find Lalla another piece of garden that she liked he could arrange an exchange. Simpson had heard in the kitchen that Lalla was not really keen on gardening, so he planned to offer her a shady little bit of ground behind a laburnum tree, which would not show much. It was not until after Aunt Claudia had left for Canada that he saw Lalla to talk about the exchange, and on that day Alec and Toby had come over to plan autumn planting. Toby had a piece of string between two sticks, and while Harriet held one end and Lalla the other he worked out how many strawberry plants the bed would hold, and Alec wrote the number down in a book. When Simpson came along he said " Good-morning " and then stopped in the loitering way of somebody who wants to be noticed and has something to say. Lalla was enjoying herself, and did not want anyone to bother her, so she spoke in her most madamish voice. Simpson had children of his own and was not going to be madamed by Lalla.

" I spoke to your auntie about veg. in my border, and she says if you was agreeable I could give you a bit of earth some other place for you to dig in."

Lalla looked at Simpson despisingly.

" Thank you. This is my garden and it's stopping my garden, and it's not a piece of earth, it's going to be a strawberry bed."

Simpson had grand ideas for next year ; he was ordering many new plants, lots of them tall, and he could see the effect of his bed would be quite spoiled by short things like strawberries. He was just going to speak his mind about this when Toby said :

" What other garden were you going to give her ? Could it be something bigger ? You see, there's not much acreage here for strawberries, and we had meant to invest in some prize plants."

At the words " acreage " and " prize plants " Simpson looked altogether different. Evidently Lalla had sensible gardening friends. He knew at once that the bit of a bed behind the laburnum would not do and thought what

" What other garden were you going to give her ? "

else he could spare. He was a gardener who grew vegetables because he must and flowers because he liked them. He had a bright idea. It would be very nice for him if he could have all the herbaceous border, and Lalla's friends would look after a bit of his vegetable garden. There was quite a long strip of vegetable garden in which he was meant to plant winter greens. He thought growing winter greens a waste of time ; cooks never seemed to want to cook them, and they were what he called "messy" if not used.

"If you'd come this way and have a look there's a nice bit I could spare which would be prime for fruit."

The moment Alec and Toby saw the piece of vegetable garden that might be Lalla's, they were thrilled. It was so large a piece that it was almost the beginning of having a market garden, but there was a snag. It would need constant attention from them both, for it was no good hoping that Lalla and Harriet would look after it properly. Alec saw the only thing to do was to take Simpson into their confidence.

"I say, this would be grand. But the thing is that Lalla lets us plant vegetables and things for market, and Mrs. King doesn't know, and if Lalla had a bit like this we'd have to come here quite a lot."

"It would have to be secret," Harriet explained. "Can you keep secrets ? "

Simpson scratched his head. He did not know Aunt Claudia very well, but he knew from the little he had seen of her and from what he had heard in the kitchen that she was not the sort of person to like things done that she did not know about. But gardening was a nice healthy occupation and he could not think Mrs. King would object to Lalla going in for it with her friends. It would suit him, and Mrs. King never came into the kitchen garden, and what the eye did not see the heart didn't grieve after.

"I reckon I can. You won't want to be setting the strawberries yet awhile, and then I suppose it'd be when you're not in school and that. If you tip me off when you want to come I could get you in by the side gate."

When Simpson had gone the most tremendous measuring went on and after the measuring Toby worked out a long sum. It was not the sort of sum which anybody else wanted to do. It was in rods, poles and perches. If a piece of land was so long and so wide and in each square foot of it you could plant a strawberry, and each strawberry plant cost so much, how much would it cost to lay out the whole plot? When he had finished they had thought so much about strawberries that to all four of them it seemed as if the strawberries had been planted and were getting ripe.

Toby said :

" We must net them. We don't want your capital eaten by birds, Alec."

Lalla saw the beds scarlet with fruit.

" And me and Harriet can sneak out before lessons and pick them ready for you to sell."

Alec shook his head.

" They'll have to be picked overnight. Harriet will have to bring them home with her. Toby will have to meet her and help to carry them, while I'm doing the paper round."

Harriet liked the idea of her and Toby staggering home under basket loads of fruit, but she saw difficulties ahead.

" But I go straight home from skating lots of days. What shall we do then ? "

Alec turned to Lalla.

" Those days you'll have to pick them, and we'll have to find a way for Toby to come and fetch them. Nobody must see him take them, or your aunt will think we're stealing her fruit."

" That'll be all right. If I'm working hard at my skating Aunt Claudia won't be cross about anything."

Then Lalla bounced because she was pleased. "Isn't it gorgeous. Giggerty-geggerty, fancy me being the one to start the market garden."

Harriet skipped over to Alec.

"We ought to do our pledge. Will it be all right as Edward isn't here?"

Alec said he thought it would be, and he linked his little finger into Lalla's. Lalla linked her other little finger to Toby's, and Harriet linked hers to Alec's and Toby's.

Alec spoke in his solemn, growly voice.

"We Johnsons and Lalla, but without Edward, swear on the stomach of our Uncle never to divulge what has taken place to-day."

They lifted their hands.

"Guzzle guzzle guzzle, quack quack quack."

CHAPTER XII

LOOPS

★

HARRIET was glad when September came. It had been hot and crowded in their part of London in August. Being on the outside of London where it was easy to hire a boat and go on the river, crowds of people came down every day on bicycles, in buses and in trains, and it was not nice for the people who lived in the neighbourhood, because all the best parts of the river were taken up by visitors. Although there were nice things to do because the boys were having holidays, she missed the rink, and though she tried to practise skating in her head it was not the same thing. Because she missed Lalla, and skating, and because it was hot, she began to look rather daddy-long-leggish again.

Olivia worried about her.

" You're a miserable little scrap, my pet. I don't want you to go backwards, you were looking so much better. I wish you could go away, but the next best thing is for you to be out all day."

Harriet would have liked to have helped in the shop, or in the house, but as she was not allowed to, when she was not out with the boys, she went down to the river and watched the boats go by, and read Lalla's postcards saying how lovely it was in the Isle of Wight and wished for the term to begin.

The day the rink re-opened her family noticed that she looked different. Edward was the first to mention it. They were having breakfast at the time.

"Harriet's looking like me this morning, not so good-looking but pleased, like I do."

After everybody had told Edward what they thought of him they looked at Harriet.

"As a matter of fact," said Alec, "you do look as if you'd had a present."

"Nothing came by the post," said Toby, "not even a postcard from Lalla."

George took a look at Harriet.

"Funny. I was worrying because you were so pasty. You've quite a colour this morning."

Olivia smiled.

"You do look better, pet, and I can't think why, for it's just as hot and just as dusty. Have you children planned something nice for to-day?"

Toby helped himself to some stewed plums, which they were having to eat with every meal just then, as a lot of unripe ones were coming from Uncle William.

"We're going to The Tower of London, but Harriet won't come because the rink is re-opening."

"Nonsense!" said George. "Of course she must go to The Tower. There's no need for you to start skating till Lalla comes back, Harriet."

Olivia was looking at Harriet.

"Would you rather go to the rink? You are a funny child. I should have thought it would be terribly boring for you all alone."

"I wouldn't have thought anybody could want to go round and round ice," said Edward, "when they could look at the Traitor's Gate."

But Olivia could see that for some reason Harriet would rather go to the rink.

"Whatever you might like, Edward, Harriet would rather skate, so that settles it."

Coming back to the rink after a whole month of not being at it, seemed to Harriet almost the nicest moment she ever remembered. The first person she saw was Sam. She had not seen much of him since she had her own skates and boots. He gave her a nice welcome.

"Hallo, duckie, here we are again. Sit down, and let me have a feel of these calves. My, my, we are getting on. Whoever would have thought these muscles were the bits of putty I first felt."

"You promised me I'd have proper little skater's legs like Lalla's."

Sam nodded.

"So you have too, and I hear you're making quite a skater."

Harriet stared at him.

"Me! Who told you that?"

Sam winked.

"A little bird I know. I got a whole flock of little birds in this place; nothin 'appens on this rink but one of them pops along to tell me. How's Lalla?"

"On the Isle of Wight for another week. She won't come here until Max Lindblom comes back, then she starts training very hard."

"'aving another go at her silver I 'eard. Oh well, many takes a lot of shots at that."

"Sam! She's not going to take a lot of shots, she's going to pass this time. She would have last time only . . ."

Sam held up a hand.

"Don't tell me, I know. She didn't work. My birds

told me about that too. I don't often get a dekko at her
these days but you tell her from me not to take it too
hard if she fails again. Her Dad—one of the nicest men
I ever knew—wouldn't have wanted his kid getting in a
state about figure skating, I do know that."

Harriet was very fond of Sam, but she thought that
kind of talk would be bad for Lalla.

" If you don't mind my saying so, I wouldn't say that
to her, it's most important she should pass this time. You
see, she's more or less promised her Aunt Claudia she
will, and I think if she doesn't her Aunt Claudia will
think it's my fault."

Sam let out a great roar of laughter.

" That's a good one that is. It's not a year yet you've
been on this ice. I can see you now, being half carried
by your Mum down those stairs, and now you tell me
it'll be your fault if your friend doesn't get her silver
medal, that's good that is."

Harriet saw Sam did not understand, so she changed
the subject.

" Has one of your birds told you that I'm going in for
my preliminary and my bronze after Christmas ? "

" They have. A whole flock of them told me, and
some other things too."

" What other things ? "

" Nothing I shall tell you now. You come to me in
two years' time and I'll tell you if they was right."

It took Lalla some time to settle down after the Isle of
Wight, but when she did settle she worked well. There
were days when she was mad-doggish at practice, and was
funny on the ice, instead of practising her figures, but
most days she tried hard and, as a result, her tracings
grew better. One reason why she worked hard was that

Aunt Claudia took to popping in unexpectedly to watch her lessons and practice. Lalla might tease Nana about Aunt Claudia, and mimic her, but she was the sort of audience she liked when she was skating. Nobody else watched her in the same thrilled way as Aunt Claudia did. Aunt Claudia could be strict. " I don't think that was good, Lalla, you held yourself wrongly, didn't you ? " but often it was " Splendid, dear, now all over again. Work, work, that's our motto, isn't it ? "

One reason why Aunt Claudia came to watch Lalla skating was that, as soon as she had passed her silver test Mr. Matthews was arranging for her to give more skating exhibitions. Whenever Max heard the word exhibitions, he looked most disapproving, but Aunt Claudia simply did not care. She knew Lalla enjoyed giving skating exhibitions, she knew she liked being Lalla's aunt when she gave skating exhibitions, and, provided Lalla passed her silver test, she was not going to let Max spoil their fun.

Harriet always felt awkward and nervous when Aunt Claudia was at the rink, for she was not sure what she was expected to do. She tried at first to watch Lalla, as she supposed she was meant to do, but she found that this was wrong.

" My dear child, what are you mooning about for ? I thought you were having lessons so that you could be a companion to Lalla. Surely there's some little exercise you ought to be practising."

When Harriet went off and practised as directed, that sometimes annoyed Aunt Claudia too.

" Funny child, you've no idea how serious you look. You would think you had to work at skating, this is meant to be fun, you know. You've got to enjoy yourself, and enjoy watching Lalla."

Max beckoned to Harriet to leave the private rink

One day when Aunt Claudia was at the rink Max beckoned to Harriet to leave the private rink and come outside and talk to him. He sat down and patted the seat next to him. He looked so serious that Harriet, already very subdued by Aunt Claudia, was sure she had done something wrong.

"Harriet, I have decided that you shall take your preliminary and bronze tests when Lalla takes her silver."

Harriet thought of Aunt Claudia's face and had a sinking feeling inside.

"I couldn't. Please, I'd rather not, I'm only here to keep Lalla company. You said after Christmas and then it was only because . . ."

Max spoke in a very sure voice.

"You will take them when Lalla takes her silver in three weeks' time, and you will pass them. When you have passed them we will work together hard for your inter-silver, which you will attempt next May. I do not know, but I think it may be that if Lalla passes her silver test this time, she shall make her first attempt at the inter-gold in May; she may not pass, but it is better she should work than waste her time at the exhibitions."

Harriet felt most peculiar in front. She pressed the place that felt peculiar with her two hands.

" Max, not the inter-silver, you know I don't know any of the figures. You are only saying that, I know, because you think it will be good for Lalla, but however good it is for Lalla I couldn't take it, I absolutely couldn't."

Max flicked his fingers, a way he had when he wished to dismiss difficulties.

" There are six months for us to work, that should be enough." He turned to face Harriet. " I am very pleased with you, you have talent, my child."

Harriet peered into Max's eyes, trying to make out if he really thought she had talent, or was just saying it to make her think she could go in for the inter-silver to annoy Lalla and make her work.

" You don't mean that, you know you don't ; you don't really think I'll be a skater, you know I'm only learning to make my legs strong, and because it's good for Lalla to have somebody of her own age for a friend."

" It is impossible at your age to say how good a skater you will be, but if you progress as you are progressing now, who can tell ? But for you it is necessary you should enter for tests. You must gain confidence. You must forget this Aunt Claudia of Lalla's, that you had weak legs, and are a companion for Lalla, and must hit yourself like this," Max gave his chest a hearty smack and said :

" Me. Harriet. I have a great skating career in front of me."

Harriet laid a hand on Max's knee.

" Please don't talk like that, Max. It isn't really the sort of thing I could ever say, and you know it, and honestly, if I did say it and Lalla's Aunt Claudia heard me, I'm sure I wouldn't be allowed any more lessons, or ever to come to the rink again. Only Lalla can say things like that."

Max got up. He made another flicking, dismissing gesture with his fingers.

" Me. I do not care what the aunt thinks; I know what I know, and that is what is right for you, and what is right for Lalla."

Harriet went back to the small rink. Aunt Claudia was still there watching Lalla practise. She did not seem to have noticed that Harriet had left the rink, which did not surprise Harriet, who was never sure, unless spoken to, that Aunt Claudia knew she was on the ice. Nana, sitting several seats away from Aunt Claudia, had noticed. She looked up, gave Harriet a little approving nod as if to say, " That's right, back again, dear," and went back to her knitting. Harriet chose a piece of ice as far as possible from Aunt Claudia and Lalla, and practised her eights and changes of edge. She did them badly, because she was not thinking about what she was doing. " Inter-silver next May !" She couldn't enter, and even if she could, whatever would Lalla say ? Lalla was not the sort of person to like her friend taking the skating tests she had taken. Nobody had ever meant her to be a skater. If only Max knew Lalla's house better, he would understand. Nobody but Lalla went in for proper skating in her house.

Presently Aunt Claudia got up to go. It was a moment

when Harriet was thinking about everything but her feet. She was doing a change of edge as Aunt Claudia passed, and slipped and fell. She had no tights, so was wearing long stockings. When she stood up her stockings and pants met ; when she fell there was an ugly gap showing bare leg. Aunt Claudia paused beside Nana; her crisp, sharp voice rang round the rink.

" That poor child ! She doesn't seem to be getting on very well. Still, I suppose she enjoys herself, and if Lalla likes having her it can't do any harm her learning."

The moment Aunt Claudia was off the rink Lalla flew across the ice to Harriet.

" You are an idiot, Harriet. You know you can skate better than that. I was simply terrified that Aunt Claudia was going to say it was no good having you taught any more, and if she had I couldn't have blamed her." She giggled. " You would choose the one moment she's looking at you to fall down on your tail."

Nana looked up from her knitting.

" That's not the way to talk, Lalla dear. We can't all have the same gifts, and I'm sure Harriet does her best. There's no need to be unkind just because she fell over, she might have hurt herself. You've fallen over plenty of times, and you haven't caught me laughing at you."

Harriet took Lalla's hand and skated round the rink beside her. She spoke in a low voice so that Nana should not hear.

" You'd have skated badly if you'd been me. Max says I've got to take my preliminary and my bronze when you take your silver."

Lalla squeezed Harriet's hand.

" Don't worry, they aren't difficult. I'll help you if I can. Anyway it doesn't matter if you pass or not, does it? I mean, no one's expecting you to be a champion grim."

Harriet swallowed before she answered.

"That's not all. If I pass them Max wants me to try for my inter-silver in May."

The enormity of daring to try for the inter-silver, which Lalla had only passed a year ago, made Harriet's voice end in a batlike squeak. Lalla was as shocked as Harriet.

"Inter-silver next May! But you couldn't! Whatever is Max thinking of? I call it mean of him, and I'll tell him so. Poor Harriet, as if you could!"

Although Lalla said it was mean of Max to plan that Harriet should try for her inter-silver in May, inside she was cross and worried. It made things all upside down having Harriet going in for tests. Tests were her things and test days ought to be her special days. She had not minded Harriet taking her preliminary and bronze tests in the spring, for by then she would have got her silver and be working for her inter-gold, but it was a different thing letting her take them this autumn, so that she could work to take her inter-silver in the spring. She knew Harriet could not pass an inter-silver test, but she did not like to think of her working for it. But the fact that Harriet was to work for it, if she passed her preliminary and bronze, made Lalla absolutely determined that she would pass her silver with good marks. But, although she was working extra hard, she made time to look at Harriet's skating in a thinking way, which she had never done before. Harriet was not the sort of skater anyone would think about, she never did things which caught the eye, she was always in some corner, or, when they were on the big rink in the centre, working away by herself, practising and practising, and studying her tracings. Lalla made time to look at some of those tracings, and what she saw made her go back to her brackets, feeling surprised. "She'll pass those tests," she thought, "of course she'll pass them." Then her mind added comfortably, "Anybody would pass those easy sort of tests who works as hard as she does." Inside she was mixed up, one piece of her feeling resentful, and another piece ashamed of feeling like that. The resentful piece felt that Harriet had sneaked up to being good at skating without saying anything about it, and the nice part said, "Don't be silly, you've been watching her all the time, you could have found out how she was getting on if you'd wanted to."

Harriet passed her preliminary and bronze quite easily. She did not get as good marks as Lalla had when she had taken the tests, for she was stiff and lost marks for style. Harriet's passing her tests only interested herself, Lalla, and Max, for nobody else knew anything about them. Miss Goldthorpe was present, and knew, of course, that Harriet was taking tests, but when Harriet said : "They're just baby exams, everybody takes them," she believed her, and did not bother to watch her while she was in front of the examiners, but settled back in the Forest of Arden and had a nice time with Rosalind and Celia. Something, she had no idea what, made Harriet hide that she was taking tests from her family. Not being sure whether Max thought really that she might make a skater made her shy of talking about her skating, and the shyness had got worse since Aunt Claudia had taken to coming to the rink. Harriet thought it quite likely she would not pass, and she didn't want to come home and tell her family she had failed. They would be nice but she was sure they would say, when she was not there, " Poor old Harriet, let's hope she hasn't ideas she's going to turn into a Lalla." She had not any ideas like that, and she didn't want anyone to think she had.

Aunt Claudia turned up in time for Lalla's silver test. She stood as near the judges as she could, looking smart, proud and disdainful. The judges, a man and a woman, did not seem to know she was there, which Harriet thought must be very annoying for Aunt Claudia. The moment Aunt Claudia arrived Miss Goldthorpe and Harriet moved as far away from her as possible. Miss Goldthorpe sat on her handkerchief and Harriet held her thumbs. This time the thumb-holding and the handkerchief worked. Lalla passed. But only just ; once again Max managed to get her marks, she needed fifty-four to pass and what she got was fifty-five point two. Aunt Claudia was so glad that Lalla had got what she called " that silly test " behind her, she did not mention her low markings.

" Don't worry, dear, I dare say those judges . . . what curious clothes . . . are not very experienced. You've passed and that's what matters. You will, of course, have to work hard at those figures ; they must be perfect by the time you enter for open championships, but I'm very pleased with you."

In spite of all Max felt about it, Lalla gave four skating exhibitions that Christmas. He had an argument with Aunt Claudia, but he lost. He arrived at Aunt Claudia's side where she was watching Lalla practise, in a mood to speak his mind ; but when it came to mind-speaking it was difficult to be as good at it as Aunt Claudia. She watched Max thumping his chest, saw his eyes flash, heard what he said about it being bad for Lalla, who was not a child whose work was improved by applause, heard that he wished her to work for her inter-gold only and not be distracted, with an amused expression in her eyes.

" My dear man, there's nothing to get excited about. All work and no play is bad for any child. Lalla is now eleven, and it is important she gets used to public appearances. It will not be long before I shall be travelling with her all over the world for open championships, as indeed so will you. I never interfere with your skating lessons, but over these public appearances you will please allow me to be the best judge."

Max took a deep breath, and opened his mouth. It was as if he were trying to say something important, and yet was afraid of saying it. Then he shut his mouth, shrugged his shoulders and walked away.

That Christmas Aunt Claudia and Uncle David again went away and Lalla spent Christmas Day with the Johnsons. On Boxing Day she was allowed to invite the Johnsons to her house, to see scenes from " Alice." Aunt Claudia supposed only Lalla and Harriet were acting, but Miss Goldthorpe thought that would be dull, so there were scenes for the boys too. Harriet was Alice, partly because she had the sort of hair, but mostly because she could rehearse the boys' scenes at home. The boys acted the mad tea party with Alec as the Mad Hatter, Toby the March Hare, and Edward the Dormouse, and the Walrus and the Carpenter scene with Alec the Walrus, Toby the Carpenter and Edward a very gay, dancing oyster. Lalla played lots of parts. She was the Red Queen. She was the White Knight riding on her rocking horse, and she was the Caterpillar. Lalla was very funny ; the audience of Olivia, George, Cook, Wilson, Helen and Nana laughed and laughed. Lalla's gift for mimicking people made her feel she was the person or creature she

was acting. She knew just the right way to say Lewis
Carroll's words to make them sound as funny as they
truly were. As the Caterpillar she had been sewn by
Miss Goldthorpe into a green eiderdown, and her face,
looking out, with the hookah hanging from her mouth,
was almost as funny as the words. When she had climbed
off the piano stool which Nana had trimmed as a toadstool, and crawled out of sight, Cook said :

" She is a caution ! "

" Better than going to the pictures," Wilson agreed.

Olivia turned to Nana.

" I never knew she was an actress, bless her."

Nana thought acting " Alice in Wonderland " in the
drawing-room at home at Christmas was the very thing
for Lalla to be doing, and she was pleased she had made
a success of it.

" She was always a rare mimic. Of course I stop her
at once if she starts it, but you ought to see the way she
takes off her aunt, the very image of her she is."

When Christmas was over, there was the excitement of
Lalla's four galas. Lalla enjoyed these more even than
she had the year before, because now that she was eleven
she was not sent home after her performance with Nana,
but stayed till the end, sitting beside Aunt Claudia,
hearing the nice things people had to say about her.
Aunt Claudia too enjoyed Lalla's exhibitions more than
ever ; it was fun having Lalla with her ; there was no
doubt about it that she was not only attractive to look
at, but had the sort of personality that made people
remember her. She was usually amusing and gay, but
when she was on the ice to give an exhibition, she seemed
to be saying " Look at me, isn't it lovely to be me ? I
find skating such fun." After the last of her public

performances, Aunt Claudia said, as she kissed her good-night :

" I'm so proud of you, dear. Do hurry up and pass all those nasty tests, so that you can be entered for open championships. We shall have such fun. We'll take Miss Goldthorpe with us and Nana to look after your clothes, and Max Lindblom. Won't it be exciting ? "

Lalla, carried away by the success of the evening and Aunt Claudia's enthusiasm, did something very unusual. She flung her arms round Aunt Claudia, gave her a hug, and said, " Won't it be ? I just can't wait."

After that night things began to go wrong. First Lalla's house had influenza, and then Harriet's. When everybody got over influenza, the weather turned bitterly cold, and though the rink was warm and they wore plenty of Nana's knitted underclothes, both Lalla and Harriet got cold and stiff if they stopped working for a moment, and both Miss Goldthorpe and Nana got chilblains and snivelling colds from sitting at the rink, and were inclined to be snappish in consequence. Worst of all, Lalla's skating went wrong. This time the going wrong was not because she would not work. For her inter-gold she had to do figures called change edge loops. Change edge loops needed the sort of skating which was not Lalla's. They needed control, and rhythm, both of which she had sometimes, but as well they needed immense concentration, and that was not a quality Lalla possessed when she was skating figures. Somehow, however hard she fought to stop it, her mind would slip off what her feet were doing, and this showed on the ice in a bad tracing. Because of her success at exhibition skating, and Aunt Claudia's promises of the fun they would have when she was through with her tests, Lalla really had meant to startle everybody by

passing her inter-gold test that May. Always before she
had been sure she could do a figure if she worked at it,
but this time she had to learn a figure she simply could
not get right. Max was sorry for her, as well as worried.

"You must relax, Lalla, this is not difficult for you,
you know how it should be, but each day those tracings
are worse." He knelt down on the ice and pointed to her
circles. "Look at this ! And this ! "

Lalla, because she was unaccustomed to not being able
to do something, became unusually silent for her, and
inclined to be sulky.

"I can't help it. I try and try. I don't know why I
can't do this stupid old figure. I wish you'd leave me
alone."

Max did not mind her sounding cross because he
understood it.

"You must not worry, Lalla. We will leave the loops
for two or three weeks. If, when we try them again, they
are still difficult, we will give ourselves longer. You will
not try for the inter-gold until the autumn."

"I'm trying for the inter-gold this May. You know I
know how to do the beastly things, and that I always do
better in tests than in practice."

Max nodded, and agreed this was true, but if Lalla
could not get better tracings after a rest he thought she
had better leave the test for the time being.

Lalla did not give up her loops; she had no lessons
on them for two weeks, but she never stopped practising
them, until at last she began practising them in her sleep.
Sometimes she would wake up with a jump, thinking she
had just finished a loop and done it wrong ; sometimes
she just went on practising in her head all night. Which-
ever way it happened it was bad for her, and instead of

looking round-faced and gay with shining eyes, she began to look thin and pale, and her curls hung lankly, and she had a hang-dog look in her eyes. Miss Goldthorpe and Nana were very worried.

" I don't know what it is, Miss Goldthorpe dear," Nana said. " Of course there's this taking the test again, but then there's always one of those. Last time it was the brackets bothered her, and this time, from what I can gather, it's something called the circles, but she's not one to let skating get on her mind."

" Is it her diet ? "

Nana made scornful, clicking noises.

" Diet ! Me let a child in my nursery diet looking the way she does ? If there's anything she fancies to eat, she has it, and as much of it as she likes, and has done ever since she had the influenza. Not that she eats as she should, only picks at her food, and if there's a thing I can't abide, it's seeing a child pick at her food."

" You know Mr. King better than I do, could you talk to him ? "

Nana was knitting a new pattern of a jersey, and had to count her stitches. In the pause she thought about Uncle David.

" What would I say ? I dare say he'd get Mrs. King to have the doctor along, but he'd only give her a tonic same as he did after the flu."

" Couldn't you get Mr. King to have a talk to Lalla, she's fond of him ? And he might get to the bottom of what's troubling her."

Nana considered it.

" Well, of course, I always say it's better going to a gentleman when you want advice. Seem to have more sense than a lady. I might do that. She doesn't see much of him really, being only her step-uncle and one to laugh at the skating and all. But it was him that told Lalla to speak her mind about having Harriet to work with her." She turned over the problem a little longer. " I'll do that, Miss Goldthorpe, I can't say when, me not going much in their part of the house, but I'll manage it somehow."

" And I'll have a talk with Max Lindblom ; I'll see him sometime when the children aren't there, and ask whether there's any need for her to take that examination just now. Then I might have a talk with Harriet's mother, she's a very sensible woman, she might have an idea of what's upsetting the child. Harriet may have said something."

Nana shook her head.

" Never. Harriet's Miss Quiet in my nursery, you never know what she's thinking. But you see Mrs. Johnson, dear ; it can't do any harm and it might do good. Anything's worth trying ; it properly upsets me to see my blessed lamb the way she's looking now."

CHAPTER XIII

THE QUARREL

★

MISS GOLDTHORPE saw Max Lindblom one evening. He was giving a lesson when she reached the rink, but she waited until he had finished, then asked him if he could spare a moment.

" This is nothing to do with me, and I don't know what Mrs. King would say if she knew I was seeing you, but Lalla isn't herself at all. She's quiet at her lessons, which is quite unlike her, and she gets cross easily, and that's unlike her too. She always was a child who liked to have her own way, and order people about, but she never does that now, almost I wish she would. You know, I think this test is worrying her."

Max did not answer at once. He led Miss Goldthorpe to a seat where nobody could hear what they were saying.

" I do not wish her to try for this inter-gold test. There is no need ; she is still very young, why should there be this rush ? "

" I think she wants to get it over and done with. You know what great plans there are for her when she has finished with these tests."

Max made an angry, growling noise.

" It has been wrong from the beginning. The child has talent, yes. She has a good personality, yes. But these things do not necessarily make the great skater."

" I couldn't agree with you more. I think it wretched that she feels that she must be a skater and nothing else. But she has been brought up to believe in a great future ever since she was a baby, and, except of course for that one time when she failed to pass a test, it's all been coming true. But now I gather there is something she can't do. I learn from Harriet she's working terribly hard, and still she can't do whatever it is."

" She will do it, but not yet. The aunt should forbid skating for many months. Let us forget it, she should say, let us go away. You, I think, should tell the aunt to say these things."

Miss Goldthorpe sighed. What a foolish young man he was !

" Mr. Lindblom, I've told you before it's quite impossible for me to say anything like that to Mrs. King. Last time when you asked me to say something to her I explained that if I did it would mean that I would be given notice, and I have no intention of being given notice. I'm not a vain woman, but I do think that I'm useful to Lalla, and I therefore would do nothing to risk offending Mrs. King."

Max shrugged his shoulders.

" Then nothing can be done. I have told Lalla she should not attempt her inter-gold this spring."

" Have you told Mrs. King ? "

Max lit a cigarette.

" The trouble is Harriet."

Miss Goldthorpe's eyes opened very wide.

" Harriet ! What has Harriet got to do with it ? "

" Skating is a very expensive thing. To work properly you must have what Lalla gives Harriet : the good governess like yourself, the outside classes, everything specially arranged to fit in with the training. It is impossible to train properly and to attend a school. If I say to Mrs. King give Lalla six months, and no skating, that will mean six months without lessons for Harriet."

Miss Goldthorpe switched her mind from Lalla to Harriet. Harriet was stronger now ; in spite of influenza and the cold winter she seemed well ; she was always frail-looking compared to Lalla but that did not mean she was delicate.

" I don't think you need worry about Harriet. Of course skating has done wonders for her, poor child, but she's much stronger now and she could practise if she wanted to. Mr. Matthews, you know, very kindly lets her come here free of charge."

Max looked pityingly at Miss Goldthorpe, as if he were thinking, " How can I make this poor, ignorant woman see what is so clear to me ? " Then he saw his next pupil was waiting. He got up, said good-night, and went back on the ice.

It was a nasty night, with driving rain. Outside the rink Miss Goldthorpe put up her umbrella and walked towards her bus stop, but before she reached it a gust of wind caught the umbrella and turned it inside out. While she was struggling with it she felt it taken from her hands, and when she blinked away the rain which was in her eyes, she saw that her rescuer was Alec. Alec had the bag which had held papers over his arm, for he had just finished his evening round.

" Hullo, Miss Goldthorpe, were you coming to see us ? "

Miss Goldthorpe had been thinking of nothing but how nice it would be to sit in front of a fire and read a book, but now that Alec suggested it, she saw that this was the obvious moment to call on Mrs. Johnson.

Miss Goldthorpe got a lovely welcome from the Johnsons, especially from Harriet, but Olivia guessed she would not have come to see them on a nasty wet night without some reason. She told Toby to take Miss Goldthorpe's wet coat and umbrella and put them in the bathroom, and when she saw George pushing a chair up to the living-room fire she stopped him.

"Miss Goldthorpe is staying to supper with us and I'm going to ask her to help me cook it. I'm afraid it's a poor feeding night. March never seems a lucky month for William."

George was not hearing his brother William run down.

"You can't say that. There were five duck eggs yesterday as well as all those splendid winter greens."

Toby looked up from his homework.

"People don't come to us for duck eggs, and the greens weren't splendid, the brussels-sprouts had gone bad."

Harriet was playing snap with Edward.

"There were some turnips as well, I saw Mummy washing them."

Edward looked reproachfully at his father.

"You can say what you like, about Uncle William, but nobody can't say that soup, soup, soup every evening is nice, and that's what we have to eat, made with his old vegetables. A lady said to me to-day I was looking pale, and I told her that was because I ate too much soup."

Olivia laughed.

"What nonsense! You don't look pale and you don't have soup every evening, and you know it. As a matter of fact to-night it's curried duck eggs and vegetables, and you know you'll like that. Come along, Miss Goldthorpe, don't listen to these grumblers."

In the kitchen Olivia shut the door and gave Miss Goldthorpe a chair while she went about her work. The kitchen-dining-room was so cosy that in no time Miss Goldthorpe had told Olivia all about Lalla ; how worried she and Nana were, of how she had seen Max, and what he had said.

Olivia had by this time boiled the duck eggs hard ; she gave them to Miss Goldthorpe and asked her to take off their shells.

" It seems to me a lot of fuss about nothing. If it was one of my children I wouldn't let them go near a rink again if I thought it was worrying them. But I suppose Lalla is different ; as they are determined to make a skater of her I suppose she has got to pass these wretched tests. Is there no one who can make the child see it's silly to go in for it now, as her instructor thinks she shouldn't ? "

Miss Goldthorpe carefully shelled an egg.

" To have to tell her aunt that, would seem to Lalla admitting that she was not the success she's expected to be."

Olivia gave her curry sauce a savage stir.

" If only I could speak my mind just once to Mrs. King. I'm a mild woman, but you'd be surprised what I would say."

" I wouldn't. I've never really lost my temper, it has never seemed worth while. But, do you know, sometimes when I think of the way Mrs. King has brought up poor Lalla I wish I could whip her. Extraordinary, for I don't hold with corporal punishment."

" What about Mr. King ? George says he's nice, can't he do anything ? "

Miss Goldthorpe explained that Nana was seeing him,

but how difficult it was for him to interfere. Then she said :

"I wondered if you would see Lalla. I've been planning a treat for her on Saturday. I've taken seats for a musical entertainment ; the advertisements say it's funny ; I was not inviting Harriet as I know you like to have her on Saturday afternoons, and from what I read this comedy couldn't do her any good educationally. . . . I wonder, would you use my seat and take Lalla, and have a talk with her ? It would be a great kindness."

"Bless you, of course I will. I shall enjoy it. I love musical comedies, and hardly ever get a chance to see one. And of course I'll talk to Lalla, but I don't know if I can help. I haven't seen her for weeks, what with influenza and the foul weather, and last time I saw her she was on top of the world. I can't imagine that child except on top of the world."

"That, I think, may be the trouble ; she can't imagine herself in any other place."

Miss Goldthorpe was a poor liar. On Saturday, in the car driving to the theatre, she told Lalla a halting story of a book she had to return, and of how, as Mrs. Johnson was in the West-end, she was using her seat. Lalla laughed at her.

"It's no good telling me that, Goldie. Harriet's mother never would be this end of London on a Saturday with all of them home, and you know it. I bet it's just you so hated to see a musical comedy you gave your seat away. Isn't that it ? "

Miss Goldthorpe was glad Lalla had hit on something near the truth.

"Well, dear, I don't like musical plays."

Lalla put her arm through Miss Goldthorpe's and rubbed her cheek on her shoulder.

" And you paid for the seats. You didn't dare tell Aunt Claudia this was educational, did you ? "

" It was a little present for you."

Lalla hugged Miss Goldthorpe's arm closer.

" Dear Goldie, you're an angel, and however much a beast I seem, I truly love you."

Olivia was shocked at Lalla's appearance. The round, gay, bouncing Lalla she knew had disappeared, and in her place was a thinner, almost serious Lalla, with most of the bounce gone out of her. Olivia was thankful to find that the gayness and the bounce were not quite gone, for the play was very funny and Lalla not only got bouncing and gay from laughing, but in the intervals made Olivia laugh by her imitations of the actors. Miss Goldthorpe had arranged that Olivia should take Lalla home in a taxi, but Olivia thought a taxi would be too quick over the journey, for her and Lalla to have a proper talk.

" How about going home on the top of a bus ? "

Lalla was charmed.

" Could we ? Do you know, I've hardly ever been on a bus. Aunt Claudia is afraid of germs."

Olivia looked pityingly at Lalla. Poor lamb ! Even a bus was a treat. If only she could steal her and take her home with her.

Olivia was not a mother who asked her children to tell her things. She tried to make them feel she was always interested in anything they would like to tell her, but if they did not want to talk about something that was their own affair. Because of this, it was difficult for her to make Lalla talk, but in the theatre she had planned a way to do it. She started by telling her she was thinner, and asking if it was her diet, and when Lalla explained that the dieting had finished, she said she wondered if she was outgrowing her strength, which was something which easily happened at her age.

"It happened to me. Do you know, I was nearly as tall as I am now when I was not much older than you are."

"But I'm not much taller, only thinner."

"It's the same thing. It means using a lot of energy in growing up, and then there isn't as much energy for other things. I was brought up in South Africa, you know, and riding was my thing. I loved horses more than anything else in the world, and was supposed to be a marvellous horsewoman, but outgrowing my strength affected my riding. I suppose my horses could feel I wasn't as full of pep as usual."

Lalla looked suspiciously at Olivia out of the corner of her eyes. Had Harriet told her about how she could not do loops? Olivia did not look like somebody saying something on purpose. In fact she had stopped talking about outgrowing your strength and was talking about the funny man in the play. Lalla joined in and soon was acting for Olivia most of the parts, and they were both laughing again at the jokes. But underneath what she was saying, and underneath her laughing, Lalla knew something nice had happened. It was as if there had been a tight, hard band round her middle, and somehow Olivia had loosened it and made her feel better. Presently she asked a question.

"What did you do for outgrowing your strength?"

"Saw a doctor. He cured me."

At Lalla's gate Olivia kissed her good-bye.

"I have enjoyed my afternoon. I wish sometimes you could arrange for Miss Goldthorpe to give us another afternoon out."

That night Lalla slept really well. As she was slipping into sleep she thought, "How silly I've been. It isn't that I can't do those loops. It's I need a tonic. I'll tell Nana to buy me a bottle." And then, cosily, "And if she won't Harriet's mother will. It's nice going out with Harriet's mother, I hope I'll be allowed to do it again."

There were no secrets between Miss Goldthorpe and Nana, so Lalla had told Nana about the matinée. At breakfast the next morning she told her what Olivia had said about outgrowing her strength. Nana tried not to look ruffled, but inside she felt it. She might tell Miss Goldthorpe something ought to be done about Lalla, who was not eating and did not look well, but that did not mean she wanted Lalla asking for a bottle of tonic. Children should not think about their health, that was for grown-ups to do for them. She gave Lalla halibut oil in the winter to keep off colds, and salts now and then in the summer if she had spots, and she made her take the tonic the doctor ordered after her influenza, but health talk from children was not right and she did not hold with it. Then she looked at Lalla and her heart softened. Harriet's mother had done her good. She seemed much more herself this morning, and was eating a good breakfast without being told.

"That tonic was for the influenza and wouldn't do good for anything else. You'll have to see the doctor."

Lalla helped herself to honey.

"I wish I could see Harriet's doctor. Ours is so old and grumpy. Harriet's one said she would get well if she skated. I should think a doctor who said that would know something gorgeous to make you stop outgrowing your strength."

After breakfast Nana saw Uncle David walking up and

down the lawn smoking. Nana did not hold with gardens in early March, but it was a lovely morning, a good moment to catch him alone, for Lalla was working in her garden, and Aunt Claudia was still in bed. Nana dressed as warmly as if it were a cold day in mid-winter, and went out.

Uncle David was glad to see Nana because he had just been talking to Lalla, and was thinking about her.

" That child of yours has been looking under the weather lately. What are you doing to her ? "

Nana glanced up at Aunt Claudia's windows to be sure they were shut.

" That's what I've come out about, sir. She's got another of these tests coming on for the skating. That Mr. Lindblom doesn't want her to take it, but Lalla won't be put off."

Uncle David made a despairing gesture with his shoulders.

" Blast that skating ! But I can't do a thing unless Lalla asks me to ; if I interfere on my own I shall be eaten alive, not only by Mrs. King but by Lalla, and as well I'd lose the child's trust."

" I know, sir. But it seems Mrs. Johnson has told Lalla she might be outgrowing her strength, not that she is, but thinking it might be that and not something she can't do at the skating seems to have cheered her up. Childlike she fancies a bottle of medicine would put her right, and she's taken to the idea that she would like to be given it by the doctor that looks after Harriet and ordered skating for her."

" You think it would be a good idea ? "

Nana did not think it a good idea that Lalla should want to see a doctor. She did not believe in illness unless there was something to show for it like spots or a temperature. But Lalla was not herself, not eating properly, getting thin. If Nana had her way she would have suggested a fortnight by the sea at Easter, nothing like sea air for building children up ; but Lalla would not go to the sea, she would talk about her test and refuse to miss her lessons on that nasty cold ice.

" I don't know what to say, sir, I'm sure. I try to treat her like I'd treat any child, which is what her mother would have wished, but with the skating and all I can't. Maybe if she's taken a fancy to Harriet's doctor it can't do any harm, though I doubt it does any good."

Uncle David smiled sympathetically.

" Don't worry too much. I'll have a talk with her and try and find out what's on her mind."

Lalla, as instructed by Alec, was raking between the rows of strawberries. The March wind had put colour into her cheeks and the good smell of growing, coming out of the earth, made her eyes shine, but she still did not look as she ought to look. Uncle David's eyes twinkled when he saw what she was doing.

" You know, poppet, I'll never believe you planted those strawberries. I bet Simpson put them in."

Lalla leant on her rake.

" You're wrong, he didn't."

" But neither did you."

Lalla gave an imitation of Nana.

" Those who ask no questions won't be told no lies."

Uncle David laughed.

" I've just seen her. I told her you looked as if she was starving and beating you, and she tells me you think Harriet's doctor would be the one to cure you. Is that right ? "

Lalla laid down her rake and joined Uncle David.

" Yes."

Uncle David took her hand. They walked down the path.

" What's the matter with you ? "

Before yesterday afternoon Lalla would not have answered that, but now, certain a bottle of tonic from the right doctor was all she needed, she explained about the loops that would not come right ; how she even tried to do them in her sleep ; how fussed she had been, but now that she knew that nothing had gone wrong with her skating, but only outgrown strength, she was not worrying any more.

Uncle David watched Lalla while she talked. She was not big for somebody of eleven, in fact she was short for her age, he doubted if any doctor would think outgrown strength was the trouble.

" I expect you've been overworking. Isn't the child wonder taking another skating test ? "

" Yes. The inter-gold in May."

" I dare say the doctor will suggest less tests. It's a way they have."

Lalla stood still, all the pink made by the wind leaving her face, and the gayness disappearing from her eyes.

" Then I won't see him. I've got to pass that test, absolutely got to."

" Why this May ? Wouldn't next year do ? "

Lalla tried hard to explain.

" No. It must be now, so I know I can do it. If I have to wait I'll think and think I can't. And I simply couldn't bear that."

Uncle David gave her a friendly pat on the back.

" What rot ! You know you and your aunt between

you are making martyrs of yourselves for this skating ; simply couldn't bear it because you might be told not to take a test for a month or two. Really, Lalla ! "

Lalla kicked a stone off the path.

" Silly Uncle David, you don't understand." Lalla's voice wobbled. " It was awful that time I failed my silver, more awfuller than anybody knew. People looked sorry ; nobody ever looked sorry for me before and I hated it. When people look at me without looking proud of me I feel I'm not Lalla Moore any more."

Uncle David lit another cigarette. He lit it very slowly to give him time to think of what he had better say.

" It sounds as though we must try and fix for this doctor of Harriet's to give you a bottle of champion-skater mixture, if that's what you want. But you've got your ideas all upside down. The Lalla I know is an amusing child, and I believe could make her mark in the world without ever putting skates on again. There's a saying, ' There are more ways than one of killing a cat,' and I think there are more talents than one belonging to Lalla Moore, but I know neither you nor your aunt will believe it."

Uncle David knew it was impossible to get Aunt Claudia to agree to Lalla seeing a new doctor ; he would be asked what Lalla's doctor had to do with him. Aunt Claudia usually left Lalla's health to Nana, and sent for the doctor only when Nana asked her to. She might have noticed Lalla was looking peaky and be thinking of her seeing the doctor, but she certainly would not want Uncle David suggesting it. The only thing to do was to ring up Olivia and ask her to arrange it.

Olivia did arrange it. She saw Dr. Phillipson and told him all about Lalla, and he and she made a plan. It was

arranged that the next Saturday Miss Goldthorpe, instead
of taking Lalla to a theatre, should take her to see a
film at a local cinema, and afterwards they would have
tea at the Doctor's house.

That next Saturday Miss Goldthorpe talked to Mrs.
Phillipson in the drawing-room while Dr. Phillipson
talked to Lalla in his surgery. He explained it could be
only talking ; Lalla was not his patient, but he might
find out what sort of medicine she needed just by talking.
He was, Lalla found, easy to talk to and enormously
interested in skating. He wanted to know all about her
training from the very beginning, all about tests, what
you had to do at them ; it was almost as if he wanted to
skate himself, everything she said absorbed him. To make
figures clear to him Lalla drew them for him. The last
she drew was loops.

" These are what I have to do in May and they've
been going wrong ; I've fussed and fussed because I'm
not used to not being able to do a figure. So that's why
Goldie has brought me to tea because I was sure a man
like you who thought of skating to cure Harriet's legs
being cotton-wool, would know what to give me for
outgrown strength which makes my loops go wrong."

Dr. Phillipson seemed to be studying Lalla's drawings.
Inside his head he was wondering how best to help her.
It seemed as if what she most needed was to believe it
was any reason, except that they were too difficult, which
was making her fail at loops. After a bit he sat down,
took a piece of notepaper and began writing.

" I can't guarantee this, but have it made up, take it
regularly, and it might do the trick."

Lalla looked at the sheet of paper. Most of it she
couldn't understand for it was written in doctor-writing,

but at the top was printed in big letters, " Skating Mixture for Lalla Moore. One tablespoon to be taken daily before visiting rink."

The medicine worked. Lalla felt better, and so worried less, and so her loops were better. Then, so slowly she hardly noticed it, the effect of the medicine began to wear off. Max Lindblom could have explained that if she was judging the medicine by her loop tracings it was bound to stop helping her, for her loops were as good as she was going to get them for the present, and no medicine would make them any better ; but Lalla had not told Max about the medicine ; she wanted him to think she did her loops marvellously without help, so when they stopped getting better she could not talk to him or anybody about it, but just felt more fussed and bothered than ever, all by herself. As each day she got more miserable and more anxious her tracings got worse and worse, and as the tracings got worse so did Lalla's health. She slept worse because she spent her night practising, and in the morning felt too tired to eat or do lessons, and the result was she grew crosser and crosser, and if anyone even hinted that she might leave taking her test until the autumn, she was angry for hours, so though everybody was sorry for her, nobody knew how to help her.

" She's like a reel of cotton come unfixed in a work-basket," Nana said, " tied into knots round everything, you don't know where to start to look for an end to start rewinding."

Aunt Claudia was as bothered about Lalla as everybody else, but her bothering over her, though she did not know it, got Lalla into a worse state, even than doing a bad tracing. Aunt Claudia thought Lalla was suffering from quite unnecessary nerves.

" Cheer up, dear, it's not like the Lalla Moore I know to worry. Where's that champion grim got to, I wonder ? "

Lalla usually refused to answer, but sometimes she would be rude.

" Don't talk like that ! I'm not a baby."

That would make Aunt Claudia try to be especially understanding.

" Of course you aren't. Eleven and a half is a big girl. Don't think I mind for myself if you're a little rude, I know that's just a sign that you have temperament, and a skater must have that, but my Lalla mustn't forget a great skater has also to be her country's ambassadress."

Once Aunt Claudia suggested that perhaps Lalla should see the doctor.

" You're getting thin, darling. Perhaps the doctor would give you something to make you fatter."

" My goodness ! I thought you wanted me thinner. All those months no potatoes, no cakes, no nothing nice. Now you want me to see a doctor because I've got thinner. Well, I won't see him, so there. I'm not Alice in Wonderland eating things all the time to make me grow littler and bigger."

Aunt Claudia did not mention a doctor again to Lalla, but she did to Nana.

" I think Lalla ought to see a doctor. She seems a little nervous, but I won't worry her until after her test."

Nana said politely, " Just as you say, ma'am," but her tone showed that she did not think much of what Aunt Claudia had said.

Aunt Claudia was not particularly worried about the test, because she did not know how Lalla was doing, for the moment the effect of the medicine began, as Lalla thought, to wear off, she told her she was not to come to the rink. Nana heard her tell Aunt Claudia this and was terribly shocked.

" A child your age speaking that way to your aunt ! You won't have her coming indeed ! The nursery is now the schoolroom, but from the sound of you it ought to be in my nursery again. I'd teach you how a little lady ought to behave."

Aunt Claudia was shocked too, and also hurt.

" Not come ! But you know how I love watching you skate. And now that we are nearing the time when you can enter for amateur championships you must get used to me watching you. Just think, Lalla, if you get your inter-gold this time, there is only the gold left, and then our fun starts, but it's our fun, we're going to share your triumphs, aren't we ? "

Lalla's inside felt as if it rolled over. Inter-gold this time ! Only the gold left ! Share our triumphs ! If only it was happening. It had got to happen. It had been promised her since she was a baby, and she had to go on being promised it. Aunt Claudia was not going to watch her, and perhaps go and whisper to Max afterwards. Somehow she would pass her inter-gold, and then Aunt Claudia would never know she nearly had not been able to do loops.

" I don't want you to come until I ask you."

" But why not, dear ? "

" Because I don't." Lalla remembered how she had made Aunt Claudia let Harriet go on sharing classes. " If you come, I won't skate, I'll go home."

That settled that. Nana opened the door for Aunt Claudia and saw her downstairs. When she came back her face was red.

" That I should hear a child of mine speak that way.
It's not altogether your fault, you've been brought up
very foolishly in many ways, and so I've always said, and
through it you've become a shocking little madam, but
you'll suffer for it, pride comes before a fall, you'll
see."

Lalla swallowed a lump in her throat. If only Nana
would understand it was not she was being a madam,
but Nana could not, it was no good trying to explain.
She turned away to the window, blinking to keep back
tears which wanted to run down her cheeks. It made
things more awful than ever if Nana was turning against
her.

It was not only Nana who seemed to Lalla to be
turning against her, it was everybody, and the worst
turner-against was Harriet. Harriet had done her best.
It was not easy being friendly with Lalla when she was
in a state. If she talked about skating Lalla would
probably say something like " What do you know about
it anyway ? " and if she did not talk about skating she
got suspicious. " Why do you try and not talk about my
test ? I suppose Max has told you not to. You two are
always talking to each other, jabber, jabber, jabber. I
guessed you were talking about me." In the few weeks
while Lalla thought her medicine was working it had been
all right. Harriet had her usual fun with her, they talked
all the time when they were not at lessons, and rushed
out every day to look at Alec's strawberries, but when the
effect of the medicine finished Harriet found the only
thing to do was to keep out of Lalla's way as much as
possible, and talk to her as little as possible. She did not
want to have a row with her, and she knew she would in
the end. Nobody could go on giving soft answers that

were supposed to turn away wrath, when the wrath went on coming at you just the same.

As it happened as her inter-silver test day came nearer, Harriet did not feel talkish. During the last six months the little-girl Harriet, without her noticing it, had disappeared and a new Harriet had taken her place. A Harriet who looked much the same outside, but was more of a person inside. Everybody else noticed it. Miss Goldthorpe told Nana it was a pleasure having Harriet about, she was becoming interesting to talk to. Nana said she didn't know about talking, but Harriet was paying more for dressing, she looked really nice now at the rink, in the new things she had knitted for her, and when she had first had her it hadn't mattered what she had put on her, she had never looked more than three-halfpence worth of nothing. Alonso Vittori, watching Harriet, murmured, " It's a funny little personality but she's got something, that child." Monsieur Cordon said of Harriet to Miss Goldthorpe, " Un type curieux ! " At the rink she stopped being just the little girl Mr. Matthews allowed to skate free, or the child Lalla Moore's aunt had taken up, and became Harriet Johnson, one of Max Lindblom's promising pupils. As the day of the test came nearer Harriet was more and more wrapped up in skating, and less and less noticing what people were thinking or saying. She had private plans. If she passed the inter-silver, and she knew it was a big " if," she would tell the family. They knew about an inter-silver test, for they had heard about it when Lalla went in for it. It would be fun to come home and say, just as if it was nothing, " I passed my inter-silver test to-day." How surprised they would be. They would laugh of course. Her mother would say, " Darling ! *You* have ? I didn't know you could skate properly." Toby was sure to tell her not to get cocky, that if Lalla's chances were less than one in a thousand, then hers were less than one in fifty thousand. But telling them would be the beginning of her idea. If she passed, she held her thumbs when she thought of it, perhaps this autumn she could try for the silver, and, if she passed that, the next spring the inter-gold, and have a try for the gold six months later. That would mean if she got on as fast as that, she would have her first try for the gold the autumn she was thirteen, and, allowing for lots of failures, she might have passed everything by the time she was fifteen. Even if she didn't pass them all she would have a lovely career for when she was old enough. She would be a professional skater like that poster of the girl in the ballet skirt skating on one foot, which she had seen just before it was first planned she should go to the rink. Nobody must know what she was planning or they would laugh at her, which was natural, while she was no better than she was now, but she was sure if she worked she would get better, and then she would surprise the boys by earning money much sooner than they could.

Harriet's was a very full day. Every morning she caught the bus in time to reach Lalla's house by a quarter to nine. The moment Wilson let her in she rushed up to Nana to change and was in the schoolroom by nine. After lessons there was ballet, fencing, a walk sometimes, gardening or shopping for Lalla. Then lunch. Then the rink, Max's lessons, and hard practice. Then home and homework, for now she and Lalla were eleven and a half, more lessons had to be squeezed in, so having tea with each other had to come to an end. After lessons there was supper and bed. When, as well, there was thinking and planning a future there was not much room for other people's troubles, and that was how the quarrel with Lalla started.

Rinks draw press photographers. Lalla was so used to being photographed that she broke off whatever she was doing, posed charmingly, and skated off as casually as if she had only stopped to sneeze. But one day a photographer noticed Harriet.

"Who's the little ginger girl?"

Somebody explained.

"A pupil of Max Lindblom's. Only been skating about eighteen months. He thinks a lot of her."

The photographer took an action photograph of Harriet practising a back change. It was a lucky photograph, Harriet looked charmingly serious. The photographer's paper published it, over the caption "Little Harriet Johnson, for whom a great future is predicted." It was an evening paper, and of course somebody saw the photograph. Harriet was having a lesson at the time, so the picture was shown to Lalla. Lalla said how nice it was, and she must buy a copy for Harriet, but inside she was furious. Harriet! Poor little Harriet who wore her clothes, and had her lessons paid for to keep her company, sneaking around and getting her photograph taken! The bit about her future was, of course, only idiotic, Harriet had no future. It was the meanness of it she minded, Harriet had only been photographed to be annoying; she knew that just before a test, if anyone's photograph was published it had to be hers. Now she came to think of it Harriet was being mean all round. She was pretending to be so quiet and mousey, and all the time playing up to people like Alonso Vittori, Monsieur Cordon, and Max, trying to show them how good and hardworking she was. As the angry thoughts flew round in Lalla's head, so she skated faster and faster, until it was as if she was in for a relay race. " Mean ! Mean ! Mean ! " But if Harriet was going to treat her like that she would show her.

When Harriet, knowing nothing about the photograph, skated back on to the private rink, Lalla, her face scarlet, dragged her into a corner.

" Look at that ! "

Harriet stared at the photograph. Her ! Her in a paper ! Then she saw what the paper had written.

" *Look at that !* "

" Oh, bother ! I never knew it was being taken, or I wouldn't have let them."

" Why not ? "

" Because the family might see it, and I don't want to tell them I'm taking tests or anything, I want to surprise them."

Lalla looked at Harriet, and a stab shot through her. Surprise them ! Suppose she did ! Suppose she could ! Suppose . . . but she would not think of that. She was frightened at her half-thought, and so worried and miserable she could have cried, but she was too proud to do that in public, and anyway she knew something better, something to make Harriet feel as awful as she was feeling.

"You'd better keep this photograph, for it's most likely the only one they'll ever take of you, for if you pass your inter-silver I'll tell Aunt Claudia I don't want you to work with me any more."

CHAPTER XIV

THE THERMOMETER RISES

★

HARRIET felt as an insect must feel who flies round and round a room unable to find a way out. What was she to do? If she told Max she would not enter for her inter-silver he would just flick his fingers, and tell her not to be silly. She could not explain to Miss Goldthorpe or Nana, they would be furious with Lalla, who would think her a mean beast to tell tales, which she would be. In any case it would do no good; neither Nana, Goldie nor anyone else could make Aunt Claudia let her go on sharing things with Lalla if Lalla said she didn't want her. Nor could she tell her family. First of all they wouldn't understand; they had never heard she was going in for her inter-silver, so all they would say would be, " Well, don't enter for the inter-silver if Lalla's cross about it," not seeing that if you learnt from Max Lindblom you couldn't just say " I'm not entering," without making him understand why. As well, she couldn't tell her family because of Lalla. They thought Lalla was sometimes a bit grand; she might have been much worse seeing the silly way she had been brought up, but they all liked her, and talked about her as if she was part of the family. It would be horrible to have to tell them what Lalla had threatened and why. It would make the boys turn against her, they probably wouldn't even pick the strawberries they had grown in her garden. Olivia, who not only liked but really loved Lalla, would find it hard to forgive her. The terrible thing was that Harriet had to make up her mind quickly. Having made her threat Lalla wouldn't speak any more. It had been possible, Harriet hoped, to hide from Nana that she and Lalla weren't speaking. They had both practised at different ends of the private rink until it was time to go home. When Nana called they went to the changing room speaking only to Nana. Outside the rink Nana said good-bye to Harriet and Harriet said good-bye to Nana ; it had not been notice-able, Harriet thought, that Lalla did not say " See you to-morrow " or " Bet I get my homework finished sooner than you do," or something usual of that sort.

To make up her mind what to do Harriet walked home by the longest way she knew, and just before she reached home she found the answer. She couldn't tell Max she would not try for her inter-silver after he had worked so hard to make it possible, and she couldn't let Lalla tell Aunt Claudia she didn't want her to learn things from her. It would not be true, Lalla would be miserable doing things all alone again, but being Lalla, having said she would say something, she would say it, even if it hurt her. Harriet got a lump in her throat when she thought of not learning things with Lalla. No more Nana! No more Goldie ! Never to see Lalla again ! It couldn't be. No more dancing ! No more fencing ! It was at that thought, although it was not a cold evening, that Harriet shivered. No more skating ! She could go to the rink and practise, but she knew she never would. What good would practising be to her when she had dreamed of being good enough to be a professional ? How could she practise at the rink where Lalla was ? How visit a rink just to practise, after having daily lessons from Max? It was not to be thought of. Lalla must be given in to, and no one but Lalla must know why she was unable to take the test.

When Harriet reached home only Olivia was in. She was in the kitchen.

"Hallo, darling. You're first. Edward's gone to tea with one of his admiring old ladies. Toby's in the shop with Daddy, and Alec, of course, is doing his papers."

Harriet leant against the kitchen door.

"I'm going up to bed."

Olivia was cutting a loaf. She put down the knife and came to Harriet.

"Are you ill, pet?"

Harriet hated lying to Olivia.

"I feel sort of funny-ish."

"Where?"

"Just all-overish."

Olivia took Harriet's satchel of books from her.

"Let me help you up to your room, darling. I dare say it's nothing. I expect you're over-tired; I was only saying to Daddy last night what a busy life you led, and how I hoped it wouldn't be too much for you."

Lying in bed, trying to look ill, and feeling mean at being waited on, when she was perfectly well, Harriet heard the rest of the family return one by one.

First Toby and George, talking cheerfully as they came upstairs, then silence, then whispers. Olivia would be telling them about her, and to keep quiet in case she was asleep. Presently Edward came home.

"Mummy! Mummy! I've had a gorgeous tea, and Mrs. Pinker said she wished she could adopt me."

Toby came out, his whisper was as carrying as Edward's shout.

" Shut up. Harriet's ill. I should think Dad and Mum would be glad if Mrs. Pinker would take a conceited little rat like you."

It was when Alec came home that everybody forgot to be quiet. He raced up the stairs shouting :

" Mum ! Dad ! Everybody ! Look at this. Where's Harriet ? "

They all talked at once.

" Let me look, Toby, I'm shorter than you, so you can see over me."

" All right, Edward, but don't shove or you'll tear it."

Olivia reading out loud :

" ' Little Harriet Johnson for whom a great future is predicted.' "

George's amazed :

" That's never my Harriet ? "

Then Olivia's :

" She's not well, poor pet, but I think this will cheer her up. I'll see if she's awake."

The photograph ! Because of the quarrel with Lalla Harriet had quite forgotten the photograph. But of course Alec would see it. It was on the front of the paper, he would notice it as he folded the papers to put them in the letter-boxes.

It was dreadfully difficult to pretend to be ill when all the family sat round the bed looking proud and admiring.

" But what's all this, darling, about the future ? " Olivia asked. " I didn't know you could skate properly yet."

" I can't, it's just something to say."

Alec re-read the caption.

"Somebody must have said you had a great future."
Toby's brain was working.

"How many girls go to your rink, Harriet?"

"I don't know, dozens and dozens."

"Well, if five dozen girls skate at a rink, and a photographer photographs the eight most promising . . ."

"Don't bother the child with mathematics," said Olivia. "It's obvious, though she won't say so, that somebody does think she's promising."

Alec sat down on the bed.

"What about those tests Lalla does? Will you have to do those?"

Harriet felt a huge lump form in her throat. What fun this evening would have been if she could have said she was taking her inter-silver at the beginning of next month.

"I took my preliminary and bronze before Christmas."

There was a family howl.

"Slyboots," said Alec.

Edward looked reproving.

"If it was me who was passing tests, I'd tell everybody."

"I bet you would," said Toby, "but Harriet's not a bragger like you, thank goodness."

"What comes next?" asked George. "I mean, there's a silver something Lalla passed, isn't there?"

"Yes, pet," said Olivia, "what comes next? Tell us everything. We're so full of pride and curiosity."

Everything? Oh, if she only could! Harriet tried to say inter-silver, and that perhaps she would try for it in the autumn. But would she? Would Lalla ever let her try for it? She struggled hard against the wave of misery that flowed over her, but it was no use. Her eyes

" How did you know I wasn't ill ? "

filled with tears, she rolled over on her pillows and cried dreadfully.

Olivia, finding that Harriet had no temperature, decided she was just tired and a day or two in bed would put her right, so she rang up Lalla's house and asked Wilson, who answered the telephone, to let Nana and Miss Goldthorpe know. But when it came to the fourth day, and Harriet just lay in bed and wouldn't attempt to get up, she became worried.

" It's so unlike her," she said to George, " I'm going to get Dr. Phillipson to have a look at her."

Harriet had been afraid of that ; Dr. Phillipson was not a doctor to like people who were well stopping in bed. She made a plan. As soon as Olivia went down to see what Uncle William had sent for the shop which would not sell, and so she would have to cook, Harriet nipped down to the kitchen, boiled a kettle, and filled a hot-water bottle. When Dr. Phillipson arrived he did what he usually did, put his thermometer in Harriet's mouth, and while it was there, talked to Olivia. That was Harriet's chance. She took the thermometer out of her mouth, and laid it on the hot-water bottle.

Dr. Phillipson seemed to be able to time taking temperatures without looking at a watch. Harriet trembled as she saw he was going to take the thermometer out of her mouth. Would it have gone up enough degrees for him to say she was ill?

Dr. Phillipson looked at the thermometer for longer than usual. Then he looked at Harriet. Then he gave the thermometer a shake. Then he rummaged in his case and handed some instruments to Olivia.

" I shall examine her. Would you boil these for ten minutes."

When the door had shut behind Olivia, Dr. Phillipson sat down on the bed. He spoke in a friendly whisper.

" What's up ? " Harriet tried to look as if she did not know what he meant, but she failed dismally. He took one of her hands. " I thought we were friends. You may as well confide in me, because if you want to stay in bed you'll need co-operation."

" How did you know I wasn't ill ? "

" I thought you were all right when I looked at you, but when I found your temperature was so high the quicksilver had run up out of sight, I knew you must be malingering, for if the thermometer was speaking the truth you'd be dead."

Harriet saw she was caught. It was no good trying to

deceive Dr. Phillipson, and it was true he was a friend.

" If I tell you what's happened you must swear not to tell anybody. It's something really terrible."

The relief of telling everything made Harriet feel happier than she had since the quarrel. When she had finished Dr. Phillipson got up and walked to the window thinking hard. After a bit he made up his mind.

" I think it might be possible to sort things out for Lalla, as well as for yourself ; and she needs help badly, poor child."

Harriet was surprised that Dr. Phillipson was nice about Lalla ; she had expected him to say she had behaved like a little beast.

" It wouldn't mean her telling Aunt Claudia I'm not to learn with her any more ? "

" No. But it will mean several people will have to know what's happened."

Harriet did not like that.

" Will I have to tell them ? Lalla will think me an awful sneak."

The Doctor rumpled her hair.

" Lalla will do most of the telling. Now take that worried look off your face and trust me."

Lalla had been as bothered as Harriet had been about meeting after the quarrel. She did not want Goldie or Nana knowing there had been a quarrel. " Not that I mind what they think," she told herself, " they're sure to side with Harriet, everybody sides with Harriet just because she's so mimsy-pimsy and good." But telling herself that sort of thing didn't help. A voice in her head, which she could not talk down, told her that she would mind dreadfully if Nana and Goldie knew what she had said to Harriet, because they would both be ashamed of her. It was a relief when Wilson came up the next morning with Olivia's message. It was sensible of Harriet to pretend she was ill. Lalla even had to admit to herself it was clever of her. If Harriet said she was ill she wouldn't be allowed to go in for her inter-silver test, and when it was certain she was not going in, she would be nice to her again.

In spite of the voice in her head which nagged at her, telling her how badly she had behaved, Lalla got through the next three days pretty well, she thought. She answered inquiries about Harriet in an ordinary voice, and was sure nobody suspected it was anything to do with her that was making Harriet stay in bed. Then on the fourth day she had a shock. Each morning Miss Goldthorpe rang up and asked how Harriet was, and each morning Olivia said in a casual way there was nothing much the matter, she would probably be up the next day, but on the fourth morning Olivia sounded worried.

" She seems all right, but I can't get her out of bed, so I'm getting Dr. Phillipson to look at her."

When Lalla heard this a cold feeling like drips of icy water ran down her back. Dr. Phillipson ! His medicine had not done much good but she knew he was clever. He wouldn't be fooled into thinking a person was ill when they were not, and he wouldn't say Harriet was not to take a test, unless he thought she was ill. What was Harriet going to do now ? She couldn't be such a mean dog as to tell the truth. All the morning the thought of Harriet seeing the doctor made her inside feel wobbly and her hands damp. Not that she was ashamed of what she had said, of course she wasn't, but she wouldn't want everybody knowing, they didn't understand about skating, and so wouldn't see how sly Harriet had been

At the end of lessons she said in as uninterested a voice as she could manage:

"While I'm putting on my coat would you telephone Mrs. Johnson, Goldie dear, and ask what the doctor said."

When Lalla came back to the schoolroom dressed to go out Miss Goldthorpe seemed sad and grave.

"I'm afraid it's bad news, dear. Harriet's dreadfully ill. The doctor told Mrs. Johnson he had never known anybody live whose temperature showed so high a reading."

Lalla gaped at Miss Goldthorpe. Harriet very ill! Harriet with so high a temperature she might be going to die! It couldn't be true. Harriet had been perfectly well five days ago. She wasn't ill now, only pretending because she wanted a reason not to take her inter-silver.

"What's the matter with her?"

"The doctor can't say. Mrs. Johnson asked if she had been working too hard. She says she's worrying about something. She's talked a lot about you, and an inter-silver test."

Lalla licked her lips which had gone very dry.

"What did she say about me?"

"Mrs. Johnson didn't say. Rambling, I expect, poor child."

Lalla felt most peculiar. Worrying! Inter-silver! What had she done? She heard bells ringing somewhere and Goldie was behaving in a very odd way, far off one minute, and near the next. Then everything spun round, and she felt herself falling.

Lalla opened her eyes to find herself lying on her bed; Nana was dabbing eau-de-Cologne on her forehead.

"There, there! This won't do. It won't help Harriet if you get ill."

Slowly everything came back to Lalla. Tears oozed in a tired way out of her eyes.

"She's terribly ill, Nana. She's got so high a temperature she might die."

"Nonsense, dear, you weren't meant to take it so serious. For all she's so frail-looking, Harriet's tough. You look more like dying, green as a lettuce you are."

Miss Goldthorpe came hurrying in carrying a glass.

"Here's the brandy. I've rung the doctor, he'll be along in a minute."

Lalla, though she still felt very come and go-ish, sat up.

"I won't see the doctor. He'll say I've to stop in to-day, and I won't. I must see Harriet."

Miss Goldthorpe put an arm round her and held the brandy to her lips.

"Sip this. You couldn't see Harriet anyway. Her doctor said you weren't to see her unless he gave you permission."

Lalla choked over the brandy.

"I must. This is disgusting stuff."

Nana took the glass from Miss Goldthorpe.

"Nonsense, dear. You drink it up. I don't hold with spirits as a rule, but for fainting brandy's good."

Lalla knew it was no good arguing with Nana about medicine, if she said "swallow" then swallow it was. She finished the brandy and at once felt better.

"If I see the doctor, will you ring Harriet's doctor, Goldie, and say I must, absolutely must, see Harriet?"

"Very well, dear, but it can't be to-day. I'm sure you've got to stop in bed to-day."

"Of course you have," Nana agreed. "Fainting indeed! That's something quite uncalled for and not what I like from a child of mine."

Lalla's doctor was old and rather grumpy, but he was a good doctor; when he saw Lalla he was not at all pleased; he told Nana to undress her and he would thoroughly overhaul her. The overhauling took a long time; it seemed to Lalla that there was no bit of her he was not interested in. At last she got cross.

" I've nothing the matter with my eyes, so there's no need to pull them about, and my knees are quite well, so there's no need hitting them to see if my legs bounce."

But Lalla might just as well have kept quiet. The doctor did not care what she said but went on calmly with his examination. At the end he packed his case.

" She's to stay there, Nurse, until I give her leave to get up. Now, where's Mrs. King, I want to see her ? "

Lalla spoke pleadingly.

" Don't be all doctor-ish. What are you going to tell Aunt Claudia ? "

The doctor came back to the bed. He pointed at the boots and skates in the glass case, and to the text.

" There's to be no more of that business for quite a time. You're thoroughly run down, young woman. I'm telling your aunt you're to go away somewhere bracing."

" I can't just now, my friend Harriet's ill, and I've got a skating test."

The doctor made a tush noise.

" There will be no more skating tests for many months. I can promise you that."

Nana went out of the room with the doctor. Lalla lay as still in bed as if she had been carved in wood, waiting to feel all over her the frightful words the doctor had said. When that happened she would do something, dash downstairs, make a scene, tell Aunt Claudia not to listen, that she was going to take her test no matter what anybody said. But although she lay as still as still for a long time, and understood in every inch of her what the doctor had ordered, she didn't get angry, or dash anywhere; instead she felt as if she had been carrying a weight on her back which was far too heavy for her, and somebody had quietly lifted it off and said, " Don't bother with that. Sit down and rest." She had not given in to any-body about the test. The doctor didn't even know about her trouble with loops. She had fainted. She was run down. She wasn't to skate, she was to go away for a holiday. In the autumn, after the holiday, she would take the test. There would be nobody whispering, " Lalla isn't taking her test because she isn't ready for it." Nobody saying, " Lalla Moore's not doing as well as everybody expected, is she ? " Nobody could say anything but the truth : " Lalla isn't taking her test because she's terribly run down. She fainted, absolutely unconscious." Almost, as in imagination she heard the dramatic story of her faint passed round the rink, Lalla said, " Giggerty-geggerty " but before the " gig " was in her head she remembered Harriet. Harriet with the highest temperature anybody ever had all because of what she had said to her. Poor, poor Harriet, and they wouldn't let her see her, wouldn't let her say she was sorry and that of course she could take the inter-silver if only she'd get well.

Miss Goldthorpe came in. She drew a chair up to the bed. She sat down looking cosy and like somebody not in a hurry.

" This is upsetting. No skating for a bit."

Lalla brushed the skating aside.

" Goldie, I've got to see Harriet, absolutely got to."

" Why, dear ? "

Lalla wriggled.

" I can't explain why but I've got to."

" I can't help you then. I thought perhaps you could send a message by me to Mrs. Johnson. She could have passed on whatever it is you want to say to Harriet, if she thinks she's well enough to hear it, but if it's a secret it will have to wait until both you and Harriet are better."

Lalla bounced in the bed with impatience.

" I'm not ill. I fainted, which I never did before, but that's not having the highest temperature anyone ever had without being dead."

Miss Goldthorpe looked fondly at Lalla.

" Don't you think you could trust me and Harriet's mother with the message? It can't be as secret as all that, is it? "

Lalla saw she would have to admit at least part of the truth.

" It's something I said that's made her ill."

" You ! What did you say ? "

Lalla was still peculiar after her faint, and deadly worried. Her voice rose in a howl.

" Oh, Goldie, I've been an awful beast, the nastiest beast that ever, ever was. You'll despise me for ever and ever, you see . . ."

Miss Goldthorpe sat on the bed, her arms round Lalla and heard the shocking story. It was difficult to hear it through Lalla's chokes and sobs. At the end she lent Lalla her handkerchief, and brushed her hair off her face.

" You'd better tell Mrs. Johnson all this, and she can tell Harriet how sorry you are, and I'm afraid you'll have to tell Nana. You see, the doctor said you were to be kept quiet and Nana won't let Mrs. Johnson in unless she knows how important it is."

Lalla gave her nose an enormous blow.

"All right. I'll tell Nana too. I'll tell everybody anybody likes. I'll even tell Harriet's brothers if she wants me to, and that would be awful, especially Toby, who's always been a bit despising."

Nana sat by Lalla's bed knitting and heard the confession. Occasionally she shook her head or made a clicking noise with her tongue against her teeth. At the end she said :

"It was wrong of you, dear, and you know it, but if Harriet's well in time she can take that test, and no harm done."

"But she couldn't be well in time, not with the highest temperature in the world."

Nana went back to her knitting.

"I shouldn't wonder, funny things temperatures. Now you stop fretting and it'll all be Sir Garnet. You'll see."

Olivia had been shocked to hear of Lalla's faint, and came round as quickly as possible. Although she had to keep her promise to Dr. Phillipson and not tell Lalla that Harriet wasn't ill at all, she couldn't let her go on worrying.

"Harriet's better, pet."

"Oh good ! Will you tell her I'm awfully sorry. I didn't mean what I said, at least I did then, but I don't any more, and please tell her she can do her inter-silver test if she's well in time, do you think she will be ? "

"I shouldn't wonder." Olivia took off her coat and gloves and sat down. "Suppose you tell me all about it." Not by a flick of an eyelash did Olivia let Lalla know she already knew the story. She wanted to hear it again, for only that way could she help Lalla. At the end she asked: "Why did you mind about the photograph ? You've had so many taken."

Lalla pleated her eiderdown while she tried to explain.

" It wasn't the photograph . . . it was those loops I told you about . . . I hoped I couldn't do them because I'd outgrown my strength, like you said, but it wasn't that . . ."

" What was it ? "

Lalla struggled with herself. It was what she had never admitted, and had never meant to admit.

" I just couldn't do them. They were too difficult."

Olivia jumped up and kissed her.

" Bless you, my pet, I've been longing to hear you say that."

Lalla wriggled away.

" Why ? "

" Don't be cross. I don't know anything about skating ; you may be the great skater of the future, I don't know, but since that matinée we went to together I do know you're worrying too much about it. Miss Goldthorpe tells me you're not to skate for a while, and I think it very good news. You might find it isn't the only thing you want to do."

Lalla threw her chin into the air.

" I won't. You see, I've got to be something important and how else would I be except skating ? "

Olivia put on her coat.

" I must get back to Harriet. I don't know, but I have an idea that if, for a little, you would stop thinking about being a skating champion, you might find out that it wasn't so important as you thought."

CHAPTER XV

THE FUTURE

*

AUNT CLAUDIA rented a cottage on a lonely part of the south-east coast, and into it moved Lalla, Harriet, Miss Goldthorpe and Nana. The doctor said there were to be very few lessons for Lalla, so sitting-round-the-table lessons only happened on wet days, and on fine days she and Harriet went about doing just what they liked, wearing hardly any clothes, and getting browner and browner every day. Every night Lalla went to sleep the moment her head touched the pillow, and she did not wake until Nana came in and drew back her curtains. She ate the most enormous amount of food, including all the things Aunt Claudia had said made a person fat, and although she got fatter nobody cared.

" Anyway," Lalla said, " I don't go on getting fatter. I just got fatter to start with and now I've stuck that size."

Harriet too had an enormous appetite but she remained thin, and nobody minded that either.

" You're that kind, dear," Nana said. " You won't fatten not if you ate forty meals a day."

To begin with Harriet was told to try not to talk about skating to Lalla, but that soon wore off, for Lalla would talk about it. She had not watched Harriet when she had passed her inter-silver test, but she loved teasing her and showing her how she must have looked taking it. She would pull down the corners of her mouth.

" Watch me, Harriet. This is you waiting to begin. Now this is you doing your back change. Here's you doing your threes. This is your one foot eight. And this is you trying not to show how much you want to look at your tracings."

Lalla was funny enough imitating skating on ice, but with bare feet on wet sand she was so silly that Harriet would laugh so much that it hurt, and then Lalla would laugh too, and they would have to lie down or they would have fallen over.

But as she got better and gayer Lalla began to think. Not the frightened dashing from side to side thinking, but sensible thinking, and what she thought came out in things she said to Harriet.

" I shan't try for my inter-gold until Max says I'm ready . . . Down here where Aunt Claudia isn't I see it's silly to rush, and get in a state . . . I don't think even working hard from September I'll get those loathsome change loops right this year. I don't care a bit if I wait till May. . . ." Then suddenly one morning she said : " Harriet, d'you know what I'm going to do? I'm going to write to Uncle David, at his office so Aunt Claudia won't know I've written, and get him to see Max and ask him when he thinks I'll be ready to take the inter-gold. I'd rather know than not know. If Max says not till May, Uncle David can tell Aunt Claudia for me while they're in Canada in August. Canada's a gloriously long way off, I wouldn't know what she was saying and I wouldn't care."

There was no answer for quite a while to Lalla's letter

to Uncle David, except a postcard saying "O.K., poppet." Then suddenly he telephoned. Lalla answered the phone ; they could tell by her excited squeaks something nice was going to happen.

"All of them ! What fun ! Lucky them, I wish we could. In the car ! Giggerty-geggerty, I must tell Harriet, I can't wait."

It was wonderful news. Uncle David had taken rooms near the cottage for Olivia and George for a week, and for himself for a night. For the boys a tent was coming and they were camping in it all of August. Uncle David was bringing the Johnsons by car.

A week later they all arrived. At first there was such a lot to say that it seemed they would never catch up with each other's news. Over the tent putting-up, at which Lalla and Harriet helped, Alec told of the wonderful thing that had happened to him. Mr. Pulton had seen George and said he would like to send Alec to an agricultural college, and when he had finished training he would invest some money in a market garden. He had said that he would like to help make somebody else's dream come true, because it was too late now to find his own.

"And I'll tell you one reason why he said that," said Toby, "it's because Alec took him some of our strawberries. My word, Lalla, they've been stupendous. Simpson's been marvellous, he's picked them for us every day and had them ready when Edward and I went to fetch them."

Harriet was terribly pleased about Alec.

"That'll mean more chance for you, Toby, you can go somewhere like Oxford and be a professor at mathematics, for Alec won't cost anything."

Edward was knocking in a tent peg. At this he stopped and looked in a pained way at Harriet.

"There is me. I shan't go to a university because by then I'll be a film star . . ."

The rest of what Edward had to say was lost. They all fell on him and rolled him in the sand.

That night it was fine. They had supper on the beach. While it was being cooked Lalla and Uncle David went

A week later they all arrived

for a walk. Lalla, in spite of trying not to care, felt wormish inside.

"What did Max say?"

Uncle David lit a cigarette.

"There's no thought of you going in for that test you were working for until next year."

Lalla was frightened to ask, but she made herself.

"Did he say anything else?"

Uncle David took her hand.

" Prepare yourself for a shock, poppet. He doesn't see you as a world champion. He says you'll never be a good enough figure skater."

Lalla stopped. Her eyes were frightened.

." But I couldn't just be ordinary, I'm not used to it."

Uncle David laughed.

" You won't be. We've got ideas, that Max of yours and I. Anyway there's nothing for you to worry about. You go back to your skating as usual in the autumn."

Lalla could hear Uncle David was happy about her.

" Tell me what you and Max have thought of, I can feel it's something nice."

" There's something else first which you've got to know. It's about Harriet. Max thinks she's a find."

Lalla gasped.

" Harriet ! Do you mean it might be her who's a champion grim and not me ? "

" Might. It's too early yet to say. But don't think that means you're out of the picture. You're not. You'll like Max Lindblom's idea for you."

Lalla was impatient.

" Well, why don't you tell me what it is ? "

" I've got your Aunt Claudia to talk round. You know, it's been tough on her not being allowed to discuss skating with you."

" But I ought to know, it's my future."

" Don't take that tone with me, young woman, or I'll drop you in the sea. Now listen. How would you like to be a professional skater ? "

When Lalla and Uncle David got back to the picnic, supper was almost cooked. Olivia and Nana were tasting some soup they were boiling over a fire of driftwood.

" There you are, Lalla," George called out. " Harriet says you'll give us an imitation of her on the ice."

Lalla was delighted, she felt so gay, just in the mood to make people laugh. An audience again ! It made her tingle as if it was Christmas Eve. She ran on to the sand and not only imitated Harriet, but Max, a fat judge trying to keep warm, and Mr. Matthews nearly falling over as he presented a bouquet. She had a perfect audience ; everybody laughed until they could not laugh any more.

" You must stop, Lalla darling," said Olivia, drying her eyes, " or I shall upset the soup."

Lalla knelt by Olivia and looked at the soup.

" I wish that was a witches' brew, and you could see things that are going to happen. Uncle David says he's told you Harriet's more likely to be a champion grim than me."

Edward peered into the soup.

" See that bubble. That's you, Lalla, getting awfully important."

Uncle David had a look at the bubble.

" I shouldn't wonder. I can see Lalla as a professional. She's got what it takes, and she can be funny too. The world is short of funny queens of the ice."

Edward gave a squeak.

" Look at that piece of carrot that's come to the top. That's Harriet skating with one leg stuck out behind her."

Olivia gave the piece of carrot a little push.

" My Harriet skating to the stars, I can't see that happening."

Lalla looked in the soup.

" I can. I expect Aunt Claudia will help."

Harriet could hardly believe all she had heard. Max

thought she might make a star skater ! Lalla not minding!

"I feel curiouser and curiouser, nearly twelve, which is old enough to start proper training, and perhaps something gorgeous going to happen."

Lalla felt mad-doggish with gayness. A professional ! She would have to be able to do all the figures of course, but after that, free skating for ever and ever, and an audience to watch her do it.

"Giggerty-geggerty, I can't wait. Imagine if that soup could show the future. Don't you all want to know what happens to Harriet and me ? Because I do."

THE END

BALLET SHOES FOR ANNA

For Jeremy, Bridget and Andrew Brooke
Third Generation Rhodesians

Darlings,
I learned what it was like to live through an
earthquake sitting on your granny's verandah in
Rhodesia. So I thought this book belonged
especially to you.

Love,
NOEL

First published in Great Britain by
William Collins Sons & Co. Ltd 1972

Prologue

Anna sat on the caravan steps. She was dressed for her dancing lesson in a white tunic. She was tying on her pink dancing slippers. When the shoes were on she glanced up and saw what she thought was something extraordinary. It was birds, hundreds, perhaps thousands of them, all collecting on the hill above the village. Living in a caravan, Anna was always travelling so she accepted that in Turkey, where she now was, birds perhaps behaved differently from birds in other countries. For in her experience when birds migrated it was never in the very middle of summer, yet migrate was what these birds were clearly going to do. There was the usual bustle and excitement migrating birds always seemed to create. Then suddenly, as if someone had fired a starting pistol for a race, the birds took to the air and, looking like a black cloud, flew away. Not a bird stayed behind – not a single one.

Never at her dancing lessons with her grandfather did Anna let her mind wander. The lessons were held in the main room of Jardek's little white cottage. Against one wall he had put up a barre made and polished by himself. Always lessons

7

started the same way. Jardek would say "Demi plié, Anna. Twelve very beautiful."

That day, though she tried not to think about it, at the back of Anna's mind was a question: "Why did the birds fly away?"

After her lesson Anna went back to the caravan. She stood on the steps and gazed in all directions. Nowhere, on the ground, in the trees, on the roofs or in the air was one bird. Not a bird anywhere.

1. The Story Begins

To the children Grandfather and Grandmother's little house in Turkey was home. This was because it was the only proper house they ever stayed in.

Francesco, the eldest of the three children, had said to his grandmother:

"It is so good that you never move anything. Always we know when we stay with you that all will be as we left it."

Augustus, the second boy who was known as Gussie, had agreed fervently – Gussie was often fervent.

"Nothing, absolutely nothing, can be more beautiful than that."

Anna was the youngest. She added softly:

"Nothing – nothing ever."

The children did not call their grandparents Grandfather and Grandmother because they were the father and mother of their mother Olga who was Polish. Instead they called them Jardek and Babka. This was not the proper spelling but it was how the words sounded to the children. They had never seen them written down.

The children were British because that was what

their father was, but they had never been to England. Their father was an artist called Christopher Docksay. Even when he was quite small it was clear that Christopher was meant to be an artist; but his father refused to admit this, hoping that if he ignored the child's talent it would die out of him. Mr Docksay worked in a bank and it was his ambition to become a bank manager. He thought being a bank manager was a splendid secure life so he wanted his sons, Cecil and Christopher, to grow up to be bank managers too.

Cecil was very like his father so he agreed with him that the best career in the world was to work in a bank. At school he studied hard – especially at mathematics – which he thought would help him to become a bank manager, and as soon as he was old enough he left school and joined a bank. Christopher, who was many years younger than Cecil, hardly worked at his lessons at all, spending much time filling his exercise books with drawings, and when he should have been doing his homework he was painting.

The teachers at the school where Christopher went of course knew all about his wanting to be an artist, and the headmaster did his best to get the boy's father to allow him to try for a scholarship to an art school.

"Your son has real talent, Mr Docksay, he should be given his chance. I'm sure he'd win a scholarship."

But Mr Docksay would not listen. He made a noise like a horse makes when he gets chaff up his nose.

"Art! Nonsense! No future in it!"

Then one day when he was fifteen, Christopher decided he could bear life no longer. He must find someone to teach him to paint and he must live amongst painters. He searched the house for things that would sell, then he flew away to Paris. That, as far as his mother and father were concerned, was that, for he never heard from them again. But he did try. For the first two years after he had run away he drew what he thought were very funny pictures of himself on Christmas cards and sent them home, but he got no answer though he was careful to give his address.

"I suppose they're still sulking about the few bits and pieces I took, to pay my fare to Paris," Christopher grumbled to his friends, "but they shouldn't, the old man can put it against anything he may be going to leave me in his will."

Christopher had a very hard time in Paris and often he nearly starved, but he achieved his ambition. He became not only an artist but also a very good one. He had a rare gift for getting on to canvas light and heat such as you see and feel in hot countries. So by degrees his name became known and his pictures sold.

In order to paint the sort of pictures he liked painting Christopher was always moving about. He believed in being mobile so he bought an old gipsy caravan and a piebald horse called Togo and for many years drove wherever the mood took him. In those days he thought himself the luckiest fellow in the world. But that was before he drove into the little village in Turkey where he learnt what real happiness could be.

It was a very tumbledown little village on the side of a hill – just a few whitewashed cottages with their roofs held down by strong branches cut from trees, for the wind could be so savage it could blow the roofs off. There was also a shop, a very small mosque and a tea house. But what made Christopher pull Togo up outside the smallest of the cottages was the light. For some reason it shimmered and danced on that village in a way he had not seen before, and the cottages threw back the heat so violently it was as if it had substance so could be touched. Then, while he was gazing at the effects of heat and light, the door of the cottage outside which the caravan was standing opened and out came what Christopher thought was the loveliest girl he had ever seen. She was Olga.

Naturally, after seeing Olga together with the glorious light on the village, Christopher decided to stay. He made an arrangement for Togo to share a field with some cows, parked his caravan on the side of the road and settled down for a visit which should last until Olga agreed to marry him, which he knew might take time. Why should Olga wish to marry a man so much older than herself?

The marriage happened six months later. That was when, if the children were about when the story was being told, they would join in.

"One year after that when we are in Iran I was born," Francesco would say.

Then Gussie would burst out:

"I was born farthest away. I was born in India."

"Only just," his mother would say, smiling at Christopher. "One more day and you would have been born in Pakistan, but you were in such a hurry to arrive."

Anna knew she was the lucky one.

"Me, I was born in Turkey staying with Jardek and Babka, so I was the only one not born in our caravan."

Jardek and Babka had not been born in Turkey, they had come there as refugees from Poland during the last world war. In those days Jardek had worked in the underground helping people to escape from Poland. In the end someone had betrayed him and he and Babka had to escape themselves. They had very little money, for by profession Jardek was a teacher of dancing and during the war there had not been many who wanted to learn to dance. So when they found the little tumbledown whitewashed cottage in the Turkish village, which cost almost nothing, they were grateful and settled down. At once Jardek, who was clever with his hands, set about repairing the cottage outside, while Babka put the inside in order. This took some time. Then, just as everything was tidy, Olga was born.

"Praise be to God," Jardek had said. "Now we have everything – a home and a child." He said this in Polish because at that time it was the only language that he spoke and in fact he never managed more than a few words of any other.

The year this story begins was the year that Francesco was ten, Gussie was nine and Anna was eight. The summer was a very special summer for they were staying two whole months with Jardek and Babka. This was because in the autumn Christopher was having an exhibition of his pictures at the other end of Turkey. Two months would give him time to get his pictures framed and a few more painted. More important, it would give Togo a real rest, which he would need if he was to pull the caravan to the other end of Turkey, for it was a journey of many, many miles and he was not young any more.

The two months in the village would also give time to discuss an important plan. Jardek, when the children stayed in his cottage had, as a matter of course, given them all dancing lessons. What was the use of having a highly skilled ballet teacher for a grandfather if you did not learn to dance? Jardek had no success with the boys; they danced better than most boys because they had been properly taught, but that special little spark for which Jardek searched was not there.

It was different, though, with Anna. From the time she could walk she had only to hear music and she had to dance. When she was little Jardek had just played tunes on his violin and let Anna dance to amuse herself. When she was six he had begun to give her lessons. Nothing strenuous – just the five positions and exercises and simple steps. But he had always known that here, in his own grandchild, was that rare special spark for which he had always searched.

Family discussions were noisy and there was much laughter because only Olga spoke everyone's language. Christopher refused to speak any language but English except when he was in France, when he would, if pushed, speak French, but with a strong English accent. This English accent was quite unnecessary for he could, as his children knew, speak perfect French. Olga had fairly correct English but spoke with a strong Polish accent. Christopher insisted that his children should speak English so, as Olga taught them their lessons, she spoke English most of the time. But Jardek and Babka spoke a mixture, mostly it was Polish but with English or Turkish words thrown in.

The discussion that summer was of course about Anna. It was no longer right, Jardek had decided, that Anna should only have dancing lessons when they stayed at the cottage. It was now time she began serious work. This year, when Christopher took his family to his exhibition, Anna must be left behind.

Anna could not think of her family going away without tears coming into her eyes. However, she knew of course that as she was to be a dancer – anything else was unthinkable – sacrifices must be made. Besides, though she loved her mother and father most, she also loved Jardek and Babka.

That Anna must have more dancing lessons was accepted by Christopher and Olga. Christopher, remembering his own stormy childhood when no one would allow him to learn to be an artist, would as soon as shot Togo as think of depriving Anna of her dancing lessons.

Because everything was more or less settled about Anna, that did not stop the endless discussions for as a family they all loved discussions and the more excited they got the better. But that summer morning when this story starts, although all the family were at breakfast, almost nothing was said. This was because it was so dreadfully hot. Never before had any of them known such stifling heat or such odd-looking weather. The sun was hidden behind a sulphur-coloured sky. Nobody felt like food but Olga insisted each child finished their yoghourt and ate one slice of bread with olives.

The children were to take one of Christopher's pictures to be framed. The frame maker lived in a village over the next hill about three miles away. There was no suggestion that they need not all go for they had always done everything together. Christopher looked up at the molten sky.

"I would take the caravan but I don't like spoiling poor old Togo's holiday by harnessing him up in this heat, and though the light is vile I must work today."

The children did not answer, they had all they could do forcing down their bread and olives.

"Perhaps," Olga suggested, "the children could the picture take tomorrow. Then today we will have school."

That settled it, nobody wanted the long walk in the sun, but they wanted lessons less. Anna felt this particularly for she knew Jardek was feeling too hot to give her a dancing lesson that day, but she hoped it might be cooler tomorrow. Christopher felt in his pocket and gave Francesco some money.

"Get some fruit and cold drinks and don't attempt to come back until the late afternoon."

The children got up and put on their hats. Then something – they did not know what – made them all turn just to look at Christopher, Olga, Jardek and Babka where they sat drinking their tea.

17

2. The Village That Went Away

My goodness, it was hot walking to the next village! Used as the children were to heat they streamed with perspiration until they were wet all over. To make them hotter there was just a dirt track to the other village, so the dust was terrible. As they walked in single file, Francesco leading and carrying the canvas, Gussie next and Anna last, Anna particularly became brown with the dust that stuck to her.

When they got to the village it almost seemed like a wasted walk for the picture framer was asleep on his bed. He did open one eye but he refused to take an interest in any picture. So Francesco leant the canvas against the wall, feeling certain the picture framer would remember it when he woke up, for he was very fond of earning money and a great admirer of Christopher's paintings.

The children bought some figs, a vine leaf of mulberries for each of them, and a bottle apiece of lemonade. Then they looked for a place in the shade where they could have a picnic.

"It's rather a long way," said Francesco, "but I think we climb up the hill as far as those cactuses, they're the best shade there is. It's much too hot to stay in this village."

Gussie groaned.

"If I don't lie down soon I'll drop down."

But Anna sided with Francesco.

"He's right, Gussie, that cactus hedge is quite thick, it's real proper shade."

When the children reached the cactus trees they were so hot and tired that they just flopped down in the shade panting, unable even to take a drink of lemonade. Then after a long time, Francesco said in a puzzled voice:

"Have you noticed something? How is it there aren't any birds?"

Gussie stared round.

"I expect they've gone somewhere cooler, and I don't blame them."

"This is the third day they've been gone," Anna told them. "Two days ago before my dancing lesson I am putting on my shoes and on our hill there were thousands of birds. Then they all flew away and they haven't come back."

Gussie reached out for his bottle of lemonade and his vine leaf of mulberries. It was then he noticed a horse in the next field.

"Look" I think that horse has gone mad."

Francesco and Anna looked where Gussie was pointing. The horse was old and thin but it was behaving as if it was a foal, rushing round bucking. The children stared at the horse in amazement.

19

"You can go mad when it's hot," Gussie stated. "Somewhere I am reading that dogs can."

"You can't get hydrophobia just because it's hot," Francesco told him, "but perhaps if it's very hot like today it can make you a bit strange."

Anna suddenly burst out in a voice which sounded as if she easily might cry.

"I don't like it; everything feels strange. I didn't like the birds going away, now the sky looks odd and now that horse."

Francesco thought Anna was being silly.

"Drink some lemonade, it's just that you're thirsty and it's so hot."

It was as Francesco said this that it began to happen. There was a roaring sound as if a very fast train was coming out of a tunnel pushing blazing hot air in front of it. Then the earth behaved as if it was the sea. It rocked to and fro like waves, and as it rocked the children were rolled and tossed around. Over and over they went. Then, after what seemed like ages, just as suddenly as it had started to move, the earth stood still again.

For a long time the children lay just where the earth had thrown them. Then one after another they sat up and at once noticed two extraordinary things. First the hillside, which had been smooth except for the dirt path, was now cut up as if a giant had stamped and had cracked it open. The other thing they noticed was that now, instead of being hot, it was turning cold, much colder than the children, who had always lived in hot countries, had known it could be.

It seemed as if the strange terrible thing that had happened had taken from the children the power of speech. Gussie did ask:

"What happened?"

And Francesco did answer:

"I don't know."

Then, without any more talking, as best they could because of the cracks in the earth, the children hurried up the hill towards home. At the top of the hill they stopped. Opposite them they should have seen the village quite distinctly. Jardek and Babka's little cottage with Togo in the field opposite which he shared with some cows and a donkey. The other cottages, the shops, the tea house, and the little mosque. But none of it was there. Where the village had been there was nothing — nothing at all.

3. Sir William

Sir William Hoogle was a famous archaeologist and writer. He was travelling in Turkey when the earthquake happened which destroyed Jardek and Babka's village, in fact he was near enough to feel the earth tremors himself. On the radio he heard how terrible an earthquake it had been for those living at the centre of the disaster. He learned about the village which had disappeared, and of how difficult it was to carry out rescue work because the ground was so full of fissures that no aeroplane could land. Such help as was reaching the afflicted areas was being dropped by parachute.

Now Sir William not only spoke Turkish but also understood most of the local dialects. In his mind he could see the planes flying over the scene of the earthquake, dropping bundles by parachute on people almost certainly too shocked by what had happened to know how to use what they were being given. There were of course doctors and nurses being dropped but would they have time to help anybody but the injured?

"I think I could be of use," Sir William told himself. "Anyhow, I shall go and find out."

All round the areas affected by the earthquake, railway lines had become twisted, the roads had fissures across them and were blocked by piles of rubble which had once been buildings. If there is one kind of help no country wants in times of national disaster it is unskilled labour. So when Sir William asked officials how he could be transported to the scene of the earthquake he was told politely – for he was very distinguished – but firmly he could not go. As soon as aeroplanes could land help was coming, meanwhile those on the spot were doing all that could be done.

Sir William quite understood the officials. After all, he was not a specialist in disaster work, but all the same he was still convinced he could be of use. So he bought a camel – he turned out to be very bad-tempered – called Muzzaffer, filled a light case with his toilet articles and a change of clothes and things he thought might be useful and rode off in the direction of the afflicted part of the country.

It was a long way for Sir William to ride for he had to make constant detours to avoid fissures. His journey was not helped by Muzzaffer, who complained loudly the whole way that Sir William and the case were too heavy for him – which was not true – and that he hated earthquakes. All the same he carried Sir William safely first to the village where the children had taken Christopher's picture to be framed, and then to the centre of the disaster area.

From the moment they saw their village had gone a sort of silent frenzy had come over the children, then, without saying a word, they stumbled and ran all the way to where they thought the little house had been. There they knelt down and dug and dug with their fingers. But though they dug without stopping they could not find any sign of their family – just nothing – nothing at all.

Nor was the place where their own little house had been the only place where the children dug, they dug in the field Togo had shared with the cows and the donkey. They dug where they thought the tea house had been. They dug where the shop had once stood. They dug for the other cottages and the mosque. On they went, dig, dig, dig until their nails were broken and their hands covered in blood. And still they never spoke.

Although the children's own village was gone others were not, but the damage everywhere was terrible and very widespread so each district had to help itself. To begin with all who were not injured tried to get the wounded out from under fallen buildings. Presently the first of the aeroplanes arrived and a doctor, a nurse and a tent came down by parachute. Later came more doctors and nurses and piles of blankets and packets of food. It was when the blankets arrived that the people noticed how cold it was. By now the tent was up and all the wounded that could be found had been taken into it. The doctors then decided that as it would soon be dark looking for wounded must stop for that day, that the women should build a fire and cook a meal, but that everyone else should put a blanket round them and search the countryside for any people who might be homeless and bring them to the tent.

It was only by accident that the children were found, for who would look for people in a village which had disappeared? But a man and a boy decided to climb the hill to see if anyone was about on the other side. That was how they fell over the children. At no time did the children speak much Turkish and now they couldn't speak at all, they couldn't even hear, they just went on dig, dig, dig. The man, who had a big voice, roared for help and presently two more men turned up and after discussion the three men took off their blankets, rolled the children in them, picked them up, slung them over their shoulders and, sending the boy ahead to tell the doctors what they had found, they marched off towards the tent.

The children knew nothing of what happened after that, for the doctor who examined them almost at once gave them an injection and laid them in the hospital part of the tent covered in blankets.

The arrival of Sir William two days later on Muzzaffer caused quite a sensation in what was now called "Camp A". By that time help of every kind had arrived: troops to mend and clear the roads, helicopters to fly wounded to the hospitals, rescue squads to dig in the ruins and help of other types, particularly clothes, food and medicines. A very important man who knew the neighbourhood was in charge of relief work so it was to him Sir William, with a parcel under his arm, presented himself. He explained who he was and asked if there was any way in which he could be of service.

"you are British?" asked the official.

Sir William nodded.

"I am."

"Then you may be able to help me. We have in the camp three children. We believe them to be British."

Sir William liked the facts.

"Why?"

The official opened a drawer and took out a large envelope. "The children do not know this. But caught in a crater we found the remains of what probably was a caravan, there was little left of it but this." He took out of the envelope a British passport. "This belonged, as you can see, to a man called Christopher Docksay. His wife's name was Olga and there are three children listed – Francesco, Augustus and Anna."

"Did Christopher Docksay live here?" Sir William asked.

"No, not live," the official explained. "But the locals say that Madame Docksay was the daughter of an old Pole who, with his wife, lived in that village which has gone. This daughter, whose name was Olga, married this Christopher Docksay and every year they came to stay, travelling by caravan. He was an artist."

"He was indeed," Sir William agreed. "He'll be a great loss. You say the locals told you all about the family, but what do the children say?"

The official threw up his hands.

"The doctors say it is shock and will pass, but so far the children have said nothing, not to each other, not to us. They just sit, well-behaved you understand, but like deaf mutes. They were found digging with their fingers for their family where that village once stood. The doctors say the children do not yet want to remember, when they do they will talk."

Sir William thought for a moment, then he showed the official the parcel under his arm.

"I found this today. It is a picture of Christopher Docksay's, the children took it to the village over that hill to be framed on the day of the earthquake. The picture framer was showing it to everybody because the painting is of the village which has gone. I paid him for his work and promised to see that the picture was delivered to Christopher Docksay's executors, whoever they may be. If the doctors permit I shall show this picture to the children. It might get through to them."

The children could not stop shivering. They sat on the floor of the tent with blankets round them.

One of the nurses had combed their hair and washed their faces and they had been fed with soup. They paid no attention when a doctor led Sir William over to them. Nor were they interested when Sir William sat down opposite to them and opened a flat parcel. Then he spun the contents of the parcel round so that it faced them.

There was the little house just as they had last seen it except that on the porch only Olga, Jardek and Babka were drinking tea for, of course, Christopher was painting the picture. There was a second's pause, then Francesco fainted, Gussie was sick and Anna screamed.

4. The Uncle

Cecil Docksay lived with his wife Mabel in Essex. His house was in a place called Fyton. Much of Essex is very pretty but Fyton was not because it was mostly badly designed new houses which crowded round the church, a village green and three thatched cottages. But Cecil Docksay thought his house perfect because, as he was always saying, it was so labour-saving and therefore easy to run.

It was a neat house outside and in. Upstairs it had three bedrooms: one the big main room which they shared, two small spare rooms in which everything was always in dust-sheets because they never had a visitor to stay. There was, too, a magnificent bathroom.

Downstairs there was a big room which they called the lounge. This was full of green velvet furniture and had a white wallpaper with a design on it of trellis work up which climbed ivy. On the walls there were no pictures but a trail of ceramic geese in full flight.

The lounge looked on to the garden, which was even more labour-saving than the house for everything in it was made of plastic. The garden was covered in concrete pretending to be crazy paving. In the middle of the concrete there was a small pool by which sat two scarlet gnomes apparently fishing, only there were no fish in the pool, not even a tadpole in the spring. Instead of flower beds there were metal containers and in these lived plastic plants which were changed to suit the season. In the spring they were full of daffodils and hyacinths. Then those were sponged and put away and out came rose trees and other summer flowers. When the autumn came it was goodbye to the summer flowers and a splendid show of plastic chrysanthemums took their place. Everybody else living in Fyton grew real flowers and, though their gardens were small, they worked very hard to make them look and smell beautiful.

"So foolish," Cecil Docksay would say to Mabel as he watched their neighbours struggling with greenfly or dead-heading their real chrysan- themums. "What I say is why make work?"

Mabel did not answer for she liked real flowers but to say so would only mean an argument.

At the front of the house was the dining room, in which the table and chairs were made of something which looked like wood but was unmarkable, because it was heat-resisting, dirt- resisting – in fact there was nothing it did not resist including being nice to look at.

The kitchen was Mabel's pride. It was quite a

large room and had been bought exactly as it stood at an exhibition called "The Home Beautiful". It was the most labour-saving kitchen ever invented. The house was called Dunroamin.

The day the letter arrived was wet and stormy. Cecil and Mabel Docksay were having breakfast, Cecil looking with pride at the way their plastic rose tree stood stiff and resistant to the rain and wind, while their neighbours' roses, which had been beautiful, took on that sad stuck-together look which roses have on wet days.

Mabel Docksay had always been a shy person. Her mother had been good-looking and popular with a large circle of friends. She would have liked to have a pretty little girl of whom she could have been proud. So it was annoying for her that she had a child who tried to make herself smaller than she was so that she would not be noticed. If her father had been about he would have understood and sympathized with Mabel for he was shy himself, but he was out at work all day so had never seen much of his daughter.

Mabel had worked hard at school but she was more a plodder than clever, so she was not able to fulfil her dream which was to be sent to a university, which would mean living away from home. Instead she had settled for a job in the local bank. "Well, I suppose at least it's a safe job," her mother had said to her friends, "and she needs a safe job, poor darling, for she's so shy and I'm afraid rather dull, so she will never marry." Of course Mabel knew this was what her mother believed so she thought herself the luckiest girl in the world when the assistant manager at the bank, Cecil Docksay, asked her to marry him. She was so grateful to be asked, which meant getting away from home and living in a house of her own, that she mistook gratitude for love. Her father did worry about the marriage for he thought Cecil Docksay a terribly dull man.

"You're very young, Mabel," he had said. "Don't rush into anything you might regret."

Mabel with shining eyes had replied:

"I'm rushing to do what I want to do."

Just about the time Cecil Docksay, by then manager, retired from the bank his father and mother died so, since Christopher was forgotten, he inherited all the money there was and was able to buy Dunroamin. Mabel thought Dunroamin was a pleasant house and knew she should be happy to live in it and grateful to dear Cecil for buying it, but somehow she didn't feel any of these things — only rather depressed.

Who wants two silly gnomes? she thought resentfully and secretly looked enviously out of her windows at other people's children. Oh, if only she and Cecil had had a child!

On the wet and stormy morning when the postman knocked on the door Mabel jumped up to get the post, for Cecil was not the sort of man whom anyone would ask to open a front door.

There was only the one letter — a long white envelope with Turkish stamps. Cecil opened the envelope carefully with a knife for it was a good envelope which could be used again, and he was nothing if not careful. He noticed it had been sent from a hotel in Istanbul. Then he looked at the end of the letter to see who had signed it but he couldn't read the signature. But the hotel secretary who had typed the letter had typed at the bottom "Sir William Hoogle". Cecil knew that name for having been a bank manager he prided himself on knowing who was who.

All the papers had carried the news that Christopher Docksay had been killed in the earthquake. To Cecil, Christopher's name was not one to be mentioned, for having run away to Paris with his father's possessions he was a thief so best forgotten. In Fyton it had not yet crossed anyone's mind that the odd Mr and Mrs Docksay who lived in Dunroamin and planted plastic flowers instead of real ones could possibly be related to anyone famous, especially not to a famous artist.

On the radio the newscaster had said that of recent years Christopher's pictures had fetched a lot of money, which had made Mabel ask:

"Are you his heir, dear?"

"I suppose so," Cecil had agreed. "No doubt someone will communicate in time." Now, as he started to read his letter, he said to Mabel: "This is from Turkey, no doubt about Christopher's estate. Wonderful how quick they were finding my address."

But as Cecil read the letter a great change came over him. He made so many grunts and growls that Mabel trembled. That was how she saw his colour change from yellow (he was a pasty man) to red and finally to purple. When he came to the last word he thumped his fist on the table so hard that if anything could have marked it that would have.

"I won't have it. Prying busybody! Why should he take it upon himself to find my address? How does he dare dictate to me what I should do or not do?"

"Who, dear?" Mabel asked.

Cecil could hardly speak he was so angry.

"Sir William Hoogle. It seems Christopher was married to some Polish woman and they had three children."

Mabel did not know who Sir William Hoogle was, or what Cecil was so angry about, so she said, trying not to sound as thrilled as she felt:

"Three children!"

Cecil could have hit Mabel repeating every word he said. He'd give her something to repeat.

"Listen!" he roared. "This is the last paragraph of the letter: 'I plan to deliver the children to you at the end of the week. I will cable the time of our arrival.'"

The day after Sir William arrived at Camp A the children were better. The terrible cold which followed the earthquake was gone, so they sat in the sun outside the hospital tent to eat their breakfast and that's where Sir William found them. They looked, he thought, a pathetic lot of little ragamuffins, for you can't be thrown about by an earthquake and finish up either clean or tidy.

"You lot want some new clothes," he said. "We must go shopping."

Anna looked surprised at such ignorance.

"There are not shops here and the clothes at the relief places are not yet for children."

"Some will be coming," Gussie explained. "The nurse told us."

"I don't think we'll wait for that," said Sir William. "Let's go to Istanbul. Good shops there."

The children stared at him. Of course they had heard of Istanbul but they had never been there. Christopher had never gone to a town unless he had to. Towns were tiresome about parking a caravan. Francesco, used to travelling at a speed chosen by Togo, suggested:

"Isn't Istanbul rather a long way away?"

Sir William took a cigar from his pocket and lit it.

"A long way away from where?" he asked.

Well, that was a question. It brought all three children slap up against the things they did not want to think about. Where now was home?

Everybody was gone – Christopher, Olga, Jardek, Babka and Togo, the little house and the caravan. When they went away from where they were now they had no place at all to come back to.

Francesco gave a shiver as if it was cold again. Gussie looked as if he might be going to be sick, which he had been off and on since the earthquake, and two tears trickled down Anna's cheeks.

"I'm sorry," she choked, "but you shouldn't have asked that."

"Nonsense!" retorted Sir William. "You can't live in a hospital tent for ever. You have been given into my charge for the time being and I don't intend to let you out of my sight until I see you settled. Now, Francesco, you are the eldest. Tell me what you know of your family."

Francesco wanted to be helpful but all the family he knew were dead. However, Sir William was aware of that so he must mean farther away relations.

Then Gussie said:

"There was the father of our father." He turned to Francesco and Anna. "He was that horrible man who would not let Christopher paint."

Francesco remembered, for Christopher had often told the story. He looked at Sir William.

"So our father had to take things from the house to sell for the air fare to Paris where he must learn to paint."

Sir William nodded.

36

"Good thing he did, for he became a very fine painter. Do you know where this grandfather of yours lived?"

All the children shook their heads. Never once had they heard a place mentioned and, never having been to England, they would not have remembered if they had. Then another piece of information came into Gussie's memory.

"The brother of our father was already in a bank while Christopher is in a school." He looked triumphantly at Francesco and Anna. "You remember Christopher telling us that?"

They did indeed. Riding along a yellow dusty road in Pakistan. It was not said to them but to Olga.

"This is the life, Olga. I love it. The sun to beat on your head, the smell of spices up your nose and a caravan for a home. And to think if my father had had his way I'd be shut up in a bank. I might even be on the road to becoming a bank manager. I suppose Cecil is one by now unless he's retired."

Recalling that scene hurt so much the children would have wished to change the subject, but they liked Sir William and he was trying to help so Francesco said to the others:

"I suppose Cecil is a bank manager now."

Sir William was not the sort of man who missed anything anybody said.

"Who is Cecil?"

Christopher had told so many funny stories

about his brother Cecil it seemed strange anybody didn't know who he was.

"He is the brother of our father. He is The Uncle," Gussie explained. "He is already in a bank when Christopher is at school."

"Is he married?" Sir William asked.

The children shook their heads.

"We do not know, he was in a bank when our father is first leaving to paint in Paris," Francesco explained. "For two years our father sends his father and mother a Christmas card."

"With funny drawings of himself on them," Gussie added.

"And his address," Anna reminded them.

"But the father is still angry," said Francesco. "He never answered. Never at all."

Sir William saw he had got all there was to know out of the children. He had plenty of influence and Docksay was an uncommon name. If any of the family were alive he would run them to earth.

"The army say the runway will be open tomorrow, in which case we should get a plane for Istanbul. From there I will telephone London to inquire after your relations."

"But they don't sound very nice," said Gussie.

Sir William smiled comfortingly.

"If we find them you can try them out. I shan't be far away, I'll keep in touch."

Francesco remembered that Sir William did not know the important thing.

"Anna has to learn to dance."

"Real proper learning," Gussie added. "For Jardek, our mother's father, was a great teacher and he said Anna was special, she was going to be such a dancer as he had always prayed he would teach."

Sir William knew very little about dancing, but he was an optimist and did not believe in imagining difficulties — time enough to worry when they cropped up.

"I feel sure dancing classes can be arranged," he said calmly. "But the first thing is to find out if you have relations and where."

Sir William did his best to give the children a splendid time in Istanbul. He also bought them new clothes, such as they had never owned: grey flannel shorts for the boys with shirts and ties, and two good cotton frocks for Anna. Also there were pullovers for them all in case it turned cold. Then, on the fourth day, Sir William had a telephone call from London. He told the children the news at once.

"You have got relations. Your grandparents are dead but your Uncle Cecil is alive and you have an Aunt Mabel. They live in a house called Dunroamin in a place called Fyton. I am writing to them today to explain the situation and to say I will deliver you to them at the end of the week."

5. The Decision

It was a stormy morning inside as well as out in Dunroamin after the letter arrived. Angry words flew round the dining room like hailstones.

"We'll go away, Mabel. We'll lock up the house."

"We couldn't do that for long, dear," said Mabel. "I mean, it's our home, where should we go?"

"I'll send a cable to Istanbul to say you are ill, something infectious so we are unable even to see the children."

"But," squeaked Mabel, who had almost lost her voice trying to be heard over Cecil's shouts, "everybody knows I'm not ill. They see me shopping every day."

"I'll see my solicitor, I'm sure nobody can be forced to take in their brother's children, especially a brother who is a thief."

Mabel thought of something he would care about.

"Wouldn't it look very bad if it came out that we'd refused to have them?"

"How can it come out? The children are in Turkey. I suppose there are orphanages in Turkey."

"Not for British children, dear."

Cecil looked back at his letter.

"They are only half British, their mother was a Pole. Why don't their Polish relations have them?"

"Perhaps there aren't any," said Mabel. "Anyway, I don't see how you can suggest that. I mean, wouldn't this Sir William think it was odd?"

In the end, though very grudgingly, Cecil accepted that for the time being he was beaten. He simply could not cable Sir William to say, "No. I won't have the children."

"We must just hope there is some money," he said. "Then we can pack the lot off to boarding schools; the papers have been saying his pictures sold well."

"Yes, dear, they did," said Mabel, thankful to be able to agree about one thing at least, though secretly not accepting the boarding schools.

The Cecil thought of something new to be cross about.

"If only we had bought a smaller house with no spare bedrooms, we couldn't have had the children. That was your fault, Mabel, you would have that kitchen."

Mabel was used to being blamed for things she had not done, so it was no surprise to her to hear it was her fault Cecil had bought Dunroamin. Though actually the first she had known of the purchase was when Cecil had said: "I have bought a house."

So she changed the subject.

"What shall we do if this Sir William wants to stay the night?"

"We can't have him, thank goodness. In his letter he says there are two boys and a girl. That uses up the two rooms; in any case I have no intention of this Sir William or any other busybody crossing the threshold. If I have to bring up my brother's children I shall do it in my own way. I shall fly to Istanbul and collect the children. Imagine Sir William writing 'I will cable time of arrival'! Who does he think he is? Any cabling time of arrival will be done by me."

While all this arguing was going on in Dunroamin the children were getting to know Sir William, whom they called S'William, for they had never known a "Sir" and never seen the name written, and the more they got to know him the more they liked him. He was so sensible and unfussy. Without being told he knew they could not eat proper food since the earthquake, so he let them have what they liked. If all Anna wanted was hard boiled eggs and olives in a sandwich that was all she liked so why argue? If Gussie mostly fancied fruit and fizzy lemonade then let him live on them. Black coffee with perhaps an ice cream was not Sir William's idea of a nourishing meal but if it was Francesco's that was his business. He only made one food rule.

"I don't mind what you kids eat, but it's not much, so see there's always some of what you like to hand. After all, what's to prevent you being hungry in the middle of the night? And, believe me, if all else fails two or three buns at midnight are a splendidly filling meal."

After one midnight meal of figs, buns and bars of chocolate Gussie said to Francesco:

"I think things to eat in bed is a good idea, in fact only eating when you want to is a good idea. I plan to go on doing that when we get to The Uncle."

"An uncle, especially a British uncle, eats food at proper times, S'William told me," replied Francesco.

"I expect we can make him see our way is simpler," Gussie said. "After all, he ought to be glad, for it saves cooking and laying tables and all that."

Francesco was getting sleepy – buns at night do have that effect.

"S'William said he expected living with The Uncle would turn out all right, that things often do. So perhaps he'll understand about food."

Sir William, who was seldom surprised by anything, was amazed when the cable arrived. For a man who lived in a house called Dunroamin did not sound as if, without a word of warning, he would roam as far as Istanbul. He was also annoyed for he did not want an unknown companion landed on him for the flight home, so he bought four tickets in an aeroplane going to London and wired the flight number and time of arrival to Uncle Cecil. Then he called the children.

"Go and pack, kids. We leave for London in two hours."

He gave an envelope to Francesco. "I don't expect you'll ever need this but if you do, write to me at this address. No doubt your Uncle Cecil is a splendid fellow but sometimes an outsider can help. Don't worry if, having written to me, it's weeks before you get an answer for I am always travelling, in fact I'm only going to say one night in London then I'm off to Alaska. And, by the way, I'm holding on to your father's picture for you. Some more may turn up but in the meantime it seems to be all you possess, so I should keep it a secret if I were you. Proper wolves there are in the picture business."

It's impossible for anything to happen slowly at an airport. The children had only just got their breath back from the excitement of the journey when they found themselves staring at a strange man who was almost like Christopher only somehow quite opposite.

The man said:

"I am your Uncle Cecil. Wait over there while I talk to Sir William."

Over there, which was by an advice counter, Anna whispered to the boys:

"I wish he didn't look like Christopher because

I don't think I'm going to like him."

"He speaks," Gussie said, "like a very old dry biscuit."

Sir William during the flight had told Francesco a lot of things including the fact that they might not take to their uncle right away — nor he to them — there would have to be give and take on both sides. So now Francesco tried to explain this to the others.

"S'William said we mightn't like The Uncle at first but we must give time."

"I don't need time," Gussie retorted. "I hate him now this very minute."

Sir William was thinking that very same thing. He simply loathed leaving the children with their uncle but what could he do? This Uncle Cecil was their legal guardian. In any case in his travelling life there was no place for three children. So he did the best he could. He cut the goodbyes short.

"Goodbye, kids," he called out. "Let's hear from you some time." Then he waved, turned and was swallowed up in the crowd.

6. The Aunt

The boys, who shared the larger of the two bedrooms, woke up early the next morning.

Gussie sat up and looked round.

"What a horrible room!"

Francesco sat up too.

"I think it's just so clean and we aren't used to rooms that are as clean as this."

"The hotel room in Istanbul was very clean," Gussie argued, "but it didn't look like this."

Francesco saw suddenly something that was wrong with the room.

"There aren't any pictures, even the hotel in Istanbul had pictures, not very nice but they had them. As a matter of fact there aren't any in the whole house."

"I wish," said Gussie, "we'd kept our picture, it would be something of us, now there is nothing."

"S'William was right though, if it was here it would be sold."

"What, by wolves like he said?"

Francesco lowered his voice to a whisper.

"No. By The Uncle. I do not think he is pleased we have no money."

Gussie tried to remember last night but it was a blur.

"I remember The Uncle driving us in his motorcar, it was a long way and I went to sleep."

"When we got to this house The Aunt was in the hall and she said supper was ready and we should wash," Francesco prompted him.

"And did we?" Gussie asked.

"Yes, and then we went into a room for eating and there was a dish rolled up in thick grey stuff like a blanket. The Aunt said it was steak and kidney pudding. You looked at it and at once you were sick so you went to bed."

"Fancy, and I do not remember," said Gussie. "But then I've been sick a lot lately."

Francesco went on.

"Anna began to cry, just a little at first but then louder and louder so she went to bed. The Aunt took her."

"And you?" Gussie asked. "You stayed?"

"Yes, not to eat, that I could not, but The Aunt gave me a glass of milk with chocolate in it. The Uncle said she should not give in, children should eat what they were given, but she said it wouldn't hurt for once, it had been a tiring day."

"What else did The Uncle say?"

Francesco clasped his hands round his knees.

"He said we spoke English very bad, you remember Christopher said that too. That now it is the summer holiday but soon we all go to school."

"Where?"

"There is a school in this place."

"For Anna too?"

Francesco nodded.

"That is the bad thing. I told him Anna could not go to an ordinary school, she must go where there is good training to dance, but he made a sort of spitting sound and then he said: 'I don't hold with dancing nor ever will.'"

Gussie was shocked.

"Did you explain what Jardek had said?"

"Every single word and on each word he made more spitting noises. It is no good hoping, Gussie. The Uncle will not pay for Anna to learn to dance."

Gussie was so shocked he did not answer for quite a while. Then he got out of bed and began putting on his clothes.

"Quick, we must hurry."

Francesco watched him.

"Hurry where?"

"To S'William, of course, to sell our picture to pay for Anna to learn. We must get it before he goes to Alaska."

Francesco shook his head.

"Do you think I did not think of that? S'William is in London, we are a long way from there, we should have to take a train, and we have no money, no money at all."

Often when there was to be a picture exhibition

Christopher had driven the caravan to a place where there was a telephone. Gussie remembered this.

"Then we must telephone."

Francesco felt under his pillow and brought out Sir William's envelope. He passed it to Gussie.

"I thought of that but look, there is only an address."

Gussie took out the piece of paper inside the envelope and saw this was true. There was just an address scrawled across it but no telephone number. He put the paper back in the envelope and gave it to Francesco.

"Then what shall we do?"

"First take off your clothes and get back into bed. In this house all is arranged. I think we will bath before we dress. The Aunt said so. Then we must learn this address by heart in case we lose the envelope."

"Can't we hide it somewhere?"

Francesco looked round the room.

"Where?"

Gussie had undressed again. Now he put on his pyjamas.

"Let's look."

At that moment they heard someone coming up the stairs so, quick as a grasshopper, Gussie got back into bed while Francesco shoved the envelope under his pillow.

Aunt Mabel opened the door. None of them had

taken Aunt Mabel in last night for Gussie and Anna were both too wretched and too tired to notice anybody, and Francesco was talking to his uncle. But now the boys had a chance to study her and very odd they thought she was. "Like a mouse," Gussie described her later, "afraid to move in case a cat is coming."

The oddest thing about Aunt Mabel was her voice. It was as if she had to push at her words to make them sound at all, and if she said much she seemed to run out of breath.

To look at, too, she was to the children surprising. Dressed in a shapeless flowered dress and an apron which seemed to hold her together. She had hair which, though no doubt she had put pins in it, seemed to be falling down. As a result the general effect was crumpled. This amazed the boys for the only British woman they had looked at was the Queen, whose picture Olga stuck up with a pin during lessons. The picture was of the Queen at the Flower Show and was much admired by the three children, who had supposed that was how all British ladies looked.

"Good morning, dears," Aunt Mabel puffed. "Time for baths. You can go now, Francesco, for your uncle has finished with the bathroom. You will have to run along as you are as you have no dressing-gowns."

In the caravan or when staying with Jardek and Babka, there had been no use for dressing-gowns,

50

though Christopher had an old one he occasionally put on. Bathing had happened when it could. Sometimes water was heated and poured into a tub and was used by all the family in turn. More often they bathed where everybody else did, in a wayside stream, a lake or perhaps a river. For ordinary washing there was always cold water and a tin basin.

Francesco wondered if The Aunt was blaming S'William for not buying them dressing-gowns.

"In the hotel in Istanbul we had no use for dressing-gowns for in each bedroom was a bath which was ours alone."

The glory of that memory rang in Francesco's voice.

Aunt Mabel was obviously impressed, in fact she seemed unable to answer for her mouth just opened and shut like a fish's.

"S'William bought us all the beautiful clothes we have," said Gussie.

Aunt Mabel's voice sounded more faint and jerky than ever.

"Oh dear, I hope your uncle does not know that for he would feel he ought to pay him."

Gussie was shocked.

"A present is a present, it is rude to wish to pay."

Aunt Mabel, as if her legs would no longer hold her upright, sank on to the end of Francesco's bed. She spoke in a whisper:

"In time you will understand your uncle" — she did not sound as if that was a promise. "But until you do, dears, will you try not to annoy him?"

"What is it that annoys him?" Gussie asked.

Aunt Mabel squeezed her hands together.

"Please, please, dears, don't ask him to let Anna dance. You see, to him dancing is not right."

The boys gaped at her. Naturally, with a grandfather like Jardek, dancing was like painting or any art – a gift from God to be treasured and worked at. Had not Olga explained this to them almost every day? Gussie supposed The Aunt did not understand.

"Jardek – he was the father of our mother – was a great teacher of ballet in Warsaw. When he had to leave and come to Turkey he taught us. Francesco and me we have no gift but Anna has."

Francesco added:

"Always Jardek knew this. 'She has the real special spark,' he said: 'always I have searched and now I am rewarded to find it in my own granddaughter.'"

"Not to let her learn," said Gussie firmly, "is a sin – a bad sin."

The voice of Uncle Cecil roared up the stairs.

"What's going on, Mabel? Those children should be bathed and dressed by now."

Aunt Mabel scuttled to the door.

"Hurry, boys," she gasped. "Hurry."

Francesco and Gussie looked at each other then Francesco gave Gussie Sir William's envelope.

"Hide it somewhere while I have my bath.

52

Afterwards we will talk for it is us who must arrange that Anna learns to dance."

7. *Money*

When the children sat down to breakfast Uncle Cecil said:

"I make it a rule at meals that nothing is said unless it is important or uplifting."

This was so off-putting that the children could only look at each other out of the corners of their eyes to say what they thought. When they had lived in the caravan or stayed with Jardek and Babka everyone had so much to say that all talked at once and seldom minded if no one was listening. Of course sometimes Christopher would bang on the table and shout "I will have hush" or something like that. Mostly this happened when a picture was going wrong, then the last way to describe what Christopher said was either important or uplifting.

By good luck the food was what the children liked and could eat – a cereal followed by boiled eggs – and though Anna left half her egg in its shell Uncle Cecil did not notice so there was no trouble.

After breakfast the children were told by Uncle Cecil to go to their rooms to give their aunt a hand with the tidying up.

"Old beast!" Gussie muttered as they climbed

the stairs. "He ought to have seen the way we helped Babka. I think he thinks we can't even make a bed."

Anna said to Francesco:

"If I bring a piece of ribbon will you plait my hair?"

Francesco was surprised.

"Why plait it, you never do?"

"It'll look awful plaited," said Gussie.

Anna darted into her bedroom and came out with a piece of red ribbon to match the red check cotton frock she was wearing which Sir William had bought for her. Anna had dark hair and big dark eyes, so even when she was too pale, which she was at that moment, red suited her.

"I wore my hair loose in Istanbul because I couldn't do it on top of my head" – she didn't need to say "as Olga did it" because the boys knew – "but I think this is a plait sort of house. I mean a plait is neat and this is a very neat place."

Francesco plaited her hair and tied the red bow on the end of the plait. It was a sad sort of thing to do for it reminded him of Togo who, on birthdays and at Christmas, had always had his tail plaited. But of course he did not tell the others what he was thinking. Instead he said to Anna:

"I'm glad you came in. Gussie and I have much to tell you. The Uncle will not let you learn to dance, he thinks it is wrong."

Anna swung round to face Francesco. Her face

was whiter than ever, especially round the mouth.

"I do not care what The Uncle thinks. I do not like him and I will dance. I must dance, you know what Jardek said."

Francesco remembered what he had told Gussie to do.

"Where did you put the envelope with S'William's address?

That calmed Anna down.

"Good. I had forgotten we had his address. We will go now and tell him. He will understand and arrange everything."

Gussie showed Francesco the built-in cupboard.

"In such a house even a bottom shelf which is not used is covered with paper." He opened the cupboard door so the others could see. Each shelf was covered with a pale green washable lining paper with a pattern of leaves on it. "Under there at the back," he pointed to the bottom shelf, "is S'William's envelope. The Aunt will never look there."

"Good," said Francesco. Then he turned back to Anna. "This place is far from London where S'William is, and today he goes to Alaska. If he was in London, even if I had to walk, I would have gone to him and asked him to sell our picture."

Anna was not her father's daughter for nothing. There was desperation in her voice.

"I must learn," she said, "and from the best teacher. If we cannot sell the picture we must sell things from this house."

Francesco suddenly felt very much the eldest.

"No," he said firmly. "That we will never do. Olga taught to steal is wrong you remember."

"I do," Gussie agreed. "That catechism we had to learn. It said 'Thou shalt not steal' and Olga said it was not truly stealing that Christopher did because it was from his own father."

"This would be from our own uncle," Anna argued.

"No," said Francesco. "You shall learn to dance but no one will steal."

Gussie thumped his chest.

"Francesco and me — we will earn the money. How do you think boys earn money in Britain?"

A procession of ways of earning money passed through the children's minds. Loading donkeys with wood, leading a camel from one place to another, calling conveyances for people, running errands; there were, especially in towns, a hundred ways of earning small coins and small coins added up.

"First," said Francesco, "we have to find the best place for learning dancing."

"Who would know?" asked Gussie. "The Uncle doesn't and I shouldn't think. The Aunt does. Would a priest?"

Francesco was doubtful.

"This I don't know, but we could try. But while we are trying, Anna, you must practise."

Anna nodded.

"I did in Istanbul holding on to the end of the bed. But I can't do much. Exercises done wrong can do harm. Then I have no shoes and it is difficult to be right when you only wear socks."

No shoes! The boys had not thought of that. Anna had had soft pink shoes tied on with ribbons. Jardek ordered them from a shop in Italy. But of course they were gone with everything else.

"I think shoes should be the first thing we should buy," said Gussie. "Then we find out where Anna must go to learn."

Aunt Mabel took the children shopping that first morning to give them some idea of Fyton. To the children, who had never been out of the Near or Far East, it was confusing for everything was different. Fyton, which had been a village, was growing into what is called "a new town". As a result it was full of young married couples. It seemed to the children that everybody owned a fat pink and white baby in a pram. There were older children as well, all well dressed and rushing about with shopping bags. They were amazed at the supermarket.

"These British must be very honest," Anna whispered to Francesco. "Imagine everything out where anybody can steal!"

"I think also they are very rich," said Francesco. "We have seen no beggars — no beggars at all."

Aunt Mabel wanted to get home to cook the

lunch but she had come to a conclusion about the children. If there was to be any peace in the house she must keep them out of Cecil's way as much as possible. Fortunately, he was out a good deal serving on committees and organizing things, but he was at home that morning so the children must stay out. Mabel opened her purse and took two tenpenny pieces out of it. She had no idea how she was going to explain where the two tenpenny pieces had gone for Cecil went through the accounts daily, but she would think of something and for the moment peace was more important. She showed the children the turning to Dunroamin and the clock on the Town Hall.

"You must start home at twelve-thirty, dears, so that you have time to wash before lunch which is at one o'clock sharp. These," she gave the two tenpenny pieces to Francesco, "will buy you all ice creams."

When Aunt Mabel had pushed her way out of sight between perambulators the children examined the tenpenny pieces, which was the first English money they had seen. Anna clasped her hands together ecstatically.

"Perhaps The Aunt each day will give us such money for ices. Then soon I will have my shoes."

"It is a start," Francesco agreed, "but for dancing classes much money will be wanted."

Gussie again thumped his chest.

"Me, I have thought of a way."

"How?" asked Francesco and Anna.

"Up that road," Gussie pointed to the place he meant, "there is a little market, not like a big bazaar but things are sold from stalls."

"But we've nothing to sell," Francesco reminded him.

"Oh yes we have," said Gussie. "S'William gave two of everything for each. All we need is one, we can wear a blanket while the one is washed."

Anna saw the idea.

"And our suitcases. Our beautiful new suitcases! People must give money for those."

Francesco was carried away by the enthusiasm of the other two.

"No one, not even The Uncle, could mind that we sell what is ours. Now all we must do is find out how we can borrow a little stall."

8. Wally

The children went to have a look at the little market. They were connoisseurs of markets of every description; they thought very poorly of this one.

"No cooked food," Gussie grumbled. "There should always be cooked food in a market, it smells well so people come."

"But they do sell clothes," Francesco said, pointing to a stall which had clothes all round it on coat hangers.

They went up to the stall. Anna fingered a coat.

"But not good clothes like the ones S'William gave us."

"What you kids want?" a voice asked. The children looked round and at first could not see who had spoken because he was behind the clothes. Then a boy about Francesco's age with bright red hair came round the stall. "This is me mum's stall but I'm lookin' arter it."

Gussie liked the look of the boy and, anyway, he expected everybody to be friends, at least he had until he met The Uncle.

"We aren't wanting to buy anything, we were

wishing to know how you can have a little stall."

The boy stared at Gussie.

"You talk funny. Foreign, are you?"

"No," said Francesco, "we are British but we have not lived here until yesterday."

"Where did you live then?" the boy asked.

"Just now it was Turkey though me I was born in Iran," Francesco explained.

"Me I was born in India," said Gussie.

To say these things was too near all they wanted to forget. Anna's voice became a whisper and her eyes filled with tears.

"Me I was the only one not born in the caravan."

The boy was puzzled. If they lived in a caravan they must be gipsies, but they didn't look like gipsies.

"What's your name then? Mine's Wally — well, Walter really, but everyone calls me Wally."

Francesco introduced them.

"Me I am Francesco, this is Gussie and this is Anna."

"Where you living then?"

"In a road called The Crescent," said Gussie. "The house is called Dunroamin and we want a stall to sell some clothes."

"And three suitcases," Anna reminded him.

"Good clothes, Anna's other frock which is blue, and we have flannel shorts and a shirt each," Francesco explained.

To Wally the three children seemed as helpless as

62

babies. He knew The Crescent. There were nice houses up there. Not the sort where the owners booked a stall to sell clothes.

"Look 'ere," he said in the voice he would have used to a baby. "Me mum will be back in a minute and she don't fancy people standing round, not unless they're buyin' anythin'. Now there is a seat down there, go and sit on it until I come. You can't 'ave a stall but maybe I'll think of a way round thin's."

Wally did not keep the children waiting long, for he arrived on a rattling old bicycle which was much quicker than using his feet.

"Mum's back," he said, propping his bicycle against the seat. Then he sat down between Francesco and Anna. "Now, let's 'ave the whole boilin'. Why, livin' in The Crescent, do you want to sell your clothes?"

Anna answered.

"Because of me. I must learn to dance."

"Jardek — he was our mother's father — was a very great teacher of dancing in Warsaw and he said Anna has the real special spark," Francesco explained.

Gussie joined in.

"When there is a great gift not to learn is a sin. But The Uncle we now live with says it is to dance that is the sin."

To Wally the children might have come from another planet. He was fascinated by them, and at the same time felt protective about them. He had found them, they were his to look after.

"You got to get one thin' in your 'eads. This is England and in England kids your age can't work, it's against the law. If you was to set up a stall you'd 'ave the coppers after you. Nor you can't 'ave a paper round nor nothin' like that."

Francesco studied Wally. Wally was bigger built than he was but he didn't look much older.

"But you are working. How old are you?"

Wally shook his head sadly at such ignorance.

"I'm ten but I'm not workin', just standin' in for me mum while she had a cuppa. The coppers knows us, they knows it's just on account of it's the school 'olidays, they'd be around all right if I was helping me mum of a term time."

Anna had an idea.

"Do you think it would be possible for our things to be sold on your stall?"

Wally thought about that.

"I'd 'ave to talk to me mum. You see, your uncle might think your clothes was his like, then he would call it stealin'. Me mum wouldn't 'ave nothin' to do with that. 'Ow much money was you wanting?"

"We have these," Francesco showed Wally the tenpenny pieces, "but we want much more for it is for dancing shoes."

"Mine," Anna explained, "were lost in the earthquake with all else."

64

At that moment the Town Hall clock struck 12.30. The children got up.

"We must go," Francesco explained. "We have to be very punctual or The Uncle will be angry."

Wally could not bear to let them go. They had been fascinating before but now with Anna saying her shoes were lost in an earthquake they were like something on the telly.

"Now look," he said, "I gotta 'ave time to think what's best to be done. Can you be back 'ere by 'alf past two?"

To the children, used to roaming where they would, this presented no difficulties.

"Of course," said Gussie, "we've nothing to do."

Wally watched them walk down the hill. He hated to see them go.

"Watch it now," he called after them, "see you two-thirty."

Sir William had not been at all happy about leaving the children at Fyton. He had taken an instant dislike to Cecil, who seemed to him both prim and smug. He had in the short while he had known them become fond of the children. But what could he do? Without doubt Cecil Docksay was Christopher Docksay's only brother and, therefore, legal guardian to the children. He could not have been said to be exactly welcoming when he met them at the airport, but on the other hand he had not suggested he did not want them. Suppose the

65

children were wretchedly unhappy with their uncle, could anything be done?

Sir William was so worried about the children that he asked an old friend who was a barrister to dinner, and to him poured out his anxieties.

The barrister listened with interest, for he knew about pictures and had admired Christopher Docksay's work.

"I should try and see the children as often as you can. It's about all you can do, unless of course you think they are neglected."

"But there are other forms of neglect besides what is legally meant by the word, aren't there?" Sir William asked. "I mean, the children have lost everyone they loved, they need that replaced."

"You're on a difficult wicket there. Much the best thing you can do is keep in touch. You could see them when you are in England, couldn't you, and write to them when you are away? Children love getting letters."

Sir William had never written to a child in his life. Now he looked in a worried way at his friend.

"Write about what?"

The barrister, who had brought up four children and who now had nine grandchildren, laughed.

"You old bachelor, you. You've had the children with you for over a week, you must have some idea what interests them."

It was then Sir William remembered the talk he had had with the children in Istanbul.

"The girl Anna wants to learn to dance."

"All girls go through that stage," said the barrister. "It doesn't last."

Sir William tried to catch an atmosphere.

"These aren't ordinary children. They have been brought up with a deep respect for art in any form. It seems their maternal grandfather taught dancing in Warsaw. He was teaching the girl whom, according to the children, he thought was the real thing."

"Well, that's a good start for a letter to the children. Ask if they've fixed on a dancing teacher."

"If they haven't, who is the best?"

The barrister thought.

"None of my brood was anywhere near first-class but I remember talk. There is a Madame Scarletti, who must be very old now, but I believe she is still going. Now she was a Pole, she married an Italian called Scarletti. You could find the address of her studio in the telephone book."

9. Hair

The Crescent was buzzing with the news. One paper had said Christopher Docksay had left three children. Another had said they had been in hospital but had left for England in the care of Sir William Hoogle. No paper had said the children had been brought to Fyton to live with their uncle, but it had taken no one in The Crescent long to put two and two together. Yesterday children with suitcases had been seen getting out of "that odd Mr Docksay's" car. This morning three children had been seen going out shopping with Mrs Docksay. Many people in The Crescent had children of their own, others had grandchildren, but all, whether they had families or not, said:

"Poor children! We must see what we can do to help."

Cecil Docksay had been working all the morning. Though he had retired from his bank he was still a busy man, for, being good at figures – which is something bank managers have to be – he was in demand to be the treasurer of charities. It could not be said he was liked for he was unsociable, but it was admitted he was useful.

Now, his work over, he was in his garden looking proudly at his plastic flowers when, out of the corner of his eye, he saw what he described to himself as "some fool" in the next garden watering his real flowers. He paid no attention because he was not the sort of man neighbours talked to over garden fences, but that day he had a surprise. The neighbour spoke to him.

"I believe Christopher Docksay was your brother. I'm so sorry. Terrible tragedy. Don't know much about pictures myself but the papers say he was a wonderful artist." Cecil muttered something that just might have been "thank you". "My wife," the neighbour went on, "met three children out with Mrs Docksay this morning. Are they your brother's kids? Saw in the paper there were three coming to England."

Cecil was livid at what he considered inquisitiveness but he had to answer.

"That's right. They're living here."

The neighbour swallowed back the "Heaven help them" which sprang to his lips. Instead he said:

"We were wondering if the children would like to come to tea one day. We've got twins, you know – a boy and a girl. They're eleven."

Cecil was speechless with rage. Ever since they had lived in Dunroamin he and Mabel had kept themselves to themselves.

Now, after one night in the house, the children

were being asked out to tea. It was unbearable.

"Not going out at the moment," he growled and strode back into his house and shut the door. At the same time he looked at his watch, three minutes to one, the children had better be punctual or he'd show them who was master here.

There can be few things more annoying when you are feeling cross than that those with whom you are cross should take the wind out of your sails by doing exactly what you had meant to scold them for not doing. Exactly at one o'clock the three children, washed and tidy, walked into the dining room.

The idea was Francesco's. Walking home, he had been thinking about his uncle. Upstairs, he told his thoughts to the others.

"If we take care never to do anything in anger, and if we try not to speak at meals, it will be much better for The Uncle will leave us alone."

"Why should we?" Gussie expostulated. "I like talking at meals like we always have, and if I'm angry I do things at once without thinking."

Anna agreed with Francesco. She had come into the boys' room to have her hair plaited.

"He's quite right, Gussie. It is not nice here but we must try while S'William is in Alaska. When he comes back perhaps he will sell our picture, them something better could be managed.

To add to the tidy washed look Francesco felt was expected of them he tried to do something with Gussie's hair. They all had thick dark hair but Gussie's had a slight curl in his which made it stand up. Francesco, much to Gussie's annoyance, took a wet comb to it.

"Why should I comb my hair to please The Uncle?" he grumbled. "I do not like him so I don't care how it looks. Anyway, it was cut and washed in Istanbul."

On their first day in Istanbul Sir William had sent all three children to a hairdresser.

"You boys look like a couple of savages," he had said, "and Anna is not much better."

"Our hair is usually much better than now," Gussie had told him. "It is the earthquake, it makes a terrible dust."

"Our mother was always washing and cutting our hair," Francesco had added. "For Anna she tied it on top of her head with a ribbon so her neck was cool."

This was so vivid a picture that none of the children could bear to think of it.

Sir William saw this.

"I didn't suppose your hair was always a mess. You must remember I was never in an earthquake. But yours does need washing and perhaps a bit of cutting. What length you wear it is your business, but you might have it trimmed."

But that was a week ago and Gussie's hair, though clean, was on end again. Francesco slicked it down with a wet comb which was unbecoming but effective.

"Now we all wash," he said. "Then we watch over the stairs and the moment The Aunt comes out of the kitchen with the food we walk down the stairs."

Cecil looked at the children to find something about them on which he could rub off his anger. But there was nothing. They were not a credit to him because, having lived so long in hot countries, they were pale compared with ordinary English children, and they had dark circles under their eyes as a result of all they had suffered. Then he noticed Gussie's hair. The wet comb had not only made the hair lie down neatly but also had made it look longer. If there was one thing Cecil hated it was boys with long hair.

"You need your hair cut, Augustus," he said. "You can have it done this afternoon."

Gussie clean forgot what had been decided in the bedroom.

"Cut! Cut! Cut!" he said. "Everybody speaks about cutting. It was cut last week in Istanbul."

Mabel was putting helpings of fish pie on the plates. This meant her back was to the table, but even from that position she could feel a diversion was necessary if Cecil was not to get angry.

"Don't worry, dear," she said to Cecil. "I'll see Gussie goes to the barber's." Then, to keep Gussie quiet, she added: "Would you two boys come and hand round the plates?"

Francesco could see Gussie was longing to go on

arguing, so as he gave his uncle his plate of fish pie he asked:

"How much in England is it to have the hair cut?"

"Too much by a long chalk," said Cecil. "Probably twenty-five pence. Everything costs too much these days."

That silenced Gussie. Twenty-five pence would be more than those ten pences. If only The Aunt did not come with them surely they could find a way to keep the money.

It was lucky the children had had a busy morning for it had made them hungry, so somehow they forced down the fish pie which they all – used to highly seasoned food – thought disgusting. The fish pie was followed by what Mabel called a summer pudding. It was made of bread and blackcurrants and though, as the children agreed later, not nice it was good for taking away the taste of the fish pie. At the end of the meal Cecil put his hand in his pocket and took out some change and passed it over to Francesco.

"There's twenty-five but you may get it done for twenty. If you do, bring me the change. And see Augustus's hair is cut really short, he looks like a girl as he is, and anyway I'm not made of money, this cut had got to last a long time."

Fortunately Mabel had no intention of going with the children to the hairdresser. She told them where the barber's shop was, then she turned her worried mouselike face to Francesco.

"I trust you, dear, to see it really is cut short. You don't want unpleasantness, do you?"

Gussie only waited to get the other two alone before he burst out:

"I do want unpleasantness. I won't have my hair cut. Christopher liked it, Olga liked it and so I think did Jardek and Babka – at least, they never said they didn't. If anyone tries to cut my hair I'll run away."

Francesco and Anna knew that when Gussie got cross he could talk louder and louder until he was almost screaming.

"You know we can't have your hair cut," said Francesco, "this twenty-five is for Anna's shoes."

"Then what will The Uncle say?" Gussie demanded.

"This I do not know," Francesco admitted. "But we will tell all to Wally and he will find an answer."

10. Wally's Mum

Wally was already sitting on the seat when the children arrived. This time he had not brought his bicycle. He was so pleased to see them he bounced off the seat and rushed to meet them.

"There you are! You gotta come to me mum's stall. I told 'er how Anna had lost her dancing shoes in the earthquake and she's ever so interested. She says she read about you in the paper, you know, your dad and mum and that being killed. She says you come and talk to 'er an' she's sure thin's can be sorted out so's you've enough for Anna's shoes. What's an earthquake like?"

Francesco did not want Gussie to be sick or Anna to cry so he said:

"I'll tell you some day but just now we want a way to cut Gussie's hair without spending money."

"You see," Anna explained, "The Uncle has given twenty-five pence for it to be cut, but we need the money for my dancing shoes."

Gussie caught hold of Wally's sleeve.

"I don't want it cut. It's all right the way it is. Anyway, I do not like The Uncle so I won't do things to please him."

Wally was not sure how his mother would react to this hair business. She might think taking twenty-five pence, meant for hair cutting, to buy shoes was cheating. So all he said was:

"We'll ask mum, she'll know what's best."

Wally's mum was waiting for them behind her stall. Her name was Mrs Wall. The children took to her right away. She had red hair like Wally and, though she was not old, she had a fat cosy look. They had not seen anybody fat and cosy since Babka and, now they saw fat and cosiness again, they knew how badly they had missed her.

"This is them," said Wally in a proud voice, rather as if he was introducing three TV stars.

Wally's mum saw the pale faces and the shadows under the eyes and she felt so sorry for the children that it hurt. She pulled Anna to her and gave her a hug.

"So it's you who wants to learn the dancin'."

That hug was too much for Anna. It was just the way Babka had hugged. Ever since Sir William had looked after them all three children had tried not to think of things which reminded them of the little house that went away. And most of the time they had succeeded, pushing other things on top of what they were trying to forget. Now, with one hug, Wally's mum had brought everything back. It was like a dam breaking. All the pushed-away hopeless misery came tumbling out. First Anna was crying, then Gussie and finally Francesco.

Wally's mum was a great believer in having a good cry.

"That's right," she said in her warm cosy voice. "No good bottlin' thin's up." Then, over the heads of the three children for by now she had them all in her arms, she called out to Wally:

"Get the stall packed, dear, then we'll go 'ome and I'll make a nice cuppa tea. Nothing like a cuppa when you're feeling low."

The children cried for quite a long time for they had a lot of held-in crying to get out of them. But when they had reached the occasional hiccupping-sob stage Wally's mum said:

"Now, blow your noses and we'll get movin'. Wally's packed the pram."

It had not struck the children to wonder how Wally's mum transported her goods to her stall. They had often watched stalls put up, and knew that at the end of the day someone would come and help carry away the baskets and boxes. Or perhaps a boy would arrive with a donkey. But a perambulator was something new.

"How is it you have the perambulator?" Gussie asked in the sniffy voice of someone who has been crying.

Wally's mum laughed.

"You'd never think it but it's Wally's old pram. His dad said he'd sell it when Wally got past it, but I had a feeling it would come in useful and it has."

"You see, me dad he was a lorry driver," Wally

explained, "and he was in a smash. Well, he can't do much now so that's why me mum has the stall, and the perambulator's grand for getting the stuff along."

"Wally comes to push the perambulator 'ome after school, he never misses," Wally's mum said proudly.

The boys helped Wally push the perambulator and as they walked the children told Wally's mum about their troubles.

"The Uncle is a terrible man," Gussie explained. "He says to dance is a sin."

Wally's mum, though sorry for the children, still held to her views on what was right.

"Well, the one who pays the piper calls the tune," she said, "and you can't go against that."

"You do not see that I must dance?" Anna asked, appalled.

Wally's mum put an arm around Anna and gave her a squeeze.

"I never said that. Of course you must dance if you 'ave the gift. But this uncle – well, he has taken you in and he's feedin' you and that, so it's his right to say if he don't hold with dancing."

Then they told her about the ice cream ten pences and the twenty-five pence for the hair cutting.

"We do not know how much the shoes will cost," Anna explained, "but forty-five pence must help."

Wally's mum thought about that.

"The tens you were given for the ice cream, that's all right, but I don't know about that twenty-five that was given for hair cuttin' and nothin' else."

"But I won't have it cut," said Gussie. "I like it the way it is, everybody liked it, there is only The Uncle who wants it short."

Wally's mum looked at Gussie with a twinkle in her eye.

"I see I'll 'ave to say to you what I says to Wally — 'want will 'ave to be your master'."

"But, Mum," said Wally, "couldn't Dad . . ."

His mum silenced him with a gesture.

"We'll see what we'll see. Now come in, dears, and I'll put on the kettle."

They had stopped outside a small house sitting by itself in a field. In the field there were a lot of hens and one cock and a sty from which came the grunting of a pig.

"You have a farm," said Francesco. "We had many friends who had farms."

Wally's mum laughed.

"It's 'ardly a farm but Wally's dad always fancied pig-keepin' and when 'e got compensation for his accident we spent it on this place. 'E can't do much from 'is wheelchair but Wally 'elps and the pig is company for 'is dad when we're out."

"Come on," Wally told the children. "We keeps the pram back of the pig sty. We'll tell Dad we're 'ome."

Wally's dad was in his wheelchair. He seemed to have lost both legs in his motor accident but he was a very cheerful man.

"Meet our Bess," he said, pointing to the very fat pig in the sty. "Makes a lovely pet Bessie does."

Wally did the honours.

"This is Francesco and this is Gussie and this is Anna, they were in an earthquake."

Wally's dad had also read his newspaper. He gave the children a quick look, then he changed the subject.

"Is your mum making a cuppa then? Looks like we could all do with it."

Over tea and a splendid cake Wally's dad was told about Anna's dancing and the twenty-five pence for Gussie to have his hair cut. That made him look at Gussie.

"Well, you could do with a cut."

"But I don't want it done," Gussie protested, "and we need the money for Anna's shoes. She can't practise properly in socks."

Mr Wall looked at his wife.

"You get out the basin and me scissors."

Wally's mum got up.

"Lovely hair cutter he is. Just amateur like. But there's quite a few come to him."

Wally's dad beamed at Gussie.

"Then you gives me the twenty-five for the 'air cut and I gives it back to you and everybody's 'appy."

"Except me," Gussie growled.

"Even you, I shouldn't wonder," said Wally's dad. "It's a marvel the way I can keep cuttin' and still leave the 'air looking OK."

Wally's mum put a stool for Gussie beside the wheelchair and wrapped a towel round him, then Mr Wall put a pudding basin on Gussie's head and clipped at the hair that was outside it.

"It's not just the shoes, is it?" Wally's mum asked Anna and Francesco. "Wally was telling me you wanted to sell some clothes."

"They are ours – given us by S'William, so absolutely nothing to do with The Uncle," Gussie shouted.

"You sit still and don't talk," said Mr Wall, "or I'll 'ave a ear off of you."

"We have a suitcase each and Anna has another frock and we have shorts and shirts," Francesco explained. "But we do not know of a teacher so we cannot tell how much it will cost."

Wally's mum looked at Wally.

"Isn't there someone the girls go to of a Saturday?"

Wally nodded.

"Miss Audrey de Veane. Lovely teacher they say she is."

"Puts on shows for charity and that, doesn't she?" his mother asked.

"Them as is old enough gets work in pantomimes," said Wally. "Wouldn't fancy it meself, but she's well spoke of."

81

"You know any girl what learns off of 'er?"

Wally sighed.

"Well, that Doreen does, you know — her down by the church. Silly sort she is but she does learn the dancing."

"You'll go on your bike first thing tomorrow. Just ask her what this Miss de Veane charges. No need to tell her why — just ask."

The children had to go home soon after that. Gussie's hair was finished, it looked rather peculiar for it was much shorter at the back than at the front, though there was still a lot on the top of his head.

"Aren't they lovely people?" Francesco said.

Gussie skipped on ahead.

"Wouldn't it be good if we could live there instead of with The Uncle?"

Francesco felt the twenty-five pence in his pocket.

"And what a day! We have more money for the shoes. We have found someone who teaches dancing and Wally's mum will sell what we need to pay her. Are you pleased, Anna?"

Anna hesitated.

"Yes. Of course I am glad if the lady can teach as Jardek did. But until I know that I cannot say if I will learn with her." She looked anxiously at Francesco. "Will you explain this to Wally's mum? I would rather die than she should think I am not grateful."

Francesco sighed. There was so much he had to do now he was head of the family.

"Do not worry," he told Anna. "If you cannot learn from this lady it is I who will explain."

11. Suitcases

The shoes Anna needed would cost £1.40. The children went to a shoe shop to find out. The lady in the shop offered to order the shoes right away but Francesco would not allow that.

"No, first we will pay then you will order."

Outside the shop Gussie and Anna started to argue.

"I wish you'd have let her order," Anna said, "because we know how we will get the money, and I do need the shoes."

"I thought it was silly," Gussie agreed, "for we'll most likely have the money tonight if we give Wally's mum our things to sell today."

Francesco did not answer at once for he was making a plan. It was odd, he thought, how, now he had to be the one to make decisions, he was learning just to make them and did not mind what the other two said.

That day was a good one for getting the things they had to sell to Wally's mum, for it was a day when Uncle Cecil had to go to London for a meeting.

"Today," said Francesco, "we will only take the suitcases to sell."

"Why only suitcases?" asked Gussie. "With The Uncle out we can take everything. Even if The Aunt saw us I don't think she'd say anything, and anyway they are ours."

"No, just the suitcases," said Francesco. "Those we could not need for we are not going away and, if we did go away, we could use a box, but our clothes we do need. Already The Aunt has washed them, it will be easier if we do not need to sell the clothes."

"If we need more money," Anna suggested, "it may be difficult to take the clothes. Today they could travel in the suitcases."

Francesco thought they were being very stupid.

"But, don't you see, if we sell the clothes and then do not need the money, The Uncle cannot be given the money so he has to spend his money on our clothes. Well, we do not want this for as soon as S'William is home he will sell our picture, then we can pay."

"Oh, very well," said Gussie. "Come on, let's get the suitcases."

Always when Cecil went to London Mable turned out the house. So when the children ran upstairs to fetch their cases the boys were horrified to find her in their bedroom. She was wearing a big apron and had her hair tied up in a tea cloth. She was polishing the floor with a hairy thing on the end of a long stick. The boys had made their beds and left the room, as they thought, reasonably tidy before they went out, so they saw no need for her presence.

"Let me do that," Gussie said, trying to take the polisher from her.

"We always have helped clean since we were very little," Francesco explained.

Mable looked more like a frightened mouse than usual. When she spoke she seemed terribly out of breath.

"I haven't touched anything. I have left the envelope under the paper."

Francesco thought he would try and explain.

"It is only S'William's address. We thought that was a safe place."

"It is safe," Mable puffed. "I shall never touch it or say it is there." She gave a nervous smile. "There is no need to be afraid of me, dears."

Mabel looked as if she was going to say more, but at that second Anna came into the room carrying her suitcase.

It was a horrid moment for nobody knew what to say. Anna stared at Mabel as if she had turned into a dragon. Mabel gazed at the suitcase as if hypnotized. The boys just stood, both trying to think of some reason why Anna was carrying her suitcase.

"We thought . . ." Francesco began.

"Well, it's always useful to have a case with you," Gussie said in a rush. "You know, to put things in."

Then Mabel surprised them. She leant her

polisher against the wall and sat down on Francesco's bed. She had great difficulty pushing out her words.

"Your uncle is a fine man but he likes to be alone, he does not want strangers in his house."

"I wouldn't call two nephews and a niece strangers," said Gussie.

Mabel went on as if he had not spoken.

"For me your uncle always comes first, but when I can help you I will. We must work together to keep things peaceful. I do not interfere. If you wish to take out a suitcase that is nothing to me."

Francesco thought The Aunt's candour deserved candour in return.

"Really we are taking all three. It's to sell, you see we need money for something."

"Much money?" Mabel asked.

"To us a lot," said Gussie. "We've got forty-five pence but we need one pound and forty pence."

Mabel seemed so reasonable Francesco was beginning to wonder if they should tell her more, but evidently that was not what she wanted for suddenly she got up, picked up her polisher and darted out of the room.

Gussie looked after her in astonishment.

"Did you see? It was just as if she was a mouse and a cat was after her."

Francesco took the two suitcases out of the cupboard. He gave Gussie his.

"Come on, let's take them to Wally's mum."

"Of course," said Gussie when they reached the road, "we have never known an aunt. Do you suppose they are all like that?"

"Perhaps British ones," Anna suggested.

Francesco felt somehow better inside because of what Mabel had said.

"It is not the way it was with us – I mean, before the earthquake, where everybody said everything they thought, but I think for her it was a lot, almost I think she meant she was a friend."

Gussie refused to change his view of Mabel.

"To me she is just a mouse. She'd never be a friend if The Uncle is angry, like a mouse she'd run into her hole."

Anna had put her hand into Francesco's.

"I agree with you. Anyway, for us who have almost no friends, it is nice to have a mouse."

Wally was on the lookout for them. He rushed to meet them.

"I thought you were never coming." He looked admiringly at the suitcases. "Cor! They're a bit of all right, aren't they?"

Wally's mum was serving a customer but she gave the children a gorgeous smile.

"Shan't be long," she called out. "Wally's got something to tell you."

"I almost forgot," said Wally. "That Doreen, her that goes dancing of a Saturday. Well, that Miss de Veane she charges two pounds and ten pence for a term and there's extra when you take an exam. The term begins when school does and that's the week after next, so you did orter take Anna long to see 'er right away."

Wally's mum was thrilled with the suitcases.

"Now, let's see 'ow much you need and let's see if we can get it."

Francesco held up three fingers.

"Ninety-five pence for the shoes and two pounds and ten pence for the lessons, that's three pounds and five pence altogether."

" 'Ark at you!" said Wally's Mum. "Proper adder you are, I was always shockin' at sums and this decimal money drives me up the wall. Give me back the old 'alf crown, that's what I say."

Gussie was not going to allow Francesco to get all the praise.

"We can all add. Olga taught us."

Wally's mum examined the suitcases.

"We did ought to work for a bit over for there may be postage on the shoes and ribbons and that. Suppose I was to try for one pound twenty-five for each? It would give us a nice bit in 'and."

"But we gotta sell 'em, mum," Wally reminded her. "I mean, Anna can't wait about, that Doreen said she orter see the dancin' teacher right away, and she can't do that not without she's got some shoes."

Wally's mum opened her purse and took out a pound note.

"Go an' order them," she said. "When I says I can sell somethin' I can sell it."

Gussie and Wally took Anna to the shoe shop to order her shoes. Francesco stayed behind to explain to Wally's mum that Anna would not learn from Audrey de Veane if she was not as good as Jardek.

"It could be," he said, "that this Miss de Veane is not what Anna is needing. You see, Jardek was a wonderful teacher."

Wally's mum was making room for the suitcases on her stall.

"Who was this Jardek?"

"The father of our mother."

"Oh, your grandpa. Well, I never knew a grandpa in the dancing line, but I wouldn't suppose 'e'd be better than a lady brought up to it like, would you?"

Francesco screwed up his face, trying to find a way to explain.

"Only Anna will know. So if Anna says she cannot learn from this lady you will not think she is not grateful?"

Wally's mum put a hand on his shoulder.

"Look, son, there's things you've got to understand. This Audrey de Veane is the only one that teaches here."

"But there could be others in some other place."

Wally's mum turned Francesco so that he faced her.

"Not in Fyton there isn't, so Anna, as thin's are, has to learn in Fyton."

"Why?"

"Because that's where the school is. I know you ain't lived in England and so don't know what's what. But you can take it from me that not you, nor Anna, nor Gussie – not even the Queen 'erself, can alter the school laws. Come the week after next you 'ave to go to school. So it's Miss de Veane of a Saturday for Anna or no dancin' and that's flat."

12. Miss Audrey de Veane

Sir William, when he was a child, had been a keen stamp collector, so he decided the children probably were too, so he wrote to them on the aeroplane. It never crossed his mind there was any urgency. He thought the chances were that there was an established dancing teacher near Fyton and quite possibly Anna's lessons were already arranged. So he wrote the children a friendly letter telling them that he would not be away long, and that when he came back he would ask permission from their uncle to take them out. At the end of the letter he said:

"If, Anna, you are not fixed up with a suitable dancing teacher I hear very good accounts of a Madame Scarletti. I looked her up in the telephone book. She has a studio at 45 Bemberton Street, Chelsea, London. I gather she is very old but still one of the best teachers in the world." Then Sir William licked up the letter, put it in his pocket to post on arrival and forgot all about it for the next six weeks, when by chance he wore that coat again and found the letter in a pocket.

Wally's mum got £1.25 for each suitcase and

Wally arranged that Doreen, who lived by the church, should take Anna to Miss de Veane's studio.

"She's a right silly type, that Doreen," he told the children. "Giggles at nothin', but she's been with Miss de Veane since she was ever so small, so she's in with her like so could get her to see Anna."

This was not at all what Anna wanted.

"But it's I who wish to see Miss de Veane. Until I see how she teaches I do not know if it is with her I wish to learn."

"But, Anna," Francesco pleaded, "if she is the only one could you not learn from her just until S'William comes home?"

"I think it is what Jardek would have wished," said Gussie. "Great harm cannot come from one lesson each Saturday."

Anna stamped her foot she was so cross.

"Great harm can come. Wrong positions, wrong use of muscles and my legs may be ruined for ever and ever."

Gussie shrugged and turned to Francesco.

"I do not know why we sold the suitcases. Wally's mum says all must go to school or The Uncle may go to prison. This would I think be a good idea but he will not wish to go. So Anna can only dance when there is no school and there is only one to teach. What more can we do? In London perhaps there are many who teach well but how can Anna go to London? The Uncle will not take her in his car for he thinks to dance is a sin."

Francesco agreed.

"He's quite right, Anna, it's Miss de Veane or nobody at all. Go and see the lady and if she will teach you then try how it goes."

"But if it goes wrong?" said Anna. "She will have all the money for our suitcases, and we have no more money."

"If we must we will get more," Gussie promised, "but go in hope that this lady is such a one as Jardek would approve."

So two days later the boys took Anna, with her shoes in a paper bag – which Mabel gave her without asking why she wanted it – to the house by the church where Doreen lived.

Wally was quite right. Doreen was a very giggling girl, but she was kind-hearted so took complete charge of Anna.

"Now you don't want to be nervous like, she's ever so kind really." Then Doreen giggled. "Course it's different for me, I been with her ever so long so I dance solos and that for her shows."

Doreen was a plump little girl with brown ringlets. She did not, Anna thought, look a dancer, at least she did not look like the girls Jardek had taught of whom he had shown her photographs.

"Which solos do you dance?"

Doreen giggled again.

"All sorts, ever so pretty the costumes I've worn. Once I was a fairy and another time a butterfly and another time the spirit of winter. I wore a big white bonnet for that with a robin on it. Of course mostly it's musical comedy or tap that I do."

Anna had no idea what Doreen was talking about, but it didn't sound the sort of dancing Jardek taught.

The studio door was opened by Miss de Veane. She was a long thin woman with orange-coloured hair which at the roots showed it was really dark. She wore a very tight-fitting black dress and white boots. Anna, as she had been taught to do by Olga to any grown-up, dropped a polite little curtsey.

This made Doreen giggle.

"She's part foreign. That's why she does that, she does it to everyone."

Miss de Veane, perhaps because she had called out orders at dancing classes for so long, had an oddly hoarse voice.

"Very nice, too, I wish you'd all curtsey. I had to when I was a student. Come into the studio. Sit down, Doreen, and try not to giggle. Come here, child. Now put on your shoes."

"Yes, Madame," said Anna.

She sat on the floor and put on her pink canvas shoes on to which Wally's mum had sewn pink ribbons.

"I have a gramophone," Miss de Veane said. "Could you dance to some little thing to show me what you can do?"

Anna looked shocked.

"I was not allowed to do anything but exercises, Madame."

Miss de Veane looked at Anna's tightly plaited hair, her pale heart-shaped face, at the plain but well-cut blue cotton frock she was wearing – an unusual child and, remembering the curtsey, she wondered. Surely in this Fyton into which she had drifted she had not been sent a dancer? Well, even if she had it was too late now, she had lost interest.

"All right," she agreed, "go to the barre. We will start with six demi-pliés."

For ten minutes Miss de Veane rapped out orders, some for exercises at the barre, some to be done in the middle of the room. They were simple enough, such as she taught to those of her girls who wanted to enter for exams. But Anna was younger. When she had finished with her she asked:

"How old are you?"

"Eight, Madame."

Miss de Veane noticed the "Madame" and the foreign accent.

"And your name?"

"Anna Docksay."

"Well, Anna, I will take you as a pupil. My class is at ten on Saturday mornings, that is, tap and ballet. I teach musical comedy to the juniors on Thursday evenings but that's extra."

Anna had not properly understood.

"I only wish for a class for ballet exercises. So I

do not make faults which could remain."

Audrey de Veane thought back to her childhood when she had been a promising child dancer. Goodness knows where she might have risen to if she had been carefully trained. But she had been forced through every type of dancing until at twelve she was old enough to join a troupe. Why should this child be picked out for special attention? *She* had never been. Then something stirred in her, a flicker of the old ambition, even if she herself was past dancing she could at least train a good dancer.

"I do take a few special pupils, usually to coach for a public performance. But I suppose I might squeeze you in. Each lesson will cost fifty pence for half an hour."

Anna had not been in England long enough to be good at understanding the money. She looked anxiously over her shoulder at Doreen who had taken in every word of the conversation. Doreen got up and joined Anna and Miss de Veane.

"That means you could have about four lessons private for what it would cost for a whole term," she explained to Anna.

Anna did not know what to do. Four lessons was very little, but four like the ten minutes she had just done was better than a class which was not all ballet but was also this something that Madame called tap. Among the many things that Jardek had told Anna in mixed Polish and English was that a dancer must live for nothing but dancing, that anything which came between a dancer and dancing, must be forgotten absolutely. Anna saw now what Jardek had meant, that after the four lessons were over how to find the fifty pence each week was a thing she must forget entirely. She must trust in God and it would come.

"Thank you, Madame," Anna said firmly. "I think it best I have the private lessons."

13. Twins

Nobody could settle down in Dunroamin, it wasn't that sort of house, but while Anna was with Miss de Veane the boys for the first time since they had arrived had time to look round and see where they had come to live.

When they first realized that there was nothing they had to do they felt they must have forgotten something. But going over things in their bedroom they found they had not. Anna had got her shoes. At this minute they were on her feet. Enough money had been made when Wally's mum sold the suitcases for a whole term's dancing lessons to be paid for.

"It seemed as if there was a lot to do," Francesco explained to Gussie, "because everything took so long. I mean, there was four days between taking Anna to the shop to be measured for shoes and them coming."

"And what a four days," Gussie groaned. "With eating all that terrible food and my hair being cut."

"I never have known why The Uncle didn't get angry about your hair. Of course it had to be because we needed the twenty-five pence but, though I know Wally's dad tried, it certainly does look most peculiar."

"A crying scandal," Gussie agreed. This was an expression of Christopher's which his family had adopted.

"Yet The Uncle, though he frowned and made snorting noises, said nothing — nothing at all," Francesco marvelled.

Gussie had an idea about this.

"I think that was because, if he didn't like it, the only thing he could do was to pay again and this he will not do. I think he is one with a closed purse."

"Perhaps he is poor," Francesco suggested.

This made Gussie laugh so much that he rolled on his bed.

"Poor! In India, Pakistan, Iran, Iraq, Ethiopia, Egypt — every place we have seen poor. Poor is to swell in the wrong places, to seek for scraps from the gutter, to beg. It is not to eat three meals a day sitting at a table in a good blue suit with a clean starched shirt and have a motor-car in the garage."

"Perhaps there is two kinds of poor," Francesco suggested. "The Uncle has perhaps enough for him and The Aunt but not for the three of us."

Gussie made a rude noise.

"He has a closed purse and I dislike him very much and he eats terrible food."

Francesco sighed.

"Cabbage — that is a dreadful vegetable."

Gussie shuddered.

100

"Cooked to taste like dirty water. No garlic, no curry — all food here is as if eating paper. But perhaps, because it is never hot in Britain, I am getting hungry like we were before the earthquake so, however bad the food, I now eat."

Francesco had moved to the window.

"I'm beginning to too and so is Anna. Do you know we have been here five days and never gone into the garden."

Gussie joined him and stared admiringly at the gnomes.

"Those are elegant. I never before saw statues painted red. I wonder what it is for which those little men fish."

"We'll look," said Francesco. "The Uncle is gone."

The boys ran down the stairs and went into the lounge. They had not seen this room before because it was in there that Cecil worked. They were spellbound at the sight of it.

"Velvet like in a palace," Francesco gasped. "Imagine sitting every day on green velvet."

Gussie examined the ivy climbing up the trellis work on the wallpaper.

"And such beautiful paper on the walls. It is good we cannot come in here unless The Uncle is out. It would be terrible if we made a dirty mark on such a wall."

There were French windows through to the garden so the boys stepped out and at once saw what a strange garden it was. Not that they had ever owned a garden themselves but they had seen the gardens of others, so they knew what to expect.

"Nothing is real," Gussie exclaimed. "Feel this rose, it is made of stuff like clothes."

Francesco was stroking a plastic spray of orange-coloured climbing nasturtiums.

"Do you remember that Christopher said there were no gardens in the world so beautiful as the gardens of England? This must be what he meant."

Gussie was for once almost speechless he was so full of admiration.

"Such an ideal! No flower ever dies."

"No earth anywhere at all," Francesco marvelled. "You could be all day in such a garden and be as clean as when you started."

"Hi!" said two voices. The boys spun round, and over the wall they saw two faces looking at them – a boy and a girl. Both had blue eyes and straight fair hair.

"Hi!" they replied.

"We are twins," the boy said. "We're Jonathan and Priscilla Allan."

"We are Francesco and Gussie Docksay."

"We know," said Priscilla. "We read about you in the paper. My father asked your uncle if you could come to tea with us."

"I am sorry, we did not know," Francesco apologized. "The Uncle does not talk much."

"Is he better when you know him?" Priscilla asked. "We think he's horrible."

"That's what I think," said Gussie. "We may not speak at meals unless it is important or uplifting."

Jonathan giggled.

"If we had a rule like that in our house nobody would ever speak at all."

"That is how it is with us," Gussie agreed. "Nobody does speak at all. It is not nice. Before we came here everyone talked mostly all at once."

"Could you come to tea today?" Priscilla asked.

Francesco shook his head.

"Today our sister Anna goes to Miss de Veane to see if she wishes to learn from her, then we go to tell Wally's mum what has happened as she sold our suitcases to pay for her lessons. She always gives us tea when we go there."

"Miss de Veane's all right," said Priscilla. "I go to her on Saturdays. Why did you have to sell your suitcases? Wouldn't your uncle pay for your sister to learn?"

"He thinks to dance is sinful," Francesco explained.

"And I think he does not like to spend money," Gussie added.

"Well, he'll have to spend some soon," said Jonathan. "I suppose you're going to school, aren't you?"

"In the week after this," Francesco agreed.

"Then you'll need uniform," Priscilla told them.

"Grey skirts for us girls and shorts for the boys and purple blazers. You've got the shorts but you'll need blazers."

Francesco and Gussie looked at each other.

"There has been no talk of clothes," said Gussie. "Do all have to wear this?"

"I don't think they can make you," said Priscilla. "But you'll look pretty odd if you don't for everyone does."

"I think this we should tell The Aunt," Francesco told Gussie, Then he remembered his manners. "Thank you for asking us to tea, but we do not know if it is possible. The Uncle does not seem to know people."

"Then come tomorrow," said Priscilla, "and we'll get the gang along, there's lots of us in The Crescent."

Cecil was still out so the boys rushed into the kitchen where Mabel was making a cottage pie for lunch.

"Next door," said Gussie, "there are twins called Jonathan and Priscilla and they say we have to have uniform for the school."

"The grey shorts we have," said Francesco, "but we have to wear something purple, I do not know what."

"And Anna will need a grey skirt."

Mabel left the pie and sank on to a chair.

"Uniform?" she panted. "Yes, all the children here wear it. Grey with purple blazers. Oh dear, I suppose I should speak to your uncle."

Francesco felt sorry for Mabel for she was so obviously scared.

"If there is no money for the uniform I do not think it matters. Priscilla did not think we must wear it only we would look" — he turned to Gussie — "how did she say?"

"Pretty odd," said Gussie, "if we didn't, but we don't mind looking odd if there is no money."

Mabel made several efforts to get her words out.

"It is not that there's no money," she explained at last, "but your uncle feels it should be used for promoting special causes, you know he has special causes? He's very generous to them."

To the boys nothing could matter less than what clothes they wore. Francesco, feeling Mabel was still looking fussed, gave her arm a friendly pat.

"Forget the uniform. It is not nice for The Uncle to have us when he does not want us. It is better we do not aggravate."

Mabel seemed as if from somewhere she was getting courage. There was pink in her cheeks and her voice was stronger than usual.

"Your uncle doesn't know about this so you mustn't say anything, but I have some savings and there is money from the State. It's very wrong of me to have savings without telling him, but there it is — I have them. So leave it to me, by the time school starts you'll all be wearing uniforms."

14. Neighbours

The boys saw Anna coming home and went to the gate to meet her. Her news was not what they wanted to hear. It had been almost like old times to wander where they fancied, talking to whom they fancied without having Anna's dancing lessons or dancing shoes or the ribbon for the shoes to worry about. So when she came home and told them what she had arranged Gussie couldn't control his disgust.

"All that money for just four lessons! Then fifty pence wanted each week!" He slid to the ground and lay flat on his back. "Just thinking of it exhausts me."

Francesco pulled Gussie to his feet.

"Will you never learn? In Britain nobody lies down in the street. And outside the house of The Uncle!' Then he turned to Anna. Where dancing was concerned he trusted her absolutely so if she had said she must have private lessons, private lessons – bad news though it was – it had to be. "We must talk to Wally and his father and mother, they will know how a child earns money in England."

"Could it not be," Anna suggested, "that after

four weeks S'William is home? Then he will sell the picture."

"We will of course write," Francesco agreed, "but we must make plans in case he does not arrive."

That afternoon they went as arranged to what they called Wally's farm. By now they were on patting terms with Bess, the pig, but they were making no headway with the hens and the cock.

"I wish they would like us," Anna said. "When you have few friends even a hen can be a comfort."

Wally's mum heard them coming.

"Come along in, dears. Well, Anna, will Miss de Veane 'ave you?"

The family were sitting round the table on which were the tea things and a cake. There were three empty chairs waiting for the children. Gussie drew one to the table and sat down.

"She would have," he said, "but Anna thinks it better she should have private lessons."

Wally and his mum and dad gazed at Anna as if she were the Loch Ness monster. Each was thinking of what trouble everyone had taken to get the shoes and raise the money for the term's classes, and here was Anna saying she needed private lessons.

"Private lessons!" said Wally's mum. "Won't they be pricey?"

Gussie accepted a slice of cake from Wally's dad. He nodded.

"Fifty new pence for one half hour each Wednesday after school."

"This means," Francesco explained, "we have money enough for five lessons so Gussie and I we must earn this money each week."

Gussie took the cup of tea Wally's mum passed to him.

"In Britain no one has a donkey to load or a camel to lead, nor a store to mind while they sleep."

Wally, Wally's dad and Wally's mum were all shocked that a child of Anna's age should think she needed private dancing lessons at the terrible price of fifty pence for half an hour each week. But they knew the boys were fussing about Anna learning to dance so they spoke cautiously.

"I suppose," Wally's mum suggested, "you couldn't try the Saturday morning class for just one term, could you, Anna?"

Anna turned her big dark eyes to Wally's mum.

"Miss de Veane said things right. Six demi-pliés in each position. But my shoes are new so in the fifth position my shoe slipped so my foot is not turned out right. And at once the Madame said: 'Watch that back foot.' That is how Jardek would speak but not of course in English words. In a big class the Madame cannot watch every foot so it is better one half hour alone, then I work in my bedroom on the other days. Then if faults come she will see at my next lesson."

As far as Wally and his mum and dad were concerned Anna might have been speaking in a foreign language. But evidently Francesco and Gussie understood.

"So you see," Gussie said, "these private lessons is how it must be."

"And they cannot stop after five lessons," Francesco added, "so we must always earn the money."

Gussie turned to Francesco.

"I have an idea. If we could borrow some old very poor clothes we could beg." He held up both hands and whined: "Alms for the love of Allah."

Wally's dad laughed.

"You do that, son, and you'll find the police after you. Nobody can't beg in this country."

"Not real beggin'," Wally's mum explained. "There's some way of getting a licence to sell matches and such like."

"But you wouldn't get a licence," said Wally. "You're too young."

Gussie sighed.

"It is a pity. I have seen many beg so I know how this is done.

To Wally the children were still something out of a fairy tale. So if Anna had to have fifty new pence every week – scandalous waste of money though it seemed to him – she had to have it.

"Don;t worry," he said. "I'll 'ave a word with some of the boys, maybe they'll know of a way."

Wally's dad, during his years as a lorry driver, had known of many methods by which money was made – sometimes by children – which he thought odd if not downright dishonest. These children who had lived such a strange roving life ought to have an eye kept on them, especially young Gussie who was, he thought, less sensible than the other two.

"Tell you what, if Wally can hear of anything you could do decent, like weeding a garden or cleanin' a car or that it's OK, but anythin' out of the ordinary you come to me. We don't want you gettin' into any trouble, do we?'

The journey to London seemed to have given Uncle Cecil time to think, or perhaps at his meeting he had met a stodgy friend who had encouraged him by thinking the same as he did, for that night after supper he said:

"I wish to talk to you three. Come into the lounge."

Even Gussie quailed. Clearly The Uncle had found out they had sold the suitcases and what he would do was past imagining. To add to Gussie's troubles the food that night seemed to them all particularly revolting. A reddish sort of meat with yellow fat served with balls made of what the children thought was a form of blanket. There was also cabbage. Gussie, after a few mouthfuls, had leant towards Mabel.

"Always I am eating," he whispered to Mabel, "what I do not like, but this is impossible."

Mabel, gasping and puffing, had whispered back:

"It's boiled silverside and dumplings, dear. It is a great favourite of your uncle's."

Gussie, who believed he would be poisoned if he ate what was on his plate, turned thankfully to his uncle and pushed his plate towards him.

"You like it. You have it. For me, if it is possible, I would like bread and butter and olives."

From the way the uncle and aunt stared at Gussie he might have asked him for some extravagant dainty instead of for the simplest food of which he knew.

At last, after a terrible pause, Uncle Cecil said in a voice like the inside of a refrigerator:

"Take away his plate, Mabel. Augustus will eat nothing tonight."

So it was with their hearts in their mouths that the three children followed Uncle Cecil into the lounge and sat down facing him on the sofa. Anna, scared though she was, had to smile when she felt the sofa.

"At what are you smiling, Anna?" her uncle demanded.

Anna stopped smiling.

"It is this so beautiful sofa," she whispered. "I do not think I have sat on velvet before."

Uncle Cecil did not seem interested.

"I shall pass over your ill-behaviour, Augustus, in

not eating your dinner," he said. "Your punishment is that you will go to bed hungry. What I wish to talk to you about is my neighbours. When we first settled here we decided, your aunt and I, to keep ourselves to ourselves. We had no wish to waste time on idle gossip. So the same rule will apply to you. You will meet the local children at school but your friendship will finish there. You will not go inside their homes and of course you will never invite any of them here."

Francesco thought of Jonathan and Priscilla.

"There are twins who live the other side of the wall. They were asking us to tea."

"You will say no," said Uncle Cecil.

Gussie felt, as he was in disgrace already, a little more wouldn't hurt.

"Why can't we go to tea?"

Uncle Cecil looked at Gussie and that he disliked him showed.

"Because your English is atrocious. When the term starts with school and homework plus a lesson in English from me, when I am free, your days will be full. I do not want you wasting your time and injuring your eyesight staring at television and chattering with the neighbourhood children."

The children has never seen television. There was a set at Wally's farm but it was never turned on when they were there so it meant nothing to them. But they had always talked to everybody they met as best they could in their mixed languages, so they were incapable of believing their uncle meant what he said or, if he did, that it would really happen. People always talked to each other. What really mattered in this conversation was the awful news that Uncle Cecil intended to teach them English. That was terrifying. And when? Would it interfere with Anna's dancing lessons? However, nothing could be done that night so Francesco got up. He bowed to his uncle.

"Thank you for telling us," he said politely.

Gussie gave less of a bow and spoke in rather a growly voice.

"Thank you."

Anna gave her little bob curtsey.

"Thank you, Uncle Cecil. Good night."

But outside the lounge when the door was shut Gussie made a rude face at it.

"And I shan't go hungry to bed. The Aunt will see I eat."

And Gussie was quite right. There was a splendid cheese sandwich under his pillow.

15. What the Uncle Thinks

The next morning after breakfast Francesco followed Aunt Mabel into her kitchen. Each time he saw the kitchen he was filled with fresh admiration. There had not really been a kitchen in the caravan for the stove on which the food was cooked was usually put outside. In Jardek and Babka's little house the kitchen had been a very small sort of outhouse. He gave a great satisfied sigh.

"This room is beautiful," he told Mabel. "Almost too good for using."

Mabel in bed the night before had worried about the children's food. It was true they were eating better but she could see they seldom liked what she cooked.

"What sort of food did you eat when . . . well, I mean, before the earthquake?" she puffed.

Francesco tried to remember.

"Nothing had a name, there was much stews and rice and all is tasting very good with garlic, and often there is a curry so hot it makes tears in the eyes and . . ."

Mabel gasped as if she was tasting the curry.

114

"I'm afraid your uncle wouldn't like that sort of food at all."

"If perhaps some food might be left on the plate," Francesco suggested. "That is a terrible thing that cabbage."

"Next time your uncle goes to London," Mabel whispered, "we will have mushrooms. You'll like those."

Francesco remembered why he was there.

"The Uncle says we may not talk to the children who live next door but they were asking us to tea. Since we may not speak have you perhaps a piece of paper and an envelope so we may write to explain why?"

Aunt Mabel, who had been washing up, stopped and went to sit in a chair. She pointed to the door.

"Shut that please." Francesco shut the door and Aunt Mabel pointed to another chair. "Sit down, there, dear. I want to try and make you understand something." Francesco sat and Aunt Mabel, very puffily, went on. "Your uncle is a good man but he does not like children, so it's hard for him that you are here, but he does his duty – he gives you a home."

"We did not ask to come," Francesco reminded her.

"I know," Aunt Mabel agreed, "and I am very glad you are here. But for your uncle it is different. You see, though he was working when your father went away and he was told by your grandfather that he was . . ." she broke off unable to finish.

115

Francesco was totally unembarrassed, so often he had heard his father roaring with laughter describing his escape from England so that he could paint. He tried to put his aunt at ease.

"Christopher's father said he stole but all he took was enough to sell to take him to Paris where he must paint. Some day he knew he would have money and when that day came, of his share he must lose what he had taken. This is not to steal, it is to borrow, that is all."

Aunt Mabel nodded.

"Yes, dear, but your uncle does not see it like that. He was brought up to believe his brother was a thief. So now he feels it is necessary to take special care of you three so nothing bad can influence you. That is really why you may not know the local children, you see you might watch something unsuitable on television. You know, Westerns and things like that."

Francesco had no idea what a Western was, but what his aunt had said had set up a little worry in his mind. If just borrowing enough things to sell to pay your fare to Paris was something that in Britain made you a thief, perhaps special care should be taken of Gussie who was in so many ways so like Christopher. Care too should perhaps be taken of Anna who, if money was needed for dancing lessons, might take anything. But those were not thoughts with which to trouble The Aunt.

"I understand and I will make the others

understand. Now perhaps I could have the paper and the envelope?"

Aunt Mabel opened a drawer in the dresser and showed him notepaper and envelopes. Then she picked up a little box.

"And if you should ever want to write a letter that needs stamps, I keep them in here."

The letter was the work of all three children. They wrote it lying on the floor in Anna's bedroom. Francesco did the writing prompted by Gussie and Anna, all remembering carefully Olga's lessons on letter writing and how the difficult words should be spelt.

"My dear Twins" – they had to put that for they had no idea how to spell Jonathan and Priscilla – "we send you greetings. We regret we cannot accept your kind invitation for The Uncle wishes us to study for we speak English very bad but we shall meet you at school with sincere felicitations. Francesco. Gussie. Anna."

The next question was how the letter should be delivered.

"I think we should fix it to a stone and throw it over the wall," Gussie suggested.

"That cannot be," Francesco pointed out. "The Uncle sits in the lounge and he will see. No, one of us must go to the house and knock."

"To knock we need not," said Anna. "In Britain all houses have a slit in the door for letters, and like here there is always a bell."

In the end it was decided Anna should take the letter.

"But do not ring the bell," Francesco told her. "Go soft as a little cat to the house and just put it through the slit in the door."

Anna, though secretly scared in case The Uncle saw her, carried out her mission successfully and the envelope lay safely on the next door house's mat.

That afternoon was Anna's first dancing lesson. Francesco and Gussie took her to the studio for Wally's mum thought she should not walk about on her own. At the studio door, Francesco gave Anna the fifty pence for her lesson.

"Try and make her write down you have paid in case she asks twice," he said, "for fifty pence is a lot of money."

Miss de Veane was alone when Anna arrived. Anna gave her little bob and handed over the fifty pence piece.

"Here is the money, Madame."

Audrey de Veane gazed down at Anna and felt a curious sensation, it was a feeling of tenderness, which she did not recognize for it was so many years since she had felt it. She had looked not unlike this little girl once. But hard times and the need to work had soon knocked sense into her. Then she had married and come to live in Fyton where she had thought to live as an ordinary housewife for the rest of her days. It was not to be,

118

her husband had died leaving her a house but very little money, so she had earned what she needed in the only way she knew – teaching dancing. Even in Fyton she supposed there might be somebody worth teaching. But there never had been. What she had taught was a long line of Doreens all giggles and curls without as much talent as would fill a salt-spoon. Then out of the blue had come this child. Was it possible? Then she gave herself a mental shake. She must be getting soppy in her old age, she told herself.

"Thank you, Anna," she said putting away the fifty pence piece. "Not put on your shoes while I write out the receipt." By now, through gossip and the papers, she knew who Anna was. "Whom do I make it out to? Your uncle?"

Anna, bent over her shoes, kept her head.

"No. Mr Francesco Docksay."

Outside the boys waited, leaning against the wall.

"One lesson gone," said Francesco, "and only four left and still it is we do not know how it is we may earn fifty pence each week."

"Perhaps," Gussie suggested, "Anna is not liking Miss de Veane. Then we must wait until S'William comes home and can sell the picture and tell us where it is Anna should learn."

Francesco looked sadly down the road.

"If only in Fyton there was donkeys and camels to be watched or messages to run. But here there is nothing, all is ordered and arranged."

Gussie slid to the ground and stretched out flat on the pavement.

"All is too honest here, you cannot bargain in the shops, so how can you make a little money on the side?"

Francesco caught hold of Gussie by his jersey.

"Get up. Each day I am telling you on the streets in Britain, you cannot lie."

Gussie sat up.

"Why not? Why should I stand for half an house? I was in nobody's way."

Francesco pulled Gussie to his feet.

"I do not know why but I do know care should be taken. Today I am talking to The Aunt and she is saying The Uncle is believing Christopher was a thief."

Gussie turned pink with rage.

"He was not. He only borrowed a few things to take him to Paris so he could paint. Some day money would be his and then what he had borrowed would be returned. This is not to steal."

"Not to us or to Christopher," Francesco agreed. "But to The Uncle – yes. So he was told by his father and so he believes."

"But what has this to do with resting in a road?" Gussie asked.

Francesco tried to explain.

"Because of The Uncle. As he thinks Christopher was a thief, then to him it could seem there is bad in us too which must be watched, so always we must try to do well. This is why we may not know other children. They could show us something which is a Western where we could learn to do wrong."

Gussie was much quicker than Francesco when it came to picking up odds and ends of information.

"That is a box called The Telly which is in Wally's farm. I think it is like a small movie. The harm is because when such a picture is showing called a Western Wally will not go to bed."

Francesco, as so often when talking to Gussie, felt what he was trying to say slip away from him.

"But you do see, Gussie, if that is how The Uncle feels we must try very hard not to offend. We need to be much more careful than when . . ." he broke off, while both boys in their minds watched Togo pull their caravan along roads covered in dust while Christopher sang songs which made Olga say: "No, Christopher. Not in front of the children."

"Than when," Francesco said at last, "we had our caravan."

Inside the studio Anna was happy in a way she had not been since the earthquake. Dancing terms seemed to be the same in all languages and so was the correct positioning of the body, arms and feet. Only over one point did she and Miss de Veane differ. It was after Anna had performed a small enchaînement in the centre of the studio.

"When those shoes wear out," Miss de Veane said, "I will start you off on pointe work."

When she had said this to her other pupils there was tremendous rejoicing. For to dance on their pointes was every girl's ambition. Anna was not pleased at all – in fact she was shocked.

"That cannot be," she told Miss de Veane. "Jardek was saying I would have my first shoes with the blocked toes when I was eleven. Now I am eight."

Miss de Veane, who, during the class, had seen in her mind's eye Anna at her next public show dancing "The Dying Swan" swallowed what she would like to have said. This was an unusual child and needed handling carefully. She collected herself inside her black dress.

"Oh well," she said to herself, "two years will soon pass."

Anna was only eight but she was sensitive and there was something in Miss de Veane's hoarse statement she did not like. So when at the end of her class she joined the boys at the door and Gussie asked how the lesson had gone she said doubtfully:

"It was good. Very good. But I do not know yet if Miss de Veane is such a teacher as Jardek would wish."

16. Uniforms

The children thought the school uniforms very elegant. The boys had purple blazers with the school crest on the pocket, grey socks with purple turnovers, grey shirts and purple ties and a purple school cap. Anna wore the same except she wore a grey pleated skirt and instead of a cap, since it was the autumn term, a grey felt hat with a purple ribbon round it.

Aunt Mabel had been clever. She was determined their three children should be as well turned out as all the other children, but if she bought all they needed it would use up her entire savings so she had to get Uncle Cecil to pay part of the money. Asking Cecil for money always threw her into a state so she was huffing and puffing worse than usual when she came into the lounge to speak to him.

"Ce – Ce – Cecil," she gasped. "The children start school next week and they need uniforms."

Mabel had chosen a bad moment for Cecil was in the middle of adding a column of figures. He carefully wrote down a figure and marked where he had got to, then he put down his pen and glared at Mabel.

"The children seem adequately dressed to me. Why should they have uniforms? They can attend school in what they have."

Mabel knew it was a waste of time to say "all the other children in The Crescent wear uniform, we don't want our three to look different". Such an argument would carry no weight at all with Cecil so she had planned another.

"The boys have only cotton shirts and Anna cotton dresses. They have jerseys but since they are used to hot climates, for the autumn they should have thick coats or they will catch cold – even pneumonia."

Mabel had chosen a good argument. Cecil hated illness, and he certainly did not want talk in the neighbourhood. He opened a drawer and took out his cheque book.

"How much will overcoats cost?"

Mabel had worked out how much she needed.

"The coats should be big so they will last and they will need thick shoes. I couldn't do with less than fifty pounds."

Cecil looked as if he might have a fit.

"Fifty pounds! It's a fortune. My dear mother did not spend that much on my clothes in a year."

Mabel nodded.

"I know, dear. But fifty pounds today goes nowhere."

The children, when Mabel took them to the

shops where the uniforms were sold, took their uncle's point of view.

"Why," Gussie demanded, "do we need all these clothes? We have our jerseys when like today it is cold."

"This is not what we call cold, dear," Mabel explained. "But later in the autumn and when winter comes it can be very cold and very damp and you are not used to it."

Anna suddenly remembered real cold.

"After the earthquake the cold was terrible. Even in a rug my teeth is rattling."

The assistant who was fitting out the boys pricked up her ears. These must be the children of the artist who was killed in the earthquake. The manager should know they were here. It was the clear the children's had not unlimited money, perhaps under such circumstances help and advice would be forthcoming, even a slight reduction.

The assistant was quite right. The manager too had read all about the Docksay children. Glowing with good feeling, he arrived at Mabel's elbow.

"Ah, Mrs Docksay, I heard you were here, and these are the three little people who escaped. Now, let me see how I can help you."

The manager did help. He seemed to know exactly how much children would grow before next summer. He knew of an exchange scheme in the school which meant outgrown uniforms could be sold. He was wonderful about overcoats, sending the assistant downstairs to bring up what he called "my special stock".

While all this was going on the children stood patiently having different garments fitted on to them. Never, even during S'William's wild outburst of extravagance in Istanbul, had they known such spending. Before the earthquake Olga would sometimes tell Christopher she must visit a bazaar because clothes were needed. But that had never meant more than a frock for Anna or some shirts or shorts for the boys. Once or twice on some celebration day Christopher would take Olga to a shop and a meal afterwards and Olga would come home giggling and wearing something very exotic, but serious top to bottom shopping they had never known. Now amazed, but stunned into patience, they found themselves with new warm underwear, school uniforms, overcoats, mackintoshes, shoes, rubber boots, new pyjamas and each a splendid dressing-gown.

"It is too much," Francesco whispered to the other two.

"Such money would pay for the most beautiful dancing classes," Anna moaned.

Gussie said nothing for he was studying the situation. In his opinion where there was so much apparently to be had without trouble there should be pickings for those who were buying. Such an arrangement was usual when much money was spent.

When all the shopping was over the manager said:

"I am sure these little people are tired. May I offer you all tea?" Then he smiled at the children and added: "With perhaps ice creams."

The invitation accepted, Gussie hung back and, when no one was looking, took a scarf, two pairs of woollen gloves and a tie out of his pockets and laid them on the counter.

"That is the worst of Britain," he thought, "all behave too well so it is not possible to take more. It is better in Eastern countries."

Then he hurried after the others.

But Francesco had noticed Gussie was not with them. So when he caught up he whispered anxiously:

"You didn't take anything, did you?"

Gussie's face expressed shock amazement.

"Me! Take a squeeze when the man offers ices! Such an idea!"

17. School

Before school started Wally's dad had a talk with Wally. They were down by Bess's sty. Wally was cleaning out.

"When I was in that smash with me lorry," Wally's Dad said, "I couldn't bring meself to talk about it, not for months I couldn't, even the insurance could only get what 'appened out of me slow like. I reckon the three Docksay kids is like that. It's not 'alf goin' to upset them if the children at the school asks too many questions."

Wally leant on his rake which he was using to clean the sty.

"I know, but what can I do about it? Maybe Francesco and me might be in the same class but the other two won't so I can't see what's 'appenin' to them."

Wally's dad wheeled his chair closer to the sty, as if he was afraid someone would hear what he said though there was only Bess there.

"I was thinkin' you might 'ave a word with the 'ead."

Wally nearly fell into the pig sty,

"The 'ead! Why, I never spoken to 'im and I

'ope I never will."

His dad went on calmly as if Wally had not spoken.

"I was goin' to see if your mum would go, but you know how she is, like enough just seein' the 'ead and she'll talk about you."

Wally did see. Too well he knew that his mum believed he was not properly appreciated in the school. Not promising anything, he asked:

"If I was to see the 'ead what would I say like?"

In the evenings Wally's dad sometimes went down to a pub called The George and Dragon for a pint. There the publican had a boy of Wally's age who was clever, and often the publican talked to Wally's dad about the headmaster and what an understanding man he was.

"You can do it all right, son. Just tell 'im what a state the kids get in when they remember what 'appened, 'e'll understand all right."

Wally had no idea how you saw a headmaster, but the next day he got on his bike and went to the school. He knew the headmaster would not be there, but the school keeper would and might know where he lived.

The school keeper was loading some coke into the boiler room to be ready for when central heating started. He knew Wally by sight.

"'Ullo!" he said. "Not like you to come to school when you don't 'ave to."

"It's a message I got for the 'eadmaster," Wally

explained. "D'you know where 'e 'angs out?"

"You're in luck," said the school keeper, "he's inside seeing some new bookshelves what has come for the library."

The headmaster was equally surprised to see Wally.

"Hullo! Wally Wall, isn't it? What can I do for you?"

Wally swallowed twice then burst without pause into his story.

"It's these Docksay kids what's coming next term. Me dad says you did oughter know what a state they gets in if anyone asks them questions. When we first sees them it was shockin' the way they cries, you see, they 'aven't nobody left not except an uncle an' an aunt, who does right by them but they don't get on like an' . . ."

The headmaster was a tall man. Now he laid a hand on Wally's shoulder.

"Not so fast. Let's sit down and talk this over. I think your father was quite right to tell you to see me. But what we have to think about is how best to do what needs to be done."

As a result of Wally's talk it was arranged that as soon as the children arrived for their first day at school he should take them for a guided tour round the school and the playing field. Meanwhile the headmaster would talk to the rest of the school and tell the children that the Docksay children were not to be questioned. That some day they would talk about what had happened but until then they were to be left alone.

"You try to imagine," he told the school, "what it would be like to go for a walk and come home to find your father, your mother, your brothers and sisters — all your pets and your house had just disappeared. One or two of the teachers know because it could happen in the last war, but if it did, even now all these years later, it's not a thing we talk about. So you treat Francesco, Augustus and Anna just as if nothing had happened to them. I know it's hard, for we'd all like to know what it's like to be in an earthquake, but we must wait and perhaps some day they will tell us. Hands up those who understand." Every hand in the room shot up.

Francesco, Gussie and Anna liked school. It was, they found, easier than doing lessons with Olga for each worked in a separate class, whereas Olga had to try and teach all three at once though none of them was studying at the same level. The children had taken for granted Olga had taught then well, but really it was surprising for Olga's English was bad and, though she had been well educated in Turkey, she was not trained as a teacher, yet the children passed the little tests given them with, on the whole, flying colours.

The headmaster told them the results.

"You have done well, especially in arithmetic, reading and geography."

"Arithmetic we must know," Gussie explained.

"When every two, three weeks it is another country and another money you must learn to add in all."

"Geography is I think easier when always you are travelling," Francesco pointed out. "But it is the Near and the Far East which is good, where a country is cold we never work."

Anna saw the caravan in her memory with Olga in her broken English reading to them from *Alice in Wonderland* or *The Wind in the Willows*.

"Because we must read Christopher buys a big box of books called *Children's Classics*. I do not remember when we could not read."

The headmaster heard a tremble in Anna's voice so he gave them all a big smile.

"But nobody taught you how to speak English." Francesco nodded.

"Everyone said our English was bad. Christopher said it was terrible."

"So did S'William," Gussie put in, "and so does The Uncle. He is going to give us lessons and this we do not like."

"Well, I must say you can do with some lessons," the headmaster said. "Now I'll tell you what I'm going to do. I'm going to put you this term to work with people of your own ages, then later on we'll see."

The children liked school, not always the actual lesson times but the play times were fun. They soon got to know all the children in The Crescent and

Francesco made friends with Jonathan and Priscilla who were in his class. But though Gussie in particular was always asking questions, neither he nor Francesco could find out how to earn fifty pence a week. They were in a junior school where the children were too young to be allowed to work. Older children, they discovered, could earn such money easily on paper rounds or helping in a shop on Saturday mornings, but for children of their age working was not permitted.

"Don't you get pocket money?" Priscilla asked Francesco. "All children do."

"How is pocket money?" Francesco asked.

All the children in the school were trying to improve Francesco's English.

"Not 'how is?' " Jonathan said. "It's 'what is?' Anyway it's money you are given every week to spend."

Francesco was thrilled.

"Who gives such money?"

Priscilla could hear the sentence was wrong but she did not know how.

"Our father gives ours, I suppose your uncle would give yours."

Francesco knew the answer to that.

"He would not. The Aunt perhaps if she could, but I do not think she has much."

However, he passed on the news to Gussie in case he had any ideas.

"Now that we have the English lessons on

Tuesdays and Thursdays could we perhaps talk about pocket money?"

The Uncle's English lessons were always conversations. He would pick out one of the children and say: "Describe what you did this morning" or "Describe what you do at recreation". Francesco always tried hard to answer correctly. Gussie wouldn't try at all and Anna was so scared of making a mistake she only spoke in a whisper. To do Uncle Cecil justice he was very patient, he merely corrected, never scolded, but there was that about his patience that made Gussie describe it as "too full a cupboard out of which any minute all would fall".

Now Gussie thought over what Francesco had said.

"It is true all but we have pocket money. Each week they give a new penny to buy a lifeboat or for a dog to lead a person who is blind. Us they do not ask because they know we have nothing."

"Some pay for school meals," said Anna. "For this they have much money to pay, in one week more I think than the whole dancing class."

Gussie gave Anna a dirty look.

"If you think I am going to starve for your lessons you are wrong."

"Nor will The Uncle pay for the school dinners," Francesco pointed out. "He says sandwiches is better. And I think so too, it is terrible what they had yesterday, that thing called a cottage pie and prunes covered in custard."

"Always the sandwiches are not good,"
Francesco agreed, "but often they are and The
Aunt cuts pages out of papers to find new things to
put in them which taste good to eat."

"We must try the pocket money," Gussie said.
"Today is the lesson, let us agree the first one he
asks a question of talks of pocket money."

"Oh no," Anna pleaded, "not if it's me. I will do
it wrong."

Gussie looked at Francesco.

"So she would. The first of us two. It is agreed."

"I suppose so," Francesco said gloomily.

That evening when the children came into the
lounge and sat on the sofa it so happened The
Uncle started with Gussie.

"Describe to me, Augustus, your school library."

"It is a room by itself and each day two boys
is . . ."

"Are," said The Uncle.

"Two boys are looking after it. We go at the
dinner break and change a book."

"The books are free?" The Uncle asked. This
was of course Gussie's chance.

"Yes, otherwise all in the school . . ."

"Everyone in the school," The Uncle corrected.

"Would get books except us, we would have no
books because we have no pocket money."

Uncle Cecil was silent for a moment. The truth
was he had forgotten pocket money. But when he

had been a boy there had been some. A penny for church on Sunday. Three pennies towards school charities and two pennies for himself. Christopher, when he was old enough for school, had only pretended to put a penny in the bag on Sundays and had never given a farthing to school charities, but had secretly spent his whole sixpence on painting materials. Uncle Cecil turned to Francesco.

"If you had pocket money, Francesco, on what would you spend it?"

Francesco told the other two afterwards he so longed to say "on dancing lessons for Anna" that he nearly did. Then, just in time, he stopped himself. Trying desperately to speak good English so as not to offend he said:

"As the other children do. There is – I mean are – many school charities to which all give. This week I think we will buy a lifeboat."

Uncle Cecil of course understood that money today would not go as far as it had when he was at school, so, feeling very generous, he decided to double what he had received.

"Every week," he said in a grand voice, "each of you will receive five pence."

18. Francesco's Turn

Of course the children could not use their pocket money either for school charities or for themselves. Every penny would be needed for Anna's dancing classes, and obviously fifteen pence a week would not be a great help. All the same, it still left a lot to be found and not one word from S'William. Not knowing that Sir William was capable of leaving an unposted letter in his pocket for six weeks the children worried, for of course they knew how easy it was to be well and happy in the morning and to have vanished for ever by the evening.

One night in bed Francesco said to Gussie:

"No one has said something has happened in Alaska. I asked Wally to ask his dad, for he reads two papers but he says there has been nothing in the news."

There was now only one week's money left to pay for Anna's classes. Gussie found it hard never to have sweets when others did.

"I was thinking that our five pence should be saved for a week when we have earned nothing. Then some weeks we might not need it."

Francesco sat up in bed.

"I do not know yet of a week when we can earn anything. Not unless Wally hears of something. He is trying hard."

"What I think," said Gussie, "is that we should take turns – you the first week, me the second. Then it could be sometimes we have our pocket money to ourselves. Not perhaps Anna as she is causing us to work but you and me."

Francesco was suspicious.

"Have you a plan?"

Gussie sounded cautious.

"No. But – I have ideas."

Francesco leant over towards Gussie's bed.

"Do tell me before you do anything. There is not the same rules in Britain as there was in the places we knew. Then to beg was honourable and to take a squeeze from the shopping correct, but here it is not so."

Gussie smiled in the darkness.

"Do you think I don't know! You get the fifty pence your way and I will find a way to get mine."

Francesco found it hard to sleep that night. If only he knew what Gussie was planning. But since they had been going to school Gussie had gone his own way and made his own friends and Francesco was not sure they were good friends for him. Wally had put this idea into his head.

"Young Gus has picked up with The Gang."

Francesco's English was improving rapidly. So he

swallowed back "how is a gang?" and instead asked what it was.

"It's them from the new block of flats. They're what's called re'oused from farther off an' by what's said they're a rough lot. You know, breaking public telephones and that for fun."

"Why is that fun?" Francesco had asked.

Wally couldn't explain exactly.

"Just for somethin' to do, I reckon, but young Gus did ought to watch out, for the coppers 'ave their eyes on a lot like that."

Now, tossing in bed, Francesco thought of what Gussie had said. "You get fifty pence your way and I'll find a way to get mine." But what would be Gussie's way? Oh dear, if only S'William were back. Then he had an idea and it was this which sent him to sleep. Tomorrow he would write to S'William so at least he would get a letter the moment he returned to England.

The one person who never appeared to worry at all where fifty pence was coming from was Anna. It was true that she spent most of her free time thinking about her dancing, and working at exercises in her bedroom, but the truth was that she had a secret worry of her own as well. She was almost sure that Miss de Veane, though she had not said so, was planning that she dance in her public performance at Christmas. After a lesson she would say:

"Before you go, Anna, do this enchaînement for

me. Wait, I will put some music on the gramophone."

And then Anna was given a series of steps which she could guess was part of a dance. It was lovely to do and made her feel much more that she was really dancing than exercises did, but she knew it was wrong. Jardek would never have allowed it. But what was she to do if Miss de Veane ordered her to dance? She had learnt a lot since she came to Fyton, and one of the things she had learnt was that until S'William returned and the picture could be sold she must learn from Miss de Veane, for she was the only teacher there was. There would be other teachers in London but London was many miles away and she had no means of getting there.

It was natural now for Anna to go to Francesco when she had a problem, so she went to him about her dancing lessons. He should know what she most feared. In the last two weeks only Francesco had taken Anna to her class. Gussie, on the days when they did not learn English with Uncle Cecil, had taken to slipping off after school with his friends. This Wednesday, on the way home from her dancing class, Anna said to Francesco:

"That was the last of our money. Will you have another fifty pence for next week?"

Francesco had no idea where his fifty pence was coming from but he did not want to worry Anna.

"It will be ready for next Wednesday."

Anna tried to explain what was troubling her.

"I think perhaps if Miss de Veane knew we have no money she would teach me for nothing."

Francesco could have jumped like a kangaroo. For nothing! No more worrying where fifty pence was coming from! However, he spoke cautiously for there was no knowing what Anna felt.

"Why should she?"

Anna looked up at him and her eyes were full of anxiety.

"I think perhaps Jardek taught better even than we knew. At Christmas Miss de Veane gives a great performance in a concert hall, it is for some charity. At such a concert all she has taught, dance — girls like Doreen. I think she would wish me to dance so all would think it was not Jardek who had taught me but that she had. So more pupils come."

Francesco was shocked.

"But you are only eight. Jardek would never permit this."

"I am nearly nine," Anna reminded him. "And Jardek is no longer here."

This was so miserable a thought that they walked in silence for a moment, almost on tiptoe so that what little they still had of Jardek would not be disturbed. Then Francesco asked:

"Has she said she wishes you to dance?"

Anna shook her head.

"No. But I feel she is planning. If once she knew it was hard to find the money I think she would offer lessons, but in return I must do in all things as she says."

Francesco was no stranger to such arrangements. Often when they had travelled by caravan they had met children who, in exchange for a bed, clothes and food were somebody's little slave. Sometimes it had worked well but often it had not. The thought of selling Anna into such a life appalled him.

"Miss de Veane must never, never know it is hard to find the money. You must let her think if each lesson is costing a whole pound we do not care. There is always plenty of money."

Anna took Francesco's hand and rubbed her face against his sleeve.

"When you talk so it is as if Olga is back."

She could not have said anything nicer.

But still Francesco had not got fifty pence, not if he used all their pocket money, and the next class was one week away.

19. Saturday at Wally's

What with the days growing shorter and school taking up much time, and Uncle Cecil's English lessons, the children were seeing very little of Wally's family. They did of course see Wally at school but only Francesco saw him to talk to because they were in the same class. There was never a chance that they would walk to school together because Wally rode there on his bicycle, whereas the children got there by walking up The Crescent.

"I don't like it," Wally's mum would grumble. "They was sent to us like and I'd be much happier in meself if I could keep an eye on them like."

Wally's dad agreed with her for he knew he would be much happier too, but it was hard to figure a way of seeing the children. Then that very Saturday morning, when Wally was looking after the stall, his mum had a piece of luck. She was in the supermarket, her trolley piled high with the week's shopping. At the place where you pay there was a woman stacking her shopping on the counter.

"Nice weather for the time of year," the assistant said to her.

The woman, sorting out what she had bought, seemed overcome by this casual remark. She puffed and gasped and dropped a packet of breakfast cereal and half a pound of tea on to the floor. Wally's mum stopped to help her pick the packets up and as she did so something about the woman struck her. What was it the children had said? "The Aunt seems only held together by her apron." Well, she hadn't an apron on now but she did look as if she was held together by her coat buttons. The children has also said she had hair which always looked as if it might tumble down. Well, certainly this woman had hair like it was straggling out from under her shapeless felt hat. Then Gussie had said The Aunt was like a mouse – afraid to move unless a cat was coming. "Poor lady," Wally's mum thought, "if ever anyone looked scared of a cat, she does."

The woman panted out a weak "thank you" and went back to sorting out her shopping, and it was then Wally's mum decided to take a chance. "Seemed like me duty really," she told Wally's dad when she got home.

"S'cuse me," she said, "but would you be Mrs Docksay?"

The assistant and Wally's mum put out hands to make sure Aunt Mabel did not drop anything more on to the floor. Then Aunt Mabel squeaked:

"Yes."

"Perhaps then you'd 'ave a cuppa tea with me,"

said Wally's Mum. "You see, I know the children, in fact your Francesco is in a class with my Wally at the school and they're pals like."

Presently in a nearby tea shop Wally's mum and Mabel were drinking tea.

"I know 'ow you're placed, dear," Wally's mum said. "Your 'ole man's not the only one that likes to keep 'imself to 'imself but the children won't come to any 'arm along of us. I was thinkin' it would be nice if you could let them come along of a Saturday afternoon, maybe Sundays too."

With a tremendous effort Mabel managed to explain Cecil's outlook.

"You see, he was brought up to think the children's father took what did not belong to him: of course he didn't really, he only borrowed, at least that's what he thought, but you know how it is, what you are told as a fact sticks. Anyway, he won't let our children mix with other children in case they should be a bad influence. He doesn't want them to see television."

Wally's mum laughed.

"What I always say is what the eye doesn't see the 'eart doesn't grieve after. 'Course the telly's on in our 'ouse on a Saturday – catch my ole man missing 'is football – but what's the 'arm in a game of football? Nor Wally wouldn't miss it either come to that."

Mabel had brightened up but she still spoke in jerks.

"I'm sure football would be all right. As a matter of fact, I have worried rather about Saturdays and Sundays now the days are drawing. You see, Mr Docksay likes the house quiet but it's difficult for the children to be quiet when they've nothing much to do and nowhere to go."

Wally's mum decided to get the matter fixed. She got up.

"Well, I got to go but I'll expect the children later. Can they stop to tea?"

Mabel picked her shopping bag up off the floor.

"Well, they must be home by half past five at the latest or my husband might notice they were out." She flushed. "You see, I shall let him think they're having tea in the kitchen."

The children were charmed when before lunch their aunt told them they could visit Mrs Wall.

"Such a nice woman," she said, "but you must slip out quietly and be back sharp at five-thirty."

"They've got a farm," Anna told her. "Hens and a pig called Bessie. It's lovely, they're not too tidy and everyone is pleased you are there, almost like . . ." She broke off.

Francesco helped Anna out.

"She's right. In a sort British way it is perhaps a little like it was at Jardek and Babka's."

When Wally's mum saw the children she held out her arms and gave them one gigantic hug.

"I 'ope you 'ad a word with the 'ens and Bess on the way up. You won't get out again for the

146

football's started and Mr Wall thinks, like 'e does most weeks, 'e's goin' to win the pools." She looked questioningly at Anna. "You keen on the football, dearie?"

"We've none of us seen it except when we play at school," Gussie explained.

"You go and look too, dear," Wally's mum told Anna, "but if you don't fancy it, which I don't meself, you come in the kitchen and we'll trim up the cake what I've made for tea."

Anna watched the TV for a little while but she did not understand football, nor Wally and his dad's explanations, which the boys seemed to find absorbing, so she slipped away to the kitchen.

"And I bet not one of 'em knew you'd gone," said Mrs Wall.

"No, none of them."

Mrs Wall gave Anna some cherries and nuts and told her to trim the cake.

"Well," she asked, "how's the dancin' goin'?"

Anna trusted Wally's mum.

"Sort of well. I mean Miss de Veane teaches well, I think, almost as if it is Jardek, but I do not know how she is thinking."

"How do you mean, dear?"

Anna made a pattern of nuts and cherries.

"At Christmas she is giving a show . . ."

"Oh, you mean her concert. Does one every year for a charity. That Doreen dances a special piece on her own, so I 'ear."

Anna sounded determined.

"Jardek would never allow this. I do not know but I think Miss de Veane wishes me to dance on the pointes."

Anna sounded so appalled that Wally's mum tried to feel shocked too. Only she had no idea what Anna was talking about.

"Oh, my word!"

"Imagine! And I am not yet nine and Jardek said not until I was eleven."

"But unless I got thin's wrong you can't learn with this Miss de Veane much longer. You only 'ad the money for five lessons, didn't you?"

Anna gazed at Wally's mum with horror-struck eyes.

"But I must learn with her, that is until S'William is back and we can sell our picture. You see, in this place there is no one else."

"But isn't it fifty pence a week, dear? Where's that coming from?"

Over Anna's face there seemed to fall a curtain. Wally's mum could not know that Anna was hearing Jardek say in Polish and broken English: "A dancer must live for nothing but dancing. Anything that comes between a dancer and dancing must be absolutely forgotten." So she must not think where fifty pence was coming from: it would appear. She put a final cherry on the cake. Her voice was calm and confident.

"This week Francesco pays. Next week it will be Gussie."

The football had been a great success. In fact Wally, his dad and the boys could not leave it, so they had their tea sitting round the box.

"I don't want to rush anybody," Wally's mum said, "but I did promise your auntie you'd be home by five-thirty sharp."

Looking at the boys' faces as she brought round the food Wally's mum decided Francesco did not look as well as she would like, he had those same dark smudges under his eyes all three children had had when they arrived. And he didn't eat nearly as well as Gussie, who wolfed three sandwiches with pickled onions before he started on the cake.

After tea when the children had left and Wally and she had gone out to shut up the hens, Wally's mum said:

"I don't think young Francesco's lookin' good. No trouble at the school, is there?"

Wally shoved the last of the hens into the run.

"No, not there, 'e does well at school. I think it's money, 'e's always on at me to find a way 'e can earn."

"And 'ave you 'elped 'im?"

"I don't see a way," Wally confessed. "You see, 'e's only ten. And there's no gardenin' this late in the year."

Mrs Wall fastened the door of the chicken run.

"Tell you what, when the kids come along

tomorrow get out of 'im what 'is trouble is. Shouldn't wonder if it's Anna's dancin' lesson. But whatever it is let 'im talk it over with you. For troubles shared is troubles 'alved, and 'e is your friend."

20. The Sacrifice

As Sunday turned out it was easy for Wally to get Francesco alone, for Wally's dad decided to give Gussie's hair another cut.

"Your uncle will be creatin' about it again any day now," he said. "Give us the basin and a towel, Wally."

"But if we wait until he says something," Gussie argued, "he'll give me twenty-five pence like he did before. And we need it extra bad because we spent the end of the suitcase money on Anna's last lesson."

"Because I let you take your uncle's money the once it don't mean I'm makin' a habit of it. Now sit down and don't wriggle or I'll 'ave a ear off of you."

"You come into the kitchen, Anna," said Wally's mum. "And 'ave a look at what I've got. Next week I gets me Christmas puddin's started. You ever ate a Christmas pudding?"

Anna never had nor did she know what it was. Unwillingly she pulled her mind to look at past Christmases. Christopher had always driven the caravan to Jardek and Babka's little house for Christmas. Anna could almost see them arrive, perhaps as late as the morning on Christmas Eve, with bells tied on Togo's harness and red ribbons plaited in his tail.

"I do not know a Christmas pudding but always there was cakes, piles of cakes. Babka made them."

Wally's mum saw it was hurting Anna to talk about Christmas. For everybody who has someone to miss, Christmas is the worst time for missing them. But Christmas would come just the same, so it was best the children should face it. She had an easy chair by the window. Now she sat down in it and held out her arms to Anna.

"Come and sit on my knee and tell me all about your Christmas, then I'll tell you how we keep it 'ere."

Anna climbed on to Wally's mum's cosy lap.

"Christmas Eve was as Babka and Jardek knew it when they were little and lived in Poland. Christmas Day was for Christopher but not very much except for presents, for he said there should be a turkey but often it was not possible to buy one."

"What happened on Christmas Eve?" Wally's mum asked.

Anna tried to remember it all.

"You eat fish. That is because it is a fast. When Jardek and Babka were little always after the fish were many, many more dishes but of course we did not eat like that. The first thing for the Christmas Eve dinner was when we covered the table with straw."

"Straw!" said Wally's mum. "What would you

put straw on the table for?"

Anna screwed up her face trying to remember.

"It was sort of holy straw. After we had eaten Babka took it out to Togo. She did not let Christopher see because he would laugh and it is not good to laugh at what is holy, but Babka told us such straw, if eaten by Togo, would keep him in health for a whole year."

"Well, that was nice," said Wally's mum. "Maybe I better put some straw on the table for Bess and the hens. Do you put the cloth over it?"

Anna was remembering better.

"Oh yes, the best tablecloth. Then when all were sitting Babka brought in the soup. This was always made with almonds and was beautiful. Then came the fish with so many different sauces you could not count."

"My goodness!" said Wally's mum. "I'm glad we don't do that here on Christmas Eve or I'd never get up of a Christmas morning."

Anna was almost tasting things now.

"Then comes the cakes. The best is called pirogi. This looks like a little loaf of bread but inside it is all almond paste and poppy seeds. Always Gussie had to be stopped eating them or he was sick. As well there are other cakes and fruits dried in sugar."

Wally's mum was getting confused.

"But what did you do on Christmas Day? Didn't you hang up a sock or stocking?"

Anna shook her head.

"None of us had socks or stockings till S'William bought them. And why should we hang them up?"

"Children get presents in them."

Anna leant back against Wally's mum's warm shoulder.

"But we did have presents – things Christopher had bought, but best was the outside for on each one he painted a picture, sometimes . . ."

Anna's voice had faded away. It was too much. Those parcels of Christopher's, so beautiful and often so funny. Never, never to have one again.

Wally's mum lifted Anna off her knee.

"You come over here and I'll show you what I put in me Christmas pudding."

Wally was not used to making excuses to talk to people. Whatever he had to say just came straight out. Still, his mum had said he was to let Francesco talk so he knew he had to do it.

"I got to oil me bike," he said to Francesco. "You comin'?"

The bike was kept in a lean-to which was just a piece of corrugated iron leaning against the hen house. Because Wally's bike was there, and an upturned wooden box made a kind of work bench, it had always seemed to Francesco and Gussie a most desirable place to own.

"All his very own," Gussie had said enviously, "and to have a bicycle too!"

Wally started to oil his bicycle. He hoped his mum was right, she usually was, but it seemed to him like poking his nose in where it was not wanted to ask Francesco questions. At last he said:

"What's 'appenin'? I mean about fifty pence for Anna's next lesson? Can you do it out of that pocket money?"

Francesco did not answer at once, so Wally looked up at him and saw he was swallowing as if he was trying not to cry. At last Francesco said in a voice which sounded not as if he was talking to Wally, but to anyone anywhere:

"Always things was easy. Christopher thought of nothing but pictures, but if something had to be decided then Olga took away his canvas and perhaps his paints and he could not have them back until the decision is made. Now there is nobody, only me, and I do not know what is right to do. We could perhaps with the pocket money find enough for one more lesson but one is not enough, it is each week this great sum we must have. This Wednesday I should pay and the next Gussie, but for this Wednesday, except the pocket money, I have nothing — nothing at all."

Wally tried to find the right words to ask a question.

"Will it be so shockin' bad if Anna doesn't 'ave a lesson until S'William comes 'ome and you can sell your picture?"

Francesco choked back a sob.

"But will he come? He gave us his address and I have written with the right stamp."

"What did you say?"

"I didn't know how to spell S'William so I just said 'Please to come and see us, it is urgent that we sell our picture with many felicitations love Francesco.' "

"I wouldn't worry, 'e'll come."

"But suppose he never does? You do not understand, Wally. Anna must learn, for her not to learn is a very, very bad sin."

Wally wiped down his bicycle with a rag.

"What I don't see is why you 'ave to get in a state about it. It isn't as though you could do anythin'."

Francesco looked at Wally and there were tears in his eyes.

"I had never known how it is to be the eldest. All is now in my care. There is nobody else. Nobody at all."

"Come on," said Wally, "race you to the 'ouse, we've 'ot toast with relish for tea."

The next morning in the playground at break Wally drew Francesco into a corner. There he took an envelope out of his pocket, and in it was £1.50.

"Go on, take it," he said to Francesco. "It's for you. It'll pay for three lessons and with the three Gussie's payin' for that's six weeks, and I reckon S'William'll be 'ome by then."

Francesco had turned first white and then red.

"One pound and fifty pence! Where did you get such money?"

Wally made a face at him.

"No need to look suspicious. I come by it honest." He struggled to sound casual. "If you want to know, I sold me bike."

Francesco was horrified. The bike, though old and clattery, was, as all knew, the pride of Wally's life.

"I can't take it. You must get the bicycle back."

"There's gratitude for you," Wally jeered. " 'Get it back,' he says, I know it wasn't up to much but it was dirt cheap at one fifty and 'im that bought it knows it. 'E won't give it to me back, 'e's been on at me for months to sell it to 'im."

Francesco looked at the money as if it was the crock of gold from under the rainbow.

"It is too much," he whispered, "but some day, perhaps when we sell the picture, there will be a new bicycle for you."

Wally did not believe any picture was worth the price of a bicycle but he didn't say so. Instead he changed the subject.

"Now mind you, nobody isn't to know 'ow you got the money. Nobody – not Gussie, not Anna – nobody. I just might tell me mum, for she'll see it's missin', but that's all."

Francesco, moved almost past speech by Wally's generosity, could only nod.

"I promise," he whispered.

It was on the way home from school that Gussie learnt that Francesco had raised his share of the money for Anna's lessons. Anna brought the subject up.

"I wish S'William would come home. I need a dress, Miss de Veane calls it a tunic, for dancing. School clothes is not right and I have no others."

Gussie looked at Anna rather as a mother bird must sometimes look at its ever-hungry young.

"A tunic! Here's me and Francesco not knowing how to earn fifty pence each week, it's a lot of money, and now you ask for tunics!"

"Don't worry, Anna." said Francesco. "I have enough for three lessons without using our pocket money, perhaps that could buy a tunic. Also, I think The Aunt would help."

Gussie has not got over his habit of sitting or lying down when he felt like it. Now he sat down on the pavement.

"What! You have money for three lessons! How?"

"I have it and that is enough," said Francesco. Then he opened his hand and showed them Wally's coins.

Gussie was furious. He knew in the most secret place in his soul that he was by far the smartest of the family. He had been convinced that he alone was within smelling distance of a way to raise money, and here was Francesco, so slow and so tiresome about what was right and what was wrong, with one pound fifty. In that second he knew what he must try to do. He had hesitated before but now it was certain. He got to his feet and, looking terribly proud, faced Anna and Francesco. He thumped his chest "Me, Gussie, will have enough for four lessons."

21. The Gang

Although Gussie had spoken in a bragging way about getting two pounds by Wednesday week he knew inside himself that, though he had a plan, he had very little idea how to carry it out.

At school there was quite a large group of children who lived in a block of flats just outside Fyton. These children belonged to families who had been rehoused from slum clearance areas from other parts of the country. Many of these families had settled down well and had friends all over Fyton, but there was a small element of what the police called "troublemakers". Many of this group had younger brothers and some of these were in Gussie's class. They were known as The Gang and Gussie admired them enormously.

To admire people does not mean they want to become your friends so, try as Gussie would, he had remained a kind of admiring hanger-on. What drew him to The Gang was not just that they appeared to share exciting secrets but that somehow all of them seemed to have money. It had been his ambition to work his way in and then to startle Francesco by throwing down a fifty-pence piece when his turn came, saying casually: "There is plenty more where that came from."

Now the unthinkable had happened. It was Francesco who had the money while he, clever Gussie, looked as if it was he who would have to use the pocket money when his turn came.

He was faced with having to get fifty pence. Gussie considered The Gang carefully. He had not done this before, when he felt the day when he would actually have to pay for a dancing class was miles away, and indeed might never come for surely S'William would be home soon. The Gang was mostly made up of boys of nine and ten but the leaders were big boys of eleven who would soon be moving on to a senior school. These big boys would sometimes call the younger boys into a corner of the school yard and either tell them something or give them something. Gussie, on the outskirts of the group, had never known what went on, but he had succeeded in looking as if he did and that was all that then had mattered to him. But now he had to find out what went on for he was sure that whatever it was that happened had to do with money.

Gussie was popular with his class for he did not mind what he said, and often just in the way he said things the children found him funny, but he had not yet made an especial friend unless he could count Tom. Tom was a member of The Gang. He was a pale boy with hair so fair it was almost white, pale pinkish eyes behind glasses with thick lenses and a look as if he never got enough to eat. This last was not true for Gussie knew what food Tom brought for his lunch and it was enough for six of him. Gussie had sort of made friends with Tom because Tom was very fond of his curry, something his mother never put in his sandwiches, but which Aunt Mabel, forever studying, had learnt to make for the children. So Gussie now and then swapped a curry sandwich with Tom, not because he liked Tom's meat sandwiches but because he was good-natured.

The day after Francesco's revelation that he had £1.50, there were curry sandwiches in the children's lunch boxes so in break time Gussie went straight to Tom.

"We've got curry today. It will be curried chicken for we had chicken in Sunday. Want to swap?"

Tom did, so a pact was made that the swap would take place in the classroom at dinner time. But when dinner time came Tom dashed over to Gussie.

"Come on. Swap quick. There's a buzz. I'm wanted in the playground."

Gussie was not having that.

"All right. I'll come with you. We'll swap outside."

The Gang meeting was the same as usual. Those close to the leaders. which included Tom, clustered together in a corner. The outer ring, which included Gussie, saw and heard nothing. But this time Gussie made sure he did not lose sight of Tom. The moment The Gang broke up he had him by the arm.

"Come on and swap. I'm starving."

Tom and Gussie sat together on one of the big coal bunkers which were near the school keeper's house. Gussie proudly laid out three beautiful curried chicken sandwiches; his mouth watered as he looked at them. Tom pushed forward three great sandwiches of coarsely cut bread, one full of beef, one of pork and one of cheese. Gussie shuddered but he took them.

"Bit of all right your auntie's sandwiches," said Tom with his mouth full. "But it's odd you don't 'ave school dinners like the others from The Crescent."

Gussie groaned.

"The food we eat at The Uncle's is terrible. That cabbage! But school meals — no, that is not to be endured. The Aunt knows this. What were you saying to The Gang?"

Tom took another enormous mouthful of sandwich.

"Nothin' you want. You see, you got no money. We was given some thin's to sell like."

Tom looked around to see nobody was watching them.

"Mostly thin's the girls like." He whipped a scarf

out of a pocket. It was bright green with squirly patterns on it. "This is just one, we got 'em in all colours."

"Then you sell them?"

"That's the ticket. Mind you, it's fair do's for they're cheaper than they are in the shops."

"But where do you get them from?"

Tom looked vague.

"That's up to the leaders. Maybe they're what's called rejects from a factory."

"Then if you sell them do you get the money for them?" Gussie asked.

"That's the ticket. They cost fifty pence and if I sells one I get ten for meself. It soon mounts up."

Gussie could imagine that it did. He could imagine too how many such scarves Mrs Wall might sell on her stall. Why, he only had to sell five and he would have fifty pence.

"I would like to sell such scarves," he said.

Tom looked doubtful.

"Who to?"

"Well there is The Aunt, she will buy one, and there is someone else I know who might buy many."

Tom finished the last curry sandwich and started off on a beef one.

"I can't get you scarves nor nothin' else to sell jus' like that. I got to tell somebody you're willin', then, if he says 'yes' you swears a vow to obey the leaders even in the face of death. Then they cuts your arm so your blood mixes with their blood. Then they sets you a task and if you do that OK you're in."

Gussie was enthralled. Just for the right to sell a few scarves it sounded wildly exciting.

"When can you tell the somebody? Because I want to have fifty pence earned by the Wednesday after this one."

Tom went on chewing.

"That should be easy. But mind you're sure you want to do it, for if you wasn't to keep the vow 'avin' made it they'd kill you, straight they would."

Gussie was carried away by the whole idea of joining The Gang. He thumped his chest.

"You do not worry. Me, Gussie, when I swear a vow I swear it. The vow is kept."

22. The Letter

The next day Sir William's letter came. Aunt Mabel had it in her apron pocket. She gave it to Francesco when he came in from school.

"It's from Sir William, it's got his name on the back. Take it upstairs to read. I don't know why but just hearing his name upsets your uncle. Luckily he hasn't seen it."

The three children went into the boys' bedroom. It was of course the letter Sir William had written on the aeroplane and forgotten to post for six weeks. Francesco read it out loud to the other two. The beginning part saying he would not be away long and that when he came back he would ask permission from their uncle to take them out was received with interruptions from Gussie.

"How does he mean 'not away long'? Already it is months."

"I do not believe he is ever coming back."

"Why does he say nothing of our picture?"

The last part made Anna turn quite white with excitement.

If, Anna, you are not fixed up with a suitable dancing

teacher I hear very good accounts of a Madame Scarletti.
I looked her up in the telephone book. She has a studio
at 45 Bemberton Street, Chelsea, London. I gather she
is very old but still one of the best teachers in the world.

"Madame Scarletti!" Anna whispered, as if they
were magic words. "One of the best teachers in the
world."

Gussie, who had been lying in the floor, jumped
to his feet.

"You be quiet," he shouted at Anna. "You
cannot go to Madame Scarletti until the picture is
sold. And now I do not think it ever will be sold
because I think S'William has stolen it. Always you
want something. First it is private lessons. Then it
is a tunic. Now it is a Madame who lives in London
where you cannot get . . ."

Gussie might have shouted more for he was very
angry, but the door opened and Aunt Mabel,
looking worried, peered in.

"Oh, don't quarrel, dears. We could hear you in
the lounge with the door shut, and you know how
your uncle dislikes noise."

Gussie was so angry with Anna that he might
have gone on shouting, only Anna and her one-
track mind prevented him. S'William's letter and
Gussie's shouts had reminded her of her tunic.

"Aunt Mabel, I need a tunic for dancing." At the
mention of dancing Aunt Mabel's head looked like
disappearing, for, though she knew that somehow

Anna was learning, she did not admit even to herself that she knew that she knew. But Anna was too quick for her. She darted to the door and gripped Aunt Mabel by a sleeve of her jersey. "It is simple to make and the material need cost very little, or we have our pocket money which could buy it." Gussie groaned. "But now I must have a tunic because . . ."

This time it was Francesco who interrupted for he felt sure Anna, in her excited state, was going to mention Madame Scarletti.

"She does need a tunic," he said quietly. "Perhaps she could explain after tea before the English lesson."

Aunt Mabel nodded.

"A tunic. You shall have it, Anna." Then she was gone.

This dramatic disappearance made Gussie forget he was angry.

"You see," he said. "Is she not exactly as a mouse who has seen a cat?"

Francesco opened the door of the cupboard in which they kept Sir William's address under the lining paper and put Sir William's letter beside it.

"Now we must get ready for tea and the English lesson," he said. Then he added in what he was afraid was becoming a special older brother voice: "Now don't forget, either of you, no one — no one at all must know what is in that letter. If it is necessary some day Anna may have to go to

London but no one, not even Wally's mum would agree to that if they knew."

The children always had their tea in the kitchen. This meant Cecil had his tea in peace alone with Mabel and the children, provided they kept their voices down, could talk as much as they liked. As well, in their opinion, they had much better food all of a savoury nature, whereas in the lounge there was thin bread and butter and a horrible cake full of seeds. That day of course they talked about the letter. Francesco for once did most of the talking.

"It does not matter yet, Anna, how well this Madame Scarletti teaches. You cannot see her because you cannot go to London. But when there is holidays perhaps a way can be found. Now you have Miss de Veane and that is enough."

"I should think it was," Gussie growled. "At fifty pence each week. And if you saw this Madame Scarletti I should think she would cost five pounds each week."

Anna looked trustingly at Francesco.

"It is knowing she is there that is mattering. I do not know how Miss de Veane thinks, if she thinks wrong I now know where else I can learn."

Gussie leant across the table.

"If The Uncle had heard how you spoke that English, Anna, I think he would have a fit and perhaps die, which, though a good idea, would mean you couldn't learn at all for we would have no home."

Aunt Mabel asked no questions about the tunic. She accepted the pattern Anna gave her and said when ready she would put it on her bed.

"Now be careful in your English lesson," she warned all three children. "Your uncle is still a little upset by the noise you made upstairs."

As it turned out, the noise Gussie had made had good results. As it was getting towards Christmas Uncle Cecil was getting busier, for all the charities he worked for sold things like Christmas cards at Christmas and that meant a lot of work for the Treasurer. He had come in tired that afternoon with a bit of a headache and Gussie's shouts from upstairs had been the last straw. Over tea he had thought seriously about the children's English. There was no doubt about it – all three had greatly improved. His lessons consisting of conversation on intelligent subjects, such as "Tell me what impressed you most in Istanbul?" "What do you know about the Magna Charta?" were succeeding. Gussie's replies to any question were painfully frivolous, but on the other hand his English was quite fluent. Perhaps the day had come when the lessons could be given up and he could leave the children's English to their teachers at school, so when the children were sitting in a row on the velvet sofa he said:

"Francesco, do you think your English has improved?"

Francesco felt worried. Is he said it had The

Uncle might be angry and say it was still terrible. But if he said it was still bad he might think they had not worked during his lessons.

"I hope it is better." Francesco spoke with caution. "It should be with the conversation lessons as well as school."

"And what do you think, Augustus?"

"I think we speak so good – I mean well – that soon it is us who will be giving English lessons."

"And what do you think, Anna?"

Anna was so scared during English lessons she always spoke in a whisper.

"I know I speak better, a teacher at school told me so."

Cecil could hardly resist letting out a sigh of relief. He had found the English lessons a great trial and he was thankful from the bottom of his heart that no one had made him a school teacher. He was thankful too that he and Mabel had no children, but he was still furious at the bad luck which had landed his robbing wastrel of a brother's children on him.

"I agree with your teacher, Anna," he said, "so I have decided this will be your last lesson. Instead ask your teachers for books from the school library. There is nothing like reading a good book to improve your English. Now go to your rooms and start your homework. And go quietly."

All the children crept up to the boys' room. Then, when the door was shut, stuffing their handkerchiefs in their mouths to shut out the sound of laughter, they rolled on the floor, occasionally snatching out their handkerchiefs to say "A good book!" "The last lesson!" They did not know it but it was the first time they had laughed like that since the earthquake and they didn't even notice there was no Christopher to say, "Shut up, you kids, I will have hush."

23. Wilf

Tom, though he preferred to remain in the background, did speak to The Gang leader about Gussie. This was a big boy called Wilf. He had dirty fair hair which nearly reached his shoulders and he wore a jersey with a skull and crossbones woven on to it. All the smaller boys were scared of him, for if they displeased him he didn't wait to hear an excuse but out came his fists and he was a good boxer.

There was never a teachers' meeting but Wilf's name came up, for all the teachers considered him a menace and longed for the day when he would move on to another school.

"I'm sure he's a bad influence," the headmaster was always saying. "And I shouldn't wonder if he was a thief. Any day I'm expecting to hear he's in juvenile court."

Tom had sold his scarf, so it was easy for him to speak to Wilf for he had to see him to give him the money. Passing over the money was always done when nobody was about, but Wilf had several tough friends who watched out for him to see if the coast was clear. The Gang had a pass sign of thumping one fist on the other. Tom gave this sign and was allowed into the senior classroom where Wilf was sitting alone at his desk. Tom came up to the desk and laid down forty pence.

"Where'd you sell it?" Wilf asked.

"One of the girls bought it for her mum's birthday."

"Where did you say you'd got it?"

"Sellin' it cheap, I said, for a friend what's got a shop London way."

Wilf nodded both to show he approved and to dismiss Tom, but Tom did not move so Wilf asked:

"Well? What is it?"

"There's a boy in my class called Gussie Docksay. 'E wants to join."

"'Ow does 'e know there's anythin' to join?"

"'E's one of the kids what 'angs around when we meet in the playground."

"Gussie Docksay. Isn't 'e one of the kids what was in that earthquake?"

"That's right."

There was a cunning smile on Wilf's face.

"Live up The Crescent?"

"That's right."

Wilf came to a decision.

"Go and find 'im, I'll see 'im now."

Gussie had no idea that Wilf was to be feared. He knew him by sight of course, as did everybody in the school, but he had never spoken to him. So when Tom took him to the classroom door and told him to go in he went in afraid of nothing except that Wilf might refuse to let him join The Gang.

Wilf looked at Gussie and rather liked what he saw. Gussie was small for his age but he looked tough, intelligent and noticeably unafraid.

"Why do you want to join?" Wilf asked.

"Money," Gussie explained. "It's not for me but I have a sister who must learn to dance. She has private lessons, each one costs fifty pence. This I must earn for I pay every other week. My brother Francesco has three weeks' money but I have none and this I do not like."

Wilf had not listened to half of this.

"Now an' then I gets thin's to sell. Where they comes from is none of your business, but if you was caught sellin' and asked where the stuff come from what'd you say?"

Gussie thought back to the old days.

"They was sent to me by an aunt in Baghdad."

Wilf had never heard this excuse before.

"Why Baghdad?"

Gussie made an expansive gesture.

"All happens in Baghdad and there everyone has an aunt."

Wilf's voice became stern.

"Well, you can say what you like as long as you don't mention no names. If you do" – he made a gurgling sound and drew a finger across his throat – "you know what'll 'appen."

Gussie was charmed but felt Wilf had not quite finished the story.

"Then you throw my body in the ditch where I am eaten by hyenas."

Wilf blew a sharp whistle on his fingers and at once three of his friends rushed in. Wilf pointed to Gussie.

"The kid's joinin'. Stand round. Now, Gussie, you says after me, 'I swear to obey my leader Wilf whatever he tells me to do, and I swear even in the face of death I'll never give away the name of any member of The Gang.' Anyone got a knife?"

A rather rusty knife was produced and Gussie was told to hold out his wrist. Then one of his friends made a nick on it and a nick in his own wrist and, when spots of blood appeared, rubbed them together.

"Now you are a blood brother," said Wilf, "but before you gets taught the sign you 'ave to do a test."

"Yes, I know," Gussie agreed. "Tom said I would have to. What must I do?"

The same cunning smile came over Wilf's face.

"In your uncle's garden isn't there a couple of gnomes?"

Gussie was surprised.

"I never knew they were called gnomes but there are two little men who fish. How did you know they were there? You can't see them from the road."

"You'd be surprised what I know," said Wilf. "And maybe you can 'elp me to know more, there's lots interesting about The Crescent. Now what you 'as to do is to fetch one of those gnomes an' bring it to me here. When I 'ave the gnome you're in."

"And then can I sell things and start to earn some money?" Gussie asked.

Wilf smiles his cunning smile.

"I don't know about sellin'. I might have other work for you. But when you brings that gnome I shouldn't wonder if you could 'ave fifty pence on account like."

Gussie was so cock-a-hoop at having succeeded in one try in joining The Gang that it was not until he was walking home from school that it got through to him how terribly difficult a task he had been set. A gnome might, for all he knew, be heavy. Then, even if he could take a gnome without The Uncle catching him, how was he to carry it to school? It was the kind of thing everybody would notice.

With a kind of turning-over feeling in his inside Gussie faced the awful fact that he might not be able to do his test. Perhaps Wilf had purposely set him something he couldn't do. It was a terrible thought for it meant if he did not bring a gnome to school he couldn't join The Gang so couldn't get any money.

The children were supposed to walk home together, but there was no one to see that they did and no one to complain if they did not, so quite often Francesco and Anna walked together and Gussie loitered behind, skylarking with the other boys. This day he deliberately stayed behind because he was so full of thoughts about the gnome that he wanted to be alone.

The route The Crescent children used going to and from school crossed a busy road where a lollipop lady was waiting to see them safely across. The lights were red, so Gussie lolled against a lamppost waiting for them to change and the lollipop lady to signal him over. While he stood there saying in his head "'suppose I could borrow a gnome without The Uncle seeing, how could I get it to school without anybody noticing?" he was distracted by what to him was an unusual sight. Two children came along pulling a strange figure in a sort of cart made of a box. It was wearing a mask and an old hat. While he was staring at the cart, the lollipop lady caught hold of him.

"Come on, dreamer. I've been signalling and signalling you to cross but you took not a bit of notice."

Gussie pointed to the figure sitting in the little cart.

"What's that?"

The lollipop lady led Gussie into the road and held up the traffic.

"That's a penny for the guy, of course. I'll be glad when the fifth of November's over. Blessed nuisance you kids are with your guys."

Safely across the road, Gussie gazed back at the little cart now disappearing round a corner. "A penny for the guy? The fifth of November? Blessed nuisance you kids are with your guys!" If other children could make little men and pull them about in carts why couldn't a gnome travel in the same way?

In a moment Gussie was cock-a-hoop again. He would ask Wally what a guy was. He was as good as in The Gang. He gave a hop, skip and a jump and ran home to tea.

24. The Gnome

Although the Docksay children were now part of the community, Wally still kept a proprietary eye on them all. So when the next morning in break he met Gussie looking for him he at once found a corner where they could talk.

"How is the fifth of November?" Gussie asked.

"Not ' 'ow is?' You say 'what is?' It's about the gunpowder treason and plot. There was this bloke called Guy Fawkes and 'e tried to blow up the 'ouses of Parliament but they caught 'im at it. And ever since we makes guys and burns them on bonfires on the fifth of November, which was the day he tried to do it. Then there's always fireworks."

"Can anybody make a guy?"

" 'Course. I sometimes makes one. I lug it around in the pram and asks people for a penny for the guy. The money what you get is to buy the fireworks." Then Wally remembered that Gussie had not yet got his share of Anna's dancing lesson money. "But if you was to get given any you could use it for Anna, nobody wouldn't know."

Gussie could not confide in Wally, for he had a

feeling he might disapprove of Wilf and of his joining The Gang. Yet he had to have the pram and that he wanted it had to be a secret.

"Could you lend me the pram just for tonight? I'll get it back to you before school tomorrow. And could you not tell anyone you were lending it? You see, I want to surprise Francesco when I give him fifty pence."

"Fat chance you got of gettin' fifty pence," said Wally. "You'll be doing wonderful if you get ten. People don't give like they did, they say that fireworks is dangerous and us kids shouldn't be allowed to beg."

"But is it permitted?"

"The p'lice don't stop you if that's what you mean, but me dad would wallop me if he knew I took out a guy. 'Im and me mum don't 'old with it."

All Gussie needed to know was that it was not a police offence. Of course The Uncle would be angry if he knew one of his gnomes was being shown as a guy, but that had to be risked.

"Could I borrow the pram tonight?"

Wally was doubtful.

"Why don't I come along of you? Me mum won't 'alf be after me if she 'ears you been down town on your own after dark an' that."

Gussie could be very persuasive.

"All I want is to fetch the pram after tea, push it around for not more'n an hour I should think, then

I'll bring it back to you."

Grudgingly Wally agreed.

"Well, you know where it stands, at the back of Bess's sty. But for goodness' sake walk quiet. You 'aven't seen me mum when she's creatin' and believe me you don't want to."

All the rest of the day Gussie worked on his plan. Teacher after teacher scolded him for inattention but Gussie didn't care. What he had to do was desperately important and needed careful working out; let them scold, he would attend to his lessons tomorrow.

That day after tea Gussie, without saying a word to Francesco or Anna, slipped out of the house. He knew it was a safe thing to do for though Francesco might worry he wouldn't say anything to The Aunt and of course, nobody, unless they had to, ever spoke to The Uncle.

Gussie's first objective was the pram. Usually the things from the stall were left in it overnight covered with a sheet of plastic, but Wally had promised to clear it out so that there would be room for the guy.

It felt funny creeping through Wally's farm without calling out "Hi! Can I come in?" Especially as the telly was blaring out to show the family were at home. It felt awful to sneak up behind Bess's sty without saying a word or giving her a scratch, and Bess thought so too for she seemed to recognize Gussie's smell for she gave him a surprised grunt. The pram, being old and squeaky, would not have been easy to move quietly, but luckily any noise it made was drowned out by the pop music being belted out from the TV set.

Gussie, without attracting anyone's attention, pushed the pram up The Crescent and quietly parked it outside Dunroamin. Now came the difficult part. Each house in The Crescent had a little path on one side of the house with a gate at the far end, beyond which stood the dustbins which were emptied once a week. Cecil always entered his garden through the French windows in the lounge, so he kept the gate into his garden locked except on the day when the dustmen came. This was not the dustmen's day so Gussie knew the gate would not be open. But Mr Allan, father of the twins, had no French windows so he and his family always came into their garden through the gate. Gussie, knowing this, nipped up their garden path and down into their garden.

It felt strange seeing Dunroamin from the wrong side of the wall. The lights were on in their bedrooms so Francesco and Anna were doing their homework, though more likely Anna was doing her dancing. He stood on tiptoe to peer over the wall and saw what he had expected. The curtains in the lounge were drawn, so there was no chance The Uncle could see out, and most likely The Aunt was in the kitchen cooking supper. Now all he had to do was climb over the wall.

All he had to do! The wall was straight up and with no footholds and, because there had recently been rain, a little slippery. It was then that Gussie thought of the dustbins. Standing on a dustbin he could reach the top of the wall and haul himself over. Dustbins had played no part in the children's lives before the earthquake, but they had studied them since and were filled with admiration.

"Such a system!" Francesco had marvelled when first catching the dustmen at work. "All carried away so no smell and no mess."

Gussie went to examine the Allans' dustbins. There were two, they were large and made of metal with plastic tops. But what Gussie had not suspected from the easy way the dustmen handled the bins was that they were heavy and it was only by slow stages that he managed to get one to the wall. Then, very out of breath, he climbed on to the plastic lid.

Plastic dustbin lids do not always fix on securely, they get warped by wind and rain. The Allans' dustbin had a lid like that. As a result when Gussie climbed on to the lid it tipped up, and down Gussie fell with a terrible clatter.

At once the curtains of the Allans' lounge window were drawn back and the window was opened. Two people hung out and a voice Gussie recognized as Jonathan's asked:

"Who's there?"

It was obvious to Gussie that it was no good

trying to hide from the twins so he ran over to the window.

"It's me, Gussie," he whispered. "I fell off your dustbin."

The twins were full of curiosity.

"Whatever were you doing on our dustbin?" Priscilla asked.

"Ssh!" whispered Gussie. "Don't let anyone hear. If you come out I'll tell you."

The twins were supposed to be doing their homework but they never bothered with it much and often, especially in the summer, would climb out of the window into the garden. They climbed out now.

While they were climbing out Gussie made a quick decision. He would tell the twins what he was going to do but not about Wilf or joining The Gang.

"I was going to climb the wall to take one of The Uncle's gnomes."

The twins thought that a splendid idea.

"Where are you taking it to?"

"I thought the school," said Gussie. "I have borrowed a perambulator, it will look like a penny for the guy."

"But the school's shut. Where will you put it?" Priscilla asked.

Gussie had not thought that far.

"I suppose I could hide it somewhere."

Jonathan started to giggle.

"Why hide it? Let's put it on the head's window ledge. It's quite large and the gnome could fish into the flower bed underneath the window."

Gussie thought about that. It was true Wilf had said bring the gnome in to him. but he couldn't really expect that, for how could anyone carry a gnome into the school without being seen? It was a joyous thought to put it on the head's window ledge, and even more gorgeous that Jonathan meant to help.

"All right. Can you help me on to the dustbin?"

Jonathan and Priscilla held the dustbin lid in place and Gussie, now able to reach the top of the wall, hauled himself over. On the other side he lowered himself quietly into the garden, landing on some plastic chrysanthemums. Very quietly he fumbled his way towards the gnomes.

Always Gussie had supposed the gnomes would be very heavy so he nearly spoilt everything by using too much strength to pick one up, with the result that he fell into the pool with the gnome on top of him. Luckily the lounge curtains were thick and the windows were shut, so Cecil did not hear the splash, but Jonathan and Priscilla did and in a few seconds Jonathan was hauling first the gnome and then Gussie out of the pond.

"Come on quick," he said. "I can get up the wall. Then pass the gnome up to me. Priscilla will take it, then I'll pull you up."

Except that Gussie was very wet and his teeth

chattering with cold it was all too easy. Mrs Allan was cooking on the other side of the house, and Mr Allan was out for the evening. In a matter of minutes the gnome, with his fishing rod, which they discovered was detachable, lying beside him, was in the pram. Priscilla had fetched her own and Jonathan's coats and a warm sweater for Gussie and they and the pram were halfway up The Crescent.

"Now the only place we have to be careful is crossing the main road," said Jonathan. "You better leave saying 'a penny for the guy' to me and Priscilla because we know how."

"But if we get any pennies we can't keep them," Priscilla pointed out. "Dad wouldn't mind about the gnome, he'd think it funny, but he'd be livid if we took charity money, so if we get any we'll put it in somebody's collecting box." As it happened nobody gave the children any money but neither did they pay any attention to them, there were too many guys about.

The school gate was locked but Jonathan climbed over and Priscilla passed him the gnome, then she and Gussie climbed over. The school grounds seemed very eerie that night for there were no lights in the grounds, but the twins knew their way perfectly. The only disappointment was that, having set up the gnome on his window ledge, it was too dark to see him.

"And remember," Priscilla warned, "you can't go and look at him tomorrow, Gussie. We can only go when somebody else tells us he's there. Nobody must ever know who put him there."

Outside the school grounds Gussie collected the pram and said goodnight to the twins, then he went off towards Wally's farm pushing the pram. When he got to the farm it seemed as if he had only been away five minutes. It sounded as if the same tune was roaring out from the TV and Bess gave the same surprised grunt. But Gussie did not feel the same. He'd done it. He'd taken The Uncle's gnome. Tomorrow he'd be a proper member of The Gang. Goodness, he felt proud! When he got home, in answer to Francesco's anxious questions, all he would say was:

"You find out what 'a penny for the guy' means. That's all I'll tell you."

25. Call the Police

The next morning the three children went off to school as usual, but they were not inside the school gates before they could feel something unusual had happened. All the school were milling around, shrieking with laughter and standing by the headmaster's window ledge. Presently the headmaster looked out. He roared with laughter when he saw the gnome.

"He's an unexpected visitor. Do any of you know where the little gentleman has come from?"

The children made various suggestions but none near the truth.

"Well, I must see what I can find out. I don't love gnomes myself but no doubt somebody does and is missing this little fellow."

After roll call the headmaster signalled to the school not to move. He was smiling, so evidently he still thought the gnome funny.

"Have any of you ever seen that gnome before?"

First Francesco's hand was held up, then Anna's and lastly Gussie's. Then, after a second, the twins put their hands up,

The headmaster looked at Francesco.

"Where have you seen the gnome?"

"It is The Uncle's," Francesco explained. "He has two who fish in a pond though there are no fish."

"And our visitor is one of the two?"

Francesco shook his head.

"He looks the same but perhaps all such gnomes look the same."

"And where have you two seen him?" the headmaster asked the twins.

"In Mr Docksay's garden," said Jonathan.

"We live next door," Priscilla explained.

"And you both think it's one of Mr Docksay's gnomes?"

Jonathan managed a realistic shrug of the shoulders.

"He looks the same."

The headmaster did not question Gussie or Anna.

"All right," he said. "I'll telephone Mr Docksay to see if a gnome is missing." Then, signalling to the pianist to start playing, he called out "School dismiss".

As it happened Cecil had not looked out of his windows that morning so he was very surprised at the headmaster's question in the telephone.

"A gnome! Hold on, headmaster, I will look." A second later Cecil was back on the telephone. "Indeed it is mine. Vandalism! I shall call the police."

"The gnome appears undamaged," said the

headmaster calmly. "I think it must have been intended as a joke."

Cecil almost roared.

"A joke! A joke! Do you call it a joke when somebody breaks into the privacy of your garden?"

The headmaster felt he could do no good.

"Well, if you will drive up to the school I'll see the school keeper helps you lift the gnome into your car. I'm sorry this has happened."

Cecil shouted for Mabel who came scurrying down the stairs.

"Someone has had the impertinence to take one of my gnomes up to the school."

Mabel's hand flew to her mouth.

"Oh no!" she panted. "Whoever would do that?"

"Where were the children last night?"

"In their rooms doing their homework."

"You're sure?"

"Of course, dear. Anyway how could they get into the garden, you were in the lounge?"

Cecil went to his desk and took out the key to the garden gate.

"And the gate was locked. Then someone got over the wall. I shall call the police."

Mabel gave a squeak.

"Must you, dear? I mean, if you know where it is there is not much the police can do, is there?"

"It's vandalism. An Englishman's home should be his castle."

"Yes, dear. I suppose so, dear," Mabel agreed. "If you are going to telephone the police I'll finish making the beds."

At the top of the stairs Mabel paused to listen to make sure Cecil was on the telephone, then she hurried into the boys' room. From behind the wardrobe where Gussie had hidden them she took out some very damp clothes and a strange jersey. The jersey she folded nearby then put it in his drawer where he could not fail to see it, but the clothes she put into the washing machine.

"Very naughty of him if he took it," she thought, "but I don't see how he could have. Such a little boy to carry one of those large gnomes."

Cecil was not finding the police as helpful as he expected.

"Yes, sir," the policeman at the end of the line was saying. "A gnome. I've got that. But it's been recovered, I think you said, sir, so what were you wanting us to do?"

"I want every inch of my garden examined to discover where someone broke in."

"Very well, sir. I'll tell the inspector."

"And I want your men here at once."

"I'll see what can be done," the policeman said placatingly. "Good morning, sir."

It was pouring with rain at break time so the children had to stay in. Anna was looking for Francesco or Gussie when she was caught by the arm by Doreen and dragged into a corner. Doreen was looking plumper than ever and her ringlets bobbed every time she spoke, but for once she was not giggling.

"What are you dancing in Miss de Veane's concert, Anna?"

Anna felt as if someone was squeezing her inside.

"I'm not dancing. Miss de Veane knows I cannot dance yet, I must have many years more training."

Doreen looked knowing.

"That's what you think but I'll tell you what we think. There's eight of us, with you, takes private lessons, and yesterday Miss de Veane gave us the designs of our costumes and told us what we were dancing in the fairy ballet. It's in a fairy wood and I'm a foxglove first and then a dragonfly, and all the others who learn private are flowers or a bee or that. The Saturday class are in groups – primroses and daisies and such. So we asked Miss de Veane who was to be the fairy what wakes all us flowers up and do you know what she said?"

Anna's eyes were dark with fright. This was her nightmare coming true.

"No," she whispered. "What?"

"Well, it was not said exactly – more hinted like. She said it was a very small girl who would one day be a beautiful dancer. Well, the only small one she teaches is you and my mum says it isn't fair. Here's me learnt since I was four so if anyone is to be picked out it should be me."

Anna could not think what to say for she knew

that Miss de Veane could be very determined, even determined enough perhaps to make her dance when she did not want to. Then, almost as if he were beside her, she heard Jardek's whisper in his mixed Polish and English: "Anna, my Anna, you must live for nothing but to dance. Anything which comes between you and true dancing must be forgotten." In a flash Anna had changed. She was no longer afraid of Miss de Veane. She threw her chin into the air.

"If you wish to dance this fairy you should ask to do so. There is no thought that I will dance in public nor that I shall learn much longer with Miss de Veane. I am going to learn in London."

26. Trouble

Wilf, though he would not have dreamt of saying so, was amazed at the cleverness of Gussie. "What an idea," he thought, "having got the gnome to put it on the headmaster's window ledge. But what he admired most was Gussie's discretion.

"You mean to say," he asked, "that you never told young Wally why you wanted his pram?"

Gussie was surprised.

" 'Course not. You said what would happen if I told."

"Nor you didn't tell the Allan twins neither?"

" 'Course not. They just thought it was a funny thing to do. Actually it was Jonathan who thought how it would be to put the gnome on the headmaster's window, and I thought the idea was fine because I couldn't bring it into this classroom."

"And you're dead sure your uncle won't guess you done it?"

"Why should he? He doesn't know about Wally's pram so how is he thinking I got the gnome to the school?"

"But Wally will guess why you wanted 'is pram."

Gussie dismissed that with a gesture.

"If he does he will not tell. He is our friend."

Wilf took two fifty-pence pieces from his pocket. He handed them to Gussie.

"There's plenty more where that came from. In a day or two I'll 'ave another job for you. But remember, you never say nothin' or . . ."

Gussie drew his finger across his throat with a blood-curdling noise.

"Then I am in a ditch being eaten by hyenas."

Wilf whistled for one of his friends.

"Show young Gussie the pass sign. He's in."

Gussie planned his great moment for showing Francesco and Anna his pound carefully. It was so clever of him to have earned it he must make an occasion of showing the other two that he had it. Should he just walk in and throw the money down or should he give it to Anna with a grand gesture, saying: "Here is your dancing-class money."

After school Wally joined Gussie.

"Walk a bit of the way 'ome with me. I want a word with you."

Gussie, still very much above himself for his tremendous success with Wilf, was charmed for he was sure Wally was going to tell him how clever and funny he had been, but Wally was not. As they walked along in the rain he suddenly burst out:

"I don't know nothin' about why you wanted the pram 'an I don't want'er know nothin' but anyone what joins up with Wilf's gang wants' 'is 'ead seein' to."

Gussie tried to sound puzzled.

"How is Wilf's gang?"

"Come off it. D'you think nobody don't see what's goin' on? Everybody knows about The Gang though most is too scared to speak up. D'you think I don't know you was alone with Wilf dinner time? I shouldn't wonder if taking the gnome up in the pram wasn't something to do with it."

"Why should Wilf want the gnome?"

Wally was fond of Gussie but just now he could have shaken him.

"I can't do no more than warn you like. That Wilf is up to no good, I don't know what 'e does for I don't go near 'im and you wouldn't if you 'ad any sense. I know you want money for Anna's dancin' but if you take any from Wilf you'll be sorry. I know you're scared to do it but it would be better to ask your uncle."

"Him! He will not give especially for dancing which he says is a sin. Anyway, he has a closed purse."

Wally kicked a stone up the road.

"I don't know what to say to you. I've told you to keep away from Wilf. I can't do no more not unless I was to tell me mum about you, an' I can't do that."

Gussie was furious with Wally for trying to spoil his glorious day. He did not want to hear bad things about Wilf for, somewhere pushed away inside him, was a sneaking suspicion that Wally was right.

"If you want to know, I was only talking to Wilf at dinner time about the gnome. He thought it very funny. And I'll talk to anybody I like an' you can't stop me."

As a result of this conversation with Wally, Gussie, instead of bursting with pride, came home cross. All the way home he had muttered to himself Christopher's favourite saying: "It's a crying scandal! It's a crying scandal!" He had no idea what it meant but it sounded good. However, once he was in The Crescent his spirits revived and he jingled his fifty-pence pieces together with pride.

In the house he rushed up the stairs and flung open his and Francesco's bedroom door. He was in luck, Anna was in the room. It was his big moment.

"Anna," he said. "You can stop fussing. Here is two more lessons and I will have another fifty pence whenever you want it."

It was Francesco who answered.

"Anna will no longer work with Miss de Veane. She says she must go to London to this Madame Scarletti."

Could anything be more infuriating? To have succeeded in joining The Gang just to pay for dancing classes. To have stolen a gnome so cleverly and to have made the entire school laugh. To come home with a whole pound just to be told Anna did not want it. This was too much. With a crimson face Gussie turned on Anna.

"Always there is something. First it is shoes. Then it is classes. Then it is the tunic, now you have all except enough money to pay until S'William gets home. Then, when first Francesco and then me get the money, all you say is now you must go to London to this Madame Scarletti. Well, you cannot go, for even if you could see Madame Scarletti once that is all, for how can you go each week to London?"

Francesco looked anxiously at the door.

"Do be quiet, Gussie, or The Uncle will hear and you know he does not like noise. Anna cannot learn from Miss de Veane because she will make her dance as a fairy on a stage in public."

"Well, let her be a fairy then. For just one day it will do no harm. But London is impossible."

Anna could hear Jardek speaking.

"You know I cannot dance in public or do anything but exercises. Jardek said . . ."

"Jardek said! Jardek said!" Gussie roared. "But Jardek is dead."

Francesco turned to Anna.

"Gussie's quite right. If Jardek was here now he would see it is not possible you should go to London."

"And he would see you must dance this fairy," Gussie added.

The door opened and Aunt Mabel looked in.

"Oh, please be quiet, dears. I can hear you all over the house. Fortunately your uncle is out, for if he was in he would be most annoyed." She sidled into the room. "I was going to warn you to be very quiet at supper. Your uncle is angry with the police. He is seeing a superintendent now."

There was a moment's shocked silence. All three children knew about police. Too often had police moved on the caravan. In some countries police would be pacified with money but that was unlikely in Britain.

"What has The Uncle done?" Francesco asked.

"Nothing dear, of course," Mabel puffed. "It is that gnome. You will have heard about it at school. The police came to find out which way somebody got into the garden."

Gussie felt as if cold water was trickling down his spine.

"And did they find out?"

"That's what your uncle is so angry about. They came so late that the rain had washed away all the marks. There was one chrysanthemum bent but the police did not think that was evidence."

Gussie released a deep breath. Francesco said:

"We will be very careful not to offend at supper."

The children did not speak for a moment or two after Mabel had sidled out of the room. Then Francesco said:

"You had better go to your room, Anna, to get tidy for supper." Then, when Anna had gone, he turned to Gussie. "I do not know what you are doing but even for Anna's dancing you should not do what is wrong. Jardek would not wish that."

Now that Gussie knew the police had not discovered how he had got into the garden he was his old self again.

"When you got one pound fifty pence did I say you had done what was wrong? No. But you look at my pound as if I am a thief. Now I will tell you a secret, it was me borrowed the silly old gnome but I did not hurt him so leave me alone."

27. A Load of Worries

Francesco was so full of worries he began to look quite ill. His biggest worry was Gussie, for Wally had told him about his suspicions.

"I know he doesn't look very nice, but what is it bad that this Wilf is doing?"

Wally struggled to explain.

"Nobody outside his gang don't know nothin', not for sure, but he's always givin' little kids thin's to sell."

"In Britain that is wrong?" Francesco asked.

" 'Course not, if they're come by honest, but what they say is they're pinched." He saw Francesco did not understand. "Stole like."

Francesco was shocked.

"Stole! To steal is a sin."

Wally thought he might have exaggerated.

"If not stole they're come by funny, what's called rejects from a factory what someone's got 'old of. Anyway, you don't want young Gussie mixed up in anything like that."

Francesco agreed fervently. Too well he knew how easily Gussie might get mixed up in something bad, not because he was bad but because, like Christopher, he liked excitement.

"I do not know what I can do," he told Wally. "Because I am the eldest, now almost eleven, I can try to look after Gussie and Anna, but it is hard to be Jardek, Babka, Christopher and Olga all together. You see, there is only me now."

Wally wondered if he should have bothered Francesco.

"I wouldn't get into a state about it. After all, we don't know, not for certain, about Wilf's gang. But it wouldn't do no 'arm to keep an eye open and if you see young Gussie selling anythin' then you can do somethin'. Maybe go to the headmaster."

Go to the headmaster! Francesco classed him with The Uncle. To talk to either was impossible.

"Thank you for telling me," he said. Then he turned away so that Wally never knew there were tears in Francesco's eyes.

Then there was Anna. Anna, so good and gentle until there was interference in her dancing. Francesco did not believe that S'William had let them down. Gussie's idea that he had stolen their picture was fantastic. On the other hand he certainly was being slow coming home.

If only S'William would arrive, Francesco thought, it would be as if a great stone rolled off his back, for S'William was the kind of man who took charge and saw no difficulties anywhere. Never would Francesco forget the way he had said to Anna: "Nonsense. You can't live in a hospital tent

202

for ever. You have been given into my charge for the time being and I don't intend to let you out of my sight until I see you settled."

Of course, from S'William's point of view, that was just what had happened. He had found them an uncle and an aunt and they had good clothes and, though often nasty, especially cabbage, plenty to eat. All in fact should have been well. How could S'William know that in their school there would be Wilf and his gang? How could he know that Miss de Veane should wish Anna to dance in public? How could he know the trouble he had caused by writing about Madame Scarletti?

What Francesco supposed had happened was that S'William, for reasons to do with his work, had delayed coming home and, if he thought about them at all, supposed they were safe and well. In any case he might think they were old enough to look after themselves for all their birthdays were near Christmas, which meant he would soon be eleven, Gussie ten and Anna nine. Perhaps in Britain at such ages you were no longer considered a child.

The next Wednesday Anna went to her dancing class with her plans clearly made.

"I shall say nothing," she promised Francesco, "unless she tries to teach me a dance. Then I shall say 'no' – exercises only. I pay so I decide."

"Try not to finish with Miss de Veane," Francesco begged. "Some day you shall see this

Madame Scarletti, but not now, and in Fyton Miss de Veane is all that there is."

Outside the studio it was bitterly cold, with a fine stinging rain in the wind. This gave Francesco an idea.

"Perhaps," he said, "as it is so cold I could come inside."

Anna was not sure she liked that suggestion.

"It is not a very big studio."

"But it is so cold," Francesco pleaded. "Already my teeth knock together."

Anna was very cold herself but Francesco looked blue, so she relented.

"Come in. I will ask."

Anna went across the studio and gave her bob.

"Today is so cold," she said, "is it permitted my brother stays inside while he waits to take me home?"

Miss de Veane gave Anna what was meant to be a friendly smile but actually looked more like the smile the wolf gave Red Riding Hood.

"Of course, dear. Now, hurry away and change for I have something new for you to learn."

Francesco gazed spellbound at Miss de Veane. Her orange-coloured hair with black roots. Her black dress which was far too tight over the chest and hips, though it did finish up in a short pleated skirt so that she could dance, though how anyone could dance in white boots Francesco could not imagine. He thought of Jardek in his neat blouse and full trousers with his violin tucked under his chin and felt sick. "Poor Anna," he thought. "Even though perhaps the teaching is good she cannot like working with this lady."

Quite soon Anna was back. Mabel had made her a very neat tunic and she looked charming in it with her plaits pinned up on top of her head. She went straight to the barre, held on to it and turned out her feet.

"No, dear," said Miss de Veane. "We are not starting with exercises today. I have an enchaînement I want you to learn."

Anna did not move.

"What for?"

Miss de Veane hesitated, it was clear she was not used to having her orders questioned, but eventually she decided to make Anna an exception.

"We, that is all the children in my little school, are going to try to raise enough money to buy a guide dog for a blind person. We are giving a dancing matinée. The ballet, which is half the programme, takes place in a fairy wood in which live many flowers. A fairy dances through the wood to wake the flowers. You would not mind being the fairy to help a blind person, would you?"

Anna did not move or change the position of her feet.

"Of course I would wish to help the blind. Always when we lived in a caravan we saw many, many blind and always Christopher gave money.

But I will not dance this fairy, there is much work I must do before I can dance such a role."

"That, I think," said Miss de Veane, her hoarse voice sounding as if she had chipped ice in her throat, "is for me to decide."

Anna shook her head.

"No — me. It has been hard for my brothers to earn the money for my lessons, but it has been earned so now it is I who decide what I will learn and I do not dance that solo."

Miss de Veane would not have allowed any other pupil to speak to her like that. She was only allowing it now because she knew that in Anna she had something as precious as a jewel. If could be persuaded to dance she would dance well for she was incapable of dancing badly. Then one look at Anna dancing and every mum in the audience would think, if I sent my Sally or Marlene or Caroline to learn dancing she will dance like that. So, swallowing her temper which made her feel as if she was swallowing red hot coals, she said:

"I think you are forgetting the blind person, dear, who is waiting for a guide dog."

Francesco did not know what a guide dog was so he was sure Anna did not. He got up and came over to Anna and Miss de Veane. He gave Miss de Veane a little bow.

"Always we have lived abroad where such dogs are not. Perhaps if you could tell Anna about such a dog she will understand."

Miss de Veane had a desk in the corner of the studio. She went to it and took out a folder. On the front was a picture of a splendid Alsatian wearing his special guide dog harness. She gave the folder to the children.

"Imagine, if you were blind, what it would mean to you to be looked after by a dog like that."

Both children were most impressed.

"We never had a dog," said Francesco, "only our horse, he was called Togo. It would be wonderful to have a dog, Anna, to lead you if you were blind."

But Anna was not to be moved by pity.

"Is is good a blind person should have such a dog," she agreed. "The blind we have known are looked after by the children of the family but maybe a dog is better. But my dancing will not buy a dog, some other pupil will dance the fairy. But because the dog is needed I will ask The Aunt to buy a ticket."

Francesco and Miss de Veane exchanged looks.

Francesco's look said: "I'm afraid it's no good asking her but please go on teaching her for I do not know how to get her to London." Miss de Veane's look said: "See what you can do to make your sister dance, for if she refuses I shall not teach her and then what will you do?"

28. Plans

The next week was the half-term holiday. Wally had explained this to the Docksays and so had most of the children living in The Crescent, for of course walking to and from school nobody paid any attention to Cecil's silly rules so they were all friends. The only rule the children kept was not accepting invitations for tea and television – that, in their own street, was asking for trouble.

"We're goin' away," Wally had told Francesco. "But we'll be back at the weekend so Mum says she'll expect you Saturday and Sunday same as usual."

"Where are you going to?" Francesco asked.

"Me dad's sister, my auntie that is. Lives in London, she does. It's interestin' where she hangs out because it's near the river an' I watches them loadin' an unloadin' the ships."

Francesco, as Wally told him this, felt a horrible wave of unhappiness sweep over him. In his mind he was in Turkey. Christopher was trying to get a curious light effect he said he could only find on the Bosphorus. Olga was having trouble with police who wanted the caravan moved. Olga could not give lessons because of arguing with the police, so he, Gussie and Anna had gone to the waterside and watched the ships. They had remembered they had some money so they had climbed into a boat which was going to the Golden Horn. At the end of their journey they had bought cakes and ice cream and made friends with a dancing bear and listened to the muezzin calling the faithful to prayer, a real proper muezzin – not one of those gramophone records which made Christopher swear. Nothing special happened. They took another boat home where they found Christopher having drinks with the police. It was just one of those days which, from England on a grey November morning, made a lump come into your throat.

"Me dad was saying maybe you three would see to Bess and the hens while we was away. Mum'll show you where we keeps the key. It's only Tuesday to Friday, for we'll see to them Monday before we goes."

All the children loved Wally's farm so naturally Francesco agreed.

"It will be nice to have something to do for of course we will go nowhere."

Other people beside Wally had plans for the half-term. Tom, looking rather like a scared white mouse wearing glasses, sidled up to Gussie in the morning break to whisper:

"Wilf wants to see you dinner time. Same place as before."

Gussie was delighted. He had been disappointed in The Gang. He thought once he had joined them life would be full of excitement but nothing had happened at all. So at dinner time he almost ran to the senior classroom, only pausing to give a good dramatic version of the pass sign. Wilf, looking dirtier and more scruffy than usual, was sitting at his desk.

"Shut the door," he told Gussie, "for what I got to say is special private."

Gussie shut the door then stood expectantly beside Wilf waiting for orders.

"What I'm plannin' will be a bit of fun like for the 'alf-term."

Gussie was delighted, he was all in favour of fun.

"What am I to do?"

Wilf chose his words carefully.

"There's many more what belongs to The Gang than what you see in this school. Some's quite old — maybe twenty an' more. Well, I was telling them of the way you brought your uncle's gnome to the school and they wouldn't believe it."

"Well, it was difficult," Gussie boasted, "and nobody but me ever knew why I took it to the school. You ought to have seen The Uncle. He was terribly angry and sent for the policemen."

Wilf nodded.

"Well, next Tuesday will be dead easy, I'm bringing two of the leaders like to see the gnomes, they thought they'd paint them different colours."

Gussie giggled.

"I cannot imagine The Uncle when he sees them changed. I think he could explode like a firework. How will you get in?"

"Now listen careful," said Wilf, "for I don't like sayin' things twice. Can you find a way to stay awake?"

"I never tried," Gussie admitted, "but I expect I could find a way."

"You don't 'ave to find no way for I've got it. You ties a long piece of string to your big toe and 'angs it out of the winder, then when we gets there I gives it a pull."

"But how have you got into the garden?" Gussie asked.

"Same way as you did. Through the gate and over the twins' wall."

"When I am awake what do I do?" Gussie asked.

"You sneak down the stairs and comes out into the garden to 'elp paint the gnomes."

"Through the lounge, you mean. This will be easy."

"That's right," Wilf agreed. "I told you it was dead easy. Now let's see you got it right."

Gussie took a deep breath.

"Next Tuesday before I go to sleep I tie a long piece of string to my toe and out the end out of the window. That is easy for my bed is by the window. In the night you pull the string, I wake up and creep very, very quietly down into the hall and through the lounge into the garden where you will be painting the gnomes."

Wilf sounded pleased.

"You got it."

"What colour shall the gnomes be?"

Wilf smiled his cunning smile.

"We've not gone into that, not yet. Suppose you choose."

Gussie was flattered.

"I think bright blue would be nice."

"Blue it is," Wilf agreed. "And I don't 'ave to remind you not one word of this to anybody."

"Not one word," Gussie agreed, " or . . ." and he drew a finger across his throat, and made a bloodthirsty noise.

Anna was not happy after the dancing class at which Francesco was present for she did not feel that he understood. Walking home he had told her how wonderful for a person who was blind it must be have a dog. How perhaps just one dance would not hurt. He did not speak about Jardek in words for he hated to do, but underneath all he did say was: "If Jardek was here now I think he would understand." On one point Anna found Francesco did agree with her. He thought Miss de Veane terrible.

"I wish," he had said, "that it was possible to take you to the Madame Scarletti, but for this I think we must wait for S'William."

Anna did not feel she could wait for anyone. If

someone who was the best dancer in the world said they would teach her then nobody, not even The Uncle who thought to dance was a sin, could stop her from learning.

It was a terrible thing, Anna considered, for her to act on her own. This was something which before the earthquake had never happened. But now it had to happen. Francesco and Gussie would not agree so she must go to London alone to see Madame Scarletti. She knew where the money was for the fare. Under the paper beside S'William's address. Next week when there was a holiday she would take the money and, carrying her shoes and tunic in a bag, she would visit this Madame Scarletti and ask her to watch her work.

29. Madame Scarletti

On the Tuesday Gussie woke up feeling very happy and above himself. It would be such fun to get up in the middle of the night. It made him want to laugh out loud when he thought of The Uncle's face in the morning. It also made him feel proud that two gang leaders were coming to see how one boy had carried a gnome all the way to school.

Mabel was trying to make the half-term pleasant. "Your uncle will be very busy all day," she told the children. "As you know. he's treasurer to various charities and today he has to divide a lot of money up which people get at Christmas." Mabel puffed after so long a speech. "So I thought you'd like to have your lunch out and then go to a film. I will give you a pound but your uncle must not know."

Francesco and Gussie liked the idea of lunch out. In Fyton there was a Chinese restaurant called "The Lotus Bud" and they had wanted to eat there ever since they came to live in The Crescent.

"For I bet they never have cabbage," Gussie had said.

Surprisingly it was Anna who was not keen to try "The Lotus Bud".

"I wish to practise my dancing," she explained.

Gussie looked at her in disgust.

"You are getting to be a very tiresome girl," he told her. "You can't practise dancing all through the day, you must eat somewhere."

"Suppose Gussie and I go out this morning and feed Bessie and the hens then come back to fetch you to this 'Lotus Bud'," Francesco suggested.

Anna did not look as if she liked the idea, but she said grudgingly:

"Very well. But not too early. The Aunt must finish my room before I can practise."

Francesco and Gussie went to the farm soon after breakfast. Bessie seemed delighted to see them for she was evidently missing her family. The boys tried to think the hens were pleased to see them too but they knew really that they were not.

"I think perhaps hens do not need friends," Francesco said, "which is a pity."

Doing the farm took quite a long time for Bessie had to have a warmed-up mixture to eat, and there were the eggs to collect and of course the hens to be fed. All the time they were working while Gussie was jabbering away about anything which came into his head, Francesco was uneasy. He could not think why but he felt unhappy about Anna. Why had she decided she must practise that morning? She was hiding something, he was sure of it.

"Come on, Gussie," he said. "Let's lock up and then we can fetch Anna."

Gussie was surprised.

"She won't be ready yet. I do not think The Aunt has even finished her room. Let's stay here and turn on the telly."

'We cannot do that,' Francesco said firmly. "We don't know how and they would not like it, and anyway I do not think there are pictures in the morning."

Gussie scowled.

"Always nowadays you are saying 'No! No! No!' all the time. You never used to do this."

Francesco was sorry.

"I am the eldest and someone must say it. You know Wally's dad would not wish us to touch his telly."

Gussie did know, but he did not want to hear about it.

"Then let's go down in town, there's sure to be some boys from the school about."

Francesco shook his head.

"You do as you wish, but me I am going to fetch Anna. I do not mind waiting until she is ready. I will bring her to 'The Lotus Bud' at half past twelve."

Gussie did not mind a morning in his own. If he met some of his friends they might have fun.

"OK," he said. "And you can go now if you wish. I will lock up."

The keys to the Walls' house lived under a grating near the pigsty. All three children knew where it lived but Francesco was officially in charge of it.

"You promise you will put the key in the right place?"

Gussie was insulted.

"Of course I will. Nobody but you is so sure I will not do things I should."

Francesco was ashamed.

"I know and I am sorry but somehow in Britain I feel there is only me, at least until S'William comes back. That makes me say 'no' when I do not mean it."

Francesco, without meaning to, ran almost all the way back to Dunroamin. He could hear The Aunt in the kitchen and knew The Uncle would be counting money behind the shut lounge door. He ran quietly up the stairs, meaning to go to Anna's room, but instead he stood on the top of the stairs staring into his and Gussie's room. The door was open and so was the door of the wardrobe in which they kept S'William's address, his letter and their money. Anna, dressed to go out, was kneeling in front of the wardrobe taking from under the lining paper S'William's letter and their money, and putting both into a paper carrier bag which was lying beside her.

Francesco moved into the doorway.

"Anna! What are you doing?"

It was almost as if Anna had expected interference and was prepared for it. She stood up holding the carrier bag in her arms.

"I go to London to see Madame Scarletti. She must see me dance. If she cannot see what Jardek saw then I will dance that fairy to buy a dog for someone who is blind. If she can see then she will teach me. This is sure."

"How were you going?"

"I go to the railway where I buy one ticket, it is called day return half price. Priscilla, who lives next door, told me this."

Francesco could see it was no good arguing.

"Then I will go too. I have here the pound The Aunt gave. But I have told Gussie to meet us at 'The Lotus Bud' at twelve-thirty and he has no money."

Anna seemed pleased to have Francesco's company.

"Gussie will find money when he needs it. That is how Gussie is."

As it happened Gussie only looked in at "The Lotus Bud" to tell the other two he would not be staying for lunch. He had been invited to friends and there would be television afterwards. Not finding Francesco and Anna in the restaurant he rejoined his friends and thought no more about them.

Even if you knew London well, 45 Bemberton

Street, Chelsea, was not easy to find. It was a little street tucked in amongst other streets, so close to the Thames you could hear the tugs hooting. Francesco and Anna never would have found it on their own. Fortunately for them, Christopher had often dropped bits of information about Britain into his conversation and one was: "Nothing to touch an English bobby if you want help." And then he would sing "If you want to know the time ask a policeman." So at the station when they arrived they had found a policeman and showed him S'William's letter and had been told to get to Sloane Square on the Underground, and then to take a bus to Chelsea Town Hall.

"When you get there," the policeman had said, "ask again."

So at the Town Hall they had asked again. They chose an old man selling newspapers.

"Funny you should ask me," he said, " 'cause I don't suppose many about here knows where it is." Then out of a pocket he took a piece of paper and a pencil and drew them a little map. "Stick to that an' you can't miss it. Foreign, aren't you?"

"Not now," Francesco explained. "Now we are British but it is not long we have lived here."

"You'll be all right in Bemberton Street," the paper man promised. "Proper. United Nations up that way." Then he went back to selling his papers.

Bemberton Street was very shabby-looking. Paint was peeling off the wall, windows were cracked and so were the two steps leading to the front door of number 45. But to Anna the house was a fairy palace for in it lived Madame Scarletti. Francesco rang the bell, which was not answered, so he rang again. This time after a pause a grown-up girl wearing a black tunic and ballet shoes opened the door.

"We wish," Francesco said politely, "to see Madame Scarletti."

The girl looked amused.

"Many people wish to see Madame. They come from all over the world. But Madame sees no one without an appointment."

Francesco was appalled. He had agreed to the journey because Anna could not go alone, but it had not occurred to him that having got here Madame Scarletti would refuse to see them.

"Would you perhaps beg for us a few minutes, you see we come a long way and we will not have the money to do this twice. At least not till S'William gets home. Look!" He fumbled in his pocket and took out the envelope containing Sir William's letter. "You see, we are told to come here." He handed the girl the envelope and when she had opened the letter he pointed to the portion addressed to Anna.

The girl read what Sir William had written. Then she looked at the envelope, then turned it over and read "Sir William Hoogle" on the back.

"Docksay," she said. "Would you be the children

Sir William Hoogle rescued after an earthquake?"

"We are two of them," Francesco agreed. "There is another called Gussie but he is not here."

The girl came to a decision.

"Wait here. I will show Madame this letter."

It seemed to Francesco a long wait but Anna was not worried, she had reached Madame Scarletti's doorstep, it never crossed her mind she might get no further.

Anna was right to have faith. Presently the girl came back.

"Come along," she said. "Madame will see you."

Madame Scarletti was indeed very old but, as so often with dancers, she had kept her figure. She was small and looked as if she were made of frail porcelain. She had immense gleaming black eyes and her white hair was piled in intricate plaits on the top of her head. She was wearing a long taffeta dress and round her shoulders was a vivid scarlet shawl. On her feet were ballet shoes.

Madame Scarletti was sitting on a high-backed chair. Beside her was a long cane with an ivory top. Francesco and Anna approached her, then Francesco bowed and Anna, instead of her usual bob, made a lovely obeisance right down to the floor.

Madame Scarletti's voice was surprisingly strong for anyone so old. She looked only at Anna.

"Your father was Christopher Docksay."

Anna felt she ought to curtsey again but she didn't.

"Yes, Madame."

"And he married Olga Popouska."

Anna looked at Francesco.

"Was Olga called Popouska?" she asked him.

Francesco did not know.

"I do not think we knew. She was just Olga and our father was Christopher, and our grandfather and grandmother were Jardek and Babka and our horse Togo."

"But I know," said Madame Scarletti. "Many, many years ago in Warsaw there was a great teacher of dancing. His name was Ivan Popouski. I did not know what happened to him until I read in a newspaper about the Turkish earthquake." She turned to the girl in the black tunic. "This is Maria, my keeper and guardian, without whom I could not live. Did I not say to you, Maria, that the grandfather who was killed in the earthquake must be Ivan Popouski?"

"That's right," Maria agreed. "That's why I wanted you to see these two." She looked at Francesco and Anna. "Which is the dancer for I suppose one of you is?"

Madame made an impatient tch-tch-ing sound. She looked scornfully at Maria.

"Where are your eyes, girl? Do you not recognize the face of a dancer when you see one? I knew this little girl could dance the moment she entered the studio." Then she turned to Anna. "You have shoes with you?"

"And my tunic," Anna agreed.

Madame waved a hand gracefully towards the door.

"Take the child where she can change."

Then she looked at Francesco.

"Come and sit down." She pointed to a footstool. "I can see you have suffered. Tell me about it. Every small thing, it is much better not to shut things away inside, keep them outside where you can see them."

So Francesco told her. He started on the day of the earthquake. The terrible heat. The odd-looking yellowish sky.

"It was so hot that nobody is talking, and only because Olga said we must could we eat any breakfast – yoghourt and a slice of bread with black olives."

Then Francesco explained about the picture. How Christopher had said he would have taken it to the picture framer in the caravan but it would spoil Togo's holiday.

"You see, he was old and it would be a long way right across Turkey to the picture exhibition. Christopher could not take his picture to be framed because he must work. It was only three miles over the hill so we went. It was, I think, the only day when Jardek said it was too hot for Anna's dancing lesson."

Francesco paused there, seeing again the little house as they had last seen it, with Christopher,

Olga, Jardek and Babka drinking tea.

After a moment Madame Scarletti gave him a friendly pat.

"Go on. Every small thing. Lay it all out."

So Francesco went on. He described the terrible heat climbing over the hill so they were wet all over. How the picture framer was asleep on his bed so they had to leave the picture for him to see when he woke up. How they had bought figs, a leaf of mulberries and lemonade. How they had carried the food and drink halfway up the hill to picnic in the shade of some cacti. How it was then he noticed there were no birds. No birds at all. How Anna had told them the birds had left two days before, she had seen hundreds of them fly away.

There was another small pause while Francesco tried to remember. During this Anna, changed into her tunic, came back into the room with Maria. Francesco did not see them so Madame Scarletti put a finger to her lips and they quietly sat down.

"I think it was then Gussie saw the horse. As it seemed then it appeared to have gone mad, but I know now the horse knew just as the birds had known what was to happen, it was only us who did not know."

"Then it happened?" Madame Scarletti asked. Francesco nodded.

"In the camp, men asked us often how it was but we could not say. Now I cam remember a great noise and hot air, then the earth moved and we were thrown everywhere. Afterwards we got to the top of the hill and looked. All was gone. The little house. Jardek, Babka, Christopher, Olga and Togo, as if they had never been."

Madame Scarletti seemed to know the end of the story.

"Then Sir William Hoogle found you and soon he discovered your uncle and your aunt with whom you are now living."

That was when Anna joined in.

"They are not nice. The Uncle thinks to dance is wrong."

Francesco tried to be fair.

"The Aunt tried to be kind but she is afraid of The Uncle. When S'William comes back I hope he will arrange things better."

Madame Scarletti beckoned to Anna.

"Go to the barre and we will see what you have learnt." Then she smiled at Francesco.

"There is good news for you. Sir William has arrived in England. *The Times* newspaper printed this. Now he is home I believe you can be a little boy again."

30. Dial 999

Madame Scarletti had a car. She told Maria to drive the children to the station and to see them on the right train.

"I shall write to Sir William," she told Francesco, "and arrangements will be made for Anna. It may be she will live here with me."

These words were like a Te Deum to Francesco. Madame would write to Sir William. Madame would make all the arrangements. Madame might even have Anna to live with her.

Because of being taken by car to the station, the children were home in good time, but Gussie was home before them. He had felt annoyed at this, for he wanted to tell them about a film he had see on TV and he must do it before supper, for the last thing he wanted was Francesco and Anna being late going to bed. If he was to wake up in the middle of the night he should go to sleep early.

"Where have you been?" he demanded.

"To see Madame Scarletti," said Anna.

Anna spoke in so pleased a voice it maddened Gussie.

"And what for? Who is to pay for lessons in

London?" Then he turned to Francesco. "Why did you let her go? It had been hard to get fifty pence for that Miss de Veane, to get enough for Madame Scarletti and to get Anna to London is impossible."

Francesco was too happy to mind what Gussie said.

"Imagine! S'William is in England. It is in *The Times* newspaper. Have you been to the farm to put Bessie and the hens to bed?"

Gussie would have loved to say "Yes, I have!" but he couldn't. Rushing home to tell the others about the television he had seen and the food he had eaten he had forgotten the farm in his annoyance at finding the other two out.

"No. But I will go now."

"Both will go now," said Francesco. "If we run we should not be back late for supper. But if we are, do not worry, Anna, keep saying 'S'William is back', then nothing The Uncle says will matter."

The boys ran all the way to the farm. It was dark when they got there so the hens were waiting to come into their coop. Bessie, of course, could get into her sty but there was a padlock on her door at night, the key of which was kept under the grating with the house key. Wally had lent them a torch.

"If S'William answers my letter soon," Francesco said, "have you a plan? I mean, we know about Anna but what about us? What do we want if the picture sells for much money?"

"I do not wish to live with The Uncle," said Gussie.

"I do not wish either," Francesco agreed. "But where else do we wish to go?"

Gussie fixed Bessie's lock.

"If it was possible I would like a caravan. Not of course as before — that can never be — or perhaps a little house like Babka and Jardek had, but I do not think that is possible in Britain. There will be police and laws about children living alone."

Francesco held out his hand for Bessie's key and turned the torch on to the grating.

"The only rule in Britain that we know is the one of which Christopher always spoke. Do you not remember how, if we made an extra noise when he was working, he would say 'I will have 'ush. If you kids lived where I was brought up I'd refuse to keep you, then they'd clap the lot of you into a home'?"

Gussie felt a sort of heave in his inside.

"Suppose The Uncle did not want us. Could he put us in a home?"

"Not unless we did something bad. But he does not have to have us. You remember how The Aunt said: 'He does not like children so it is hard for him that you are here, but he does his duty, he gives you a home.'"

Gussie, wondering if painting a gnome was so bad you could be clapped in a home said:

"And you said: 'We did not ask to come.'"

Francesco put away the keys.

"We are not going to do anything bad, but it is good that when we see S'William we tell him where it is we wish to live."

Gussie did not say much on the way back to Dunroamin. He wished now he had not agreed to paint a gnome blue, especially as there was no money in it, but it was too late now to do anything about it.

It had seemed to Gussie that evening that Francesco was never going to sleep. He was so excited about S'William coming home he had to talk about it. At last Gussie in desperation pretended to be asleep, in fact he pretended so well he was almost asleep when something reminded him of what he had to do. He sat up in bed and looked towards Francesco's bed. He certainly did seem to be asleep. Very quietly, Gussie slipped out of bed. The window was already open so, fixing a loop of the length of string Wilf had given him round his left big toe, he dropped the other end, which had a small weight on it, out of the window, got back into bed and promptly fell asleep.

What seemed to Gussie hours and hours later he was woken up by a continual tugging at his left toe. For a moment he could not remember what was happening, then it all came back to him. He felt down the bed for the string, took the loop off his toe, gave three tugs of the string as Wilf had told him, put on his dressing-gown and bedroom slippers and sneaked down the stairs. Very quietly he opened the lounge door, fumbled his way across the room to the French windows, unlocked them and he was in the garden. There he heard Wilf say "This is 'im". Then a sack was put over his head and he was rolled over on his face. Then once more he heard Wilf's voice.

"Now you lie still and nothin' won't 'appen to you. But if you tries anythin' you know what to expect."

Gussie, tied inside the sack, could not draw his finger across his throat but he knew all right. Just for a few moments he was puzzles. He expected to hear whispers and perhaps the movement of a pot of paint. He could not imagine why Wilf had tied him up in a sack instead of letting him paint one of the gnomes. Then a new thought came to him. Why was there no sound? Why did nobody move about, not even to give him a kick? The horrible answer soon came to him. The Gang were not wanting to paint a gnome. they had got him out into the garden so that he would leave the French windows open. They were going to steal from The Uncle.

The sack was uncomfortable and dirty but there was plenty of air inside it so Gussie could breathe. He rolled over on to his back and thought what to do. If he called for help Wilf and his friends would stop him, and anyway muffled in a sack The Uncle wouldn't hear, sleeping the other side of the house.

But Gussie was agile as an eel. He rolled up and down the concrete paths, which pretended they were crazy paving, and at last he was rewarded, the rope which had held his arms to his sides shifted to his feet. Then it was a matter of seconds for Gussie to sit up, push off the rope and wriggle out of the sack. Then what? He could not shout for help for The Gang members would hear. Then he had an idea. On his hands and knees he crept up to the lounge door and peered in.

There seemed to be three of them – Wilf and two others. Wilf was holding a torch and the other two were trying to open a safe let into the wall. Gussie did not know it was a safe but he could hear what they whispered to each other. A rough voice growled:

"You never said that 'e kept the money in a safe, Wilf."

Wilf didn't sound his tough self at all, in fact he almost whined.

"I didn't know, did I?"

A third voice said:

"Better give it up. We 'aven't the tools to open that."

"'Oo says we 'aven't?" the rough voice retorted. "I never bin beaten by a safe yet and this should be dead easy."

While they were talking Gussie had got to his feet. Very quietly he took the key out of the inside of the lounge door. Then softly he shut the door and locked it on the outside. Then he ran to the twins' wall and yelled:

"Help! Help! Thieves!"

He made such a noise that both twins woke up and shoved their heads out of their windows.

"Who is it?" Jonathan asked.

"It's me, Gussie. How is it when you need policemen? There are three thieves in the house."

It seemed no time after that before sirens were blowing and policemen all over the place. In most houses Wilf and his friends would have got away, but they did not know Cecil. The locks and chains on his front door were splendid, so Wilf and his friends were caught red-handed.

When the thieves, including a very cowed-looking Wilf, had been driven to the police station, the police sergeant who was in charge asked everybody to come into the lounge, including Mr Allan and the twins as well as Mabel, Francesco and Anna. By that time it was established that nothing had been stolen and no one had broken into the house.

"Now," said the police sergeant looking at Gussie, "you say you were in the garden. Had you left the French windows open?"

Gussie's thoughts were running around like a cage full of mice.

"Yes."

"So you let the thieves in. Did you do it on purpose?"

"No. I was tied in a sack."

"But what brought you down into the garden in the middle of the night?"

Gussie felt there was nothing for it but the truth.

"I was to paint a gnome blue."

"Disgraceful!" said Cecil.

"Paint a gnome blue!" The sergeant was puzzled. "I'm afraid you want a better story than that."

That annoyed Gussie.

"It's true. I was to paint a gnome blue."

The sergeant sounded very unbelieving.

"You were meeting the thieves to paint a gnome blue. Then you know who they were."

Too clearly Gussie could hear Wilf making a gurgling sound and drawing his finger across his throat.

"Only one and I can't tell you his name."

Priscilla tried to help.

"We know one of them. He's Wilf who goes to our school."

In a very angry voice, The Uncle said:

"I'm afraid you'll get no help from my nephew, Sergeant. Result of a bad upbringing."

None of the children was standing for that. Francesco said:

"No one shall say we had a bad upbringing. It was a beautiful upbringing before the earthquake."

"Beautiful," Anna agreed. "It is only now that Gussie does something bad – never before."

Gussie was furious.

"I don't see that I have done something bad now. It was me who got out of the sack and shouted to the twins to send for policemen, and it was me who managed to lock the thieves in. If I had not done that they would not have been caught."

The sergeant looked at the constable, who was taking notes.

"Take a torch and go out into the garden and see if you can find a sack and a length of rope."

While the constable was gone Mr Allan said:

"I must say, Sergeant, if what the boy says is true — and I suspect it is — I should think he ought to get a reward. It was a stout effort getting that key out of the door, for if the thieves had caught him I hate to think what might have happened."

Before anyone could answer, and it was clear from the furious look on Cecil's face that he was going to, the constable was back with the sack and the rope.

"There," said Gussie, "you see, I was telling the truth."

Gussie looked almost fat with pride. It was more than Cecil could bear.

"If the sergeant has done with you, go up to bed, Augustus. I will deal with you in the morning."

"And you go too, dears," Mabels told Francesco and Anna. "I will be up with hot drinks for you all in a minute."

Cecil almost roared.

"Not for Augustus."

Then a very odd thing happened. Mabel, looking more than usually held together, this time by the sash of her shapeless dressing-gown, with her hair not falling down but meant to be down, puffed out:

"Augustus needs a hot drink more than the other two. He has been out in the night air in his dressing-gown, and he is certainly over-excited, which well he may be for, as Mr Allan said, he has been a very brave little boy. So if you will excuse us, Sergeant." Then, without looking at Cecil, she swept the children in front of her and marched out of the lounge.

31. The Story Ends

Even if you were up in the middle of the night rules were never changed in Dunroamin. So the children were called the same time as usual and were still half asleep when it was time to go down for breakfast.

Gussie was not feeling as pleased with himself as he had been during the night.

"Do you think," he whispered to Francesco, "that having meant to paint a gnome blue is enough for The Uncle to put me in a home?"

Francesco had no idea, but until S'William appeared he was still in charge.

"I do not think so. Anyway, if he does I will go too. I think Madame Scarletti will find room for Anna."

It was an even more awful breakfast than usual. If anyone had to speak it was in a whisper. Gussie afterwards said The Uncle looked like a sky looks before there is thunder. And The Aunt, not as if a cat is catching her but as if it had caught her.

Breakfast over Cecil made a pronouncement.

"You will stay in your room this morning, Augustus. The police may need to see you."

On the way upstairs Francesco whispered to Gussie:

"Thank goodness it is only you who has to stay in your room. I had thought it would be all of us so I was worried about Bessie and the hens."

"I thought of that too," Gussie agreed. "But I did not think he would lock our doors so we could have sneaked out."

Francesco looked sadly at Gussie.

"That was a bad thought. Sometimes I think you will never learn how things are in Britain."

After Francesco and Anna had gone to the farm and Mabel had done the bedrooms, Gussie was very bored. He hung out of the window and thought about the excitement of last night and wondered how a gnome would look painted blue. Presently he heard the doorbell ring and guessed it was the police. He hoped they would send him for it would be something to do, but nothing happened. Then the front-door bell rang again. This time Gussie tiptoed into the passage to see who it was. Mabel, who had evidently been cooking, came along the passage drying her hands on her apron. She opened the door wide, but Gussie could not see who was there. Then a voice said:

"Good morning, Mrs Docksay."

Gussie made one rush and he was down the stairs clutching Sir William round the waist.

"Oh, it's so good you are home. Anna is needing

to learn with that Madame Scarletti. Francesco is becoming like a cross old man and I may be sent to a home because I have trouble with thieves."

Sir William seemed never to change wherever he was. He had not now got Muzzaffer, the camel, on which he had arrived at Camp A. But otherwise he was exactly the same.

"I met Francesco and Anna at the end of the road. I have suggested we lunch together." He turned to Mabel. "I would like a few words with Mr Docksay if I might. Then, with his permission, I will take Gussie to join the others at a restaurant, they say it is called 'The Lotus Bud'."

At "The Lotus Bud" Sir William, by refusing to allow more than one child to speak at a time, managed to get more or less the whole story of their stay in Dunroamin. At the end, he turned to Francesco.

"One way and another you seem to have managed well. Your uncle has agreed to the sale of your picture and in the meantime I will advance what is needed. I think you should buy a bicycle right away for Wally. It would be pleasant if it was waiting for him when he returns home."

To Anna he said:

"So you may become a great ballerina. Madame Scarletti spoke to me on the telephone last night. She will train you, and for the time being take you into her home. She has someone called Maria who will look after you."

Then he turned to Gussie.

"It was silly of you to want to paint your uncle's gnome blue, but I gather the police have decided that was your only crime. You know your uncle does not like children and you seem to have done nothing to make him change that opinion. What I would suggest is that I look around for a boarding school for you boys; there are some good ones about where you could both have fun as well as learn. But what we have to think about is the holidays, for Anna too will have holidays. Of course you could go to Dunroamin." The children groaned. "In fact, you must see your aunt, for she is very fond of you. Anyone got any ideas?"

It is strange how things happen. Where no ideas were before suddenly there was the same idea in all three children's heads.

"A caravan," said Francesco.

"Not one pulled by a horse like Togo," Gussie explained. "But one that stays where it is."

Anna nodded.

"On Wally's dad's farm. There would perhaps be room for me in the house but not for the boys."

Sir William seemed pleased. He spoke in exactly the same voice as he used when he had stated: "The army say the runway will be open tomorrow, in which case we should get a plane for Istanbul." Now he said:

"Good. I will see Wally's dad as soon as he gets home. If he agrees, that sounds fine. Anyway, you can try things out, and if they don't work I shan't be far away. I'll keep in touch."

Francesco smiled at him.

"I hope you do. It is a great consolation to know where you are."

THURSDAY'S CHILD

Dedicated to an
American penfriend, Kathy Retan,
with love

First published in Great Britain by
William Collins Sons & Co. Ltd 1970

1. The Choice

Margaret had been discovering all her life that grown-ups were disappointing conversationalists. So now that she was ten she was quite prepared to carry on a conversation by herself. That January afternoon as she walked – or sometimes, forgetting it was a crime – skipped home beside Hannah, she argued about boots.

"I know you say and Miss Sylvia and Miss Selina say that boots are economical because they last longer but I don't think that's true. All the other girls at school wear shoes and they say they don't wear out quickly and they ought to know. And what nobody understands is what wearing boots does to me – they humiliate my legs. If I wasn't me but a different person they would humiliate me all over, but not even boots can do that. I am Margaret Thursday and unhumiliatable."

Hannah, her mind worrying round like a squirrel in a cage, had not been listening to a word Margaret said. Now she pulled her to a halt in a shop doorway.

"Let's have a look at you, dear. You are to have tea with the rector."

7

Hannah was a bony woman, made bonier by wearing long stiff all-embracing corsets which creaked. She had worked for Miss Sylvia and Miss Selina Cameron most of her life, having first come to the house when she was thirteen as a between maid. She had sobbed herself sick before she went, much to her mother's annoyance.

"Give over, do," she had said. "What have you to cry about with everything so nice?"

The "everything" had been packed in Hannah's wicker basket, material provided by Mrs Cameron but sewn by Hannah and her mother. Such riches! Print dresses, black dresses for the afternoon, aprons, caps and, of course, an outfit for church on Sundays.

The Camerons had been kind to her, which was why Hannah had stayed with the family. There had been periods when she had got so far as walking-out with one or other of the menservants, but things had happened. First, Mr Cameron had died. Mrs Cameron was the helpless type and she had clung to Hannah, who had by then risen to being parlourmaid, as though to a rock. For some reason, which Hannah had never understood, after Mr Cameron's death there was less and less money. Slowly, changes had to be made. Not at once but over the years. First the menservants, then the cook and her assistants were given notice, until finally — except for a man once a week for the garden — there was only Hannah.

When Hannah had first come to work for the Camerons, Miss Sylvia had been twenty and Miss Selina eighteen. In those days they had been known as "Those pretty Cameron girls". Now Hannah was over sixty, so Miss Sylvia was over seventy and Miss Selina rising seventy, and they were known as "The old Cameron ladies".

Hannah had, almost since she was a baby, carefully taught Margaret how to be a good housewife. Her efforts had little effect for Margaret loathed dusting, polishing and sweeping, and as for laundry she just would not try. But Hannah's efforts were not altogether a failure for she had taught Margaret to cook. Often Hannah found herself so tired at the end of the day she could scarcely drag herself up to bed, but it had never crossed her mind to give in her notice. Miss Sylvia, always the delicate one, was getting very frail, and poor Miss Selina ever so hazy in her mind. Anyway, Saltmarsh House, where they lived, was her home. She could not imagine living anywhere else.

Now Hannah's bony, work-roughened fingers attempted to tidy Margaret's hair. This was chestnut-coloured and very curly, so not at all easy to control.

Margaret tried to wriggle out of Hannah's reach. She loved the rector but was surprised to be going to tea with him, for he was not the sort of man to give sudden invitations.

"Why am I going to tea with the rector?" she

asked, still trying to pull away from Hannah. "Please leave my hair alone, you know the rector isn't the sort of person who cares how people look."

"Tidiness shows respect," said Hannah. She stood away from Margaret to see the whole effect. Margaret was dressed as simply-brought-up children were dressed in the winter at the beginning of the century. A blue pleated skirt, a darker blue jersey and a red coat. On her head was a red tam-o'-shanter. On her legs black woollen stockings and the boots.

Hannah sighed, conscious that all Margaret's clothes were darned and could do with a sponge.

"I suppose you'll have to do, but if only we'd had warning you could have worn your Sunday green."

"Thank goodness you didn't know," said Margaret, "because I hate wearing my green for you've patched the elbows with stuff that doesn't match."

Hannah gave her a sad smile.

"Beggars can't be choosers. Come on or I'll be late getting my ladies' tea."

Margaret liked going to the rectory for Mr Hanslow, the rector, was, excluding Hannah, her greatest friend. The rectory could have been a beautiful house, but the rector was very poor so both it and his garden were neglected. He was looked after by a Mr and Mrs Price who lived in a cottage down the road. Mr Price was really the

10

verger, but he managed to combine his church work with a bit of gardening and cutting wood for the rector. Mrs Price cooked abominably and did what little housework was done.

Margaret never rang the rectory bell, she just opened the front door and shouted.

"Can I come in? It's me – Margaret."

The study door opened and the rector came smiling into the passage. He gave Margaret a kiss.

"There you are, my pet. Come in. Mrs Price has made toast for our tea."

Over burnt toast and stewed tea, Margaret chattered away as usual, bringing the rector up to date with home and school news. Then, when Mrs Price had cleared away the tea things, she stuck out her legs.

"Do you think you could speak to Miss Sylvia about these boots? Truly nobody wears boots any more. All the girls at school have laced-up shoes."

Mr Hanslow did not look at the boots but straight into Margaret's eyes.

"I have always thought you were a sensible child, which is why I have asked you here today to discuss your future."

Margaret was surprised. What future? Nothing ever changed in Saltmarsh House. It must, she decided, be something to do with the little school for the daughters of gentlemen which she attended.

"Is it about school?"

"That is one of the things we have to talk about," said the rector. "You remember, of course, the details of how you came to live here."

Margaret was proud of her history.

"Of course I do. One Thursday you found me on the steps of the church when I was a teeny-weeny baby. And with me in my basket there were three of everything, all of the very best quality."

"And a note," the rector reminded her.

"Oh yes. Printed so no one would know who had written it. It said: THIS IS MARGARET WHOM I ENTRUST TO YOUR CARE. EACH YEAR FIFTY-TWO POUNDS WILL BE SENT FOR HER KEEP AND SCHOOL-ING. SHE HAS NOT YET BEEN CHRISTENED."

The rector nodded, smiling at the memory.

"You were a beautiful baby and if screams were anything to go by you certainly got the devil out of you at your christening. I would have dearly loved to take you in, but Mrs Price could not sleep in and an old bachelor did not seem a suitable guardian for you, so. . ."

"So," Margaret prompted him, for she thought he was being rather slow telling the well-known story, "you asked the Miss Camerons to have me as they were the only people hereabouts with a big enough house and they said 'yes'."

"God bless them," said the rector, "for there was no one else in the parish suitable and it did work out very nicely, but now things have gone wrong. This Christmas no money arrived for your keep."

"No money!" Margaret gasped, for always the money had arrived with the utmost regularity. It came each year between Christmas Eve and New Year's Day. It was put in a bag somewhere in the church — fifty-two golden sovereigns. The bag was never found in the same place twice and no one had ever seen the money arrive. "Do you think it came and someone stole it?"

The rector took a card out of his breast pocket and passed it to Margaret.

"This was found in the font."

Like the card which had come with her when she was a baby, this one was printed. It said "NO MORE MONEY FOR MARGARET".

Margaret was shocked.

"How very mean! You would think a mother would manage something. Have you told Miss Sylvia and Miss Selina?"

The rector hesitated.

"Really this card has hastened something which had got to happen sooner or later. Miss Selina is getting very old."

Margaret giggled.

"She's getting more and more like a baby every day. Now Hannah has to dress her and undress her."

"Very sad," said the rector, "but it is also very worrying. You see, with the old ladies needing so much attention, Hannah has too much to do. It has broken her heart to admit this but it is true. So even before Christmas I had agreed to find you a new home."

Margaret felt like Alice must have felt as she fell down the rabbit hole. A new home! But Saltmarsh House was her home, her only home. How could she be going to a new one — children never did that.

"I suppose you didn't know," she said, "but I help Hannah. Often and often I cook the supper and I do lots of other things — not as well as I cook, but I do them."

The rector took one of Margaret's hands.

"It is not a question of helping in the house, it's everything. The two old ladies are all Hannah can manage. She admitted this before Christmas and we discussed plans, thinking you still had an income of fifty-two pounds a year. But now the situation has changed. The Miss Camerons are, as you know, very far from rich, and now you have no money. . ." The rector broke off, looking at Margaret with great love but also with a childlike confusion.

The rector's worried face pulled Margaret together.

"If I still had fifty-two pounds a year where were you going to send me?"

"Nothing was decided, but we had thought of a boarding-school."

"Well, I'm glad I haven't got the money for that for I'd hate it. Couldn't I live with you? I could do all the things Mrs Price does and I'd work in the garden as well as I'd eat very little."

The rector looked more worried than ever.

"I thought of that, but Mrs Price refused to consider it. She is a great sufferer with bad legs and. . ."

Margaret had her own opinion about Mrs Price's bad legs, which she thought were used as an excuse not to work.

"Well, send her away. I can look after both of us – truly I can."

The rector gave a little groan.

"It can't be done, pet. You see, there's Mr Price. He doesn't really charge me, as you know, he throws me in, as it were, with his position of verger. But I did speak to the archdeacon about you, asking his opinion as to whether you could possibly live here. But he said he thought an old bachelor like myself was a most unsuitable guardian for a little girl."

Margaret made a face.

"How silly of the archdeacon. Well, if I'm not staying at Saltmarsh House and I'm not staying here, where am I going?"

The rector had spent many hours on his knees asking God for advice and help in handling this interview. He was convinced help and advice would be given to him if only he was spiritually able to receive it. Now, with Margaret's brown eyes gazing up at him, he felt painfully inadequate and ashamed. Why was he so ineffectual a man that he had not risen in the world so that he had the wherewithal to succour children such as Margaret?

"I'm afraid, pet, you are not going to care for either of the two solutions I have to offer. You are, I know, a brave child, but now you will need all your fortitude."

Margaret stiffened to take what was coming.

"Whatever it is," she said, "I'm still me — Margaret Thursday. Go on, tell me."

Since Margaret had no surname it was the rector who had chosen Thursday, the day on which he had found her. He thought it touching that she was so proud of it.

"I have, of course, tried everywhere to find you a home in this parish. I have succeeded in only one case. Your school. I know you do not much care for your teacher, but though perhaps she has a difficult nature she is a good Christian woman."

"I have never seen anything very Christian about her," said Margaret. "I think she's hateful."

The rector shook his head.

"You must not make such harsh judgements, pet, especially now that she is trying to help. She has offered you a home in the school. Her suggestion is that you should do schoolwork in the mornings and housework in the afternoons and. . ."

But there the rector stopped for Margaret, her eyes flashing, had jumped to her feet.

"I'd never live there, I'd rather die. You should see that poor Martha who works there now. I think she beats her and there are black beetles in the kitchen. Anyway, do you think I'd be a maid in my own school where, whatever anybody else thinks, I know I'm not just as good as anybody else but a lot better? Remember I came with three of everything and of the very best quality."

The rector screwed himself up to tell Margaret his alternative suggestion.

"The archdeacon has told me of an institution of which his brother is a governor. It is an orphanage, but an exceptionally pleasant place, I understand. He has offered to speak to his brother about you."

Margaret swallowed hard, determined not to cry.

"Where is it?"

"Staffordshire."

Margaret tried to recall the globe in the school classroom. She was now in Essex, surely Staffordshire was miles away.

"Near Scotland?" she suggested.

"Oh, not so far as that. The orphanage is near a town called Wolverhampton. I do not know it myself."

Margaret was so dispirited her voice was a whisper.

"Would they take me for nothing?"

"Yes."

"And I would be treated like all the other girls?"

"Girls and boys – orphanages take both."

Margaret gulped hard but she would not cry.

"Then that's where I'll go. If I can't stay here I'd rather go to a place where I am treated as a proper person."

2. Packing Up

The orphanage – called St Luke's – was, so pamphlets pleading for funds said, "A home for one hundred boys and girls of Christian background". The building had been given and endowed by a wealthy business man who had died in 1802. He had stipulated in his will that though the actual building was near Wolverhampton no child from any part of the country who was an orphan and a Christian was to be refused a vacancy provided they were recommended by a clergyman of the Established Church.

"So splendid of the archdeacon to recommend you," the rector said to Margaret, "for he carries more weight than I could hope to do, and then, of course, there is his brother who is a governor."

One of the worries of the committee who ran St Luke's was how to collect their children. Most of them were too young to travel alone, especially if the journey included changing trains and crossing London. So a system had been devised by which new arrivals were collected in groups. When possible, new entrants were delivered to London by their relatives or sponsors, and there they were met by someone from the orphanage.

The rector came up to Saltmarsh House each time there was news about Margaret, but it was March before he arrived with definite information. Hannah always considered it unseemly that the rector should come into the kitchen, so he was led into the drawing room, which was cold, for neither Miss Sylvia nor Miss Selina came down until teatime so the fire was never lit until after luncheon.

"Stay and hear the news," the rector told Hannah, "for it concerns you." He opened a letter from the archdeacon and read.

I have now heard from the chairman of the committee of good ladies who run the domestic affairs of the orphanage. She says there are two members of one family to be admitted at the same time as your protégée Margaret Thursday. They are to meet in the third class waiting-room at Paddington Station on the 27th of this month at 1 p.m. The train does not leave until 2.10, but the children will be given some sort of meal. They say Margaret Thursday should bring no baggage as all will be provided.

Hannah was appalled.

"No baggage indeed! That's a nice way for a young lady to travel. Margaret came to us with three of everything and she is leaving us the same way, not to mention something extra I've made for Sundays."

"I think," the rector explained, "the orphans wear some kind of uniform."

"So they said on that first form they sent," Hannah agreed, "but there was no mention of underneath." Then she blushed. "You will forgive me mentioning such things, sir."

The rector dropped the subject of underneath.

Do you think arrangements could be made for someone to stay with your ladies for one day while you take Margaret to Paddington Station? I would take her myself, but the archdeacon says . . ." He broke off, embarrassed. Hannah understood.

"No, better I should go. It's not a gentleman's job. We'll have to book on the carrier's cart to the railway junction for London."

The rector was glad to do something.

"I shall see to that, indeed, I will arrange everything. All you have to do is to be ready by the 27th. Can you manage that, Margaret, my pet?"

Margaret had been waiting for a chance to speak.

"Can I take my baby clothes with me?"

"Whatever for?" gasped Hannah.

"I don't quite see. . ." the rector started to say, but Margaret interrupted him.

"I don't want to get to this St Luke's looking like a charity child. If I show my baby clothes – three of everything and of the very best quality – they'll know I'm somebody."

The rector looked at Margaret's flashing eyes. He

spoke firmly for he wanted her to remember his words.

"If you behave like somebody you will be treated like somebody. Never allow anyone to suggest that because you do not know who your parents were you are in any way inferior to others more fortunately placed."

"You needn't worry," said Margaret. "I never will. But what I think is that it will help if everybody can see I'm someone who has a mother who cared that her baby was properly dressed. How can people know that if they don't see the clothes?"

The rector held out a hand to Margaret and she came to him.

"It is my hope that some day your mother will come and claim you. You do not know and I do not know what terrible thing happened to her that forced her to leave her baby on the church steps. Nor do we know what new misfortune has deprived her of money, but I believe — and I pray for this night and morning — that one day her fortunes will change and then she will come to me and say: 'Where is my Margaret?' Then I shall ask: 'First, madam, describe the baby clothes you left for the child, otherwise how do I know you are her mother?'"

"Well, truthfully," said Margaret, "it's not likely the wrong mother would want me. What for?"

The rector smiled.

"How do we know?" he teased her. "Some day

21

you may prove to be the heir to a great fortune. Remember Thursday's child has far to go."

"Or," Hannah suggested, "you might become famous. I'm always telling her, sir, she might write a book. You ought to hear the stories she tells me of an evening, and all out of her head."

"So you see," said the rector, "I must keep the baby clothes for the day when your mother claims you." He got up. "Now I must get on with your affairs. I will arrange for the carrier to call here on the 27th."

Hannah still had the wicker basket which she had brought to Saltmarsh House. Now she gave it to Margaret. To make her and "underneath" trousseau she had raided the old ladies' cupboards. There she had discovered an unused length of flannel, part of a roll bought to sew Miss Selina into one winter when she had pleurisy, and there was a voluminous cambric petticoat once worn by Miss Sylvia and other useful bits and pieces. She had sewn the clothes at night after Margaret was in bed, so it was the night before she left that Margaret saw them for the first time after they were packed in the wicker basket.

"Three of everything," Hannah said proudly, lifting layers of tissue paper. "Three plain cambric petticoats. Three pairs of drawers with feather stitching. Three scalloped flannel petticoats. Three linings in case at that orphanage they make you wear dark knickers. Three liberty bodices and three nightdresses – all fine tucked." Then Hannah drew back yet one more piece of tissue paper. "And here for Sundays is a petticoat and a pair of drawers edged with lace."

Margaret gasped. Then she threw her arms round Hannah.

"Lace! Oh, darling Hannah, thank you. It's like being a princess. When we go to church on Sundays I'll be sure to see my frock sticks on my heel so everyone can see the lace."

Hannah was shocked.

"You'll do nothing of the sort. What you have to remember is you were spoke for by an archdeacon so don't shame him." Then she turned back to the wicker basket. "Your Bible and Prayer Book are in the bottom. I've tucked your stockings in wherever there is room, but on the top are your hankies, your brush and comb, your toothbrush and one nightie so you can get at them easy if you arrive late. And in a corner down at the bottom is that tin of mine with the cat on it you're fond of. I've filled it with toffees."

Suddenly it all seemed terribly final. Although most of Margaret had accepted that she was going to the orphanage, another part of her had refused to believe it. Could she really be going away from the rector and Hannah and all the people she knew and loved? With a howl she threw herself at Hannah.

"Must I go? I'll work in the house much more

than I ever have before. I'll like dusting, truly I will, and I'll hardly eat anything at all."

Hannah, her eyes dimmed by tears, gave Margaret a little push.

"Don't, my darling. Don't. It won't do no good." Then she knelt down and closed the wicker basket and fastened round it a leather strap.

3. The Journey

The orphanage was poor. The endowment, which a hundred years before had seemed more than sufficient to dress, feed and house a hundred orphans, was now quite inadequate. Charitable people subscribed and sometimes held bazaars and jumble sales to raise funds, but there was still barely enough to keep the home going. The matron, who was a hard woman and in any case disapproved of spoiled orphans, kept the expenses down as low as they would go, largely by saving on food. "What won't fatten will fill" was one of her favourite sayings. As a result, Miss Jones, called assistant nurse but really assistant everything, who had been sent to meet Margaret and the other children, was very conscious of the lightness of the bag in which was her own and the orphans' dinners to be eaten in the waiting room. A stale loaf of bread, some margarine, one ounce of cheese per person and a bottle of water.

Miss Jones was already in the waiting room when Hannah and Margaret arrived. She scarcely looked at them but fixed horrified eyes on the wicker basket.

"I hope that is not the child's luggage. You were informed no luggage was to be brought."

Hannah had measured up Miss Jones. "That's a jumped-up Miss Nobody," she thought. Out loud she said:

"No young lady I have charge of goes away without baggage and they're not doing so now, and don't forget Margaret is no common orphan, she was spoken for by the archdeacon whose brother is one of the orphanage governors."

Miss Jones never saw the governors, her life was ruled by Matron, of whom she was terrified. But it was common knowledge in the orphanage that even Matron had to listen to the governors. Perhaps if this child – to whom she had taken an instant dislike – knew a governor it was better to leave the question of her baggage to Matron. She looked coldly at Margaret.

"You are, I suppose, Margaret Thursday."

"That's right," Margaret agreed. "Of course, Thursday isn't my real name. I was called that because that was the day the rector found me and . . ."

Miss Jones pointed to the bench on which she was sitting.

"That's enough talking, sit down quietly." Then she said to Hannah: "You can go now."

Both Margaret and Hannah forgot Miss Jones. They gazed at each other with stricken faces.

"Oh, my dear pet!" said Hannah, holding out her arms. "Oh, my dear pet!"

Margaret put down the basket and ran to her.

"Hannah! Hannah! Don't leave me."

Hannah, with tears rolling down her face, knelt and hugged her.

"You got some stamps," she whispered, "the rector gave you. Bear it if you can, dear, but if you can't you write and something might be thought of."

Margaret hugged Hannah tighter.

"Don't leave me. You can't! You can't!"

Hannah knew every minute she stayed made things worse for Margaret. She freed herself from her clinging arms and, blinded by tears, stumbled towards the door. Margaret tried to run after her, but Miss Jones had stood enough. She grabbed Margaret by the wrist and picked up the wicker basket.

"Sit down and behave yourself. I never saw such a display. You wait until Matron hears of this."

"Hannah! Hannah!" screamed Margaret.

But Hannah was gone and the door had shut behind her.

Miss Jones was furious. There were others in the waiting room and they were looking pityingly at Margaret. It was too much, making her look like the wicked stepmother in a fairytale when really she should be admired.

"Be quiet," she said in an angry whisper. Then, raising her voice for the benefit of the others in the room: "This is a very ungrateful way to behave for you are a lucky girl to be going to St Luke's."

At that moment there was a diversion. The waiting-room door opened and three more children came in – a girl and two boys. They were shabbily dressed in black and each was as golden-haired as Margaret was brown. The eldest, who was the girl, led her brothers towards Miss Jones. In spite of the shabby clothes, she had evidently known better days for she spoke in the clear voice of the well-educated.

"Are you the lady from St Luke's?"

Miss Jones nodded.

"You must be the three Beresford children."

"That is correct," the girl agreed. "I am Lavinia. This" – she pulled the elder boy forward – "is Peter, and this" – she tried to pull forward her younger brother – "is Horatio," but Horatio refused to be pulled.

"Don't like that lady," he announced. "Horry wants to go home."

Miss Jones made tch-tching noises. This really was her unlucky day. Now another child was going to make a scene. But she had reckoned without Lavinia.

She let go of Horatio's hand and felt in her coat pocket and brought out a sweet and put it in the little boy's mouth.

"You mustn't mind him," she told Miss Jones. "He's only little, but he'll settle down."

Miss Jones opened her coat to look at her watch,

which was fixed to her blouse with a gunmetal bow. Thankfully she saw it was time to eat.

"Now sit down, all of you, and have some dinner. We have a long journey ahead of us." She opened the dinner bag and took out the food and a knife. She cut five slices of bread, smeared on a little margarine, then on each slice she placed a small knob of very dry cheese. She passed a slice to each of the children. Horatio looked in disgust at his slice.

"Is this meant to be dinner?" he asked.

Lavinia put an arm round him.

"Eat it, darling," she whispered. "Then you shall have a sweetie."

Margaret had received her slice but she made no effort to eat. She had succeeded in stopping crying except for an occasional hiccuping sob, but she had such a lump in her throat she knew she couldn't swallow anything.

Lavinia, taking advantage of a moment when Miss Jones was repacking the food and the knife, leant across to Peter.

"Put the little girl's slice in your pocket," she whispered. "She'll be hungry later on."

Somehow the other children had got the food down them. Miss Jones took another look at her watch. She got up.

"Come along," she said. "Pick up that basket, Margaret, and hold my hand. You three," she told the Beresfords, "follow me and be sure to keep close."

In the train Margaret began to feel better. Presently she felt so much better she was able to eat her bread and cheese, now rather hairy after being in Peter's pocket. They had a reserved compartment and Miss Jones sat in a corner as far from the children as possible, so in a whisper Lavinia and Margaret exchanged information.

"I'm not going to St Luke's except for a few days," Lavinia explained. "There were only vacancies for the boys. Anyway I'm fourteen, so I'm going into service somewhere near so I can see the boys on my half days."

Margaret could not imagine Lavinia in service, she was not a bit like Hannah or that poor Martha at the school.

"Will you like being in service?"

"I want to learn how to run a house," Lavinia explained.

Peter broke in.

"Our mother said you could never give orders if you didn't know how a house should be run."

Margaret had not supposed orphans gave orders, so Peter's statement cheered her. She knew that she would be a giving-orders sort of person, but it was nice to think she would not be alone. Then she had another cheering thought. Perhaps if she made friends with these children Lavinia would see her as well as her brothers on her half days.

"I'm ten, nearly eleven," Peter told her. "How old are you?"

"I'm nearly eleven too," said Margaret. "How old is he?" She pointed to Horatio.

"It's rude to point," said Horatio, "but if you want to know I'm six."

Peter was determined Margaret should be well informed.

"Our mother's dead," he announced.

"Yes, I suppose she is, and your father too," Margaret agreed, "or you wouldn't be orphans."

Peter started to answer that, but Lavinia evidently didn't want him to.

"No, we wouldn't be, would we? Now tell us about you."

"Well," said Margaret, "I'm not properly an orphan. I was found on a Thursday in a basket on the church steps with three of everything of the very best quality."

The Beresfords were thrilled.

"How romantic!" said Lavinia.

Peter looked admiringly at Margaret.

"So you could be absolutely anybody?"

"That's right," Margaret agreed.

"And until this Christmas every year gold money was left in the church in a bag to keep me."

"And nobody saw who left it?" Lavinia asked.

"Never.

"My goodness," said Peter, "it's like a book!"

Lavinia looked across at Miss Jones and saw she was asleep.

"Peter is going to write books when he grows

up," she whispered to Margaret. "He's very clever, he never stops reading."

"I keep hoping there'll be books in the orphanage," said Peter, "then I won't mind how awful it is."

Horatio looked as though he might cry.

"It won't be awful, Vinia, will it?"

Lavinia sighed.

"Why did you say that?" she said to Peter. "Now he's going to cry and I've no sweets left."

That was Margaret's moment. She climbed quietly on to the seat and took her wicker basket off the rack.

"But I have," she said. "A whole box of toffees. Let's share them out before she wakes, for I bet they won't let us eat them when we get there."

4. The Orphanage

The train did not arrive at Wolverhampton until nearly six o'clock and then there was a long drive in a horse-drawn omnibus. As a result the children, who since breakfast had only eaten the slice of bread and the morsel of cheese, were so exhausted that they scarcely took in the orphanage.

To make everything more muddling the orphans appeared to be wearing fancy dress. They were having supper when the children first saw them. Forty-nine girls at one table, forty-eight boys at another, eating, the children noticed sadly, only bread and margarine and drinking what looked like cocoa.

"Oh dear!" Lavinia whispered to Margaret. "I did hope it would be soup and perhaps eggs."

The "fancy dress" was, the children were to learn, ordinary orphanage wear. It had been designed when the orphanage had first opened over a hundred years before and had never been changed. For the girls there were brown cloth dresses to the ankles, white caps and long aprons. For the boys there were loose brown trousers and short matching coats. Out of doors both girls and boys had brown capes. On Sundays the girls had white muslin scarves folded into their dresses and the boys wore white collars.

That first night the children seemed to see nothing but brown everywhere they looked — brown out of which rose the noticeably pale faces of the orphans. As the children stood in the doorway swaying with tiredness and hunger, they were startled by the harsh voice of the matron.

"Don't stand there gaping, sit down. There is room for you two boys there and you girls here."

Lavinia pulled herself together.

"I think perhaps," she suggested in her quiet but authoritative voice, "I had better sit beside my little brother just for tonight. He is so tired he may need some help. . ."

She got no further for she was confronted by Matron, a stout woman who looked as if she had been poured into her black dress and then had set inside it, so upholstered did she look. She had sandy reddish hair and a fierce red face.

"I am matron here, young woman," she said, "and I give the orders. Off you go, boys, and you two girls sit. And do not forget to thank God for your good food."

The bread was stale and hard to get down, but the children were ravenous, and the cocoa — if it was cocoa, for it tasted of nothing — was hot.

"We can have two slices each," a little girl next to Margaret whispered to her, "and sometimes, if there's any over, a drop more cocoa."

Lavinia strained round to see how Horatio was getting on. Fortunately he was not crying for he was nearly asleep, but he was swallowing the pieces of bread soaked in cocoa which Peter was pushing into his mouth. Then she saw that Miss Jones, who was talking to Matron, was pointing to Margaret.

"Expect a storm," she whispered to Margaret. "I've a feeling Miss Jones is telling Matron about your basket."

Miss Jones was, and presently Matron came striding over to Margaret, her black, upholstered chest heaving with what appeared to be rage. She clapped her hands.

"Silence, everybody," she roared. "What, children, is the orphanage rule about luggage?"

"Bring no luggage," the children chanted, "everything needed will be provided."

"And is it provided?" Matron asked.

"Yes," answered the children.

"But here we have a new orphan who has quite deliberately disregarded the committee's rule." Matron beckoned to Miss Jones. "Bring Margaret Thursday's basket."

Miss Jones — a much meeker Miss Jones than the one who had met the children — scuttled out and was soon back carrying, as if it were a bomb, Hannah's wicker basket. At the sight of it in Miss Jones's arms, Margaret nearly broke out crying. Was it only last night that Hannah had so proudly shown her what she had packed? Lavinia slipped a hand into Margaret's.

"Don't give that Matron the pleasure of seeing that you mind. I bet she likes seeing people cry."

Clearly Matron was surprised, in fact, almost pleased, at the beautifully made and packed clothes. She had placed the basket on the end of the girls' table and had tossed aside the tissue paper. But as she took out one garment after another she made no comment except an occasional mutter to Miss Jones. "Ridiculous." "Much too good for an orphan," and finally, "Lace! Look, Jones, lace!" But as she repacked the little basket she laid a few things on one side.

"Come here, Margaret," she said.

Giving Margaret's hand a last squeeze, Lavinia moved to let Margaret get off the bench. Margaret, having scrambled over the bench, raised her chin in the air and marched over to Matron.

"I have not yet decided what shall be done with these clothes, but you may keep your Bible and Prayer Book and your toothbrush. What is this tin for?"

Matron held out the now empty toffee tin. The much-loved cat's head seemed almost to smile at Margaret. She swallowed a sob.

"It's to keep things in. It was a goodbye present."

Perhaps because she had no use for it, for it could not have been from kindness, Matron laid the tin beside the Bible, Prayer Book and toothbrush.

"You can go back to your seat. Take these things with you. Now stand, children. Grace."

The orphans pushed back the benches and stood, hands folded, heads bent. Then they sang Bishop Ken's Doxology.

Praise God, from whom all blessings flow.
Praise Him, all creatures here below,
Praise Him above, ye heavenly host,
Praise Father, Son, and Holy Ghost.

"Yes, indeed," said Matron. "Never forget how fortunate you are and how much you have for which to praise God. See them up to the dormitories, Jones, but leave Lavinia Beresford with me."

"Oh, couldn't I see Horatio to bed?" Lavinia pleaded. "He's so little and so tired."

Lavinia, from the tone of Matron's voice, might have suggested having a bath in public.

"Go into the boys' dormitory! Are you mad, girl? Quick, children, march."

The boys went first, each one as he passed Matron bowing his head as if before a shrine. At the end, dragged along by Peter, came Horatio. He was, Lavinia saw, really walking in his sleep so he at least would not suffer. The girls followed the boys, but they, as they passed Matron, each had to curtsey.

"I won't curtsey to anybody," Margaret muttered to Lavinia.

"Don't be a fool," Lavinia retorted. "What is the point of putting her back up?"

Margaret respected Lavinia's opinion and anyway she was too tired and too miserable to have much fight in her. So, clutching her possessions, she followed the last girl and, in spite of having her arms full, succeeded in making the necessary bob.

"I don't like the look of that girl," Matron observed to Miss Jones, who was following the children. "She has a proud air, she must be humbled."

"Quite so, Matron," Miss Jones agreed. "I thought the same the moment I saw her, and the scene she made in the waiting room was disgraceful."

Lavinia followed Matron into her sitting room. It was, she noticed, a surprisingly comfortable room to find in that desolate place, and though it was March there was a cheerful fire burning in the grate. Drawn up to the fire was a table laid for a meal. Evidently, thought Lavinia, she is going to have her supper. Matron sat down at her table, but she did not ask Lavinia to sit.

"I have good news for you," she said. "The Countess of Corkberry, who has always taken a kindly interest in this place, needs a scullery maid. You are to receive five pounds a year, but Her Ladyship has agreed to advance part of that sum so that you may have a respectable wardrobe. I understand you have a tin trunk at the railway station.

Does it contain any clothes suitable for a scullery maid?"

"I don't really know what a scullery maid wears," Lavinia confessed, "but I have some plain frocks, perhaps they will do."

"Nonsense!" said Matron. "You will need print dresses, aprons and caps and a black outfit for Sundays. All the staff have to attend church." She looked at Lavinia's fair plaits. "And of course you must put your hair up."

"My hair up!" Lavinia gasped. "I'm only just fourteen."

"Fortunately in sewing classes our girls work at wardrobes for our leavers who are going into service, so you can be fitted out — at your expense, of course. I should think two days will be enough to provide everything. A carrier will bring your box here tomorrow."

"Two days!" said Lavinia. "I had hoped perhaps a week to see the boys settled in."

"Two days," said Matron. "We have no room for you here. For tonight a mattress has been put on the floor at the end of the girls' dormitory. . ." Matron stopped for there was a knock on the door. "Come in."

The knock had been made by a girl who looked no older than Margaret. She was wearing the orphanage uniform but her hair was screwed up inside her cap. She was carrying a laden tray.

"Ah, Winifred! Supper," said Matron. "Good."

Winifred put in front of Matron a large steak, a dish of potatoes and another of cauliflower. Then from a cupboard she fetched a bottle of porter.

Lavinia felt saliva collecting in her mouth at the sight of such good food.

"That will be all, Lavinia," said Matron. "Winifred will direct you to the girls' dormitory."

Margaret, shivering with tiredness and lack of food, had accepted without question the bed pointed out to her. She had followed the other girls into an inadequate washroom in which were jugs of cold water and tin basins, in one of which they all cleaned their teeth. She had been shown a tiny shelf over her bed on which she was told to put her toothbrush and mug, her Bible and Prayer Book.

"And when Miss Jones says 'Pray' you stop whatever you are doing and kneel by your bed," her guide whispered, "or she hits you with a hairbrush."

Margaret had just pulled on the ugly coarse greyish-coloured nightdress, which was lying on her bed, when the order came for prayer. She hurriedly dropped to her knees and buried her face in her hands. Evidently it was Miss Jones who decided how long prayers should be, for a few moments later there was another bark from her. "Up, girls, and into your beds."

Margaret had hidden the tin Hannah had given her in her bed. In the dark she hugged it to her. It was a little bit of Hannah. Putting her head under the scratchy inadequate bedclothes, she stifled her sobs.

"I can't bear it. They've taken all my clothes. I'll never wear lace on Sundays. Oh, Hannah! Hannah!"

But when a little later Lavinia crept up to the dormitory and found Margaret, though her face was wet with tears, she was asleep.

5. First Day

When Margaret woke up the next morning she could not at first think where she could be. Accustomed to a room of her own, she was puzzled by the sleeping sounds which came from the orphans. Then, as if a cold heavy weight had dropped on to her solar plexus, she remembered. This was the orphanage. St Luke's Orphanage that the archdeacon had told the rector was "an exceptionally pleasant place". Pleasant! Rage filled Margaret. Then she remembered she had three carefully hidden stamps – wait until she wrote to the rector and told him what the archdeacon had dared to describe as exceptionally pleasant.

Margaret sat up and looked down the dormitory. There was not much light because the curtains were drawn, but peering over the twenty-five beds which lined each wall she could see at the far end of the room a mattress on the floor covered, as were the beds, with a grey blanket. "That," she thought, "must be Lavinia. I bet she won't mind if I wake her up."

To think of something meant for Margaret doing it immediately. In a second she was out of her bed and, holding up her long greyish nightgown, was running down the dormitory. She sat down by the hump under the blanket which was Lavinia.

"Lavinia! Lavinia! Wake up. It's me. Margaret. What shall I do? I can't stay in this dreadful place. You won't leave Peter or Horatio here, will you?"

Lavinia had the gift of waking up clear-headed.

"You'd better go back to your bed," she whispered. "I'm sure you aren't allowed to be here."

Up went Margaret's chin.

"I don't care. I'm doing no harm. Did you hear what I said? I'm running away. I can't stop here."

Lavinia sat up.

"I'm only going to be here for two days. I'm to be scullery maid for somebody called the Countess of Corkberry."

"Two days!" said Margaret. "I thought you said a week."

"I did, and that's what I hoped, but it's not to be, but I'll be back every other Sunday."

"They said you could?"

Lavinia spoke with quiet authority.

"Either I have every other Sunday or I won't work for the Countess."

Margaret looked approving. That was the way to talk.

"I wish I could be a scullery maid. I'm a good cook and it's sure to be better than being here because it couldn't be worse."

"Well, you can't be," said Lavinia, "you're too young. You would have to pass a labour exam before you could go out to work. I quite see that you want to run away, but please stick it out for a bit. You see, I want you to keep an eye on Peter and Horatio."

Margaret weakened. She wanted to leave that morning. But perhaps she could bear a week or two, especially knowing Lavinia would come back every other Sunday.

"Well, I might stick it out for a bit, but. . ."

Margaret got no further for Miss Jones had flung open the door and was clanging a huge bell. She stopped in mid-clang, her mouth gaping, unable to believe what her eyes told her.

"Margaret Thursday! What are you doing out of your bed?"

Margaret got to her feet.

"Talking to Lavinia. She's my friend."

"Go back to your bed at once," Miss Jones thundered. Then she gave another clang on the bell. "Up, girls, up. Form a line for the washroom." She looked again at Margaret, who had not moved. "Now what is it?"

"You said I was to go back to bed. Then you said 'Up, girls, up', and now you say form a line for the washroom. What do you want me to do?"

Miss Jones was more sure than ever that she did not like Margaret Thursday.

"You will get your toothbrush and mug and join

that line there for the washroom."

It was a slow shuffling walk to get washed, made the more dismal by the shrieks of the small children who were being washed by Miss Jones and an assistant.

"They put soap in their eyes," a small girl who was in front of Margaret told her. "It happens every day. It used to happen to me."

"Beasts!" said Margaret.

Lavinia, who had taken her place behind Margaret, whispered:

"I do hope Peter has managed to wash Horry. He'd kick anyone who put soap in his eyes."

Margaret found her clothes had disappeared and in their place were her orphanage clothes: a vest, a bodice, coarse long straight-legged drawers, a grey winceyette petticoat, the uniform dress, an apron and a cap. The only thing left of her own clothes were her boots.

"It would be them," she thought resentfully, "knowing I always hated them." Then there were tears in her eyes. Even the despised boots were something of home.

None of the clothes were new and none fitted, but Margaret was given some good advice by an older girl whom Miss Jones sent to show her how the uniform cap should be worn.

"Don't say anything doesn't fit," she whispered, "for you'll be made to alter it yourself in what they call 'free time' – we don't get much of that."

There was no such thing as a looking-glass in the dormitory, so Margaret could only guess at her appearance. She could see, however, how the others looked and that was enough.

"My goodness!" she thought. "Suppose Hannah could see me now!"

As a matter of fact, Margaret was wrong. Of course the clothes were a hundred years out of date and they felt ridiculous to her, used to skirts to her knees, but grown-up people thought the orphanage children looked picturesque. The cap really did suit Margaret. It was made of white cotton with a drawstring at the back which held it tightly in position. The children were supposed to strain their hair out of sight under the caps, but Margaret's curls refused to be controlled and spiralled out round her face.

Breakfast was another depressing meal. Each child had a bowl of lumpy porridge served with a mere splash of milk and no sugar. This was followed by one slice of bread and margarine and a cup of weak tea.

The orphans were not taught in the orphanage but, wrapped in their brown cloaks, they were marched two-and-two down to the village school.

"At school don't they laugh at us in these clothes?" Margaret asked the girl who was paired with her, whose name was Susan.

Susan shook her head.

"No. They're used to us, and anyway I think

46

they are sorry for us. Sometimes they give us things. Once I had a whole apple."

Margaret, used to the large overgrown garden at Saltmarsh House where she could have all the fruit there was for the picking, felt even more depressed. Imagine speaking of an apple like that — something to be remembered!

"Don't we ever get fruit at the orphanage?"

"Oh yes," said Susan. "Always at Christmas we are given an orange."

An orange! It was not just that an orange a year was all she was to expect, but Susan's calm acceptance that outraged Margaret. But she had other questions to ask. One had been worrying her since she had been given her uniform for nobody could run far dressed in it.

"What do they do with our own clothes?"

Susan looked scared, peering round to see that Miss Jones was not within hearing distance.

"We don't know."

"But they must be kept somewhere."

Susan whispered so low that Margaret had to strain to hear.

"Some of them say Matron sells them."

"For herself?"

Susan nodded.

"But that's only what they say. We don't know."

"They won't sell mine," said Margaret. "I'll ask Matron for them."

Susan clutched at Margaret's arm.

"Don't. Just for asking you get a terrible punishment, you could. . ."

They were outside the school playground. Miss Jones, red-faced, was standing by Susan.

"What were you saying? You know talking is forbidden."

Susan might look meek, but she evidently knew how to fool Miss Jones.

"I was only telling Margaret what work we shall do in school this morning."

"Oh!" Miss Jones turned away. "Quick march. Straight to the classrooms, children. No playing in the yard."

6. School

A Miss Snelston was head of the village school and from the first the children liked her. It was not easy with only one pupil-teacher to assist her to teach children of all ages in two rooms, but somehow she managed.

Most of the pupils other than the orphans were the children of farm labourers, red-cheeked and solidly built on a diet largely composed of vegetables, eggs, milk and bread, for at that time farm labourers' wages were very low so meat was a rarity. All the children, urged on by their parents, had one aim which was to pass the labour exam as early as possible so that the girls could go into service and the boys get work on the farms. Miss Snelston, of course, knew this was their ambition and she accepted it. "After all," she would say to her pupil-teacher, Polly Jenkin, "they may as well leave when they are twelve for you and I know, however long we keep them here, very few would learn any more, and of course it's hard for the parents to find the school money." School money was twopence a week, which in those days was paid as school fees.

It was Miss Snelston's hope each time there was a new batch of orphans that a really intelligent child would turn up. That was how she had found Polly Jenkin. She had taught her since she came to the orphanage at the age of four and had discovered in her a real fondness for learning, so the moment she had passed her labour exam she had applied to the governors for her. She arranged that Polly was to receive two-and-sixpence a month and would live in her cottage, in return for which she would help with the housework.

The school morning started with prayers and a hymn, then, leaving Polly to get the school work started, Miss Snelston called Margaret, Peter and Horatio into her little office and gave them their slates.

"These are your very own," she explained. "You must look after them carefully for on them you do your sums and sometimes dictation. My aim is to see four sums right on every slate." She smiled at the three children, hiding from them her deep pity for well she knew how hard their lives would be. "You," she said to Peter, "must be Peter Beresford and this must be Horatio."

Horatio, looking very tiny in his brown uniform, which was at least two sizes too large for him, smiled back at Miss Snelston.

"That man that washed me put soap in my eyes," he told her.

"I'm sure he did," Miss Snelston thought,

looking at Horatio's still bloodshot eyes and tear-stained cheeks. She turned up the sleeves of his jacket which entirely hid his hands.

"Dear me, that suit is very big for you." She turned to Peter. "Bring him in here in middle morning break and I'll stitch the sleeves up." Then she looked at the trousers flapping round the child's ankles. "Do you think Matron would mind if I shortened the trousers?"

Peter was a good-looking boy with large blue eyes. Now he turned these anxiously to Margaret.

"Would she mind?"

Margaret felt something she had never felt before. A sort of warm feeling round her heart. All her life people had looked after her, now somebody needed her. It was nice to be needed.

"I shouldn't think she'd notice."

Miss Snelston evidently thought that sensible.

"You are Margaret Thursday?"

"That's right," Margaret agreed. "It's not my real surname. You see it was a Thursday when the rector found me. I was in a basket with three of everything packed with me, all of the very best quality. And there was a card which said my name was Margaret and that fifty-two pounds would come every year to keep me — and so it did until last Christmas."

Miss Snelston would like to have heard more but the school needed her.

"Can you read and write?"

Margaret thought that a foolish question.

"Yes."

Miss Snelston turned to Peter.

"And you?"

"Oh yes, of course."

There was something about the way Peter answered that caught Miss Snelston's ear.

"What do you read?"

"What I can get. Before. . ." Peter hesitated, then said: "Before we were sent here I was reading *David Copperfield*."

Miss Snelston held out a hand to Horatio.

"You and Margaret can sit next to each other," she told Peter. "Horatio will be in the next room with the little ones — or can you read too, Horatio?"

Horatio shook his head.

"But I can draw pictures."

"Good," said Miss Snelston, longing to give him a hug. "If you draw a good picture we will put it up on the wall."

Back at the orphanage, Lavinia had been sent to what was called the linen room. There on a trestle table were piles of print dresses, aprons and caps made in sewing time by what Miss Jones described as "the female orphans". She held a dress up against Lavinia.

"Mostly these fit anyone," she said. "The apron ties them in."

Lavinia turned the dresses over. "There are so

many pretty prints in the shops," she thought. "I wonder why they have to choose such ugly ones."

"I think I'll just take two dresses," she said. "They'll do to start with and I can buy some prettier ones later on."

Miss Jones jumped as if she had been bitten by a snake.

"Prettier! Prettier! Who do you think you are? Pretty indeed! It is not prettiness that Her Ladyship is expecting from her scullery maid."

But Lavinia was not easily cowed.

"Did you never hear the proverb, 'He who pays the piper calls the tune'? Just now I am paying the piper and I say I only want two print frocks. I have a black dress and coat which will do for Sundays, but I will take four aprons and caps."

Miss Jones could have shaken her. It was, she thought, foolish of Matron to have told Lavinia she had to pay for the dresses. Better to have fitted her out and then sent the bill to Lady Corkberry's housekeeper for payment to be deducted from her wages.

"Very well," she snapped. "Take what you want and then follow me. I will show you where you can sew."

The orphans came home at twelve for their dinner. This was the big meal of the day. A regular amount of food was allowed for each orphan each week and from this ration Matron was supposed to select the meals. But Matron was fond of her food so she made a point of never weighing the meat the butcher sent or the fish from the poulterer's, well knowing she would be rewarded by tasty steaks and delicate soles. As a result the main meal, though eaten to the last lick, usually left the orphans hungry. That day the meal was a stew which should have contained at least a quarter of a pound of meat per child, but in fact was mostly turnips, parsnips and potatoes, with fragments of meat floating around. However, there had been complaints that the children went back to school hungry, so the stew was followed by a slice of suet pudding served with a teaspoonful of treacle. The suet puddings were so solid it was said if you threw one against the wall it would not break up but would bounce back to the thrower.

Margaret and Lavinia succeeded in sitting next to each other and in exchanging a little conversation.

"The school's nice," Margaret whispered. "Miss Snelston turned up Horry's suit. Nobody can read as well as Peter. We are made to point to each word as we read it."

"I'm going tomorrow," Lavinia told Margaret. "My trunk is coming this afternoon and there are things in it I want to tell you about. I'll have to wait until everybody is asleep, but I'll come and talk to you tonight."

Afternoon school was given up to the lighter subjects. First there was dancing, which Margaret loved, then there was two-part singing and finally drawing. "If only it was all school and we never had to go to the orphanage, wouldn't it be lovely?" Margaret thought, but soon school was over and Miss Jones was outside shouting "Get into line. One two. One two. No talking." Sadly, out of the corners of their eyes, the orphans watched the village children laughing and pushing each other about as they ran home to their teas.

For the orphans, work was not over for the day. After tea, which was a slice of bread and margarine and a cup of milk and water, there were what were called "tasks". Some of the girls were sent to sew, others to the kitchen to peel potatoes. For the boys there was wood to cut and bring in and what was called "repairs", which meant mending any piece of furniture which needed it.

The youngest children, of whom Horatio was one, were turned loose during this time to play. There were no toys in the so-called playroom, but the children managed without, so almost at once Horatio was seized on by two small girls who told him he was their little boy for they were going to play "Home". "Home" was an immensely popular game with the smaller children, who could spend hours pretending they were mothers and fathers — creatures few of them had seen.

Margaret, because it was an unpopular task, was sent by Miss Jones to the scullery to peel potatoes. This was supposed to be done in silence, but the cook and her assistant were out so only Winifred was in charge, and of course nobody paid any attention to her. Occasionally she squeaked:

"Oh, be quiet, do. If Matron was to hear she wouldn't half wrought me," but mostly she kept darting to the scullery door to hear what was going on, for she was only thirteen and had, before Matron took her on to work in the kitchen, been an orphan herself.

Margaret was holding the floor. Apart from the fact that she was new so no one knew her story, she loved an audience and knew how to keep them amused. Of course she told the story of her arrival in a basket, but on this occasion she added a few touches.

"And every one of my baby clothes was embroidered with — what do you think?" It was clear the little girls couldn't think. "A coronet. And amongst my baby clothes was a beautiful diamond brooch."

Susan was amongst the potato peelers.

"Oh, Margaret, you are a fibber!"

"I'm not then," said Margaret. "I'll write to the rector to tell you it's true. Then you'll see."

"Who do you think you might be, then?" another child asked.

Margaret had so often wondered about this she had dozens of suggestions to offer.

"Well. . ." she said, "I might be. . ." From that night onwards Margaret was established as the queen of story-tellers.

Margaret was almost asleep by the time Lavinia felt it safe to come to her bed. She brought with her two books, *David Copperfield* and *A Tale of Two Cities*.

"These are Peter's. I can't get them to him as I can't get into the boys' dormitory. Anyhow, I don't believe he'd know how to hide them. Could you?"

"I can try. I made my tin box into my bed this morning and nobody noticed, but I don't know if they look sometimes. Really I ought to get them to school, they can be safe in Peter's desk."

"Well, do what you can." Lavinia put the books into Margaret's bed. "He must have something to read. He'd rather read than eat. And here," she put a piece of paper into Margaret's hand, "is my address. If anything goes really wrong get a message to me there. Perhaps that Miss Snelston would help, she sounds nice."

Margaret rummaged round and found her tin box and opened it.

"I'll keep it in here. I may take this to school. I'll see. It depends if they search our beds."

Lavinia found and held Margaret's hands.

"Don't run away, will you? It's awful enough going off and leaving Peter and Horry, but if you weren't here I think I'd die."

"I won't run away without telling you, I promise you that. But you will come every other Sunday? Promise."

Lavinia kissed her.

"I promise, or at least, if they won't give me every other Sunday, I'll find another place to work. I can promise you that."

"Good," said Margaret. She lay down again and, hugging her box to her, she was soon asleep.

7. *Lavinia*

Lavinia drove away the next morning in an estate cart belonging to the Corkberrys. The children did not see her go as they were at school. The young man who drove the cart shouldered her tin box and, though Miss Jones saw her drive away, she neither waved nor smiled. It was a dismal departure.

Lavinia tried hard not to cry but she had to gaze out over the fields so the driver would not see that her eyes were brimming with tears. But if he could not see the young man guessed.

"Don't 'ee take on now," he said. "You'll like it up to Sedgecombe Place. They be good employers, His Lordship and Her Ladyship. And the grub's good — far better than you would get in that old orphanage. Cruel hard on the little 'uns they say that be."

The driver told Lavinia his name was Jem and he worked with the horses. He was a cheerful youth and made Lavinia feel better.

"Do you think I shall see Lady Corkberry today?"

Jem shook his head.

"No – not her. There be a Mrs Tanner, she be the one you'll see. She be the housekeeper. Bit of a dragon seemingly, but they say if you do your work right she'm fair."

Lavinia's heart sank. Would Mrs Tanner want to see if she worked well before she promised her every other Sunday?

"Is it far from Sedgecombe Place – I mean from the orphanage? You see, I want to get back there on my time off, I've two little brothers there."

"Not far," said Jem, "maybe four miles – not more. Walk it easy, pretty walk too all along the canal bank."

Lavinia looked round.

"I can't see a canal."

"Not from here," Jem agreed, "but this is canal country, it's near here where the Shropshire Union Canal runs into the Staffordshire and Wiltshire Canal. I did ought to know for I was born on a canal boat."

"Were you? What made you leave it to work at Sedgecombe Place?"

"The pneumonia," Jem explained. "Cruel sick I was and down at a place called Autherley my dad had to call the doctor. Well, there wasn't no hospital near so the doctor told her ladyship about me and she fixed it so I was put to bed in the house. Well, when I was better like, the doctor he said I wasn't to go back on the canal no more, so that's how I come to work with the horses. I see me dad and mum often enough when they're passin'. All the way to London my dad does."

Lavinia knew nothing about canals. She thought it very odd to be born on a boat.

"Have you got a lot of brothers and sisters?"

"Five. Tight squeeze it was when we was all there, but now my eldest brother he has his own boat and the next he give up same as me, then me two sisters got married so now there's only young Tom left, eleven he is, he leads the horse – not the same one, of course, but the one they give you at the stables."

"Doesn't Tom have to go to school?" Lavinia asked.

"No – canal people don't go to school. I can make me mark because one of the men I work with showed me. Young Tom would have gone to school if he could have been spared, but a course 'e couldn't be, not with there bein' nobody else for the 'orse. He don't like the canal life, Tom don't. Dad's dead scared he'll run off some time."

"I must get someone to show me the canal path," said Lavinia. "It will be nice walking by the water now the spring's coming."

"You'll see me around," Jem promised, "and if you tell me when you have time off I'll put you on your way."

At the next bend in the road they could see Sedgecombe Place – a grey battlemented building lying in a great park.

"My word!" said Lavinia. "It is a big place, there must be a lot of servants needed to keep it right."

Jem whipped up the horse.

"You've said it." He did not speak again until he drove the cart through some wrought-iron gates. "We go up this path here, it leads to the back door."

Just as Jem had predicted, Lavinia was taken at once to be interviewed by Mrs Tanner. She was a tall rather severe-looking woman in a black dress with a black silk apron over it. Round her waist was a chain on which hung a bunch of keys. The housekeeper's room in which she saw Lavinia was, however, cosy, with pretty curtains and primroses in a vase, so perhaps, Lavinia thought, she is gentler than she looks. Mrs Tanner sat upright in a stiff chair while Lavinia stood just inside the door.

"You are Lavinia Beresford?"

Lavinia curtseyed.

"Yes, ma'am."

"Have you worked in a kitchen before?"

"No, ma'am. This is my first place."

"I see. This is a big place and we all have to work hard. You will receive five pounds a year less what you have had advanced for your uniform. You will share a room with the under kitchen-maid. Between you there will be your room to do and you have to look after the rooms of three footmen. You will rise at six for, as Mrs Smedley the cook will explain, you will have the kitchen range to see to so that the water is hot by the time she comes down. Otherwise your work is to wait on her and, of course, wash up. At night, before you go to bed, there will be the range to blacklead and the kitchen and scullery to hearthstone. At all times you will call Mrs Smedley ma'am. That is all, do your duty and you should be very happy with us."

Lavinia could see she was meant to curtsey and say "Thank you", and she wished she could have, but she must arrange her days off.

"Please, ma'am," she said, "what about my time off?"

Mrs Tanner frowned.

"Her Ladyship does not give time off to you young girls, but sometimes, if there are no guests, you may go out together in the afternoon providing you do not leave the grounds."

Lavinia swallowed nervously.

"I quite understand, ma'am, but you see I have two little brothers at the orphanage. The younger is only six. So I can only take a place where I am permitted to visit them. I had thought perhaps every other Sunday."

Mrs Tanner, as she told Lady Corkberry later, was so surprised she did not know how to answer.

"A personable young woman, M'Lady, very nicely spoken. I did not know what to answer because I understand she wants to keep an eye on the brothers. Still, it wasn't for me to go against your rules so I said I would speak to you."

Lady Corkberry was a good woman. Taking Jem into her house when he had pneumonia was not an isolated kindness. She expected to serve her fellow men when the opportunity offered; that, in her opinion, was what great positions and possessions were for. It was not her custom to meet her junior maids for she left their care to those immediately in charge of them, but this was an exceptional case.

"Very well, Tanner, I will see the young woman in the morning room after breakfast tomorrow."

Although it was her first day, Lavinia found that after she had unpacked and changed she was expected to work, but not before she had eaten. Midday dinner was over in the servants' hall, but there was plenty of food about. Mrs Smedley, a large red-faced woman, pointed to a table by the window.

"Sit there." She nodded at a dark-haired, anxious-looking girl. "This is Clara. You share her room. Give her some dinner, Clara."

Lavinia remembered her instructions.

"Thank you, ma'am." She sat while Clara put in front of her a huge plate of cold meat with a large potato in its jacket, a jar of pickles, a loaf of bread, at least a pound of butter and a great hunk of cheese.

"Eat up, girl," said Mrs Smedley. "You'll find you need to keep your strength up here."

After the food she had eaten at the orphanage Lavinia needed no encouragement.

"My goodness," she thought, "if all the meals are like this it will be a great temptation to take some leavings in my pocket for the boys."

Mrs Smedley was right about Lavinia needing to keep her strength up for she did find herself very tired before she stumbled behind Clara up to their attic. There had been guests for dinner, and after running to and fro waiting on Mrs Smedley all the evening there had been a great mound of washing-up to do in the scullery. Then, after a supper taken standing, the girls set to at their housework. Black-leading the range, hearthstoning the kitchen and scullery floors and a long passage.

"Terrible, isn't it?" Clara groaned. "And we've been one short until you came. Sometimes I've been that tired I haven't known how to get up the stairs."

But in spite of going to bed late and rising early, Lavinia looked, Lady Corkberry thought, remarkably fresh and pretty when Mrs Tanner brought her to her the next morning.

"The young person Beresford, m'lady," Mrs Tanner said, giving a curtsey.

It was clear Mrs Tanner meant to stay, but Lady Corkberry did not permit that.

"Thank you, Tanner. You may leave us. Your name is Lavinia Beresford?" she asked.

Lavinia curtseyed.

"Yes, m'lady."

"And you have two brothers in the orphanage?"

"Yes, m'lady. Which is why I asked if I could have time off every other Sunday. I must see they are all right."

Several things were puzzling Lady Corkberry.

"You speak very nicely. Where were you at school?"

Pain showed in Lavinia's face.

"We did lessons at home with my mother."

Lady Corkberry looked sympathetic.

"She taught you well. A pretty speaking voice is a great advantage." She hesitated. "You say you must see your brothers are all right. Surely you know they are all right at the orphanage. It is highly spoken of."

Lavinia did not know how to answer. She did not want Lady Corkberry descending on the place for Matron would, of course, guess who had talked, which might make things harder for the boys. So she hedged.

"It's not what they are used to. It will be better when they settle down."

Lady Corkberry could feel Lavinia was hiding something, but she did not want to bully the child.

"Very well," she said. "Every other Sunday." Then she smiled. "Perhaps one day in the summer I might have the little boys here for a treat. You would like that?"

A flush spread over Lavinia's face.

"Oh, I would, m'lady. It will be something for them to look forward to."

"Very well. Now go back to your work. I will see what can be arranged."

8. A Letter

Because she enjoyed the school and truly was getting to love both Miss Snelston and Polly Jenkin, Margaret, though she still meant to run away, had no immediate plans to do so. This was not only because of her promise to Lavinia and that she was growing fond of Peter and Horry, but also because of her Sunday underclothes. Whenever she thought of that lace-edged petticoat and those drawers she was so full of rage she felt she could not run away until in some way she had paid Matron back. Poor Susan, on the walk to school, would have been bored to exhaustion with the lace on Margaret's Sunday underclothes only Margaret was always inventing new things she would like to do to Matron and Susan enjoyed hearing about those.

"I would like a great enormous saucepan full of frying fat," Margaret would whisper through the hood of her cape, "and I'd push her in and fry her and fry her until she was dead," or, another day: "I thought of something in bed last night. I would shut her up in a cupboard with thousands and thousands of hungry rats so they would eat every bit of her."

But Margaret did not only plan horrible ends for Matron, she collected information about her from the children, particularly those who had been in the orphanage since they were babies. As a result, she gradually built up a picture of the way Matron managed things. She learnt that in May each year Matron had a holiday. She went up north, it was said, to visit a brother, and that was when — so the story went — she sold any clothes belonging to new orphans which were worth selling.

"She goes away with a great big box," a child called Chloe told Margaret, "and it weighs ever such a lot because Mr Toms has to carry it" — Mr Toms was the Beadle — "and he swears ever so, but when she comes back it's so light anyone could carry it."

"Clothes wouldn't weigh all that lot," said Margaret.

"It's not only clothes," Chloe whispered, "it's food. Our food. Last year we nearly starved before she went so she could take a huge joint of beef to her brother, and sausages and pounds of cheese and that."

"How do you know?" Margaret asked.

"Winifred, of course. They think because she works in the kitchen she's one of them, but she never is, she's still one of us."

Margaret, turning over these scraps of information in her head, saw that they made a pattern. Somehow, before Matron went away in

May, she must get back the clothes Hannah had made for her. And somehow she must get hold of her jersey and skirt before she ran away.

Meanwhile, Margaret did what she could to look after Peter and Horry, often getting punished for it. Punishments in the orphanage were tough. They ranged from being sent to bed without supper to beatings, but in between there were other terrors, such as being locked in a cupboard, being tied to a tree in the garden or being shamed by being sent to church on Sundays without a white fichu or, in the case of the boys, a white collar; this told the whole congregation a child was in disgrace. By suggestion, the children had learnt to look upon being disgraced in church as the worst punishment of all.

The very morning Lavinia left Margaret had secreted Peter's two books under her cape and carried them to school. At school she had put them in his desk.

"You can read all through playtime," she told him, "and other times, perhaps, if you ask Miss Snelston."

Peter was delighted to see his books again, but he absolutely refused to keep both in his desk.

"I must have a book in the orphanage, Margaret, it's awful as it is, but with no book I think I'd die."

"But when could you read?" Margaret asked him. "I know we are supposed to have free time every day, but mostly we don't."

"It's better for us boys, I think," Peter explained. "At least that's what the boys say. They say Mr Toms doesn't seem to mind if they don't do much as long as Matron doesn't know. They say he hates Matron."

"I bet he does. Who wouldn't?" Margaret agreed. "But where will you keep a book?"

"I'll find a place," said Peter confidently. "Out of doors somewhere, but of course safe from rain."

Margaret looked in surprise at Peter. He was such a thin, pale little boy, most of his face seemed to be eyes. Yet he wasn't at all weak, at least he wasn't about things he cared about – like books. She had been thinking of him as a small boy, but now she remembered he was as old as she was.

"Will you take a book home tonight?"

"Of course," said Peter calmly. "Those horrible cloaks aren't good for anything except hiding things in."

But in spite of Peter's confidence, Margaret felt responsible for him, so after tea she nipped out before tasks to see where the book was to be hidden. Peter had been ordered to act as donkey to the big lawnmower, tugging it along by ropes worn over each shoulder while another boy pushed. This suited Peter perfectly.

"This is grand," he told Margaret. "Harry" – he indicated the other boy – "says it's all right if I read while I'm doing it, he'll shout if I go crooked."

That was the first time Margaret was caught and

punished. She was slipping back into the orphanage when she ran slap into Miss Jones, who turned puce with rage.

"Margaret Thursday! Where have you been? I distinctly heard Matron say you were to help in the kitchen."

Margaret thought quickly. Whatever happened she must not mention Peter.

"I thought I heard a cat crying."

"A cat!" Miss Jones's face turned even more puce. "We have no cats here, with a hundred orphans to feed and clothe we cannot afford to keep a cat."

"Thank goodness!" thought Margaret. "Poor cat, it would starve in this place." Out loud she said: "May I go to the kitchen?"

"At once," Miss Jones ordered, "but this will, of course, be reported to Matron and you will be punished."

"I think that's mean when I was only trying to help a cat that wasn't there," said Margaret, and dashed off to the kitchen.

Miss Jones, on her way to Matron's office, muttered: "That is a very unpleasant child. There is something impertinent about her."

Matron, when told about Margaret and the supposed cat, agreed with Miss Jones about the unpleasantness of Margaret.

"One of these independent children," she agreed. "It will take time before she is moulded to our shape. Send her to me when she comes in from school tomorrow, she shall have ten strokes on each hand. That will teach her who is the ruler in this establishment."

It was very difficult to help Horatio, but he so badly needed help Margaret did all that she could. There were two periods when he needed her most. One was morning washing time and the other was his free time when he came home from school. Two ex-orphans not suitable for farm work were employed on the boys' side of the home to help keep discipline and to wash the little boys. They were loutish types in their late teens who enjoyed their small power and showed it by bullying and taking pleasure in being rough. It made Margaret mad to see poor Horry come into the dining room, his eyes red from soap, his cheeks shiny from tears. But Margaret, though seething with rage, kept her temper. She could do nothing for the time being for it was past imagining what the punishment would be if a girl was found in the boys' dormitory.

"Most likely I'd be beaten so hard I'd die," she thought, "and that wouldn't help Horry."

Then she had an idea. When on the train she had opened her wicker basket to give everybody toffee, she had told Lavinia she had three stamps. Lavinia already had a pretty shrewd idea what the orphanage was going to be like.

"Hide them," she advised. "Stick them inside one of your boots, they won't find them there." So far Margaret had not used a stamp for she did not want to write to Hannah or the rector with news which must depress them, for what could they do? And she certainly was not going to tell Hannah what had happened to her underclothes. But that meant she still had her three stamps and one of these she used to write to Lavinia. She took off the boot in which the stamps were stuck to the inside of the toe and took one out, then Miss Snelston gave her a piece of lined paper and an envelope and promised to post the letter.

Margaret had never received a letter. Although she did not know it, she would have been receiving letters regularly from the rector, had not the archdeacon warned him that it had been found that letters upset the orphans and so they were discouraged, so Margaret was very hazy how a letter should be worded. However, she did her best and at last she got over what she wanted to say. She wrote:

Margaret Thursday says when you come on Sunday she would be obliged if you could bring some sweets to bribe that beast Ben who washes Horatio very faithfully Margaret Thursday.

9. Plans for Sunday

Quite by chance, Margaret learnt where Matron kept the orphans' own clothes. It was through a girl at school called Sally, whose father had met with an accident and as a result could only do part-time work, so Sally's mother helped out taking any little job she could get. One morning in break Sally said to Margaret:

"My ma is goin' up to your old orphanage next week."

"What for?" Margaret asked.

"It's work she does for the matron — dead scared of your matron my ma is."

"I don't wonder," said Margaret. "I think most everybody is."

"It's washin' and mendin' and that she does," Sally explained.

Margaret was amazed.

"Washing! I can't think why Matron pays your mother to do that, for all us female orphans do it all day Saturdays. Cruelly hard it is, especially the ironing, you try washing for one hundred orphans, and the senior girls have to do Matron's caps as well, and all the week at 'tasks' some of us mend."

"It's not what you wear my ma does," Sally explained. "It's special stuff. Kept locked up at the top of the house my ma says. When it's done my ma has to pack it ready to travel when your matron goes on her holiday."

Sally had moved away so she did not see how Margaret's eyes flashed and her chin shot into the air. Getting Sally's mother to pack the clothes Hannah had made for her, was she! Mean beast! But Margaret kept her head. Nobody — nobody at all must guess what she planned, though think as she would she could not imagine what she would do with her lace-edged petticoat and drawers when she got them, she just knew that somehow she must get them back. Hannah's lovely present was not going up north for Matron to sell.

Lady Corkberry, although she was a very busy person, had not forgotten her nicely-spoken scullery maid. In the week before Lavinia's first half-day she spoke about her to the housekeeper when she came for orders.

"Good morning, Tanner. Before I forget, that new scullery maid, Lavinia Beresford, is to be allowed to visit her brothers in the orphanage this coming Sunday. She must be home before dark so she may leave immediately after church. Will you see a generous lunch is packed with some sweet cakes which she will no doubt wish to share with the little boys."

Mrs Tanner was very fond of her mistress and used to her ways. She thought it amazing that a great lady should remember the half-day of a new scullery maid, but she was like that. So she made a note on her pad. Then she had an idea.

"I was hearing there is something for us at the station at Wolverhampton, m'lady — garden stuff, I believe. It wouldn't be much farther for the cart to go on to the orphanage to tell them the girl will be coming on Sunday, it would be a pity if her brothers were out."

"What a capital idea!" said Lady Corkberry. "Will you see to it?"

"Of course, m'lady," Mrs Tanner agreed.

That was the day when Margaret's letter for Lavinia arrived. She read it, amused at its formality, but worried by its contents. She had no money to buy sweets and she did not know when she would be paid the balance of the five pounds a year. Over washing-up, she asked advice of her room-mate Clara.

Clara, as usual, looked worried.

"I wish I could help, but my mother has all my money; sometimes she gives me a tanner for myself, but I haven't got anything now and won't have till old mother Smedley gives me my penny for the plate on Sunday."

Each Sunday before the staff left for church, the heads of departments saw that their juniors were properly dressed, had clean handkerchiefs and money for the plate.

"My penny for the plate!" said Lavinia. "That would buy sweets."

Clara, who was drying, nearly dropped a bowl.

"Lavinia Beresford! You wouldn't dare take money from the church. Why, you might be struck dead."

Lavinia laughed.

"I wouldn't be, you know. Jesus loves children and he wouldn't grudge me keeping my penny if it was to help Horatio."

"Don't do it," Clara implored. "Even if you aren't struck dead, Mrs Smedley or someone might see, which would be almost as bad."

Lavinia laughed again, but what Clara had said gave her an idea.

"All right, I won't take my church penny. I'll tell Mrs Smedley why I want it and ask her for a little advance."

Lavinia got her chance to speak to Mrs Smedley when that lady came down from her room for her afternoon tea. Although, of course, the cakes and scones for the drawing room were made in the kitchen, Mrs Smedley had nothing to do with the actual meal, for food such as scones was collected from the under-cook by one of the footmen, but the cakes were arranged and sandwiches were cut by the butler who, with the footmen, served the tea. So at about five o'clock Mrs Smedley, refreshed by a good sleep, could come down to a kitchen scrubbed and cleaned by her juniors, to find her tea waiting on the table.

Kitchen tea was far more substantial than drawing-room tea. There was always a tasty dish of some sort as well as dripping toast and large slices of rich fruit cake. This meal was eaten by all the kitchen staff, for usually there was a busy night ahead with at least six courses to be served for dinner, so there was no time for them to eat until quite late.

Tea over, Mrs Smedley would change from the cheerful woman who had come down for her tea into a fury. Not that she felt like a fury, but she considered that it was part of her rôle to let everybody know who was who as far as the kitchen was concerned. So the moment tea was cleared away she would give out her orders with the rapidity of a machine gun. But though she was very much the general commanding the battle when there was dinner to be cooked, she never really lost her warm heart. For whenever there were guests, which meant extra hard work for everybody, she would open the cooking sherry and pour out for each of her staff a good glassful and see that they drank it.

"Now, no faces," she would say to the girls who hated sherry. "Drink it up, it's a tonic and you'll need it before the night is out."

That day Lavinia caught Mrs Smedley at her tea, beaming and rosy fresh from her sleep and enjoying a couple of juicy kippers.

"Well, dear," she asked, "what can I do for you?"

Lavinia, seeing how good-humoured Mrs Smedley looked, decided to take her into her confidence as far as she could – that is to say, without actually complaining of the orphanage. For she knew Mrs Smedley was the sort of woman who, if she suspected cruelty, would dash straight to Mrs Tanner demanding that someone visit the orphanage immediately, and how would that help poor Peter and Horry?

"It's a note I had from a girl at the orphanage, ma'am. She asked me if, when I go on Sunday, I could bring some sweets. You see, my little brother Horatio is only six and he needs a bit of help I expect at washing and dressing, and this girl thought it would help if I brought some sweets that could be handed out as a sort of thank-you to those who help him."

Mrs Smedley looked up from her kipper and her shrewd eyes studied Lavinia.

"There's stories told about that orphanage. Are they true?"

Lavinia hesitated.

"I was there only one night. It was all right as far as I could see."

Mrs Smedley went back to her kippers.

"Each Saturday before your Sunday off remind me you're going. I'll see there's a nice basket to take with you so you can have a picnic. Now, about these sweets. You want some money, I suppose?

Remind me tomorrow when I've got my purse. You can have a shilling."

At exactly this time back at the orphanage Jem was pulling up the horse who pulled the cart outside the entrance. He hitched the reins over a paling and ran up the steps. Miss Jones answered the bell.

"Yes?" she said.

Jem handed her an envelope.

"It's from Sedgecombe Place."

"I suppose that girl we sent is giving trouble," Miss Jones thought. Out loud she said: "Wait here, I will see if there is an answer."

Matron was in her office. She cut open the stiff envelope and drew out a sheet of crested paper. The letter was from Mrs Tanner.

"I am asked to inform you that on this Sunday next Lavinia Beresford will visit the orphanage in the afternoon for the purpose of seeing her brothers. Her Ladyship would be obliged if the little boys could be waiting for her and some place found where they can be by themselves. A. Tanner (Housekeeper)."

But Mrs Tanner had talked to Lavinia before she sent the letter so there was a postscript. "Her Ladyship would be glad if you would also allow Margaret Thursday to see Lavinia as she has shown kindness to the two little boys."

Matron muttered: "Tell him the children will be waiting," which sent Miss Jones scurrying back to

Jem. Alone she looked at the letter as if she could have bitten it. "Her Ladyship would be obliged if the little boys could be waiting." The nerve of it! She didn't want that Lavinia coming back here. Carrying tales she'd be, as like as not. And why Margaret Thursday? What kindness had she ever shown Peter or Horatio? It was a sneaking, low-down way of getting the orphanage talked about, that's what it was. But if there was talk she'd know where it started and she'd have the hide off Margaret Thursday if it was the last thing she did.

10. Half a Sunday

Sunday was a lovely day. All the household at Sedgecombe Place got up an hour later than usual on Sundays, so Clara and Lavinia had not to be down until seven. Lavinia, when she woke, ran straight to the window and looked out.

"Oh, Clara! The sky's as blue as blue and that field over there is gold with buttercups."

Clara came yawning to the window.

"I'm glad it's fine for you, but you wouldn't catch me walking all that way on me half-day. I always say to me mum when I get home all I want is to put me feet up."

Clara's mother had been in service in Sedgecombe Place and had married one of the under-gardeners. They lived in a cottage on the estate, so Clara was allowed home most Sundays.

"Does your mother let you put your feet up?" Lavinia asked.

Clara gave Lavinia a friendly dig with her elbow.

"Give over! Is it likely with ten little 'uns to look after? Why, I'm not inside the door before it's 'Clara do this'. 'Clara do that'."

Lavinia leant against the window.

"I do wish I had something pretty to wear to match the weather, it's not a day for black."

It was a rule of the house that all the servants wore black for church on Sundays.

"Can't you change?" Clara suggested.

"No, I was told specially I could leave right after church."

"Tell you what," Clara suggested. "When 'They'" — "They" was how the staff usually referred to the family — "have gone, take off your titfer and give it to me. Proper figure of fun we look in them.".

All the women servants had to wear small black hats to church or else black bonnets. The hats, which were provided, were made of unbendable chipped straw with a band of narrow ribbon round them. It was said in the servants' hall that they were chosen because they were guaranteed to suit nobody.

Lavinia poured some cold water from a jug into a tin basin and started to wash.

"What a good idea! I was going to put it in my basket with my lunch, but if you'll take it home it'll be lots better. I'll let my hair loose, I hate it up."

As the village church was not far away, on fine Sundays the staff walked to Matins through the grounds. When it was wet they were driven in a brake with the hood up. That Sunday Lavinia, walking last as became her humble position, almost danced down the drive. She was carrying the basket

Mrs Smedley had given her and, though she had no time to look inside, it was so heavy she was sure it was full of good things. On top of it she had put the bag of sweets, chosen with care to prove irresistible to the Ben who washed Horry. Suddenly she heard a whistle and there was Jem looking round a rhododendron bush. Lavinia, on an afternoon walk in the grounds, had told him this was her Sunday to visit the orphanage, but he had not known then how much free time he would have, though he had promised to set her on her path. Now he had good news.

"I got the half-day, too, see, so I can walk most of the way with you. I'll wait on the canal bank – I'd like a word with them on the canal boats on account they may have seen my dad, see? Then I can take you home."

Lavinia was delighted.

"Could you really? I would like that. I have to be back at the house before dark, but it's a long walk and I'd enjoy your company."

Jem thought this very fancy talk so all he said was:

"See you after church," and disappeared back behind the rhododendron.

Every weekday at Sedgecombe Place there were family prayers. These were taken by Lord Corkberry and all the staff had to attend in strict order of precedence, starting with the butler and finishing with Lavinia. Sunday morning service was, Lavinia thought, very like family prayers, for again they lined up behind the butler and sat in pews in strict precedence, again finishing with herself. That Sunday she was glad that she came last because it gave her a chance to hand the verger her precious basket and ask him to look after it.

It was peaceful in the little church, with the smell of wallflowers blowing in through the door and doves cooing on the roof. In the ordinary way, Lavinia would have enjoyed the service, glad of the chance to sit down and join in singing favourite hymns to well-known tunes. But that day she could not get her mind off Peter and Horry. Had they been told yet that she was coming? In spite of being asked for by Mrs Tanner, would she be allowed to see Margaret?

After church all the staff had to form up in two lines on either side of the churchyard path. Then, as Lord and Lady Corkberry and any guests they might have passed, all the men had to raise their hats and the women to curtsey. Usually the Corkberrys would nod and smile in reply, though sometimes they would pause to speak. That morning Lady Corkberry stopped in front of Lavinia.

"Have they given you a good packed lunch?"

Lavinia gave another curtsey.

"Oh yes, m'lady. I haven't looked but it feels heavy."

Lord Corkberry was a man who liked to spend

his life on a horse, though he would as a change shoot game, or fish. He left the running of his house entirely to his wife and seldom spoke to the indoor servants. Now, to Lady Corkberry's surprise, he spoke to Lavinia.

"And where have you secreted this packed lunch which you have not seen but which feels heavy?"

Poor Lavinia, with all the servants' eyes on her, turned pink. She gave yet another curtsey.

"I – asked the verger to look after it, m'lord."

Lady Corkberry smiled.

"Have a pleasant day." Then she moved on.

When they were out of earshot, Lord Corkberry asked his wife:

"Who is that girl, Rose?"

Lady Corkberry was surprised at his interest.

"The new scullery maid. She has two little brothers at the orphanage whom she is going to visit."

"Funny," said Lord Corkberry, "she's the dead spittin' image of somebody. Can't remember who, but it will come back."

The Corkberrys and the heads of staff out of sight, Lavinia dashed into the church to retrieve her basket, tossed her despised hat to Clara and joined Jem at the church gate.

At all times a canal bank is a fascinating place. That morning in April it seemed to Lavinia to have magic about it. There were primroses and cuckoo flowers along the banks, and in the woods she could see celandines and wood anemones. Jem could not understand her excitement.

"They'm pretty all right, but you don't have time for no prettiness when you have to lead the horse what pulls the boat. Very contrary critters canal 'orses can be."

Lavinia forced herself to attend to Jem.

"Fancy being born on a boat, it must have been odd."

"Not really. It's what you're used to, I suppose, but it was a tight squeeze. Our boat, the *Crusader*, she's called, like all canal boats is only seven feet. There's two cabins like, one fore and one aft, with a cross-bed for me dad and mum. Well, you can see with six of us there wasn't much room for larkin' or that."

Lavinia looked at the canal, so quiet with trees reflected in it, while a mother moorhen taught her babies their way around, and a heron flashed low over the water looking for a fish.

"I wonder why you and your brothers hated the canal life, it looks fun to me. I'd love to walk along leading a horse."

Jem sniffed.

"Think you'd love it, do you? That's all you know. You try it all weathers. Mind you, though it's cruel 'ard on the boys, it's worse on the 'orses. There's stables all up and down the canal and we 'ires them from there. A canal boat loaded weighs maybe twenty, maybe thirty ton, and the 'orse he has to pull that weight eighteen maybe twenty hour a day, and when he has to start the boat movin' it's wicked for there's the weight of the water added."

"Poor horses!" Lavinia agreed, but her mind was only half with Jem, the weather was lovely and so soon she would see the boys.

Jem left Lavinia about a mile from the orphanage.

"I shall wait here," he said. "Should be a boat along any time now. See you later."

"Dear Jem, thank you so much," said Lavinia, and hurried off along the path.

11. The Picnic

Matron did not mention to Margaret, Peter or Horatio that Lavinia was coming until after midday dinner. Sunday dinner was the big meal of the week, so it was enormously looked forward to by the orphans. Sometimes it was boiled silverside with dumplings and on another Sunday a round of beef with Yorkshire pudding. Actually, whatever was served, there was more of the dumplings or pudding on each plate than meat, but the orphans didn't mind – suet or pudding made you feel full and that was something they seldom felt.

After grace had been sung, Matron held up a hand for silence.

"Seeing the day is so fine you may all take your Prayer Books into the garden for an hour and learn the collect for the day outside. I shall hear you repeat this myself this evening. You little ones who cannot read can look at the Bible picture books. When the hour is up, Miss Jones will give you all Sunday tasks, during which you will take turns to read out loud *The Pilgrim's Progress*. I wish to speak to Peter and Horatio Beresford and Margaret Thursday."

All day Margaret had been waiting for a message. This was Lavinia's half-Sunday. She didn't suppose she would be allowed to see her, but she meant to have a good try, and anyway she would bring sweets for that awful Ben.

Matron waited until the orphans had filed out, then she ordered Peter, Horatio and Margaret to stand in front of her. She fixed her eyes on Peter.

"I have received a letter from Sedgecombe Place. Your sister Lavinia is being allowed to visit you this afternoon. As an exception I am allowing her to take you and Horatio for a walk."

Nobody ever went outside the orphanage except to school or church. Even Peter, vague as he was, knew this. A walk with Lavinia! It was a glorious promise. His eyes shone.

"Oh, thank you, Matron."

Matron turned to Margaret.

"Lady Corkberry is under the illusion that you have been of service to Peter and Horatio so she asks that you may be allowed to join the party. I was much inclined to refuse this request for I am far from satisfied with your behaviour, but as the suggestion comes from Lady Corkberry I have decided – unwillingly – to allow this great treat, so you may join the Beresford boys on their walk with Lavinia."

Margaret had to hold her tongue between her teeth to prevent herself from answering. She longed to say: "Thank you – but I don't want any favours

91

from you." Instead, splendidly conscious that she had arrived on the church steps with three of everything all of the very best quality, whereas Matron when a baby was most likely dressed in passed-down woollens which were grey with age, she gave a curtsey. Then, smiling sweetly, she said:

"Thank you kindly, Matron."

Matron could feel that somehow Margaret was making fun of her, impertinent child that she was, but she could say nothing, so she strode out of the dining room calling over her shoulder:

"Get ready now, you can sit in the hall until Lavinia arrives."

The Sunday fichus on the girls and white collars on the boys gave the orphans a cared-for look. But even in their Sunday clothes Lavinia was shocked when she saw Margaret and Peter. Horry, she noticed thankfully, was much as usual. But Peter's face had shrunk and his eyes seemed to have grown bigger. Margaret seemed to be much paler and her hair, though still curling under her cap, was less defiant. Lavinia put down her basket and knelt in the hall hugging all three to her while she murmured: "My darlings! My poor darlings!"

Margaret said:

"Matron said we could go for a walk with you."

Lavinia was delighted.

"We'll have a picnic. I saw a wood not far off and I've got the food in this basket."

For a picnic the despised brown cloaks came into

their own. Lavinia spread them out so there was room for them all to sprawl on them without getting damp. As the children had just eaten their dinners she decided to leave the meal until as late as possible so they could enjoy it. "After all," she thought, "I eat well every day so it won't hurt me to have my dinner late for once."

"Vinia," Horatio demanded, "I think there's wolves in this wood, can I go and look?"

Lavinia took off his Sunday collar.

"Of course you can, and if you find a friendly one you might bring it back with you. Give me your collar, Peter. We mustn't mess them up and you can go wolf-hunting too."

Peter obediently took off his collar.

"Did you bring me a book? I'm reading as slow as slow, but I've nearly finished *A Tale of Two Cities* and I'm over halfway through *David Copperfield*."

"Not this week I didn't but I'll see if I can get hold of anything for next time. Aren't there any books in the orphanage?"

"Just *The Pilgrim's Progress* and some Bible picture books, and they are kept in Matron's room," Margaret explained.

Lavinia, having no idea how she would manage it, repeated her promise to try to get hold of something, which seemed to satisfy Peter for he ran off with Horatio.

"Are you happy to stay here," Lavinia asked Margaret, "or would you like to pick primroses?"

Margaret stared at her, surprised that anyone so sensible could ask so silly a question.

"What could I do with primroses?"

"I suppose, even in the orphanage, there must be a jam-jar."

Margaret took off her fichu in case she should crumple it.

"I should have thought even in the little time you were there you would know orphans don't have flowers, in fact, orphans don't have anything. I've still got that box Hannah gave me that the toffees were in. I keep it in my bed, but they'd take it away if they knew and I'd be punished."

"How do they punish you?"

Margaret held out a hand which had red marks across the palm where she had been given ten strokes with a switch.

Lavinia drew in her breath.

"Do Peter and Horry get beaten like that?"

"Neither of them have got punished yet. The things Peter does, like reading when he's pulling the mowing machine, they don't know, and the little ones get more slaps than real punishments."

Lavinia took Margaret's hand and looked at it.

"Mean beasts!"

"Truly, I'd rather have my hands hit than some of the other punishments. I hate being locked in a cupboard and it's pretty awful being sent to bed without supper because you are so hungry you can't sleep."

"You and Peter look as if you were usually hungry – Horry doesn't look so bad."

"That is because of Polly Jenkin. She helps Miss Snelston who is head teacher, they are both awfully nice. Polly is very fond of Horatio and she sneaks things to him when the others aren't looking. Good things like sandwiches full of meat and hardboiled eggs, and often he gets a glass of milk."

"God bless Polly!" said Lavinia. "I do hope some day I can thank her."

Margaret looked worried.

"I know Peter is getting thin, but it's difficult to help him. You see, the boys and the female orphans don't often meet. Sometimes I sneak out to talk to Peter, but if I'm caught I'm punished. But I've got a plan." She lowered her voice as if even there Matron could hear. "The cook – she's called Mrs Bones, and it's a good name for her for all we get is bones – well, she has to cook Matron's supper, but if she knew I could cook I think she'd be glad to let me do it for she says she's on her feet all day and they hurt something chronic. Well, I'm working on Winifred, who was an orphan but now is in the kitchen, to tell Mrs Bones about me, and if I get a chance to cook I'll get some pickings, and I don't care what punishments I get I'll share them with Peter and Horry."

Lavinia looked fondly at Margaret.

"You are a kind girl."

"Not really," said Margaret. "Mostly it's sort of

revenge. I despise Matron so much I don't care what I do to annoy her."

The picnic was a wild success. There were such delicious things in the basket. Sandwiches of all sorts, a fruit pie, cakes, biscuits and a slab of chocolate. With cries of delight, the hungry children fell on the food until there was not a crumb left. They were so busy eating they did not notice Lavinia gave them everything, eating nothing herself.

"What's in that bag, Vinia?" Horatio demanded.

Lavinia handed the bag to Margaret.

"It's sweets. Peter is going to give one to Ben every day so that he does not put soap in your eyes."

"Where shall we hide them?" Peter asked.

"At school," said Margaret. "You can bring one back every day."

Lavinia was very silent on the walk home to Sedgecombe Place. It had made her cry to leave the children at the orphanage. Surely somewhere there was a better place that would take them in?

Jem was used to being on his own so he respected Lavinia's silence and walked on ahead whistling.

When Lavinia got in Mrs Smedley was starting to prepare Sunday supper. She looked out of the window where the sun was setting.

"Just in time," she said. "There's a good girl. I'm giving them macaroni cheese for a hot dish so, as my girl's out, you can grate the cheese for me." Then she noticed that Lavinia looked tired. "But have some tea first."

In the kitchen there was a cupboard called "The Housemaids' Cupboard". This was always bulging with snacks: game, cold chicken, cold meats, as well as fruit puddings and cakes. Any of the staff could help themselves from that cupboard whenever they felt hungry. Lavinia took a plate and piled on to it a rich assortment of food, then, fetching a knife and fork, she sat down at the table in the window and ate the lot.

Mrs Smedley watched her. She had packed her luncheon basket herself so she knew what had been in it. At last she asked:

"Was the dinner all right?"

Lavinia looked up apologetically from her plate.

"Lovely. I was able to share it with the boys and Margaret."

"Share nothing," thought Mrs Smedley. "I think you thought the children were hungry and gave them the lot. I'll have a word with Mrs Tanner about that orphanage and maybe she'll find a way to pass it on."

12. A Night Adventure

Margaret, by tactful questioning, managed to get out of Sally some news.

"My mum is going up to your old orphanage after dinner Tuesday."

It was all very well to have the information, but Margaret could not imagine how she would use it. But she was determined that somehow she would. So on the Monday after the picnic she decided, as a first step, to find out where the room was in which Sally's mother would work. Sally had said "at the top of the house" – a part of the building no orphan had ever seen, but Margaret, by talking to Winifred, had collected a little information.

"I sleep on top under the roof with Mary," Winifred had said – Mary was Mrs Bones's kitchen maid. "Funny little room it is, with the water tank in the corner what makes noises like an old man with the wheezes. Still, it's not so bad on account there's only us so we can do what we like up there. Mrs Bones wouldn't half take a turn if she could see what we sneaks up for our suppers."

"Lucky you!" Margaret had said. "I'd love to sleep in the only room at the top of the house, it's awful sharing with forty-nine other girls."

"Don't I remember!" Winifred had agreed. "Sniffin' and snuffin', not to say throwin' up at times." She had lowered her voice. "But it's not the only room. There's another where Matron keeps you know what."

Margaret had hidden that she was bursting with interest.

"Have you ever seen inside?"

Winifred shook her head.

"Not likely!" There had been drama in her voice. "I wouldn't dare go in. It wouldn't surprise me if, as well as the clothes what we know are there, there wasn't some dead orphans poked away in a cupboard."

Margaret carefully planned her time for exploring. Winifred had to carry in Matron's supper the moment the last orphan had gone up the stairs to bed. Miss Jones, having put out the lights in the girls' dormitory, retired to her room, which was just off the passage outside. She, like all the staff except Matron, had eaten her supper with the orphans. As bread, margarine and cocoa were barely enough to keep the orphans alive, it was likely that somehow Miss Jones got hold of something extra and ate it in her room. So just after lights out was the ideal time, but the snag was that just after lights out few of the orphans were asleep. No one dared to get out of bed for fear Miss Jones would reappear, which sometimes she did, but there was a lot of whispering and giggling from bed to bed. If the orphans saw Margaret get out of bed and go out of the dormitory one of them would be certain to tell-tale for tale-bearing was rewarded, usually with an extra slice of bread and margarine, though sometimes with a real luxury like a piece of cheese. But Margaret had it all planned. Softly as a kitten jumping, she eased herself out of her bed and then lay flat on the floor; from there she rolled from bed to bed until she reached the end of the room next to the door.

Miss Jones always wedged the dormitory door open so that she could hear if there was any disturbance. There was a gas jet in the passage, but it was turned very low so there was little light. Fortunately the child in the bed by the door, called Violet, had her back to it when Margaret reached the door, for she was whispering to her next-door neighbour, so, still flat on the ground, Margaret was able to crawl out. But as she crawled she passed over a loose board which gave a loud creak. Had anybody heard? Violet in the end bed had. She shot up, stifling a scream.

"There's a burglar outside, I'm sure there is," Margaret heard her whisper.

"What would a burglar come here for?" another girl replied. "D'you think he's after our uniforms or maybe he'd fancy my nightie?"

This witticism was relayed up and down the dormitory, causing explosions of laughter.

"I'd better move," thought Margaret. "If that noise doesn't bring old Jones nothing will."

Margaret got to her feet and ran down the corridor to the stairs and was just going to climb them when she heard Miss Jones open her door. Quickly, she lay down flat against the banisters.

From where she was she could see Miss Jones, who had not yet undressed, go to the dormitory door.

"Who was laughing?" she asked.

In a frightened squeak, Violet answered:

"Please'm, I mean Miss Jones'm, I thought I heard a burglar."

Miss Jones expressed astonishment by using the word "burglar" like a piano. She started on a low note and rose almost an octave.

"A burglar? And what, pray, would a burglar want here?"

Violet was evidently nearly in tears.

"I don't know, Miss Jones."

Miss Jones had not come to the dormitory unarmed. Out of her pocket she took a hairbrush.

"A girl who keeps others awake must be punished," she said.

Margaret could hear no more except muffled cries. Too well she knew what was happening. Poor Violet was being beaten on her behind with a hairbrush, and very painful it was. Margaret was sorry and decided, as it was her fault, to give Violet one of Ben's sweets in school tomorrow. Then, taking advantage of Miss Jones being by Violet's bed, she ran up the stairs.

The boys' dormitory was over the girls' room. Here the same system prevailed. The dormitory door was fixed open, there was a low gas left on all night, but the room which on the floor below belonged to Miss Jones was on the boys' floor occupied by Mr Toms, the Beadle. It was orphanage gossip that he liked a glass or two of porter at night and did not expect to be disturbed unless an orphan was so ill death might be expected. Margaret, relying on this gossip being true, ran up the passage and climbed the last flight of stairs.

There was not a sound on the top floor except the wheezing of the water tank. Margaret was not surprised at the quiet, for she knew Mary and Winifred would not be up yet for they had the stove to blacklead and Matron's supper to wash up before they could go to bed. There were two doors just as Winifred had described, and she knew which was the room she wanted because behind the other door she could hear the wheezing tank. Quietly she turned the handle. To her surprise the door opened, for she had expected it to be locked. She closed it softly behind her and looked around. There was a moon that night and by its light she could just see that the door being unlocked was going to do her no good for the room was empty except for a table, a chair and two large cupboards standing side by side just away from the wall. Margaret tugged and pulled at the doors of the cupboards, but they held firm. She was wasting her time for both were locked.

"I can't break them open," thought Margaret, "so I must get the keys or I must get up here when Sally's mother is working and try to fool her that Matron wants her or something."

It was no good hanging about, for she still had the adventurous journey back to her bed. So she went to the door and had just opened it when she heard heavy breathing and steps climbing the stairs, and there was the flickering light of a candle.

"Matron!" thought Margaret. Softly she closed the door, then she dashed across the room and squeezed herself behind the cupboards.

13. By Moonlight

Evidently Matron, too, did not want to be seen. Margaret heard her pause outside and was certain she was making sure Mary and Winifred had not yet finished in the kitchen. Then, just as quietly as Margaret had done, she opened the door, and equally quietly shut it behind her.

Margaret, squeezed behind the cupboards, could only guess what Matron was doing. She was so frightened she could hear her heart beating and wondered Matron could not hear it too. "Oh, dear God," she prayed, "don't let me sneeze – please don't let me for I think if Matron finds me here she'll kill me, truly I do. I don't know how. Maybe she'll throw me out of the window and say I jumped, or lock me up for ever and ever with no food."

From what she could hear, Margaret guessed that Matron was unlocking the cupboards then taking things out and putting them on the table.

"I guess she's putting things ready for Sally's mother," thought Margaret. "Oh, I wish I could see what she's put out. I wonder if my Sunday clothes with lace on them are there."

Matron seemed to be lifting things or perhaps stretching up to the top shelves for something, for Margaret could hear some agonised squeaking from her corset bones, for Matron, conscious she was fat, was always laced into tight corsets.

After what seemed to take an hour but was really twenty minutes, Matron had evidently finished what she had come to do for Margaret heard her go to the door, open it quietly then close it behind her. Then she heard another sound – a key being fitted in the lock. Then, with awful finality, it was turned.

Margaret heard the key pulled out. Then she heard the stairs creak as Matron went down them with, no doubt, the key in her pocket.

Margaret wriggled out from behind the cupboards. The moon had temporarily disappeared behind a cloud so she could see nothing. For a moment she panicked and might have flung herself against the door and screamed, but just in time she pulled herself together. "I must wait," she told herself, "until the moon comes back, then I can see what I can do. There must be a way I can get out, there absolutely must."

A minute later and the moon reappeared. It was nearly full and seemed to be shining straight in at the window. It lit up the table so now Margaret could see what Matron had been doing. On the table there was a pile of clothes, all in miserable condition, dirty and torn, evidently the clothes

Sally's mother had to wash and mend. But of her clothes and her wicker basket there wasn't a sign. "I expect they're in these cupboards," Margaret thought, and turned to look at them, which gave her a surprise. For some reason, perhaps because when Sally's mother had finished washing and mending the clothes they were to go back in the cupboards, Margaret saw they were now both open. She looked in first one cupboard and then the other. In the second cupboard she saw her underneath wardrobe laid out on one shelf and her wicker basket on another.

It was so exciting to see the clothes again that, for a moment, it made Margaret forget the terrible position she was in. Suddenly it was as if Hannah was in the room with her. "Three of everything," Margaret heard her say. "Three plain cambric petticoats. Three pairs of drawers with feather stitching. Three scalloped flannel petticoats. Three linings in case at that orphanage you wear dark knickers. Three liberty bodices and three nightdresses all fine tucked, and here for Sundays is a petticoat and a pair of drawers edged with lace."

Margaret carefully counted everything. It was all there, as well as the stockings and handkerchiefs, all unworn, just as Hannah had packed them. Margaret hugged the clothes to her.

"Darling, darling, Hannah!" she whispered. "I'll find a way to get them, Matron shan't sell them." Then she remembered where she was. It was all very well to say she would find a way to get the clothes, but first how would she find a way to get out of the room?

As she stood there hugging her clothes she heard Mary and Winifred come up the stairs.

"Lucky, lucky them," thought Margaret. "If only I was the other side of that door!"

She heard the girls go into their room and shut the door. They would probably help her if they could, but how could they break down a door without waking the whole orphanage?

"But I won't give in," Margaret decided. "I'd rather jump out of the window than Matron should find me here."

Thinking about the window, Margaret moved across to it and looked out. Even the sad-looking garden looked exciting in the moonlight for the shadows were so black. Then Margaret's attention was caught by something. In the garden there was an oak tree, now covered with the beginning of little new leaves. She had always known about the tree but had never thought about it before, it was just a tree with wire netting round it to prevent the orphans from climbing it. But now she saw that it was so tall its top branches were on a level with the first floor. "If only I could get near that tree," Margaret thought, "I would climb down it and then I might find a window open and climb in."

Very quietly so as not to be heard by Mary and Winifred, she opened the window and leant out.

Then she saw a most extraordinary thing, so extraordinary that it seemed like an answer to prayer. There was a ladder to the right of the window tied in place by a rope. She could not see where the bottom of the ladder went, but it was clear some sort of work was being done on the roof.

"And," thought Margaret, "if a workman can climb up then I can climb down."

Out of the cupboard she took her wicker basket. "I wonder where she put my skirt and jersey," she thought, "for now I've found a way to get out I shall take everything." Gingerly she turned over the grubby clothes on the table, but her clothes were not among them. So she went back to the cupboards. It was not easy to see what was there, but by fumbling she found there were several garments hung on hooks, and amongst them were her pleated skirt and overcoat, the jersey was at the back of a shelf. Regretfully Margaret hung the coat back on its peg. "I hate leaving it," she thought, "for Matron to sell, but I'd never get it into my basket."

It took no time to pack the basket for the underclothes were already folded. When she had finished Margaret fastened the leather strap, then, carrying it in one hand while hitching up her detested orphanage nightgown with the other, she sat on the window ledge, swung her legs outside and studied the ladder.

"If I hadn't this basket," she thought, "I could lean over and hold the ladder with one hand and pull the other half of me on to it. But with the basket I can't." Then she looked at the oak tree. If she wriggled away from the ladder to the other end of the window-sill she would be above the oak tree. Why shouldn't it look after her basket till she could climb up and get it back?

Margaret was so full of schemes that she did not feel frightened. She did not realize how easily she could be killed so, holding the basket in one hand, she eased herself along the window ledge until she was over the oak tree. Gripping the ledge with her other hand, she threw the basket as hard as she could and, miraculously, it landed safely in the oak tree branches. Fortunately for her a wicker basket, even if it hits an oak tree, does not make much noise so no windows were opened to ask what was going on.

Getting on to the ladder Margaret found was more difficult than she had expected. She was, after all, not yet eleven so her legs were not very long. It was more by luck than anything else that, when finally despairing of doing it any other way, she propelled herself towards the ladder, caught a rung and somehow held on.

Climbing down the ladder was easy but, wondered Margaret, where was she going? All too soon she found out. The end of the ladder was on a ledge somewhere, Margaret guessed, near the boys' dormitory. She knelt on the ledge and looked down.

"I expect," Margaret thought, "they push another ladder up to here, but they put it away at night." She leant forward and studied the front of the house. It looked terribly flat with nothing to hold on to.

"I suppose I'll have to stay here until the morning," Margaret thought. "Perhaps the workmen start early and will help me down."

It was then for the first time that Margaret looked up. Just above her there was a window and it was open. In a flash she was up the ladder again and had eased the window farther open and climbed in.

The window was at the far end of the corridor on which was the boys' dormitory. It would have been easy for Margaret from there to have slipped down the stairs to the girls' dormitory and then, by rolling along the floor, have found herself back in her own bed. But that was not good enough for her. She had found the clothes and she meant to hold on to them. So instead of going back to the girls' dormitory she went to the ground floor and let herself out through a side door into the garden.

Getting over the wire netting and climbing the oak tree − especially wearing her voluminous nightdress − was not easy. But Margaret, having succeeded so far, was not going to lose her treasure now, and at the fourth attempt she succeeded in catching hold of the strap, and pulling the basket with her she reached the ground.

But now what? Where could she hide a basket? If only she knew where Peter kept *David Copperfield*, but all he had said was "out of doors somewhere but safe from the rain". Where would you find a place like that in the orphanage? The answer was you wouldn't – at least not big enough for a wicker basket. However, something had to be done with it.

"Just for tonight I'll put it amongst the garden tools," Margaret decided. "I don't believe those are used until the boys get home from school."

The journey back to bed seemed easy after all Margaret had been through. She had a little difficulty in re-locking the door into the house for it was stiff, and then she was scared to death because a door opened just as she was climbing the stairs. However, whoever it was did not see her, so almost before she could believe it she was rolling along the dormitory floor to reach her own bed.

"Margaret Thursday!" her neighbour Chloe whispered. "Where you been? You been gone ever so long."

"No, I haven't," said Margaret, "you've been dreaming." Then, hugging her tin box, she turned over and almost at once she was asleep.

14. The Archdeacon's Brother

Through Mrs Tanner the news did reach Lady Corkberry that perhaps all was not as well food-wise as it should be at the orphanage.

"Mrs Smedley says she packed enough food for a small army, m'lady, yet when Lavinia came back it was clear she had eaten nothing. Ate like a wolf she did, Mrs Smedley says."

Lady Corkberry was worried. She herself had nothing to do with the orphanage, but it was a local charity and, as such, everybody's concern. She and her friends got their girls from there who were to be trained for domestic work and their boys for the stables and garden. But she knew how easy it was to start gossip, so she said quietly:

"Thank you for telling me, Tanner, I will talk to his lordship and see if inquiries should be made. I daresay there is nothing in it, at Lavinia's age there is no need to have missed a meal in order to eat like a wolf."

That evening after dinner Lady Corkberry told Lord Corkberry what Mrs Tanner had told her.

"That the girl was hungry after her walk home would not have worried me, but I had a feeling when

Lavinia asked to visit the orphanage every other Sunday that she was anxious about her brothers."

"Is that the girl you spoke to after church?" Lord Corkberry asked.

"That is right."

"I was going to tell you about her. You know I said she was the spittin' image of somebody, well, only this morning it came to me who it was. Do you remember Delaware's daughter, Phoebe?"

Lady Phoebe, Lord Delaware's daughter, had caused a great sensation in her day by eloping with one of her father's grooms, but Lady Corkberry, though she had met Phoebe, could not remember what she looked like.

"You knew her better than I did for you stayed with them in Ireland for some hunting."

"That's right," Lord Corkberry agreed. "Sixteen she was then, wonderful seat on a horse and pretty as a June rose and wild as a hawk. I told her father, 'You'll have to keep your eye on her,' I said, 'or she'll kick her heels and be off.' And she did, with a groom."

"What happened to them?"

"Nobody knows. Ned Delaware wouldn't have his daughter inside the house – cut her off without a penny. The groom was a bad lot so I heard."

"Is Lavinia really like her?"

Lord Corkberry nodded.

"Spittin' image. I could see it in spite of that shockin' hat you make the girls wear."

"Curious," said Lady Corkberry. "I wonder if she could be a daughter."

Lord Corkberry shook his head.

"Don't suppose she'd know. Proud as the devil they say Phoebe was. After her father cut her off never spoke of her family again."

"Then we shall never know. Poor Lavinia, if she is a daughter of Phoebe it's a sad story. But what I was wondering was, just in case there is anything that needs looking into at that orphanage, if we know anybody who is a governor."

Though they had finished dinner they were still at the dinner table, so Lord Corkberry poured himself out another glass of port. While he was sipping it he thought over his wife's question.

"I believe old Thomas Windle is."

Thomas Windle was a retired lawyer who lived on land belonging to the Corkberrys.

Lady Corkberry was pleased.

"Good. Then I could call on him and see if he can help."

"I don't really know the fellow except as a tenant," said Lord Corkberry. "But you had better choose your time for they say he never leaves his precious library. Great bookworm the fellow is."

Lady Corkberry sent over a note to Mr Windle the next morning. She asked if it would be convenient for her to call the following afternoon.

"It is in connection with St Luke's orphanage

that I wish to see you for I understand that you are a governor."

People never refused to see Lady Corkberry so Mr Windle sent back a note to say he would be delighted to receive her ladyship. But when the note was gone instead of going straight back to the book he was reading he thought about the orphanage. There were governors' meetings four times a year which he attended faithfully, so it wasn't that which was worrying him but something else. Now what? Then it came to him. His brother, the archdeacon. He had asked him to sponsor an orphan. Now what was its name, was it a girl or a boy? He went to his desk and searched for his brother's letters. There they were. Margaret Thursday, of course! He had written several times about the child's admittance. She must be in the orphanage by now. Could Lady Corkberry have come across her and felt he had been remiss? He did hope not for he believed he took his duties as a governor seriously. Oh well, he would know tomorrow and if he had been remiss he would atone for it in any way Lady Corkberry might suggest.

When Lady Corkberry drove over the next afternoon Mr Windle met her on the doorstep. After greeting her, he said:

"My library is the most pleasant room in the house. Should we talk in there?"

It was a delicious day with birds singing and the

smell of flowers blowing on a light breeze.

"Why," she suggested, "should we go indoors? I see you have a seat under these delightful lilac trees. Why do we not sit there?"

Under the lilac trees Lady Corkberry explained why she was worried. Then she said:

"The orphanage as such is none of my business, but orphaned children are the business of us all. Are you satisfied with the way the place is run?"

Mr Windle was a thin man, pale from spending too much time in his library. Now he nervously rubbed his hands together, which made the joints crack.

"I must explain that we governors only meet four times a year. These meetings are largely concerned with finance. It costs a great deal of money to feed and house a hundred orphans."

"I am sure," Lady Corkberry agreed. "I will tell Lord Corkberry we must increase our subscription."

"Too kind," murmured Mr Windle. "Of course we see the matron, whom they say is an admirable woman." He sighed. "I'm ashamed to say she frightens me."

"And you only see her — nobody else?"

"No. Matron reports on conditions generally and the boys and girls who have gone out to work. You see, Lady Corkberry, there is a ladies' committee, it meets monthly and it is they who inspect the home and hear about the individual children. I thought perhaps you had come about that for I sponsored a child called Margaret Thursday. She was highly recommended by my brother. He is an archdeacon."

Mrs Tanner had not added the postscript about Margaret Thursday without asking Lady Corkberry's permission.

"How curious! Margaret Thursday is a friend of my new scullery maid, Lavinia Beresford, who has two brothers in the orphanage. I am sure there is no excuse for the uneasiness I feel, but all the same would it not be pleasant to know we had nothing to be uneasy about? Do you think we could hatch a little plot together? As this child is your responsibility, could you perhaps invite her here to your house? Children talk so much more freely away from an institutional background."

Mr Windle was appalled.

"A child here! I'm afraid I'm an old bachelor, Lady Corkberry, and have no idea how to entertain a child."

Lady Corkberry almost patted his hand.

"I would not suggest she came alone, in fact that Lavinia — she is my scullery maid — should be invited too is part of the scheme. I believe the younger boy is very small and small children confide in one in a way older children would not. Now if you could invite Margaret Thursday and the Beresford boys on a Sunday afternoon I could arrange that the elder sister, Lavinia, could have time off to meet them. I and Lord Corkberry might look in during the afternoon."

What could poor Mr Windle do? Lady Corkberry was not a person to whom you said "No". So when half an hour later she drove away he was holding a piece of paper on which was written:

Margaret Thursday and the Beresford boys. Tea one Sunday. Purpose — inquiring into feeding in the orphanage. Lady C. says she will provide cakes.

15. The Invitation

Margaret found it very hard to get up on the morning after her adventure. She had not noticed at the time how much behaving like a monkey she had been forced to do, so was surprised at how many parts of her ached. Chloe, who was sure she had not been dreaming but that Margaret really had left the dormitory during the night, looked at her suspiciously.

"What's the matter? Why don't you get up? Old Jones won't half create if she sees you."

Stifling groans, Margaret got as far as sitting on the edge of the bed.

"I don't feel too good."

"Shall I tell old Jones you're sick?"

That suggestion got Margaret out of bed and, toothbrush and mug in hand, into the washroom queue.

"I was only pretending," she told Chloe. To herself she said: "If I was half dead I'd get to the school somehow. I don't want to be here when Matron finds that basket is missing."

As it turned out, the basket had to stay hidden under the gardener's tools for it was a relentlessly wet morning, so there was no possible excuse for anyone to go near the garden. But the moment she reached school Margaret told Peter about it.

"Well, after I got my basket I couldn't think where to put it so I put it under the garden tools. Nobody will touch those before you boys do, will they?"

Peter, who had been listening to Margaret's story with the spellbound interest he gave to reading, woke up at that.

"Oh yes. Mr Toms does." Then he looked at the window, "but not today he wouldn't, not in this rain. He keeps special jobs, he says, for wet days."

"Could you get it do you think?"

"I expect so," Peter agreed, "but where would I put it?"

The children looked at each other. Where could Margaret hide it? Even if she unpacked the basket there was nowhere safe from Matron and Miss Jones's prying eyes.

"In those sheds where you boys cut wood is there hay or anything like that?"

Polly was ringing the bell, so there could be no more talk until break. Peter, to Margaret's surprise, gave her arm a nice kind of squeeze as if to say "don't worry". He said:

"Leave it to me. I'll tell you in break."

By break Peter, again to Margaret's surprise for he was usually such a dreamy boy, pulled her into a corner of the schoolroom for it was too wet to go outside. It was easy for the orphans to talk to each other undisturbed during break for the village children usually sat together eating what they called "Beavers", which was a mid-morning snack.

"I think I know where I can put it," Peter whispered. "It's not hay exactly, more sort of dried sticks which I think Mr Toms uses when he grows peas. It's under them I keep *David Copperfield*. I think Mr Toms knows and doesn't mind."

"Could you get it there at dinner-time? For I expect by the time we get home this afternoon Matron will find it's gone and there won't half be a search."

Peter considered that.

"If it goes on raining it's all right where it is until tomorrow. Directly it's fine I can move it because it's one of my tasks to clean and polish the spades, so I can say I was doing that."

Margaret hated to leave the basket where somebody might find it by accident, but Peter seemed to know what he was talking about. In fact, Peter that morning stopped being a little boy and felt older than she did. So, unusually meekly for her, Margaret said:

"All right. I'll leave it to you."

To Margaret's surprise there was no excitement when they got back to the orphanage that afternoon. Why wasn't there, she wondered? Hadn't Sally's mother told Matron there was no basket in the cupboard? Then she found a reason. Most likely Matron had only told Sally's mother to mend and wash the clothes on the table. It could be she never even looked in the cupboards. Anyway, whatever had happened, it was clear there was no search going on. But thought there was no search there was obviously something else in the air for Matron, during tea, gave Margaret what she described later to Chloe as bite-you-in-the-back looks.

After tea as usual Matron gave out chores. Some of the boys, Margaret noticed, were given repair jobs to do in the house, but others were to put on their cloaks and run to the outhouse where Mr Toms had work for them to do.

"We have had," Matron said, "as possibly some of you have noticed, workmen repairing the roof. This is now finished and Mr Toms will order some of you to clean the ladder the men used."

"My goodness!" thought Margaret. "Wasn't I lucky! If it was tonight I was getting my basket the ladder wouldn't have been there and it would have been raining."

The girls' tasks were much as usual, though that evening there was a sewing class, which meant that those, like Margaret, directed to peeling potatoes had less time in which to do it.

"But," said Matron, "though you may have less time I shall expect every potato peeled, so no talking. Any girl found talking will have to deal with me. Dismiss — but will you, Margaret Thursday, stay here. I want to speak to you."

In pity, Margaret's friends — and she had many by now — looked at her. What had she done? What would her punishment be? For themselves the potato peelers felt punished already, for potato peeling, which had become popular since Margaret had come to the orphanage, would be very dull without her stories to keep them going.

Margaret felt as if cold water was trickling down her spine. So Matron had found out, goodness knows how! Now what would she do to her? Did she know an even more awful punishment than those she had already had?

Matron, more red-faced than usual, beckoned Margaret to stand in front of her.

"I suppose you have no idea what I am going to say to you?"

Margaret tried to hide how frightened she was. She stuck her chin in the air.

"No."

"You came to us, if you remember, through the recommendation of one of our governors — Mr Windle."

Margaret turned a mental somersault. Mr Windle! So this wasn't about the missing basket!

"Well, really," she explained, "it wasn't because of Mr Windle but because of my rector, he was the one who found me with three of everything of the very best quality on the church steps — his archdeacon wrote to his brother and it's him who is Mr Windle."

Matron's rather beady black eyes gave a sort of snap.

"You talk too much. Kindly listen in silence when I am speaking. Mr Windle feels it is time he saw you since he sponsored you. Today a servant rode over with a note. He wishes you and — at I understand the request of Lady Corkberry — the two Beresford boys to take tea with him on Sunday. A conveyance will be sent for you at 2.30."

Margaret gaped at Matron. Going out to tea! A conveyance might mean a carriage! How glorious to go out to tea in a carriage. She would feel like a princess. Then she remembered what Matron was waiting for. She gave a little bob curtsey.

"Thank you, Matron."

"Do not thank me," said Matron. "You are one of my most unsatisfactory children and if I had my way you would have no treats at all, I disapprove utterly of you being allowed out two Sundays running. But since Mr Windle is a governor I must respect his wishes. One thing I must demand of you — under no circumstances discuss orphanage affairs. Just say, 'I am very happy'. If you say more be sure I shall hear of it."

Margaret thought, "Catch me telling a lie like that, and I'm certain Peter and Horatio won't either," but, looking as meek as she knew how, she gave another bob.

"Yes, Matron. I quite understand, Matron."

In the scullery over the potatoes in whispers she confided with embellishments to her fellow-peelers what Matron had said. When she came to "Just say 'I am very happy'", the children giggled so much that a terrified Mary, who was in charge, rushed into the scullery.

"Oh, do be quiet or someone will hear, and if they do Matron will take it out on me. You know she will."

That evening after sewing, Margaret, as she often did, sneaked into the playroom to see how Horatio was getting on. He was managing much better now that Ben was given sweets by Peter not to put soap in his eyes. He seldom came down to breakfast red-eyed and shiny with tears. He was too, getting on well with the other children, for being small for his age he was in great demand to be the baby when the little girls played "Home". He was that evening when Margaret came in being the baby rocked to sleep in a chair. But he stopped being the baby when he saw Margaret and ran to her. He pulled at her arm to make her lean down so he could whisper.

"Peter said if I saw you I was to say. . ." Horatio took a deep breath and recited like a budgerigar: "He got it out and he has hidden it."

Margaret kissed him.

"Thank you, darling. Do you know we are going out to tea again this Sunday? I must go now or

Matron will catch me."

The little girls came for Horatio to put him back in his pretend bed. He beamed at them.

"Do you know last Sunday when Vinia came we had so much to eat we couldn't eat any more and now Margaret says it's going to happen again. Next Sunday."

The peaky, pinched–looking little girls were pleased for him.

"Lucky you!" one of them said. "I never had so much to eat I couldn't eat no more. It must be a lovely feeling."

Horatio patted his tummy.

"Oh, it is, it's the bestest feeling in all the whole world."

16. *Questions*

Lavinia was delighted when Mrs Tanner told her the news about Mr Windle's tea party.

"There's a trap being sent for the children at half past two," Mrs Tanner explained. "So her ladyship said to tell you if you left the house about three you should be there in nice time. You're a very lucky girl, Lavinia, it isn't many in your position would be allowed out two Sundays running."

"Oh, I do know that, Mrs Tanner, ma'am," Lavinia agreed. "I do indeed. Would you thank her ladyship for me?"

Mrs Tanner was herself puzzled by what she had to say next. She never criticised anything Lady Corkberry did, but this time she felt her charity was going too far. That this was how she felt showed in her voice.

"You will have the opportunity to do that yourself. Her ladyship has stated she wishes to see you in her sitting room at 2.30 this afternoon. One of the men will show you the way."

Lavinia was as puzzled as Mrs Tanner. Why should Lady Corkberry wish to see her? The new scullery maid. It didn't make sense. She spoke her thoughts out loud.

"Perhaps I am to be told who this Mr Windle may be and why he has invited myself and the boys for the afternoon, for truly, Mrs Tanner, ma'am, I have never heard of him."

"No doubt," Mrs Tanner agreed, though what she thought was, if telling things to a maid needs to be done it should be done through me. Out loud she said: "Now back to your work and do not forget, the sitting room at 2.30 sharp in a clean apron and, of course, a cap."

Caps were the bane of Lavinia's life. They were seldom worn in the kitchen, but they had to be at hand for morning prayers and in case Lady Corkberry came in person to speak to Mrs Smedley. They were not the starched caps worn by the parlour and housemaids, but a little round piece of linen edged with lace. Lavinia did try always to put her cap where she could find it, but more often than not it got mislaid and all too often trodden under foot. As a result, often before prayers she had to wash it out and dry it on a toasting fork in front of the stove.

That morning she took Clara into her confidence.

"I must give my cap a wash," she said as she searched the back of the scullery door. "I'm sure I hung it here after prayers."

Clara came to help.

"What you want it for now?"

Lavinia pounced on her cap which had fallen on the floor and got caught under the door.

"Oh, look at it! Like a dish rag!" She ran to the sink and began washing it. "I have to go to the sitting room to see Lady Corkberry at half past two."

Clara nearly dropped the mincer she was cleaning.

"Whatever for? What you done? Never once have I been sent to speak to her ladyship, and if I had been sent for me mum wouldn't half wallop me."

Lavinia went on washing her cap.

"I don't think I've done anything, it's about Sunday. A man called Mr Windle has invited my brothers for Sunday afternoon and I'm to go too, and Mrs Tanner said when I saw her ladyship to be sure to wear a clean apron and a cap."

Clara was surprised.

"Mr Windle! He lives in what they call the Dower House. My dad says he's got ever such a lot of money but he spends it all on books. He doesn't care about nothin' else. Catch me buying books if I had a lot of money!"

Lavinia had washed the cap.

"I'll just slip out and peg it up outside. It should be dry long before dinner-time."

At 2.30 sharp one of the footmen opened Lady Corkberry's sitting-room door.

"It is the young person from the scullery, m'lady."

Lady Corkberry was writing letters. She got up from her desk and sat in an armchair.

"Come in, Lavinia." She nodded to the footman. "You can go, Henry."

Lavinia, in a clean print dress and an apron so starched it crackled and her cap pinned to the top of her head, stood after her curtsey respectfully just inside the door. She thought she had never seen a more beautiful room. There were huge windows with rose-sprigged curtains and a rose-coloured carpet. The furniture shone so that it reflected back the sunlight. On all suitable furniture there were bowls of flowers, and many of the chairs and the sofa were covered in the same material as the curtains.

Lady Corkberry cleared her throat. She had been feeling that Lavinia was on her conscience since Lord Corkberry had told her whose daughter she might be, so she wanted to find out what Lavinia knew about her background, but she did not know where to start.

"You have been told about the tea party at Mr Windle's to which your brothers have been invited?"

Lavinia, taking the advice of the Red Queen, gave another curtsey.

"Yes, m'lady. It is so good of him for I do not think he has ever heard of my brothers."

Lady Corkberry thought, "She really could be Lord Delaware's grand-daughter."

"No, indeed. It is your little friend Margaret Thursday whom he knows. The brother is, I understand, an archdeacon, it was he who suggested sending Margaret Thursday to the orphanage."

"That was a mean thing to do," thought Lavinia. Out loud she said:

"I see, m'lady."

Lady Corkberry thought she saw an opening.

"You sound doubtful if it was a kindness. Do you not care for the orphanage?"

Lavinia was not going to risk any trouble coming to the boys while they were under Matron's care, and there would be trouble if Matron thought she had been making complaints.

"I daresay it's very good, m'lady," she said, "but of course it's not like being in your own home."

Lady Corkberry nodded.

"No, indeed. Have you children been orphaned long?"

Lavinia thought before she answered and chose her words with care.

"Our mother died at Christmas. From that time until the boys went to the orphanage I managed our home."

"But it was too much for a young girl?" Lady Corkberry suggested.

Lavinia saw their home again. It had been small,

but her mother had kept it wonderfully and somehow, in spite of their poor furniture, had managed a sort of elegance and, still more remarkable since they lived in London, there were nearly always some flowers. Lavinia had done her best to keep the house as spotless as her mother had done and to continue the boys' lessons, but the money had given out. Her mother had managed to keep the home going by selling such nice things as she had, but when she died there were no nice things left and almost no money.

"Your mother starved herself to keep you children going," the doctor had told Lavinia, "which was why she had no strength to fight an illness. You can't manage on your own, you know."

Desperate at the thought of breaking up the family, Lavinia had pleaded with the doctor.

"I can manage. I can get work, I'm very strong."

Unwillingly the doctor had given in, but only temporarily.

"I won't interfere now, I'll give you a month, but if at the end of that time you aren't fixed up I must see that some arrangement is made for you."

At the end of the month when the doctor called things were no better – in fact, worse. Lavinia had not found regular work and Horatio was crying because he was hungry.

"I've had a talk with the vicar of this parish, whom you know," the doctor told Lavinia. "He knows of an orphanage that will take the boys and find you a place in service nearby. Meanwhile, I will lend you the money to live on. After you have left I can sell what is in the house to pay me back so do not worry about that."

The vicar made all the arrangements. He had not known Mrs Beresford except by sight when she brought the children to church on Sundays, but he could say with truth that the boys appeared entirely suitable for a church orphanage.

"There is just one point," the vicar had told Lavinia. "To go to St Luke's the boys must be orphans. When did your father die? I don't remember seeing him."

Lavinia had turned a little white, but she spoke out bravely.

"No, you would not have. He never came to church. He died nearly a year before my mother."

Lavinia came back to Lady Corkberry. What was it she had asked? Oh yes, she had asked if they had given up their home because it had been too much for her to run.

"No, m'lady. But it was not a neighbourhood where there was much work so the money was finished."

"Had your mother worked?"

Lavinia thought again of her mother and the thinking brought tears to her eyes. She looked at the floor hoping Lady Corkberry would not notice.

"No, m'lady, but she taught us all our lessons,

that's why my brother Peter is such a reader. Somehow she always managed to get him books."

Lady Corkberry felt she was asking too many questions and she could see that questions about her mother upset Lavinia, but she had to persist.

"Was your mother widowed long?"

Lavinia again gazed at the floor, but this time it was for fear her expression would give away something.

"No, not long."

Lady Corkberry sighed, she had found out nothing and perhaps upset the girl, which was a mistake if she was hiding things she should say about the orphanage. She gave Lavinia a dismissing nod.

"Well, I must not keep you from your duties. It is possible that his lordship and I may be at Mr Windle's on Sunday, in which case I may see you then."

"What did her ladyship want?" Clara asked the moment Lavinia got back to the kitchen.

Lavinia took off her cap and clean apron.

"I don't know really, except to say how it was my brothers are asked to Mr Windle's place. It's on account of another orphan called Margaret Thursday. I suppose he thought it would be easier seeing her if she had other children to play with."

"She was a long time telling you that," said Clara.

Lavinia thought over her interview.

"Well, she asked a lot of questions, you know — about where we lived before the orphanage and all that."

Clara nodded.

"The gentry are all like that, if they was us they'd be called nosy. Come on, old mother Smedley said we could go out in the grounds for an hour."

17. Sunday with Mr Windle

Jem was sent to fetch the children, for the coachmen liked to have their Sundays off. The coachmen at Sedgecombe Place were always very well turned out in fawn coats, white breeches and black top hats with what looked like a little windmill on the side. Jem had no uniform as such for he never drove the Corkberrys, but the head coachman had strong views on how his stable lads should appear when in public. So, since he was driving, it was a spruced-up Jem who drew up the trap smartly outside the orphanage. He was dressed in a navy coat with brass buttons which had belonged to the head groom and had been cut down for him, and a blue cap with a peak rather like chauffeurs wear today.

The children, hopping from one foot to the other with excitement, were waiting for him, but as the trap stopped, like a Jack-in-the-box Miss Jones flew out of the front door.

"Quietly, children," she said in her most repressive voice. "Horatio, you will sit in front with the driver and you two will sit in the back. And no talking or you will take this young man's attention from his work."

Jem, like anybody else given charge of a vehicle, looked upon it while he drove it as his property. He had not until Miss Jones spoke cared twopence who sat where, but she had rubbed him up the wrong way and he decided not to put up with the old cat's interference. Speaking as though he had been given orders by Lady Corkberry herself, he said:

"It's the little girl who is to come in front, the boys are to sit at the back."

Miss Jones was furious but she said nothing. "It was extraordinary," she thought, "how things were always working out well for Margaret Thursday, but let her wait, one day they would knock the spirit out of her."

As they drove off, Margaret looked at Jem out of the corners of her eyes and decided that she liked him, but she wanted to be sure he didn't despise her for living in an orphanage. She spread her brown skirt out as elegantly as she could.

"You mustn't think I'm an ordinary orphan," she explained. "You see, I was found on a Thursday on the steps of the church with three of everything of the very best quality."

Jem grinned.

"I wasn't. I was born in a canal boat and I'd be there still if I hadn't had the pneumonia."

Margaret was thrilled.

"In a boat! Do you know it's the first time I ever

met anybody born in a boat: Doesn't it make you feel special?"

Jem grinned again.

"No, why should it? Six of us there is, but we've all left the boat now except my young brother Tom and he'd like to but he can't get away."

"Why can't he?"

"A canal boat is pulled by a 'orse, see? Well, with me dad steering someone 'as to lead the 'orse and Tom's all that's left."

"Doesn't he like leading the horse?"

Jem shook his head.

"Would you like to be a legger — that's what we call 'em? Hour after hour leadin' the 'orse in all weathers? Cruel it can be when there's wind and rain. But when it snows!"

"I wouldn't mind," said Margaret. "I wouldn't mind anything as much as living in that old orphanage. Some day I'll run away."

Jem looked at her clothes.

"You wouldn't get far dolled up like that."

For a second Margaret nearly told him about her basket, but caution won.

"I've got plans," she said.

Jem had decided Margaret was a proper card so he teased her.

"Well, when you run away give me a knock and I'll start you on your road."

Quite seriously Margaret answered:

"I will. What is your name and where do you live?"

Still amused by her, Jem told her.

"I'm Jem. There's bedrooms over the stables. I'm the last so you can't miss it. I've 'ung a 'orseshoe over the door."

Mr Windle was used to appearing in the law courts, but not to entertaining children. Nevertheless he came out the moment his manservant reported that the trap had arrived. He had the sort of face people connect with the law – a mixture of cleverness and shrewdness overlaid by a mask, so that whoever he was cross-examining would not know what to expect. Now he had tried to drop his mask and appear pleased, but it was not a great success for he still looked what the rector used to describe to Margaret when speaking of his churchwarden, "a cold fish".

He gave Margaret his hands to help her down.

"Welcome, my child!"

Then he turned to lift down Horatio.

"And how are you, my little man?"

"Not very well at this moment," said Horatio. "I think if the drive had gone on any longer I should have been as sick as sick."

"I think it's driving back to the horses, sir," Peter explained. "You know, seeing the road running away from you. I felt peculiar myself."

The manservant was helping Peter down. He did not care for charity children and looked as though he didn't.

"Don't you trouble, sir. I'll take them round to

the back to tidy themselves."

Mr Windle looked relieved for certainly the boys did appear pale and it really would be distressing if they were sick in the drive.

"Very good, Gregson, and tell Mrs Gregson to look after Margaret. Afterwards send them out in the garden to play. I will go back to the library."

Peter looked after him longingly.

"Has he a library?" he asked Gregson. "I mean, a real one full of books?"

Gregson looked down his nose.

"We have some thousands of books here. We have the finest library in the county."

Jem winked at the children, then he tossed them their capes.

"I don't suppose you'll need those, but you may as well have them just in case."

The children, washed and brushed, had only just reached the garden via the back door when Lavinia arrived. She was looking pretty for she had taken down her hair and wore it tied back with a ribbon, and she had taken off her Sunday black and was wearing a green dress her mother had made for her. It was a little tight and short, but it still suited her.

"Darlings!" she called. "Come here and let me look at you all."

Horatio flung himself at her.

"Vinia! Vinia! I was nearly sick driving here but I'm all better now."

Lavinia was carrying a basket. She drew back a cloth which covered its contents.

"Just as well you're all better for look at what there is for tea."

The children gasped for the basket contained the most wonderful assortment of cakes.

"Could we have just one now?" Horatio begged.

But Lavinia pulled the cloth back into place.

"No. You'd get me the sack. Mrs Smedley – she's the head cook – packed the basket herself and said I was to take it straight to Mrs Gregson. Do you know where I find her?"

"I'll show you," Margaret offered. "We go in at the back door, she says the front door is not for the likes of us."

Lavinia laughed.

"What do we care! Are you boys coming too?"

To Lavinia's surprise it was Peter who said "No".

"I thought Horry and I would explore."

Lavinia looked round. It was a very tidy sort of garden. Neat flower-beds at the moment full of tulips, wallflowers and forget-me-nots, all of which looked as if the distance between them had been measured with a yard measure. The wide lawns were neatly mowed and the paths spotlessly kept. There was no run-about garden at all.

"There's not much to explore," Lavinia said doubtfully. "I think it's the sort of place where you sit out of the wind and talk. Imagine how awful it would be if you fell over and broke a rose tree."

Horatio had sharp eyes, he pointed to the bottom of the garden.

"I can see a place to explore. There's a little gate in that wall."

Lavinia accepted that.

"All right – off you go. Come on, Margaret."

To Horatio's disappointment, Peter refused to go to the gate in the wall.

"We'll go there presently, but now I want to walk round the house."

"What for?"

Peter was vague.

"Just to look. I want to know where the rooms are."

Mrs Gregson unbent a little towards Lavinia for she loved news of what went on at Sedgecombe Place. With admiration she unpacked the cakes.

"Wonderful hand with cakes, Mrs Smedley has. I could, of course, have made them here, but there's enough work for me without fancy stuff. I suppose she gets her fancy stuff started early, I mean meringues and that?"

Lavinia wanted to get out to join the boys, but she did not intend to make an enemy for after all, Mr Windle was a governor at the orphanage, so she stayed for a few minutes chatting.

Outside, Margaret said to her:

"Don't call the boys for a minute. I must, I absolutely must tell you about what's happened. I've got my basket back and all my clothes."

Margaret's story was so enthralling, for she made it sound even more exciting than it had actually been, that neither she nor Lavinia saw Lord and Lady Corkberry come in through a gate which led into their own park, nor did they hear them as they crossed the lawn. So both jumped when Lady Corkberry said:

"There you are, Lavinia, and this must be Margaret Thursday."

Both girls gave a curtsey.

"Yes, m'lady," Lavinia said hurriedly, feeling sure that Margaret would not know who Lady Corkberry was or how to address her.

"Where are your brothers?" Lady Corkberry asked.

Lavinia looked round.

"I don't know, m'lady, but they can't be far, it isn't a very big garden." Then she raised her voice and called: "Peter! Horry!"

Just out of sight Horatio tugged at Peter's arm.

"Come on, Peter, Vinia's calling us, and anyway, it's very rude to stand on tiptoe so you can see into someone's window. Mummy told me that."

"You go," Peter whispered. "I must see a little more. I won't be a minute, I promise you. But don't tell Lavinia what I'm doing."

Obediently, Horatio trotted round the corner.

"There you are," said Lavinia. "Where's Peter?"

"Coming." Horatio gazed at Lord Corkberry. "Who are you?"

Lord Corkberry put his hand under Horatio's chin and stared down at him.

"I'm Lord Corkberry, but the question is — who are you?"

"I am Horatio Beresford," Horry explained.

Lord Corkberry turned to Lady Corkberry.

"He's Ned to the life. Never saw anythin' like it."

As Lady Corkberry had hoped, Horatio proved easy to get information out of. She soon learnt that he wanted to see what was the other side of the gate in the wall so she offered to show him. Hand in hand they walked across the lawn, while Lord Corkberry went to greet Mr Windle.

"Do you like living in the orphanage, Horatio?"

Horatio looked surprised.

"Of course not. Nobody does."

"Why? Are they unkind?"

Horatio thought about that.

"Ben was. He always put soap in my eyes on purpose until Vinia sent him sweets not to."

"Do you get plenty to eat?"

Horatio was amazed at such ignorance.

"In the orphanage there is hardly nothing to eat. There's very nasty porridge, all lumps, for breakfast, and teeny-weeny milk and never any sugar. Then for dinner there's meant to be meat but mostly it's carrots and things. For supper there's just two pieces of stale bread and cocoa."

Lady Corkberry hoped that perhaps Horatio was

exaggerating, it was natural for children to complain about food.

"You don't look starved."

"That is school," Horatio explained. "I eat there. Polly Jenkin brings me things."

"And who is Polly Jenkin?"

Horatio was surprised.

"I thought everybody knew her. She helps Miss Snelston."

Lady Corkberry saw daylight.

"And Miss Snelston is your schoolteacher?"

"Of course she is."

They had reached the gate so Horatio peered through. Outside was the canal bank and by squinting sideways Horatio could see quite a lot of the canal. Lady Corkberry shook the gate.

"I'm afraid Mr Windle keeps this locked, and very wise too, for you never know who's about near canals. Do you like the matron at the orphanage?"

Horatio swung round. His eyes, Lady Corkberry noticed, had dilated with fear.

"No," he whispered, as if even in this garden Matron could hear. "She frightens everybody. She beats Margaret and locks her in a dark cupboard full of black beetles. All us orphans know it's because of Matron that everyone is so miserable."

From Margaret, Peter and Horatio's point of view the tea was magnificent, but they ate so much and took so long over it that as soon as it was

145

finished Lord and Lady Corkberry and Lavinia — though by a different route — had to leave. This meant that Mr Windle, much to his dismay, was in charge of the children for a quarter of an hour until Jem brought the trap round. Fortunately for him, Horatio asked if he had a key to the gate to the canal bank. He had so he, Horatio and Margaret had a look at the canal and were rewarded by seeing a dabchick and all her babies swim by.

"Where's your brother?" Mr Windle asked Horatio.

What Horatio might have answered Mr Windle never knew for Margaret, always the first to reply, said:

"Oh, he will be mooning about somewhere, he's a terrible dreamer but he's never lost."

Walking home, Lady Corkberry said to Lord Corkberry:

"I've talked to the little boy. There is something wrong at that orphanage. Next week I shall call upon the schoolmistress and see what she knows or suspects. I have a feeling from what little Horatio said that the matron is a bad woman, in which case she must be punished."

Lord Corkberry nodded:

"And I have a feelin' I shall have to go to Ireland and have it out with Ned Delaware. If young Horatio isn't his grandson I'll eat my hat."

18. Trouble

To avoid further trouble with his insides, Horatio was put in the front seat between Margaret and Jem. Margaret offered to give her seat to Peter, but he wouldn't have it. He was in his most dreamy mood and scarcely seemed to be conscious of his surroundings. He settled down in the back seat muffled in his brown cloak, and only after a nudge from Margaret and much fumbling did he produce his hand for Mr Windle to shake.

Horatio slept all the way home, and even Margaret, because she was full of good food and air, was almost silent. It was not until they could see the orphanage that she became her animated self.

"Doesn't it look awful, Jem, but it's much awfuller inside? I shouldn't wonder if Matron was waiting to pounce on me for something I haven't done the second I get in. Thank goodness I'm still full of tea, so I shan't mind if I have to go to bed without supper."

Horatio had woken up and clung pathetically to Margaret.

"Must we go into that horrid place? I wish we could have stayed with Vinia."

Margaret hugged him and tried to think of something to say to comfort him. She turned round to Peter.

"Do you suppose directly we get in Matron will find us Sunday tasks or do you think I could look after Horatio?"

"Matron's not going to get a chance with me," Peter answered. "I'm going straight to the shed to see if the others are working. If Matron asks you that is where I am, but I am sure you will get a task."

At the orphanage door Margaret said goodbye to Jem.

"Thank you very much for driving us and telling me about living on a canal boat." She lowered her voice. "And if ever I do run away I'll come to you first. The last bedroom over the stables."

Jem, though he was certain Margaret did not mean it, winked in a pretend conspiratorial way.

"And don't forget — feel for me 'orseshoe over the door."

The moment she and Horatio were inside the orphanage Margaret could smell trouble. By the rules laid down by the ladies' committee there should not have been ordinary tasks on Sundays, but there usually were for Matron was a firm believer in Satan finding mischief for idle hands. Margaret, having hung her own and Horatio's cloaks in the cloakroom, was wondering if she dared slip into the little ones' playroom when Violet, looking as scared as the white rabbit when he was keeping the Duchess waiting, sidled into the room.

Margaret despised Violet, considering her a poor spiritless thing, but she had given her one of the sweets meant for Ben to make up for having had her whipped when she had mistaken her for a burglar, so she approached her as a friend.

"What's up? Where is everybody?"

Violet reduced her voice to a scared squeak.

"I don't know where everybody is but Matron's proper upset. I think you're meant to be in the scullery."

Margaret took Horatio into the hall and gave him a push towards the playroom.

"In there, darling. Go and play 'Home' until supper."

In the scullery sure enough she found the usual potato peelers, including Susan and Chloe, only today they were not peeling potatoes but sitting round a tub scrubbing swedes. They were all pleased to see Margaret.

"Did you 'ave a good time?" Susan whispered.

In an almost inaudible voice another girl said:

"Tell us about the eats."

Margaret saw the other girls had taken off their Sunday fichus and had rolled up their sleeves so she did the same.

"There is no need to whisper," she said cheerfully. "There's no one in the kitchen, not even Winifred."

The girls were sitting on benches; they made room for Margaret on one.

"You better go careful," they told her. "Matron's in a terrible taking."

Margaret kicked the basket of swedes.

"Where did this lot come from?"

"One of the farmers sent them in," Chloe explained. "I think he grew them for the lambing but he had this lot over."

Margaret inspected the swedes.

"I guess the sheep wouldn't eat them and I don't blame them – half of them are rotten."

"What won't fatten will fill," said Susan.

This was such a favourite statement of Matron's that the girls giggled.

"What's Matron in a taking about?" Margaret asked.

"We don't rightly know," Chloe said. "We think from the way she carried on something's been stolen from up there." She jerked her thumb towards the roof.

"You know," one of the other girls whispered. "It's that room up top opposite where Mary and Winifred sleep. It's where Matron keeps you know what."

Margaret was able to get away with a nod in reply, which was lucky for her heart was beating so hard she could scarcely speak. At last she managed:

"Who is she creating about? Did she say?"

"No," the girls told her. "She just created about

everything. It was Winifred told us something was missing. She heard her banging around in the room upstairs mutterin' something awful."

Chloe nudged Margaret.

"And we said lucky Margaret's out or Matron would take it out on her same as she always does."

Susan said:

"Come on, Margaret, tell us what it was like and what you 'ad to eat."

Margaret somehow pulled herself together. The girls had looked forward to her getting back and she was not going to let them down.

"Well, first the carriage came for us with a man dressed all proper driving. Old Jones didn't half look mad to see me sitting up beside him."

"Tell us about what you ate," Chloe pleaded.

"You wait," said Margaret. "Well, we came to the house and there was Mr Windle and a manservant waiting. And do you know what? The maid curtseyed to me and said 'Good afternoon, Miss Thursday'."

The girls giggled, well aware Margaret was making things up, but enjoying it just the same.

"Then," Margaret went on, "after we'd washed and that we were sent to play in the garden. You never saw a garden like it. Why, it was so big you could lose yourself. And the flowers! Roses and lilies and everything."

Winifred poked her head round the door.

"Funny sort of garden in April, but do talk quiet,

Matron's creatin' somethin' shockin' and she'll kill me if she hears you talking."

Margaret lowered her voice to the smallest whisper.

"The tea! Well, there was rolls with real cream and jam on them and then cakes. Well, you never saw anything like it, all iced and with cherries on and that, there was some covered in chocolate and inside was whipped cream."

It was too much for the girls. Together they let out an envious "Ooh!"

Matron must have been passing for in one second she was in the scullery, her face redder than usual and her hair seemed to be standing on end.

"Who dared to make that noise?" She looked round at the girls and saw Margaret. "I did not tell you to come in here. You should have reported to Miss Jones as soon as you came in and she would have told you that I wished to see you. Come with me."

Matron strode out of the room, and with apparent meekness Margaret followed, though making time to give the girls a wink to cover the fact that her knees were shaking.

Matron led Margaret into her office and, shutting the door, sat down behind her desk.

"Lift up your skirt, Margaret," she ordered.

Margaret, scared as she was, found it hard not to smile. So that was what Matron wanted. Was she really hoping to see a petticoat edged with lace? She lifted her skirt to display her grey winceyette orphanage petticoat.

"It was clean this morning."

The orphans always had clean underclothes on Sundays so Matron ignored that.

"Now lift up that petticoat."

Margaret's chin shot into the air. This was really going too far, drawers weren't clothes you showed people. However, it was not worth being beaten for, so, slowly, she lifted her petticoat to show her coarse long straight-legged drawers.

Even Matron could not believe there was anything hidden under them for they were tight as well as straight. Politely, Margaret held out one leg.

"Would you like me to take off my boots?"

Matron, though she had tried to fool herself that Margaret had stolen the wicker basket, had never really believed that she had. How would she have known where it was and, having found it, where could she have hidden it? No, without doubt the culprit must be that woman she had employed to wash and mend the old clothes she was taking north to sell. But it was not going to be easy to prove. How could the woman have carried a basket out of the orphanage without being spotted? And if she was accused without evidence to whom might she not complain? Suppose she complained to the ladies' committee, how was she to explain why at her own expense she was having the clothes repaired? As usual she turned her bad temper on to Margaret.

"You can put down your skirt. It was you, of course, who led the girls on to make that noise in the scullery — it is always you. We have had nothing but trouble since you came to the orphanage."

Margaret, furious at having been made to stand in front of Matron in a pair of shameful orphanage drawers, felt as if that mother whom she had never known was encouraging her to assert herself. Chin high and cheeks flushed, she retorted:

"I do not mean to cause trouble, I think it's just that I am used to better things. You may not know, but when my mother left me on the church steps I had three of everything of the very best quality embroidered with crowns" — this was a new invention and pleased her — "there were crowns on everything and each year gold money was left to keep me."

Matron asked in an icy voice:

"And what happens to the money now?"

"It stopped. You see my mother got quite poor, for my father, who was an admiral, was drowned on the High Seas."

Matron had had enough. She seized Margaret by the arm and led her back to the scullery. There she snatched a greasy, dirty dishrag from the sink and shoved it into Margaret's mouth. Then she turned to the other little girls.

"That will happen to anyone who dares to tell lies to me. When you have cleaned out your mouth, Margaret, you will go to bed without your supper."

Margaret took the dishrag from her mouth and flung it into the sink.

"Thank you, I will go now, and anyway I wasn't wanting any supper."

Although Margaret stumped bravely up the stairs she wasn't feeling brave inside for well she knew going to bed supperless would not be the end of her punishment.

When with her toothbrush she had cleaned the taste of dishrag from her mouth and was ready for bed, she found her tin box and hugged it to her.

"Oh, Hannah! Hannah!" she sobbed. "How am I to bear it? It gets worse here – not better."

But in the morning, as usually happens, things did look better. The sun was shining and even Matron could not prevent a child from going to school. And it was Margaret's favourite school day for in the afternoon it was dancing and they were learning a fan dance, which they were promised the best six would dance at the end of term concert. It never crossed Margaret's mind that she might not be one of the six best.

The day was full of niceness. Miss Snelston was interested in their afternoon with Mr Windle and a girl who had had a birthday on Saturday gave Margaret a little piece of her birthday cake. Then it happened. The children were playing in the yard before afternoon school. Margaret was skipping with some other girls who had a skipping rope when Miss Snelston called her.

"I have a job for you, dear." She held out some primroses. "One of the little ones picked these for me. Will you put them in water?"

Margaret ran into the schoolroom. It was empty except for Peter reading at his desk. She filled a pot with water from the tap behind the door and, arranging the primroses, put the pot on Miss Snelston's desk. Passing Peter on the way out she gave the top of his head a friendly pat. He looked up, startled, and the book closed. Margaret saw the title — it was *Bleak House*. She snatched it up, it opened at the front page. Inside there was a bookplate, though Margaret did not know that was what it was, but she could read clearly the name THOMAS AUGUSTUS WINDLE.

"Did you steal any more?" she asked Peter.

"I didn't steal them," Peter protested. "They're only borrowed, I'm giving them back."

"How many did you take?"

Peter opened his desk. Inside on top of *Tale of Two Cities* lay Sir Walter Scott's *Ivanhoe* and his *Kenilworth*. Feeling sick, Margaret opened both. As she expected, both belonged to Mr Windle.

Margaret put *Bleak House* in the desk.

"Get a pencil and a piece of paper," she ordered Peter. He found a piece of drawing paper and a pencil.

"I only borrowed. . ." he started to say, but Margaret stopped him.

"Write this: 'Miss Snelston Mam will you see

these books which I borrowed get back to Mister Windle and oblige goodbye Peter.'"

"Why goodbye?" Peter asked. "I shall see her tomorrow."

Margaret shook her head.

"You leave that on top of the books after school. You won't see her never no more for we have got to run away. It will have to be tonight before Mr Windle finds the books are missing and sets the coppers on you."

19. Escape

Margaret felt as if a top were spinning inside her head. There were so many plans to make and so little time. In fact, it might be too late already if the police were at the orphanage.

To run away was one thing, but where should they run to? She could change her clothes, but Peter had nothing to change into, so anyone who saw him would know where he came from. Then what about Horatio? Could they leave him alone in the orphanage?

By the time afternoon school was over Margaret had cleared her thoughts a little, but at the expense of her lessons — even of her beloved fan dance.

"What is the matter, dear?" Miss Snelston asked. "You've been very inattentive this afternoon, which is not like you. Are you tired after yesterday?"

Margaret longed to throw her arms round her and tell her everything but she believed she could not. If the police came for Peter it must be best if Miss Snelston knew nothing.

On the walk home Susan was puzzled at first because Margaret would not whisper to her as usual, but Margaret found an excuse.

"I'm in bad with Matron so I don't dare risk talking today."

It was on the walk home that Margaret found one answer to her problems. What to do with the two boys. She would take not only Peter but Horatio as well to Lavinia. On an enormous property like Sedgecombe Place there must be somewhere Lavinia could hide the boys, and from what she had told them it should be easy to sneak out food to them. The next problem was how to find Sedgecombe Place.

"I know the thing to do is to get on the canal bank because there's that bit of the canal at the bottom of Mr Windle's garden," she told herself, "and his garden is part of Sedgecombe Place. Then the only thing is to find Lavinia. Then when I've given her the boys I can go off by myself, which will be easy. Maybe I could get a place as a cook and when I do I'll write and tell Hannah and the rector where I am. I've got two stamps still inside my boot."

There were no police at the orphanage, Margaret was glad to see, but there was the usual difficulty of how to speak to Peter. Margaret dared not risk being caught doing anything wrong for Matron would be sure to give her an extra bad punishment, perhaps locking her in a cupboard for hours, which tonight would be a disaster. But after tea she had a little bit of luck. As it was a lovely evening twenty of the girls, of which Margaret was one, were ordered to take what Matron grandly called "the linen" out and peg it on a line to air. It was while Margaret was doing this that she heard the big lawnmower and saw Peter — reading as usual — being the donkey, while his partner steered the mower.

A wave of temper swept over Margaret. Look at Peter just reading a book as if nothing had happened and there she was worrying herself sick about how to keep him out of prison. However, she had to speak to him and scolding him now would do no good, the great thing was to get him as quickly as possible to Lavinia and let her do the scolding.

"I must speak to Peter Beresford," she said to Susan, who was beside her. "If Matron comes out could you scream?"

"What about?" Susan asked.

Margaret, not for the first time, sighed at the dullness of Susan. If it had been her who had been asked to scream she could have thought of a dozen reasons.

"Say a wasp stung you."

Susan looked round.

"There aren't any wasps."

"Well, say you saw a mouse. You could because there are outdoor mice as well as the indoor sort."

"I'll try," said Susan unwillingly. "But do be quick."

Margaret nodded and slipped behind bushes to

the lawn Peter was helping to mow. He was so deep in his book he did not hear her so she clutched at his arm.

"Listen, and for goodness' sake do exactly what I tell you. Tonight, after Mr Toms has gone to his room, taking your clothes with you roll under the beds until you get to Horatio's. Wake him up and, first getting his clothes, get him on the floor, then both of you roll under the beds until you get to the last one. Then, if all is quiet, crawl out into the passage. There you'll find me or if I'm not there wait for me. I shall be coming. It's quite easy rolling, I've done it before so I know."

"Where are we going?" Peter asked.

"To Lavinia. When she knows about you taking the books she'll hide you, she can't let you go to prison."

"Can you go to prison for borrowing books?"

"Mr Windle won't think you borrowed, he'll think you stole and you can go to prison for much less things than that. Now go on, tell me what I've told you to do."

Peter seemed to have understood but then he said:

"What happens if I go to sleep before Mr Toms shuts his door?"

That maddened Margaret.

"You really are a soppy boy. Here's me and Horatio running away all because of your beastly books and all you can say is" – she imitated him –

"what happens if I go to sleep before Mr Toms shuts his door?"

Peter turned pink.

"I wasn't meaning it like that. Truly, I am very grateful you are keeping me out of prison. I just meant how do you make yourself stay awake?"

"I don't know," said Margaret. "I just know I did it and if I can do it you can do it for we're the same age." She shut his book. "And don't read any more . . ." She broke off with a gasp for the book was *Bleak House*. "Oh, Peter! How could you! Now if we're caught you will have stolen property on you."

Peter turned his strange blue eyes on Margaret.

"You don't understand. I had finished *David Copperfield* and I have always wanted to read *Bleak House*. Mummy was trying to get a copy for me. If I have to go to prison I will think it worthwhile if I have read *Bleak House* first."

"And the other two?"

"I left them in my desk. I knew I couldn't run away with three books."

From the clothesline came a scream.

"I must go," Margaret said. "See you tonight with Horatio in the passage outside your dormitory."

The scream from Susan was not a warning at the approach of Matron but because the girls had finished pegging up the sheets and were going indoors.

"Thank you," Margaret whispered to Susan. "I would have been caught if you'd gone in without me. When nobody is looking sneak to my desk tomorrow, you'll find some sweets in a bag. Take them."

Sweets were so rare that Susan could not believe her ears.

"Take them! More than one, do you mean?"

"Yes, take them all. You earned them, that was a good scream."

Margaret had no difficulty in keeping awake. She had still a lot of planning to do, in fact, it came to her as a shock when she heard Miss Jones say "pray" and then, after the girls had scrambled up from their knees into their beds, "Good night, girls", as she wedged open the dormitory door before marching off to her bedroom.

When the time came to slip out of bed and leave the orphanage for ever Margaret found she had a problem, Hannah's box, the tin box with a picture of a cat on it which she had loved since she was a little girl. And Hannah had given it to her. How could she leave it in her bed to be taken by Matron? But rolling under beds by yourself was one thing and rolling with a tin box was another. So Margaret changed her plans. It would be easier and quicker to roll, but as she had her box she must crawl.

Afterwards Margaret never knew how she had done it, for crawling in a long nightgown was difficult and crawling silently almost impossible.

But somehow she succeeded and, stepping carefully over the board outside the dormitory which squeaked, she was in the passage on the way to the stairs which led up to the boys' dormitory.

Peter, though so dreamy-looking a boy, was very far from being stupid. After his time at the mowing machine was over he had hidden *Bleak House* where he could easily lay his hands on it in the dark and hurried into the orphanage to have a word with Horatio. Although Margaret did not know it, Peter had managed a series of arrangements which gave him a chance to speak to his little brother. One was making himself responsible for Horatio washing before and after meals. At such times the cloakrooms were always crowded so they couldn't say much, but seeing Horatio was washed was one tiny link with the home they had once known. Peter as usual found Horatio being cherished by two little girls in a game of "Home". He held out his hand.

"Come on. Wash time."

Horatio obediently joined Peter.

"That Emily," he confided, "is a very silly girl. She wants me to promise that when we play I will always be her little boy and belong to nobody else."

Peter drew Horatio into a corner outside the cloakroom door.

"Would you like to see Lavinia?"

Horatio beamed.

"'Course I would. Where is she?"

Peter leant down so Horatio could hear his whisper.

"This is a terribly important secret, you mustn't tell anybody."

"I won't," said Horatio. "I know all about secrets."

"We're going to see her tonight."

Horatio was surprised.

"Doesn't Matron mind?"

"She doesn't know and she mustn't know. It's a secret between you, me and Margaret."

Horatio seemed suddenly much older than six.

"What do you want me to do?"

Peter put his mouth to Horatio's ear.

"You know after the Beadle has said 'pray' how we get into bed as he turns the lights out?"

"I know," Horatio agreed.

"Do you think, just as the light goes out, instead of getting into bed you could get underneath it?"

"I could," Horatio agreed. "Then what do I do?"

"Nothing. Just wait there until I come for you and we have to get your clothes. Then we roll under the beds all the way to the door. Margaret says she will be in the passage."

Horatio saw nothing to get excited about in these arrangements.

"I like rolling."

"Good," Peter said. "Now come and wash."

Everything went so easily as planned that it

seemed strange to Margaret that all the orphans did not run away. Margaret met the boys in the passage and all crept down the two flights of stairs to the hall.

In the orphanage all the boots and shoes were cleaned as a before-breakfast task by boys who had earned a minor punishment. Overnight they were left downstairs by the orphans in rows in the passage outside the kitchen. So before escaping the children had to find their boots, which was not easy in a dark passage amongst ninety-seven other pairs. Margaret found hers by the stamps stuck inside the toe and Peter knew his by feel, but Horatio could not be sure his pair were his own but they fitted and that was all that mattered. They escaped into the garden by the side door Margaret had used before.

Outside it was Peter who took charge. Oddly, considering how vague he always seemed, he led the way to the shed where he had hidden Margaret's basket and his book as easily as if it were daylight, and he thought of things she might have forgotten.

"When Horatio and I have changed," he said, "what shall we do with our nightshirts?"

It was a dark night for the moon was behind a cloud. Margaret fumbled amongst her clothes. "I wish I could wear my lace," she thought, "but I can't because Hannah said Sunday and this is Monday."

"By the time I've changed there could be room in my basket. I shan't take this awful old nightdress, I shall tie up a stone in it and sink it in the canal."

"I'd like that," Horatio said. "Peter, can I sink my nightshirt?"

"Better not," Peter decided. "It's all we've got to sleep in and Lavinia won't have any more to give us."

It felt wonderful to Margaret to wear proper clothes again. She could not see herself but she could feel the liberty bodice, the scallops on the flannel petticoat, the feather stitching on the drawers and the crisp cambric of her petticoat. She had never been particularly attached to her pleated skirt and blue jersey, but it was nice to wear short skirts again and even nicer to be free. If she had not been afraid of her boots making a noise she would have skipped. "No more horrible meals," she thought. "No more Matron. No more Miss Jones. No more awful orphanage clothes."

Peter came across the shed to her. He and Horatio had changed so he was carrying their nightshirts. He gave them to Margaret who folded them and put them and her tin into the basket.

"We can take turns to carry it," Peter said, "for all I have got is my book."

Margaret marvelled that he could speak so calmly of stolen property. *His* book indeed! However, this was no time for quarrelling, the sooner they were away from the orphanage the better.

"We ought to get started then, for I don't know the way."

Peter was surprised.

"Don't you? I do. We go down that lane before we get to the school and then across a field and there's the canal bank. Then we turn left and walk along it until we get to Mr Windle's gate."

Margaret had taken it for granted that she would be the leader so for a second she was annoyed, then she saw how silly that was as she didn't know the way and Peter did.

"All right," she said. "You lead. Come on, Horatio."

20. Jem

It was a strange, spooky walk. The wind rustled last year's sedges on the canal bank, birds and animals let out odd little sounds and once all three children nearly screamed when a cow put her head over a hedge to look at them. Peter had told Horatio they would pretend they were Pale-faces being chased by Redskins so they must be as quiet as possible, but Horatio needed no game to help him to be quiet. Without a word he stumbled along behind Peter, grateful to know it was Margaret who was on his heels. Even the sinking of Margaret's nightdress was carried out in silence, for Margaret merely rolled it round the biggest stone they could find and let it slide into the water.

Because they could not hurry in the dark it was over two hours before the children reached the little gate in Mr Windle's wall which led to the canal bank. Margaret had been afraid they might miss it, but Peter knew what he was doing. He stopped suddenly.

"This is Mr Windle's wall," he whispered. "If we go on to the end of the wall we come to the wood that is part of Sedgecombe Place. There's a path if we could find it, Lavinia said so."

Four miles is a long walk for a six-year-old, especially in the middle of the night. In fact, it was a long walk for them all.

"Before we go into the wood," Margaret suggested, "couldn't we sit down for a little? Horatio is tired."

Horatio was not having that.

"I'm only a little bit tired, I can still walk for hours and hours."

Peter, whose turn it had been to carry the basket, gave it to Margaret.

"You two wait here while I find the path. Lavinia said it led straight to the house. Do you know where she sleeps?"

Margaret felt along the bank for a comfortable place to sit down.

"No, but Jem will. We have to find the stables. His is the last room and it has a horseshoe over the door."

"Right," said Peter. "You can find him. Now wait here, I shan't be long finding the path."

As the uniform cloaks lived in the cloakroom at the orphanage the boys had not brought them with them, so when they sat down Margaret noticed that it was cold. She wished that somehow she had managed to get her coat out. She put an arm round Horatio.

"Let's keep each other warm until Peter gets back."

"Let's," said Horatio, and immediately went to sleep. One minute later so did Margaret.

They were woken by Peter shaking them.

"Come on. I've not only found the path but where the stables are. Follow me."

Because they had been asleep neither Margaret nor Horatio had noticed how long Peter had been away. So they were surprised as they followed him through the wood what a distance it was to the house and stables. But at last Peter stopped.

"This path on the right leads to the stables," he whispered. "They are cobbled so we'd better not all go in because of noise. You go, Margaret, but you had better leave your boots here."

Margaret was not nearly as good as Peter at finding her way about in the dark. "The last bedroom over the stables," Jem had said. It was easy to tell she was in the stables for there was a nice horse smell and an occasional small stamp as a horse moved in its sleep. The trouble was, where were the staff's bedrooms? The horses' stalls were on both sides, so which was the last? Then quite by accident she found something, her hand touched some steps which she could feel climbed up above the horses' stalls. Margaret, her heart in her mouth in case she made a noise, climbed the steps and found herself on what seemed to be a landing. There was no question she had reached the grooms' bedrooms for from behind each door – and there seemed to be four of them – came shattering snores. Carefully Margaret felt her way along to the end, then she lifted her hands to the top of the door. At first she thought she was outside the wrong room then her fingers felt the cold of metal – it was Jem's horseshoe. The door was fastened by a latch. Softly and slowly she lifted it.

Jem was dreaming he was riding the winner of the Grand National when he felt a hand on his face and heard a whisper.

"Wake up, Jem. Wake up. It's me – Margaret."

Jem had been used most of his life to being woken up at unexpected moments. On the canal all types of emergencies could occur so his father had expected all his children to spring out of their sleep at a shout. But this was different. Margaret? Who was Margaret?

"What d'you want?" he asked. "Who are you?"

Margaret patted what she guessed would be Jem's shoulder under the blanket.

"You remember. You fetched me and Peter and Horatio from the orphanage."

With a sinking heart Jem did remember.

"To take you to Mr Windle's. You 'aven't run away, 'ave you?"

Margaret sat on the bed while in a whisper she poured out her story.

"So you see we simply had to get away. I couldn't let them put Peter in prison."

Jem had an inborn fear of the police. Since he was a baby his father had threatened that if he did this or that the coppers would have him, so he accepted at once that Peter had to be hidden.

"But what can I do? I couldn't 'ide a cat, not in these parts."

Margaret settled more comfortably on the bed.

"I don't want you to do anything. All I want is for you to go into the house and fetch Lavinia."

Margaret had been going to say more but Jem was so shocked at her suggestion of fetching Lavinia that he bounced up in bed so violently he nearly threw her on to the floor.

"Inside the 'ouse! Me! I ain't never been inside since I 'ad pneumonia. If I was caught inside it'd be me what the coppers are after."

Margaret saw her whole plan falling in ruins.

"But you must go inside sometimes. Where do you eat?"

"One of the groom's wives does for us and a right good cook she is."

"So you truthfully don't know where Lavinia sleeps? Now what shall I do? I suppose we had better wait outside the kitchen until she gets up in the morning. I suppose you can show us where the kitchen is?"

Jem was appalled. He was happy in the stables and now, thanks to this orphan, he could see himself being dismissed without a character. He could imagine the questions there would be if Margaret and the two boys were found outside the kitchen in the morning, and he had no doubt that it would soon be known that Margaret had been to his room. He shivered with fright.

"You can't sit outside the kitchen door. Proper state everyone will be in."

"It's what I'm going to do," said Margaret. "I can't hide the boys. For one thing they are dressed in the orphanage uniform, and you know what that looks like."

Jem had to agree to that.

"Proper figures of fun."

"So if you can't show me which is the kitchen someone else will have to. Who sleeps in the next room?"

Jem leant forward in the bed and clutched at where he supposed Margaret was sitting. He caught her by the arm.

"Oh no! You dursent do that. You'll get me the sack, true as life you will. I tell you straight, if you wake up the other lads they'll rouse the 'ouse and that'll bring the coppers 'ere as quick as their bicycles will take 'em."

"Well, then, what am I to do?"

Margaret was desperate and this showed in her voice. It matched the desperation Jem was feeling.

"Now sit quiet like while I think. You can't go to the 'ouse an' that's flat so we got to think of somethin' else."

"What else?"

Slowly − for nothing came quickly to Jem − an idea was being born.

"Quiet now, lass." Then, after a pause: "And it might work too, it might an' all."

Margaret hated to be kept waiting.

"What might?"

Jem had his idea clear now.

"My dad's boat is tied up two miles up the canal. So I see'd 'em tonight. When I left my brother, young Tom, he steps a bit of the way along of me. 'E says 'e's 'ad it, 'e won't leg the 'orses no more. 'E said 'e was runnin' away."

Margaret leapt ahead of Jem.

"You mean Peter could leg instead of Tom?"

"That's the idea."

"But what about me and Horatio?"

Now Jem had a plan he was keen to carry it out.

"You nip along back to the boys. Stay in the bushes outside the stable entrance. When I come back I'll give a whistle."

"But what about me and Horatio?" Margaret asked again. "Now we've run away we'll have to stay run away. Matron would kill us if we went back."

Jem was tired of questions.

"You nip along. I'm 'avin' a word with me ma. Shouldn't wonder if she'll manage with the lot of you. Powerful fond of our Tom, our ma is. Do a lot she would to give 'im 'is chance to get away."

21. Polly Makes a Discovery

So scared were the orphans of being blamed for
something they had not done that none of the
children mentioned that Margaret, Peter and
Horatio were missing. But in the girls' dormitory
Miss Jones, counting heads before the children
were marched down to breakfast, missed Margaret,
and in the boys' dormitory Ben, expecting to wash
Horatio, spotted he was not there and this led to
the fact that Peter was also missing.

There had not been a morning like it in the
memory of Winifred, who though not now a
proper orphan had been under the orphanage roof
longer than any of the other children. It was
rumoured afterwards that Miss Jones screamed all
the way to Matron's office. The boys swore that
Ben had rushed into Mr Toms's room without
knocking and so caught him still in bed. But
whatever the truth, it was certain that the
orphanage was shaken from head to foot. So shaken
that Mary and Winifred were called in to serve the
breakfast and, forgetting the rules in all the
excitement, tipped each porridge plate full of milk
and slammed down plates of bread on the tables

and told the children to help themselves. As a result the children went better fed to school than they had ever been before.

When the orphans were lined up ready to march to school Matron came out of her office. Her face was no longer red but a sort of greeny-yellow, and her upholstered chest inside her black dress was heaving as if she had run upstairs.

"You will have heard that Miss Margaret Thursday and the Beresford boys are missing. This matter is being dealt with by the police, who will no doubt bring the culprits back within an hour." She paused there. "I need not tell you children that the runaways will be very severely punished." The children shivered. "And should there prove to be a ringleader" – again Matron paused and all the children thought "Margaret" – "there will be such punishment as will be remembered as long as this orphanage stands. Now this is an order. There is to be no mention at school that Margaret, Peter and Horatio are missing. The matter will be handled by the police and I do not want talk in the village. I have my ways of finding out if any one of you children disobeys me and I can promise you that if I am disobeyed the offender will spend the whole evening locked in the under-stairs cupboard and then go supperless to bed. You may go now. Quick march!"

Matron's words were taken to heart by even the smallest orphans so nothing was said about

Margaret, Peter and Horatio, but Miss Jones spoke to Miss Snelston about their absence.

"They have a slight rash so Matron has kept them at home. Probably due to overeating at Mr Windle's on Sunday."

Miss Snelston received this news with misgiving. Both she and Polly in the past had cared for orphans who had been marched to school when so ill that the proper place for them was bed. So it was strange to hear of three children being kept away for a slight rash.

"I don't like the sound of it," Miss Snelston told Polly. "I suspect we're in for an epidemic of something. Matron would never keep those children at home for an ordinary rash."

It turned out to be an unusual morning in another way for after the children had gone home to their dinners the Countess of Corkberry's carriage drove up to the school gate.

Polly was just laying out her own and Miss Snelston's lunch when the Countess walked into the schoolroom.

"Oh dear!" she said, looking at the food. "I've come at a bad moment."

Miss Snelston gave Polly a look to tell her to clear away the lunch and offered the Countess a chair.

"Not a bad moment at all. We only have something light and cold, our big meal is in the evening."

Polly carried the lunch into the other schoolroom. The Countess waited until she had shut the door.

"I am the Countess of Corkberry," the Countess explained, "and I have called on you at this time because I knew the orphans would be absent. I have a girl from the orphanage working in my scullery – or rather she has two brothers at the orphanage. She has said nothing but I and some of my senior staff have the impression that she feels the boys do not get enough to eat. In fact, the younger boy, Horatio, described the menu and it did sound inadequate. I realize, of course, that children often complain about food without cause, but I must admit I feel disturbed."

Miss Snelston had sometimes dreamt of something like this happening. Someone influential – someone who cared – looking into the affairs of the orphanage. She was so thankful to see Lady Corkberry she could – had she dared – have kissed her.

"Oh, Lady Corkberry, I cannot tell you how glad I am you have come to me. I have been at this school now for five years and never a day but I have worried about those orphans."

Lady Corkberry was puzzled.

"But if that is the case why could you not go to the ladies' committee or talk to one of the governors?"

"None of the ladies on the committee belong to

this village, I do not even know their names. The women here say that the ladies' committee have dust thrown in their eyes by the matron. I am afraid she is a hard woman. Many of my children come to school with their hands badly scarred through beatings and I suspect they are scarred in other places too."

"And the children are hungry?"

"Always, I fear. We do what we can and so do the village mothers. They often send an extra apple and sometimes a cake. But you know how it is, times are hard for farm labourers so what food there is they need for themselves, and schoolteachers are not well paid."

Lady Corkberry nodded sympathetically.

"I understood from Horatio that Polly Jenkin fed him."

Miss Snelston looked towards the other room. She spoke apologetically.

"She is my little assistant and was an orphan herself so she knows what it is like. Horatio is a dear little boy and nicely spoken. Of course, it's not fair to help one child and not another but, you see, there are one hundred orphans."

"I do indeed see." Lady Corkberry got up. "I must not keep you any longer from your luncheon. But I can promise you I will somehow look thoroughly into affairs at the orphanage and see that what is wrong is put right."

Miss Snelston also got up.

"I feel you must wonder why I have done nothing though suspecting so much. But apart from knowing nobody on the committee interference from me might easily have caused my dismissal and I should regret that, for at least I know the orphans are happy while under my care and I think perhaps I give them all the love they have ever known."

Lady Corkberry held out her hand.

"Goodbye. I am sure of that. And please don't blame yourself, it is people like myself who have the means and the time to help but who passed by on the other side. It is we who are to blame."

Polly, her eyes goggling with interest, came back with the lunch as soon as she heard Lady Corkberry drive away.

"That was the Countess, wasn't it? Such a lovely carriage, I saw it from the window."

"Yes, she does a lot of good work, but she doesn't often come this way for this isn't Corkberry land. I have seen her several times, though, and once I went to Sedgecombe Place for they threw the grounds open — it was some political affair and I went along with one of the farmers and his wife."

Polly helped herself to a sandwich.

"What did she want?"

Miss Snelston longed to confide in Polly but she didn't dare. There would be enough talk about Lady Corkberry calling as it was. She thought quickly for an explanation which would satisfy not only Polly but the whole village.

"She is interested in a charity. Maybe when the summer comes there will be a fête or something and our children might do some dancing."

Polly glowed.

"Wouldn't that be fun! That maypole dance is ever so pretty."

Miss Snelston wanted to change the subject. She looked down the classroom. On each desk but two lay scrubbed slates ready for the afternoon's work. Her eyes fell upon Peter's desk.

"I wonder what Peter keeps in his desk. Do you see, it doesn't shut properly."

"I'll look," said Polly. "I expect it's that book he's always reading — *A Tale of Two Cities* — he says it's exciting so I'm going to read it when he's through." She had reached Peter's desk and threw it open. After a pause she came back holding Peter's note and the two books. She gave the note to Miss Snelston.

"'Will you see these books. . .'" Miss Snelston read out aloud, then she broke off. "Why does he say 'Goodbye'?"

Polly looked blank.

"I don't know. That's funny, he couldn't have known he was going to have a rash."

Miss Snelston had turned quite pale.

"It's more than funny. Oh, Polly, where are Peter, Margaret and Horatio? I have a feeling something is very wong."

22. The Nightdress

The stone the children had found was not big enough or sufficiently securely fastened to the nightdress to cause it to sink for long. At some time during the night it had got free and had risen from the bottom of the canal to get tangled in some of last year's reeds. In the ordinary way it would have clung there unnoticed unless one of the canal women had seen it and pulled it on board hoping to make use of it, but that morning, as soon as the children had left for school, the Beadle had been sent hurrying to fetch the local policeman.

Police Constable Perkins was rather a slow man. There was almost no crime in the village for him to bother about except on days when there was a fair in the neighbourhood, when there might be a few drunks about and maybe a fight or two, so mostly life was easy. In fact, how the village usually saw their policeman was bent double in his kitchen garden, where he grew onions which were the admiration of all. So it was in his kitchen garden that the Beadle found him when he panted up to his gate.

"Matron up at the orphanage wants to see you

immediately," he gasped, for he was unused to running.

"What's up, then?" Perkins asked.

Mr Toms was not giving anything away.

"You'll know soon enough and you better 'urry."

So Police Constable Perkins put on his uniform jacket, clipped his trouser legs, mounted his bicycle and rode off to the orphanage.

Like most of the villagers, Police Constable Perkins was scared of Matron, so scared that he had never encouraged local gossip about the orphanage.

"Now, now," he would say when one of the village women would hint things weren't right. "There's a committee of ladies looks after that place and if they are satisfied reckon we should be, it's not for us to criticize what's done by our betters."

Matron saw Perkins in her office.

"How the children got out of their dormitories I cannot imagine. The escape from the house is quite clear, a side door has been found open. I have no doubt at all where they have gone. The sister of the two boys works in Sedgecombe Place so all three are almost certainly with her."

Perkins was writing all this down. He stopped when Matron mentioned Sedgecombe Place.

"Sedgecombe Place isn't rightly on my beat. I should 'ave to pass that on to the police constable in Sedgecombe village."

"Don't talk nonsense!" Matron snapped. "This orphanage is on your beat. All you have to do is to go to Sedgecombe Place and ask to see the scullery maid. Her name is Lavinia Beresford. I will spell that for you. Demand from her where she has hidden the children, then bring them back here to me."

Perkins wrote everything down.

"Would I ask her ladyship if I could see the young woman Beresford?"

Matron struggled to control her temper.

"Of course not. You will go to the back door and ask to see the girl. I do not anticipate that you will have any difficulty with her. It is likely she will be thankful to hand back the children for she knows they have a good home here and how happy they have been. Do not tell anyone except the girl why you are there, the fewer people who know about this the better."

Police Constable Perkins got back on his bicycle and via a footpath across a field he reached the canal bank. There he rode slowly along thinking not of missing orphans but of summer days and fishing.

It was because the nightdress was hanging on the reeds at a place where two summers ago he had caught a monster carp that Perkins chanced to see it. He got off his bicycle, leant it against the hedge and carefully, for the bank was slippery, hauled in the nightdress. It was an unattractive sight, soaked in water and stained with mud, so that he would probably have thrown it back if he had not seen on the inside of the neck in large ink letters ST LUKE'S ORPHANAGE.

"Oh my! Oh my!" he murmured. "'Just go to the back door,' she said, but this is more than that. This is a great deal more than that. This is a dredging matter."

He rolled up the nightdress and tied it to his handlebars, got back on his bicycle and, pedalling furiously this time, rode not to Sedgecombe Place but to Police Constable Frinton's cottage in Sedgecombe village. He was pedalling so hard and his head was so full of what he had to tell Constable Frinton that he scarcely saw a canal boat called the *Crusader* gliding by, and though he had to wait to let them pass he paid no attention to a small boy who was leading a horse, even though the small boy was attempting at the same time to read a book.

Although telephones had been invented, in the country areas very few houses had them so news did not reach people in a few seconds. But that did not mean that news did not get around, so the first person who saw Constable Frinton and Constable Perkins set off to the canal carrying waders and pitchforks rushed round Sedgecombe village spreading the news.

"Someone's drownded in the canal. Must be over t'other side for 'twas Constable Perkins who came to fetch Constable Frinton."

Of course the gossip reached Sedgecombe Place.

It came via one of the stable lads who had taken a horse to the blacksmith.

"Someone's drownded in the canal," he told the stable.

"Someone's drownded in the canal," one of the grooms told a gardener.

"Someone's drownded in the canal," the gardener told Mrs Smedley when he brought in the house vegetables.

"Hear that, girls?" Mrs Smedley called out. "Someone's drowned themselves in the canal, poor soul."

Lavinia, scrubbing potatoes at the sink, said to Clara:

"Who would do a thing like that? I'm glad it didn't happen on my Sunday off. I would hate to see the poor soul do it."

The only person who took the news personally was Jem. Margaret had told him she had got rid of her nightdress in the canal. Immediately he heard someone was supposed to be drowned he put two and two together and came out in a cold sweat. That silly girl! If the police thought someone was drowned it wouldn't be just a matter of three orphans missing, which wouldn't have caused much concern, but a real thorough search would be made. A big search was almost certain to include the canal boats, and if it did could his mother, smart as she was, hide three children she couldn't account for?

"Oh dear!" worried Jem. "I wish I'd never set eyes on young Margaret. She'll get me the sack yet, I know she will."

Meanwhile the news was spreading to Constable Perkins's own village, but now with more detail. For in spite of Matron's strictures the news had leaked out that three orphans were missing. So the moment it was known that the constables were raking up the bottom of the canal the village put two and two together. Doors were flung open and the women gathered in knots.

"Those poor little children drownded."

"Nor I don't wonder, beaten black and blue shouldn't be surprised. That Matron ought to be behind bars, that's where she oughter be."

"Rough musicking that's what her needs."

"And that's what her is going to get this very night."

Rough music, as it was called, was a country way of expressing public disapproval. After it was dark the whole village would turn out to beat on pots, kettles, anything that would make a noise. Then they would form a procession and march for perhaps two hours round the offender's cottage. It was an effective punishment for ill-doers for the noise carried for miles, so the next day "Who was rough musicked last night?" was the question on everybody's lips. As a rule, shame brought the offenders to their senses. To rough music Matron would serve a double purpose, it would not only bring shame on her but it was an immensely effective way of seeing that attention was focused on the orphanage.

At the orphanage Matron was almost frantic with worry. Of course the news had been brought to her that the police were dredging the canal, and close on top of that someone had passed on the news that Lady Corkberry had called at the school. Ever since she had been at the orphanage she had been dishonestly squeezing a little money here and a little money there so that she could have a nest-egg for her retirement. Was everything to be lost because of three worthless orphans? "If Margaret were to come in now," she told herself, "I would strangle her with my bare hands." Then worse thoughts came. Suppose, just suppose the children were drowned, would matters finish there? Would local ladies like Lady Corkberry poke in their noses and start asking questions?

It was the longest day Matron had ever known. She sent the Beadle to Police Constable Perkins to know if he had any news, but he was out. His wife who, with the rest of the village, was against Matron, would only say:

"You tell 'er there's no news and Mr Perkins 'e wouldn't wonder if this time no news was bad news."

It was just after the orphans had gone to bed that the rough musicking started. The men, when they came in from work, had been solidly behind their womenfolk.

"Bin talk about that old orphanage since that matron come."

"Time she was taught a lesson."

"Doan't want no more orphans trying to drownded theirselves."

So as soon as it was dark the village went to the orphanage and the noise started. Matron went to her window, drew aside the curtain and peered out. It was a frightening sight for the villagers were angry. There was moonlight and by it she could see the expressions on their faces as they beat on their pots and pans. The noise rose and rose and was accompanied by an angry murmur. Matron lost her head. She dropped the curtain and ran from wall to wall, beating against each one as if she were a moth trapped by a light. As she ran she moaned:

"Oh no! Don't let them in. They'll kill me. I know they'll kill me."

When at last the rough music finished Matron was unconscious on the floor.

23. Ma Smith

Jem was lucky that the night he had to see his mother the boat was tied up for it did not happen every trip. It was quite usual for his father, the Captain, as all owners of canal boats are called, to make a straight trip to London without a stop. Each trip took ten days and it was quite commonplace during those ten days for neither the Captain nor his wife to rest long enough to take their clothes off. So on many a trip Jem's only chance to see his family was when they were going through a lock. The reason for the tie-up that night was that the boat needed a minor repair.

Jem's mother had not yet gone to bed when he had crept back on board. She had been in the galley boiling a kettle so that there would be a cup of tea ready for her husband when he had finished his job of work. She had been startled when Jem had come in.

"Our Jem! What's brought you back this time of night?"

Jem had jerked his head aft towards the cabin where Tom was sleeping.

"Young Tom stepped along of me after I left 'ere.

Ma, 'e won't be a legger no more. 'E'll run away."

His mother had nodded.

"I knew it was comin'. Each day I thank Gawd when I find 'e's still 'ere of a mornin'.'"

"'E wants to live along of Bert," Jem had said.

Bert was the brother who had run away from working on the canal. He had made friends with another young man and together they owned a quite prosperous rag and bone business in Wolverhampton.

"'Tisn't the rag and bone business," his mother had told Jem. "It's the schoolin'. The Captain gives 'im his twopence a week regular for the school each end of a trip an I send 'im lookin' ever so nice with 'is slate on 'is back. But that ain't enough, for our Tom wants to go every day. Well, our Bert 'e says Tom oughter 'ave 'is chance and 'e can live along of 'im and go to school."

"But you can't manage without 'im."

His mother had fixed her large dark eyes on Jem.

"'Ow can we? That Ebeneezer we 'ave to 'elp the Captain 'asn't got no more brains than a sparrer. I done what I could – many's the night I been the legger while Tom got a sleep. An' so 'e should, a growin' boy like 'im."

Jem had moved nearer to his mother. He had lowered his voice.

"Listen, Ma. I think I've found a way round things."

Out had poured the story Margaret had told

192

him, repeated as far as he could remember in Margaret's own words. When he had finished he had stood quietly watching his mother's face. There was a candle and by its light he could see her thoughts racing across it like cloud shadows across a field of corn. At last she had said:

"Is the boy what the coppers are after dark like our Tom?"

"No. 'Air the colour of barley 'e 'as but you could fix 'im up to be dark."

His mother had given a slight bow of the head to show she accepted that.

"And the young boy, is 'e tough? For 'e'll need to be a legger too. Why, Tom 'e couldn't manage on 'is own so a green young 'un couldn't."

Jem could see his mother was going to accept the children.

"I'll fetch 'em. Should be back 'ere in less than an hour."

His mother had held up a warning finger.

"When you get back listen for the Captain snoring before you come on the boat. I shall say nothin' to 'im tonight. When we start tomorrer Tom will 'ave gone and the other kids will be 'ere. It'll be easier that way. Creep up on 'im, sort of."

When about three-quarters of an hour later Jem and the children had arrived on the bank beside the boat there had been no need to listen for the Captain's snores. They reverberated like thunder along the canal bank. Jem had made a sign to the children to stay where they were while he had crept quietly on board.

Jem's mother had decided it would be safer if she came ashore to meet the children, for any noise on board might wake the Captain.

Margaret was never to forget her first sight of Jem's mother. She had loomed up out of the night, so enormous a woman it was as if a huge animal was standing beside her. She had carried a lantern so by its light Margaret had been able to see more or less what she looked like. The mass of dark hair with a trilby hat on top of it tied under her chin by a scarf. The wide voluminous black dress. The vivid coloured shawl which was round her shoulders.

"I'm Mrs Smith, Jem's ma," the woman had explained. "You'll 'ear me called Ma Smith up and down the canal but to you I am Mrs Smith."

"Yes, ma'am," Peter and Margaret had said together. Horatio was almost asleep so he had not answered.

"Nor I don't want no ma'ams," Mrs Smith had said firmly. "We're plain canal folk what don't believe in airs and graces." She had moved the lantern so the light fell on Peter. "'E don't look the cut of a gaolbird to me," she had said to Jem. "You better take 'im on the boat and do something with 'is face and 'air if 'e's to pass for our Tom. There's some walnut juice top shelf in the galley and I've put out on the table that black dye what I bought at Lostock Fair." She had swung the lantern over to Margaret. "I meant to use it for meself where I'm goin' grey but I've never got round to it. You come with me, girl. I'll 'ave to cut your 'air off and fix you up in togs of our Tom's for you'll 'ave to be the legger when we start for 'is" — she looked at Peter — "'air won't be dry. You better fetch our Tom, Jem, tell 'im 'e can go. We 'aven't long, for the Captain wants to start real early, which is good for it'll be dark so 'e won't see who is leggin', an' by the time the sun's up the boy can 'ave took over as legger and I'll 'ave told the Captain what's been arranged."

Mrs Smith had taken Margaret to the galley. There she had sat her down and with large scissors had chopped off her hair.

"Pity," she had said. "Lovely 'air but there it is, from the cut of 'im that boy won't 'ave the strength of our Tom so you'll 'ave to 'elp out. Time I've put some walnut on your face and togged you out in Tom's clothes you'll pass for a boy anywhere."

"Has Tom lots of clothes?" Margaret had asked. "Because Peter and Horatio will need clothes too. I expect you couldn't see in the dark, but they've got on their orphanage uniforms which are very odd-looking."

"I saw," Mrs Smith had said. "We'll manage. Throw nothin' away has always been my motto. Comes in 'andy at times like now."

Mrs Smith was daubing Margaret's face with

walnut juice when Tom came into the galley. Margaret couldn't see him for he was behind her and Mrs Smith did not pause in her daubing.

"You off, son?"

"Yes, Ma."

"Come and see us next time we're passing Wolverhampton."

"'Course," Tom had agreed and then apparently gone, for he had said no more.

Mrs Smith had said no more either. Then, sounding rather as if she had a cold, she had fumbled in her pocket.

"It's the walnut juice," she had said, "makes me eyes water."

Soon afterwards Mrs Smith had led Margaret to a small cabin. It had several bunks in it, on one of which Horatio was asleep.

"This is the for'ard cabin," Mrs Smith had explained. "Ebeneezer − 'e's the hired man − 'e slept aft along of Tom. You better doss down quick for it won't be long now before the Captain wants to start."

To Margaret it had seemed not more than five minutes before Mrs Smith had shaken her awake.

"Come on, dearie. Put on these clothes."

The clothes were a pair of dark trousers, a knitted jersey and a battered old soft hat.

Margaret had not undressed before going to bed so she undressed now.

"Shall I keep on my bodice?" she had asked.

"The suspenders will keep my stockings up."

Mrs Smith was folding the clothes Margaret had taken off.

"No, you can't wear no stockings nor socks neither, the men and boys on the canal boats never do. Just your boots. Cruel 'ard it'll be at first but you'll get used to it." She had stroked Margaret's petticoat. "My, they dressed you fine at that orphanage. Lovely work this is."

Margaret had nearly burst with rage.

"Those clothes aren't orphanage clothes, they're mine, and there's more in that basket, one set with real lace. If we hadn't run away Matron was going to steal my clothes."

Mrs Smith had kept her mind on the business in hand.

"You tuck the jersey into the trousers and put this belt round." Then she had looked at Margaret's basket. "We'll keep you dressed as a boy for the time bein' so I'll pack this stuff away. Now come on, I'll show you 'ow to 'arness the 'orse."

Margaret had seen nothing of a horse.

"Where is he?"

"Tied up down the bank. Reckon it's one of the best nights the poor old fellow ever 'ad. 'Owever 'ard you 'ave to work on this boat, Margaret, you remind yourself the 'orse works 'arder."

24. Wilberforce

Jem was no actor so on the day the children escaped he had found life hard in the stables. Rumours had flown around like bees about to swarm. Jem had been expected not only to react but to gossip about each one with the other lads.

"They say the matron pushed them into the canal and drownded them." "Three little 'uns is missin'." "Mr Frinton and Mr Perkins is dredging for them now."

A quick calculation told Jem the *Crusader* should be safely past the dredging operations. Knowing where the children were it was hard to sound horrified. He leant down to pick up a cleaning leather.

"Did oughter be 'orse whipped that matron," another lad said, "or maybe 'anged."

Later there was more news relayed by the postman.

"The police constable couldn't find the bodies. They say they are going to ask for help from Scotland Yard. Just imagine that now! Never had Scotland Yard here before, us haven't."

Then came the rumours as to where the children

had been seen. In Wolverhampton. On trains. In a carrier's cart. In a gipsy encampment.

"Not a mention of the *Crusader*," thought Jem thankfully and, because he was thankful, he managed suitable replies.

"Well I never!" "Gone to Wolverhampton!" "So the gypsies got 'em!" "Mr Frinton will soon 'ave them back then."

From the stable point of view the most startling news came, via his valet, from Lord Corkberry.

"We're going to Ireland," the valet said to the head coachman. "Stayin' with the Marquis of Delaware."

The head coachman and the valet were old friends.

"Now!" said the head coachman. "Whatever for? There's no huntin' now."

The valet tapped the side of his nose in a meaning way.

"I think there's more in these missing orphans than meets the eye. If you ask me it's mixed up some way with Ireland. Anyway we leave tomorrow. You're driving us to the boat in the brake."

Off went the head coachman to give his orders. The brake, which was spotless, was to be brought out and polished. The harness for the horses was to shine like diamonds.

"His lordship," the head coachman confided to the second coachman, "is leavin' for Ireland. I'm driving him to the coast in the brake."

That was like putting a match to dry bracken. The rumours flew out of the stable all over the estate to the village.

"The orphans have been seen in Ireland. His lordship is going himself to fetch them back."

Jem felt wretched. He had been forced to refuse Margaret's request to give Lavinia a message to say the boys were safe. He knew Margaret had not understood that in his position there was no excuse for him to go near the house. And if he ran into Lavinia in the grounds, as he sometimes did, given a message like that who knew what a girl might do? Screech out or faint dead away most like. And one thing was certain sure, when it was known it was he who had given Lavinia the message they would have the truth out of him in the swish of a cow's tail, and that would mean the rozzers on board the *Crusader*, which would not only bring terrible trouble on his ma and dad but would be the end of his fine job in the stables.

However, Jem was a good-hearted boy, so though unwilling he had allowed Peter to write a note. They had no proper paper but they found a small piece in which sweets had been wrapped and there was a stub of pencil in Peter's pocket. Peter had written: "Dear Lavinia we are with Margaret and quite safe do not show this to anyone love Peter and Horatio." He had folded this over and written "Miss Lavinia Beresford" on the back.

"I'm not makin' no promises, mind," Jem had said as he had put the note in a pocket. "I can't give it to Lavinia but if I can find somewhere to leave it like, so someone else picks it up and gives it to her then I will."

The wilder the rumours got the more that note from Peter weighed in Jem's pocket. What had Lavinia heard? Did she believe the boys were drowned? Was she crying her eyes out?

Then after his dinner Jem got some real news, from Clara, with whom Lavinia shared a bedroom. She had woken that morning with raging toothache so Mrs Tanner, hearing all normal remedies had been of no avail, ordered the trap to be brought round to take Clara to the dentist. Jem was told to drive it.

On the outward journey Clara had said nothing, only clasped a woollen shawl to her face and groaned, but on the return journey, free from pain for the tooth had been removed, she was, for her, full of talk.

"Nobody hasn't been allowed to tell Lavinia, not yet. That was an order from her ladyship herself."

"I suppose Lavinia will be upset when they do tell her," Jem had suggested.

Clara had swung round to gape at him.

"Upset! With two brothers drownded or worse! Why, those brothers are all she thinks about. I reckon when she knows she'll go stark starin' mad."

Having delivered Clara to the back door, Jem

drove the trap back to the stable and, being free, after he had stabled the horse and helped put away the trap, he went up to his room and sat down to do something he rarely did – think.

Where in the whole of Sedgecombe Place estate could you put a note someone was certain to find? Dozens of ideas went through his head but none of them made sense. Then, as if it was given him as a sign, a dog barked.

Sedgecombe Place was full of dogs. There were four retrievers for the shooting which lived with the head keeper. Two puppy hounds lived in the stables. A spotted dog which ran under the dogcart was looked after by a gardener. But as well there were several house dogs, including a small white fluffy dog which belonged to Lady Corkberry. This dog was supposed to stay in the house but, though small, it had the courage of a lion and would roam where the fancy took it, including into the stables, which is where Jem had met it. It was the business of one of the footmen each afternoon to find the dog and take it back to the house at tea-time, for Lady Corkberry liked it to share her afternoon tea. The dog's name was Wilberforce – it was given a lot of other names by the staff, none of which were polite. Now Jem knew who should carry Peter's note – it was Wilberforce.

Well fed though he was, Wilberforce was fond of a snack of garbage. There was a splendid garbage heap at the end of the kitchen garden ready to be burned in an incinerator. Strolling casually as if admiring the vegetables, Jem walked through the kitchen garden. He was in luck. The gardeners were planting out seedlings in the greenhouses so there was no one about. The garbage heap was at the end of the kitchen garden which was handiest for the kitchen. Gingerly, Jem walked towards it. Would Wilberforce have chosen somewhere else to go that afternoon? Then Jem's heart leapt. Sticking out of the rubbish heap was a wagging tail attached to something white.

It was a quick job. Jem picked up Wilberforce. Then, talking to him gently to prevent him yapping, he tied the note securely to his soft pale blue collar.

"Now you be careful," he said as he put Wilberforce down, "it would be ever so easy to tear that bit of paper off of you."

Then, as secretly as he had come, Jem slipped out of the kitchen garden.

When half an hour later Lord Corkberry joined Lady Corkberry for tea, the butler came in carrying Wilberforce.

"M'lady, Henry fetched Wilberforce, as he always does, from the garden — or rather I would gather from the odour — from the garbage heap — and he saw this hanging from his collar."

"This" was Peter's note, now terribly dirty and torn.

Lord Corkberry laughed.

"Been gettin' love letters, old man?" he asked Wilberforce.

The butler held the grimy note away from him as if it would bite.

"It is addressed, m'lord, to the young woman in the scullery whose brothers are missing from the orphanage."

Lord Corkberry held out a hand.

"Is it, by jove!" He took the note and turned it over. "That's right. Now what do we do? If it's bad news don't like just to shove the note at the girl."

The butler cleared his throat.

"It is not sealed, m'lord, just folded."

Lord Corkberry gave him a shrewd glance.

"So Henry had a look and I daresay you did too."

Lady Corkberry broke in.

"I think we must read it for if it's bad news the shock might make the child ill." She turned to the butler. "Ask Mrs Smedley to be so good as to send Lavinia Beresford up here immediately."

25. First Morning

The Captain found Peter and Horatio a glorious
joke. Mrs Smith, choosing a moment when there
was no one about either on land or on the water,
brought them up to meet her husband, who was
steering the boat. She had done what she could to
change the boys' appearance but the dye for their
hair had come out wrong. What promised on the
bottle to restore greying hair to its original rich
chestnut had turned Peter and Horatio's fair hair a
strange dark green. Their far too pale faces for
canal boys had been daubed with walnut juice, but
it had not gone on smoothly all over so they had a
mottled look. Since they could not wear their
orphanage clothes, Mrs Smith had dug out of a
chest clothes that had belonged to her sons when
they were small. Evidently at all ages the Smith
boys had been far broader than Peter and Horatio
for the clothes hung on them in folds which,
together with their green hair, gave them an odd
scarecrow look.

"These are the boys," Mrs Smith said. "This is
Peter and this is Horatio. The girl is leggin'. Boys,
this is Cap'n Smith."

The boys, not having hats to take off, gave slight bows and said:

"Good morning, sir."

Horatio felt this was not enough greeting for a man who had taken them all on to his boat so he added:

"I hope you are well, sir, and had a pleasant night."

The Captain could not have been more surprised if a grasshopper had spoken. He opened his mouth and let out great roars of laughter. Presently he mopped his eyes.

"Did you get a load of that, mate?" — all canal boatmen call their wives mate — "Couldn't 'ave spoken nicer if 'e was the king hisself." Then he looked at Peter and let out another roar. When his laugh was over he gasped: "That's never the boy the rozzers is after?"

Mrs Smith, seen in the daylight, though still enormous, looked larger than she actually was because of the fullness of her skirt and taller because of her headgear. The trilby hat Margaret had noticed the night before was not her only head covering for she wore a rather battered straw bonnet with the trilby hat tied on top of it. Now in answer to her husband she nodded, which made the trilby wobble.

"The very same. Stole books 'e did, at least that is what will be said, but young Margaret says 'e only borrowed them."

The Captain looked at Peter.

"An' what do you say? Speak the truth, boy. I won't 'ave no liars on my boat."

"Truly, sir, I only borrowed them. You see, one was *Bleak House*, well, I had to read it, you do see that."

The Captain again shook with laughter.

"'Ark at 'im, mate. 'E reads books! No, son, I don't see why you 'ave to read this *Bleak 'Ouse*. I never learnt to read and never felt the loss of it, but I can make me mark. Now see, boys, we don't want no sirs on this boat. I'm the Cap'n and that's what you call me. For work you takes your turn as leggers. Seeing there's three of you it shouldn't be too 'ard. While they're still out lookin' for you, Peter, none of you won't work no locks where there's a lock-keeper. Ebeneezer or me'll do that. Me mate will show you about the tunnels." He had finished with them and was turning away when he had another look at the green hair and the baggy suits. Once more he let out a roar of laughter. "If they don't beat cock fightin'. Couple of guys for Guy Fawkes's day if ever I saw them, then they open their mouths an' no duke could speak prettier. Take 'em away, mate, before I split a gut laughin'."

Margaret found that as she led the horse she threw off feeling sleepy so she was able to make plans. From what Mrs Smith had said while she was cutting off her hair and staining her face she did not mind who led the horse as long as one of them did, so she could work out a scheme. There were stables Mrs Smith told her every five or six miles to which horses were returned and from which new ones were hired. But that did not mean their horse was returned to a stable every five or six miles; from what she had gathered about the unusualness of their being tied up last night and from what Jem had told her she was afraid the poor horse often had an eighteen- to twenty-hour day and that meant so did the leggers — if not a twenty-four-hour day. Even dividing the day and the night into short shifts, could Peter and Horatio walk that far?

Margaret's thoughts were disturbed by Mrs Smith, who came along the canal bank to join her.

"We're comin' to a tunnel an' I want to show you what you do so you can teach the boys."

Margaret looked at Mrs Smith striding along beside her, her voluminous skirts brushing flat the young grass.

"Did you teach all your boys to be leggers?"

"Only me eldest then 'e taught the next and so on down to Tom. They each started leggin' the day they was five. Mind you, when they was little 'uns I usually lent a 'and with the locks, they're 'eavy for small ones."

Margaret tried to picture the massive Mrs Smith helping out when the work was extra hard.

"And for you, too, I should think."

Mrs Smith hitched her brilliantly coloured shawl more securely on to her shoulders.

"You're thinkin' I'm too fat for much work" — she slapped her thighs — "but it's not all me, it's me petticoats what makes me look so big. The cold is cruel on the canals of a winter and often into the spring. Last winter when it froze I wore nine flannel petticoats and three pairs of flannel knickers, me own, a pair what belonged to me ma and a pair what belonged to me old gran. Of course now the nice weather's comin' I don't wear so many, just the one pair of knickers, but I still wear four petticoats. Can't be too careful. Ne'er cast a clout till May be out."

At the tunnel Margaret learnt that she had to what Mrs Smith called "unpeg" the horse. This meant untying his lead rope from the canal boat. Then she had to lead the horse along the bank to the other end of the tunnel and there wait for the boat to come through.

"But how does the boat come through without the horse to pull it?" Margaret asked.

"The Captain and Ebeneezer leg it," Mrs Smith explained. "You can tie up the 'orse at the end of the tunnel. I'll send young Peter down, 'e can carry on till dinner-time. When we say 'leg it' through the tunnel it means the men lie on their backs on two boards what are fixed to the stern either side of what we calls the stud, that's a piece of wood shaped like the letter T. Well, lyin' on their backs on these 'ere boards they push the boat through the tunnel with their feet."

"My goodness!" said Margaret. "Isn't it terribly hard work?"

"Shockin' sometimes," Mrs Smith agreed. "You ought to see the Hare and Castle tunnel on the Trent and Mersey that is, three-quarters of a mile of it and bricks fallin' on the men, and many a time they've been stuck inside for as much as three days. They say motors is comin' to drive canal boats but I say so's Christmas. Well, you go on, dear, tie up the 'orse and show young Peter what 'e 'as to do when 'e comes. Then it's on board for you to 'ave a bite of breakfast."

Breakfast was bread and jam and strong black tea.

"Meat's our food," Mrs Smith explained. "Before a trip I buy a twenty-pound lump of beef or pork and another mid-week. Then dinner-time I puts it on the table. Then all on the boat take their cut to suit theirselves, but it 'as to be enough for their dinner and their supper for they won't see no meat again till tomorrow dinner-time."

Happily tucking in to unlimited bread and jam, Margaret asked:

"But why don't you put the meat back on the table for supper?"

"Because we don't. It's canal ways. Canal folk say sleep on a meal and work on a meal and that means meat. So afore we take a kip we eat what we cut off for our suppers and there's always plenty of tea and bread and jam. So come dinner-time cut what you need and see the boys do the same or you'll go hungry."

That morning Margaret worked out a shift system.

If the Captain decided not to stop, each of them would walk the horse for four hours at a stretch. Horatio would do two shifts – eight to twelve in the mornings and four to eight in the evenings, which would give him plenty of time in bed. She decided she had better be the one to leg from eight to midnight because stabling the horse and fetching the new horse would come in that time. Her sharp eyes had spotted where Mrs Smith kept the feed – chopped oats and bran – for the horses, "and I bet I can sneak an extra bit," she thought, "so the horse doesn't go hungry to bed for he has a terrible day."

The first morning passed peacefully. If anyone was out looking for the children there was no sign of them for all they saw was a policeman riding a bicycle who never gave them a look. Then just before dark, as Ebeneezer was helping Peter with the gates of a lock, another policeman, this time pushing his bicycle, appeared. Peter, to the policeman's eyes, looked like any one of the hundred or so children leggers he had seen at one time and another working on the canal bank so he didn't bother with him but addressed the Captain.

"You seen three children dressed queer-like in orphanage uniform?"

The Captain did not like policemen.

"No."

The policeman opened his notebook and read out:

"'Two boys name of Beresford aged eleven and six and a girl name of Thursday aged eleven.'"

"No," said the Captain again.

"What they wanted for?" Mrs Smith asked.

The policeman did not know for Constable Perkins had not told him. But he was not going to admit that.

"That's as maybe." Then he again read from his notebook.

"'The boys are very fair, noticeable so. The girl is darkish with curls.'"

At supper-time the Captain was just going to take his first enormous mouthful of meat when out of the corner of his eye he saw Peter. Once more he shook with laughter.

"Mate," he said to Mrs Smith, "I don't know what we let ourselves in for but I can swear I ain't seen no boys with noticeable fair 'air." Then he looked at Margaret. "Nor I 'aven't seen no girl neither."

Mrs Smith laughed with him.

"Nor me." Then she turned to Peter. "You'll 'ave to eat up, young man, for it's time you was doing the leggin' and young Horatio was 'avin' his supper. And mind you don't speak to nobody for where there's one rozzer next thin' we know there'll be six."

26. In the Drawing Room

Lavinia was amazed to find herself in the drawing room where Lord and Lady Corkberry were having tea. Nor was she standing, as befitted her position, but sitting in a chair as if she were a friend of the family. Because she felt shy she stared down at the dirty little piece of sweet paper on which Peter had written his message, though by now she knew by heart what was written on it.

"We kept it from you that the children were missing," Lady Corkberry explained, "because a nightdress from the orphanage was found in the canal."

"Our constable and the one near the orphanage thought it might be a case of drownin'," Lord Corkberry said. "Never believed it myself, of course, the police found nothin' and now this note proves there was nothin' to find."

"Have you any idea, Lavinia, where the children might have gone?" Lady Corkberry asked.

Lavinia shook her head.

"No, m'lady. We haven't any friends in these parts nor anywhere, and anyhow I don't see how the children could get far in that uniform. I think they must be hiding close by."

"The police have searched pretty thoroughly," Lord Corkberry said. "Now suppose you tell us what you know about yourself, maybe that'll give them a lead."

Lavinia pretended to have another look at Peter's letter.

"There's nothing to tell."

"But you remember your parents, don't you?" said Lady Corkberry gently. "Did not your mother ever speak to you about the place where she was born? Perhaps the boys might have gone there."

Lavinia again shook her head.

"They couldn't go there for it was in Ireland and she never named a place."

It was all Lord Corkberry could do not to give his wife an I-told-you-so look. Instead he asked Lavinia:

"What about your father? Was he from Ireland too?"

A slow flush crept up Lavinia's cheeks.

"We never heard him speak of where he came from."

Lady Corkberry saw that Lavinia for some reason did not like speaking of her father so she changed the subject.

"I wonder if Margaret Thursday has any friends?"

Lavinia's face lit up.

"Yes, she has, m'lady. She was found in a basket

on the steps of a village church by the rector, not a poor baby for she had three of everything of the very best quality, and until last Christmas fifty-two pounds was left in the church each year for her keep."

"God bless my soul!" Lord Corkberry exclaimed. "What a romantic story! Do you think the little baggage made it up?"

"No, I'm certain she didn't," Lavinia protested, "for she told us a lot about that rector and about Hannah who brought her up. She loves them both very dearly."

"I suppose the orphanage would have their addresses," Lady Corkberry suggested.

Lavinia tried to remember all Margaret had told them on the train journey.

"The house she lived in belonged to two old ladies and it was called Saltmarsh House. I think she said Saltmarsh was the name of the village."

Lady Corkberry looked at Lord Corkberry.

"Better send someone for the constable, he should hear all this."

Lord Corkberry nodded.

"I'll see to it. You stay here with her ladyship, Lavinia, until the constable arrives."

Lady Corkberry could see that Lavinia didn't like to think of policemen looking for her brothers.

"Do not worry too much, dear. I am sure they will be found in no time for, as you reminded us, how could they get far in those clothes?"

"What I'm wondering is, why they ran away," Lavinia said. "Margaret talked of it but I thought it was just talk, but the boys never thought of it and if they had they would have come to me."

Lady Corkberry wished that she could get on a more friendly basis with Lavinia. It was so difficult, she thought, to get confidences out of a girl who could not forget she was your scullery maid, yet she must try and get information about the orphanage.

"I had a talk with Miss Snelston this morning at the village school."

For the first time since she had come into the drawing room Lavinia smiled.

"The children say she is very kind. Do you know, her assistant called Polly Jenkin gives Horatio food. I mean, she did give Horatio. . ." Lavinia broke off, her face crimson. What had she said? When the children were found they would, of course, be taken back to the orphanage and how much worse things would be for them if Matron found out there had been talk about how the orphanage was run.

Lady Corkberry guessed what Lavinia was thinking.

"I want you to tell me all you know about the orphanage for I can promise you it will not, when they are found, bring more trouble on the missing children. You see, I saw Mr Windle today, he is a governor of the orphanage, as you know, and he tells me they will be delighted to have me on the ladies' committee. This means I can go in and out as I choose and I can assure you no child will in future be punished without my knowledge."

Lavinia looked at Lady Corkberry doubtfully. Could anyone, even Lady Corkberry, make Matron do anything she did not want to do?

"I suppose that might make a difference."

Lady Corkberry patted the seat beside her on the sofa.

"Come and sit here. I need your help, Lavinia. If, as I am afraid is the case, the orphans are neglected and ill-treated matters must be put right, and how can they be put straight unless people like myself know the truth?"

Once Lavinia started to tell Lady Corkberry about the orphanage she needed no prompting. She described everything as she had seen it from their first meeting with Miss Jones in the third-class waiting room at Paddington. Then, having told all she knew personally, she repeated what she had heard from Peter, Horatio and particularly from Margaret.

"She's the one I heard most from because Margaret's not afraid of anyone – not even of Matron. I know she had all the punishments there are, beatings and being locked in a cupboard where there are black beetles and going to bed without supper. She was getting very thin, in fact, she looked quite different from when she came, but she never gave in and she never would have. I think she would have let Matron beat her to death first."

"And yet," puzzled Lady Corkberry, "she ran away. Why? What drove the children to do that?"

The butler, with difficulty restraining himself from a start of shocked surprise at seeing the scullery maid sitting on the sofa beside Lady Corkberry, came into the room.

"Mr Windle asks to see you urgently, m'lady. There is a lady with him — a Miss Snelston."

Thomas Windle did not look a cold fish that afternoon, he looked what he felt — a truly worried man. He showed this by cutting out his usual formal manners and speaking almost as he came through the door.

"Oh, Lady Corkberry, since I saw you this afternoon about serving on the ladies' committee I have had a visit from Miss Snelston, whom I hear you know. Most distressing, most. If only the boy had come to me."

Lady Corkberry said:

"Do sit down, Miss Snelston, and you too, Mr Windle. This is the missing boys' sister, Lavinia. Now tell me, you have some news?"

Mr Windle looked at Miss Snelston.

"Indeed, yes. Tell her ladyship, Miss Snelston."

Miss Snelston felt in her pocket and brought out the message written on drawing paper that Polly had found in Peter's desk. She passed it to Lady Corkberry. Lady Corkberry read the message out loud:

"'Miss Snelston Mam will you see these books which I borrowed get back to Mister Windle and oblige goodbye Peter.' What books?"

"*Ivanhoe* and *Kenilworth* by Sir Walter Scott," said Miss Snelston.

"Both from my library," Mr Windle stated, "and a third book is missing – *Bleak House.*"

Lavinia said:

"That piece of paper, m'lady, could I see it?" Lady Corkberry passed it to her. Lavinia studied it. "Peter wrote this but it's not what he would say. I think Margaret told him what to write."

Mr Windle looked unhappily at Lady Corkberry.

"Miss Snelston fears that these missing books are the reason why the children have run away. She thinks they think that I have informed the police that they have been stolen. Oh dear, if only the boy had confided to me his wish to read I should have been delighted and none of this would have happened."

Lady Corkberry turned to Lavinia.

"Has Peter had an unhappy experience with the police?"

Lavinia looked and felt shocked.

"Oh no, m'lady, he's just a dreamy boy always buried in a book."

"That is true," Miss Snelston broke in. "A most remarkable reader for his age. I allowed him to read in playtime – the children have little or no time to themselves in the orphanage."

Lady Corkberry was still looking at Lavinia.

"But if Peter has had no trouble with the police, why should he run away? Why did he not tell Miss Snelston he had borrowed the books and asked her how he should return them?"

Lavinia looked apologetic.

"I'm afraid he wouldn't have returned them until he had read them, books are all he cares about." Then, almost as if she had been there, she saw what must have happened. "I am sure it was Margaret who thought they ought to run away. Margaret makes stories out of everything, it would be just like her to think the police thought Peter was a thief and were chasing him. And she would have taken Horatio too because I'd asked her to look after the boys so she wouldn't have left him behind."

Miss Snelston nodded approvingly.

"That is what I believe happened, Lady Corkberry. Margaret is a remarkable child but, as Lavinia says, inclined to dramatise things. Now what I would suggest is that the police concentrate on larders. Although I am sure Margaret would not touch food which does not belong to her for herself I think she might steal for the boys."

"So you feel they are still in this area?" Mr Windle asked.

"Positive," said Miss Snelston. "That uniform may be picturesque but it is also noticeable. Everybody round here knows the children are missing so one sight of the uniform and they will be found. But the police will have to have their eyes about them if they want to find Margaret Thursday."

Lavinia was not attending to what Miss Snelston was saying. Ever since she had been given Peter's note it had been nagging at her. There was something queer about it. Peter would not have fastened it to Wilberforce's collar for he did not know there was a Wilberforce nor to whom he belonged. Then it couldn't have been fastened to Wilberforce for long or it would have come off; that meant somebody must have had the note quite recently, somebody who, for some reason, could not bring it to the back door. But who?

27. Rain

From the beginning the Captain could see his trip would have to be slowed down to fit in with the powers of his new leggers.

"Won't do us no 'arm, mate," he said to Mrs Smith, "to take it easy for the once. If we works those boys too 'ard they'll only fall flat on their faces and then where are we?"

"They're triers," said Mrs Smith, "no sayin' they're not, an' never a grumble, but you're right, it won't do none of us no 'arm to get a good night's sleep."

So a new timetable was arranged. The boat was tied up before midnight each evening and did not move again until after five in the morning.

The children were more than thankful to work shorter hours, for though they walked slowly because of the weight the horse had to pull, before the Captain tied up at night each had walked a considerable number of miles. Then there were the locks. Though, to prevent the children being seen, Ebeneezer worked the locks where there were lock-keepers, one of them had to run down and help him at all the other locks, and what a lot of locks there seemed to be. And what a weight the lock gates were, even leaning on them with all their weight the children found them cruelly hard to move.

But there were compensations; they all liked the Captain and loved Mrs Smith. They tried to be friends with Ebeneezer but he, poor fellow, was weak-minded and had never really understood that Tom was gone and the children had taken his place. Then it was glorious to eat as much as you liked. For the first few days on board Margaret and Peter could not take full advantage of unlimited food as their insides had shrunk while they lived at the orphanage, but when they caught up they made up for lost time, much encouraged by the Captain and Mrs Smith.

"That's a proper cut of meat." "That's what I like to see." "You'll never come to no harm if you looks after your stomick."

Another great pleasure were the tunnels. Often it took the Captain and Ebeneezer a long time to leg through them for it was easy to get stuck, for steering was awkward lying on your back pushing the boat along with your feet. This meant that whoever the legger was, when they met a tunnel, had a lovely rest, the child stretched out flat on the bank and the horse quietly and gratefully nibbled at anything within reach.

"All the horses know about tunnels," Horatio told the others. "They always give me a sort of smile when we come to one."

Because they had to keep out of sight the children spent a lot of time on their bunks. This meant plenty of reading time for Peter, who was so enjoying *Bleak House* that he seemed almost drunk after a long read, and plenty of sleeping time for Horatio. Margaret, after a rest on her bunk and perhaps a short sleep, would slip along to the galley to see if Mrs Smith was there and, if she was, settle down for a talk.

"For she's the sensiblest person I ever knew," she told Peter, "even sensibler than Hannah and I never thought anyone would be that."

Although, except for the policemen and some lock-keepers, they had seen few people on the banks since the children came aboard, there was another danger of which both the Captain and Mrs Smith were constantly warning them. This, which happened quite frequently, was when the *Crusader* passed another canal boat.

"You see," the Captain explained to the children, "all of us canal people know each other so it wouldn't do no good us saying we got three grandchildren on board because they'd know it wasn't true. Then if that rozzer asks them if they seen three children they wouldn't know what to say, see?"

There was not as a rule any need to hide the children when a canal boat was passed because the two that were not legging were in their bunks, but they did have to keep a sharp look-out at the locks when one of the children was sent to give a hand to Ebeneezer. The real danger was if someone spotted that the child legger was not Tom, although when this happened Mrs Smith had a story ready.

When two canal boats approached each other conversation started as soon as they were within hailing distance.

"How's thin's? What's your cargo?" Groans of sympathy greeted the news that the *Crusader* was carrying ironmongery for this was heavy stuff and back-breaking to unload at the journey's end.

As the boats drew nearer somebody – usually the woman – might look round and spot the legger. Then she would roar:

"That's never Tom. Who is it then?"

"Our Tom's along of Bert," Mrs Smith would yell back, "'avin' some schoolin'. You remember old Enoch what used to work for the Captain when my boys were little 'uns?"

There had been an Enoch just as now there was an Ebeneezer, so often the woman on the other canal boat would help out. She would shout to her husband:

"You remember Enoch. Well, the Smiths have got 'is grandson leggin' for them. Tom's gone to get some schoolin'."

But the greatest pleasure of canal life, especially on the morning shifts when they were not too tired to enjoy it, was the canal and the bank. On the bank may was coming into flower and through the hedges they could see fields golden with buttercups. Each day they would bring back, like presents, news to the others of what they had seen. Herons, water-rats, frogs, field mice, fish — there was no end to the excitements, and naturally each wanted to outdo the others. Peter, who from his first shift had realized you could not read and lead a horse, learnt to be almost as sharp-eyed as Horatio and Margaret. Even on the day when they had what the Captain called a bacca hoss, which the children learnt was a horse who did not need leading because he knew his own way, Peter did not take *Bleak House* with him when he took over his shift for fear of missing something.

There was one thing about their legging the children thought was a secret, though it never was for Mrs Smith's sharp eyes had spotted what was going on. They never wore their boots except on the boat. Margaret had discovered that they couldn't on her very first shift.

"Take off your boots," she had told Horatio when he had come to relieve her, "hang them round your neck. As we mayn't wear socks you get awful blisters otherwise. Look," and she had showed him blistered heels. "But put your boots on again when you get on the boat for Mrs Smith says canal boys always wear them."

Horatio had sat down and taken off his boots and had been pleased with the result.

"The grass feels all squidgy between my toes."

On the boat Margaret had given the same instructions to Peter.

"But for goodness' sake don't forget to wear them on the boat for if Mrs Smith sees us carrying them I'm sure she'll make us wear them, she says all canal men and boys wear boots."

Without any warning the children's pleasure in the canal bank came to an end. Mrs Smith broke the news when she woke Margaret for the first shift.

"Terrible weather, dear." Margaret looked at her sleepily and saw she had discarded her pretty shawl and instead wore a sack round her shoulders. Then she heard the dismal patter and gurgle of the rain on the cabin roof. "I got a sack you can have, it'll keep the worst off of your shoulders, but you'll all three have to share it as it's the only spare I've got."

Margaret sat up, took off her nightdress and pulled on her trousers. Mrs Smith handed her her jersey.

"I know it's hard but you'll have to wear your boots today."

Margaret's head popped out of the neck of her jersey.

"I didn't know you knew we weren't wearing them. I get awful blisters if I put them on."

"You'll wear 'em and so will the boys wear theirs," Mrs Smith said firmly. "It wouldn't matter who you was to meet this weather they'd know you weren't no proper legger squelching along in the

227

mud in bare feet. Now come and 'ave a cup of tea and I'll tell you how to cure blisters. What you want is hungry water."

Margaret followed Mrs Smith to the galley.

"Hungry what?"

Mrs Smith poured Margaret a strong cup of tea and told her to help herself to bread and jam.

"It's made of rosemary tops and home-brewed wine. Cure any blister that would."

"Goodness!" said Margaret, much impressed. "I didn't know you knew about medicines."

"Bless you yes, ducks, all us canal women 'ave to. There's never a fine day but you'll see us on the canal banks picking what we need. 'Course a doctor's fine in an emergency and so's a 'orspital but they aren't always there. So us canal women makes our own medicines. Why, I never brew a cup of tea but I put in a pinch of hayriff."

"What's that?"

"Just a wild plant, but it keeps away the rheumatics. Then there's featherfew — wonderful for the liver and kidneys."

Afterwards Margaret swore that when that morning she fetched the horse from the stable and tied him to the boat she heard him sob. Certainly he knew how wickedly hard his work would be on so wet a morning, slipping and sliding as he dragged his dreadfully heavy load.

"Be brave," Margaret told him, "and I'll help all I can. But it's going to be pretty awful for me too because I've got to wear my boots and that means blisters."

Margaret had a dreadful four hours. The wet grass slapped at her bare legs. She slipped and slithered on mud. In spite of the sack she was soaked to the skin and could scarcely see where she was going for the rain cascading off the communal hat. But these troubles were as nothing to her heels. Very early on she had blisters, and soon at each step she felt as if a knife was cutting into her heels. She longed to take off her boots, but each time she looked at the boat she could see Mrs Smith keeping an eye on her.

When at last Horatio relieved her, Margaret could have cried with thankfulness. But instead she nearly cried for Horatio. He looked so terribly small and already so very wet. She put the wet hat on his damp green hair.

"Oh, Horry, it's dreadful out this morning and your boots will hurt. If you can't bear it shout and I'll finish your time – I'm not a bit tired."

Horatio put the sack round his small shoulders.

"I'll be all right." He looked up at the black clouds overhead. "Perhaps presently the sun will come out."

Surprisingly all their blisters did get better, soaked in hungry water before and after each shift, but the work remained desperately hard for it rained and rained day after day as if it would never stop. Then on the fifth wet afternoon when Peter was legging the boat just stopped and then crashed into the canal bank.

"Now then! Now then!" the Captain roared. "What's to do?" He leant over the side of his boat, peering through the blinding rain. "Peter! Peter. . ." Then he broke off to shout "Mate! Mate! Send one of the others to get 'old of that hoss. Young Peter's fainted."

28. New Plans

Peter was carried on board by Mrs Smith and Ebeneezer and laid in his bunk. Because she needed Margaret's help, Mrs Smith woke Horatio, who was asleep, and sent him to look after the horse.

"You don't need to walk 'im, Horatio," Mrs Smith explained. "Just keep 'im from chewing the 'edge, 'is doing that is what made the boat bump into the bank."

By now an experienced legger, Horatio, though half asleep, picked up the communal sack and hat, put them on and without fuss jumped ashore. There he pulled the horse back on to the path.

"It's all right," he explained to him, "I don't mind you eating anything but you must keep on the path because otherwise the boat goes into the bank with an awful bump."

The horse, grateful for a stop whatever the reason, seemed to understand for he came obediently back on to the path where he nibbled at the wet grass.

In the for'ard cabin Mrs Smith was issuing commands to Margaret:

"Get those wet clothes off of 'im. Put on 'is nightshirt. Cover 'im up good. I'll mix 'im a cup of tansy tea — rare tonic that is, 'ave 'im sittin' up in no time."

Actually Peter came round before Mrs Smith was back with the tansy tea. He opened his eyes and stared, puzzled, at Margaret.

"What's happened?"

Margaret collected his wet clothes off the floor.

"You fainted so of course the horse went to eat the hedge which made the boat bump into the bank. That's how the Captain knew what had happened."

Peter was surprised and slightly proud for he had never fainted before though he had read about it happening in books.

"Why did I faint?"

"Just tired, I expect. You walked a long way today because there weren't any tunnels."

Peter thought about that.

"Tunnels aren't much fun when it's raining — I mean, it's too wet to lie on the bank."

Mrs Smith came back with the tansy tea.

"That's better," she said, "though you still look as if you'd been dragged through a 'edge backwards. Now you feed 'im this tansy tea, Margaret, and see 'e drinks every drop while it's 'ot. I'm goin' to 'ave a word with the Cap'n."

As the boat was stationary the Captain was sitting under cover smoking his pipe.

"This is a rum trip, mate," he said when his wife joined him. "We started out to do a flyer in ten days, now the rate we're goin' looks like it might be three weeks."

Mrs Smith sat down on a box of hardware.

"It's no good, I've known it was no good ever since the rain come — before that really. I been havin' my eye on the kids, especial Peter. You can't see 'im proper on account of the walnut juice, but under it 'e's a shockin' colour. Then none of 'em — not even Margaret — has ate their vittals right since the rain come. They ain't used to it an' it's hard goin' an' that's a fact, though I never saw kids with a better 'eart for it. Never a peep out of the one of them. We'll 'ave to let them go."

The Captain was shocked.

"You mean give 'em to the rozzers?"

Mrs Smith positively bounced on her box. It was such a bounce that the enormous earrings that she wore swung out from under the scarf that tied on her trilby hat.

"The rozzers! They'd send them back to that orphanage! Over my dead body. I reckon that matron is a real bad lot and I 'ope she gets what's comin' to 'er."

"Then what shall we do with the kids? If they can't do the work I'll 'ave to get another legger."

Mrs Smith leant towards him.

"I been thinkin'. Suppose we give Ebeneezer the leggin' and take on a new man to 'elp you."

The Captain thought about that.

"Then what about the kids? We couldn't keep and feed them as passengers like."

"I got a better idea. Your sister Ida."

The Captain had a great respect for his wife but this time he could not imagine what she was thinking about.

"My sister Ida! Why, I hasn't 'eard from 'er save at Christmas, not in years. I wouldn't know where to find her."

Mrs Smith felt in her pocket and triumphantly produced a Christmas card with a picture on it of a robin in the snow.

"I kep' it on account it's pretty." She opened the card and read out loud: "'Doing all right hope this finds you in the pink as it leaves me doing panto as per for now but shall be round Chatham till June love Ida same address as usual.'"

"Chatham!" said the Captain thoughtfully. "Chatham. Well, we 'ave to pass there but I don't see how we'd find 'er nor how she'd 'elp if we did."

Mrs Smith had long ago accepted that the Captain took time to absorb new ideas.

"You forget the last time we see'd her. Lostock Fair it was. Remember what she said?"

The Captain tried. Then he shook his head.

"No."

"She said not to forget if Tom, he was only a little 'un then, fancied a change as they had always a place for a little boy."

The Captain slapped his knee.

"So she did. You thinking she might fancy Horatio?"

"Sure of it. Ever so nice spoken 'e is, and small, not much bigger nor a shrimp."

"What'll we do with Peter and Margaret then?"

"I reckon Ida will make room for Peter. I wouldn't mind keeping Margaret 'ere. Makes 'erself useful she does and she's comp'ny. The stories she tells — you did ought to hear 'er."

The Captain saw no objection.

"How we going to write to Ida? Neither on us can write a letter."

Mrs Smith got up.

"The kids can write — leastways Margaret and Peter can. I'll buy a piece of paper and a henvelope and a stamp and that."

Back in the for'ard cabin Peter had with difficulty swallowed his tansy tea, for he thought it was revolting.

"Never you mind how it tastes," said Mrs Smith. "It's a tonic, which is what you need. Now I'm going to cover you up with all we've got so you sweat nice, that'll send you to sleep. I don't want a sound out of you till supper time."

"But what about the legging?" Peter asked. "Margaret and Horatio can't do more than they're doing."

"Nor I 'aven't 'eard anyone askin' them to," Mrs Smith retorted. "You leave the legging to me.

Maybe the Captain will tie up now seein' we've stopped — and maybe he won't. What you got to do is sweat nice and go to sleep."

Mrs Smith and Margaret went into the galley where Mrs Smith let down the table and put on it a bowl and one of her water jugs which, like the boat itself, was gaily painted with castles, roses and diamonds. Then off a shelf she took what Margaret had supposed was a white rope which she had seen hanging aft and often wondered what it was for.

"What is that?"

Mrs Smith poured some water into the bowl.

"A cow's tail, dear. We 'angs it aft for luck. The knot under it we calls the Turk's Head. It 'as to be washed reg'lar in pure water on account that soap turns it yellow. I suppose really it's the same as our paintings like on this jug and on the boat, it's just for fanciness, but you won't see no canal boat what 'asn't its cow's tail aft and isn't painted pretty."

Mrs Smith didn't like being interrupted when she was working, so Margaret waited until the cow's tail was washed and hanging up to dry before she said:

"Will Peter be all right to leg tomorrow because if he isn't I could do some of his time?"

Mrs Smith sat down at the table and gestured to Margaret to do the same.

"Peter's not cut out to be a legger nor Horatio neither."

Margaret was half out of the chair.

"But they can't go back to the orphanage for Peter would go to prison. . ."

Mrs Smith held up an imperious hand.

"Quiet, now. Nobody hasn't said nothing about sending the boys back. What me and the Captain 'as in mind is the stage. The Captain 'as one sister by name of Ida. Well, she married away from the canal — and the fellow she married is an actor — well, he's a bit more than that, he's a manager of what they calls a fit-up."

"What's that?"

"I don't rightly know," Mrs Smith confessed, "but from what they said I don't think they acts in a real theatre, more fixes up a theatre theirselves in 'alls and that. Well, we think they might find a place for Horatio."

Margaret had never been inside a theatre in her life, but she had touched the fringe of the theatre world. In her school several girls had collections of postcards with photographs on them of the leading actors and actresses of the day which sometimes, as a great favour, she had been allowed to look at. But she couldn't imagine Horatio amongst such gorgeous creatures.

"I don't think Horatio can act."

Mrs Smith knew no more about theatres than Margaret did.

"I expect he could learn same as he has learnt to be a legger."

"But if we go to the Captain's sister Ida, who will be your legger?"

"We was thinkin' of makin' Ebeneezer the legger and gettin' a new man to work with the Cap'n. And we was thinkin' maybe if I got paper and that and a stamp you'd write a letter to the Cap'n's sister."

"Of course I would," Margaret agreed. "And you needn't buy a stamp. I've got two. I had three but I used one to write to Lavinia. I used to hide them in the toe of my boot at the orphanage but since I've been here where you needn't hide things I've kept them in my tin box that Hannah gave me. They are a bit scrumply and we may need extra glue, but they're still good stamps."

Mrs Smith, inclining her head, accepted the stamp.

"There's a Tommy shop not so far along, we can get some ink and a piece of paper an' a henvelope."

Tommy shops catered for the canal boats. Margaret had not been in one because of the need to keep out of sight, but she had often seen Mrs Smith go ashore to shop in them.

"Peter has a pencil. That would be better for I'm not so good at ink writing. Are you going to tell the Captain's sister all about us? I mean about the orphanage and Peter having taken the books?"

Mrs Smith did not believe in beating about the bush.

"We was thinkin', the Cap'n and me, that Ida

might want Horatio but as well she might take Peter. We was thinkin' you could stay along of me for. . ."

Mrs Smith got no further than that for Margaret, her chin in the air and her eyes flashing, was on her feet.

"I don't care where we go but you're not dividing us up. Lavinia asked me to look after the boys and I said I would and I always will." Then Margaret ran round the table and threw her arms round Mrs Smith's neck. "It's not, dear, darling Mrs Smith, that I wouldn't like to stay with you — truly I would. But I made Lavinia an absolute promise and I must keep it. Oh please, Mrs Smith, do, do understand."

29. Goodbye to Matron

Lady Corkberry was not the kind of person who started things but did not finish them. She had been prepared to find it hard work putting the affairs of the orphanage in order for she had expected opposition from the existing members of the ladies' committee. But as things turned out she was welcomed with open arms.

"Oh, dear Lady Corkberry," the chairman of the ladies' committee said to her, "how glad we shall be of your help. We – no doubt foolishly – believed everything that Matron told us and now look what's happened. She was so disliked locally that she was rough musicked by the village. The shame of it!"

Lady Corkberry and the chairman visited Matron intending to tell her that not only must she leave but so must Miss Jones. They found there was no need to say anything. Like most bullies Matron, when turned on, had become like a pricked penny balloon, all she could do was cry and plead to be allowed to go.

"It was horrible, horrible," she sobbed. "I could not believe people could be so cruel. Imagine rough musicking me!"

Lady Corkberry remembered what Lavinia had told her.

"You may leave by all means, in fact, we were intending to tell you to do so. But first there are things we want to know. Where do you keep the children's own possessions?"

Matron sobbed louder than ever.

"It's that Margaret Thursday. She has been talking. Nothing has gone right since that dreadful child came here. It's lies, all lies. I've not taken anything that did not belong to me."

But of course that story was no good for Mrs Bones was still in the kitchen and, since she had always disliked Matron, was only too willing to tell tales against her. Soon Lady Corkberry and the chairman knew how much of the orphans' food Matron had not ordered so that luxuries could be delivered for herself, and how much good food had travelled up north with her each May.

"I will arrange for a conveyance to drive you and Miss Jones to the London junction this afternoon," Lady Corkberry said coldly. Then she held out her hand. "May we have your keys, please."

Matron handed over the keys.

"What about our money?"

"That will be a matter for the lawyers," Lady Corkberry said. "I should not imagine you will receive anything, considering how consistently you have robbed the children. You are a lucky woman we are not taking you to court."

Matron and Miss Jones left that afternoon at a time when the children should have been in school, but the children learnt from Winifred what was happening. So, soon after afternoon school had started, without saying a word to Miss Snelston or to Polly, the orphans streamed out of the school back to the orphanage. There they hid in the bushes both inside the orphanage entrance and down the road. Afterwards Miss Snelston gave them a lecture on not being unkind to those who were already feeling low and miserable. But the children were not ashamed. Throwing everything they could lay hands on at Matron and Miss Jones had been utterly delightful and, though Miss Snelston might say they had behaved badly, the children knew they felt better inside because they had in a way paid Matron back for every moment they had been hungry and for all the punishments they had suffered.

Actually the orphans soon forgot the bad old days of Matron and Miss Jones. A new matron came whom they all loved, and so much money was raised by the governors and the ladies' committee that the food became wonderful – so wonderful that Miss Snelston had to organize extra games to prevent the orphans from becoming too fat.

Meanwhile the search for the children went on. The local police in Essex visited both Margaret's rector and Hannah, but they of course knew nothing.

"Margaret had stamps," the rector said. "I gave them to her myself. But she did not write and neither, to my grief, did I write to her. You see, I was told the authorities thought receiving or sending letters tended to upset the children, so much against my will, I had to accept their ruling."

Hannah surprised the police by the calm way she took the news that Margaret was missing.

"Margaret wouldn't have run away," she said calmly, "if there wasn't cause. But now she has run she wouldn't come here for she knows we tried every way to keep her. Very independent type Margaret is, when she's ready to tell us where she is we'll get a letter."

A few days later the rector received a letter from the archdeacon which backed up what Hannah had said.

"I hear from my brother, Thomas Windle, that the child, Margaret Thursday, and two boys have run away from the orphanage. I hear too that I owe you an apology. Far from the happy place I believed the orphanage to be, it seems there was a cruel matron — since dismissed. All is well at the orphanage now so I pray Margaret Thursday will soon be found."

"Pity he didn't find out about the matron before we sent Margaret there," Hannah sniffed, "but there's no need to worry. Margaret will be looking after herself and the two boys too, shouldn't wonder."

Lavinia, too, was searching for the missing children, but her method of searching was different from that of the police. Hers was a question and answer system. Who on the estate would be afraid to bring a note to the back door? For days the answer was nobody, then suddenly she got a clue. One of the boys exercising a horse fell off and was concussed. The doctor was sent for and it was decided that while he had to be kept quiet the boy should be nursed in the house. Talking of this to her staff, Mrs Smedley gave Lavinia the clue.

"Her ladyship is too good the way she takes the stable boys in. No reason they can't be nursed in their own rooms."

"I suppose there's no one to nurse them," Lavinia suggested.

"Nonsense!" said Mrs Smedley. "Tough as old rope those boys are and what I say is, have them in when they're ill and the next thing you know they'll be in every day."

Lavinia was surprised.

"Don't they come in?"

"I should hope not indeed – only for the party at Christmas – I don't want a lot of stable boys smelling of horses in and out of my kitchen. Let one so much as come to the back door and he'd go away with a flea in his ear."

"So that was it," thought Lavinia. "A stable boy! But which?" Then she had her answer. Jem, of course. Who else had the children met? Somehow she decided she must talk to Jem. Not easy for she had no excuse to go to the stables and when she met him it was by accident in the grounds. She had seen him on the day when Clara went to the dentist, but it was a long time since she had spoken to him. But now she had to find him however difficult it might be. "I don't care what happens to me," she told herself, "but I must see Jem. I absolutely must."

30. The Tunnel

The boat was tied up beside the Tommy shop, and having watched Mrs Smith go ashore to buy the notepaper Margaret went to the for'ard cabin for the stamp. Peter seemed to be asleep and so was Horatio, so very quietly she went to her bunk under which was her basket. She had not seen her tin box since she came on board for as she was happy she no longer slept with it in her arms. The cat painted on it appeared like an old friend and it brought Hannah so vividly to her mind that it was almost as if she could see her. Was it only in March that Hannah had said, speaking of the basket: "In a corner down at the bottom is that tin of mine with the cat on it you're fond of. I've filled it with toffees"? It seemed years ago and yet it was only weeks. Could it be only weeks since Hannah and she had said goodbye in that simply awful waiting room? "Oh, my dear pet!" Hannah had said. "Oh, my dear pet! You got some stamps the rector gave you. Bear it if you can, but if you can't you write and something might be thought of." Of course nothing could be thought of – Hannah had only said that to comfort her, but now that things were better should she write?

Sitting on her bunk staring at the tin box, Margaret felt such a longing to see Hannah that tears came to her eyes and trickled down her cheeks. She was brought back to the present by Peter. He was sitting up in his bunk.

"Why are you crying?"

Angrily, Margaret brushed away her tears.

"I wasn't. I never cry. Why should I cry? I'm Margaret Thursday and I only need me so I've nothing to cry about."

Peter was not a prying boy. Margaret had cried but if she liked to say she hadn't that was her business. He turned politely to his own affairs.

"Can I leg tomorrow?"

"I don't think so, anyway Ebeneezer is going to do most of the legging."

Peter thought about that.

"But if we don't leg what are we going to do? They can't keep us here if we don't work because the Captain only gets thirty-six shillings for a trip and, though that sounds an awful lot of money, it isn't really with all that has to be bought. The Captain told me so, he said it was cruel hard to put anything by."

"We're not staying on the boat. Horatio is going to be an actor. Mrs Smith has gone to get notepaper so I can write to the Captain's sister about it. That's why I was getting out a stamp."

"Will the stamp still work after being such ages in your boot?"

"I think so, anyway the Captain has glue if it won't stick."

"So you'll have one stamp left. Are you going to write to Lavinia? She would like to know that Horatio is going to be an actor."

"I don't know. I should think it would be better to wait until we get to London. You see, when Horatio is an actor I think I might get a job as cook and perhaps you could work in a bookshop — at least, you could if you don't take the books — and then we might have a little home of our own."

At this glorious vision Peter's face lit up as if he had a bright star in his head.

"Could we? Then we could write to Lavinia and tell her where we were and she could come and live with us."

Margaret was equally carried away. Of course that would be the right time to write to Hannah and the rector.

"And I'll write to Hannah and invite her and the rector to tea. Imagine tea in our very own little house!"

Peter came back to the present.

"I must be a legger until we get to London, do make Mrs Smith see that."

Margaret was certain Mrs Smith wouldn't let Peter leg. In spite of the tansy tea and a long sleep he still looked very peculiar. However, it was no good upsetting him so she gave him a nod, which might mean anything or nothing, then skipped off to the galley ready to write the letter.

The letter Margaret wrote to Mrs Smith's dictation was not well worded or elegant but no one worried about that. The miracle was that Ida, who had never been to school as a child, had picked up sufficient education since so that she could read a letter. Under Mrs Smith's direction Margaret first addressed the envelope.

"Put Mrs Ida Fortescue."

"How do I spell that?" Margaret asked.

"I don't know, dear. How it sounds, I suppose. It isn't their real name, that's Robinson, but Ida says Fortescue has got more class to it and it seems that matters to actors. The address is a public house, it's called The Bull. They're so well known there I reckon if you just wrote 'Ida' on the henvelope it would find her."

To dictate, or what she considered dictating, was a great effort to Mrs Smith. She untied her trilby hat and laid it on the table, which gave Margaret her first sight of the little black straw bonnet she wore under it. She put her arms on the table and, breathing heavily, said:

"Tell Ida that the Cap'n an' me hopes this finds her in the pink as it leaves us. Then say the Cap'n an' me is bringing you a little boy for an actor called Horatio. Tell 'er how 'e speaks very pretty. Then tell 'er the Cap'n reckons he should 'ave discharged 'is cargo this next Saturday so we'll meet them in The Bull Sunday night bringing Horatio along of us."

"What about me and Peter? You haven't said anything about us," Margaret protested.

"Don't want to put Ida off, do we?" Mrs Smith reminded her. "Bringing Horatio is one thing, maybe she'll be pleased to have him, but tell 'er I'm bringing three kids and they mightn't show up at all."

In the end Margaret got a letter of a sort written, the Captain provided glue to stick on the stamp and Ebeneezer was sent ashore to post it.

The next day very early in the morning the boat got moving, with Ebeneezer leading the horse. To Ebeneezer being a legger was a dream come true. He was tough and did not mind how many miles he walked provided no one asked him to think. Thinking was something Ebeneezer could not manage. Mrs Smith, watching him, nodded her head understandingly.

"I reckon Ebeneezer will do all right with the leggin'," she told Margaret. "You can take over from 'im when he needs a lay-off for his dinner an' that. Now what I want you to do is stand by the Cap'n. Help at the locks and maybe 'e'll let you do a bit of steerin'. Of course, come a tunnel you must take the 'orse from Ebeneezer so 'e can leg through it with the Cap'n."

Margaret did not want the boys to appear merely passengers.

"Horatio can lead the horse at tunnels. He likes doing that."

"I got other plans for Horatio," said Mrs Smith. "It's no good my askin' Ida to take 'im for an actor with green 'air. I gotter work on 'im to get him back to fair before she sees 'im."

The boys' green hair seemed permanent for all the rain of the last days had not affected it.

"How will you do that?" Margaret asked.

Mrs Smith looked mysterious.

"I know 'ow. There's a wash my old gran made up, there is camomile and costmary in it an' I don't know what else but I got it all. When I've put that on the boys' 'eads a time or two there'll be no more green, I promise you that."

Mrs Smith's cure for green hair was not quick in action. Twice that day and twice the next she made up a paste and plastered it on to the boys' heads and twice a day she washed it off. In between she covered their faces with an ointment which slowly removed the walnut juice.

Meanwhile Margaret was becoming a thoroughly competent assistant to the Captain. She saw a lock coming and had jumped down and was working the gates before he had time to yell for her. Under his tuition she learnt to steer, and she was ashore and had hold of the horse at the tunnels before the Captain had time to whistle for Ebeneezer.

The day after Peter's fainting attack the weather

at last had begun to clear up, but by now they had left the real countryside behind. There were still long stretches of green, and in places there were fields of buttercups, but slowly London was sticking out its tentacles, clawing in the countryside in order to build factories and rows of sad, black-looking houses.

Margaret thought the change was horrible. She missed the green and the flashes of gold where marsh marigolds grew at the water's edge, but such things meant nothing to Ebeneezer. He never looked right nor left but, sucking a piece of grass, plodded on, caring not at all whether the path on which he walked was fresh young green or black and cindery. As he walked he hummed tunelessly which, had anyone understood him, showed he was supremely contented. So contented that he was blind and deaf to other sounds, which was why, when Margaret was having an early dinner in the galley, when the Captain yelled: "Ebeneezer. Tunnel coming up," Ebeneezer heard nothing and when he was brought to a stop by the tunnel itself, forgetting that he should be on the boat, he unhitched the horse and walked on with him up the path to the far end of the tunnel.

The Captain made such a noise shouting at Ebeneezer that Mrs Smith and all three children rushed out to see what was wrong. The sight of the boys with their heads tied up in towels made the Captain madder than ever.

"Get down below, you boys. How do you know who's comin' through the tunnel? One look at you and we've 'ad it."

"Skip it, boys," said Mrs Smith. Then she joined the Captain. "Let Margaret run after him. She won't take long."

The Captain leant over the side of his boat to look at Ebeneezer.

"Won't take long! If Ebeneezer walks back the pace 'e's goin' now we'll never be unloaded Saturday."

Margaret had an idea.

"It's not a very long tunnel. Couldn't I leg through it instead of Ebeneezer then we won't waste any time?"

The Captain laughed.

"You leg it! Why, your little legs couldn't reach the tunnel side."

"You couldn't do it, dear," Mrs Smith agreed, "it's dangerous, you could easy fall in, then like enough you'd be crushed between the boat and the tunnel wall."

Margaret was determined to prove not only her worth but that she, representing Peter and Horatio, was a proper canal worker. She stuck her chin in the air.

"Don't be silly! Margaret Thursday is as good a legger through a tunnel as any Ebeneezer and so would Peter and Horatio be if you'd let them do it." She turned to Mrs Smith. "If you'd let me put the pillows off my bunk on the boards they will lift me up enough for my legs to reach the wall. It's a very narrow tunnel."

It was a narrow tunnel and not long as tunnels went and the Captain was in a hurry so, though unwillingly, he gave in to Margaret. Seizing the planks that were used for tunnel legging, he laid them across the bows.

"Get the pillows," he told Mrs Smith. "Now come here, Margaret, and I'll show you how."

Margaret was never to forget that tunnel. Never could she have imagined how heavy a boat was to move when pushed along by human feet. Then it was so spooky inside. Icy cold water dripped on to her face. Bats flew so low she thought they would get into her hair. Even helped out by pillows it was all her legs could do to reach the tunnel wall, and the pain in her thighs grew more and more excruciating. She was so intent on sticking it out and being every bit as good a legger as Ebeneezer that she did not see what every legger watched for – the pinpoint of light which meant the tunnel end, so it was a glorious surprise when suddenly the tunnel came to an end and the sun was shining on her face.

The Captain helped Margaret to her feet.

"You're a rum 'un, Margaret Thursday," he said. "Pity you weren't born a boy, you'd 'ave finished up an admiral or such, I shouldn't wonder."

Margaret was pleased but she hid it.

"Thank you, but I don't want to be anybody but me. I'm going to make Margaret Thursday a name everybody is going to remember. You see if I don't."

31. At The Bull

All day on Sunday before they left for The Bull Mrs Smith worked hard to make the boys, particularly Horatio, presentable. Their hair was now even fairer than it normally was and their faces quite clear of walnut juice.

"I would've liked 'Oratio to wear a 'at," Mrs Smith sighed. "It would be pretty if he could take it off when 'e meets Ida and Mr Fortescue."

"He'll bow," said Peter. "Mother taught us, she told us it was polite when you met a lady."

Margaret was once more dressed in her skirt and jersey but deliciously conscious that, because it was Sunday, she was wearing lace underneath. She was even more anxious for Horatio's success than Mrs Smith for if Horatio were not accepted as an actor where were they to go?

"Do it now, Horatio. Show us how you'll do it."

Horatio got to his feet and stood in front of Mrs Smith. He gave a beautiful bow.

"Good evening, Mrs Ida ma'am. I hope you are feeling well."

Mrs Smith was overcome with admiration.

"Oh my! Well, I never did! Oh my, isn't he the little gentleman!"

"Shouldn't he say Mrs Fortescue ma'am?" Peter asked.

"Rightly, I suppose he should," Mrs Smith agreed. "But you do the best you can, Horatio, ducks. Why, I shouldn't wonder but what you was took on for the acting right away."

"What's to happen after they've seen Horatio?" Margaret asked. "Do Peter and I just walk up to you or do you call us?"

This was the part of the plan that was worrying Margaret, and she had reason to be anxious. After she was dressed in her girl's clothes she had re-packed her basket and had suggested to Mrs Smith that she should put in the boys' nightshirts, which were at that moment drying outside on a line. Mrs Smith was usually a very direct sort of person so when she was indirect it showed.

"Well, no, dearie, I wouldn't do that. See, I don't know what plans will be made and it could be awk'ard like if you was sleepin' in one place an' the boys another. No, I got a bit of paper an' I thought I'd make a parcel of the boys' thin's."

Now at Margaret's question Mrs Smith again looked flustered.

"We got to see 'ow thin's shapes like. What the Cap'n 'opes is that Ida or more like Mr Fortescue can use a bright boy like Peter for takin' money an' thin's."

"But you will tell them about me, won't you?" Margaret pleaded. "I don't want any work. I'll get that in somebody's kitchen, but just to begin with if I could sleep where the boys sleep. You see, I did promise Lavinia. . ."

Mrs Smith was clearly fussed.

"Now don't take on, ducks. I'm sure we can fix thin's up nice. But don't forget when we gets to The Bull you an' Peter sits one place an' the Cap'n, me and Horatio another."

The Smiths and the children arrived at The Bull before the Fortescues, so the Captain led Margaret and Peter over to a window seat.

"Now you two stay 'ere and don't move neither on you till you're called." He had grown fond of the children, particularly Margaret, and felt worried lest they never were called. "Tell you what," he said in what he hoped was a cheerful voice, "what say I buys you both a bottle of ginger pop."

The ginger pop did distract the children for a few minutes for the Captain did not bring them glasses so they had to drink out of the bottles, which was difficult to do for they had been sealed by a glass marble in their necks which got in the way when they were drinking.

"If only I could break this bottle I'd keep my marble to remind me of the Captain," Peter said. "I think he's one of the nicest men I know."

Margaret looked at the stout glass pop bottles.

"For goodness' sake don't try and smash it, there would be an awful noise. . ." She broke off and gave Peter a nudge. "Look."

Peter looked, and both he and Margaret stared at what they saw. Mr and Mrs Fortescue had arrived, and a very impressive entrance they made. Mr Fortescue was handsome in a flamboyant way. He had dark curly hair and a most impressive moustache, curling up at the corners. He was, to the children, very grandly dressed.

Mrs Fortescue – or Ida as the Smiths called her – was even more grand. She had bright red hair on top of which sat an emerald green hat with a whole green bird on it. She was dressed in a very in-and-out green silk garment which seemed to be a short coat over a long swirling dress. Close to, as the children were to find out later, the silk was cracking in places, especially where it fitted too tightly. The outfit was finished off by a high-boned net collar round which glittered what looked like a diamond necklace, and long kid gloves which had once been white.

Both the Fortescues paused in the doorway and only when everybody had seen them did they, with a start of apparent surprise, notice the Captain and Mrs Smith. Then Ida stretched both arms wide.

"Brother!" she exclaimed. "Brother, dear!"

The Captain, looking embarrassed, came forward and gave her a smacking kiss. Then he turned to his brother-in-law and shook his hand.

"Well! How's thin's? What will you 'ave? The 'ospitality is on us."

Mrs Smith, who was not the kissing type, pushed her brown cheek awkwardly against Ida's noticeably pink and white one.

"One moment, Cap'n," she said. "Ida and Mr Fortescue will want to meet the boy." She laid a hand on Horatio's shoulder. "This is Horatio Beresford."

Horatio was perfect. He gave a beautiful bow before he said:

"Good evening, ma'am, and you too, sir. I hope you are both feeling well."

"If it wasn't Horatio who was doing it," Margaret whispered to Peter, "I'd say he was showing off."

Peter saw what she meant but he stuck up for Horatio.

"He's only doing what our mother told us to."

The effect on the Fortescues of Horatio's politeness was obvious. They looked at each other with faces which clearly asked, "Would you believe it!"

"Speaks pretty, doesn't he?" said Mrs Smith. "Puts me in mind of the way you speak, Ida — ever so refined."

Margaret and Peter were afraid that when the drinking began everybody would go to the bar where the drinks were served, which would mean they would not hear a word that was said. Instead the men went to the bar to fetch the drinks and Ida, in a very grand way as if she owned The Bull, led Mrs Smith to a table.

"This is our favourite," she said. "No one else would dream of sitting here when we honour The Bull."

The table was quite close to the window seat on which Margaret and Peter were sitting, so Mrs Smith hurriedly pushed Horatio into the chair which had its back to them. He had been told he was not to speak or look at them, but there was always the chance that he might forget.

"Do you think you could find a place for Horatio?" Mrs Smith asked.

Margaret and Peter now noticed that Ida, when not trying hard, sometimes forgot her elegant voice and talked more like her brother.

"Well, dear, of course I leave all business to Mister Fortescue. We 'ave – have plans for which this boy would I should say be hon – on the small side, but I expect we'll fit him in, mostly we can use a small child."

Margaret nudged Peter.

"If they want a bigger boy," she whispered, "I expect they'll use you. Would you mind?"

"I don't know," Peter whispered back. "I haven't tried but I'd like anything if only we could have our own little house."

The men arrived with the drinks and there was a good deal of raising glasses and health drinking.

While this was going on Horatio, tired after the long day, went to sleep.

"I must say he's pretty as a picture," said Ida. She turned to her husband. "He won't cost much and he can make hisself useful."

Mr Fortescue felt things were moving too fast.

"There's a play bein' made out of a book which I shall have the honour to present. There is a boy in it, but this boy is a bit too small for Cedric, do you not think, my dear?"

Ida nodded.

"I just said the same thing. Lovely play it is, it's called *Little Lord Fauntleroy*."

"My public will eat it — just eat it," said Mr Fortescue.

"And it might 'ave been written for us," Ida added. "There's the boy's grandfather, the Earl, and I think I can say without contradiction there's no one on the boards today to touch Mr Fortescue when he is appearing as a member of the aristocracy."

Mr Fortescue gave her a bow.

"And the part of the boy's mother — Dearest, he calls her — fits Ida like a shoe."

The Captain cleared his voice.

"'Ow old a boy was you wantin'?"

Mr Fortescue gave his moustache an upward brush.

"Well, I'm not particular, he is seven in the book, eight when it finishes."

"There you go!" Margaret whispered to Peter.

"You may be just eleven but you can look seven. Oh, I wonder if they'll mind me coming too."

A moment later Peter was called.

"As it 'appens Horatio 'as a brother," the Captain said. "Peter, come here a moment."

Peter came to the table. He bowed to Ida.

"Good evening, ma'am."

Ida turned to the Captain.

"Where did you find them? These aren't canal kids."

"Cedric to the life," said Mr Fortescue. "But I tell you what, Ida, the little one will do for Tom, the false heir."

Margaret lost track of the conversation for a bit for first more drinks were fetched and after that the talk was about business arrangements. It seemed that both boys were to be something called apprenticed. She stretched forward, hoping to hear what they were to be paid, but there was no mention of money, only "all found," which Margaret was afraid meant a home and clothes and food. "Oh dear," she thought, "it doesn't sound as if we can have a little house just yet."

Presently the men got up to fetch yet another round of drinks, and while they were gone Mrs Smith said:

"Ida, dear. Could you do me a favour?"

"If I can," Ida agreed.

"Well, there's a girl. She's not a sister to the boys but she's like a sister, isn't she, Peter?"

Peter was nearly asleep but he jerked his head up. "Yes. Just like a sister."

"Margaret. Margaret," Mrs Smith called. "Come here a minute, dearie."

Margaret slid off the window seat and came to the table. She gave Ida a polite bob curtsey.

"Good evening, ma'am."

Ida turned to Mrs Smith.

"What d'you think we are — a baby farm? We don't want a girl. Six a penny they are. We got a girl workin' for us, well, she's a grown woman really but ever so small she is, so when we want a girl kid she plays 'em." The men came back with the drinks and Ida pointed a finger at Mrs Smith. "Thinks we're a baby farm, wants us to take this girl as well."

Mr Fortescue gave Margaret a glance then he handed Mrs Smith her drink.

"Sorry, dear, but nothing doing. The two boys — yes. We'll have them tonight. The girl — no. Why, she's not even pretty."

He sounded so condescending it was more than Margaret could bear. Up went her chin and her eyes blazed.

"Thank you very much, but I wouldn't work for you if I was starving. I don't know who you think you are but I came in a basket with three of everything all of the very best quality and marked with crowns. And every year one hundred pieces of gold money were sent to keep me. You may talk about me in a despising voice, but one day you'll be sorry because I'm Margaret Thursday who's going to be very famous. Just now I'm not sure how — I just know I am." Margaret meant to make a splendid exit, sweeping out of the public house slamming the door behind her, but she was prevented by Peter — a Peter she did not know existed, very pink in the face, his blue eyes looking as though there was fire in them. He flung his arm round Margaret.

"How dare you be rude to Margaret? We think her very pretty. And she's brave as brave. It was Margaret who arranged all about our running away, and me and Horatio are not going anywhere without her."

In the excitement Horatio had woken up and now he decided to join in. He got up and came to Margaret and Peter. He caught hold of one of Margaret's hands.

"Don't mind that man, Margaret. Peter and me love you next best to Lavinia and we're going with you to our own teeny-weeny house like you said we could."

Mr Fortescue was looking at Margaret with a speculating eye. Now he turned to Ida.

"The girl's quite something when her dander's up — quite something."

Ida nodded for she, too, could see in Margaret what he could see. She turned graciously to the children.

"Come and sit down, dears. Maybe both Mr Fortescue and me spoke a bit hasty." She turned to her brother. "I know you'll want to be making an early start so I'll just fix things up as best I can for tonight and tomorrow we'll manage something better."

Saying goodbye to Mrs Smith was to Margaret almost as bad as saying goodbye to Hannah had been. She would have clung to her as she had clung to Hannah, but Mrs Smith was not the clinging type.

"Goodbye, dear," she said briskly. "I shall miss you. But we'll be seeing you all again soon. Send us a line, Ida; when you're acting this Little Lord Something and tell us where you'll be, and me and the Cap'n will be along to watch."

After the Smiths had gone, the children stumbled along behind the Fortescues to their theatrical lodgings, Margaret carrying her basket and Peter the brown-paper parcel containing his and Horatio's nightshirts and Mr Windle's copy of *Bleak House*.

"Do you think it's going to be very terrible?" Peter asked Margaret. "I mean, as terrible as the orphanage?"

Up shot Margaret's chin.

"'Course not. It'll be all right, anything is all right as long as we stick together."

32. At Morning Prayers

In spite of all her efforts, Lavinia failed to find Jem. The truth was he was scared she might be looking for him, so if he went for a walk in the grounds of Sedgecombe Place he was as scary of being seen as a wild deer. Lavinia, though desperately anxious about the boys, did not know what to do. Everybody told her not to worry, the police would soon find the children, but first one week and then another went by and there was never a clue as to their whereabouts. Mrs Smedley grew quite worried about Lavinia.

"You must pull yourself together, girl," she told her. "You don't eat enough to keep a sparrow going, why you're getting so thin one day you'll be going down the plug-hole with the washing-up water."

"Wouldn't you be worried if you were me?" Lavinia retorted. "I can't help thinking something terrible has happened to the boys and I think it worse in the night and then I don't sleep."

Mrs Smedley, though kind, was brisk.

"That's being silly, considering the note Peter sent. Besides, worrying never did nobody no good. What you've got to do is stay where you are so the boys know where to find you, and keep your heart up. When you feel down try whistling – great help that is."

Lavinia did try whistling and she struggled to eat her meals, but nothing helped. Then one night in bed she came to a decision. It was being stupid to suspect that Jem would help and do nothing about it, she must tell someone that she wanted to see him. But the question was who? The right way to do a thing like that was to tell Mrs Smedley who might repeat what she had said to Mrs Tanner, who in turn might tell Lady Corkberry. But it was such a vague way of getting anything done and there was always the chance that Mrs Smedley, who thought nothing of stable boys, might not bother to tell Mrs Tanner, which meant no one would tell Lady Corkberry. Unconscious that she had done so, Lavinia spoke out loud.

"But there must be a way. There must."

Clara was nearly asleep but she sat up with a jerk.

"A way to do what?"

Lavinia had a certain respect for Clara. Being a local girl with a mother who had at one time worked in the house and whose father was one of the gardeners, she had good solid knowledge of how the whole estate was run. Though Lavinia had never thought of it before it was just possible Clara might know how she could get hold of Jem.

"If I tell you what I'm thinking, Clara, will you promise not to tell anybody else?"

Clara saw no harm in that. Lavinia heard her spit on a finger.

"See this wet. See this dry. Cut my throat, if I lie. Now go on, tell me."

"You know that note I had from my brother?"

All the household and most of the outside staff knew the words of that note by heart.

"You mean – 'dear Lavinia we are with Margaret and quite safe do not show this to anyone love Peter and Horatio'?"

"That's it," Lavinia agreed. "Well, there are two things about that note I keep thinking and thinking about. First, why should Peter write 'do not show this to anyone'? As he didn't say where they were going how could it matter who saw it?"

Clara sounded contemptuous.

"That's boys all over. Always tracking and that, I expect he just wanted to make it sound adventurous like."

"But that isn't what worries me most," Lavinia explained. "It's how I got the letter."

Clara did not follow that.

"I thought it was tied to Wilberforce's collar."

"That's just it, that is how it came. But you know Wilberforce, how he gets around, if that note had been on him long it would have come off, so it looks as if someone had just tied it on. That would have to be someone who works here for if a stranger had come someone would have seen him, and if a stranger had touched Wilberforce he'd have barked the place down, you know how he is."

"Little varmint, don't I just!" Clara agreed. "My dad says if he was his he'd put him in a water butt."

"Well, I've been thinking," Lavinia went on, "and I've decided it must have been someone in the stables and that someone I think is Jem. You see, both my brothers and Margaret know him because he drove them to tea with Mr Windle."

Clara did not answer immediately. Then she said, as if she was tasting the name:

"Jem! Jem!" If Clara could sound excited she sounded it now. "If Jem's anything to do with it then where those kids are is on Jem's dad's boat. They're canal folk."

Lavinia had not in her wildest imaginings pictured the children on a boat, but now she saw Clara might be right.

"The thing is, I must talk to Jem. How could I do that? You see, I think he's hiding from me."

"You couldn't – not without saying why like. We aren't allowed in the stables and the stable boys don't come to the house."

"I know," Lavinia agreed. "I think and think of every way to meet and each day I don't. Oh, Clara, I'm so worried about the boys."

Clara, and indeed the whole household, were truly sorry for Lavinia and longed to help her. Probably it was the longing to help which made Clara suggest something which was far beyond what she would dare do herself.

"If I were you I'd tell her ladyship. I mean, how you think Jem might know something."

"Would you? You mean ask Mrs Tanner if I could speak to her?"

"No, not this time I wouldn't. You see, old Tanner's a nosy type so she would want to know why. If you told her why she might send for Jem, who I reckon would just shut up like a rabbit trap, but if her ladyship were to talk to him that would be different. There isn't anybody who would dare not answer questions if her ladyship asked."

Lavinia decided her best chance of getting a note to Lady Corkberry was after family prayers. Now Lord Corkberry was away, prayers were taken by Lady Corkberry. The staff filed into the dining room in strict order of precedence, led by the butler, followed by Mrs Tanner and finishing with Lavinia. This meant that when prayers were over Lavinia had to open the door and hold it open until all the staff had passed through except the butler. He took over the door from her so that he might hold it open for the Corkberrys, who immediately after prayers went from the dining room to the morning room for breakfast.

"Somehow," Lavinia thought, "I ought to see a way to leave a note for her ladyship. Of course I'll be in real trouble if I'm seen, but I feel sure I'll find a way."

Lavinia had no notepaper but there was an exercise book in which Mrs Smedley wrote down any special orders for the gardeners. The next morning at six o'clock when she and Clara came down to clean and light the stove, Lavinia tore out the middle pages of the exercise book where it wouldn't show and sat down to write her note.

"There's no ink," she told Clara. "Do you think her ladyship'll mind pencil?"

"May as well be hung for a sheep as a lamb," said Clara which, if not comforting, was at least common sense.

The note was short.

"My lady, could I see you on private business to do with my brothers respectfully Lavinia Beresford."

The note finished, Lavinia put it in the pocket of the clean white apron she would wear for prayers, then, tying on her sacking apron, she got out her blackleading brush and joined Clara at the stove.

It turned out not to be a good morning for wanting to do anything out of the usual for Mrs Smedley came down in a state.

"This is going to be quite a day, girls. Her ladyship had a telegram last evening from his lordship, he's coming home tonight bringing the Marquis of Delaware with him. Mr Durham went off in the brake right away to meet them."

Mr Durham was the head coachman. Had he gone alone or had he taken a stable boy to help with the horses?

"Has Mr Durham gone alone?" Lavinia asked.

Mrs Smedley thought that a time-wasting question.

"How should I know and what business is it of yours, I'd like to know. Lucky her ladyship doesn't like much breakfast so there'll just be kidneys and bacon and the kedgeree. Get out the fish, Clara. You girls can give the men's rooms a lick and a polish today for there'll be a lot of courses for dinner tonight and likely enough very late, so everybody get a move on."

Through prayers Lavinia had to sit on her hands to prevent them trembling. Could she? Would she dare give her ladyship the note? Then prayers were over. Mechanically she got to her feet and opened the door. Through it passed the staff, the girls' aprons crackling, the men marching almost like soldiers. Then the butler was level with her and suddenly Lavinia was no longer afraid. She let the butler take hold of the door then, instead of passing out into the hall, she walked across the dining room and laid her note on the Corkberry family Bible.

33. The Theatre

Though they had slept on makeshift beds – the boys on a mattress on the floor and Margaret on a shiny horsehair sofa – they had all slept soundly for they were tired after a long day and at least they were together, so they were in good spirits when they woke up.

The landlady where the Fortescues were staying, whom they called Ma, was, the children thought, a very kind if dirty lady. But though dirty herself she let them wash in her scullery and gave them a splendid breakfast of sausages with fried bread.

"Eat up, kiddies," she said. "With theatricals you never know what time you're getting your next meal."

The theatre was a tent which moved with the company from village to village. It was set up in a field. Outside it had posters stuck all over it advertising "The return by public request of Mr and Mrs Fortescue and Company, appearing tonight in that phenomenal success *Maria Marten* or *The Murder in the Red Barn*". In the entrance to the tent there was a wooden box rather like a sentry box with "Advance Booking" painted on it, but nobody at that moment was selling or buying tickets.

Inside, the tent was full of benches for people to sit on. At the far end was the stage with a rather torn red curtain draped on each side of it. The tent, the children learnt later, belonged to the Fortescues, as did the curtains, the scenery, the props and the wardrobe. When the time came for the company to move on, a farm cart and horses were hired for the removal.

Sitting on the front benches studying their parts were the actors, but they all got to their feet when the Fortescues came in. "Morning, Chief." "Morning, sir." "Morning, Mrs F."

Mr Fortescue went on to the stage.

"Morning, all. Before we begin our labours I have an announcement to make. As you know, Mrs Fortescue and myself have been desirous to add *Little Lord Fauntleroy* to the repertoire."

There was a murmur of assent from the company, amongst which could be heard "Pack them in" and "Sweetly pretty". "Until now," Mr Fortescue went on, "we have been unable to commence rehearsals for lack of the right boy, but now we have acquired one." He looked at the back of the tent where the children were standing. "Come up here, children."

Peter seemed to be in a dream and Horatio was watching a butterfly which had flown inside the tent, so Margaret took a hand of each and led them to the platform. Mr Fortescue patted Peter on the shoulder.

"Here, ladies and gentlemen, is Little Lord Fauntleroy. Say good morning, Peter."

Peter, looking very thin in his too broad suit, bowed slightly.

"Good morning to you all," he said politely.

Though it was a small thing to say it had a great effect for the tent fairly buzzed with conversation, all of which seemed to be approving. In a moment Mr Fortescue held up his hand for silence.

"But Peter is an orphan and we must all do what we can for the fatherless, so I have agreed that Peter's brother Horatio should also join my company, and he can play little Tom, the wrongful Lord Fauntleroy."

Horatio was an enormous success for he beamed at everybody and there were cooing sounds from the women of "Little sweetheart". "Little love".

Mr Fortescue held up his hand for silence.

"One moment. These boys who were recently rescued from an orphanage so grim, so terrible I could not offend your ears by describing it, found themselves a little mother." Mr Fortescue laid a hand on Margaret's head. "Could I separate these babes?"

Horatio had been trying to follow what was going on, now he looked in a puzzled way up at Mr Fortescue.

"Margaret isn't our mother, she's our friend."

Mr Fortescue gave a slight frown for he thought Horatio had interrupted a beautiful speech, but the company thought this funny and roared with laughter, so Mr Fortescue decided it was time for work.

"That is all I have to say," he said grandly. "Now on the stage everybody concerned in Scene 1 Act 2 of *The Heart of a Mother*. And this evening parts will be handed out for *Little Lord Fauntleroy*."

The children, finding they were no longer wanted, wandered out of the tent into the field outside. It was a beautiful field full of ox-eyed daisies and buttercups with a hedge round it in which dog-rose buds were showing. Peter had, of course, brought *Bleak House* with him and, since it was a lovely morning, lay down in the grass and was immediately oblivious of anything outside his book. Margaret took Horatio's hand.

"Shall we explore?"

Horatio had no time to answer before Ida came to the tent opening.

"Can you sew?" she called out to Margaret.

"Not as well as I can cook, but Hannah taught me to sew and we never stopped sewing in the orphanage."

"Good," said Ida. "Go round the back of the tent and there you'll find Mrs Sarah Beamish. She plays character parts and sees to the wardrobe. You give her a hand and Peter can take on the advance. Where is Peter?"

Margaret pointed.

"Reading over there."

"Reading!" Ida was evidently impressed. "Fancy at his age! He shouldn't have no trouble then in selling tickets."

Margaret fetched Peter.

"You've got to sell tickets," she explained, "but don't fuss, nobody's here to buy any so I expect when you know what they cost and all that you can go on reading until anybody comes."

Because she did not know what else to do with him, Margaret took Horatio with her round to the back to look for Mrs Beamish. They found her in one of the two small tents which were used as dressing rooms. She was a short woman, almost as broad as she was high, wearing a bonnet with cherries on it. She looked up as Margaret and Horatio came in. She had a surprisingly deep hoarse voice.

"There you are, luv," she said to Margaret. "If I gave you a cake of soap would you like to wash out Mr Fortescue's things? There's a couple of pails of water outside. Pity to let a day like this go by and not wash anything, real drying weather it is."

Margaret preferred washing to sewing.

"I'd like to. Have you anything Horatio could do?"

Mrs Beamish had very twinkling eyes, now she twinkled them at Horatio.

"I want me cotton reels tidied – how about that?"

Horatio was pleased to help with the cotton reels so he sat down by Mrs Beamish while Margaret went off with the laundry. Horatio rummaged through Mrs Beamish's sewing basket.

"Do you want them wound up and the end put in the little proper place?"

Mrs Beamish was pleased.

"Who taught you to do that?"

"It wasn't me that was taught," Horatio explained. "It was my brother Peter. Our mother taught him but I watched so I remember."

Mrs Beamish looked in a puzzled way at Horatio.

"Did your mother teach you to speak that way?"

Horatio had found a reel of green cotton badly in need of attention so he was not really listening to Mrs Beamish.

"What way?"

Mrs Beamish felt around for the right words.

"Well – I don't rightly know – like a little gentleman."

Horatio nodded.

"She taught us everything. How to read – I didn't get far with that – and how to write. I can't do that either but I can draw."

Mrs Beamish felt in her pocket.

"Like a cough sweet? Sarsaparilla they are. Nothing like it for cooling the blood."

Horatio politely took a sweet and put it in his mouth. He thought it tasted horrible, but he was too polite to say so; so he decided not to suck it.

"It's delicious," he said, taking it out of his mouth and putting it in his pocket. "But I think it's difficult to talk with a sweet in your mouth – don't you?"

Mrs Beamish's eyes twinkled again.

"There's them as likes sarsaparilla and them that don't," she said. Then, changing the subject: "Will you like being an actor?"

Horatio looked up at her.

"I don't know. You see none of us know what an actor is. Even Margaret doesn't know."

Mrs Beamish laughed.

"You will time Mr F. has taught you. You must come along one day and see a play. We do a matinée Saturday. All about a Christian girl being thrown to the lions. You'd like that."

"I should," Horatio agreed. "You see, I never saw anyone thrown to the lions – in fact, I never even saw a lion. Where are the lions kept?"

Mrs Beamish laughed so much she shook like a jelly.

"You'll be the death of me! Lions indeed! Mr F. has enough trouble paying all of us without feeding lions as well."

"But I thought you said I could see a Christian girl thrown to them."

"That's just pretending like," Mrs Beamish explained. "All the men does a bit of roaring. Sounds fine."

Ida came round the tent with Peter.

"Where's the girl?" she asked. Mrs Beamish explained about the washing. "When you're through with her send her to advance bookings. I want you to measure Peter. Mr F. says we'll do *Little Lord Fauntleroy* week after next. You got that piece of black velvet what I wore in *The Cry of the Heart?* Make him a nice suit, that will, and he has to have a red sash and a lace collar."

Margaret was charmed with her job at advance bookings for very few people booked in advance, mostly they just came to the theatre out of curiosity, so she was free to watch what was happening on the stage. And very interesting she found it. Mr Fortescue, who swaggered about carrying a cane, was evidently a grand sort of person. He was trying to persuade a girl to come to London where he could get her a very good job. As well as being the grand gentleman, Mr Fortescue was showing the girl what to do and how to say her part. She was a very short rather bulgy girl called Mary. Margaret could feel Mr Fortescue was not pleased with her.

"Poor girl," she thought, "I bet she's the one who has to play children too, though I shouldn't think she ever looks like a child."

"Don't you trust me, my child?" Mr Fortescue had to say. "I speak only for your good and for the good of your poor old widowed mother. . ." Mr Fortescue broke off. "Come on, Mary, that is where you start to cry."

Obediently Mary cried — not very well, but Mr Fortescue allowed her to go on.

"I don't wish to seem ungrateful, sir," she sobbed, "but my mother wishes me to stay at home."

Ida came on to the stage and dramatically flung her arms round Mary.

"I do indeed, sir. This child is all I have. Do not, I implore you, attempt to take her from me."

Mr Fortescue held up his hand.

"Splendid, Mrs F. Now, just to fix the scene, I will take it again from the beginning up to your entrance, Ida."

"Poor Mary!" thought Margaret. "I do hope she does it right this time."

For a while it seemed as if Margaret's hope had come true, but then they came round again to Mr Fortescue's speech beginning "Don't you trust me, my child?" finishing with "your poor old widowed mother."

Mary seemed carried away by Mr Fortescue's acting for she stared at him with a sort of blind look on her face. Margaret was feeling so sorry for her she could not help herself.

"Cry," she called out. "This is where you have to cry."

A sudden hush came over the theatre. It was so quiet all those present could hear a lark singing as it rose towards the sky. Then Mr Fortescue said:

"It seems I have acquired an assistant producer. I

shall find more use for you, Margaret, than sitting at advance bookings." He looked towards the side of the stage. "Did you hear the child, Ida? We must consider how we can use her."

34. The Whole Truth

Lady Corkberry, on reading Lavinia's note, took Lavinia into the morning room with her and told her to sit down. Then, while she ate her breakfast, Lavinia explained about Jem.

"I have kept thinking and thinking and yet I can't understand about that note I had from Peter. You see, Wilberforce is such a busy sort of little dog, the note couldn't have been on his collar long or it would have come off. Then who put it on his collar? It couldn't be anyone from outside so I decided someone who works here must have done it, someone who couldn't just come to the back door and give it to me."

Lady Corkberry was equally puzzled.

"Who could that be?"

"I couldn't think at first," Lavinia explained. "Then suddenly I knew. It must be Jem. You see, he knew the children because he drove them when they came to tea with Mr Windle, and if it's Jem they could be on his father's boat."

"Jem!" said Lady Corkberry as if she was trying out the name. "Jem. So you think Peter gave him the note to give you?"

"That's right," Lavinia agreed. "That's why I think he knows where they are. I've kept trying to see him but I have never had the chance. You see, we aren't allowed in the stables and Jem can't come to the house."

Lady Corkberry got up and pulled a bell on the wall.

"You should have come to me before."

The butler came in.

"You rang, m'lady?"

"Yes, send Henry over to the stables and tell him to find Jem and bring him to me here."

That was too much for the butler. It was, in his opinion, most unsuitable that the young woman from the scullery should be sitting in the morning room — but to bring in a stable boy!

"In here, my lady?" he said with all he felt in his voice.

"In here," Lady Corkberry replied calmly. Then she buttered herself another piece of toast.

When Jem got Henry's message he felt as if he had fallen down a rabbit hole so fast he had left his inside at the top. This was it. All was discovered. It was the end of his job, and the police station like enough for his mam and the Captain.

When the butler, stiff with disapproval, had shown Jem into the morning room, Jem had known at once his worst fears were realized for sitting by the door was the girl he had tried to avoid — Lavinia. But Lady Corkberry was very good at putting people at their ease.

"Good morning, Jem," she said cheerfully. "Keeping well, I hope. No further trouble with your chest?"

Jem was so scared he had almost lost his voice.

"Oh no, m'lady."

"I've sent for you," Lady Corkberry went on, "because we want your help. You did tie that note on to Wilberforce, didn't you?"

Jem went crimson to the tips of his ears.

"Yes, m'lady."

"So you saw the missing children?"

"Yes, m'lady — not willing, m'lady. That Margaret she came in the middle of the night. Proper taking she was in an' she'm say how the rozzers — the police, m'lady — is after Peter."

Lavinia could not bear the suspense.

"Do you know where they are now?"

Jem hesitated.

"Well, I do an' I don't in a manner of speakin'."

Lady Corkberry nodded.

"Quite understandable, for I think in the kindness of your heart you hid the children on your father's boat. Didn't you, Jem?"

Really Jem was glad to confess everything for it had weighed on him, so he told Lady Corkberry and Lavinia the full story.

"I'd 'ave spoke up before like," he explained, "only I didn't want no trouble."

Lady Corkberry smiled at him kindly.

"There will be no trouble. His lordship is returning from Ireland tonight with Lord Delaware. I think they will wish to collect the children. Where should your parents' boat be at this moment?"

Jem reckoned on his fingers.

"It all depends of course 'ow fast they'm travelled — you see, the children isn't used to the leggin' — leadin' the 'orse, that is — so it might take a day or two longer, but I would say the trip's over an' most like the Cap'n's on his way back."

"Anyway, you know the boat and where it stops," said Lady Corkberry, "so hold yourself in readiness, for I expect his lordship and Lord Delaware will want you to guide them and they will make an early start tomorrow morning."

Lavinia was so puzzled that the moment Jem had left the room she said:

"Forgive me, m'lady, but why wait for his lordship? Couldn't the police pick the children up?"

Lady Corkberry pointed to a chair at the table.

"Sit there, Lavinia. I want to talk to you. One day will make no difference. The children will be quite safe on Jem's father's boat for he and his wife are good people. I would not dream of informing the police who might blame them for what was intended as a kindness."

"But why should his lordship go?" Lavinia asked.

Lady Corkberry prayed she would find the right words to explain.

"Do you know what your mother's Christian name was?"

This was such an unexpected question that for a few seconds Lavinia did not answer. Then she said:

"Yes. It was Phoebe."

Lady Corkberry nodded.

"We thought it might be. You see, when his lordship spoke to you one Sunday after church he thought he saw a likeness to your mother, whom he had known when she was a young girl. Then at Mr Windle's he met Horatio and he was convinced. Apparently the likeness is extraordinary."

"Horatio is rather like Mummy looked," Lavinia agreed.

"So his lordship went to Ireland to tell your grandfather what he suspected."

"My grandfather!" gasped Lavinia. "I never knew we had one."

"I think you have. If his lordship is right your grandfather is the Marquis of Delaware, so your mother was Lady Phoebe Milestone. She ran away from Ireland with the man she loved and your grandfather never heard of her again. What happened to your father?"

Lavinia clasped and unclasped her hands.

"We don't know exactly – at least the boys don't. I think he stole some money and used it to go to South America. I think Peter guessed something was wrong because the police came, but then Mummy got ill and that was so awful we forgot everything else. Then she died. At first I looked after the boys but I couldn't get work and that was when they got the boys into the orphanage. I never talk about it because, you see, we aren't really orphans."

Lady Corkberry did not like what she had heard of the children's father.

"I should not trouble your head about that. From the sound of things you are as good as orphans, for I am sure your father will never come back."

Lavinia got up.

"You've been very kind, m'lady. Can I go back to my work now?"

Lady Corkberry got up. She came to Lavinia and put an arm around her.

"You may if you wish. I should have liked to have had you staying with me as my guest but his lordship – Lord Corkberry, I should say – said you should be left where you were until he knew that your grandfather would acknowledge you. You see, he quarrelled with your mother when she married your father."

Lavinia laughed.

"Me a guest! I couldn't ever be that, I'd feel such a fool – I mean they all know me as the scullery maid."

That night Lord Corkberry arrived with Lord Delaware. As Mrs Smedley had expected, they were very late and demanded an enormous meal.

After it Henry was sent to fetch Lavinia. Lavinia, at Lady Corkberry's suggestion, did not put on her apron or her cap, so she was wearing just the sprigged cotton dress she had on for her washing-up.

The Corkberrys and Lord Delaware were still at the table when Lavinia came in. She stood just inside the door smiling shyly. Lord Delaware, as if he was walking in his sleep, got out of his chair and came to her. He took her in his arms.

"Phoebe!" he whispered. "You're Phoebe come back to me."

35. The Rehearsal

Margaret became assistant to Mrs Beamish.

"My old legs aren't what they were," Mrs Beamish told her, "and there's a lot of gettin' about needed. Down to the shops for a piece of material, into the theatre to fetch someone for a fitting and, of course, the everlastin' washin'."

So every morning as soon as the children got to the theatre, as they had learnt to call the tent, Margaret ran round to Mrs Beamish and so she did not see Peter's early rehearsals. Then on the third morning Mrs Beamish, instead of giving her work, said:

"Sit down a minute. I got things to say to you."

Margaret knew she worked hard and as well as she could so she was not worried. She sat down on the floor and smiled up at Mrs Beamish.

"You don't want me to tell you again how I was found in a basket, do you?"

"Not now, dear," Mrs Beamish agreed, "though one day soon I will, for in the ten or so times you told me it's always a bit different, so I want to see what you'll make up next. No, it's on account of Peter."

"Peter! What's he done?"

Mrs Beamish was repairing the dress Ida was to wear as "Dearest".

"It's more, from what I can hear, what he hasn't done. You know how it is in a stock company — you have to learn your parts quick or at least know the cues so you know when it's your turn to speak."

Margaret had not yet seen a performance at the theatre as she and the boys were left behind in the evenings to put themselves to bed, but she had watched the company at work and knew when they were not on the stage they were usually studying their parts.

"You mean Peter doesn't know his part yet. I know he doesn't, and I am trying to help him. But, you see, we've not read the book and it's awfully difficult to learn things to say when you don't know what the person who you're supposed to be talking to is talking about. All Peter has before he speaks is the end of what somebody says."

Mrs Beamish nodded.

"I know, and I should by now with all the rôles I've played, but it isn't just Peter don't know his words it's the way he says them, just flat off, so I hear, and he don't pay no attention when Mr Fortescue tells him how."

Margaret decided she had better be honest.

"He doesn't like acting much, in fact, he doesn't like it at all."

"Beggars can't be choosers," said Mrs Beamish

dryly. "Where would you three be if him and her hadn't taken you in?"

"Goodness knows," Margaret agreed. "Back in the orphanage, I shouldn't wonder."

Mrs Beamish nodded.

"That's what I think and it's my bet that's where you'll all go if young Peter don't learn to act proper. It'll be no trouble — no trouble at all for Mr Fortescue to send for the police."

The children were enjoying life with the theatre company. They slept well, for though Margaret still used the sofa in the Fortescues' lodgings the boys shared a bed in the rooms of one of the other actors nearby. None of them minded being separated for the front doors were kept open so they could run in and out of each other's rooms as they chose. Food was irregular but they never went hungry for the actors were a generous lot and shared everything they had with the children. And one of the best things about the life was the permanent feeling it gave for the actors were always talking ahead — "Next Christmas season". "Come next spring". "Might set up by the sea next summer." Now with one blow Mrs Beamish had shattered Margaret's happiness. Mr Fortescue might send for the police. Back to the orphanage. Back to Matron.

Margaret wriggled along the floor towards Mrs Beamish.

"Oh no! No! Please — we can't go back to the orphanage, not ever. And Peter wouldn't even go there – you see, he took some books, it was only to borrow them but they don't know that. . ."

Mrs Beamish stroked Margaret's hair.

"Now, now. Don't carry on so. I was only saying what might happen. Now I tell you what to do. You're as sharp as a cartload of monkeys, so you slip into the theatre and listen to what Mr Fortescue wants and then you teach it to Peter."

Margaret jumped to her feet.

"Can you spare me now?"

Mrs Beamish smiled.

"I did without you before you come so I reckon I can do without you now. Not but what I won't say you are handy to have around and quick to learn."

Margaret went to the theatre entrance. Horatio was sitting in the advance booking box. Not that he could sell tickets for he was no good with money, but he could call somebody if a customer came. He thought it terribly boring being tied to the desk so he was delighted to see Margaret. He slid off the chair.

"Can I go and play?"

Margaret put an arm round him.

"Not just yet, Horry. I have to watch Peter for a bit."

Gloomily Horatio climbed back on to the chair. He sounded sad.

"You know, Margaret, I liked it better leading the horse than sitting by myself out here."

Margaret slipped unnoticed into the back row of the theatre. Peter with Mr Fortescue and Mr Ford, who was what Mrs Beamish described as "The Comic", were on the stage. Peter, Margaret was sorry to see, looked as if his thoughts were miles away. It was clear from the way he spoke that Mr Fortescue was losing his temper.

"This is the shop, Peter, owned by your best friend Mr Hobbs. We have worked on this scene for three days and you still do not know when you come on, what you say or where you sit. What excuse have you to offer?"

Peter sounded apologetic, but Margaret was sure it was only because he didn't like to be annoying and not because he wanted to try and act better.

"Mr Ford doesn't always say the same words."

Mr Ford, though a comic, was a sad-looking little man. He was kind-hearted so he tried to help.

"Look, sonny. It don't matter to you what I does before you comes on. I'm trying out some funny business with a bit of juggling see, but I always comes to your cue and that is 'Shockin' what the world's comin' to.' Then you walks on all casual like as the guv'nor says on account you come and see me every day. You sit down on that barrel what is supposed to have apples in it, takes one and then when I sez "Ullo' you says 'Mornin''."

Mr Fortescue looked like an elastic looks when it is stretched farther than it will go. He stared wearily at Peter. "Then you say: 'Do you remember, Mr Hobbs, what we were talking about yesterday morning?' and Mr Ford replies: 'We were mentioning Queen Victoria and the aristocracy.' Now that is where you show you are embarrassed – and when I say show I mean show – and then you say: 'And – and Earls?' Now you do know why you're embarrassed about Earls, don't you?"

Margaret was miserable for Peter for she knew he had very little idea what the story was about. She clasped her hands and prayed, "Oh, please God, let him remember for I have told him about the Earl."

Margaret's prayer was heard.

Peter, not sounding at all convinced, said:

"I suppose I don't want to tell him I am Lord Fauntleroy as he doesn't like Earls."

Mr Fortescue still looked like overstretched elastic.

"It is your grandfather who is an Earl – not you. Now, Fordy, give the cue again and this time, Peter, put some life into Cedric."

It was no good. Peter did come on at the right moment. He did sit in the right place and he did take an imaginary apple but he could not act at all. He sounded, Margaret thought, as a doll might talk if it could speak. It was just a string of words meaning nothing at all. And the worst of it was it should have been a funny scene. For Mr Hobbs was so sure Cedric could not mean he was going to be an Earl that he decided he was ill and felt him all over to see if he hurt anywhere.

All the way through the scene Mr Fortescue looked grimmer and grimmer. Then they came to the line spoken by Mr Ford: "Who is your grandfather then?" to which Cedric had to reply — reading from a bit of paper taken out of his pocket — "John Arthur Molyneux Errol, Earl of Dorincourt." As Peter was reading all his lines he did not pretend to take a paper with the name written on it out of his pocket, he just read out the name as he had read the rest of the part. This seemed to have the effect of a match on a firework on Mr Fortescue. He jumped across the stage, seized Peter by the shoulders and shook him as he roared:

"You miserable boy! Of our kindness my lady wife and myself took in the fatherless and how are we repaid? By sloth, my boy, sloth. Three days and not one word have you learnt. Moreover, you are stubborn. No child could be so deplorable an actor so I am forced to believe you are not trying. Go, Fordy, and fetch me a stick. I shall see what beating can do for this wretched boy."

Margaret acted without thinking. In a moment she was off the bench, had rushed up the theatre and was on the stage. Mr Fortescue had stopped shaking Peter but he was still holding him. Margaret put a stop to that. She seized one of his hands and with all her force she bit it.

With a howl of pain Mr Fortescue let Peter go. Then he sucked his hand where Margaret had drawn blood.

"You demon child! How dare you bite me?"

"I'll bite you again," said Margaret, "and I'll go on biting if you touch Peter. It's not his fault he can't act, he's going to write books and that's more important and. . ."

Goodness knows what else Margaret might have said for she was terribly angry, but at that moment Mr Ford, carrying a little cane, came back on to the stage.

"Of course it's not my business, Guv'nor," he said, "but if I was you I wouldn't waste no more time on Peter. Let him help with the tickets and the scenery and that." He made a gesture towards Margaret. "If you ask me there is our Little Lord Fauntleroy. He's supposed to be a boy of spirit, isn't he? Well, she'll play him to the life."

36. The Crusader

The Captain had managed to pick up a man to help him temporarily on board the *Crusader*, so with Ebeneezer leading the horse and the weather turned fine life was, as the Captain put it, "fair to middling". In fact, his only trouble was that Mrs Smith would, as he described it, "go on so" about the children.

Now that it was summer Mrs Smith had taken off her trilby hat and instead on top of her straw bonnet she wore a sun bonnet. She looked a shade thinner for she had discarded all but one of her flannel petticoats. She still wore a vivid shawl over her shoulders but made of cotton, not wool. Every dinner-time it seemed to the Captain she started up the same way.

"I wonder what those kiddies are doin' now. I do 'ope Ida has remembered what I said about Peter not being too strong."

The Captain, cutting slice after slice for himself off the joint, would try and say something soothing.

"They'll be all right, mate. Livin' like lords they are after leggin'."

Mrs Smith could not openly criticize the Captain's sister but it was clear she felt uneasy.

"I suppose you're right but it's different for Ida never 'avin' 'ad none of her own."

"Now stop worriting," the Captain would say. "It don't do your stomick no good worritin' while you're eatin' your vittals."

But Mrs Smith did worry for she had become fond of the children, so she began counting the days before they were back on another trip to London where she could visit them.

Then one day the Smiths had a great surprise. They were going through a lock when on to the *Crusader* jumped Jem.

The Captain saw him first.

"Bless me Sunday trousers if it ain't our Jem," he shouted.

Mrs Smith came out of the galley wiping her hands on her apron.

"Our Jem!" she said. "What are you doing 'ere?"

Jem looked around.

"I come – at least, we all come to fetch the children."

The Captain looked grim.

"Whatcher mean we all come? You brought the rozzers?"

"In course 'e 'asn't," said Mrs Smith, "don't talk so silly. Who's with you, son, you see I got to tell whoever it is the children aren't 'ere no more."

Jem turned quite pale.

"Not 'ere! Where are they then?"

"They're all right," the Captain explained. "Young Peter 'e 'adn't the strength for the leggin'."

"And young Horatio was too small really not being born to it like," Mrs Smith added.

"Young Margaret was doin' fine," the Captain said, "an' we would — at least me mate would've liked to keep 'er — but she wouldn't leave the boys."

"Then where are they now?" Jem asked.

The Captain lit his pipe.

"You mind your Auntie Ida?"

Jem made a face.

"Don't I 'alf!"

The Captain puffed at his pipe.

"Well, she married a Mr Fortescue who is a theatrical and 'e's got a comp'ny like."

"Give 'em a fine chance it will," Mrs Smith put in. "You see, Mr Fortescue is learnin' a new play what needs a boy like Peter to be a little Lord somethin' an' there's another boy wanted what 'Oratio can do. There wasn't nothing' for Margaret but she wouldn't leave the boys so they kep' 'er like."

"But where are they?" Jem asked in a desperate voice. "I mean they got to be found an' took back."

Mrs Smith looked flabbergasted.

"To that orphanage? Over my dead body."

Jem shook his head.

"Now listen, Ma. At the 'otel up yonder is waiting 'is lordship and another lordship from Ireland and Lavinia, the boys' sister. I didn't get a lot of what they said but it seems the boys and Lavinia are the gran'children of the lord from Ireland only they never knowed it."

Mrs Smith looked triumphantly at the Captain.

"Didn't I tell you those boys spoke pretty as lords?"

"But, Ma," Jem persisted, "they're waitin' at the 'otel for the children. I been sittin' 'ere a 'ole day waitin' for you. What am I to tell 'em where the boys are?"

Mrs Smith looked at the Captain.

"We didn't 'ave no address like. You suppose The Bull would find 'em?"

The Captain shook his head.

"Not quick it wouldn't. You see, son, they don't act in a proper theatre like. They travel their own theatre and sets it down in a field. I knows more nor less where it is on account Ida told me, so me and the mate could see the children next time we're down."

Jem made up his mind.

"You stay 'ere. I'm off to the 'otel to fetch their lordships and Lavinia, they best decide what to do."

In the end, because Lavinia had insisted on coming too, Lord Corkberry had decided they had better drive to find the children. Jem, who had never lost his canal knowledge, had worked out a likely spot where – even allowing for delays – they should meet the *Crusader*. Then, by inquiring from the various lock-keepers if the *Crusader* had passed, he had checked his guess at a meeting place and found he was right. The idea had been, in order to attract no attention to the *Crusader*, that Jem alone should fetch the children. They would then be driven back to Sedgecombe Place and, when they were safely under his roof, Lord Corkberry would inform the police that they were found. Jem's unexpected news about the theatre was, of course, upsetting.

"We better go down to your father's boat," Lord Corkberry told Jem. "No good hangin' about here if the birds have flown."

"Never heard such a story in me whole life," said Lord Delaware. "Chips off the old block, my grandsons. Play actin', 'tis their mother all over."

Lavinia was the one who was upset. She had been so sure she would see her brothers that day. She was nearly crying.

"If Jem's father doesn't know where the boys are how can we find them?"

Lord Delaware had become very fond of his grand-daughter. He put an arm round her.

"Don't fret, my dear. We'll find them if we have to comb every field that is lying round London."

In the end, of course, no one combed any field. The Captain found a place where the canal widened and turned the *Crusader* round. Then on the opposite bank he engaged a fresh horse and as fast as the horse and Ebeneezer as legger could go, took his three passengers to London.

37. Curtain Down

A first night in the Fortescue company was a common event. For the more plays they had in their repertoire the longer they could stay in one place for each play brought in a different audience. But the first night of *Little Lord Fauntleroy* was rather different. The book had been popular not only with children but with their parents so, as a result, when it was known the Fortescues were adding the play to their repertoire whole families booked in advance.

"They are putting you in charge of advance bookings," Margaret told Peter. "Try and do it well because otherwise they won't keep you and that of course means we'll all have to go. I think you'll like it because nobody ever buys a ticket in advance so you'll be able to finish *Bleak House*. Mrs Beamish says if I'm good as Lord Fauntleroy, Mr Fortescue is sure to give me some money, not enough to get us a little house of our own but enough to post *Bleak House* back to Mr Windle. It will be a great relief to my mind when it's gone because then I'll know you can't go to prison."

Peter, curiously enough, did not mind selling

tickets. He liked handling money and making sure everybody had the right change. And the customers liked Peter for they could be heard, as they walked away, saying to each other, "Quite the little gentleman" or "Gentlemanly boy, wasn't he?" These things, reported to the Fortescues, made them take a slightly better view of Peter, to whom they had scarcely spoken since what was known in the company as "the big bust-up".

The little impostor Tom in the play had almost nothing to say, but Horatio looked sweet and the company spoiled him — or at least would have spoiled him only he was an independent child who did not want to spend his time on ladies' knees or be given pick-a-backs by the men.

"They treat me like a baby," Horatio complained to Margaret, "me what's been a legger. When I tell them they don't believe me."

For Margaret it was as if a door she had never known existed had opened wide. On the night when she knew she was to act Lord Fauntleroy she was allowed to take home the whole script of the play and read it. And as she read she found she understood Fauntleroy.

"It seems strange at first," she told Peter, "that he could think his grandfather nice, because he was an old beast. But nobody had told him what a beast his grandfather had been so I think he truly got to love him."

Peter was having his bedtime read of *Bleak House*

and did not want to be disturbed.

"I'm glad you like him and want to act him. I thought him an awful boy. Anyway, I don't understand about acting so I don't want to do it ever."

But Margaret did understand about acting as the company very quickly found out. There was no need to tell her that Cedric was embarrassed at having to admit to Mr Hobbs that his grandfather was an Earl — she was embarrassed and looked it. Nor was Margaret in the least put out by changes in a scene. The Fortescues knew their audiences and what they expected, so wherever possible they squeezed in a song, a dance or some funny business for one of the cast. Of course Mr Hobbs's shop was a natural for these things, not only for Mr Ford but for the maid to dance an Irish jig and Dearest to make an entrance for no other purpose than to sing a song about the dear homeland far across the foam. Margaret as Cedric was an appreciative audience for all that went on, eating an apple while she watched and listened, and clapping each artist when they had finished, but the moment Mr Ford came back to a cue Margaret was on the spot ready with Cedric's next line.

"Proper find that Margaret is," Mr Fortescue told Ida. "When she's grown a bit I can get rid of that poor Mary."

Ida liked that idea.

"Never had a mite of talent, poor girl."

Mrs Beamish was given the work of transforming Margaret into Lord Fauntleroy. Margaret's hair had grown again and though not so long as it had been it now curled to her shoulders. One evening Mrs Beamish came round to the Fortescues's lodgings with a large bottle.

"You got to be fair, dear, for his little lordship. This is peroxide. Come on, we'll give you a wash first and then I'll put it on."

For what seemed to Margaret hours Mrs Beamish put peroxide on her hair with an old toothbrush. Then for more hours she had to sit wrapped up in towels while the peroxide took, but when the operation was over both Mrs Beamish and Margaret were stunned with admiration. For in place of Margaret's brown curls there were now curls so fair they were almost white.

"Don't I look lovely!" Margaret gasped. "I always wanted to be fair. Don't you think I look pretty, Mrs Beamish?"

Mrs Beamish kissed her.

"Wonderful pretty. And I don't mind telling you I reckon you'll never let it go dark again."

The boys were much less enthusiastic.

"You look like Mrs Ida," Peter told Margaret in a disgusted voice.

"You don't look real," Horatio said, then he added doubtfully, "but I think I love you just the same."

On the first night of *Little Lord Fauntleroy* the

tent for almost the first time in its history had a full house. Perhaps it was the full house or the thought that some of it was advance booking, but the company became nervous, and some of this nervousness was caught by Margaret who up to that moment had not known what nervousness was. Mrs Beamish was helping her to dress. Margaret did not wear her black velvet suit with its red sash and lace collar until the scenes in the castle. For the opening scenes in America she had a frilled blouse and knickerbockers with a red sash and red stockings. Margaret gripped her front.

"Do you know, I feel odd here. Do you think I'm going to be sick?"

Mrs Beamish laughed.

"Not you. Just a bit of nerves, that is. Put one foot on the stage and it will all be gone."

What Mrs Beamish said proved quite true, the moment Margaret walked on to the stage all the funny feeling was gone. But much more interesting was what took its place as the evening passed. It was almost as if the audience were holding out their arms to her. For that evening she could feel that they loved her – or rather that they loved Cedric and cared dreadfully what happened to him. It was a thrilling feeling.

Margaret was so engrossed by the scene in which Cedric first met his grandfather that she did not hear a slight commotion at the back of the theatre. Mr Fortescue, even though he was acting the Earl, heard it, but when he saw it was more people squeezing in it was good news so he paid no more attention.

What had happened was that Peter counting the takings was suddenly confronted by Captain and Mrs Smith, Jem, Lord Corkberry, a strange man and Lavinia. He jumped out of the advance booking box almost upsetting it and flung himself on Lavinia.

"Vinny! Vinny! Oh, Vinny, we have missed you so dreadfully."

The strange man said:

"What's going on here? 'Twas said you were to be little Lord Fauntleroy."

"I was but I couldn't do it."

"Then Horatio is being the boy?" Lord Corkberry asked.

"No, Margaret is. Horatio is Tom, the impostor."

"We better go and see this," said Lord Corkberry. He laid a golden guinea on the desk. "Can you manage tickets for six?"

Peter shook his head and handed back the guinea.

"Standing room only and that's sixpence so I've no change for this."

"Keep it," said Lord Corkberry. "It will be a surprise for Mr Fortescue."

The Captain grinned.

"A surprise! Reckon it will give him the apoplexy."

Although none of them knew the story it was easy for the newcomers to pick up what was happening. The scenery was poor and makeshift and not in the least like what would have been found in the castle; the clothes, even helped out by footlights, were tawdry, the acting, with a few exceptions, not of a high standard. But the theatre has its own magic and soon the Captain, Mrs Smith, Jem, Lord Corkberry, Lord Delaware and Lavinia were as carried away as the most eager child in the front row. Even when Horatio came on the Fauntleroy spell was not broken, for Lord Delaware muttered when it looked as if Lord Fauntleroy was out and Tom was in:

"'Tis a dirty shame!"

When the curtain came down Margaret found herself quite a heroine. Praise was showered on her by the company and very good to her ears it sounded.

The Captain was sent round to the back of the theatre to fetch the Fortescues. They were, as most theatre people are when a play has gone well, in tremendous spirits.

Ida gave her brother a smashing kiss.

"We never knew you were in front. What did you think of the show?"

"Never enjoyed myself more," said the Captain. "Funny, I forgot the boy was Margaret really."

"Born for the theatre," Mr Fortescue boomed. "Born to it. Talent in her little finger."

The Captain then remembered why he was there.

"You got to come and meet some people. Lord Corkberry and a Lord Delaware. Seems Lord Delaware is the boys' grandfather and he wants to see Horatio."

Margaret was taking off her stage clothes when Horatio was called by Ida. A very changed Ida seemed almost shy of Horatio. She spoke in a cooing sort of voice.

"Come along, dear. There's friends to see you, bless you, and dear little Peter too."

"Dear little Peter!" thought Margaret. "That's odd. She doesn't think he's a dear."

Margaret was so curious about what Ida was up to that she hurried into her frock and ran through the theatre to see what was going on. The first person she saw was Lavinia. It was a wonderful moment. Lavinia at last come to take charge of the boys. Until that second Margaret had not realized, much as she loved them, what a load Peter and Horatio had been.

Lavinia, hugging Margaret, said:

"Oh, Margaret! You've been wonderful!"

Lord Delaware came forward.

"So this is Margaret. You made a splendid Fauntleroy, my dear."

Horatio tugged at Margaret's arm.

"He's a Lord and we're his grandsons."

"He's Lord Delaware. Our mother was his daughter, Lady Phoebe Milestone," Peter explained.

"And we're going to live in his castle in Ireland," Horatio added.

Lavinia put an arm round Margaret.

"And you're coming too, isn't she, Grandfather?"

"Of course she's coming too," said Horatio, "she's our sister now."

Peter smiled at Margaret.

"Of course you're coming too, we won't go anywhere without you."

Lord Delaware took Margaret's hands in his.

"'Tis wonderful care of my grandsons you have taken, Margaret. 'Twould be a pleasure if you came to live with me. I would treat you as a daughter."

It was that word daughter. It hit Margaret as if someone had thrown a stone at her. A daughter! How could anyone be a daughter to somebody when they had a mother of their very own and when they were a person in their own right? Her chin shot into the air.

"Thank you very much but I don't want to be anyone's daughter. I was not found like an ordinary baby. I had three of everything all marked with crowns and each year lots of money was paid to keep me. I have friends, Hannah and the rector, and I've got a stamp so I am writing to ask them to come and see me act *Little Lord Fauntleroy* and I have other friends." She smiled at the Smiths. "I could work on the *Crusader*, couldn't I?"

"Of course you could, dear, and welcome," Mrs Smith agreed.

"It's not" — Margaret turned back to Lord Delaware — "that I wouldn't like to live with Lavinia and Peter and Horatio — I would. But, you see, I am Margaret Thursday and I'm going to make my name famous. I wasn't sure how but I think now it might be as an actress."

"Undoubtedly," said Mr Fortescue.

"You show real promise, dear," Ida agreed.

Margaret looked up at Lord Delaware.

"You do see that I couldn't join somebody else's family — that I must be just me, don't you?"

Nobody answered that and yet somehow Margaret felt that they all understood and, in a way, approved. Then the Captain said:

"If I 'ad a drink in me 'and I would say to you all: 'Raise your glasses, ladies and gents, to a girl of spirit — young Margaret Thursday. May God bless her and good luck go with her.'"